Seasons of the Heart

Cynthia Freeman lives in San Francisco, where she is currently working on a new novel. Her previous best-sellers include *Come Pour the Wine, No Time for Tears* and *Illusions of Love*.

Also by Cynthia Freeman in Pan Books

Illusions of Love

Cynthia Freeman

Seasons
of the Heart

Pan Books
London and Sydney

First published in Great Britain 1986 by William Collins Sons & Co. Ltd
This edition published 1987 by Pan Books Ltd, Cavaye Place, London SW10 9PG
9 8 7 6 5 4 3 2 1
© Cynthia Freeman 1986
ISBN 0 330 29866 6
Photoset by Parker Typesetting Service, Leicester
Printed by Richard Clay Ltd, Bungay, Suffolk

To Nini, with all my love

One

The day began the same as a million others. Nothing in the universal scheme of things was any different, but by the time Ann Coulter watched the sun set low in the Pacific she knew the rest of her life had been unalterably changed. On December 23, 1969, Ann had come face to face with her own mortality.

Sitting in the shadows of early twilight, she was haunted by a hundred fantasies. Her life seemed to be made up of nothing but endings. Birth and death were inevitable, but the choices made along the way were her own. And such hard choices they had been.

What she had done this afternoon had taxed her strength to the breaking point. Placing Phillip in a nursing home was the hardest decision she had ever made. The sad images revolved in her mind until she thought she would go mad. Those long corridors filled with people in wheelchairs, the helpless men and women who had once raced to school, fallen in love, raised children of their own now reduced to total dependency. These were human beings no one seemed to want. Was this how people were expected to end their days? Ann could not come to terms with life's cruelty. She was not afraid of growing old. It was the indignities of aging she could not bear. And for Phillip to have to suffer so before he was even sixty! She would never forget his bewildered expression when she said goodbye.

Leaving him in the nursing home had been like sending him to oblivion. How could she come to terms with herself, knowing that she alone was responsible?

It was tragic to end a marriage of almost thirty years, even if those years had not all been happy ones. In a way it would have been easier if he had died. Then the decision would have been God's. She would have been sad, but surely she would have found some peace in the

7

natural process of bereavement. This way there was no peace: instead, she was plagued with guilt. It wasn't fair that life had placed that burden on her shoulders. Though she had watched Phillip's decline, she had rejected the idea of sending him away by becoming oblivious to his loss of memory, and by reacting to his vagueness with anger. But what good would it do to think about all that now?

Staring out toward the San Francisco Bay she wondered what had happened to the years. Would she ever erase the sound of his voice asking, 'Why are you doing this to me?' He knew that he was being abandoned, and at that terrible moment, she wanted to scream out, 'I'm not leaving you here!' But she knew that she couldn't do that. Dr. Cohn's words kept her from weakening. 'I know how you're feeling, Ann. Sending someone you love to a nursing home is probably the most painful decision a person can make. But, as you asked me before – no, I don't think it's wise to keep him at home any longer. His condition will only deteriorate. No matter when you do this, it isn't going to be easy.'

Wise Dr. Cohn. She knew he was right. It was no longer safe for Phillip to be home. Yet the rationale offered her no comfort. All she could do was hold him close and whisper, 'I love you, Phillip. I'm sorry, darling . . .'

Suddenly she realized that it was completely dark. Brushing aside her tears, she turned on a lamp and poured herself a brandy. Passing the coffee table, she glanced down and saw a copy of *New Horizons*. Many of her professional achievements were chronicled in those pages. She laughed bitterly. During the interview, she had tried not to reveal too much of her personal life, especially facts concerning her marriage, but the reporter had kept pressing her for details. How had Phillip dealt with her success? Had he felt threatened by it? What was their relationship like? A marriage of almost thirty years was certainly good for a little space, surely worth mentioning for its longevity alone. Ann fielded

8

most of the questions with vague but cheerful answers. On Phillip's illness, she remained silent. He was entitled to his dignity.

Picking up the magazine, she turned the pages until she came to the image of herself which stared back. It belied her forty-nine years, although today she felt as if she were a hundred. The lonely silence was more than she could bear. Quickly she got up and put on a record, 'Au Clair de Lune,' and sat back on the couch, still staring down at her picture. The caption was black and bold: MODEST AFTER HUGE SUCCESS.

A small voice within her whispered, *It's all a travesty, isn't it? I'm no more prepared to handle my life now than I was when my mother died.*

As though a veil had lifted, Ann looked back to her childhood and saw herself clinging to her father after the funeral. She had been six then, and oh, how she had loved him. She was all he had left – or so he had said. And Ann had believed him, until two years later, when he had met Stella Burke. The pain of her mother's death had hardly faded, and Ann could still hear her own pathetic sobbing as she sat alone in her room the night he'd married Stella.

All through her teens she'd continued to feel as if her father had betrayed not only her mother's memory but Ann herself. No wonder that when Phillip had come into her life she had been so eager to escape home.

Two

The year was 1941, the month was March, and the world was alive with the sounds of spring. It seemed as though fate had directed Ann to the right place at the right time. She was the maid of honor at the wedding of her dearest friend, Ruthie, and Phillip was best man for the groom, Kenny Newman. Ann's first glimpse of Phillip made her believe in the refrain to 'Love in Bloom,' which Jack Benny sang every Sunday on the radio. His tall good looks were exactly calculated to sweep a romantic, lovely, and very vulnerable girl off her feet.

It was all so simple back then. There were three rules: one fell in love, got married, and had children. Listening to the strains of *Lohengrin* as Ruthie came down the aisle, Ann dreamed of becoming Mrs. Coulter. Those were heady times for romance. America was on the brink of war, and Hollywood had taken a firm grip on the national imagination. Ann had grown up seduced by the silver screen with its instant romances and promises of happily ever after.

Whether or not Phillip Coulter resembled Robert Taylor, Ann saw him as a hero. His hair perhaps was not as dark, and his eyes not quite so blue, but she was convinced that his beautifully molded lips, which she longed to feel against hers, and his strong chin with the heartrending cleft, were identical to her idol's.

She felt as though she'd melt as she danced in his arms the night of the wedding. He *was* her prince charming who had come to take her away, make her happy, transport her to a vine-covered cottage to the tune of 'Tea for Two.'

But once the wedding was over and Phillip escorted her home, standing facing him at her front door she no longer felt quite like Cinderella. Her violet eyes misted over.

She prayed that Phillip would not sense that she was on the verge of tears. She had hoped, wished, that he would take her in his arms, kiss her lingeringly. But instead, he stood rather awkwardly, not quite knowing what to say. Finally he blurted out, 'Well, it's really been nice getting to know you.'

Ann wanted to cry. He made it sound so final. During the rehearsals and the little suppers after, she'd gotten the feeling that Phillip liked her quite a bit. At the wedding, he had danced with her more than with anyone else. Yet now, he was leaving without any mention of seeing her again.

Ann went to bed that night wondering what she'd

done wrong. If only she looked more like Veronica Lake! But she didn't, and Phillip didn't like her enough even to ask for a date. She scarcely shut her eyes that night. When the alarm went off the next morning, she wanted to throw it against the wall.

Exhausted, she dressed with more reluctance than usual for her job at the stocking counter at I. Magnin's. She envied Ruthie safely launched as a bride. Well, Ann thought, cheered somewhat by the soft spring morning, maybe he'd call. Maybe.

But a week came and went, and the phone didn't ring for her. She cried into her pillow every night. It was obvious that Phillip just didn't like her. The only comfort was Ruthie, already back from her honeymoon on romantic Santa Catalina Island. Sitting across from her at Townsend's Restaurant, Ann found some comfort in being able to pour out her misery.

'I guess I'm just awfully dumb, Ruthie, to have fallen in love with someone who doesn't even know I'm around. But I really thought he liked me.'

'I'm sure that he does, Ann. Who could help liking you?'

'Well, my stepmother for one. I don't think I'm all that lovable. And obviously I'm not very desirable, or Phillip would have called.'

'Don't put yourself down. So what if he doesn't call? There are plenty of other fish in the sea.'

But at that moment, Ann thought no one could ever love her, least of all Phillip Coulter. And he was the one she wanted.

But Ann was quite wrong. After Phillip had said goodnight that evening, he crossed the street and stood watching as the light went on in her bedroom. He leaned against a lamppost and lit a cigarette, hoping she might come to her window. When the cigarette burned to his fingers without a glimpse of her, he turned and walked away.

Although Ann couldn't know it, she had completely misread Phillip. Not only had he wanted to kiss her, he

11

had become infatuated with her in the brief time they'd known each other.

The reason he had tried to remain aloof was precisely because he liked her so much. And he couldn't possibly think about becoming seriously involved with a woman, not with his present – and future – obligation to support his parents. Although he'd been lucky enough to get a position after law school graduation working for Levin, Cahn and Smith, one of the most prestigious firms in the city, in reality he was nothing more than a glorified clerk. His salary was so pitiful that there was almost nothing left after the rent and bare necessities were paid. So how in the hell could he think of getting married? And girls like Ann expected marriage. No, he had only one choice – to put her out of his mind.

But every night for the next six weeks he lay in the dark and ached to feel her in his arms. All he could see was her face, those lovely violet eyes, that clear, porcelain skin. The harder he tried to forget her, the more difficult it became. As time passed, he decided he wanted Ann more than anything else in the world.

The truth was that there had been little time for girls in his life, since he had been so busy earning enough to put himself through college and law school. Until he'd met Ann, his celibacy had been annoying, but not a serious problem. But she had evoked a desire he could not extinguish. Where he had gotten the strength to refrain from kissing her the night of Kenny's wedding, he would never know.

Although it wasn't apparent to Ann, Phillip was very unsure of himself. He had become almost obsessed with the idea that he would never amount to anything, and as the notion of marriage continued to haunt him, he became convinced that he would never be able to offer Ann anything. For him to have to struggle financially was one thing, but to ask her to share his poverty seemed impossible.

The dilemma that Phillip found himself in was not of his making. His father had been born to a wealthy family, and as a child Phillip had every reason to expect an easy life. He had been a change-of-life baby, and after years of longing for a son, his parents had lavished attention on him and indulged him to the extreme.

It was the roaring twenties, and America was on a spending spree. Few could resist the lure of greater fortunes. One could buy stocks on the slenderest of margins. And Simon had plunged along with the rest, recklessly pledging his stores as collateral. Of course, he should have seen the gathering clouds, but he preferred to leave his investments to his broker. Then, when the dam broke, he bitterly blamed the broker as he was forced to sell his luxury shops at a fraction of their worth. By November 1929, he was wiped out, and like many other victims of the crash, he never recovered from the blow.

Phillip had only been fourteen, but he would never forget the day his father had learned that he was bankrupt. He'd seemed to age all at once and afterward could never face his son with pride. Phillip had always displayed an interest in the business, and Simon had frequently boasted that he was a born merchant.

But now all that was gone. And, without realizing it, Phillip had been emotionally scarred almost as deeply as Simon. Phillip's ambition, his zest for life, would never recover. He decided he never wanted to be rich again; it made you too damn vulnerable. It made no difference that a fortune could be made again. He had seen what its loss had done to his father – and to others, friends of the family who had killed themselves rather than try to start over. No amount of money guaranteed security, he decided. Better to accustom yourself to living without it.

Almost immediately, the house in Sea Cliff had gone on the auction block. Phillip had been shattered watching the eighteenth-century antiques, the china and paintings, being snatched up for next to nothing. Since birth he'd been taught to cherish them. They were his legacy. Try as he might, he could not keep from blaming his father for his lack of foresight. As Phillip withdrew into sullen silence, his mother's heart ached to see the rift between the boy and her husband. Eva knew Simon was already racked with guilt and prayed that he was unaware of Phillip's resentment.

But her prayers were in vain. Simon recognized his son's anger and despised himself for throwing away the legacy his family had entrusted to him to protect for the next generation. How could he have been so blind as not to see that the market could not expand forever? He almost welcomed Phillip's silent fury; it was a fitting penance.

The burden of Simon's folly was not only in what he owed to the future, but to the past. Visions of his grandfather's fury haunted him, and his sleep was frequently interrupted by dreams of the old man describing his long struggle to establish his fortune.

Israel Coulter and Phillip Coulter, his great-grandson, were the same age, fourteen, when their respective worlds shattered – except that Israel had used the blow as a stimulus to create a new life.

During an even more than usually bloody and widespread Russian pogrom, Israel Coulter's entire family had been massacred by a drunken mob. He was the only survivor, and he realized that if he remained in Russia he too would eventually be destroyed like the rest. Even in the depths of his rage and grief, he knew that God must have spared him for some reason.

With little to aid him beyond his own wits and a few miraculously salvaged coins, the boy made his way from the Crimea to Turkey, and, finally, three years later, to the shores of America and then across the country to San Francisco. At seventeen, he was already a man. With a small box of pins and needles, he set out to make his living as a tailor, a trade he'd been taught since early childhood. In a city where gold was god, he soon prospered.

He was lucky in that first year to meet a lovely Jewish girl, Sarah, whom he married, and luckier still a year later when she gave birth to a son, Daniel. Israel never forgot the vow he made at his parents' grave that their seed would never die.

Watching Daniel grow tall and unafraid in the new world, Israel thanked his God. His happiest day was when he and Daniel watched the sign go up over the first store: COULTER AND SON, 1870.

That was only the beginning. By the time Simon was born, there were over a dozen prosperous shops. America was booming, and Israel was a shrewd and prudent businessman. He lived to ninety, surviving his son, Daniel, by nearly a decade. Simon always remembered the day when Israel called him to his bedside and said, 'This is your legacy, Simon. I leave it to you with my blessings. Guard it. Keep it safe, for your sons.'

Israel could not have foreseen that the word prudence would disappear in the postwar boom of the twenties. If you had money, why not triple it, and Simon, like most of his generation, gambled recklessly and lost. He would never recover his pride. He envisioned Phillip finishing high school no closer to knowing what he was going to do without the family business than he had been on that tragic day in 1929.

It hadn't been an easy task, but somehow Simon had managed to salvage a little money from his collapsed empire. After dinner one evening, he sat across the kitchen table from Phillip and asked, 'What are your plans, Phillip, now that you're graduating?'

Phillip lowered his eyes. 'I really don't know.'

'Well, Phillip, I've thought a great deal about your future.'

For a moment, Phillip wanted to say, *Why didn't you think about me while I still had a future?* But instead he asked, 'And what have you been thinking?' hoping that his anger didn't show.

'The one thing no one can take from you is a profession. I've been able to scrape up enough money so that you can start premed at the University of California.'

It had been decided for him, Phillip thought resentfully. But he said nothing, and only stared at his father's

15

worn face. Over the past year he had been able to view his father's failure with more compassion. He did love both his mother and father deeply, in spite of everything, and lately he had begun to realize that he himself was to blame for not having been able to accept the devastating change in their fortunes. He had made his parents doubly miserable by letting them see his resentment. Like his father, Phillip realized he too lacked Israel Coulter's ambition and iron will.

Looking at Simon, Phillip knew that he could not deny his father's attempt to make amends.

'I'll do it, Dad,' he forced himself to say. 'Thanks.'

And with that, the die was cast. Phillip enrolled at U.C. But his future as a doctor was cut short the first morning he confronted a cadaver. Ice-cold perspiration rolled down his back, and his stomach heaved uncontrollably.

Although he knew that his father would be terribly hurt, Phillip knew that he had to drop medicine. As he suspected, Simon took the decision badly. He had wanted Phillip to become a doctor as much for his own sake as his son's. If Phillip were a success, Simon would not be a complete failure, so when he saw Phillip was adamant, Simon suggested law.

Ironically, he could not have forced Phillip into a more incongruous profession. To be an attorney requires great confidence as a speaker and an adviser. Phillip had none. He'd been trained from childhood to be a merchant. That was all he'd ever wanted to be. Sure, he could have gotten a job in a men's store. That was probably the only thing he had any talent for – selling socks over a counter, or perhaps Arrow shirts.

But he could not bring himself to refuse his father the only thing Simon had left: pride in his son. Phillip finally acquiesced.

Somehow he plodded through college and law school. Graduation left him with a strange feeling of relief, rather than the conviction that he had found his métier.

Dressed in a black gown, the mortarboard on his head, Phillip stood on the stage, looking out at his parents. When he saw his father take out a handkerchief and wipe his eyes, Phillip knew that whatever his feelings about his profession, he had made the only choice possible.

A year had passed since then, and the only change was that he had had another birthday – his twenty-sixth. Every time he thought of Ann, he realized how empty his life was. Unhappy in his professional life, he had allowed nothing else to touch him – not beauty, not joy, not love. One night, after six weeks of ruthlessly trying to forget her, he realized that if he continued to deny his desire, he would never become a whole human being.

Closing his mind to further doubt, he picked up the phone and dialed her number, which he'd committed to memory so many weeks ago. But when he heard it ring, it suddenly occurred to him, what if she wouldn't go out with him? What if she wasn't even interested in him? He had been so caught up in his own feelings that he hadn't even given a thought to hers. She was probably offended that he hadn't had the guts to call her. The thought of her rejection made his palms sweat. Then he heard her voice saying, 'Hello?'

'Ann – how are you? This is Phillip,' he managed to say.

'Phillip?' She sounded surprised.

'I'm sorry I haven't called sooner, but I've been out of town . . . busy on a case,' he lied awkwardly.

Ann didn't know whether to laugh or cry. All of a sudden she felt a surge of anger. She had an urge to scream, *How dare you ignore me the way you have?* But instead she swallowed the hurt and answered, 'That sounds exciting.'

The deception was almost too much for Phillip to sustain, as he held the receiver in his sweaty palm. 'Oh, yes . . . very. Tell me, how have you been?'

'Oh, wonderful, just wonderful, thank you. And you?'

Lousy, plain lousy. But he said aloud, 'Okay, I guess.'

Ann suddenly sensed Phillip's loneliness and she felt ashamed of all the ill-natured thoughts she had harbored about him. She even began excusing him for not calling.

'What are you doing Saturday night?' he was asking.

He's asking me out! she realized, her pulse beating wildly. Taking a deep breath, she said, 'Nothing. I wasn't planning anything special, that is.'

'Great. Would you care to have dinner with me?'

'Oh, Phillip, that would be lovely.'

'Do you like Chinese food?'

She didn't, but it didn't matter. 'Yes, I love it.'

'Will seven be all right?'

'Yes. And, Phillip, thanks so much for calling.'

If I hadn't been such a coward, I would have done it weeks ago, he thought. But he said only, 'I'm sorry I haven't had time sooner.'

Three

The next day Ann stood behind the hosiery counter at Magnin's, scarcely aware of what she was doing. If she'd ever been happy that she only worked a half day Saturday, it was today. She was happy even though she was missing her weekly luncheon with Ruthie. Instead, she rushed home after work, washed her hair, and then sat before the mirror making dozens of tiny pincurls. She did her nails, plucked her brows, and changed into four different dresses before he arrived.

Scrutinizing her reflection in the mirror, she sighed pensively. If only she knew his favorite color. In fact, if only she knew what he liked in general, she wouldn't be so nervous. Tonight was so important. She had to be *perfect*. Who should she pretend to be?

The forty-nine-year-old Ann, sitting in her lonely living room, laughed bitterly. Oh, the naiveté of her generation. Why hadn't it occurred to her to just be herself? But how could she have, when she'd had no idea in all the world who Ann Pollock was? Besides, to have 'been herself' would have been drab and dull.

She remembered running downstairs the second the doorbell rang, grateful her father and stepmother were out. At least there would be no awkward introductions. When he stepped into the hallway, she saw again how handsome he was and was overcome with an un-expected rush of desire.

Suddenly she had difficulty breathing evenly. She could scarcely meet his eyes for fear that he would see in them a reflection of her fantasies. She would just die if Phillip knew how she had longed for him to hold her.

Praying for composure, she said softly, 'How are you, Phillip?'

'Fine, Ann. You look lovely.'

'Thank you. Would you wait a moment while I get my coat?'

'Sure.' He watched as she went to the closet.

God, he'd been crazy to think that he could ever cut her out of his life.

His feeling for her increased as he sat in the dimly lit dining room of Chang Lee's Imperial Palace. She looked enchanting with the dark ringlets framing her delicate face.

'Good evening, sir,' said the waiter in halting English. 'You like order?'

'What do you feel like having, Ann?' Phillip asked.

'Gosh, I don't know anything about Chinese food except chow mein. Why don't you order?'

He looked at her apprehensively. 'I thought you said you loved it.'

'Oh, I do! That is – well . . . it all sounds so good. I'll let you order for us.'

She didn't like it. He could tell. *Damn it, I shouldn't have brought her here*, he thought, but it was the only decent place he could really afford. Now she was just trying to be nice. She was always *so* sweet, *so* agreeable. Those were the traits that had attracted him in the first

19

place. Beyond that, Ann was so feminine; she made him feel strong and masculine, when for such a long time he had felt weak and powerless. He needed someone like Ann to look up to him, depend on him.

The waiter brought Phillip out of his reverie. 'I come back when you decide.'

'Oh . . . oh, yes,' Phillip answered rather blankly. He looked at Ann. 'Have you looked at the menu?'

She answered seriously, as though it were the greatest decision in the world. 'Yes . . . well . . . Phillip, I really don't know. What do you suggest?'

'You won't laugh if I tell you this, will you?'

'Of course not, Phillip.'

'Well, I don't know anything about Chinese food except chow mein, either.'

They looked at one another for a long moment, then broke into gales of laughter. For the moment the tension was broken.

When Ann saw the waiter placing the plate of pork chow mein in front of her, she felt a little bit queasy. True, she hadn't been reared kosher, but – just the thought of it!

'I think this is awfully good. Don't you, Ann?' asked Phillip, adding a little more soy sauce to the steamed rice.

'Oh . . . just wonderful, Phillip. Delicious.'

'Do you mean that?'

'Oh, yes – absolutely!'

As the meal progressed, the tension between them returned. *What do we talk about now?* Ann wondered. They couldn't keep on talking about the food.

Finally she asked, 'Have you seen Ruthie and Kenny since their wedding?' She already knew the answer, of course, since she'd asked Ruthie any number of times.

'No, I haven't. I've been busy. How about you?'

'Oh, I have lunch with Ruthie every Saturday.'

Stirring her chow mein with her fork, she took a dainty bite. 'It was a beautiful wedding, wasn't it?'

'Yes, it really was.'

Although this seemed a perfect opening, Phillip couldn't muster the courage to say all the things he had been thinking. Lying in bed fantasizing a conversation was not quite the same as sitting across a table from the actual girl, a girl who would probably think you were out of your mind for asking her to marry you on the first date.

How could he explain that he felt as though he'd known her all his life? How could he tell her that she'd been constantly in his thoughts since he'd last seen her? He had no idea whether or not she even liked him. And if she did accept his proposal, would he be able to support her and his parents as well? No, he didn't have the right to ask Ann to share the burdens of his life. He still had his parents to take care of. The more he thought about it, the more guilty he felt. He simply couldn't ask her tonight.

Suddenly he looked up at Ann. She looked so beautiful in the soft light. Why the hell was he analyzing all this? Love was a spontaneous thing – it made its own luck.

While all this was running through Phillip's head, Ann was having a few daydreams of her own. As the waiter set down fortune cookies and a fresh pot of tea, she hummed 'Tea for Two' under her breath and thought of pouring coffee every morning for Phillip before he went to the office.

Ann broke open a fortune cookie, took out the slip of paper, and held her breath as she read the prophecy. *Oh, my God*, she thought. It was unbelievable, but there it was in print: 'A tall, dark, handsome stranger will spirit you off to paradise.'

Ann glanced across the table, and in that magical moment, their eyes met. It was just like in the movies! All the problems which had seemed insurmountable to Phillip a few minutes ago seemed to vanish. His emotions overwhelmed him.

'Ann,' he blurted, 'I've tried very hard to fight it, but you mean more to me than anything else in the world. I

21

love you . . . I know I don't have any right, but . . .'

He reached across the table and took her hand. 'Of course, I have no way of knowing how you feel about me.'

Ann was completely bewildered. Although he had just said the words she'd dreamed of hearing, instead of being deliriously happy, she felt a strange resentment. Why had he failed to call her all these weeks? Why had he made her suffer so? Afraid of what she might say, she pulled her hand away from his and began toying absently with the crumbs on the table.

Phillip's heart sank as he looked at her expression. Obviously she did not share his feelings.

But when Ann finally looked up, she said, 'I love you. I have from the very beginning.'

'Have you really?' Phillip stammered, happy beyond his wildest dreams.

'Yes.'

'I never would have known it tonight,' he said naively.

'Well, Phillip, you didn't even call me for almost two months! Why did it take so long?'

'I thought it would be best, Ann, if I stayed out of your life.'

'*Best?* I don't understand. I thought that falling in love was a very natural thing. Why are we complicating this?'

'That's the way it should be. But I have a lot of problems, Ann . . . problems with myself that I had to come to terms with.'

'And have you?'

'No,' Phillip said sadly. 'No, I haven't.'

'Now that we know we love each other, can't you share them with me?'

He sighed. 'You see, darling, I don't have anything to offer you. And I don't think it's right to ask you to struggle with me. Being poor can make life very difficult.'

'Just knowing you love me is – everything,' Ann whispered.

Once again he reached across the table and took her hand. 'I'd give anything in the world, Ann, to be able to marry you now. But I have an obligation to my parents. And my salary is so small, I wouldn't be able to maintain two households.'

'But, Phillip, when two people love each other, it doesn't matter if they have to struggle. I've been poor all my life; it won't matter to me if we don't have anything. We'll have each other.'

Looking at her, he realized that there was a great difference in their approach to life. Ann's poverty seemed to be the source of her strength, while his early wealth seemed to have sapped his innate drive and energy. Maybe with Ann as an inspiration he could make something of his life. Maybe he could – at last – live up to his great-grandfather's image.

'Darling,' he said more forcefully, 'we're going to have to wait. I'm sorry. But in a year or so I'll be more valuable to the firm and should receive a good raise. Would you be willing to go steady with me until then?'

A year was an eternity to Ann. She wanted to get married now! But she swallowed the hard lump in her throat. Phillip was worth waiting for.

'Yes,' she said tremulously. 'I'll wait.'

Forgetting that he was in a small, crowded restaurant, Phillip got up, pulled her from her chair and took her in his arms. Softly, he whispered, 'You've made me so happy, Ann.'

'I hope I always will.'

After Phillip left her that night, Ann stood in the front hall, thrilling to the memory of his kisses. His lips against hers had been so tender as he murmured, 'You're so beautiful, Ann. I love you so much. How did I get so lucky?'

The next morning, Ann sat up in bed with an overwhelming feeling of dread. It should have been the happiest day of her life, but instead she had to brave telling her father and stepmother. She was fairly sure her father would understand, but Stella had resented her since she was a little girl and would surely do her best to take the joy out of her happy news. Sighing,

Ann put on her robe and went downstairs.

Ben looked across the breakfast table at his daughter. Ann looked more like her mother every year, and the reminder had become increasingly painful as Ann had grown to young womanhood. He could never forgive himself for the fact that Ann had suffered so because of his marriage to Stella. At the time he believed that he was securing a mother for his child as well as a wife, but it hadn't worked out that way. Stella had been jealous of Ann from the start, and Ben often found himself siding against Ann in order to keep the peace. He hated himself for his weakness; but then, Stella was a very different woman from Ann's mother – strong and determined. It was easier to give in to her wishes than to create more dissension by asserting himself.

When he had met Stella, she had been recently widowed, and at the beginning of their relationship, Stella had appeared to be genuinely fond of Ann. He was shocked by her reaction shortly after they married when he suggested Ann call her stepmother 'Mommy.'

'How dare you suggest the child call me that. I'm not her mother – I'm your wife.'

Ann stood at the top of the stairs, listening to the loud voices below. She had been sent to bed earlier, but had been roused by the sounds of the argument; she had never heard voices raised in anger at home and it frightened her. Now, quickly, she ran back to her room and locked her door. She felt terribly guilty that she had been the cause of a fight between her daddy and his new wife. She must have been a very bad girl for Stella not to want to be her mother.

Stella had become neither Ann's mother nor even her friend. And when a year after his marriage Ben had a massive coronary, he found he was no longer in a position to modify Stella's behavior. After his illness he was unable to continue running his cleaning business, and without him it threatened to go under. Were it not for Stella, he would have lost it. But she had lent him the money necessary to stay afloat. At least he had thought it was a loan. As it turned out, she owned the plant and she owned him.

Ben was brought out of his reverie by the shrill sound of Stella's voice asking, 'What time did you get home last night?'

Nervously, Ann answered, 'Gee . . . I don't know . . . I guess about eleven o'clock.'

'It was later than that,' Stella corrected her quickly.

Ann found herself apologizing. 'You're probably right. I suppose I didn't look at the time.'

'Doesn't it ever occur to you that someone might be concerned when you're late? But of course this is nothing new. You're never on time, and you're never considerate.'

Ann's nerves were already frayed, and she wanted to scream out, *Don't treat me like a child! I'm twenty-one years old.*

But noticing the look of pain on her father's face, she once again tried to keep the peace. 'I'm sorry. I'll try to be more considerate.'

Stella nodded. 'Who did you go out with?'

'His name is Phillip Coulter.'

Stella thought her heart had stopped beating for a moment. Her fists clenched and the muscles in her neck became taut. *Coulter!* That name had been her nemesis, and life was conspiring against her once again, threatening her with the past. Almost fearfully she repeated the name to herself: Coulter.

But maybe she was just conjuring up ghosts. Even though Coulter wasn't a common name, maybe Ann's young man wasn't related to the family she hated, the family that had made her the bitter, cruel woman she was today.

'What kind of a name is Coulter?' she asked in a calm voice.

'What do you mean?'

'I mean, is it Irish?'

'No, it's Jewish.'

'Jewish?' Stella said. 'How do you know?'

25

In spite of herself, Ann laughed mirthlessly. 'I just know.'

'But Coulter is not a Jewish name.'

'Maybe not, but he comes from a distinguished Jewish family.'

'Oh? And what does this distinguished Jewish family do for a living?'

'Phillip is an attorney and his family used to own a chain of men's shops.'

Stella almost fainted. It *was* the family! Of all the men in the world, Ann had to pick Eva Coulter's son. 'Used to?' Stella said in a cold voice.

'Yes, they lost them during the Depression. Ruthie told me about it.'

Ann saw that Stella's face was almost viciously contorted. She couldn't understand. On the verge of tears, she burst out, 'Why are you doing this to me?'

'Doing *what*?'

'Interrogating me like this!'

Ben popped a nitroglycerine under his tongue. When Stella was hellbent on one of her tirades it did no good to protest. So he bit his lip and silently cursed his weakness. He wanted to clap his hands over his ears to block out the sound of her harsh voice saying, 'You see what I mean, Ben? This is what I've put up with all these years. You always accuse me of not being motherly towards Ann, and here I show a decent motherly concern over who Ann goes out with, and she resents me.'

'I don't resent your concern, Stella,' Ann said softly. 'It's the way you question me. You make me feel as though I've done something wrong.'

Stella enjoyed seeing Ann squirm. 'Well, how did you meet this young man?' she asked.

'At Ruthie's wedding.'

'At Ruthie's wedding? Why, that was months ago! You mean to say that you've been seeing him all this time and haven't said a word? Why? Were you ashamed to bring him home?'

'No, that isn't it at all. Let me explain.'

'Explain? What is there to explain?'

Ann felt hopelessly drained. Her supreme moment was not quite the scene she had fantasized. The night before, she had pictured walking into the living room hand in hand with Phillip and breathlessly announcing: 'Stella, Daddy, we're engaged!'

Now she said nervously, her heart pounding and her hands trembling, 'Stella, we're going to be married.'

The statement caught Stella off-guard. She sat with her mouth open, in complete shock. Then, quickly, her expression changed to one of unmistakable contempt.

Ann was completely bewildered. She knew Stella resented her, but her stepmother's reactions this morning seemed unreasonable even for her. Finally Ann pleaded softly, 'Please be happy for me, Stella. Please? I haven't had much happiness.'

The room was silent. Finally, Ben seemed to find his voice. 'Ann, don't you think it was only right that you bring this young man home to meet me? I am your father, after all.'

'Please, Papa, don't be angry. I didn't know how Phillip felt about me until last night. It was the first time we'd gone out. I mean, on a real date.'

Ben was about to respond when Stella said quickly, 'You want us to believe that you went out with a boy for the first time last night and now you're engaged?'

Ann fought to hold back the tears. Finding her voice, she tried to explain why Phillip had held back. Even how he said they would have to wait for at least a year before getting married. 'I guess it sounds a little unconventional,' she admitted, 'but . . . there really aren't any rules for people in love.'

'You think it sounds unconventional?' said Stella. 'I think that he's playing some kind of game.'

'That's enough, Stella!' Ben uncharacteristically interrupted his wife, making her fury even greater.

'What's wrong with you, Ben?' Stella shrilled. She knew that without knowledge of her previous relationship with the Coulters, she must appear entirely unreasonable, but she couldn't stop herself. Her gaze shifted to Ann. 'You expect us to give you our blessing? We haven't even met him. He hasn't even given you a ring, has he?' Without waiting for an answer she attacked again. 'Why won't he marry you now?'

'I just told you, Stella. He simply can't get married right now.'

'I don't care. It's just not natural when people are in love. What's he going to do in the next year, become a millionaire? Let me tell you something, Ann. If you do anything wrong, you'll never be allowed back into this house! Do you hear what I'm saying?' Stella was all but screaming.

'I'm sorry you feel you have to say that to me, Stella. But I'm not going to sit here and take this kind of abuse from you!' Tears streaming down her cheeks, Ann pushed back her chair and fled the room.

Ben sat shaking his head in despair. Stella was behaving like a madwoman, but as his angina increased he knew he didn't dare fight back. It would kill him.

'See what I've been putting up with all these years?' Stella was shouting.

Ben wanted to scream, *You should be overjoyed. You'll have the chance to get rid of her*. But instead he said gently, 'Ann's my daughter, not yours, Stella. And I'm not all that upset. Why are you?'

'Because I've tried to be a mother to her and she didn't even have the decency to tell us that she was seeing this boy.'

'But she explained that he hadn't called her for two months.'

'And you believed her? Why does this Don Juan insist on postponing marriage? For all you know, he's just using Ann.'

'What do you mean by that?' he asked with difficulty.

'That she could get pregnant.'

'What a vile thing to say! I haven't met Phillip, but I'm sure he's a fine boy.'

'A fine boy? Look, you can close your eyes to the

28

truth, but I won't. You don't see anything. How long can two young people be engaged without sleeping together?'

'Ann is *my* daughter and I trust her.'

'Well, that's wonderful,' Stella said bitingly. 'The truth is that I know more about *your* daughter than you do. She'd do anything to get away from this house. If she got pregnant, he'd have to marry her. Right, Ben?'

If Stella had struck him between the eyes, he could not have been more stunned. Without a word, Ben got up from the table and went up to see Ann. He could no longer force himself into believing that he had married Stella to provide a mother for Ann. He should have sensed the coldness under the amiable surface. He could not forgive his selfish weakness, not this morning.

Sighing, he knocked softly on Ann's door. When there was no answer, he turned the doorknob and entered. Ann was lying on her bed, sobbing. He sat down on the edge of the bed and gathered her to him, rocking her gently back and forth.

Through the tears, Ann asked, 'Papa, why does Stella hate me so much?'

Ben swallowed. 'It's not you, sweetheart. She hates herself . . . the world.'

'But it's so unreasonable. I just don't understand what it is I do that upsets her so much.'

'Ann, please don't allow Stella to spoil your happiness. This should be the happiest time of your life.'

'Papa . . .' Ann murmured brokenly. 'Papa, I'm sorry I didn't bring Phillip home, but there wasn't time. I didn't even think he liked me.'

'That's all right, sweetheart.'

'But, Papa, what am I going to do now? How can I ask him to meet my family with Stella acting like this? I can't bring him into this house, I just can't!' Ann started sobbing again.

'We'll have to figure something out, honey. But, Ann, I want you to know that I'm overjoyed for you. I don't know if I can explain to you how grateful I am that God has spared me to see you find happiness.'

'Thank you, Papa. I want so much for you to be friends with Phillip. He's the most wonderful person – I know you'll love him.'

'Of course I will. But the most important thing is that *you* love him – and that he loves you.'

'But I want you to meet him. Maybe we could all go out for lunch? That way Stella wouldn't have to know about it.'

Four

Downstairs Stella sat at the kitchen table, marshaling her forces. Life hadn't beaten her. If she could create dissension between Ann and Phillip Coulter, she would do so.

Yet, in spite of herself, she was vulnerable. The ghosts of her past still lay ready to destroy her. Stella vividly remembered herself at Ann's age. The resemblance between them was almost frightening. But the parallels in their lives that should have made Stella more compassionate did not. She was so immersed in her self-pity that it left no room for love.

Stella's mother, like Ann's, had died when she was six. But her father, unlike Ann's, had been unwilling to shoulder the responsibility of taking care of a child. He had eventually placed her in an orphanage in Seattle, where she had remained until she was eighteen. She had then found a job in a small dress shop where she had saved enough money to pursue her dream of moving to San Francisco.

When Stella stood in front of the Ferry Building and looked up Market Street, she thought, for the first time in her life, that the gods had not perhaps completely abandoned her. After settling herself into a dark, narrow room at the YWCA, she managed to get a job as an alterations lady at I. Magnin's, which allowed her to come into contact with the most elegantly dressed ladies in San Francisco. Stella had a gift: she was a brilliant seamstress. Patrons began to specially request her services.

Sitting at Ben's kitchen table, Stella remembered kneeling on the floor of Eva Coulter's bedroom, making the final adjustments to the hem of her evening gown. Perhaps it was destiny. If Mrs. Coulter had been satisfied with the original fit of her lovely gown, she would never have summoned Stella to the Coulter mansion in Sea Cliff. But Stella was there and Mrs. Coulter was a gracious patron. She not only gave Stella a sizable gratuity, she also was generous with her praise.

'You're an absolute genius, Stella. An hour ago I would have sworn that this dress would never go to the opera tonight, but you've done a splendid job.'

Glowing from the kind words, Stella was just preparing to leave when the door to the bedroom was flung open, and in strolled the most handsome man Stella had ever seen. She was transfixed by the lean, elegant figure in impeccable white flannels.

Without turning, Eva greeted her brother. 'The prodigal returns. I haven't heard from you in a week. Now hurry, dear boy, and change for the opera.'

Ignoring her reprimand, he pecked her on the cheek. 'You could say that you're glad to see me.'

Narrowing her eyes in feigned disapproval, she said, 'I'm not.'

He laughed. 'You look divine as usual, dear sister. As if you'd been poured into that gown.'

'Thank you.' Pointing to Stella, she added, 'The one responsible is this genius . . . Stella – this is my brother, Roger Haas.'

Until that moment, he hadn't noticed Stella at all. Suddenly he realized she was quite lovely, with dark hair framing her oval face and eyes the color of dark amber. Were she dressed in Eva's elegant gown, she would look equally lovely.

As Roger looked at her and smiled, Stella felt a

31

melting sensation. 'Where have they been keeping you stashed away?' he asked.

'In the back room at I. Magnin's,' Stella answered, then regretted her comment immediately; it was far too bold.

Her misgivings were well-founded. Eva looked up sharply and saw the two figures behind her reflected in her mirror. At the sight of Roger's expression, she said quickly, 'Don't dally, dear boy. I think it's time for you to dress.'

Nevertheless, one afternoon the next week as Stella walked out through the employees' service door, she found Roger Haas waiting out on the curb. He was even more handsome than she remembered.

'I just happened to be passing,' he said, 'and thought that maybe if you weren't busy for dinner this evening, I might have the pleasure of taking you out.'

She had no idea what she said, but it must have been yes, because a short time later she found herself sitting across the table from him in the dimly lit dining room of the Palace Court. It was so elegant, and Roger was so attentive, that Stella was swept off her feet. She was entirely ready to believe that he was smitten with her.

Later that evening Stella never stopped to wonder whether it was naive to allow herself to be seduced by Roger. She only knew that he thrilled and excited her more than she had ever dreamed possible. And she had every reason to suspect that Roger was in love with her. Just a few days later he declared, 'I'm mad about you, Stella. Come live with me.'

But however persuasively Roger argued, Stella couldn't bring herself to live with him publicly unless they were married. In spite of the loosening of morals that followed the first world war, Stella was basically conventional. Finally they reached a compromise: Roger found her a tiny apartment near the beach and she became his mistress. He stayed with her almost every night until the small hours of the morning, but always left before dawn.

At first it was sheer ecstasy. Months passed and everything was wonderful. Then one evening Stella said, 'Roger, there's something we have to talk about.'

'What's that, Stella, my love?'

'Well' – she smiled up at him – 'I think that the time has come for us to get married.'

He disengaged himself from her embrace, got out of bed, and slipped into his robe. 'What brought this on?' he asked.

'Roger, I just can't go on this way.'

'Oh? I thought you were happy.'

'I *am* happy when we're together, but I'm devastated whenever you leave. I love you, Roger.'

'And I love you, too, Stella. In fact, I adore you.'

'Then prove it.'

Roger poured himself a drink from the bottle of brandy on the bedside table. Why had he been foolish enough to assume that Stella would be content to go on like this indefinitely? He took a sip. 'Darling, this isn't like you at all.'

'How would you know what's like me or not?' Stella asked bitterly.

'Well, my dear, we've gotten to know each other rather well these last six months.'

'Well, then – how much longer do we have to know each other before we get married?'

'Stella, my love, I never promised you anything like that.'

'Maybe not,' Stella cried, 'but things have changed!' She had hoped that it would be unnecessary to force his hand. Roger had been so wonderful, so generous and considerate. But it seemed she would have to tell him her secret. Painfully, she blurted out, 'Roger, I'm pregnant.'

Dear God, Roger thought, *how could I have been so stupid as to fall in love with this girl?* Personally, he didn't give a damn that she had no background, no education. To him, she was as elegant and refined as any of the society girls Eva paraded before him. As lovely as Peggy

Morgenthau, to whom Eva was currently urging him to propose. But he knew Eva would have a fit if he suggested marrying Stella, and he also knew he did not have the guts to defy his sister. She had been a mother to him. She was the one who had loved him and reared him.

When he finally recovered his composure, he said gently, 'I'm sorry, Stella . . . truly. But, darling, I just cannot marry you.'

'Can't? Or won't?' she cried out. 'For God's sake, Roger! I'm pregnant, can't you understand that? This is your child!'

'I know,' he said quietly.

'Then marry me for the baby's sake.'

Roger looked at her, not saying a word.

On the verge of hysteria, she wept, 'I love you, Roger. And you said you loved me. You gave me every reason to believe it!'

'Stella, dearest, I do love you. I don't want to be cruel. But we come from different worlds. I have obligations . . .' His voice trailed off.

Stella began to sob uncontrollably. Roger put his arms around her and murmured soothingly, 'Please don't cry. I can't bear to see you cry, darling.'

Clinging to him, she cried, 'Then marry me – please marry me. I'm frightened. Please marry me.'

After a long pause, Roger seemed to find his courage and said, 'Yes, Stella. I will.'

When he left her he had every intention of doing the honorable thing. After all, it was his child. He couldn't ignore that responsibility. But the moment he faced Eva, he knew he would never be able to stand up to her.

Pacing back and forth, she shouted, 'How could you have gotten yourself into this situation? I must tell you, Roger, if you marry this girl I'll cut you off without a dime. Remember – everything Mama and Papa left is now Simon's and mine. And in due course it should come to you and Phillip.'

'Eva, I never thought you could be so ruthless. We're talking about my child.'

'I'm not being ruthless, Roger. I just won't let you ruin your life. I promised Papa I would look after you, and I intend to keep my promise.'

Roger poured himself a brandy. 'It's my child, Eva. I want to take care of it.'

Eva drew a deep breath. She knew she had to be strong enough for both of them. 'You may marry this girl if you wish, Roger, but you cannot have it both ways. You will not get one cent. I know that Mama and Papa would have wanted it that way.'

Roger looked at his sister, now standing silhouetted against the onyx fireplace. 'That child is mine, you know. But you win. You see,' he said sadly, 'I'm not strong enough to fight you, Eva. I've never been poor, and the prospect frightens me. I've never trained to do anything but play polo, and that hardly qualifies me to take care of a family.'

Once Roger had left the room, Eva sighed deeply and poured herself a stiff drink. She felt no sense of triumph. She knew what he had said was true. He was not equipped to make a living without her. He hadn't been trained for anything, and he hated Simon's business. Well, she'd make it up to him. And he would find another woman, and forget this Stella. Perhaps she could send him to the Riviera.

When Roger went back to see Stella, he felt like a cad. He was bartering her life for his, but he felt helpless to do otherwise.

'Darling, I will support you for the rest of your life. But much as I would like to, dear, I just cannot marry you.'

Quite composed, she answered, 'But you knew that from the very first night we slept together, didn't you?'

'Frankly, at first I was just overwhelmed by your beauty. But I would marry you now if I could.'

'So . . . what's stopping you?'

'Fear, Stella.'

'Fear? Of what?'

'Poverty. We'd have nothing to live on if we got married. How long do you think you'd love me then?'

'I don't understand. What's going to happen to your money?'

'If I marry you, my sister Eva says that she will cut off my trust.'

'Your sister? What about *your* money?'

'My parents left everything to Eva. While she is alive, she has control over every penny. As long as I don't marry you, I can give you and the child a generous allowance.'

'And the money is more important than the baby and I?'

'Stella, darling, if I don't marry you, I can take care of you *and* the child. You can have everything you want.'

'You're a bastard. A weak, spineless bastard!' Stella cried. 'Get out – get out!'

When Stella heard the door close behind him, she slumped to the floor, weeping uncontrollably. How could she have allowed herself to fall in love? Everyone she had ever loved had left her: first her mother, then her father, now her lover. She would never love anyone again . . . *never*.

The next week she lay in bed, bleeding profusely from the abortion. She'd gone through the ordeal alone. There was no one to help her, she felt, least of all God.

As soon as she recovered sufficiently, she took a room at the YWCA. Though she had no money of her own, she refused to take any from Roger. She floated from one demeaning job to another; for obvious reasons she could not go back to I. Magnin's.

As the months passed, Stella found that she preferred being alone. Only on occasion would she treat herself to dinner at some small, out-of-the-way restaurant, or, once in a while, she would take a streetcar out to Golden Gate Park and listen to the free concerts.

It was on one of those rare occasions that she found herself sitting next to a middle-aged man who seemed

36

much more enthralled by the music than she. They didn't speak, but when Stella rose to leave fate intervened. She dropped her purse, which the man quickly returned, using it as an excuse to start up a conversation. It seemed harmless enough, though Stella realized that he was escorting her from the park.

As she stood at the curb waiting for the streetcar, he said, 'You are such a delightful young woman. I wonder if I might buy you dinner?'

That simple request had a sobering effect on Stella. For a brief moment she remembered the first night Roger had waited for her after work. Then, in spite of herself, Stella accepted the invitation. The evening was neither pleasant nor unpleasant. Still, she found herself accepting another date, and another . . .

Six months later, they were married. Abe Gottlieb was a widower of sixty, with two grown sons and apparently modest means, which mattered little to her. He provided a roof over her head, and food in her stomach; and she didn't need to worry about satisfying his passions. He had become so accustomed to his first wife's constant headaches that he felt that part of his life was over.

Abe was kind, and at that point in Stella's life she could ask for nothing more. But as time passed she began to want more out of life than safety, and it was with relief more than sorrow that Stella woke one morning to find that Abe had passed away in his sleep. At thirty, Stella became a widow.

They had lived so frugally that she was in a state of shock after the will was read. Her reward for her years of boredom amounted to $25,000. Since Abe had kept a tight rein on the purse strings, she assumed that he had very little, and for years she had been too apathetic to long for material things. At first she was overwhelmed with joy. Then she learned that he had left over $200,000 to his sons, and the fact that she was forced to go back to work filled her with resentment. The Depression still made jobs scarce, and she was terrified that Abe's money would soon be gone and she would be powerless. There was only one way to protect that precious $25,000, she decided. She had to get married again.

When Stella met Ben, she knew that he was perfect for her. Here was a man who could be easily dominated. His business was in trouble, but she was soon convinced that it was less the fault of the economy than his own mismanagement. She was certain that in her hands the business would again thrive. Her confidence was not conceit. Life had equipped her with the toughness it took to survive.

Ben himself was unaware that he was like a lamb being led to the slaughter. At first, Stella had considered simply buying him out. But then she decided that in a man's world, a woman with the title of 'Mrs.' was in a better position to run a business, and after careful thought, she agreed to marry him.

For all of Stella's resolve never to allow herself the luxury of caring for anyone else, she found it difficult not to respond to Ben's gentle affection. In spite of herself, she fell in love.

During their courtship, Ben made her feel more important than his child. But soon after their wedding, she realized that his daughter came first in his heart. It was pretty little Ann who was her father's darling. Once again, Stella felt that she had been duped. She had allowed Ben to unleash feelings that had been frozen for over ten years, only to find that someone other than she held the key to his heart. Soon her tentative venture into love withered and Stella decided she was being used. She took care of Ben's house, Ben's child, Ben's business! And no one wanted to take care of her. Why should she try to make life easy for the adorable Ann?

And now, Ann had brought Phillip Coulter back into her life. Roger's nephew! Even after all these years, it was still so painful. Strangely, time had softened her feelings of anger at Roger and intensified those against Eva Coulter. It was Eva who had forced the weakling Roger to abandon their baby, and all because she thought that

38

Stella wasn't good enough for her precious brother.

Without volition, tears welled up in her eyes as she thought for the first time about the tragic way Roger's life had ended. Stella had pieced together what had happened through the lurid newspaper accounts.

Roger's voyage to Europe had not been a vacation, but an exile. He had joined that group of rich expatriates who flitted from Paris to the Riviera in a never-ending search for new amusement. He had gained notoriety as an occasional house guest of Zelda and F. Scott Fitzgerald, and had been visiting them in Antibes when his Bugatti had careened off the Corniche after a wild night of drinking with the wife of a Spanish diplomat. Whether or not they were having an affair Stella never could find out, but she had no pity for Eva Coulter when she saw her picture in the paper at the funeral, swathed in black, blotting her tears with a handkerchief. Eva was the one who had sent Roger into oblivion.

It had taken Roger's death to soften her anger, but it left her with some deep regrets. The greatest of which was that she had lacked the courage to have his baby and had instead been forced to raise another man's child. The thought of Ann brought her abruptly back to the present. She knew that if she were to come face to face with the Coulters, the fragile new life she had built would shatter. Eva would not hesitate to tell Ben the truth about the affair with Roger, and Stella would be left alone without pride or dignity. She knew she had no choice but to destroy Ann's love affair with Phillip Coulter. Stella would not leave herself open to attack for Ann or Ben or anyone else.

She knew her actions would appear totally unreasonable, but she intended that Phillip Coulter would never set foot in her house. If she got lucky, maybe the strain would break up their relationship. If not – well, she certainly would not attend the wedding.

Ironically, when Stella first met Ann she had been prepared to love her. It was Ben's obvious favoritism that had made her jealous of the little girl. Even today, if

Ann had brought home almost any other man, Stella would have been inwardly delighted. In fact, she would have done everything possible to encourage a relationship that might lead to marriage. For if Ann married and moved out, then, for the first time in their marriage, Ben would have to turn to her. Only the cruellest of gods could have made Ann choose the son of her worst enemy.

Five

Ann did not say anything to Phillip about the situation at home. For the first week of their betrothal, she made sure that Phillip met her directly after work. When he dropped her off at the house, she made excuses as to why she couldn't invite him in – excuses which grew increasingly lame, even to her own ears. As the weekend neared, Ann was besieged by anxiety. She wanted Phillip to believe she came from a happy, loving family. She was worried that his parents would learn that Phillip had not been invited to meet her parents and even more concerned that she and Phillip would have no place to be alone over the course of their year's engagement.

Finally, at the end of the second week, Ann decided to plead with Stella directly.

Saturday morning, before leaving for work, she summoned the courage to say, 'Stella . . . do you think that you and I could talk for a few minutes? Like two sensible people?'

'Of course,' Stella said. She poured two cups of coffee, handed one to Ann, and sat down. 'Now, what is it you want to talk about?'

'Stella, I want to apologize for the other Sunday. I know that your intentions were sincere, and I do thank you for that. But – I *am* in love with Phillip and I *am* going to marry him. More than anything, I want to be able to bring him home and introduce him to you and

Papa. Would it be asking too much if I invited Phillip here, for Sunday dinner perhaps?'

Without rancor, Stella replied, 'Quite frankly, it would.'

Ann burst into tears. She had been so sure that if she pocketed her pride and begged Stella, her stepmother would concede.

'Stella! You don't mean it!' Ann sobbed. But the grimly unyielding expression told Ann that Stella *did* mean it.

'How can you treat me this way?' Ann cried. 'It's just not fair. This is my father's house, too, you know!'

'No, my dear,' Stella retorted coolly. 'This house and everything in it belongs to me.'

'But Stella, you have no reason not to have Phillip come here. He's wonderful. Really, he is.'

'The truth is, Ann, that I am utterly opposed to this – *affair*. I think it's beneath you.'

'Affair? Stella, you're making it sound like something sordid, and it's not. Phillip and I are engaged!'

'Well, it's some fine engagement, I must say! I don't see any ring on your finger. He said he didn't want to marry you for a whole year? I don't believe he's serious.'

'Phillip can't afford to buy me a ring right now, Stella. But we are engaged – we *are*!' Ann covered her face with her hands.

Stella looked away stonily. She knew how unreasonable she was being.

Finally, Ann raised a tear-stained face and said, brokenly, 'Stella, I never thought I'd say something like this to you, but you're cruel! Why are you denying me the one thing in the world I need from you?'

'You don't need anything from me, Ann – you never have. Why are we continuing to pretend? You've never liked me, and I've never liked you. You're not my child. And you have your precious papa to dote on you.'

'Why did you marry Papa anyway, Stella? You never loved him either,' Ann said, almost inaudibly.

'Let me tell you something. He and I would have been

41

a lot happier if we hadn't had you to deal with.'

Shaken beyond tears, Ann got up from the table. There was no compromise possible; she could see that now. As she left the room she said, 'You have no reason to do this to me, Stella. No reason at all.'

Upstairs in her room, Ann stood trembling uncontrollably. What could she do? Her first thought was to move out of the house. Maybe she could share an apartment with one of the girls from Magnin's. But she didn't want to hurt her father. The knowledge that his wife had driven his daughter from under his roof would surely kill him – Ben would be willing to let her go only on her wedding day.

For the first time ever, she called in sick. She sounded so distraught that they didn't question her. Then she phoned Phillip at his office, where he spent Saturday mornings doing legal research. 'I have to talk to you,' she pleaded. 'Can you get away? Please.'

'Ann, darling, you sound awful. Are you all right?'

'I really need to see you, Phillip.'

'Of course, darling. Where shall we meet?'

'How about the Tosca Café, where we were the other night?'

'I'll be waiting for you.'

The sight of her pale, drawn face as she walked to his table made him instantly apprehensive. Was Ann having second thoughts?

'What's wrong, honey? Please tell me. I love you.'

'I don't know how to tell you this, Phillip . . .' she began.

His heart skipped a beat. She was breaking it off. 'Tell me what?'

She hesitated. 'It's my stepmother. She's making my life such a hell, Phillip.'

Phillip relaxed. Thank God it wasn't some problem about him. 'In what way, darling?'

'I don't know how to say this, but for some inexplicable reason she's opposed to our engagement. In fact, she doesn't want me to see you at all.'

'Why? She doesn't even know me,' he said, surprised.

'That's just the point. I can't even argue because I don't know what's wrong.'

'Suppose I have a talk with her?'

But Ann shook her head. 'No, Phillip. It would only make things worse. There's just no way that anyone can change her mind. It's as if she were insane on the subject.'

Phillip didn't understand, but realizing how distraught Ann was, he reached for her hand across the table. 'Don't worry about it, dear. Perhaps she'll change her mind when she understands how serious we are about each other. And if she doesn't – well, I'm marrying you, not your family.'

It had been a long time since Ann had felt as secure as she did at this moment. She allowed herself to be comforted by his words and his strong hand on hers.

'My father wants to meet you very much,' she said. 'In fact, he can hardly wait. Can we all have lunch one day this week?'

'Yes, of course. Any day.'

'Oh, Phillip – I do love you so!'

Six

Eva Coulter's objections to Phillip's proposed marriage had nothing to do with the fact that Ann Pollock was too young for her son or that Ann was Stella Burke's stepdaughter – something which she did not know. Unlike Stella, she didn't raise her voice; nonetheless her opposition was just as unwavering.

'You're much too young, Phillip,' she protested.

'Too young for what?'

'To assume the responsibilities of marriage.' She sighed. 'You know, darling, that I only want to do what is best for you.'

'Really? And are you so sure what's best for me?'

43

Phillip had seen through his mother's pretenses for as long as he could remember. He knew that Eva Coulter treated anyone she loved as a personal possession, and demanded their constant adoration.

'You don't want me to get married at all, do you, Mother,' he said, trying to make her confront the real issue.

'Why, that's not true!' Eva said aggrievedly. 'One of these days, if you found a lovely girl, I would be delighted.'

'But I *have* found a lovely girl.'

Eva was shaken by his open defiance. This just wasn't like Phillip. Summoning all her patience, she replied gently, 'Perhaps . . . but I'm sure that if you think about it, dear, you'll realize how ill-timed this is.'

'And when would be the right time, Mother? When I'm fifty or so?'

'Now, dear, you must not get angry. It has nothing to do with age.'

'What does it have to do with, then – money?'

'The country still hasn't recovered from the Depression, Phillip. And marriage is a serious undertaking.'

'Look, Mother. This really has nothing to do with finance. The truth is that you're advising me to forget the whole thing and give Ann up.'

'Why, Phillip, that isn't what I'm saying at all!'

'Mother, you forget that I'm an attorney. I make my living recognizing contradictions. First you said that I was too young; then you said that it had nothing to do with age. Then it was a question of money; then it had nothing to do with money. Make up your mind, Mother. What exactly *is* the problem?'

Eva started to protest but was silenced by Phillip's look. 'I'm not asking you for your permission, Mother. I'm planning to marry Ann as soon as possible.' He waited for her to digest the fact. 'Now, I'm bringing her home for dinner on Sunday, and I'd appreciate it greatly if you would treat her graciously and with warmth.'

Phillip's tone made it plain that he would brook no

44

opposition. He wasn't in the mood for any of Eva's games. Ann had given him back something he'd thought he'd lost: the desire to succeed. She had become his inspiration, his reason for living.

By God, he was going to work his tail off in that law firm, and in a year – no, less than that – he would be able to go to them for a big raise, one that would enable him to support Ann in the style he wanted. And no one, including Eva, was going to deny him. Looking her squarely in the eye, he said, 'Well, Mother?'

Eva tried to hide her fear. She was losing her son to another woman. But something told her that now was not the moment to press the issue. Haltingly, she said, 'Of course, dear . . . please ask her. I want very much to meet Ann.'

'That's very kind of you, Mother.' And he left the room before she had a chance to withdraw the invitation.

Simon Coulter stood in the doorway and stared uneasily at his wife's tragic expression. 'Don't you think we should talk about this, Eva?'

'I don't think there's much to say. Phillip has made up his mind that he's going to marry this girl, and no matter what we say it will do no good.'

'My dear, you know that our son would never be attracted to a young woman unless she were worth while.'

'I'm not so sure of that. Girls are so forward today. This is a different time. But the main thing is that I don't believe Phillip is ready for marriage.'

'He's twenty-six – isn't it only natural that he should want a wife?'

Eva stiffened. 'You're putting me on the defensive, Simon, and I don't like it.'

Simon sighed and looked at his wife with pity. She truly believed that she was acting in Phillip's best interests. 'I love you, Eva. I always have and I always will. But I'm not blind. You *are* a bit possessive with Phillip.'

'How dare you say such a thing! I just want what is best for my child!'

Simon did not answer immediately. He sighed. It was difficult for him to take Eva to task. But she had to understand that she was making the same mistake with Phillip that she had with her brother years ago. Finally he said very gently, 'I know you do, Eva, dear – but you also wanted what was best for Roger.'

Eva started to sob. 'I think that's dreadfully cruel of you. Don't you think I've been through enough where Roger is concerned?'

Simon gathered his wife in his arms. 'Of course you have, but sometimes we have to look at past mistakes to avoid repeating them. Phillip is no longer a little boy. You can't keep him from growing up.'

'I'm not trying to do that. Honestly I'm not!'

'I know you're not doing it deliberately, dearest. But you must be honest with yourself. You really don't want to give him up, do you?'

'That's untrue! It's just that I feel he's too young.'

'Perhaps – but you'll be making a great mistake by opposing him. You and I, Eva, have lost a great deal in our lives. If we don't want to lose Phillip as well, I would suggest that we accept this girl. Eva, you've just got to learn to let go.'

Trying to hold back her tears, Eva repeated, 'I only want what is best for Phillip.' But she recognized the truth of Simon's words. Although she had wanted Phillip to marry back into the class to which he'd been born, she did not want to lose him altogether. And she could not bear the thought of forfeiting Simon's unquestioning adoration. Wiping the tears from her eyes, she said, 'There is one thing you cannot ask of me, and that is to love Ann. Since neither my permission nor my approval was asked for, I don't feel obliged to do that. However, I will not interfere, and I will respect her – as Phillip's wife.'

Simon kissed her tenderly. 'That's a very good start, dear.'

Seven

On Sunday evening the Coulters met Ann Pollock for the first time.

Eva said all the right things, but with a reserve which made Ann feel ill at ease. It was nothing she could put her finger on, but she sensed Mrs. Coulter was having difficulty being gracious.

Sitting awkwardly on the small sofa beside Phillip, Ann looked at the portrait of Eva which hung above the mantel. Mrs. Coulter had once been a grand lady. She obviously had hoped Phillip would marry into society. Ann noticed that what remained of her possessions looked incongruous in a stuffy little flat which rented for forty-five dollars a month. The Aubusson rugs were crowded in the small rooms and the furniture seemed cramped. Above a shabby mauve silk Louis XVI sofa hung another portrait, of Mrs. Coulter with Phillip at the age of five or so. A rose marble-topped table was placed in front of the sofa. On either side of the coffee table were two worn, tapestry-covered chairs.

Until today Ann hadn't comprehended the extent of the Coulters' loss. Now she understood Eva's reticence and wondered if a shopgirl from Magnin's was good enough for Phillip.

'Will you have sherry, my dear?' Simon was asking her.

'Yes, thank you,' she answered, barely above a whisper.

Phillip watched his mother, nervously aware that Ann's background would not meet with her approval. For the last two weeks he had carefully avoided all questions, saying only, 'Ann comes from a lovely family.'

Now he realized that he had made a terrible mistake. Eva was getting ready to interrogate Ann. Before he could think of a diversion, his mother was saying sweetly, 'Tell me a little about yourself, dear.'

Ann cleared her throat and smiled nervously. 'Well . . . I was born here in San Francisco—'

Eva interrupted her. 'Pollock? Strange – I'm not familiar with that name. How long has your family been in the city?'

'Both of my parents were born here.'

'I'm amazed that we've never met! You live with your father and mother?'

'My father and stepmother.'

'Oh – you have a stepmother?'

'My mother died when I was six.'

'What a pity. And your father remarried. Aren't you fortunate?'

'Oh, yes. We're very close.' Ann prayed that her voice would not betray her.

'How nice. And what does your father do?' Eva came to the crucial point.

'He's retired.'

'From what?' Eva smiled sweetly.

'He had a cleaning plant.'

'Well, that's a very necessary business. Now I think we should go in to dinner.'

Eva decided there was no point in pursuing the subject. Phillip was going to marry this girl, cleaning business and all. Even though Eva asked no further questions during the meal, Ann continued to feel tense and awkward.

It was only as the four were saying goodnight that Ann began to relax a little. Simon Coulter took her hand and said, 'My dear, you are a lovely young woman. We are delighted to welcome you into our family.'

Ann was so grateful that she had difficulty holding back the tears. 'Thank you,' she said softly. 'Thank you very much.'

Ann turned to Mrs. Coulter, who smiled coldly and echoed, 'Yes, we're so delighted . . .'

When Phillip walked Ann up to her door, she said, 'I don't think your mother really liked me.'

'Of course she did,' Phillip lied quickly, but once back home he confronted Eva.

'I was as gracious as I know how,' she protested.

'No, you weren't, Mother.'

'I really don't know what you expect of me, Phillip.'

'I expect you to treat Ann as part of the family. She's going to be my wife – and you'd damn well better get used to that idea!'

After he slammed the door and stormed up to his bedroom, Eva was left alone, in despair. Phillip had never spoken to her that way before. It had to be Ann's influence. But Simon's warning rang in her ears. If we oppose him, we'll lose him. Well, from now on, she would pretend to love Ann even if it killed her.

Eight

This should have been the happiest time in Ann's life, but it was far from that. In spite of the fact that Phillip said he understood about Stella, Ann still found the situation highly embarrassing, and Eva's silent disapproval made Ann equally uncomfortable at the Coulters'. She felt there was nowhere she and Phillip could relax.

Several times Ann approached Stella about having Phillip home, but Stella absolutely refused to discuss the matter.

'What do you have against Phillip?' Ann would cry. 'You don't even know him!'

'I'll tell you what I have against him,' Stella would sneer. 'He's weak and spineless. Or maybe he's not so much in love with you that he can't live without you. Otherwise, why won't he marry you now?' And she repeated the words so often that Ann herself began to doubt Phillip's love.

'Good God!' Stella would cry. 'If he hasn't married you after five months, he never will. That's a long time for people in love. You're a naive child. Can't you see that he's *using* you?'

The word 'using' troubled Ann, not because it was true, but because she recognized the extent of her own sexual desires – and they frightened her. Between her own frustration and Stella's badgering, Ann found herself wondering if Stella might not be right. Was Phillip really intending to marry her? Why were they waiting? He *did* have a job, after all. And how could they go on this way without eventually ending up in bed? And Ann was not prepared for that without marriage. What if she became pregnant? She could almost hear Stella's triumph.

One night when they were having dinner she almost asked him to set a date, but when she looked at him, she was suddenly terrified. He was so good looking. He could have any woman he wanted – who was Ann Pollock to demand anything? If she pressed him now, she would lose him.

Instead of speaking, Ann withdrew into herself. Phillip took her hand. 'Is something wrong, sweetheart?'

'Nothing . . . nothing at all.'

'Ann, please talk to me. What is it?'

'It's nothing, Phillip . . .'

'Of course it is . . . The problems at home – they're becoming worse, aren't they?'

Ann had a momentary desire to say, *Yes, damn you, and it's your fault!* But she couldn't say that. He had warned her from the beginning that there was no other choice but to wait.

Suddenly she could stand the tension no longer. She jumped up and ran from the restaurant.

Phillip was flabbergasted; Ann was always so composed. He realized that their situation was becoming impossible, and he was terrified that Ann had lost patience with him.

Throwing some money on the table, Phillip followed her out to the parking lot. Enfolding her in his arms, he said, 'Don't shut me out, Ann, please. You're all I have.'

'But, Phillip, I don't really have you,' Ann sobbed.

'Darling, how can you say that? I love you!'

'And I love you, Phillip – but I just don't think I'm strong enough to go on this way.'

'I know. I've expected too much of you. There's only one answer: we're going to get married now. We'll just have to live very simply at first.'

Married! It was the magic word for which Ann had prayed, but even as her heart leaped for joy she felt a pang of guilt: had she forced Phillip into this?

'Are you sure, Phillip?' She lifted her face and looked at him searchingly. 'I'll wait if you want to.'

'No, we've done enough of that. You bet I'm sure!'

And, in his eyes, what she saw was longing, and love.

Nine

All her frustration, all her anger, all her doubts disappeared as though they had never existed. Ann was intoxicated with happiness. Stella's objections ceased to matter, along with Eva's cold acceptance. Ann was going to be Mrs. Phillip Coulter.

That Sunday afternoon they walked the streets of the Marina District with the classified ads, looking for an apartment. Everything they saw was either too dilapidated or too expensive, but finally they came across a furnished apartment on Beach Street for $42.50 a month. It was a one-bedroom, three floors up, overlooking an airshaft. The small bathroom opened off the foyer, and two cabinets separated the dining room and kitchen, but the ice box was in good repair, the landlady assured them proudly.

Just for one moment, Ann noticed the worn linoleum and the chipped paint. Then she dismissed the apartment's flaws from her mind. *But the furniture is really quite pretty*, she decided. In fact, the living room was cozy and attractive, with a green velour sofa and matching chair. A lamp sat on the end table between them, and a pastoral print hung over the sofa. A heavy, ornately carved coffee table from Grand Rapids, Michigan, sat in front of it, and in the middle of the room lay an imitation Oriental rug in brilliant colors.

'Do you like it?' Phillip whispered.

'I love it! But you best of all,' she answered, wrapping her arms around his neck and kissing him. To think of actually *living* here – with Phillip! It was her vine-covered cottage. And she and Phillip were the only two people in the world.

A month later, Ann stood in front of the mirror as she and Ruthie watched the seamstress pin the hem of Ann's skirt. She had abandoned her fantasies of floating down the aisle in yards and yards of white tulle. It was enough not to have to wait any longer, and she understood they had no money to waste on dreams. She could wear the little suit over and over again when she and Phillip were married. Feeling very practical, she said, 'Oh, Ruthie, I never thought anyone could be as happy as I am! It seems as though the days can't pass fast enough!'

But it was just a week later that she woke up to the most important day of her life. At four o'clock that afternoon she would become Mrs. Phillip Coulter. As she gazed around her bedroom, a strange emotion seized her. In spite of the fact that she had prayed for the moment when she could leave Stella and all the dissensions, the place where she had been born was still home, a familiar and safe place. And in spite of her love for Phillip, she faced married life with a certain trepidation. She was glad when Ben interrupted her thoughts with a breakfast tray.

Ann felt a lump in her throat when she saw the white rosebud. Ben had been such a loving father. Since his marriage to Stella, the sentimental side of his nature had waned and the sight of the rose was bittersweet.

'Thank you, Papa!' she cried. 'You're the dearest man who ever lived. I'll never forget this morning.'

As Ben held his daughter close, he was happy that God had let him live long enough to see her married.

His only sorrow was that Stella had unreasonably refused to attend Ann's wedding.

'You can't do this!' Ben had shouted the night before. 'What's the reason for this insanity? First you didn't want Phillip here because you were afraid he wouldn't marry Ann. Now you won't come to the wedding. Stella, do you have any idea of the embarrassment you will cause Ann? You don't have to like the Coulters; all you have to do is be civil. Is that too much to ask? Can't you just do this one thing for my sake?'

Ben had taken Stella's silence for contempt, but in reality she was battling an impulse to tell Ben the truth. In the end, pride won out over affection.

'I'm sorry, Ben,' she had said. 'I'm not going. And I won't try to make you understand my reasons. You'll all get along fine without me. Make whatever excuses you want, but – after all – I'm not Ann's mother. I'm only the wicked stepmother.'

Something in her face made Ben realize that she was not doing this just to be cruel. For a moment he had wanted to press her for the truth. Then, years of passivity made him retreat and he had resolved to simply do the best he could to make Ann enjoy her special day to the fullest.

Now, as he sat on the edge of his daughter's bed, his heart filled with joy at the thought of her happiness.

'Ann, you are the best thing I've had in my life.' He turned away and cleared his throat. 'Now, drink your coffee.'

From the moment Ann got out of bed the day seemed to pass in a dream. She seemed to float up the stairs to the sanctuary, with her father at her side. She was so joyful that she was no longer upset by Stella's absence. She told Eva that Stella had been struck with the flu, and was not even disturbed by her mother-in-law's look of obvious disbelief.

Moments later, her father was walking her down the aisle to where Phillip waited with his best man, Kenny.

Ruthie smiled rather thinly as she stood to one side as

Ann approached the altar. How sad to be married with only eight people present. She had argued, 'For heaven's sake, Ann, why not get married in the rabbi's study?'

'I've dreamed about walking down the aisle to meet my husband all my life. The number of people watching doesn't matter at all. My father will be there, and for me that will fill up the whole room. And besides, my situation is a little different from yours, Ruthie. My father gave us a thousand dollars, and most of that has to be used for setting up a household. Ruthie, I loved your wedding, but no one could be happier than Phillip and I.'

Ruthie's attention was diverted as she watched Ben kiss his daughter as he left her at the *chuppa*, the traditional wedding canopy, and returned to the empty front pew opposite the Coulters.

Whatever thoughts, feelings, or misgivings anyone had in that small assembly vanished as the rabbi began to intone the marriage ceremony.

When the short ceremony ended, Phillip took Ann into his arms. 'I'm going to spend the rest of my life making you the happiest woman in the world.'

'You already have.'

Phillip was in such a joyous state of mind as he walked up the aisle with Ann that he was oblivious to his mother's tears. Later, Simon shook hands with his son, then kissed Ann on both cheeks. 'To the loveliest daughter anyone could wish for. Mrs. Phillip Coulter – welcome to our family.'

A quarter of an hour later they were all seated at the St. Francis Hotel for the wedding luncheon. It was a rather awkward affair. Kenny toasted the bride and groom, but the other guests were a little subdued. Ann was happily oblivious to anything except the fact that she and Phillip were together. Then, before she knew it, she and Phillip were standing in front of the hotel, saying goodbye to them.

The Pine Inn at Carmel, where they were spending the

honeymoon, exceeded Ann's wildest dreams. It was just like in the movies. A fire had been lit in their room and champagne was cooling in an ice bucket. Until tonight, she hadn't quite realized how very romantic Phillip could be. There had always been so little money, but tonight he refused to let expense be an object. He had thought of everything: red roses in a crystal vase, black caviar on a bed of silvery crushed ice.

Phillip put his arms around her and whispered, 'You've made me the happiest man in the world.'

'Oh, Phillip. I hope I always will.'

Gently disengaging her embrace, he warned himself to go slowly.

'How about some champagne?'

For the life of her, Ann couldn't explain why she suddenly felt rejected, but she smiled and said, 'I'd love some, darling,' hoping that the hurt did not show.

'This is to you, sweetheart,' he said, touching his glass to hers. 'I hope that our lives will always be as happy as this night.'

Ann sipped her champagne, then went into the bedroom to change into her new white chiffon peignoir. Seeing her, Phillip realized what a fool he had been not to have married her six months ago.

Ann slipped under the covers and nervously watched as Phillip switched off the bedside lamp and took her very gently into his arms. He had waited so long that he was having trouble controlling his passion. Yet, knowing this was the first time for Ann, he waited until he felt that she was ready to receive him.

But when the ultimate moment came, she found it shockingly unlike her fantasies. No one had ever fully described the act of love, certainly not Stella, and not even Ruthie, who had extolled the joys of married life without providing any intimate details.

So, after Phillip had spent himself, the best Ann could do was pretend she had enjoyed it as much as he. Resting her head on his shoulder, feeling his arms around her, she realized that the thing she loved most was the closeness and warmth of his embrace. For her, that was better than the actual passion.

Three days later, Phillip carried her over the threshold of their apartment on Beach Street. Putting her down, he said, 'I love you more every day.' Ann blinked back her tears. Marriage was everything she'd hoped.

That afternoon they went shopping, and Ann found the five-and-dime on Chestnut Street a source of treasures. Her father's wedding gift of Wedgwood china had been stored away, as had been the set of silver from the Coulters. They would be used only for company. Now, she carefully selected a set of crockery with blue forget-me-nots on a white background and picked a set of cutlery for four as well as a saucepan, a frying pan, a small blue agate roaster, and a coffeepot.

On the way home they shopped for groceries at the Rossi Market and served dinner by candlelight. That night they fell asleep in each other's arms.

The next evening was not so relaxed. Ann invited Phillip's parents to dinner, and everything that could possibly go wrong with the meal did. After the Coulters left, she could barely sleep, and the next morning, as soon as Phillip left for work, she called Ruthie.

'Oh, God,' she wailed. 'Everything went wrong. The chicken was overcooked, the carrots were hard, the potatoes were watery. And I know it will be just as bad the next time. Phillip's mother makes me feel so unsure of myself. She doesn't like me. And the funniest thing is that she doesn't say anything that I can put my finger on.'

'Well, don't worry about it too much,' Ruthie said when Ann paused for breath. 'She'll get over it. After all, you stole her little boy.'

'Yes, I suppose – but it doesn't make it any easier, and she wants us to spend every Sunday with them. I've told Phillip that I think we should, but he told me no, Sunday is our day. So I guess she'll have something else to hold against me.'

'Just don't let it interfere with your relationship with Phillip.'

'I won't,' said Ann, but when she hung up she felt much less confident.

Still, her days soon fell into a pleasant pattern. Phillip might be bored by his job, where he was progressing less rapidly than he had hoped, but if his days were dull, Ann's were not. She had quit her job at Magnin's and busied herself keeping their tiny apartment spotless, finding inexpensive decorations, and searching out recipes. Sometimes she would spend hours in the kitchen, and the results would be disastrous: the soufflé fell, the meat loaf would be rock hard; and many times she would have to feed them to Mrs. DiVincenzo's dog and run up to Lucca's Delicatessen for a last-minute replacement. But when it turned out well, she could hardly wait for Phillip to come home from the office. Everything seemed to take on new meaning, even such chores as washing and ironing.

She was particularly happy the night they celebrated their first month's anniversary. She fell asleep certain there were no clouds on the horizon.

At 4:00 A.M. the phone rang and she heard Phillip mutter a sleepy 'hello' into the receiver.

He listened briefly and then sat staring at the receiver. 'What's wrong?' Ann asked, turning on the light.

He hung up and took Ann in his arms. Holding her very tight, he said, 'Sweetheart, there's no easy way to tell you this, but that was Stella. Your father died about an hour ago.'

Ann was too stunned to react, but when the shock wore off, she wept uncontrollably. 'There must be a mistake! There must be! He can't be gone. I just spoke to him today!'

All Phillip could do was to hold her gently until she ran out of tears.

Ten

The next morning, as Stella sat watching her step-daughter and her stepdaughter's husband as they planned the funeral, she looked at Phillip for the first time. He was the spitting image of Roger. Ironically, she realized she might as well have gone to the wedding, as there would be no way to keep the Coulters from the funeral. As usual the last laugh was on her.

'How did it happen?' Ann asked, bringing her stepmother back to the present.

'Well, as you know, your father had a bad heart.' Watching Ann's grief, she realized that all the anger she'd felt toward the girl in the past was spent. Suddenly the years of hatred seemed meaningless. She was almost glad Ann had found someone with whom to share her life. When Ann asked if her stepmother and Ben had been fighting, Stella didn't react with her usual temper.

'No – not that things were ever very good between us. There seemed to be very little to fight about since you left.'

Ann merely nodded.

'Well, to answer your question, your father went to bed about nine o'clock, and at eleven I was ready to go to my room when I realized that his light was still on. I went in and turned it off. He seemed to be sleeping peacefully.

Stella sighed. 'About an hour later, I heard a thud and got out of bed. Your father was lying on the bathroom floor.'

Ann began to cry quietly. 'Was he dead?'

'I felt for his pulse, but there was nothing. I called an ambulance, but by the time they got here, there was nothing they could do. He was gone.'

A myriad of thoughts ran through Ann's head. She wanted to scream, *He's dead because of you, not because of his heart!* But what would that accomplish? It wouldn't bring her father back to life.

Slowly, Ann got up. It had taken Ben's death for Stella to allow Phillip into the house, but now her argument with her stepmother no longer seemed important to her either.

At the door, Stella looked at Ann for a long moment. 'I'm sorry, Ann . . . truly I am.'

The sad group that gathered at the grave site was almost identical to the guests at Ann's wedding, only this time Stella was present and Ben no longer the happy father of the bride, but the cold focus of the ceremony. Stella watched Phillip put an arm around Ann as if to shelter her from the pain. Her eyes drifted past her stepdaughter to Eva Coulter. All Stella's fears about meeting the woman had evaporated like mist the moment they had met on the chapel steps. While Stella would have recognized Roger's sister anywhere, Eva had no idea who Stella was. Despite financial reverses, Eva was as regal and lovely as she had been twenty years earlier. But time had not been as kind to Stella. Her continued bitterness had narrowed her eyes and tightened her lips in a hard expression that bore little resemblance to the girl who had loved Roger. Anyway, Stella thought sorrowfully, who remembered a little chit one had only met doing alterations? What a waste. Roger's life. Hers. Her futile jealousy of Ann.

She looked up as the rabbi finished chanting Kaddish, and Ann pulled up a handful of earth to toss into the grave. It was too late to tell her she regretted her cruelty during Ann's engagement, but she touched her hand, hoping her stepdaughter would someday understand.

As she left the cemetery her eye caught Eva's. For a second it seemed to Stella that there was recognition in that fleeting glance, but then Mrs. Coulter got into her car without speaking. Stella silently stepped into the next limousine and Ben was left to rest in peace at last.

Eleven

Ann spent the next month in quiet despair. She clung to Phillip silently, unable to share her grief. She needed his closeness, but inexplicably she was unable to let him make love to her. Somehow she felt that she would not be honoring her father if she allowed herself to take pleasure in anything.

Many times Ann would wake at night crying bitterly. Phillip would comfort her, but each time he tried to draw her closer she would turn away.

He was incredibly kind and supportive. Before he left for work, he would bring her breakfast on a tray. Three or four times a day he called from the office, and almost every night he brought her a bunch of violets. When he decided she wasn't eating enough, he began to bring home boxes of candy, hoping to tempt her appetite.

Finally his patience paid off. One weekend he took her up north to the Sonoma Mission Inn. The inn was terribly run down and it rained all weekend, but that night Ann opened her heart and her body to her husband once again.

Phillip blossomed under Ann's renewed attention. He worked harder at his job and was almost ready to ask for a raise when they woke one Sunday to discover that the lives of all Americans had been permanently disrupted.

Ann was making waffles for a late breakfast when he came into the kitchen.

'These are delicious,' he said, laughing and snagging a piece before she could serve him. 'They're even better than my mother's.'

Ann feigned a scowl. 'Well, I'm glad I can do *something* better than she can.'

'You do everything better,' Phillip said, turning on the radio.

And that was when they learned the Japanese had attacked Pearl Harbor.

Ann took off her apron and walked into the living

room. Phillip sat immobile, his face drained of all color.

'Darling, Honolulu is a million miles from San Francisco.'

Phillip looked at Ann's puzzled eyes. 'Hawaii is a U.S. territory. This means that we are at war.'

Ann felt as though she were going to faint. She held on to the chair so tightly that her knuckles turned white.

'Phillip, what will this mean to us?'

'I'll either have to enlist or I'll be drafted. It makes more sense to enlist because then I can apply for officers' training.'

Ann's heart almost stopped beating. Her world was falling apart. She had just buried her father; now Phillip was going to leave her, too.

'You can't!' she cried despairingly. 'We've just gotten married. I'll be alone!'

'But, darling – I have no choice!' Even though it was the truth, Phillip felt as if he were abandoning Ann. She looked so vulnerable as she sat on the sofa, weeping. Quickly he got up, gathered her into his arms, and gently carried her into the bedroom. He lay there, Ann cradled in his arms, brushing her lovely dark hair back from her forehead. She was so beautiful, so infinitely precious to him. But once again he was powerless to protect her . . .

The next morning Phillip stood on the corner of Leavenworth and Bush and watched the men going into the recruiting office. He sighed, realizing that history had twice irrevocably changed the course of his life. First the Depression and now the war. What good did it do to plan? he wondered. He had just begun to feel that life had meaning again, that he might even achieve success as a lawyer, when his world exploded in his face.

Lighting a cigarette, he forced himself to shut off his self-pity. After all, millions of young men were going through the same torment. Squaring his shoulders, he walked across the street.

When he came out, he felt that he had made the best

of a bad deal. He was a second lieutenant in the Judge Advocate General's corps. He didn't know to whom he would be assigned, or even to which theater, but wherever he went he would be safer than in the infantry.

Ironically, after boot camp, Phillip would receive the rest of his military instruction on the University of California law campus – the very place from which he had graduated. He would be an hour away from Ann, but would not be permitted to see her even for that length of time. The best he could hope for would be a week or two of leave before being shipped out.

That morning it had taken all of Ann's strength to say goodbye to him without bursting into tears. At breakfast she had kept the conversation going with trivialities and had refused to turn on the radio for any reason whatsoever. Phillip had kissed her goodbye as if he were just going to the office. Ann held up until the front door had firmly closed behind him. Then she collapsed on the bed, sobbing.

It was nearly four that afternoon when Ann was finally able to pull herself together. Sitting up, she stared at her reflection in the mirror. Her face bore the same haunted look it had the day her father died. She couldn't let Phillip see her this way. Quickly, she went to the bathroom and showered.

After she had slipped into a blue silk dress, she appraised herself. Maybe a little more rouge might draw attention away from the dark circles under her eyes.

She went into the kitchen and turned on the oven. Taking out a small chicken from the ice box, she prepared it for baking. She had just put it into the oven when she heard Phillip's key in the latch. For a moment she panicked, trying to catch her breath. Then she took off the apron, patted her hair, and went into the hall to greet him.

'Hello, darling,' she said, leading him into the living room. 'What can I get you? A drink?'

'That would be great, sweetheart,' Phillip replied. He

sank onto the sofa while Ann poured him a scotch and soda.

'How was your day?' Phillip asked cautiously.

'Oh, I took a nap. I guess I was tired.' She paused. 'How about you?' Her voice was even but her eyes were clouded with apprehension.

'Long day . . . I'm sorry I'm late.'

'That's okay. I just put the chicken in, so it will be awhile until dinner.'

An awkward silence fell between them. Then, after what seemed like an eternity, Phillip said, 'How do you like being married to a second lieutenant?' There – it was out in the open. Phillip laughed, hoping to erase the stricken look on Ann's face. 'I just might make this my life's work. My base pay will be four hundred fifty dollars a month.'

But Ann couldn't smile. 'I think I'd better go look at the chicken.'

Sensing that she was unable to deal with all the implications of his leaving, Phillip said nothing more about the war that evening. But as the days passed and Ann asked no questions, Phillip realized that she was pretending that nothing was going to change.

Friday, after work, Phillip picked up his uniform. He took it home and tried it on, unexpectedly feeling a surge of pride. Straightening his shoulders, he walked into the living room, where Ann was reading a magazine. At the sight of him, she jumped up. 'Phillip!' *Why couldn't you have waited?* she wanted to shout. *How could you do this to me?* But she bit back the words. It wasn't Phillip who had done this to her – it was the world.

For the next two days she steeled herself for the moment of Phillip's leaving, and by Monday morning she felt strangely calm. Their separation had an air of unreality. Phillip would be so close, but he could not come home, and apparently he would be lucky to even call. But at least for the next few weeks he would be safe, and Ann was grateful for that much.

Time passed faster than she could have believed.

Phillip returned from basic training just one day before his orders arrived. They were brief and to the point: six days later he was to report at the Ferry Building on Market Street.

They had so little time left – less than a week! They were determined to savor those last precious days as though nothing threatened their lives together.

Ann cooked all his favorite dishes, wore her prettiest dresses, and joined him in bed with passion equal to his. They avoided talking about the war and spoke instead of their plans for when Phillip came home. What kind of house they would buy, how many children they would have. Four? Five? Okay, five.

On the final Saturday, Ann fussed endlessly over dinner, wanting everything to be perfect. Precisely at seven o'clock, Kenny and Ruthie arrived, followed by the Coulters. For once there was no tension between Ann and Eva. Ann forced herself to smile as her mother-in-law talked endlessly of how adorable Phillip had been as a child.

Eva insisted on describing the rainy day when four-year-old Phillip had been caught wading in the fish pond without his rubber boots. Eva had thrown open the window, shouting for him to come inside before he caught his death of cold. She had been furious until he had innocently opened his slicker, baring a swimsuit.

'It's just swimming, Mummy,' he had called and she had burst out laughing.

Now, a hard lump caught in Eva's throat. What was going to happen to her baby? Where would they send him? Tears welled up in her eyes, but she blinked them back, and even tried to include Ann in the conversation.

Ruthie and Kenny had the most cheerful news of the evening. Ruthie was expecting a baby, and even though Kenny was leaving the following week for England, she could not suppress her excitement. Phillip poured brandy and toasted the infant's safe birth.

Looking at him laughing and joking with Kenny,

Ann's heart swelled with pride. Her handsome husband was so strong, so good. Surely God would spare him. Forgetting that there was anyone else in the room, she lifted her glass. 'To you, darling. No man has ever had a wife who loved him more than I love you.'

He got up and embraced her. Life hadn't defeated him after all. Tonight he was the victor in destiny's little charade.

Shortly afterward Ruthie and Kenny left, with Ruthie promising to call every day. Then Eva and Simon got up.

'It was a wonderful dinner, Ann.' For the first time Ann heard genuine warmth in Eva's voice. She pressed Eva's hand as Simon once again applauded Phillip's choice of a wife and then hurried Eva out the door so as not to intrude on the couple's last night together.

Ann willed herself to forget that anything else existed in the world except these last precious hours with Phillip, and in bed she did everything she could to heighten his joy. They lay in each other's arms dozing until Phillip gathered her to him one last time.

At 4:30 she slipped out of bed and prepared breakfast – orange juice, smoked salmon, scrambled eggs, and coffee. When he came into the kitchen, she turned and said, 'Look how much I've improved since our wedding night.'

'In every way,' he said suggestively.

'I guess I was pretty nervous.'

'You think *you* were nervous!'

They laughed and Phillip said, lifting his orange juice, 'Let's drink to us!'

'And to Karen.'

'Karen?'

'Yes. I thought that that would be a lovely name for our first daughter, since my mother's name was Kara. What do you think?'

Phillip felt an overwhelming joy. Of course, the timing was terrible, but . . .

'My God, no!' Ann said. 'I'm sorry, I just . . .' her voice trailed off.

'Karen Coulter is a lovely name,' Phillip said. 'We'll save it for my return.'

And the terrible moment they had been avoiding descended with a crash. It was time for him to leave.

Watching Phillip button his uniform, Ann was no longer able to close her eyes to the fact that he was going to war. She could barely speak as they picked up the Coulters and drove down to the Ferry Building, where rows of olive drab trucks were lined ominously against the curb.

Phillip embraced his mother. She seemed so fragile this morning. Then he turned to his father. 'Take care of yourself.' That was not what he wanted to say at all. *I should have been a better son*, he wanted to tell Simon. But the words were left unsaid as he turned at last to Ann. For a lingering moment, he held her close. How could he find the courage to leave? Quickly he kissed her and walked to the waiting bus.

Ann waved courageously although she felt as if her heart were breaking. Then she turned and saw the Coulters desperately clinging to each other. They looked as if they had aged ten years overnight. A wave of compassion swept over her: Phillip was their only child.

'I think it's time to go home now,' she said gently.

They went back to Ann's apartment and she suggested a bite to eat. Noting Simon's drawn face, she added, 'Can I get you some brandy?'

'That's very kind of you, my dear. But could I possibly just lie down for a bit?'

'Of course.' Ann quickly went to the bedroom, turned back the spread, and plumped up the pillows. 'Now, are you sure that there isn't anything I can get for you?'

'No, thank you, no, Ann. All I need is a short rest and I'll be as good as new.'

Ann doubted that that would be the case, but closed

the door behind her softly and went to join her mother-in-law in the living room.

As the two women sat together, Ann felt an urge to reach out to Phillip's mother. Seeing Eva's grief as she bid Phillip goodbye had made Ann realize how deeply Eva loved her son. 'Mrs. Coulter, now that Phillip has gone, I've been hoping that perhaps you and I could become closer to one another. Would you mind if I called you Mother?'

Eva was so touched she had difficulty responding. 'I don't know why you would want to call me Mother,' she said. 'I've never been that kind to you.'

'Today, that really doesn't matter. The truth is, I *need* a mother. More important, I would feel so much closer to Phillip if we were a family in the true sense of the word. I know how much he loves you.'

Eva reached into her purse, took out a lace-edged handkerchief, and dabbed her eyes. 'I don't quite know what to say. I feel very guilty for having treated you the way I did.'

'Please don't. With Phillip gone, we need each other. I wanted to ask whether you would consider my moving in with you? It would mean so much to me.'

'I would love that, my dear. But you know, Phillip's old room is very small.'

'The size of the room doesn't matter. Just the fact that it is his will make me happy. Now, on a less sentimental note, I've decided to take a job in a defense plant. The pay is good, and between that and Phillip's allotment, we'll get along.'

Eva realized this was a day of revelations. Ann had given her a great gift of love, but until this moment Eva hadn't quite realized the depths of her generosity. Ann was going to assume Phillip's financial responsibility toward his parents. Since his marriage, Phillip had continued to give them a portion of his pay, but the army paid him only one-half of what he had previously earned. He had told his parents that they would simply have to draw on their meager savings for the duration of the war. He had never suggested that Ann go back to work.

'Are you sure you want to do that, Ann?' she said.

'I'm positive. I couldn't bear sitting at home with nothing to do.'

Eva leaned forward and took Ann's hand. 'My dear, you're an extraordinary woman. I can see why Phillip loves you.'

Twelve

When Ann moved in the following week, Eva had no trouble welcoming her daughter-in-law's offer to paint not just her room, but the living room and kitchen as well. Soon the apartment sparkled with soft beige and creamy white. For the first time since the crash Eva felt proud of her home.

Simon's life improved too. Since the Depression he had had a series of jobs, none of which had lasted. Now, with the shortage of young men, Simon got a job selling shoes at Florsheim's, where his skills with customers were quickly appreciated. He brought home a hundred and twenty-five dollars a month and felt rich.

Even Ann, whose work at the shipyard was often exhausting, was grateful that her job kept her mind off Phillip's absence. When she got her first paycheck, she deducted ten dollars' allowance and put the rest in the bank in Simon and Eva's name. She left the passbook on Eva's dresser with a note which said simply, 'I love you.'

Eva and Simon were deeply touched, but at first they wanted to refuse. 'Darling, we couldn't think of such a thing,' Eva said. 'It is lovely and generous of you, but it's your entire salary.'

Ann glanced at Simon. He had insisted on using his own earnings to pay for rent and food. It gave him a new sense of dignity to be the head of his household again. But how long could he continue to work? His arthritis troubled him more and more, and his eyesight was gradually failing. When Phillip came home, he might have trouble finding a job, so it made sense for the Coulters to build a small nest egg. In the end Simon agreed and Eva went along despite her guilt. If she had known how grateful Ann was at being taken into Phillip's family she might have felt better. As it was, Eva just kept writing her son telling him how lucky they all were to have Ann.

It was now March, and Ann hadn't received a letter from Phillip in over a month. She knew he was being sent somewhere in the Pacific and she avidly devoured the newspapers, wondering where he'd been stationed.

At least today was Saturday and she could look forward to lunch with Ruthie. The Newmans had been lucky. Kenny had been attached to the Allied Supreme Headquarters and was currently as safe as one could be in England. Ann tried not to be envious as she described her fears at not hearing from Phillip.

'I know it's trite,' Ruthie said, 'but no news is good news.'

'Do you really believe that, Ruthie? I wish I did. The thing that bothers me is just that I haven't heard anything. I can't even look at the map and say, "He's *there.*" And the newspapers don't say a thing about any action in the Pacific. I guess I really shouldn't torture myself. Phillip isn't in a combat unit, and I suppose if anything terrible were going on, we'd have read about it. I mean, the government would have to tell us, wouldn't they?'

'I'm sure they would. I wish I could say something to reassure you, Ann. I do believe Phillip is all right.' Ruthie spoke with more conviction than she actually felt.

'Enough about the war,' Ann said, forcing a smile. 'You look wonderful, Ruthie. Five months pregnant and you barely show.'

'My doctor has a fit if I gain any weight. Besides, I want to be gorgeous when Kenny gets back!'

Would Phillip come back? Ann just knew that something was terribly wrong. Dear God, if only she had been pregnant, at least she would have had his child. It was hard to share her friend's joy.

'The one who's happy,' Ruthie was saying, 'is my mother. She can't wait.'

On the streetcar going home Ann stared blindly at the passing buildings. *Oh, Phillip,* she thought, *what has been happening to you since you left me?*

The truth, if she had known, would have made her still more wretched.

Thirteen

Phillip had expected to debark immediately for the Pacific theater of operations, but their ancient transport, the hastily refitted U.S.S. *General Pershing*, was still undergoing last-minute hull repairs at Oakland.

The men eyed the totally unarmed World War I relic with open mistrust as they boarded. As if to confirm their bad opinion, a musty stench of disuse hit them as they descended the companionways and eventually found their damp berths far belowdecks.

The first night aboard, jammed into the uncomfortable, stacked bunks, they exchanged bitter jokes: 'Stink's gonna get us before the Japs do' was the general consensus.

For seven long days nothing happened. On the morning of the eighth day they were rousted out an hour before dawn as the ship weighed anchor. Rumor had it that they were headed for New Zealand – easy duty there.

Phillip watched the winter sun struggling to pierce the low blanket of clouds and drizzle that concealed the Bay Area. His heart ached as they left the Golden Gate Bridge behind and slowly moved into Pacific waters.

Most of the men remained on deck and, pleased and excited to be under way at last, they began to exchange information on hometowns, girlfriends, and ball teams.

A group of older men was swapping tales of World War I trench exploits against the 'Huns,' while some young recruits listened in awe, believing every word. One of them asked if America had fought the Japs back then.

Phillip's heart sank. For many of these eighteen- and nineteen-year-olds, the Pacific war represented their first time away from home. How many would return? At least he had had a chance to finish his education and marry . . .

Leaning on a railing, he closed his eyes and pictured Ann's face.

'Bored already, Lieutenant?' a mocking voice said almost in his ear.

Phillip blushed and turned around with a rueful grin. Beside him stood his commanding officer, Captain Jerrold Bugleman. Bugleman had gone through officer training at the University of Virginia, where he was noted and sometimes feared for his wit. During the dull yet anxious days while the *General Pershing* was at anchor, Phillip came to like and respect the man, who was obviously a born leader.

With his mane of auburn hair and his freckled face, Bugleman looked for all the world like an Irishman, but he had gone to Harvard under the 10 percent Jewish quota. He was an almost straight-A student and first-string quarterback for the Crimson. His size and strength were sufficient defense against all-too-common anti-Semitic taunts.

After graduation from law school, he had accepted a good job with a well-known Wall Street firm and married his childhood sweetheart, Alicia Goldstein, in one of New York's most publicized weddings of the year.

With his money and connections, Jerrold could have easily avoided the draft. However, like Phillip, his first thought when Pearl Harbor was attacked was to sign up, but for a different reason: he felt indebted to America. His family had fled the pogroms of the

71

Ukraine in the late nineteenth century, and, like the Coulters, had made their fortune in America. But the Buglemans had been shrewd enough to hold on to their money. Resisting the lure of fast profits in the bull market of the twenties, Jerrold's father had patiently expanded his chain of grocery stores – and continued to expand them even during the worst of the Depression, when businesses were failing everywhere.

There could be no question: the United States had been good to the Buglemans, and Jerrold wanted a way to help repay his obligation. He realized that he probably wouldn't be given a front-line role, but knew he would jump at the opportunity should the unexpected occur. His commitment was outspoken, and few dared question it to his face.

The two men watched in fascination as a school of whales cavorted off the starboard bow, oblivious to the rusty old transport ship with its cargo of men who had been taught to kill.

Phillip sighed. 'Maybe they could teach us something,' he said, nodding toward the whales.

Bugleman said nothing. He had studied Phillip carefully and already concluded that the man had a quick mind, and would assume responsibility if forced to do so. But he was perhaps too sensitive, too reflective, to be a real asset to a general commanding a besieged garrison of half-starved, battle-hardened troops. The man would have to be tested. Perhaps he would break. Bugleman hoped not.

Fourteen

Pearl Harbor was still a shambles. Plans had been drawn up to salvage some of the American warships, and much of the debris had been removed, but Hawaii had ceased to be the U.S. Navy's most luxurious and sought-after post.

The bored, seasick soldiers and sailors on the *General*

Pershing were allowed only two days to look for women, buy souvenirs, and get drunk. By that time the ship was refueled and had received its definitive orders: it was to proceed to Bataan and reinforce the embattled troops who were being cut to pieces by General Masaharu Homma's 14th Imperial Japanese Army.

The American and Filipino soldiers had been forced to retreat into the Bataan Peninsula. Thirty miles long and twenty miles wide at its base, Bataan jutted into Manila Bay. Heavy jungle and rugged mountains made it a good defensive position. From this natural stronghold, the Luzon forces hoped to hold out until the arrival of the American fleet.

It was a long and terrible battle, with malaria and other tropical diseases taking their toll on both sides. The Japanese bombarded the defenders with artillery based on warships, and from the air. Their advance troops cut supply lines.

On January 2, 1942, General MacArthur, whose headquarters were in the tunneled and heavily fortified island of Corregidor, which overlooks Manila Bay, had been forced to order the already hungry defenders of Bataan on half rations. Malnutrition began to add to the already heavy casualties.

Shortly after the *General Pershing* left Hawaii, the U.S. High Command changed its mind. Given the enormous number of troops that Tokyo had committed to the capture of the Philippines, the rescue mission was foredoomed. All ships heading for the Philippines were to await further orders.

Although the troops on board the *General Pershing* continued to drill for the landing, rumors began to fly about that the show was off. There was still no official confirmation, but discipline relaxed. Finally word came through that they were to head for Australia.

The sudden shift in American strategy might have meant that Phillip would miss the war entirely, but MacArthur's headquarters on Corregidor badly needed Bugleman, and Phillip was on Bugleman's staff.

Phillip was lying on his bunk, writing a letter to Ann telling her that she shouldn't worry – he would probably spend the duration of the war in someplace nice like Melbourne – when Bugleman broke the news.

'Sorry, old boy – the old man decided he needs us. Six or seven of his staff have malaria. Not dead,' he hastened to add, 'but sick enough to be out of commission.'

Phillip groaned and crumpled up the letter. He had heard that Japanese subs, mines, and patrol boats operated fairly freely around Manila Bay, and that the Imperial Air Force already controlled the skies.

Bugleman observed his glum look and slapped him on the shoulder. 'Cheer up, old boy! Just think – you'll be working for a living legend, the great Mac himself . . .'

The two men were picked up before dawn from a destroyer escort anchored in the South China Sea. The captain of the PT boat assured them that the area was 'quite safe' and that they would reach Corregidor in a few hours.

Bugleman patted the Colt automatic and the double-bladed trench knife at his belt. 'The wife should get a load of this – Terry and the Pirates.'

Phillip's nerves were taut from the rough journey on the destroyer escort. 'Captain, may I respectfully request that you shut up?'

Bugleman ignored the remark. 'Listen, Phil . . . we'll be safe with Mac. You really think he'll let *his* ass get chopped up by the Japs?'

Phillip remained silent as he strapped on his life vest and the PT boat picked up speed. Soon he was seasick. He cursed himself for forgetting his seasickness pills. Bugleman stood peering into the mist, humming to himself. He appeared to be enjoying himself.

After some three hours, the PT boat captain called out, 'Getting close now.'

Phillip breathed deeply. They were going to make it.

Suddenly the boat shuddered violently and seemed to turn on its nose.

'We've hit a reef!' Phillip remembered yelling. Then the deck dissolved under his feet and he was in the water.

The PT boat had hit a Japanese mine.

Phillip splashed about, coughing up saltwater. He tried to spot Bugleman or a crew member in the fog, but saw no one. There was another explosion and a fuel tank went up. Phillip dived to avoid being sprayed with burning fuel. When he surfaced, he looked for something to cling to, but every usable object in sight seemed to be on fire.

The captain or a surviving crew member appeared a few yards away. The man shouted something, then disappeared under the water.

A large wave with an empty steel drum balanced on its crest was bearing down on Phillip. He tried to duck, but the container hit him squarely on the forehead and he passed out.

When he came to, he was lying on his stomach, half on, half off, a large board. Bugleman was lying next to him, kicking the makeshift raft toward shore. They had arrived at Bataan.

'Awake now, buddy?' Bugleman asked. 'I was getting worried about you.'

Phillip moved his head gingerly. 'Where are we?'

'Don't know for sure,' Bugleman said, 'but I think we're just off Bataan. Or maybe further north.'

'Bataan . . .' Phillip sounded disoriented. 'Where's . . . Pershing . . .'

'The *General Pershing*? We were in a PT boat – remember? Headed for Corregidor. We were torpedoed . . . hit a mine . . . who knows . . .'

'Oh, yeah . . . PT boat gone?' Phillip couldn't clear his head, which had begun to ache horribly.

'Nothing left.'

'Where's the captain?'

'Gone. Along with the rest. You've been out for a half

hour. Must have really creamed yourself.'

Phillip groaned as a stab of pain almost made him black out.

'Look, Phil, I'm sorry if you have a little headache' – Bugleman's sardonic humor suddenly reawakened – 'but can you help kick a little? This isn't a Sunday swim, you know.' Bugleman thought it prudent not to make any wisecracks concerning sharks which he knew infested the South China Sea.

In response, Phillip only moaned.

'It's our only chance, you idiot!' Bugleman was genuinely angry now. 'The current's taking us in the wrong direction. We'll either drown or else the Japs'll use us for target practice. For God's sake help me, will you?'

He stopped kicking. 'Listen!'

Phillip heard a droning noise but couldn't tell what direction it was coming from.

'Jap patrol boat,' Bugleman said. 'If they spot us, duck!'

Even as he spoke, the tiny boat shot out of the mist. It was manned by two Japanese marines. A machine gun was mounted in the bow.

They abandoned the plank and dived simultaneously. Phillip stayed under until he thought that his lungs would burst. He heard the propeller pass over his head. Then he came up for air, inhaling seawater as he did. He retched miserably as he saw the boat turn and race back toward him as a marine prepared to fire. He dived again, and again the boat passed over his head, this time splintering the improvised raft into a thousand fragments.

Surfacing cautiously, keeping only his face above water, Phillip could hear the Japanese cursing somewhere in the mist. Their incomprehensible babble brought home to him just how deep they were in enemy territory.

The cursing stopped and the motor was turned off, then ignited, and the patrol boat abandoned the chase and disappeared.

Now their situation was even grimmer, for with no raft to hang on to, both men were tiring rapidly.

A small plane was flying overhead.

'Reconnaissance, most likely,' Bugleman gasped. 'A Mitsubishi.'

'We've got to be pretty close now,' Phillip said hopefully. His legs were starting to cramp badly and he was horribly thirsty.

They saw the outline of the jungle rising out of the mist. Powered by hope, they increased their efforts.

The Japanese plane, which had disappeared for a few moments, was back – flying slowly and much lower now. Then it was joined by three others – Zeroes, their most feared fighter plane.

Phillip wanted to dive, but Bugleman stopped him. 'They're not out for us – look!'

The planes were in fact after much more important targets. They banked steeply to the right and screamed inland.

Phillip followed their flight.

The three planes flew up and down the beach and the nearby jungle, firing their machine guns and cannon, while Japanese warships, somewhere in the distance, lobbed heavy shells at unseen targets farther inland, toward the heavily jungled mountains.

Then the defending Americans returned fire, as their anti-aircraft guns tried to down the enemy planes.

Phillip shuddered with horror as a mutilated body – friend or enemy? – was flung by an explosion out of the sea and into the air in front of him.

Bugleman, cursing now, urged him on, and they swam toward the south end of the beach.

A hundred yards from safety, two graceful fountains of water and smoke rose from the sea from shells, fired from ships anchored somewhere offshore. Then all was quiet.

Neither man had the strength to strike out in another direction, so they continued toward the beach.

They had almost reached safety when they again

heard the patrol boat engine. Both men turned their heads in the water and looked back, sure that this time the end had come. White-hot tracers streamed past Phillip's face. He ducked, surfaced, and kept swimming.

The patrol boat was coming up fast. No chance now – they would be shot like fish in a barrel or cut to pieces by the propeller. He braced his body and waited for death.

It didn't come. Instead, the boat made a full turn and headed for open water as an American heavy machine gun concealed somewhere in the foliage beyond the beach raked the water near the boat, giving him and Bugleman a few precious minutes to make it to shore.

As if to dash his last hopes, one of the Zeroes returned and bombed the beach, trying to hit the concealed gun. Disappointed, it climbed, turned, and buzzed angrily toward Corregidor.

Phillip's knee struck sand. Weeping with joy and exhaustion, he struggled to his feet, blinking the saltwater from eyes that were almost swollen shut. He turned and squinted seaward.

Where the hell is Jerry?

The captain was floundering helplessly some twenty yards from shore – apparently about to go under. A shell exploded on the beach, showering Phillip with sand. He dropped automatically to his face, then got up and headed for the water to help his friend.

Grasping Bugleman's arm, Phillip towed him to the beach, and the two men staggered toward the safety of the jungle.

There was a crackle of small-arms fire and Bugleman dropped to the sand and lay still. To his horror, Phillip saw a bright-red patch high on Bugleman's leg. He was hit – and badly.

Bugleman was barely conscious and in severe pain. 'Can't walk . . . You go on . . . Head for cover,' he muttered.

Phillip didn't answer. Instead, he gathered what remained of his strength, bent down, grabbed Bugleman by the shoulders, fell twice, then half carried, half dragged his friend toward the shelter of the trees. He didn't slow down when a burst of pain shot through his upper arm, and continued until the dunes and bamboo thickets had sheltered them from the enemy.

Sick with fear, he laid Bugleman on the ground and ripped away the bloody fabric on his leg. The Japanese bullet had gone right through the femur, shattering it. The bone was sticking out through a mass of raw flesh. Phillip turned away and vomited.

When he recovered, he strained his swollen, almost useless eyes in the unaccustomed dimness of the jungle and looked for American or Filipino troops. He was sure they were nearby. So, perhaps, were Japanese advance scouts or sharpshooters. But he had to chance it.

'Medic!' he yelled, but his voice was lost in a blast of artillery fire. When it was quiet, he called a second time, terrified that Bugleman was going to bleed to death. The captain was moaning softly.

'Help!' he cried.

One of the soldiers – they were in fact Americans – approached with an air of indifference, puffed on his cigarette, and looked down at Bugleman.

'Call a medic,' Phillip pleaded.

The soldier seemed to be reflecting. Then he said, 'I'll see what I can do, but we're in real bad shape here.'

It seemed hours before an exhausted, sweat-stained man in khaki shorts and a torn shirt knelt before Bugleman.

'I can splint him up and try and stop the bleeding,' he said. 'But in this jungle he'll probably die anyhow. Just a matter of time.'

Methodically, the medic fashioned a rough splint out of bamboo foraged from the trees behind them. Then Phillip helped him force the jagged bone back into the torn flesh of the thigh. Bugleman, still blessedly unconscious, moaned loudly, then fell silent.

Phillip swallowed hard, trying not to be sick again. He remembered that once he had been unable to touch a cadaver.

When he saw the long, dirty bandage that the medic pulled from an equally soiled hip pocket, Phillip protested. 'For Christ's sake – you're not going to wrap him up with that rag, are you?'

The medic sighed. 'Best I got.'

Phillip had no comeback. The hideous wound, the primitive first aid, and his own fatigue had left him numb. He could scarcely move, much less think.

The medic finished, left Phillip a canteen full of evil-smelling water, and went off after promising that a stretcher-bearer would be there 'soon.'

The battle was dying down. The Zeroes had disappeared in search of more visible prey, and there was only sporadic and generally ineffectual shelling from the Japanese warships.

Finally, two bedraggled and unshaven soldiers, both shivering with malaria, arrived and loaded the still unconscious Bugleman onto a stretcher. Phillip stumbled after them, up a steep ridge and deeper into the jungle.

When they reached what Phillip had been assured was a field hospital, he gasped. It was nothing more than a collection of rusty old bunk beds set up in a clearing under the trees. The 'operating room' was an ancient shed with a corrugated roof. The floor was dirt.

Bugleman was carried inside and laid on a wooden table covered with a khaki blanket. Nurses tried to brush away the flies as the surgeon, a young Filipino, explained to Phillip that the camp had run out of anesthetics several days earlier. They had been cut off for over a month, and had received thousands of casualties, many of them worse than Bugleman.

To Phillip's horror, as soon as they dressed the wound and began to manipulate the leg, the intense pain jarred Bugleman into consciousness.

At first he tried to stifle his cries, but soon he was screaming in agony. Finally Phillip couldn't stand it any longer. He left the shed and went outside, sobbing.

Men lay on cots all over the clearing. Many of them

were so thin they were virtual skeletons. Some were missing limbs. Others had suffered grossly disfiguring facial wounds.

Phillip stumbled over to a tree and leaned against it, shaking, unable to pull himself together.

There was a gentle touch on his shoulder, and slowly he raised his head. A young nurse was standing behind him. 'Are you okay, soldier?'

'Yeah . . . I'm okay.' He attempted a weak smile.

Suddenly the nurse spoke sharply. 'Why, you're wounded.'

Puzzled, Phillip looked down and saw a patch of dried blood running from his shoulder to his elbow. Thinking back to his desperate dash across the beach, he vaguely remembered a flash of pain. 'It's nothing. Forget it.'

The nurse paid no attention to him. 'Take your shirt off, soldier,' she commanded.

There was a long cut in Phillip's arm. The nurse led him to a tent where she bathed the wound and bandaged it. Then she looked at the bruise on his temple, trying to distract him from the pain by telling him her name was Fiona and what it had been like the last month on Bataan. Listening to her, Phillip was reminded of Ann. It seemed a hundred years since she had kissed him goodbye in San Francisco.

When Fiona was finished, Phillip described Bugleman's injuries and asked what she thought about his chances for recovery.

She looked grim. 'There is a terrible problem with infection here in the jungle. And we've had to evacuate three times. He has a chance, but that's all.'

After she had gone, Phillip went back to the operating hut to see how Bugleman was doing. The surgeon was just walking out. 'You his buddy?' he asked Phillip. When Phillip nodded, the doctor said, 'He came through it pretty well. If he could be flown out . . .' He walked off, leaving Phillip with his friend.

Bugleman looked terrible, but he was conscious and

even articulate. Phillip took his hand. 'How do you feel?'

'Still hanging in there. Looks like you saved my ass.'

Phillip smiled. 'But it doesn't look like I did it soon enough to get us to MacArthur. What do you think we should do now?'

'Well, I'm going to be out of commission for a while. I guess you'll have to report to the nearest combat unit. But come back for me in a week or so.'

'Yes, sir!' Phillip said, forcing a light note into his voice. 'I'll expect to see you walking around.'

One of the orderlies gave Phillip directions to an American command post. Before he left, the man handed over a pair of boots. Without being told, Phillip knew that they had come from a corpse, but he also knew that he couldn't survive without footgear. It took him an hour to reach the camp.

Phillip reported to the commanding officer, a captain – a career soldier who wasn't much impressed with second lieutenants fresh from the States. And this one in particular was too handsome, well-fed, and aristocratic for the captain's taste.

A cream puff, Cox thought to himself. *He'll last a week*.

'I'm Captain Andy Cox,' he barked. 'Well, Lieutenant Coulter, you're going to get the chance to kill some Nips. How do you feel about that, boy?'

Phillip had seen enough of Cox's type not to react. Men like Cox loved war for its own sake, and their enthusiasm had nothing to do with making the world safe for democracy or for any other ideal, for that matter.

'Well?' Cox demanded when Phillip remained silent. 'I asked you a question, Lieutenant – how do you feel about killing Japs?'

'They are the enemy and I'm a soldier . . . sir,' was all Phillip would give him.

Cox's expression became a mask. 'Get yourself a rifle. And one more thing – bands of the yellow bastards have been landing all day and hiding in the jungle. Don't fall asleep in an exposed position. You could wake up with your belly ripped open. You wouldn't like that, would you, Lieutenant?'

Phillip was issued a standard American M-1, but he noticed that most of the men carried old Springfields. 'M-1's jam up,' the bearded supply sergeant told him. We trade 'em to the Filipinos for these.'

'Or else we just take 'em when the gooks drop 'em and run,' a soldier commented sourly.

The next day there was only intermittent shelling, but the following morning saw a full-scale attack, with air support and light armored vehicles. They had been eating breakfast when someone spotted the first dark shapes appearing on the horizon.

When the first bomb hit, Phillip dived for the foxholes that lined the edge of the beach. It was his last conscious action for hours. He crouched in the shelter as the anti-aircraft guns pounded Japanese planes, feeling helpless and wishing he had been at the camp long enough to be assigned. The bombing and strafing seemed to last an eternity. Finally there was a lull, and the men were ordered to retreat back into the jungle.

For the next few weeks, Phillip's days followed the same pattern. Long periods of bombing by the Japanese were followed by another hurried retreat. It was impossible to tell from which direction the enemy would attack next. He was given odd jobs to do, but there never seemed time for him to receive instruction as an infantryman. When there was a lull in the battle, the men had only one subject of conversation: food. They discussed their favorite meals endlessly. Hamburgers, ice cream, lasagne – it was as though talking about food nourished them.

For they were slowly starving. Since January, all they had gotten to eat was a daily half-ration of rice, often full of weevils. Occasionally one of the backwoods Southern boys would catch a monkey or a rat, and they all wolfed down the meager meat. Horses and mules had long since disappeared into the cooking pots. With the exception of Phillip and the stocky CO, Cox, all the men in the unit were emaciated. Their flesh seemed to have melted away, and their eyes were hollow, with a peculiar lifeless stare.

No one bragged about what would happen to the enemy when the American fleet arrived, for they were slowly realizing that the defenders of Bataan might not be rescued after all. Not even the most confident pep-talk from Cox could raise their spirits.

From time to time, Phillip wondered how Bugleman was doing, hoping he was still alive. But after the second week, Phillip was like all the other soldiers; he could only think of the twin imperatives: food and survival.

Early one morning, several weeks after Phillip had joined the unit, they ran straight into a unit of infiltrators. They had orders to descend a ridge and help shore up a flank of the Luzon line, which ran across the southern part of the peninsula. Not anticipating an immediate attack, they were marching carelessly two abreast down an overgrown path. Suddenly seven or eight Japanese clad in black emerged from a small clearing below them, crouched, and opened fire.

The soldier next to Phillip went down. Phillip instinctively dropped flat and began shooting. In front of him a Japanese was just cresting the hill, rifle raised. Phillip gritted his teeth and pointed his M-1. It was an easy shot, but the thought of actually killing made him hesitate. Then he aimed and squeezed the trigger.

Nothing happened. The rifle was jammed. At that moment the Japanese saw Phillip.

Panic hit him like a sledgehammer. He was a sitting duck. Without a wasted motion, Phillip rolled behind the body of a dead soldier. He heard a thwack and felt the shudder as the bullet hit his shield of human flesh. He grabbed the dead man's Springfield, aimed it as best he could, and fired.

The Japanese clapped his hands to his belly and staggered back, his face a grotesque parody of surprise. He seemed unable to believe that he had been hit. Then he dropped his rifle and crumpled slowly to the ground.

Phillip was crawling backward into a bamboo thicket when he saw Captain Cox, lying facedown, blood pouring from a ghastly wound in his arm. To his horror, he realized that Cox's arm was hanging by a shred of muscle. Bullets whistled past them as Phillip dragged the captain back behind a low, rocky ridge.

Forgetting that he couldn't stand the sight of blood, Phillip pulled out his knife and with one swift, vicious stroke, severed the limb. Then he ripped his handkerchief into strips and fashioned a tourniquet around the man's upper arm, above the stump. The bleeding seemed to have stopped, but when he gently turned Cox over, he realized the CO was dead. He had taken a bullet between the eyes.

When Phillip turned back to the shooting, he saw that for once the Japanese were fleeing. One lone soldier was still firing from a prone position, but bullets from several American rifles silenced him.

Cautiously, Phillip walked back to the other survivors. They had lost six out of twenty, including Cox, and six more were severely enough injured that they would have to be evacuated to the field hospital.

Phillip suddenly realized that with Cox dead, he was the ranking officer. But nothing had prepared him to lead this ragtag band. Looking at the hopeless, starving faces around him, he realized that the only chance any of them had of surviving was to attempt to maintain military discipline.

He straightened his shoulders, drew a deep breath, and said, 'Men. Captain Cox is dead. We'll have to bury him and the rest of the men. Four of you will help the wounded back to the field hospital. We'll wait here for your return.' None of the soldiers questioned his command: they were too confused and exhausted to care who led them.

When the four returned from the hospital, Phillip learned that Bugleman was hanging on, even though he

85

had a high fever and a badly infected wound.

As the days wore on – hot, terrifying, and violent – he adjusted to his new role of responsibility, but forced himself not to speculate on how long his tiny detachment could survive.

Late one night he was dozing, shivering from a low fever, when a Filipino courier handed him a sealed, tattered envelope. He opened it and read: *On April 9, at 0600 hours, General Edward P. King surrendered the Luzon force to the Imperial Army of Japan.*

They had lost the Philippines, and all American troops and their allies were now prisoners of war. Only Corregidor was left now.

Phillip wakened his men and told them the news. Then he ordered the cook to inform the two men on sentry duty that they might as well get some rest.

The next morning they awoke to silence. No Zeroes flew overhead, searching the jungle for targets. There was no roar of artillery from either attackers or defenders, no crackle of small-arms fire.

Phillip walked over to the nearby road and squinted toward the mountains. Their sides were covered with the white flags of surrender.

Fifteen

Looking at the eight men in his charge, Phillip knew he did not want them to meet their captors looking so ragged and beaten. He had to infuse them with a renewed sense of dignity. Quietly, he called them to attention. 'Men, I want to talk frankly. This surrender is not what any of us would choose. But we have no choice. It is our duty to follow orders. But just remember – you fought hard and you fought well. And don't you let anyone tell you differently.'

He cleared his throat. 'Now shave and clean up as best you can, and when the Japs arrive, keep your heads high.'

A short time later, they were ready for inspection. Their uniforms were hopelessly dirty, and they had no helmets, but they were clean-shaven, and they carried themselves with a hint of pride. Their weapons were emptied and stacked carefully at the edge of the clearing. Maps and code books were burned. The radio transmitter was smashed.

With nothing left to do, the forlorn little group sat silently until the sun was high. The men were almost convinced that the whole thing was a mistake when, in a sudden rush from the jungle, they were surrounded by a chattering, gesticulating rabble of Japanese soldiers.

Phillip ordered his men to their feet. No one protested.

He forced himself to remain motionless while a grinning, bespectacled corporal ransacked his pockets, taking a pocket knife, a sugar ball, and a few battered cigarettes. He missed the iodine tablets used to purify water that Phillip had concealed in his boot.

Another Japanese was searching a sandy-haired American private. After he had finished, apparently enraged at having found nothing of value or interest, the Japanese picked up his rifle and hit his captive hard across the face with the butt.

Phillip's first impulse was to attack the man, but instead he stepped forward and pointed to the insignia on his shoulders, then to the private, who was kneeling, holding his broken and bleeding nose.

'I demand to see a senior officer,' Phillip said calmly.

At his words, the NCO screamed an order and several Japanese cocked and raised their rifles. Phillip expected to be shot, or perhaps to get a bayonet in the gut, but he managed to conceal his terror. There was a tense pause, then the NCO, a heavily bearded man who walked with a pronounced limp, snarled a command and the muzzles were lowered. Phillip was perspiring heavily. He now realized that the conquerors of Bataan would observe no rules of war. He and his men were in the hands of barbarians.

Suddenly the soldiers fell silent and snapped to attention as a dusty, open staff car pulled up. Five officers climbed out, all wiry, athletic-looking men. One of them seemed to be their superior officer – probably a major, Phillip thought.

He strode up to the prisoners and said in heavily accented English, 'Who is ranking officer here?'

No one spoke. Phillip looked up and down the line. None of the Americans moved. Lifting his chin, he stepped forward and saluted. 'Lieutenant Phillip Coulter, U.S. Army.'

The major did not return his salute. Instead, he pointed at Phillip's holster, from which they had taken the pistol. 'Your holster, please.'

Phillip unbuckled it and handed it over silently.

'It is empty, yes?' the Japanese asked loudly.

'Yes, it is empty,' Phillip said coolly. 'Your men have already collected our guns.'

The major looked Phillip over, then shrugged. 'That is all!' As Phillip stepped back in line, the officer placed his hands on his hips and announced. 'You men are now the prisoners of the Japanese Imperial Army. I am Major Ito. I will be in charge until you are delivered to your commandant.'

He gave a brief, contemptuous laugh, then continued harshly, 'Any attempt to escape will result in instant death!'

With that, he barked a series of orders in Japanese, then strutted back to his car as the other officers positioned themselves along the line of prisoners.

The soldiers resumed their search. When one GI refused to take off his wedding ring, an enraged Japanese slashed the man's wrist with his bayonet. Phillip stepped forward to protest, but was pushed back. Gesturing to the bleeding man, he said, 'Just let me see how badly he's hurt.'

In response the Japanese cursed and shoved Phillip to the ground. Before he could scramble to his feet, another soldier pulled off the ring, nearly taking the finger with it. He then held it up, smiling, for the admiration of his comrades.

Nauseated, dizzy, and now suffering from thirst as well, Phillip stumbled back to his place in line, where he stood, swaying in the sun.

Late that night, a group of about fifty prisoners was marched past them. Some had crude bandages around their heads; others had arms in slings or legs bound in bamboo splints. All were wounded, and all were in what appeared to be the last stages of exhaustion. Among them, limping along on makeshift crutches, was Captain Jerrold Bugleman.

Phillip's initial joy in seeing his friend disappeared in the realization that the Japanese apparently intended to march this wretched band of walking wounded to central Luzon. This was clearly contrary to the Geneva Convention, and Phillip wanted to protest. Then he remembered the robbing of the prisoners and decided he had better say nothing.

He tried to smile encouragingly at Bugleman, who grinned back from a face that was almost yellow. The group proceeded about a half mile and was then ordered to halt for the day.

The next morning, Phillip's worst fears were confirmed. They were indeed going to move the Americans and their Filipino allies on foot out of the peninsula to prison camps in central Luzon. Phillip figured that the Japanese High Command wanted them out of Bataan as quickly as possible so that they could concentrate every last soldier on blasting the last remnants of resistance from Corregidor. And guards were wasted soldiers.

The enemy set a grueling pace the first day. Phillip worked his way toward the back of the long column, where Bugleman struggled with his crutches. Phillip choked back a sob when he saw how his friend was a mere shadow of the vigorous, good-natured man who had stood and joked with him on the deck of the *General Pershing*.

Phillip tried to look straight ahead and speak without moving his lips, as he had seen it done in prison movies. 'How are you doing?'

'Been worse,' Bugleman said. The sense of humor was still there, anyway. 'You know they bombed the field hospital?' he asked quietly.

'My God,' Phillip moaned. 'But you survived. Can you keep walking? Must be forty miles to the next railroad.'

'I'll have to try, won't I, then? They sure ain't going to carry me there.'

The attempt to be lighthearted saddened Phillip. He pushed as close to Bugleman as he could without attracting attention. 'Lean on me as much as you can.'

Later that day, a guard standing by the side of the road angrily stamped his foot in the dust and pointed at Bugleman. Then he stood directly in front of the two men, indicated Bugleman's shattered leg, and said, 'No good!'

Phillip didn't understand at first. But when the guard snatched the crutches away and tossed them into a ditch, it became very clear. The man wanted an excuse to kill Bugleman.

'Lean on me,' Phillip whispered.

'If I can't make it, you go ahead,' Bugleman said. 'That's an order!'

Phillip said nothing. They both knew that Bugleman, now without his crutches, would never make it. He hopped along on his good leg, his arm around Phillip's shoulder, gritting his teeth and trying not to cry out when his broken leg touched the ground.

With the added burden, Phillip himself wasn't sure he would survive another day.

It was nearly midnight before the miserable column, which had been swollen by the addition of more and more prisoners, was allowed to rest. There was no water available, and most of Phillip's men had already emptied their canteens. Phillip had been careful to conserve some water in spite of his thirst.

The next morning they were wakened with shouts and curses and were under way when the sun came up. At first the coolness made them forget their thirst, but as the heat increased, men began to faint. Their buddies tried to carry them along, but they too were often at the breaking point. Phillip watched, horrified, as the guards first kicked the stragglers, then shot or bayoneted them, according to whim, by the side of the road.

They passed a well, but only the guards were allowed near it. The captives were permitted to watch as the guards slaked their thirst. Phillip refused to drink the last cup of water in his canteen, wanting to save it for Bugleman. It occurred to him that the Japanese wanted to be rid of their prisoners in order to save the bother of maintaining them in a camp: perhaps the brutality was calculated, not spontaneous. In any case, the column seemed to grow larger, not smaller.

Late that afternoon there was a change of guard, and the new soldiers allowed their charges to rush to a small, slow-moving stream, drink, and fill their canteens. The dehydrated men drank until they were bloated, paying no attention to the green scum on the surface. The next day almost half of them were struck with dysentery. Since stopping in the road was punished by blows or even death, they fouled themselves and kept going.

Phillip thought that the limits of hell had been reached until the third morning, when for some reason the guards ordered the column to do double time. He looked at Bugleman: the leg was worse. He and Phillip had begun the march at the head of the column, but they had gradually dropped back and were now bringing up the rear.

Phillip's heart sank as he recognized the guard for their section – it was the same one that had thrown Bugleman's crutches into the ditch. The Japanese saw them hesitating at the edge of the column and shouted something. Phillip knew that if they fell back another step, the man would kill Bugleman.

'This is it,' Bugleman said. 'I can't make it.'

Phillip unscrewed the nozzle of his canteen and shoved it under Bugleman's nose. 'Drink it,' he ordered.

'No!' Bugleman protested. 'It's all we've got.'

Phillip tilted the canteen. 'Drink it.'

Bugleman drank.

The guard was watching them closely, waiting.

'Now move it!' Phillip shouted at his friend as he propelled them both into the safety of the center of the column.

An hour later, the double-timing ceased, since even the guards couldn't stand the pace. But it was past sunset when the prisoners were finally allowed to stop.

Some days there had been no food at all, but tonight the rice pots were going. The soldiers shuffled past the giant vats, and a cup of hot rice was slapped into their cupped hands. They crammed it into their mouths on the spot, then washed it down with weak tea.

Bugleman was so ill that he had lost interest in food, and Phillip couldn't force him to join the rice line. Phillip checked the captain's leg. As he opened the bandages there was a terrible stench. The flesh was an angry red and oozing with pus.

'Gangrene,' Bugleman murmured.

'No – there's a bad infection, but it will heal.'

'I'm going to die, Phil,' Bugleman said quietly. 'I'm never going to see Alicia again, or the baby.'

'Don't say that!' Phillip cried. Abruptly he got up, fetched some water from a nearby pond, and carefully purified it with the last of his iodine tablets.

By the time he got back, Bugleman was unconscious.

Phillip knew that his friend needed fluids badly, so he dipped a corner of his shirt into the canteen and began to drip water onto Bugleman's lips. Finally Bugleman came to and drank a little more from the canteen. Then he slept.

The next day they came to a railroad junction and were told to halt. Phillip's heart leaped. If only

Bugleman could make it to the camp, he might get some decent care, though a skeptical voice warned him not to get his hopes up.

The captain seemed a little more optimistic. 'If I can just rest for a few days, I just might have a chance . . .'

But as they were shoved into the boxcars along with hundreds of other soldiers, Bugleman's face took on a ghastly hue. The sun beat down remorselessly, sending the temperature well above one hundred. Those with dysentery had no control over their bowels, and the soldiers soon found themselves locked in a stinking hell.

One man, driven beyond his endurance, began to scream at the top of his lungs. Then he changed to an eerie howl, which finally subsided into inhuman gibbering. A man next to Phillip, already far gone with fever, died standing up, trying to look out between the slats of the closed car.

Several hours later the train stopped at a siding and they were allowed to pass the dead bodies out. Phillip seized the canteen of the dead man next to him and gave it to Bugleman. Not one of the prisoners could have said how much time passed before the train stopped again and the guards opened the doors and ordered the remaining prisoners to emerge.

They literally fell from the car, stiff, cramped, trembling, and filthy, and were confronted with a bare dirt compound surrounded with corrugated iron huts and an old hangar with a sign reading MORTON AIR FIELD, which had been daubed over with black Japanese characters.

Phillip surveyed their new home. A rough wooden platform had been erected at the head of the compound. Apparently they were to hear an address from the camp commander.

After they had waited in the sun for some forty-five minutes, a diminutive figure in black, shiny riding boots strode into view. Swaggering to the exact center of the platform, he stared down at the prisoners with distaste.

'I am Captain Nakanishi, your commandant. You, the defeated, are here to await the ultimate world victory of the Japanese Imperial Armed Forces. The Japanese Empire does not recognize the so-called Geneva Convention.' His voice was filled with contempt. 'You are not prisoners of war – you are guests of the Emperor!'

Captain Hideo Nakanishi had hated Westerners long before the war. In the early thirties he had won a scholarship to Oxford, where the upper-class English had laughed openly at his poverty, his race, his accent, and above all at his short stature. He was a Jap, a 'wog,' an outcast. He had neither forgotten nor forgiven.

When he learned of Pearl Harbor he wept with joy. But now, months after that brilliant victory, he was assigned to this miserable POW camp in an outpost where the enemy had already been crushed. But at least he could vent his hatred on the vanquished.

After his speech, the prisoners who could walk were herded into their assigned huts, while the severely wounded and desperately ill were consigned to a primitive sick bay.

When Phillip went to visit Bugleman, an Australian doctor pulled him over to a corner of the hut and shook his head. Phillip refused to meet his eyes.

Phillip bent over the mat on which Bugleman was lying. 'I'll visit you when I can. Chin up – you'll make it.'

But Bugleman grew worse. He shook violently with chills and was conscious for only a few hours a day. Phillip watched in despair, which was deepened by his observation that men in even worse shape than Jerry seemed to be pulling through.

He asked a medic to confirm this: 'Am I just imagining it?'

'You're right,' the medic told him. 'The ones that get real mad seem to make it more often. The gentle ones usually give up and die.' He shook his head sadly. 'I'm afraid your friend is one of the gentle ones.'

As Bugleman's condition deteriorated, Phillip became

increasingly angry about the almost total absence of medical supplies. There weren't even any clean bandages, not to mention anesthetics, sulfa, or quinine. The doctors had considered amputating Bugleman's leg, but without sulfa it wouldn't do much good. And they wanted to spare him the pain.

Finally Phillip went to see the senior American officer, Colonel Watkins.

'Sir, I respectfully request that a request be delivered to Commander Nakanishi. We need supplies for the hospital: sulfa, quinine, whatever else he's got.'

The colonel, a burly Southerner with a pockmarked face, drawled, 'Request denied, Lieutenant.'

'But, sir! The men are dying for lack of those few simple things.'

The colonel leaned forward, his eyes hard. 'Are you blind? Nakanishi doesn't give a damn! The more of us who die, the easier his job is. If you complain, they are just going to list you as a troublemaker. They ain't going to give you any sulfa or even any Band-Aids. No way!'

Phillip watched in impotent fury as the colonel settled back into his chair and rolled a cigarette. The next time Phillip visited his friend, Bugleman was in a deep coma. Driven to despair, Phillip decided to protest, against orders. Using an old envelope, he drafted a polite letter and walked over to the commandant's headquarters. He gestured to a guard that the letter was to be delivered to Colonel Nakanishi.

The guard was gone for two or three agonizing minutes, while Phillip waited, fearful that his answer would be the order for his immediate execution. Then the guard returned, his face impassive.

Phillip walked back to his hut. Nakanishi could deny the request, or ignore it – but at least he, Phillip, had taken a stand. Perhaps in the long run it would have an effect.

He was standing in the food line with his men when the PA system whined into life and Nakanishi mounted the platform. The men were forced to stand at attention.

'Lieutenant Coulter. Step forward.'

Phillip managed to propel himself forward on trembling legs.

'It has come to my attention,' Nakanishi began, 'that you are unhappy with the conditions provided by our glorious Emperor Hirohito.'

Phillip said nothing.

Nakanishi eyed him for a moment before descending the steps to the compound. He crossed to within two feet of where Phillip stood.

'Answer my question!' The diminutive commandant was working himself into a rage.

Phillip's initial terror was replaced by a sense of inner calm. At least he would die doing what he knew was right.

The commandant stamped his foot: Phillip's silence was an insult to him, a threat to his authority – to the authority of the Emperor himself.

He pulled his heavy service revolver out of its holster and hit Phillip hard on the right cheek with the barrel. Phillip dropped to the ground. The last words he heard before passing out were: 'Be grateful for what you've got . . . pretty boy.'

Phillip lay unconscious in the middle of the compound. No one dared approach him until Nakanishi had disappeared into his quarters and slammed the door. Then Phillip's men ran to help him. Wordlessly, they picked him up and carried him to the sick bay.

That night, Phillip lay on a mat in the hut that served as officers' quarters. The wound was deep and somewhat painful, but no bones were broken. Worse was the fact that after regaining consciousness Colonel Watkins had stormed into the sick bay and chewed him out for disobeying orders.

In the dim light, Phillip noticed that someone was standing over him. He hoped the man would go away and let him sleep.

The voice that said his name spoke gently, with a Brooklyn accent. 'How ya doin' there, Coulter?'

'Not too bad,' Phillip managed. He opened his eyes and recognized their chaplain, Father Michael O'Connor. A blunt-spoken young Irish priest, he had a pair of world-weary blue eyes that nothing seemed to shock.

O'Connor *had* seen more in his short lifetime than most men. One of ten children of a fiercely Catholic family, he had grown up in a section of Brooklyn that was largely Jewish. The little O'Connors had been isolated by their Catholicism, and by their policeman father, a basically decent man who was nonetheless uncompromisingly intolerant of the Jews around them, and liked to call them 'the murderers of Our Lord' in his bad moments.

But young Michael had always been fascinated by the community and took every opportunity to learn about it. He spoke Yiddish fluently and had studied Jewish religious customs.

When he grew older, he got a job delivering suits for Abraham the tailor. His father grudgingly admitted that money was money, as long as Michael understood that he was not to mingle with 'the sheenies' any more than was absolutely necessary. O'Connor had already decided that Michael was to enter the seminary, just as he had intended his oldest daughter for the convent.

By the time Michael reached adolescence, he had established a business for himself in delivery services. But he was also deeply offended by the corruption that ran just beneath the surface of life in the little community, and doubted he could really fit in. So it was with a feeling of relief that he had entered the seminary at eighteen, just as his sister Mary Agnes had dutifully entered the convent the year before.

But the austere, scholarly life of the order didn't satisfy Michael's desire to be needed, so immediately after taking his vows, he requested to work in one of the worst slums in Brooklyn.

The downtrodden inhabitants of the neighborhood loved O'Connor, even though he often could do nothing for them. When the pressures and frustrations

97

became too much for him, he drank, and as time passed, he drank more. Sometimes he slept in the rear of a saloon, unable to make it home. The other priests knew that Father O'Connor had his little weakness, and would quietly help him home the next day.

O'Connor was almost glad when the Japanese struck Pearl Harbor. As an army chaplain he would have no time for the bottle and even less time to feel sorry for himself. From the beginning, he had been constantly in demand to console suffering men like Lieutenant Coulter. Coulter, though not badly hurt, was now staring up at him with an expression of unrelieved misery. O'Connor knew of Phillip's friendship with Bugleman, and understood that Phillip was tortured with guilt at his failure to help the captain. He probably believed that he had made things even worse by his ill-considered action.

O'Connor cleared his throat nervously. 'That was a fine thing you did, Lieutenant,' he said. When Phillip merely turned his head away he added, 'It took a lot of guts to face Nakanishi – more guts than old Watkins has.'

'Thanks,' Phillip managed to say.

'How's your buddy doing?'

'Not so good.'

O'Connor was silent for a moment. 'It's tough to see all these young guys dying. Real tough.'

Dragging himself painfully to a sitting position, Phillip asked, 'Father, do you think that God has a purpose in all this?'

'Frankly, no. I don't think God has anything to do with it.'

'You know, I'm Jewish, and even though I'm not from a very religious family, I've always felt God's presence in my life.'

O'Connor nodded.

'But how can I believe in God when he allows all these horrible things to happen? I mean, I see Jerry Bugleman – a bright, wonderful man with a beautiful wife – and because he can't get even elementary medical care, he's going to die.'

'Well, Coulter, three years of seminary didn't give me answers to such questions. I don't know why God allows bad things to happen to good people.' He reached out and rested a hand on Phillip's shoulder. 'I'm sorry. I know I'm not being much help.'

The following evening Phillip was sitting with Bugleman, trying to make conversation. The captain seemed more lucid than he had in days, and was sipping a cup of weak tea.

'You should see my wife . . . She's a princess. I knew her all my life . . . wanted to marry her since the sixth grade. And now we're having a baby. May already be born, for all I know. Hey, maybe I'm already a papa!'

He smiled softly, remembering. 'We were going to call it Sarah. Alicia was convinced that it would be a girl.'

'Well, you'll know soon, Captain,' Phillip said. 'Ann and I haven't gotten lucky yet. Maybe after the war . . .'

'Yeah, you'll go home,' Bugleman said quietly.

'So will you, Jerry!'

But Bugleman shook his head. 'No. I want you to do something for me when you get back. Go see my wife. I need you to tell her how much I love her, and that I'm sorry I can't hang on.'

'Jerry!' Phillip cried. 'Don't even say that!'

Bugleman reached out and grabbed Phillip's hand with unexpected strength. 'Will you cut the bullshit, Phil? I'm your commanding officer, remember? You'll see Alicia . . . please?' His voice trailed off weakly.

Phillip looked away for a moment, tears flooding his eyes. 'Yeah, I'll do it.'

The next day Bugleman was dead. The gravedigging detail couldn't keep up with the flood of bodies and had resorted to mass graves, but Phillip was determined that Bugleman at least be given the proper Jewish service. So he tried to round up ten Jews to say

Kaddish but came up one short. Seeing his distress, O'Connor finally approached him.

'Lieutenant, I hear that you can't find a *minyan*. I was wondering if you could forget the fact that my collar buttons in the back. I could say the Kaddish.'

'Would you be willing to do that, Father?'

'I think Our Savior would insist,' O'Connor said, smiling.

Phillip and eight other mourners stood with Father O'Connor at the graveside. The heat had ripened the corpses waiting for burial until the stench was staggering. But as Bugleman's body was laid to rest, the final words murmured over his body were the traditional Kaddish chant.

Sixteen

Wearily, Ann swung her legs over the side of the bed and walked to the window in Phillip's old bedroom. It was almost the holiday season, but staring out into the chilly gray San Francisco fog, she had very little to celebrate.

Phillip had been gone now for ten months of sheer agony, and Ann found herself cut off from all news except the radio and the daily papers, which had told of the fall of Bataan several months previously. As time passed, she came to assume that he had been killed or taken prisoner. She had received no direct word since the day the *General Pershing* had sailed.

In desperation, she made inquiries at one government department after another, but without success. No one seemed to even know where the *Pershing* was, much less care about her husband's fate. At times she wanted to scream, to *force* the rude, harassed clerks to find out something. But during that terrible period of never-ending American defeats, thousands of wives were in the same position as Ann, and the armed forces simply didn't have accurate casualty lists.

Just before Christmas Ann arrived home to find Eva slumped over on the side of the couch.

Ann ran to her. 'Eva, darling, what's wrong?'

Her mother-in-law's face was frighteningly distorted, her eyes staring unfocused. She tried to move her lips, but the sound that emerged was garbled. As Ann put her arm under Eva's shoulders to straighten her, she noticed the yellow rectangle lying on the rug.

With a cry, Ann snatched it up, taking in the message with a single horrified glance: LIEUTENANT PHILLIP COULTER... MISSING IN ACTION... NEAR CORREGIDOR.

Forgetting her mother-in-law, Ann burst into tears. Missing in action! But when the first storm of sorrow subsided, Ann told herself: *Missing in action isn't dead. Phillip may have been taken prisoner.*

Forcing herself to be calm, Ann turned back to Eva. When her mother-in-law remained motionless, Ann rushed to the phone and called the doctor.

Eva had suffered a massive stroke, which paralyzed her entire left side, undoubtedly brought on by the shock of seeing the telegram. After a quick examination, the doctor called the ambulance and had her hospitalized.

For the next few days, it was touch and go whether she would live. Ann was at the hospital 'round the clock, while Simon hovered helplessly at his wife's bedside. It was only after several days of uncertainty that Eva gradually began to improve. A week later, they were able to bring her home, but her side remained paralyzed and her speech was unintelligible.

Simon spent his days sitting by his wife and holding her hand. He had stopped going to work and seemed unable to think of anything but Eva. Ann knew that she couldn't keep her job and still take care of the two old people. Eva would need constant nursing, and Simon was virtually useless at this point. All the courageous plans she had made for taking care of their future would have to be abandoned. They would all simply have to live on Phillip's allotment.

Ann found it hard to think positively, but she knew that she was not the only one suffering. Ruthie was equally worried about Kenny, and was struggling to raise her baby, fearing he would never see his father.

On New Year's Eve the two women decided to see in 1943 together. They sat in the Coulters' living room, while Ann popped the cork of a bottle of cheap champagne. When the clock struck twelve, they lifted their glasses and drank to Phillip and Kenny. Ann went down the hall to see if Eva and Simon would join them, but the two old people were asleep.

Back in the living room, she filled their glasses again and Ann proposed another toast. 'To you, Ruthie. Thank God you're my friend.'

Seventeen

During the next year and a half, Ann knew she would never have survived without Ruthie's support. One of the few joys in her life was Ruthie's baby, Jeremy. Seeing him grow healthy and happy, Ann found the courage to believe in the future, to believe that someday Phillip would return and they could start their own family.

But by D-Day, in June 1944, Ann was beginning to think that she would have to live the rest of her life in limbo, that the war would go on forever. Even when Germany surrendered and Ruthie learned that Kenny would be returning home, the fighting in the Pacific seemed to go on and on. According to the papers, nothing short of invasion would bring Japan to its knees.

Still Ann tried to share Ruthie's joy when they went to the station to welcome Kenny. The train pulled in, and shouting GIs surged off in every direction to find their families. As Ruthie strained her eyes for a glimpse of Kenny, she was reminded of the day he had left. How similar the scene was, yet how wonderfully different. All around her people were weeping, but this time with tears of joy.

And then she was in Kenny's arms, crying unashamedly.

'Ruthie, oh, Ruthie . . .'

'Kenny, darling. Oh, darling, I can't believe you're here.' She hugged him, feeling how thin he was beneath the well-tailored captain's uniform.

Jeremy, who had been holding Ann's hand, impatiently tugged at Ruthie's skirt. 'Mommy!'

Unbelievably, Ruthie had almost forgotten her son's presence. 'Yes, darling.' Then, face glowing, she looked up at her husband and said softly, 'Kenny, this is Jeremy.'

Kenny scooped up the little boy. 'So this is my son. How are you, Jeremy?' He looked for a long moment at the dark-haired boy in his arms, regarding him with an expression of grave interest. 'He looks . . . wonderful—' He broke off, his eyes filled with tears.

Ann watched the three of them, feeling as if her own heart would break. *Oh, God, why hasn't Phillip come home like Kenny?* For a moment, she felt a stab of envy, then she forced herself to rejoice for the Newmans.

Kenny put down his little boy and turned to Ann. 'You're as beautiful as ever, Ann,' he said as he kissed her on the cheek.

'Thanks, Kenny,' Ann whispered. 'I'm so glad you're home safely. Ruthie needs you – and so does Jeremy. He's a wonderful little boy.'

Kenny smiled. 'Isn't he, though? And I want to thank you, Ann. I know from Ruthie what a wonderful friend you've been.'

Ann smiled but thought to herself, *She won't be needing me anymore now . . .*

It was true. Even though Ruthie called almost every day, she was busy now finding a new place to live, trying to make a perfect home for Kenny. Ann now had more time alone to worry about Phillip and wonder if she would ever learn what had happened to him.

Then one day she woke up to learn the United States had dropped a new kind of bomb on Nagasaki and Hiroshima. A few days later the Emperor of Japan surrendered. Ann saw pictures of him handing over his sword. *Now*, she thought, *maybe they'll tell me what happened to my husband.*

But the months passed, and the troops coming home from the Pacific docked in San Francisco or Oakland, then dispersed across America.

And still the War Department had no information for Ann.

Once again, New Year's Eve rolled around. The Newmans asked Ann to their house near Twin Peaks, where they were giving a small party. Ann had tried to decline, knowing that being surrounded by happy young couples would depress her, but Ruthie wouldn't hear of it.

'You'll just sit at home and brood, Ann. You know you will. I *insist* that you come.'

'Okay, Ruthie. But I don't feel very festive.'

Now she sat quietly in Ruthie's gaily decorated living room, watching the party swirl around her. She looked at Kenny and Alvin Sachs and Irving Cahn, listening to their laughter and easy banter. It was difficult to believe that all these high school buddies of Phillip's had gone off to war and endured untold terrors and hardship. How could they look so happy, so healthy?

Later, in the dining room, she could barely touch her steak, so she sipped at her burgundy until everything became pleasantly fuzzy. She was reaching again for the decanter, when a hand on her arm stopped her.

Looking up, she saw Kenny's concerned face. 'Can I help you, Ann?' he asked quietly.

Ann's eyes stared past him, unfocused. 'Sure . . . Bring my husband back, Kenny. That's how you can help me.'

Embarrassed, Kenny glanced over at Ruthie, who just shrugged.

'Ann, honey, I'm sure he'll be home soon.'

'But when? *Why don't you know?*' Ann said, a rising note of hysteria in her voice.

'It will take a little while to get everyone sorted out over there.'

'But, my God, Kenny – V-J Day was in August and now it's January!' The other guests stopped chatting, but by now Ann didn't care if she was spoiling the party.

'It's too early to give up hope, Ann.'

'You mean I might have to keep waiting?'

'Perhaps.'

'Maybe Phillip will never come home. Maybe he's dead.' Ann burst into tears.

Helplessly, Kenny patted her shoulder. 'Come on, now, Ann. Don't cry.' But he could offer her no real comfort.

Ann drank more wine, then brandy, trying to drown the pain. She was only dimly aware that the other guests were going home. Standing in the front hall saying goodbye, she saw the pity in Ruthie's face.

'Do you think he's dead?' Ann demanded. The moment she spoke, she was sorry. 'Never mind. I know that you don't know any more than I do.' She made a brave attempt at a smile. 'Forgive me for being a drag all evening. I'll be better tomorrow. We're spending the day together, aren't we? At my place, if you'd like.'

There was an awkward silence as the two women fumbled for the right thing to say. Taking a deep breath, Ruthie tried to explain. She and Kenny had planned a trip to Carmel – they hadn't been away together since Kenny's return. Ruthie's mother was babysitting.

Ann nodded dully. She couldn't conceal her envy. There was no escaping the fact that Kenny had come home and Phillip had not – and probably never would.

Eighteen

Ann began 1946 with little to hope for. Phillip's view of the future was equally bleak. Sitting on the edge of a hospital cot in Honolulu, he knew he was no longer the same man who had left his wife four years earlier. He stared at his image in the mirror above the sink. It was like looking at a total stranger. His eyes were haunted, and his skin was drawn tightly across his cheekbones. Looking down, he noticed that his pajamas swam around his skinny legs, and he remembered that a fall in the last months of the war had left him with a permanent limp.

Would Ann even want him back? He was so terribly changed. His hair had begun to grow in from where they had shaved it, but there was a large bald spot that refused to fill in. His face was permanently scarred from Nakanishi's blow with his gun. He was hardly the handsome young husband who had left his adoring bride.

Worse still was the change that didn't show. The long years as a prisoner of war had sapped his spirit. His ambition had faded along with his hopes for the future. All he wanted to do for the rest of his life was to sit quietly in some safe harbor.

The little room suddenly made him feel claustrophobic. Small spaces had been intolerable to him ever since his stint in the cage. When the Japanese major had wanted to punish a prisoner, he locked the offender in a tiny bamboo cage where it was impossible to stand, sit, or lie down. The victim could only shift position, desperately waiting for death or release. It was Phillip's worst memory of the war. A week's confinement had led to his decision to volunteer when the major had demanded reasonably healthy prisoners to work on the railroad the Japanese wanted to build through Burma.

Nothing could be worse than the camp, Phillip had decided, and with Bugleman's death there was no one he really minded leaving. He had lined up the next day with thirty other GIs. As they shuffled out of the camp, Phillip experienced a sense of freedom, but it faded quickly as he was jammed into a train which took them back to the coast. From there they went from bad to worse. When they got off the train they were marched to the docks and thrown into the hold of a transport. The weeks-long trip was a hell of vile water, little food, and agonizing heat. Added to that, Phillip was violently seasick. But in a way, the constant nausea and near delirium were a blessing because afterward he remembered little of the trip.

Once in Burma the men were forced to hack their way through the jungle to the site of the railroad. Phillip could not believe the sick and malnourished prisoners could work so hard. No one was spared, neither officers nor enlisted men. Phillip strained his bony shoulders under the weight of heavy ties and boxes of iron spikes, the ceaseless hammering and pounding jarring every nerve in his body.

In charge of the work gang was a sadistic officer named Oto. Like Nakanishi, he despised and loathed the white men over whom he had been given power. But unlike Nakanishi, Oto displayed a total lack of military discipline. His worst outbursts were often followed by quiet interludes when he would retreat to his tent. Later he would emerge with a vacant stare and refuse to speak to anyone for several hours.

Some of the men whispered that Oto smoked opium. Phillip neither knew nor cared. His only goal was to survive. He worked as little as possible, trying to conserve his strength, but not so little as to attract the guards' notice.

As the months passed, the death toll began to mount alarmingly. Meanwhile, pressure from the Japanese High Command increased. Oto's opium sessions decreased and his temper became more and more vicious. Impossible work quotas were imposed, which sapped the prisoners' little remaining strength. Those who didn't perform were dragged out of the work party and beaten with bamboos.

One day Oto stumbled out of his tent at noon, red-eyed and bleary. He strode to the worksite, surveyed it for a minute, then, pointing to a fair-haired soldier staggering under a load of timber, he barked a string of orders. The guards immediately seized the young soldier, who had been pulled from the line with Phillip at Morton Air Field. He had been desperately ill with malaria and had lost so much weight that he could barely walk, let alone work. The guards threw him to the ground and stripped his shirt from his back. Then they began to beat him. Frantically, Phillip made his way over to Oto, hoping to get him to stop his men, but as he approached he saw Oto's mouth curl in a faint smile.

It was that expression that made something snap inside Phillip. He had vowed that he would never again do anything to attract attention – and punishment – to himself, but he couldn't just stand there and do nothing. How could any man remain silent before such an act of barbarism?

'Captain Oto – I beg you to stop. What you are doing isn't an act of military discipline – it's cold-blooded murder,' Phillip paused for a moment to catch his breath. He was almost amazed he was still alive. He continued: 'You've heard the rumors – Japanese victory isn't sure now. You might have to answer someday for this outrage.'

Oto was dumbfounded by this act of rebellion, and his first impulse was to shoot this insolent American as an example. But in spite of his drugged state, the commandant heard an inner voice that cautioned prudence. The winds of war had indeed been shifting, and if his prisoners were abused unnecessarily, he might be held accountable by an Allied war crimes tribunal. Furthermore, he needed every available man to complete this section of the railroad. If he killed this man, he might provoke a work slowdown. Oto could read between the lines of the communiqués he was getting daily from Tokyo. If he failed in his assignment he might well be shot.

All these thoughts crowded into his mind as he stood, tapping his riding crop on his boot and reflecting.

'I will order the beating stopped. But you, my friend, will spend time in the monkey cage. I heard that your week there made you volunteer for Burma. We will see how you like my accommodations.'

Mention of the cage left Phillip stupefied with terror. He let himself be led away in a daze, unable to take satisfaction in the fact that the young soldier had been spared.

The dreaded bamboo box sat in a cloud of flies, near the middle of the compound. It was damp and fetid at night, then blazingly hot all day long. As the bars closed with chilling finality, Phillip knew in that moment that he would have done anything, said anything, betrayed anyone, sold his very soul to escape. All he could hope was to die before he went insane.

A vision he had seen on the Death March still haunted him. They had come upon a young Filipino soldier tied to a post, left by the Japanese to die, water placed just beyond his reach. He had gone mad and was running back and forth on all fours like a rabid dog.

God, don't let me end up like that. Let the end be quick, Phillip prayed.

He had been almost three weeks in the cage when the Allied forces invaded Burma and Australian soldiers liberated the camp. They had found Phillip almost catatonic. He was skeletal by then, riddled by beriberi, and his hair had fallen out in clumps. He was covered with vermin. The cage stank unbelievably, and he was so crazed by his confinement that he believed the soldiers who released him were Japanese come to further torture him. When they approached the cage, he had flown into a terror-stricken frenzy.

Kicking and clawing, Phillip had raved wildly as his rescuers dragged him out. A medic rushed over and restrained him. They hadn't released him until he reached the psychiatric hospital in Honolulu . . .

Sitting in the solarium, gazing out beyond the flowered terrace to the Pacific, Phillip took the first hesitant steps to recovery. Some part of him would have been content to spend the rest of his life in this island paradise. It was as if his soul had been permanently scarred. He doubted if he would ever ask for more than three meals a day and a soft bed in which to sleep. But later that night he confronted the task of writing to Ann. The doctors had told him if he wasn't up to it, they would tell one of the officers to send her a telegram. *That would be cruel*, he thought.

Now he looked down at the note paper and picked up a pen. Four times he started. My dearest, My dear Ann, Darling, darling, darling . . . His hand was trembling so badly that he could not form the letters. *My God, what can I say after all this time?*

Over four years had passed since he had seen her. He hadn't written since the day he had sailed for Corregidor. Did she know what had happened to him? Had the army notified her that he had been taken to a psychiatric hospital? His dog tags had disappeared somewhere along the line – Phillip couldn't remember where. God only knew what Ann had been told, if anything.

Finally he picked up the pen again.

My dearest Ann,

I don't even know how to begin. By now, they must have let you know that I am still alive and in a Honolulu hospital. They tell me that I've been here for several months, but it is only in the last few weeks that I have begun to remember who I am and how I got here.

Now that I am able to write, I am not quite sure what to say or how to say it.

Except for a period at sea, I've been a prisoner of war, first in the Philippines and then in Burma. When I was rescued I apparently wasn't lucid. I still can't remember what happened. But I was luckier than the rest of my men. None of them survived.

Well, enough of that. I have been thinking and wondering about you, Ann. You have been in my mind, day and night for over four years. The thought of you was often the only thing that kept me from giving up.

But I realize that things have probably been very different for you. Four years is a long, long time, especially for someone as young and lovely as you, Ann. And, of course, you had no way of knowing if I were still alive. It would be only natural if you had begun to plan for a future without me.

I feel I must warn you that I have changed a great deal physically. At times, I barely recognize myself. I lost about sixty pounds while I was in captivity, and though I've regained some, I am still only about 135, which is pretty skinny for six feet. My leg was broken over there and did not heal properly, so that I walk with a limp. But the worst is that I have a bad scar across my face. I have to be honest with you, Ann – it's pretty horrible.

I guess what I am telling you is that you have your whole life ahead of you, and I don't want to tie you down to a broken-down wreck of a man.

I still love you, Ann – more than anything in the world. But I will understand if you feel that we cannot pick up the threads of our lives as if nothing had happened.

If all goes well, I will be released in two weeks' time and my ship will dock in San Francisco on April 15th.

With all my love,
Phillip

Nineteen

Ann's heart almost stopped beating when she saw the writing on the envelope – shaky but unmistakably Phillip's. A wave of dizziness swept over her and she had to support herself against the wall as she made her way to the living room. For several minutes after reading the letter she sat in shock. Then, remembering her in-laws, she ran down the hall to their room.

'Eva, darling! It's Phillip! He's alive! He's coming home!'

Eva was still unable to speak, but her faded blue eyes blazed with sudden joy. Ann threw her arms around the old woman as Simon wept with joy.

'Oh, thank God, my son!'

'It's a miracle,' Ann said softly.

After a while she left them and went to call Ruthie. On hearing the news, Ruthie exclaimed, 'Oh, Ann! I'm so glad! What happened to him? Where has he been?'

Half-laughing, half-crying, Ann replied, 'Oh, Ruthie, I don't know! He said he was a prisoner of war. Just what we suspected. All I care about is that he's alive!'

There was a silence on the other end of the line. Then Ruthie said, 'I'm so glad for you, Ann. All this time I've felt guilty being happy when you were going through such agony. You know, when we went to Carmel on New Year's Day, we both felt so badly about leaving you alone that we wished we hadn't gone.'

'Ruthie, that's silly. Of course you were happy to have Kenny back – that's only natural. Listen, you were the best friend anyone could have had these last months. No one else truly understood how much I love Phillip.'

'Well, you'll have him back soon now, honey. When exactly does he arrive?'

'The letter took so long getting here that the ship will dock on the fifteenth. Can you believe it?'

Ann almost danced with impatience as the days dragged by. She occupied herself in planning fancy dishes to tempt him. If he were thin, she would need to fatten him up.

She looked at herself in the bathroom mirror. Phillip had said he looked different. To Ann, it was impossible that he could be anything but handsome. But had she changed? Her curly dark hair was shorter now: parted on one side and waved. The violet eyes were the same, but her lips had a grim set that made her look older and sadder than the twenty-one-year-old he had said good-bye to. Deliberately, she curved them into a smile. *There, that's better* . . .

Then the day arrived. Ruthie and Kenny beside her, Ann watched as the huge gray transport ship glided past them and docked at the Embarcadero. Ann contrasted the scene with Kenny's homecoming. Today there was only a sparse crowd, and no flags at all.

The first men who descended the gangplank were carried on stretchers. Others followed on crutches and in wheelchairs. Finally Phillip appeared, standing by the rail. He seemed to be hesitating.

'Phillip!' Ann cried, but he didn't appear to have heard or seen her.

She broke into a run, calling, 'Phillip! Phillip! Over here!'

He was slowly and painfully coming down the gangplank. As he approached, Ann realized that he had written the truth. He was dreadfully changed. He moved like a very old man, bent, shuffling, limping.

But once he was in her arms, Ann forgot everything but the joy of having him back.

They kissed, and when Ann pulled away to see his face, she was appalled by the lines of suffering that surrounded his eyes; far worse than the angry red scar on his cheek.

Kenny was clapping him on the back. 'Great to see you back, old buddy!'

Phillip managed a weak smile. 'Kenny . . . Good to be back.'

He turned to Ruthie and said, 'You look wonderful, Ruthie. You and Ann haven't changed a bit.'

'Except that I'm a mother now, Phillip. Wait till you see our little Jeremy – he's almost four now.'

'Phil, I'm back in my old man's firm,' Kenny said.

Phillip was trying to focus on what everyone was saying. He and Kenny had been fraternity brothers, then gone on to law school together. But he now seemed like a stranger. Phillip could comprehend the talk about children and jobs and business as usual, but the words seemed detached from reality.

'Let's get out of here,' he muttered tersely. Picking up his duffel bag, he set off toward the exit. 'Where's the car – or did you all come by bus?'

'No, sweetheart, we came in Kenny's car,' Ann said.

113

As they neared Kenny's Studebaker, Phillip stopped short. 'Ann – where are my parents? Why aren't they here?'

'They couldn't make it to the pier, Phillip. They're waiting for us at home.'

'They're all right, aren't they, Ann?' Sudden fear sharpened Phillip's tone. 'Tell me they're all right!'

'Yes, darling,' Ann replied, her heart sinking. She would have to tell the truth before he saw his mother, otherwise the shock would be too great. 'Well, that's not entirely true . . . Your mother had a stroke and she's not in perfect health anymore.'

Phillip nodded and without another word limped to Kenny's car.

The journey home was uncomfortably silent. Ann tried to describe her life with his parents. 'I gave up our apartment shortly after you left. It seemed thriftier for the three of us to live together.'

She felt rather than saw his surprise. 'Your mother and I have become very close. And Simon needs me to help take care of her.'

'Take care of her? You mean she's not able to take care of herself?'

'Well, no, sweetheart. I told you she had a stroke.'

'Yes, but you didn't say how bad!'

Ann hesitated. No, it was better that he learn in advance. 'Darling, she's paralyzed on the left side. Her speech has been affected too.'

Phillip groaned, but when they reached home he realized nothing could have prepared him for the shock of seeing his once stylish mother reduced to this broken shell.

What had he done to her? He knew that she had been stricken because of her anxiety over him. *Why did I ever volunteer?* The enormity of his crime was not diminished by the obvious answer that he would have been drafted in any case.

Turning away, Phillip found Simon hovering behind him, his face drawn and tired. 'Son, it's good to have you home. Your mother . . .'

'I know, Dad,' Phillip whispered weakly.

Poor Simon! He looked twenty years older. *Eva's illness has been the hardest on him*, Phillip thought. He had adored his beautiful wife. To see her like this must be hell . . .

He could stand no more. Murmuring that he had a headache, he went down the hall to his old room and lay down on his bed. He knew that in a little while he had to go out and face Ann, but right now he didn't feel up to any sort of decision.

He looked about his old room. It had changed since he had last seen it. Everywhere there was evidence of a feminine occupant. Well, of course! This was Ann's room now.

Suddenly the walls seemed to be closing in on him. He went to the bathroom and splashed cold water on his face. Then he went to the living room and found Ann and Simon.

Ann had invited Kenny and Ruthie to join them for dinner, but had been on the point of calling them to cancel. She hesitated for a moment, then asked Phillip whether or not it was all right with him.

He nodded, deciding the Newmans would make things easier. He was right. As they enjoyed their meal, no one seemed to notice his silence. But then the guests left. Simon went to see Eva, and Ann and Phillip were alone.

'Darling,' Ann broke the silence. 'I think it's time we went to bed.'

She shut the door of their bedroom behind them, thinking, *My God, how I still love him. It will be all right.*

But Phillip was not as sure. *I don't even really know this lovely woman who has been living in my room, who has become a daughter to my parents.*

He undressed in the bathroom, put on pajamas, and slid between the cool, clean sheets to wait for Ann. When she joined him, her touch was infinitely gentle, undemanding. But Phillip was suddenly filled with dread. His body was ugly . . . filthy . . . scarred. He

115

couldn't touch her. He drew away and turned toward the wall.

He felt her surprise, her hurt.

With an effort, he forced himself to take her in his arms. But it was no use. He couldn't make love to her.

He got out of bed and went into the bathroom, where he sat on the edge of the tub, his head in his hands. Perspiration poured off him as he faced the truth. He was impotent.

Ann lay alone for several minutes, waiting for Phillip to return. They were bound to be a little awkward at first. That was only to be expected; after all, they had been separated for over four years. But as time passed, she began to realize that something was really wrong. She had seen how upset he was by Eva's failed health and by Simon's fragility. Now she realized that his silence at dinner bore testament to a much deeper pain.

Ann took a deep breath. Then, throwing back the covers, she went to the bathroom and rapped softly. When there was no response, she opened the door and sat down beside her husband on the rim of the tub.

'Phillip, darling – it doesn't matter at all. Come back to bed. Please.'

He remained silent.

'Please, darling. I love you. Tonight isn't important. We'll have years together. Come to bed now.'

Phillip finally stood up and followed her back to their room.

For a long time they lay side by side without speaking.

Then Phillip spoke. 'I'm sorry, Ann. I guess I wasn't quite ready to come home yet.'

'I understand, sweetheart,' Ann whispered softly. 'I'm just so happy that you're finally here with me. It will get better. I know it will.'

Phillip lay awake until morning, thankful that the darkness hid his face. The war had taken away his youth and his health. Now, it seemed, it had also driven a wedge between him and his wife. He sighed and Ann

116

turned over and wrapped her arms around him, convinced that this was the real beginning of their life together.

Twenty

But months passed, and Ann slowly realized that there were to be no new beginnings. She had naively thought that after a few months Phillip would readjust to civilian life. Even though he had not been rehired by his old firm, he would soon find a good job. After all, he had a brilliant mind and had gone to one of the best law schools in the country. One night she asked him as casually as she could, 'Darling, you must be beginning to get anxious to get back to work. It must be a bore for you to be around the house all day.'

'Yes . . . in time,' he said.

Ann watched him uneasily. What was wrong? Why wouldn't he talk to her? If she tried to question him directly, he either looked blank or simply walked out of the room. She tried to understand the difficult time he was going through, but how long did it take someone to readjust?

She didn't understand that Phillip was trying to spare her: he didn't want her to know how badly he'd been traumatized. Ann began to wonder if he still loved her. The words he had written in Honolulu came back to haunt her: She need not feel tied to him, she was free to leave . . . She had ignored that part of the letter, but a seed of doubt had been planted in her mind. Maybe what he had meant was that *he* didn't want to be tied to *her* any longer. The thought was so painful that Ann pushed it to the back of her mind. She was still Phillip's wife, and it was up to her to help him.

She knew that if Phillip were to recover, he would have to get out of the house and start coping with the world again. There were no magic answers. One day

Ann had decided that if he wouldn't go out, she would simply have to bring the world to him.

With that in mind, she had planned some dinners with friends. But Phillip objected so violently that she had to cancel them, telling everyone that her husband still tired easily. She had tried to talk him into excursions to Ocean Beach or Golden Gate Park, but Phillip wouldn't even agree to walk around the block. No matter what she suggested, he refused. In her naiveté, she had thought that her loving care would be enough to heal him. But it gradually became apparent to Ann that he had been much more deeply wounded than she had thought at first. The physical injuries were the least part of it.

Looking back, she remembered a night several weeks after his return. He had awakened screaming, thinking he was once again in the monkey cage. That night, and that night only, he tried to tell her about the pain, the degradation, the fear of going totally mad . . .

After that, there had been a few nights when she had wakened to find him bathed in a cold sweat. But he had never spoken of the war again, and she assumed that the nightmare had begun to fade from his memory.

Gradually, Phillip seemed more at ease with himself. He still would not leave the house, and at times would sink into moody silence. Still, he gained a little weight, and his limp seemed to lessen slightly. But he never mentioned going back to work, and Ann found herself becoming increasingly impatient with his willingness to let her support him indefinitely. His small disability pay didn't come near feeding and housing four people. They were already behind in paying Eva's doctor bills. What would they use for money when Phillip's disability ran out? Ann sometimes couldn't sleep at night for worry.

She had been laid off from her factory job and gone back to work part time at Magnin's. Maybe she should increase her hours, but then who would cook and clean?

Finally, she could contain her fears no longer.

She broached the topic timidly, one evening after dinner. 'Phillip, darling, I don't want to push you, but I've been wondering – do you have any plans about looking for a job?'

Phillip's hand tightened so hard on his wineglass that he snapped the stem, spilling the red liquid on the tablecloth. He shoved back his chair and almost ran from the room.

In the bedroom he sat shaking uncontrollably. It had taken every ounce of his self-control to hide his fears – the panic he felt in enclosed spaces, especially elevators, the terror that surged through him at sudden sharp noises. No one knew better than he their precarious financial position; no one had to tell him that he should be providing for his wife and elderly parents. Each day he felt less of a man, yet he was literally almost unable to go outside.

When Ann followed him into the bedroom, he couldn't look up.

'Phillip, darling – darling, I'm so sorry to have brought it up,' she murmured, sitting next to him and taking his hand.

'Ann, I'll do it,' Phillip replied brokenly. 'Just give me a little more time. Please. I love you . . .'

He wanted to promise that he would look for a job soon, that somehow he would force himself to get out of the house. But his lips couldn't form the words.

They hadn't really settled anything, Ann thought later that night as she tossed and turned restlessly next to him. The next day was one she didn't go to work, and when Simon had persuaded Phillip to go to the grocery store, she came to a decision. Picking up the Yellow Pages, she looked up Newman, Ross, Simons and Newman, Attorneys-at-Law. Nervously, she dialed. She had never called Kenny at work before.

The secretary sounded intimidatingly efficient.

'Mr. Kenneth Newman, please,' Ann said, trying to sound businesslike. 'Mrs. Phillip Coulter calling.'

'Ann! How are you? What can I do for you?'

Kenny's voice was reassuringly familiar. Ann took a deep breath. 'Kenny, I need to talk to you. Would it be an imposition if I came by the office?'

'Of course not,' Kenny said. 'But I have a better idea. How about if I take you to lunch?'

'I don't want to take up your time.'

'Don't be silly, Ann, honey. I always have time for you.'

Ann silently thanked him for not acting surprised or asking her a million questions. An hour later she fixed her makeup and said goodbye to Phillip. 'Darling, if you don't mind, I'm going downtown for an hour or so.'

'Why in the world should I mind? You must do as you please, Ann,' he replied tonelessly.

Guilt made her overly sensitive, and she fled before her face could betray her. But it was for his own good, wasn't it?

Kenny had suggested Ernie's, an old-fashioned, luxurious restaurant known for its great cuisine. Ann had never been there before, and she felt keenly aware of the shabbiness of her faded blue suit as the maître d' led her to a table.

Kenny was already seated.

'How nice to have such a beautiful companion at lunch! Usually it's just dull businessmen.'

Inwardly, Kenny was apprehensive, for he had a pretty good idea what Ann wanted. He too had wondered when Phillip would bounce back and start acting like the head of a household. Looking at Ann across the table, he realized she was very ill at ease. She was such a pretty, sweet kid, with those big violet eyes and fair skin. Phillip was a lucky man, he thought with a flash of irritation. Why couldn't he pull himself together? Other men had suffered in the war.

'Let's have a drink, Ann,' he said before she could speak.

While Ann waited for her sherry, she took her first real look at the room. The velvet wall coverings, the chandeliers, the tables covered with immaculate white linen. *It must be very expensive. But apparently Kenny can afford all this.* That thought strengthened her resolve. She opened her mouth to speak, but Kenny forestalled her. 'Shall we order?'

How marvelous to be able to have anything she liked. Her menu didn't even have prices. 'Veal Doré?' she suggested timidly. Then, worried that it was too expensive, she quickly glanced at Kenny. 'Is that all right?'

Purposely misunderstanding her, Kenny said, 'It's one of their best dishes. And I'm having the scampi.'

They had a good California wine with their meal, and by dessert, Ann began to feel pleasantly lightheaded. Glancing about the room, she wondered if there really were people with nothing more on their minds than whether to have the Steak Diane or the Lobster Thermidor. How wonderful . . .

Kenny kept up a light, easy flow of conversation until Ann began to fear the meal would end before she could pose her question. After they chose dessert, Ann decided it was time to speak.

'Kenny, what I wanted to talk to you about was Phillip.'

'Oh?' Kenny asked warily.

'He's fine,' she began. Then, with an honesty born of desperation, she amended, 'No, that's not true. He's not fine at all, Kenny. I don't know what to do. He doesn't have a job and his disability payments will be ending soon. We're just running out of money and I just don't know who else to turn to except you.'

Kenny put his hand on Ann's. 'Relax, honey. You know you can count on me.' This undoubtedly was the prelude to a request for a loan – and Kenny would be happy to oblige. Ann had been so good to Ruthie and Jeremy, and it was the least he could do. 'Tell me – what can I do for you?'

'Well, Phillip doesn't seem to go out and apply for a position. It's not that he's having any real problems,' Ann lied, 'but he's been away for so long he's afraid of being turned down.'

121

Ann couldn't meet Kenny's gaze and dropped her eyes to the table. Both of them knew that she was shading the truth about Phillip's mental health.

Then she blurted out, 'Kenny, do you think you could find a place for Phillip in your firm?'

Startled, he fumbled for words. 'Ann, I—'

'All he needs is a chance, Kenny! He's a good lawyer, you know he is!'

Kenny was speechless. This was the last thing he had expected or wanted. The Coulter family wasn't his responsibility, for God's sake! And his law firm wasn't in business for charity. A few bucks were one thing, but taking on an albatross was quite another.

He sat back, no longer seeing Ann's white, pleading face, but Phillip's, the last time Kenny had seen him. Thinking back, Kenny wondered if Phillip's weakness hadn't been there all along. He remembered his inability to adjust after the Coulters had lost their money in the Crash.

If he took Phillip into the firm with him, God only knew what might happen. Theirs was a trial firm, with a reputation for aggressiveness, and Phillip was certainly in no shape to go into a courtroom or even to meet clients, for that matter.

Suddenly Kenny's conscience smote him. He knew he was being unjust. Phillip had been a POW. He had been starved and tortured. And, unlike Kenny, he had not returned to a comfortable niche in a family business. *For God's sake*, Kenny decided, *Phil is my best friend. Don't I owe him a chance when he's down and out?*

There should be things he could do competently even now. He was intelligent. He could research briefs and draft motions, and if he studied up he really couldn't do the firm any harm. It would be nothing more than a lowly clerkship. If he had any pride he would probably tell Kenny no, but in Phil's present condition, he could hardly expect anything better.

Kenny patted Ann's hand and said, 'If you think he might want to come in with us, I'll certainly speak to him.'

'Oh, thank you!' Ann cried, relief flooding through her. Then she bit her lip. 'Kenny, please don't mention to Phillip that I suggested it to you.' She paused, then continued awkwardly, 'I suppose you think I'm disloyal, going behind Phillip's back like this . . .'

'I think you're a good wife, Ann. Phil is luckier than he knows to have you. I'll call him tomorrow.'

'Oh, Kenny. I just can't tell you how grateful I am.'

'Don't thank me yet, Ann. Let's see what Phil thinks about this.'

Twenty-One

Sitting across from Kenny at Schroeder's, Phillip felt uncomfortably out of place. His friend looked so prosperous and self-assured; Phillip was miserably conscious of his ill-fitting suit, cheap tie, and scarred cheek.

Kenny broke the silence. 'How's that drink holding up?'

Phillip, startled, asked, 'What?'

'Another martini?'

'Sure, don't mind if I do.'

When the drinks came, Kenny said, 'What do you feel like eating?'

Past echoes rang eerily through Phillip's head. *I don't know – what do you want? I don't know much about Chinese food.* His and Ann's first date . . .

'Phil? You still there?'

Phillip looked at him blankly. 'Oh . . . Whatever you're having, Kenny.'

'What else? *Sauerbraten* and *Schnitzel* and *Wein – ja?*'

'*Jawohl!*' Phillip tried to join in the joke.

If the rest of the world had changed, Schroeder's had not. The dark, wood-paneled dining room with the huge brass-railed bar was exactly the same as the last time Phillip had seen it some six years earlier. He actually found himself relaxing and enjoying the delicious meal.

123

It was only as the waiter brought their coffee that Kenny made his offer.

Phillip set his cup down abruptly and stared at his friend. On the one hand, the job was a godsend. No need to pound the streets, no need to endure nerve-racking interviews. On the other hand, it was galling – a lifeline thrown to a miserable slob who couldn't make it on his own.

Phillip felt a spurt of anger that fate had placed Kenny in a position to act as benefactor and himself in the role of supplicant. Kenny's father had been in practice in San Francisco for almost fifty years and had built a thriving practice. All Kenny had had to do was show up the day after graduation and be escorted to a plush office with his name newly lettered on the door. Nathan Newman hadn't squandered Kenny's future the way Simon had ruined Phillip's chances. It wasn't just.

Then Phillip reminded himself that he was being unreasonable. Kenny was doing him a favor. The real question he had to face was whether he could handle the stress of any job, let alone a legal practice. The thought of trying and failing terrified him, especially under Kenny's eyes. But how could he say no?

'You really need my help?'

Kenny chose his words carefully. 'We always need a good researcher, and right now we especially need someone good in pretrial procedure. I remember you were the best in the class at that back in Boalt.'

'That was a long time ago, Kenny.'

'It'll come back to you, Phil. Come on, how about it?'

Phillip lit a cigarette. 'Okay. We'll give it a whirl.'

Kenny smiled. 'Good man!'

Phillip looked at him, and for a moment it was as if the years since law school had never passed. With real confidence, he set his starting date and started off toward home. He could do it! Given this opportunity with a good law firm, he could be a success! He would be able to give Ann everything she wanted; he would recapture the enthusiasm and energy he had felt when he had first married her.

As Phillip turned at Union Square, he glimpsed his reflection in a shop window and was momentarily taken aback. What a sight he was in his shabby suit with its baggy prewar cut! Across the square was Bullock and Jones. It was an expensive men's store, but why not? He had a job, didn't he? The time had come to start living like a human being once again.

Before he could lose his nerve, he walked inside. Turning to the racks of fine worsteds with an unconsciously professional air, he quickly made a selection and, before he knew it, he was in front of a three-way mirror in an impeccable three-piece gray flannel suit. He straightened his shoulders and instantly the suit fell into line: no need even for a tailor. He didn't look bad at all, did he? In the well-cut suit, his thinness became an asset.

'I'll take it,' he announced, suddenly decisive. 'And six white button-down shirts.'

By the time he was through, he had acquired not only a navy rep tie and a discreet burgundy silk, but a pair of polished black calf wing-tips.

'I'll need to set up a charge account.' After giving his home address, he listed his business with a touch of pride: Newman, Ross, Simons, and Newman.

As Ann heard the key in the front door, she hurried from the kitchen, stripping off her apron and smoothing her hair.

'Phillip . . .' She stopped to hide her surprise. 'You've gotten some new clothes, sweetheart. How wonderful!'

'Ann, you'll never guess. Kenny has offered me a position. I start work on Monday.'

'And you've accepted. Oh, Phillip, I'm so happy for you!'

They flew into each other's arms and hugged each other tightly.

Kissing her, he whispered, 'Ann, darling, I love you

so. You've been so patient with me. Now everything will be fine, I promise.'

Laughing, crying, Ann hugged him again. 'Sweetheart, I *know* you'll be great.'

'You know, I was a bit surprised. Kenny hadn't given any hint he was thinking of hiring me before today.'

'He was probably waiting for you to get your strength back,' Ann said quickly.

'I suppose that was it,' Phillip agreed, a trifle doubtfully.

'Well, I always knew you were a genius, Phillip, and I guess Kenny knows it too . . .'

That night, when for the first time since his return, Phillip was able to make love to her, she was certain they were embarking on a bright new future.

Twenty-Two

When Phillip looked at his wife pouring out his coffee the next morning, he knew that he could conquer the world with one hand tied behind his back. The feeling of euphoria sustained him all the way to the office. Even the elegance of the Mills Building on Montgomery Street, in the heart of San Francisco's financial district, failed to shake his self-confidence.

It was only when he actually stood in front of the huge, gleaming wood door of the fifth floor office that he began to tremble slightly. Taking a handkerchief from his back pocket, he wiped his forehead. His newly born confidence was replaced by the familiar terrible feelings of inadequacy. But he had come too far to back down now.

He took a deep breath and opened the door. The receptionist seemed startled by his appearance. *It's the scar*, Phillip thought without emotion. *That's just something I've got to get used to.*

'Good morning,' he said evenly. 'My name is Phillip Coulter.'

126

Unexpectedly, she smiled. 'Mr Coulter – how nice to meet you. Mr. Newman is expecting you.'

Rising from her desk, she escorted him down the hall to Kenny's luxurious office. His friend was talking on the phone.

'They'll settle for fifty thousand. We've snowed 'em with so much paper, they don't know what hit 'em . . . they won't be able to afford to keep fighting us.'

As Phillip waited, the thought flashed into his head that this was all for his benefit. Kenny could put his caller on hold for a moment, couldn't he? But then he decided there was no reason Kenny should play wheeler-dealer for him. A moment later Kenny said, 'Got to go now. Speak to you later.' He hung up, a broad smile on his face. 'Phil! Sorry to keep you waiting, old buddy. I was talking to Sam Levy. You'll meet him one of these days. We've got a settlement cooking on a big case.'

'Sounds good to me.'

'Well – welcome aboard! Come on, I want you to meet the rest of the gang. We've got a conference in five minutes you can sit in on.'

At first Phillip felt ill at ease, sitting at the big oval conference table, but after a while the arguments began to make sense and he became absorbed in the pretrial planning.

As the conference broke up, the other lawyers briefly greeted him. One of them said, 'So you're the new clerk, eh? Don't let them work you to death.'

Phillip felt a burning sense of humiliation. With all his experience, he was coming in as a beginner. Kenny hadn't spelled it out, but Phillip had assumed that he was being hired as an associate. Now he realized that he and Kenny hadn't even discussed salary, let alone his title. Well, he was sure Kenny hadn't intended a slight. Perhaps within a few months, if he did well, he would be given some trial work.

His next shock was his office. After Kenny's, with its paneled walls and plush red carpeting, Phillip had expected that his own, though smaller, would be attractive. Instead, he was shown to a dingy cubbyhole with a linoleum floor.

He did his best to keep his face impassive as Kenny said, 'The library is down the hall. Do you work on a typewriter?' At Phillip's nod, he continued. 'We'll try to get you one. Meanwhile, I'm sure our other clerk will share with you.' He paused. 'Do you have any other questions?'

'No.'

'Good.' Kenny clapped him on the back. 'It will be great having you here.'

Phillip sank into the desk chair and lit a cigarette, trying not to let the small space make him feel claustrophobic. He knew he was going to have to control his resentment, but for the moment he wondered how he could endure such humiliation. Who was Kenny to lord it over him?

Phillip tried to remind himself that he was lucky to have a job at all. Two days ago, he was unemployed, almost unable to leave his house. *Face it, Phil – you were floundering and Kenny gave you a break.*

He began to leaf through the file on his desk. His eye caught a novel procedural motion and he soon found his old interest in civil procedure reawakening.

Before he knew it, the secretary was rapping on the door, asking if he wanted a sandwich sent in. Phillip looked at his watch and realized with a start that it was long past lunch.

'Pastrami on rye if you don't mind, Nancy.' He smiled. 'I'm just going to work straight through today.'

By five o'clock, Phillip was certain the job would work out. It was good to put his legal training to use again. He could become a success. He knew he could.

That evening, as Ann listened to Phillip's account of his first day, she decided she would never doubt God's mercy again.

As time passed, he became more assured. He turned out briefs, memos, and motions, always carefully researched and written, always on time. Often, he worked late in order to finish some project, and Ann became accustomed to hearing the phone ring at five minutes to six. She would pretend to be disappointed, but in reality she rejoiced at this evidence of Phillip's determination. He was bound to get ahead, working at this rate. So far, he earned a pittance, but they could manage for the time being, especially if he received a raise in the near future. Perhaps they could move to a bigger apartment, maybe a new dress or two for herself . . .

Phillip himself felt more and more confident with every assignment he completed. His moments of panic and self-doubt came less and less frequently, and he was certain that he would soon be ready for trial work. In fact, he was less nervous now about appearing in court than he had been before the war. After facing the likes of Nakanishi and Oto, a mere judge and jury held little terror for him.

Twenty-Three

In the months that followed, Phillip was in his office promptly at nine every morning. At first, he was busy catching up on new laws and concepts, but one day, after he had been with the firm for some ten months, he broached the subject with Kenny.

'You think that you're ready to go into court?' Kenny's tone held disbelief.

'I think I am,' Phillip said as firmly as he could.

Kenny hesitated, then spoke with care. 'Phil, listen. You're my buddy and I hate to be the one to say this to you. Less than a year ago, you were an emotional basket case. I just can't believe that in less than a year you've recovered enough to face a jury. That's a hell of a lot tougher than just grinding out paperwork.'

'I think I can handle it, Kenny.'

Kenny stared hard at him, his expression sober and

concerned. Finally he spoke. 'I think we'd better give it a little more time, Phil. You've got plenty to keep you busy right now, don't you?'

Phillip nodded, uncertain how to press his case further. If he couldn't win an argument with his only real friend, how could he take on hostile counsel?

'All right,' Kenny said when Phillip didn't reply. 'We'll talk more about this later.'

It was a dismissal and Phillip turned and left without speaking. It never occurred to him that Kenny subconsciously might not have wanted him to succeed. Kenny still remembered envying his friend's background in high school, his startling good looks, his quick brilliance, even the fact he was a war hero. Now, though Kenny didn't realize it, he tended to block Phillip's progress in the firm, and since the other partners knew the two were lifelong friends, if Kenny said Coulter wasn't ready for a promotion, they continued to hire from the outside.

Each time Phillip accepted the decision, but after another eighteen months, he confronted Kenny again.

'Kenny, when you hired me, very frankly I was just happy to be working again, and the salary was unimportant. Lately, though, I'm having a harder and harder time getting along on my paycheck. Even more, I feel I'm ready for more responsibility. I'm capable of more. I want to be considered for an associate's position, at least.'

Kenny hadn't expected Phillip to put it to him so bluntly.

'Well, it's not that your name hasn't come under consideration, Phil . . .'

'You mean that I've been considered and rejected? Would you mind very much telling me why?'

'Phil, litigation is our specialty, and all of our associates have to be able to perform well in open court. I don't want to upset you, but quite frankly no one feels you're quite ready for that.'

'How can anyone tell what I'm capable of? You've

never let me go into court at all, not even on the most minor matter. I couldn't be more underchallenged.'

Kenny regarded him kindly. 'Phil. This is between friends?'

'Of course.'

'Phil, I've seen you when you're tired or under stress. Your limp is more noticeable. Your face shows the strain. For God's sake, look at your hand – it's shaking.'

Phillip looked down. Was his hand shaking? He hadn't noticed it. But it was true that his limp worsened when he was tired. Once again, he felt helpless to protest that he was perfectly fine. He obviously didn't look it, and appearances were what counted in a courtroom.

'Okay,' he said at last. 'I'll accept that verdict for the time being. But I'd like to go on record as saying that I can't go on indefinitely like this.'

'If you feel you can find another place where you'll be happier . . .'

A moment of panic struck Phillip. He couldn't afford to go without even one paycheck, and if he looked as bad as Kenny seemed to imply, he might not find anything else.

'I wasn't threatening to quit, Kenny,' he said quickly.

Kenny idly toyed with a paper on his desk. 'I'll tell you what, Phil. Let me see if I can't get you a raise. Perhaps that will help.'

'I'd appreciate it.'

In the weeks that followed, Phillip tried not to let Kenny's opinion get to him, but doubts started to haunt him. He found it harder to be enthusiastic about his assignments and he no longer volunteered for extra work.

Ann was happy to find him on time for dinner and was not concerned about his salary. She assumed that all lawyers were underpaid until they made partner. She refused to even consider the possibility that Phillip might fail. In fact, the only cloud on the horizon that she saw was Eva's failing health. Each week Eva seemed to fade a little more. Simon and Ann did everything they

131

could to tempt her to eat and to distract her during the long days. Ann had given up her part-time job and devoted herself to Eva's comfort, but as the holidays rolled around, Eva became less and less responsive, until one January morning she slipped into a coma. By the time Phillip could race home from the office, she had died.

Ann could not believe how much she would miss her mother-in-law. The years of worry during the war had brought them closer than most real mothers and daughters. Now she felt almost as bereft as Simon. Phillip at least had his work, but Ann and Simon found their days had lost their focus.

Ann was so upset that she didn't notice that her period was late by nearly two months. For another three weeks she was so afraid she might not be pregnant that she postponed calling the doctor. When she finally went in and had the test, she practically held her breath until he called her with the news.

'No, Mrs. Coulter, there's no mistake about it. You're going to have a baby. In September, I'd say.'

Ann's joy was shadowed only by the fact that Eva was not there to share it. This was the miracle for which they had both prayed. Ann could hardly wait for Phillip to come home.

When he opened the door that night, she flew into his arms.

'Heavens, did I forget something?' Phillip laughed. 'A birthday? An anniversary, perhaps?'

'A birthday in September. Oh, Phillip, we're going to have a baby.'

Ann had not seen Phillip so unreservedly happy since the early days of their marriage. Even Simon lost the sad, drawn look his face had worn since Eva's death.

Phillip now worked with renewed ambition, while Ann and Simon spent their days readying the apartment for the child.

On September 6, 1949, Ann gave birth to a baby girl.

They named her Eva Louise, but she almost immediately became Evie. Simon wept unashamedly at the sight of the baby. It was as though his beloved Eva had been reborn in the granddaughter she hadn't lived long enough to see. Simon had almost willed himself to die along with Eva, but looking down at Evie, he now felt he had a reason to go on living. In that moment, a blind adoration for her was born in him that would endure for the rest of his life.

When Phillip was finally allowed to see his daughter for the first time, he was overwhelmed with a love like no other he had ever experienced. If he did nothing else in his life, he could be proud of fathering this beautiful baby. 'Evie,' he whispered, giving her the necklace she would always wear, 'you are my future.'

From that moment, Evie became the center of Phillip's world. Although Ann, too, had longed for this child, vowing never to allow her to be abused the way Ann had been in her childhood, Phillip felt that his life had been transformed. His days were filled with happy expectation of the moment he could pick her up, and his nights no longer were troubled by horrible dreams about the war.

As she grew from tiny infant to plump smiling baby, he insisted on feeding her dinner and playing with her on the living room floor.

From the very first her face lit up at the sight of Daddy. Ann watched the two of them with an occasional stab of jealousy. It was wonderful, of course, that Phillip took fatherhood so seriously, but there were limits. After all, wasn't she the one who spent her days taking care of Evie? Yet the minute Evie saw her father's face she had eyes for no one else. Ann didn't understand that deep down inside herself there dwelt a lonely child who wanted to be indulged and pampered just as Evie was.

Still, her twinges of jealousy were short-lived, and she laughed at her own foolishness. Phillip *was* a perfect father. When Evie had colic, he walked the floor with her, soothing her cries. When she fell down, he put on the Band-Aids. When she had a high fever at the age of one, Phillip stayed home from work for four days fussing over her like a mother hen.

'Darling, can they do without you for this long?' Ann asked, worried that he was taking advantage of Kenny. 'Evie's not in any danger.'

'Why don't you let me worry about that, Ann?' he said, a trace of irritation in his voice.

How could he tell her how unimportant he was to Newman, Ross, Simons, and Newman? They could probably hire a second-year law student to do what he did. Nothing had really changed since his conversation with Kenny. He had gotten a small raise, but he had not been assigned more challenging work. From time to time he thought of leaving, but was always stopped by the thought that if he couldn't make it under Kenny's aegis, then he'd never make it elsewhere. Without realizing it, he was beginning to see himself the way Kenny did.

It hurt him to think that Evie couldn't have every material thing she might want, and in an effort to compensate, he smothered her with love and spent whatever extra money he could scrape together on her. Nothing was too good for Evie Coulter.

Twenty-Four

It was December of 1952. Evie was three years old, and positively enchanting. For the first time she was old enough to understand what the holiday was about, and the only thing she could talk about was 'Santy Claus.'

For the last week, Ann and Phillip had been promising to take her downtown to Macy's to see this magical figure in person, to sit on his lap and tell him what she would like for Christmas.

Saturday morning, Ann woke up feeling weak and feverish. She had been fighting off a cold for several days, and now it seemed to have hit full force.

Struggling out of bed, she threw on a wrapper and went into the kitchen to find Phillip and Evie already eating bowls of oatmeal with brown sugar.

Looking up from her breakfast, Evie chirped happily, 'We're going to see Santy Claus today! Huh, Mommy?'

But Phillip, noticing Ann's flushed face and glassy eyes, asked, 'Honey, are you feeling okay?'

'I'm all right.'

Phillip was unconvinced 'You don't look so good, sweetheart. You'd better go back to bed.'

'I can't, Phillip. We're taking Evie to see Santa today; she has her heart set on it.'

'Well . . . listen, Ann, how about if I take Evie alone? There's no need for you to drag yourself down there feeling the way you do.'

'Are you sure?'

'Absolutely. It will be fun having Evie all to myself for a day. And you can get some rest.'

Feeling too sick to protest, she dressed Evie in a cotton sailor dress. Ann wished she had something warmer, but Evie had been growing so fast that most of her clothes didn't fit.

'Put her coat on, Phillip,' Ann said.

Phillip went to the closet. Taking out the little brown cloth coat, he stared at it for a moment. It seemed so shabby.

Sighing, he told Evie, 'Stick your arms out, sweetheart.'

Evie obediently stuck out both arms and Phillip wrestled her into the coat. Then he buttoned it up and stood back to survey her. Phillip had never paid much attention to children's clothes before, but somehow Evie didn't look quite right. The coat was worn and too short besides. Luckily, Evie didn't seem to mind at all.

'Bye-bye, Mommy,' she was calling from the doorway. 'I'll say hello to Santy Claus for you.'

Holding Evie by the hand, Phillip stood in line with all the mothers and children. When it was Evie's turn, she

135

just stared, big-eyed, at Santa's flowing white beard and ermine-trimmed red hat.

'Ho, ho, ho!' he said, lifting her onto his lap. 'And what would you like for Christmas, little girl?'

Reassured by the twinkle in his eyes, Evie smiled, but was still tongue-tied with shyness. Phillip just watched. How adorable she was. How far superior she was to all these other ordinary-looking children. He ordered ten copies of the picture the store took of each child without stopping to think what he'd do with them all.

When she hopped down and raced to him, he scooped her up in his arms and kissed her. 'You were great, Evie, darling.'

She curled her arms about his neck, whispering breathlessly, 'I saw Santy, Daddy!'

'Did you tell him what you wanted?'

She shook her head.

'Well, then, princess, you'll just have to tell Daddy, and Daddy will tell Santa for you.'

They wandered through aisles bedecked with sparkling lights and glittering tinsel garlands and banks of red poinsettias. It was a fairyland and Evie's eyes were like stars. But as Phillip looked down at her, something snapped inside him. All the other little girls were so festively attired – red velveteen jumpers over ruffled blouses, or starched organdy dresses with blue satin sashes. He felt like he was letting Evie down. She had a right to everything other children had.

Purposefully, he took her by the hand and led her away from the toy department down the escalator and out of the store. A blast of cold air hit them on Stockton Street and he felt Evie shiver. They waited on the corner for the signal to change, then crossed the street to the City of Paris. The imposing store, with its lacy black ironwork, was crowned by a replica of the Eiffel Tower. Eva had always bought his good suits there when he was a little boy. Before they knew it, he and Evie were in the children's department.

'I would like to see a coat for my daughter,' he said to the silver-haired saleslady.

'What color do you like, my dear?' she asked.

'Blue, please,' Evie said, dimpling.

'I think I have just the thing,' she said, taking down a hanger from the rack.

When Phillip saw his child dressed in the blue flannel coat, with its prim pearl buttons, her cherubic face framed by a matching bonnet, he was so completely carried away that he just said, 'We'll take it. How much is it?'

'Seventy-five dollars, sir,' the saleslady replied. 'Will that be cash or charge?'

'I'll write a check,' Phillip said, swallowing hard. Seventy-five dollars! That was a lot of money, but damn it, Evie was worth it. And why *shouldn't* his daughter have a decent coat?

Covertly, he checked his balance – a hundred dollars – and wrote out the check.

'Thank you, Mr. Coulter,' the saleslady said, then stopped. 'Phillip Coulter! Why, I remember when you used to come in with your mother – must be thirty years ago or more!'

'I imagine it must be,' Phillip said.

'So this is your little girl! Isn't that wonderful. She is just adorable.'

'Thank you,' Phillip said, smiling. 'Well, you'll have to excuse us, we have some more shopping to do. Merry Christmas!' he said as he and Evie took their package.

Phillip walked away, feeling unexpectedly warmed. He remembered how nice it had been going places as a child with Eva when money was never mentioned, because it was never a problem.

Suddenly he made a decision. He was going to open up a charge account. Evie was going to have a Christmas to remember. 'I need it activated immediately,' he told them upstairs in the credit department.

Something extraordinary happened to Phillip that day. Armed with his new card, he bought and bought

137

as though there were no tomorrow. Then they lunched at Blum's. Phillip allowed Evie to order anything she wanted . . . a hot dog . . . an ice-cream sundae with chocolate sauce, controlling his urge to insist on hot chicken soup and noodles.

As Phillip watched Evie happily eating ice cream, he thought she looked like a little princess even in her old clothes.

'Daddy, can we bring Mommy a box of candy?' she asked as they were ready to go.

'Of course, Evie. It's too bad Mommy couldn't come with us today, but we'll bring her candy, and something nice for Christmas, too.'

He tried to think what would make Ann happy. A nightgown? One of those frilly pink things he had glimpsed at City of Paris? No, a glamorous nightgown was entirely too frivolous. Ann had become so practical and thrifty these days, she would probably return it. He remembered that just yesterday she had been saying she needed a new toaster. He went outside, holding Evie's hand tightly in his own.

It was four on the kitchen clock. Since early that afternoon Ann had the gnawing feeling that something was wrong. Maybe Evie had gotten sick, or maybe they had had an accident. When she finally heard the key in the lock, she sprang to the door.

Evie had fallen asleep in the car and Phillip carried her into her room and laid her on the bed without waking her. He closed her door, walked into the living room, and tried to kiss Ann, but she backed away.

'My God, Phillip, I've been so worried! You've been gone since nine o'clock. Evie hasn't had her nap or anything!'

'Well, she's asleep now,' Phillip replied defensively.

'I should think so! What did you find to do with a small child for so many hours?'

'We've been shopping.'

'Shopping?'

'Wait till you see what I bought. Everything is in the car; let me go get it.'

It took three trips for him to bring in the tricycle, the panda bigger than Evie herself, the dollhouse – plus a new doll. Ann sat in a state of shock.

'You bought all this?' she asked incredulously.

'Yes. And wait until I show you the clothes.' He triumphantly pulled the lids off several boxes.

Ann looked from the pair of black patent leather shoes to a pair of white ones, three pairs of tights, lace-trimmed socks, two elaborate party dresses, and the French coat and bonnet. She shook her head as he smoothed the folds from the coat.

'We had an incredible time, darling! I only wish you could have been there. You should have seen Evie's face.'

Ann just sat there, speechless. The floor was piled with things that Evie didn't need, while Phillip stood in the middle, surveying them proudly.

'Phillip, how did you pay for all of this?' Ann asked, finding her voice. When he didn't answer, she picked up a sales slip which had fluttered to the floor. 'Since when do we have a charge account with the City of Paris?' Her eyes widened. 'My God. Seventy-five dollars for a coat! Oh, Phillip! How could you have done anything so ridiculous?'

Without the atmosphere of carols and tinsel, here in his shabby living room, it did seem absurd.

'Ann—' he tried to explain.

But she wasn't listening. 'Why, for God's sake, there must be over four hundred dollars' worth of stuff here, Phillip! You must have lost your mind. How could you have done this?'

He suddenly remembered that Ann hadn't had a new dress in God only knew how long.

'I guess I went a little overboard . . .'

'Overboard? Insane is more like it! Here we are, having such a difficult time with money, and you buy all this for Evie. Where is she going to wear two party dresses, anyway?'

Rather sheepishly, Phillip said, 'I just wanted to give Evie a Christmas to remember.'

'That's the most ridiculous thing I've ever heard. She's only three.'

He was about to respond when Ann opened another bag. 'Oh . . . and what is this? A toaster. Is that for Evie, too?'

'No, that's my tribute to you,' Phillip said, knowing that he was being unfair. 'You're the one who's been bitching about the burnt toast.'

'Oh, I see. So this is my present?' she cried. 'I had no idea how insensitive you could be! You have never bought me any kind of meaningful gift in all the years we've been married. I *do* count for something – and if you don't mind my saying it, I think that I'm as important as Evie is!'

The day that had started out so enchantingly for Phillip had turned to ashes. He knew he was in the wrong, and that only made him angrier. 'I can't believe you begrudge your own daughter a happy holiday. I think you're jealous, Ann.'

'Jealous!' she cried, on the verge of tears. 'How dare you say that to me! It's unfair. I am *not* complaining about your buying Evie clothes – God only knows she needs them. But you didn't have to go to the City of Paris. Look at these prices! A tricycle for sixty-five dollars. My God, Phillip, can't you see how ridiculous that is? And if you had just asked, I would have told you that Ruthie was going to give me Jeremy's old one.'

'Damn it!' Phillip exploded. 'Don't dictate to me what I should and shouldn't do. If I want to buy my child toys, I'll buy her toys. I am still the head of this household.'

'So you want me to give you a medal?'

Like so many arguments between husband and wife, this one went far beyond the cause. Both Ann and Phillip dredged up real and imagined wrongs. They uttered the most brutal things they could think of to wound each other, until Ann finally burst out, 'I know what you're trying to prove, Phillip – that you're not a failure.'

Phillip dropped the little blue coat he'd been holding. 'Is that what you think, Ann?' He didn't know how the fight had escalated. He just had to get away from Ann's tear-stained face. Without another word, he grabbed his jacket and walked out the front door. Ann's words had cut him to the quick. She believed that he never would be able to provide for them properly. And in his heart of hearts, he knew she was right. As Kenny had suspected, he was a loser.

And how could he blame her for being angry? It was not just his extravagance today, she must have been disgusted with him for years.

Ann was suffering equal remorse. As soon as the door slammed behind him, she burst into sobs. *My God, I sounded just like Stella. I've turned into a bitch*. She knew Phillip tried his best and that he needed her support. She cringed when she remembered how she'd belittled him. She would have given anything to take back the words. She sat, the tears drying on her cheeks, until she heard the front door open again.

They came into each other's arms before either could speak. Who was right and who was wrong no longer mattered.

It was Ann who broke the silence, holding his face between her hands. 'Let's try never to say such things to each other again. It hurts too much.'

'Never,' he whispered back.

And in that moment both believed their promise.

Twenty-Five

They put the quarrel behind them. Ann's days were filled with the house, cooking, and taking Evie to the park, the zoo, and the pediatrician. She rarely had time to stop and think.

Then one day when Evie was almost four the doctor

141

recommended Ann enroll her in a play group. 'She spends too much time with adults. She's with you and Simon all day and Phillip at night. She needs playmates her own age.'

Ann took the advice, but the first day when Ann and her father-in-law took Evie to the church where the group met, the little girl refused to go in.

'I don't want to stay here, Mommy. Can't I go home with you and Grandpa?'

'Honey, look at all the toys they have here. Won't it be fun to play with them?'

Evie shook her head, burying her face in Ann's skirts.

'Evie, honey . . .' Ann said helplessly.

'How about if Grandpa stays here with you?' Simon asked. 'Would you like that?'

Ann glanced at him. Wouldn't it be too much of a burden for him, to be surrounded by all these noisy children? But he seemed delighted when Evie looked up at him hopefully. 'Oh, yes, Grandpa, that would be much better! Will you stay here the whole time?'

They had come home that afternoon all smiles, and Grandpa had accompanied her the next day, and the next. Evie soon lost her fear of the play group, and the teacher asked if Simon would like to stay on as an aide. He was delighted, so every day the two of them trotted off together.

His new role gave Simon a new sense of self-worth. The children looked forward to seeing him, and Simon found a whole new world for himself. Best of all, he and Evie developed a special relationship.

Ann was delighted to see her father-in-law so happy, but with Evie out all morning and Simon gone as well, she found herself for the first time in years with time on her hands. Cleaning the small rooms and fixing supper left her with long hours to think about the future. She began to wonder if they would ever have the money to buy a house or even just redecorate the Coulters' old apartment. She and Phillip had moved into the one real bedroom, Evie had Phillip's old cubbyhole, and Simon slept on a rollaway bed in the living room.

Having been poor all her life, Ann had assured Phillip when they married that she would be perfectly content with whatever material things he could give her. In those days, she had been so in love that she would have been happy living in a tent. Now she wondered if their finances would ever improve. Since that terrible Christmas, they had never quarreled over money, but Ann knew someday they would have to face facts: Phillip was thirty-eight years old. He had worked for Kenny for seven years, and there was no reason to believe he would ever be more than a clerk. Meanwhile Evie was growing up, and Ann knew only too well what it was like to be a young girl without pretty clothes, without a nice home to bring friends to. More important, she wanted to save so Evie could go to college. Phillip didn't seem to share these worries, and Ann knew she was becoming resentful.

Most of the girls Ann had known in high school had lovely houses; some had moved down the Peninsula to country places with pools and tennis courts. Their husbands all seemed to have done well in the postwar boom. Ann no longer met them for a day in town. The Coulters' budget couldn't stand lunching out, and Ann's old school friends now shopped in fancier places than she could afford.

She and Phillip didn't even socialize with Ruthie and Kenny anymore. A definite constraint had developed in their relationship. Ann didn't blame Kenny for Phillip's failure to advance, but her loyalty to her husband made her loath to discuss it with Ruthie.

The result was that Ann kept everything bottled up inside her. She and Phillip hardly communicated at all. They talked around things, or avoided them. He had long since ceased to share his dreams with her – if he still had any.

The few times she had brought up the subject of a raise, or the possibility of changing jobs, he had

143

snapped, 'I'm doing the best I can, Ann. I can't do more than that.'

It always reduced her to tears.

Later, more calmly, all he would say was that he didn't care about 'keeping up with the Joneses – or the Goldbergs,' and Ann would try to put thoughts about moving to a nicer place out of her mind until the next incident arose to trigger her discontent.

It was late in the spring of 1954 that Ann received an invitation from the Newmans to a housewarming. She hadn't even known they had bought a new house. She glanced at the address – Washington and Cherry – the heart of Pacific Heights!

That was moving up with a vengeance! Kenny apparently was taking in a pretty profit from the firm to be able to afford that house. Funny, she had gotten the impression from Phillip that business was pretty stagnant. Or had he implied that simply to keep her from asking awkward questions about his own prospects?

The party was in full swing by the time Phillip and Ann pulled up in front of the house, which was aglow with lights. A very correct French maid in a black uniform with a crisp, organdy-frilled apron took their coats. Ann and Phillip stared about the imposing hall with its cathedral ceiling. Crystal chandeliers glittered overhead, and candles highlighted spectacular arrangements of roses and orchids placed at intervals on the sweeping staircase. Ann tried and failed to picture the little Ruthie she had grown up with descending those stairs. The house was so formal, so ornate. But when her friend rushed over to greet them, she realized Ruthie had changed too. She had bleached her hair a soft blond, and her beaded gown showed off a much more svelte figure than Ann remembered.

'You look lovely,' Ann murmured, trying not to feel envious. 'And the house is magnificent.'

'We like it,' Kenny said, coming over and welcoming them. 'Go in and make yourselves at home. Give the bartender a little business.' He took Ruthie's arm and went off, leaving Ann to nervously face the crowd. She glanced at Phillip and noticing his grimly set jaw, realized he was no more relaxed than she. As they waited at the bar for drinks, Ann began to notice some familiar faces. Wasn't that Polly Schwartz – no, Polly Greenberg now – with her husband, Ron? He was balding but well-dressed and prosperous looking. Ron and Polly had moved to Atherton, with their three children. Ron was a vice-president of a bank he and a partner had started shortly after the war. Polly was blond now, like Ruthie. Blond hair must be in this year, but it looked great on Polly. You'd never know she had three children – her figure was stunning.

And there was Sheila Levy. She still had dark hair, but she looked so chic in a vivid red dress and ruby earrings. Her husband, Morris, was a stockbroker, and Ann had heard they had bought a new house in Burlingame.

Ann remembered when she and Ruthie and Polly and Sheila were still in school, how they had giggled and whispered and passed notes during class. In those days none of them had any money. They had all worn hand-me-down clothes, and saved up for movies and sodas. Seeing them now, Ann realized just how far behind she had been left. She glanced at Phillip, who was still the handsomest man in the room, scar or no scar. But if Ann could have read his mind, she would have realized that he was having more trouble facing his friends' new-found affluence than she was. He remembered Sea Cliff, with its old-world charm, and knew that these new mansions weren't what he wanted. He also knew he was judged by his own lack of success.

So what if they're rich? he thought, looking at Kenny's luxuriously decorated living room. *Is money really all that important?* Then he noticed Ann, looking like a sparrow among peacocks in her old beige dress. It would be nice to dress her the way she deserved. But even in this crowd of impeccably coifed and expensively dressed women, she was the most beautiful one in the room. He

145

went over and put his arm around her, noticing that her smile seemed strained. Two hours later she sighed with relief when he suggested it was time to leave.

Later, when they were home in bed, Ann kept wondering why she and Phillip seemed to have missed out on so many of the things Ruthie and Kenny enjoyed. It wasn't just the big house and fancy clothes. She and Phillip were so isolated. As a girl she had always had friends, and she'd enjoyed entertaining when they were first married, even though they were poor. What had happened? Of all his classmates, Phillip had had the most potential – everyone always said so. He was brilliant, handsome, gifted – but since he'd returned from the Pacific, he'd lost his ambition. Ann didn't want a lot of things, but tonight, as she lay awake almost until dawn, she knew she wanted more out of life than she had had the last few years. And if Phillip wouldn't or couldn't help her, well then, she'd do it herself. She had worked for years and had enjoyed the challenge. With Evie starting school this September, Ann made a decision. She would look for a job.

The next morning after Phillip left for work, Ann dressed with extra care. As she brushed on mascara and lipstick, she told herself she had made the only choice possible. Even if Phillip's pride was hurt, she was going to get a job, but she quailed, remembering how much he had hated her working at Magnin's.

In the kitchen, Simon was washing the breakfast dishes and Evie was drying them. Watching them, Ann felt a pang of guilt at the prospect of not always being there for her daughter. Then her eyes wandered around the dark little kitchen, with the brown linoleum and dingy and spotted paint. It had been years since she and Eva had decorated. Now the sight of those walls steeled her resolve. There was a price to be paid for everything, and if their finances were ever to improve, she was the one who would have to do it. But, given that dismal bit of philosophy, Ann determined to make the reward worth the price.

She kissed Simon on the cheek, then picked Evie up and hugged her tightly. 'Mommy's going out for a while today.'

'Can I go with you?'

'Not this time, darling. I want you to stay here with Grandpa.'

'Why, Mommy? Where are you going?'

'Uh . . . to the beauty shop, Evie.'

'I like the beauty shop, Mommy. Can't I go with you? I'll be good.'

'No, Evie. I've already said I can't take you with me.' Ann turned away from Evie's hurt expression and Simon's puzzled one. Going out the door, she added, 'I'll be home around noon.'

Waiting for the bus, she took out an ad she'd clipped from yesterday's paper.

When she reached the office, she took a deep breath before going inside. There didn't seem to be a receptionist, and everyone in sight was extraordinarily busy, talking on the phone or writing furiously on note pads spread in front of them. For a moment Ann hesitated. Then she spotted the desk with a brass sign which spelled out VIOLET CUN-NINGHAM.

Miss Cunningham was in the middle of a phone conversation, and Ann had a moment to observe her. She wore a beige cashmere sweater set, with a short string of pearls. Her hair was combed into an impeccable salt and pepper page boy. When she finally put down the phone, she made a series of swift notes, then looked up at Ann inquiringly.

'Hello, Miss Cunningham. My name is Ann Coulter. I saw your ad and I'd like to apply for the job.'

'It's a pleasure to meet you, Mrs. Coulter,' Violet said, smiling. 'Please have a seat and tell me if you have any experience in real estate.'

'Well, no. But I'm very anxious to get into the field. I'm sure I can learn very fast. All my life I've wanted to be an agent,' she lied. 'You know, like some people want to be movie stars.'

Violet listened, her shrewd eyes sizing Ann up. The young woman had probably never had a job before in her life. She was beautiful, all right, and undoubtedly had married young. It was only plain women like Violet Cunningham who remained single, so why did Ann Coulter want to work now? Her suit was certainly outdated and shabby, so Violet guessed she needed the money. Well, need was a great motivator, and Violet decided she might as well take a chance. Pay was by commission, so if Coulter didn't work out, it wouldn't cost the agency anything except minor expenses.

She smiled at Ann. 'Tell me,' Violet asked, 'how familiar are you with the Marina?'

'Very,' Ann said eagerly. 'I lived there when I was first married, and I've lived in San Francisco all my life. As a matter of fact, I remember when a lot of it was just bare land, still left after they tore down the Panama-Pacific Exposition.'

Violet knew that Ann was trying to impress her, but she valued her enthusiasm.

'Well, I'm glad you like the Marina because we specialize in that district. Demand is consistent, and values are constantly climbing. We handle both sales and rentals. Rentals won't make you rich, but they're your bread and butter. Flats sell relatively quickly, but single-family homes don't. Sometimes you sit on a house for months. Other times you have a client ready to buy and the bank turns them down on the mortgage. The upshot is that you end up wasting a lot of time. Are you prepared for that kind of frustration?'

Ann knew all about frustration. Calmly, she said, 'Naturally, I'd be disappointed. But I would hardly be ready to go jump off the Golden Gate Bridge. It's just in the nature of the real estate business, I guess.'

Violet laughed, pleased with the response. 'Now, just so that I don't discourage you altogether, rentals are easy. There's a waiting list a mile long because, even though the Marina's expensive, everyone wants to live there. It's close to downtown and it's a community for raising children. Prices have almost doubled in the last ten years. Rentals go from about eighty to one hundred fifty, flats sell for eighteen hundred to twenty-eight hundred, and houses for ten thousand to thirty thousand.'

The prices staggered Ann. If she and Phillip had ten thousand dollars, they would feel like millionaires. But she nodded knowledgeably as if she were fully conversant with such prices.

'Now, Ann,' Violet Cunningham said, 'if I take you on and you work out, when I get through training you you'll be a pro. I'll expect you to stay with me.'

Ann scarcely noticed the implied threat. All that penetrated was that she had a job.

'You must understand,' Violet continued, 'that although we have one of the liveliest offices in the city, you aren't going to make much money at first. It takes at least three months or so to begin to develop a clientele, and it isn't until you start to get referrals that the commissions really roll in.' Violet watched Ann for her reaction.

Lifting her chin, Ann said, 'Well, fortunately my husband is a lawyer, so I don't mind waiting.'

Violet was too clever to be fooled by Ann's words. Mr. Coulter might be an attorney, but she was too eager for this job for it to be simply a hobby. No, Ann's husband must not be doing too well – or maybe the two of them weren't getting along these days – but a little pressure would make her work a little harder, stay a little later.

The more she thought about it, the more Violet was convinced that she was making a good move hiring Ann. 'All right, then. When would you like to start? Tomorrow?'

'Oh, I can't!' Ann exclaimed unhappily. She had had no idea that Violet might want her immediately. 'I have a little girl who's beginning school next Monday. Could I possibly come in a week from Tuesday?'

Violet hid a smile. Ann had an engaging lack of sophistication. 'That will be fine.'

'Thank you so much, Mrs Cunningham. I can't tell you how excited I am about coming to work for you.'

As Ann turned to leave, Violet, already back on the telephone, covered the receiver and called out, 'Be sure to get your license, Ann, and bring it in for me to sign on Tuesday.'

Not having the vaguest idea what license Violet was referring to, or how she was to go about getting one, Ann just said, 'I will – and thank you again.'

Trying to calm herself down, she went into a nearby cafeteria and ordered a cup of coffee and a doughnut. Phillip would know where to get the license, but fearing his reaction when she told him about her new job, she decided she better do some investigating on her own. She would have to go to city hall. She glanced at her watch. Seeing it was after twelve, she decided she'd better call home.

A minute later, she heard Evie's voice say, 'Coulter residence.'

'It's Mommy, darling. How are you?'

'I'm fine, but Grandpa and I want you to come home now, Mommy.'

'I can't right now, Evie.'

'Are you at the beauty shop?'

'Y-yes, Evie. I'm not done yet. Now let me talk to Grandpa.'

'Ann, my dear, how are you?'

'I'm just fine, Dad, but I'll be late. I hope you don't mind getting Evie's lunch.'

150

'No trouble at all, Ann dear. Please don't worry about a thing.'

'Thanks, Dad. I'm going to be tied up for another hour or so. My – hair isn't quite dry.'

Ann felt petty deceiving Simon. But it couldn't be helped. She needed to get that license quickly, before she lost her nerve.

Back in the 1950s, it was as easy to be issued a real estate agent's license as a dog license. Ann found the signboard in city hall that directed her to a second-floor clerk's office. Fifteen minutes later, after filling out a form, she received the precious permit.

Nothing in her life had given her a greater sense of pride than reading, 'The State of California hereby grants to ANN COULTER the right to act as agent in the sale of real property.' There was a good deal of fine print, but she could read no further than her own name. Ann Coulter, not Mrs. Phillip Coulter. In the eyes of the State of California, she could stand on her own merits.

Later that afternoon, she splurged on a special dinner. Cracked crab salad with genuine Roquefort dressing, sourdough bread, and stuffed capon with the wild rice they virtually never bought. She set the table with candles and roses from the flower vendor in front of Rossi's market.

The moment Phillip saw the dining room he asked, 'What's the special occasion? I know it's not our anniversary.'

'Well, no. I just thought we all deserved a treat.'

'It's certainly delicious,' said Phillip, attacking his crab with gusto.

Ann took a deep breath and relaxed slightly.

Then Phillip said, 'Eat, Evie. What's the matter, don't you like your crab?'

'I don't like the shells!'

'Mommy has taken all the crab out of the shells for you, Evie darling,' Ann told her.

Evie made a face and, trying a diversionary tactic,

she announced, 'Daddy, Mommy went to the beauty shop today. Do you like her hair?'

Phillip looked up. 'Did you have your hair done, Ann? I have to confess, I don't see any difference.'

Ann was unable to continue her deception. 'No, Phillip, I didn't. I didn't go to the beauty shop at all.'

'Yes you did, Mommy! You said so!'

'Well, darling, I – I changed my mind. I had something else to do.'

She looked at Phillip, and at the question in his eyes, all her well-rehearsed, tactful phrasings were forgotten. 'I got a job today,' she blurted out.

Phillip stared at her. 'Is that the reason for the celebration?'

'I suppose so,' Ann answered guiltily.

Phillip didn't immediately respond. He appeared unmoved by the news, but actually he was furious. Ann had set him up for this, putting on a fancy dinner and then making her pronouncement. If she had simply come to him and said, 'Phillip, I'd like to get a job,' he would have been less upset. He would have liked it a lot better.

'Why didn't you consult me first, Ann?'

'Phillip, you have always been adamant about my not working. Would you really have liked it better if I'd told you first?'

No – damn it, he wouldn't have liked it at all, no matter when she approached him. He hated the idea that Ann had to go to work because he was unable to make an adequate living. But that was the truth. His salary *wasn't* enough to support them. It was a bitter pill to swallow, but Ann *did* need to go to work. There was no point in arguing the matter.

'What are you going to do, Ann?' he asked quietly.

'It's a job in a real estate office in the Marina.'

'And how do you plan to handle the house and a job at the same time?'

'When you want something badly enough, you make the effort,' Ann said with only a slight edge to her voice.

152

Simon, who had watched this interchange with some distress, helped Evie down from the table even before she finished her chicken and took her off for a bedtime story. He felt his son and his wife needed to be alone. Simon was one hundred percent behind his daughter-in-law. For years she had carried the entire Coulter family on her slim shoulders. She couldn't be faulted as a mother or wife. More than that, Ann was the emotional center of all their lives, the source of strength, the heart. If she felt that this was for the good of the family, then Simon would support her all the way.

Phillip had barely noticed Simon's leaving. 'I'm sorry about your having to go to work, Ann.'

Ann knew how painful the admission was. 'I'm sorry, too,' she said. 'The reason I didn't tell you beforehand was I knew you would be upset. The fact of the matter is that much as I love you, I just can't go on like this any longer. Evie is beginning to grow up. Someday I'd like to buy a house. And what about her college education? These things concern both of us – and I don't see any reason why I shouldn't do what I can to help make them possible.'

'It's my fault, Ann. I should be the one providing for our needs,' Phillip muttered.

'Phillip, it's not a question of fault. We're in this together, aren't we?'

But even as she spoke, she could see that her words were having no effect. That night when they went to bed he turned his back on her, and though he didn't mention the subject again, she knew it would be a long time before he forgave this blow to his pride.

Twenty-Six

Although Evie went off to first grade as blithely as if she'd been attending school all her life, Ann started work with a heavy heart. Phillip's accusatory looks had convinced her she was abandoning her child, even though Simon had promised to walk Evie to school each day and be there waiting the moment she got out. Still, from the second Ann gave Miss Cunningham her new license, she was kept so busy she didn't have time to think. And on the way home, she couldn't help feeling a certain pride, but she was careful when Phillip came home not to let him notice anything had changed.

When Phillip came in the door she asked about his day. Dinner was on the table promptly at 6:30 and conversation centered as usual on Evie. Did she like kickball? Would she prefer peanut butter or bologna for lunch tomorrow? Afterward, Phillip watched television while Simon put Evie to bed and Ann washed the dishes. He never mentioned her job at all, and Ann went to bed, her triumph somewhat diminished by Phillip's silence.

For the next three days, Ann sat at her desk trying to appear busy while the other agents' phones rang constantly. Even though she reminded herself that it was only her first week, she couldn't help becoming anxious.

Violet casually reassured her. 'It'll come, don't worry about it for the first week or two.' But Ann still worried.

A new problem arose during the second week. It seemed that the agents were required to take turns working Sundays, answering the phone, and Ann was told she was on call the next weekend. Fearful of Phillip's reaction, she said nothing until Sunday at breakfast. This time she felt that however angry he got, he was justified. Families *always* spent Sundays together – at least happy families did.

'I have to go to the office,' she said guiltily when she finished her coffee. Phillip actually took the announcement calmly, but Evie said, 'Gee, Mommy, you're never home anymore.'

Ann tried to sound cheerful. 'Well, Evie, you can have fun with Daddy and Grandpa. You know you always do.'

'But it would be more fun if you were here too, Mommy.'

Fighting back tears, Ann smiled and said, 'Next Sunday. Is that okay?'

Evie, usually so amenable, wore a mutinous expression. 'No, it's *not* okay.'

After breakfast, when Phillip took Evie off to pick up the paper, Ann said to Simon, 'Evie is really upset about my going to the office today.'

'Well, Ann, there have been a lot of changes for her recently.'

'I guess my working has been pretty hard on her.'

'She also has started school.'

'Well, that's true, but I don't think that's it. She loves first grade, Simon. I'm amazed how well she has adjusted. I had been afraid that as an only child she had been too sheltered. No, it's my working that's bothering her, and I feel awful about it.'

'Maybe I shouldn't say this, Ann, but I feel as if Evie is taking her cue from Phillip. It's so obvious that he hates your working.'

'Oh, no, Simon! He hasn't actually said anything.'

'Evie is a sensitive little girl, and close to her father. I think she's just echoing what she senses in Phillip.'

Ann was silent for a minute. Then she said, 'Even if that's true, the tension between Phillip and me is still bad for her.'

Simon reached out and covered Ann's hand with his own. 'Ann, all children have to learn life isn't perfect. So what if Evie knows that you and Phillip occasionally differ? There's nothing wrong with your working. You're doing it for all our sakes. I just wish I could do more,' he finished a little sadly.

'Oh, Dad, please! I couldn't even think about working unless I knew I could leave Evie with you.' She threw her arms around Simon's neck and hugged him.

Although it was heartening to know that she had Simon's support, Ann was still feeling blue when she reached the office. She barely glanced up when a young couple came in asking about a flat that the agency had advertised for rent on Baker Street.

155

Nervously, Ann dialed the owners and asked if it was available for viewing. It was and before Ann knew it, the couple was signing on the dotted line. Ann felt as though she had climbed Mount Everest.

That night, at dinner, she couldn't help exclaiming, 'Guess what? I made my first commission today.'

'Wonderful, Ann!' Simon cried.

'Congratulations, honey,' Phillip said quietly.

Friday of the following week, Ann brought home her first check. After splitting the 5 percent commission with the office, she received the munificent sum of $20.00. She didn't know whether to laugh or cry. Twenty dollars certainly was not worth the sacrifices she was making, but it was a beginning.

As time passed, life at the Coulters' seemed to settle down. If Evie and Phillip weren't thrilled with her job and long hours, they were at least resigned to it.

The first month she made $80. The month after she made $150. In her third month on the job, Ann sold her first house. The commission on that, along with those from the rental of two large stores and several flats, made Ann's pay envelope gratifyingly thick, even after splitting her 5 percent with Violet. It looked like she was going to be a success in her new career.

She discovered she loved the challenge of making deals and had a real talent for negotiating. One night she came home with a savings bank book and asked Phillip to sign the joint account. She wanted him to understand that anything she was doing was for the two of them.

Phillip took the book and in a quick, slashing motion signed his name. Then he silently handed it back. Ann sighed, but she refused to let him spoil her mood. If he didn't appreciate her efforts then, he would later. She was finding that she could handle the demands of both her job and her family far better than she would have imagined. Except for the Sundays she had to work, Phillip hardly noticed that his wife had a job at all. Weekends when she was home they planned all sorts of family outings. When the weather was warm they often went to Ocean Beach, where Evie could dip her toes in the icy waves and build sand castles. Other times, they took a picnic lunch to Golden Gate Park, and once they capped a day of exploring on foot with a rare dinner out, at Chang Lee's Imperial Palace.

Looking around at the happy faces, Ann began to hope that things might work out after all. During the week she continued at her job with increasing enthusiasm. She observed and copied the other agents' techniques, while listening carefully to everything that went on in the office. She began to make call after call, following up every lead. No longer was she content to sit and wait for clients to come to her. Leaving nothing to chance, she contacted all the merchants in the area, so that they would start to give her tips on commercial properties.

There were other agents who were equally aggressive, but Ann Coulter had a sweetness which disarmed both clients and competitors. Within months, she was outselling every other agent at Cunningham's except Violet herself. Violet watched her, pleased at the success of her 'find,' and began to consider making her office manager.

Ann, however, had come to a decision. She realized she was never going to get rich working for someone else. Not only was she in competition with the other seven agents in the office, she had to split all her commissions with Violet, though she was the one making all the sales. Without telling anyone Ann resolved to get a brokerage business and eventually go out on her own. She bought several books on real estate law and financing and began to study diligently. To avoid upsetting Phillip, she would wait each night until he had fallen asleep, and go out to the kitchen to read until her eyes ached from the harsh light on the white pages. When she worked alone on Sundays, Ann pored over the files and made lists of contacts which might be helpful in the future.

She became even more efficient at work, and Violet began to experience a twinge of doubt about her protégée. Who would have thought this pretty, gentle housewife might turn into a threat?

Meanwhile, Ann was hoping to work out better transportation for herself so she could investigate more properties.

'Phillip, darling,' she began one night at dinner, 'I've been thinking. You know, you don't really use your car during the day all that much. Most of the time you just park it in the morning and don't touch it until you're ready to go home.'

'So?'

'I was wondering if you'd mind if I started to use it. I could take you to work and pick you up at the end of the day. That way I could use the car to take clients around, and it wouldn't inconvenience you at all. Would you mind that?'

'Yes, as a matter of fact, I would mind.'

'But, Phillip! I really need a car – lots of clients don't have one. Besides, it looks more professional for me to use my own.'

'Perhaps you are not aware of it, my dear, but I am a lawyer and I don't care for the idea of your dropping me off each morning as if I were a kid being driven to school.'

Ann was suddenly angry, hearing the smugness and finality in his voice. There was nothing demeaning in what she was suggesting; they weren't the only family in town who had to share one car. She tried again, as patiently as possible. 'Phillip, lots of men are driven to work by their wives. Since I need the car and you don't, I really can't see why I can't use it.'

'You don't have to see why. You just can't.' He got up from the table, grabbed his coat, and slammed the door as he stormed out of the apartment.

For a while, as Phillip strode down Geary Boulevard, he refused to acknowledge that he was being unreasonable. Damn it, he wasn't going to let Ann push him around. The car was his! He was doing his best to make a living, and if it wasn't enough for Ann, she could leave and find someone else. But as he began to calm down, he was forced to admit he was in the wrong. Little as he wanted to know about Ann's job, the fact was that she had one. She was working hard and she never taunted him about his inadequacies. Instead, she continued to perform all her roles as wife, mother, helpmeet, as well as ever, and without complaining. Turning, he ran nearly all the way home, where he found Ann in the living room, her eyes red from crying.

Quickly, he went to her and took her in his arms. 'Darling, I'm sorry. I was wrong. Of course you can have the car. I apologize for being nasty about it.'

Ann clung to him and said penitently, 'Oh, Phillip, don't make me feel worse than I already do. It was wrong of me to think of taking it.'

'No, Ann—' Phillip began, but she continued.

'I've thought it over and I've got a better idea. Let's just buy another car. We've got enough in our savings account for a down payment, and I think that after all these years, we deserve to treat ourselves a little.'

Phillip noticed with a pang that she said 'our' not 'my' savings account. The next morning he took her to a dealer where she bought a shiny maroon used Chevrolet, for which she paid eight hundred dollars cash. Ann disliked raiding her precious savings account, but she reminded herself that the car would boost sales and translate into increased commissions.

She was right – it did. And Ann was able to turn her attention to her primary goal – buying a house. Ever since she had been a little girl she had dreamed of a home of her own. Now she realized that the only way they would ever achieve a little security was to stop pouring rent money down the drain every month.

In her spare time, Ann began checking all the inexpensive houses that came on the market. There was little she and Phillip could afford, but then one day a miracle happened. Ann had become very friendly with the manager of a bank branch on Chestnut Street. Often, he had given her tips on various properties in financial trouble, and in return she had steered many of her clients to him. Now he told her there was a fabulous deal about to become available. The owner of a small house near Fort Mason had defaulted on his payments, and the bank had taken possession of it. Although the house had been sold him for $10,000, the outstandng mortgage was for only $6,500, and since in the present depressed market it was not likely to sell for much more, Ann might be able to get it simply by taking over the mortgage – with little or no down payment necessary.

Ann was almost beside herself with joy. She didn't stop to wonder whether Phillip would share her excitement. The moment they had finished eating dinner, she said, 'Darling, something wonderful has happened.' Excitedly, she described the many virtues of the house, and explained how cheaply it could be purchased.

'So, darling,' she said, 'would you like to see the house tonight?'

'Tonight?'

Somehow he didn't seem as excited as she had thought he would. Anxiously, she said, 'I think we should, Phillip. It's such a good deal that we need to move fast.'

Evie jumped off her chair and ran to Ann. 'Can Grandpa and I go too, Mommy?'

Ann hugged her. 'Of course, darling. This house will be for all of us.'

They drove over to Bay Street and in the soft evening light the house looked even better the second time around. A red-tile roofed stucco bungalow, it was typical for the Marina area. There was a living room with an Italianate composition marble fireplace, a kitchen and breakfast room giving onto a dining room, three bedrooms, and a single bathroom leading off the central hall. Best of all was the sunroom which looked out into the backyard, where dahlias grew along the fence.

When they finished wandering from room to room, Ann realized Phillip had not made any comment at all.

'Darling, you haven't said a word! What do you think?' Her voice was so eager and excited, her face so alive, Phillip didn't see how he could say no even though he felt the mortgage payments might be more than they could handle, even with Ann's earnings. Just then they heard Evie shout, 'Grandpa! Look at this jungle gym!'

What could Phillip say? Thank you, I'm indebted to you? No, there must be no hint of resentment in his words. He couldn't deny her this happiness. Forcing enthusiasm into his voice, he said, 'I think it's a hell of a buy, Ann.'

'It is, isn't it? So you think we should take it?'

'You've already set your heart on it, haven't you?'

Ann nodded ruefully. 'I guess I have.'

'Okay. What can I say?'

'Oh, Phillip!' Ann threw her arms around her husband, never noticing the defeated look in his eyes.

A month later, the Coulter family had moved in. Evie was thrilled with the backyard and Simon reveled in his new room. Even Phillip was so pleased with the space and privacy that he almost forgot that the house had been Ann's idea, not his.

That night before going up to bed they stood arm in arm in the garden. 'I don't think I've told you lately how much I love you, Phillip,' Ann said, smiling up at him. 'Do you know something? I think we must be the luckiest people in the whole world.'

Phillip gazed into her eyes. All he could see there was sincerity. She really did believe her words. She bore him no ill will for any of his failings.

So why couldn't he believe it too?

Twenty-Seven

As soon as they were settled, Ann turned her attention back to her career. She was almost ready to take her broker's exam. Meanwhile, she carefully studied the market. It was 1957 – a period of nationwide recession. Realtors were keeping going mainly through their rentals. Houses and flats were still selling reasonably well in the Marina, but buyers were resistant and choosy. Ann reasoned that that meant it was generally a buyer's market, and outside the Marina there might be great opportunities to pick up property cheaply. What she hoped to find was a piece of property she could buy and then rent until it appreciated in value. Then she would sell. Each day she read the papers, searching out foreclosures, but nothing seemed quite right. She considered a storefront with two upstairs apartments on Union before deciding it was a bit overpriced.

For several years the Union Street area had been sprouting boutiques and specialty stores which were supplanting the old groceries and shoe repair shops. Perhaps it had already passed the point where one could get in on the ground floor and make a killing.

Yet, for weeks afterward, Ann kicked herself for passing up the deal. Perhaps she was being foolishly cautious. It didn't help that she couldn't discuss the prospect with Phillip, but she knew that it would only open up the sensitive subject of who controlled their finances. She hesitated talking to Violet too, though she trusted the older woman's judgment. Ann wondered from time to time if Violet really liked her or just tolerated her because she was a good agent. While Violet was never unpleasant, there seemed to be a sharp note in her voice after Ann had closed a particularly difficult deal.

She would have been astonished to realize that Violet was envious. Here she had knocked herself out for almost thirty years, and Ann Coulter had come along and set the office on its ear in three. The strange thing was that Violet couldn't help but like Ann, who, to give her credit, never seemed to trade on her looks or charm when dealing with people.

Ann had almost decided to go to Violet with her problem when the exact piece of property came on the market. As New York was known for its brownstones, San Francisco had its Victorians, their pointed, elegant silhouettes clinging to the contours of its fabled hills. But since the twenties, many of these charming houses had fallen into disrepair. Between the late 1930s and the 1950s, people ignored them in favor of the new buildings with all the modern conveniences, and the smart money moved to the Peninsula and Marin County.

Ann had an instinctive feeling that ultimately the notion of living right in the city would revive. She noticed that urban renewal had become a political issue and that the city council was talking about preserving 'our heritage.'

Late one afternoon, Ann was walking through the Western Addition. She had been checking out foreclosures, and, looking up from the list, she saw a huge Victorian house. The façade was incredible, with graceful bay windows, a profusion of fretwork, and a curved portico supported by columns, all of which somehow created a harmony of exuberant excess. To Ann's discerning gaze the house was magnificent, for all the broken windows, the grime, and the ominously sagging front porch.

She picked her way around the back, avoiding the old tires and oil cans which littered its gravelled driveway. It had a stone foundation, so it probably hadn't settled too much. The plumbing had probably never been modernized, but at least from the outside, it didn't look hopeless.

An old woman shuffled out from the house next door and called out, 'What are you doing? Going to buy that old wreck?'

Ann smiled pleasantly without replying.

'That's the old Hampton house, you know,' the

woman said. 'Used to take up the whole block. He was in hardware.'

'Oh, yes, Hampton Hardware! I remember that from when I was a little girl.'

'Well, that's where the old moneybags lived. James Hampton, his name was. The house is real pretty inside. Brass hardware, beautiful floors. That is, if the folks who've been living here haven't put big holes in it. They must have had ten kids.'

With that the woman shuffled back into the house, shaking her head and coughing loudly.

Ann was a little startled by the woman's words, but she went on making notes. The house's history had further intrigued her. The next day, she got the key and went inside. As the old lady had said, the tenants had made a shambles of the place. The fine hardwood floors were gouged and scuffed, and there were gaping holes in the plaster. But a closer look showed Ann that the damage was mainly on the surface. The roof seemed intact, and structurally the house appeared sound.

The rooms were of fine proportions, but more important to Ann, they were so arranged as to be easily subdivided into four attractive apartments. Some previous owner had made a half-hearted attempt to subdivide the house into two flats, installing a cheap gas cooker and primitive sink upstairs, but they could be removed. There would be at least one major expense: dividing the lower kitchen into two back-to-back modern kitchens and adding two kitchens upstairs. Miraculously, old James Hampton had been a devotee of modern plumbing, and each proposed quadrant of the house already had a bathroom. Three of the four units had fireplaces, and all would have bay windows in the living rooms.

In short, the more Ann thought about it, the more perfect an investment the house seemed to be.

She went to Gil Cooley, the bank manager who had found the Coulters' small house, and laid out her proposal.

'Do you think it could work?' she asked him nervously. 'Tell me the truth, Gil.'

Gil shrugged. 'Hard to say, Ann. It sure looks good on paper. But the renovation is either going to take a lot of money – or a heck of a lot of work. Is your husband good at this sort of thing?'

Ann gave him a rueful glance. 'Not particularly. But still, I think we can do it.'

'Well, you shouldn't have any problem putting a second mortgage on your house. Prices are soaring. Actually, Ann, I think you can do just about anything you set out to do. You're a remarkable woman. You know I'll do my best for you when your loan application comes through.'

He saw her to the door, then watched her walk off with a hint of regret on his face. He had fallen for Ann Coulter at their first meeting, but he knew from discreet inquiry that she was devoted to her husband and small daughter. Still, he would see to it that she got that loan even if he had to twist some important arms to do it.

Ann was so excited she couldn't wait until Phillip got home to tell him what she hoped to do. Without hesitation she jumped onto a bus headed downtown.

The door of the law firm now read Newman, Newman, Brice & Gould. With a pang Ann realized it would never read '& Coulter.' Pushing it open, she asked the receptionist if she could see Mr. Coulter. 'I hope he's available,' Ann added. 'He's not in conference, is he?'

'I don't think so,' the woman drawled, hiding a sly smile. No one conferred with Mr. Coulter. 'Just a moment, please.'

As the receptionist rang Phillip's desk, Ann perched nervously on the edge of the leather sofa. What *would* Phillip say? They never discussed Ann's work, not even in a general discussion of the postwar housing boom.

'You can go in,' the receptionist said, interrupting Ann's thoughts. 'End of the hall on the left.'

Ann had been to Phillip's office only twice, both times during his first year at the firm. Although she knew that he had not been promoted, it was something of a shock to see that he was still working in the same dingy little cubbyhole.

He pushed back his chair the moment he saw Ann at the door. 'Sweetheart – how nice to see you. Were you downtown?'

'Phillip, I need your thoughts on something. May I sit down?'

Ann told Phillip all about her plans for the Hampton house. By the time she finished, she could no longer hide her eager excitement. 'So tell me what you think.'

Instead of answering, he rocked back and forth in his chair. Ann grew edgy wondering what he was thinking.

'Well, Ann,' the verdict finally came, 'I think you should forget it.'

'Why?'

'Do you have any idea of the cost of repairs these days? Most of those old barns are riddled with dry rot and have leaky roofs and rusty plumbing. And then there's the remodeling. Putting a kitchen in each unit would cost a fortune. Anyway, I don't think those areas are going to come back as residential addresses. We're not a country that believes in tradition.'

Seeing Ann's growing disappointment, Phillip reached across the table to take her hand, but Ann kept them stubbornly in her lap. His gesture seemed patronizing somehow.

In a voice meant to be kindly but authoritative, Phillip said, 'Ann, that kind of real estate is just too speculative for amateurs to dabble in. A lot of experts feel that the market is headed lower, and then where will you be? You won't be able to rent the place or sell it. Look, I know how hard you've worked, and how much you've accomplished. But you're trying to go too far too fast with this deal. It's just too risky. I'm sorry, sweetheart, but that's my honest opinion.'

Ann weighed her words carefully. 'I am aware that there is some risk involved, Phillip, but also there could be a lot of potential gain. Actually, I've looked into it pretty thoroughly and it may not be quite as risky as you think. Most of the realtors I know predict an upturn by the first quarter of next year, as long as the government doesn't tighten up on credit. The house is in good shape structurally, according to the inspector, and I've already found someone to do the remodeling. Nonunion.'

'Who?'

'Guido Verona.'

Phillip looked confused. 'You mean Guido the grocery boy? Ann, you've got to be kidding!'

Frightened by his wife's persistence, he got up and looked hard at her. His face was flushed. 'Honey, can't you see this deal is just too risky for us? Maybe real estate is your career, but it's our mutual financial future you're talking about.'

'I know, Phillip, but can't you see that it's a *calculated* risk? If we never take any chances, we're never going to have any real security.'

'Look, Ann, you asked me for my advice, and I've given it to you.'

'But you're wrong!' Ann burst out before she could stop herself. 'All you've done is make doomsday predictions.'

'You didn't really want my advice at all, did you, Ann?' Phillip said quietly. 'You just wanted my blessing.'

'That's not true, Phillip!'

'But *you* think the risk is worth taking. Isn't that true?'

'Well – yes, I guess I do.'

'Well, then, why did you bother to ask me?'

'Maybe we should talk more about this later,' Ann said, picking up her pocketbook.

Phillip nodded without speaking and watched her go.

Sinking back in his chair, he ran his hand through his hair. He was torn by emotions he didn't understand. On the one hand he had some perfectly legitimate objections to Ann's scheme. On the other hand, those objections had nothing to do with his decision to say no. The real reason he hated the idea was that it was *hers*.

If Ann had only understood Phillip's terror, she might have been able to empathize with him. Instead, walking to the bus stop, she was aware only of a burning frustration. Phillip hadn't even seemed to listen to her. All he'd done was make her lose confidence. Maybe he *was* right and she *was* making a big mistake. Phillip was a lawyer, after all . . .

All that evening, her fears and doubts mounted. At one point she was almost ready to go into the living room and tell him that she had changed her mind, but something made her remain silent. She was a good agent and she had learned a lot about the real estate market. It was just as likely that her analysis was right and Phillip's was wrong.

The next morning over breakfast, Phillip's face was set. Ann was sure that he was still determined to oppose her. But, unexpectedly, as he was getting ready to leave, he paused and said briefly, 'Go ahead with the deal, Ann. Just bring home the papers when they're ready and tell me where to sign.'

'Thank you, Phillip!' Ann exclaimed. Then, quickly, she added, 'Of course, I still don't know if I'll get the loan.'

He stared at her for a long moment. 'You'll get it. You know you will.' Turning, he went out the door.

There was an agonizing wait while the bank processed Ann's loan application. She knew that there were a number of factors against it. The Coulters had owned their house for such a short time. Phillip's salary was relatively low, and banks were loath to grant loans based on a woman's contribution to the family income.

Ann was right to be anxious. If it hadn't been for Gil Cooley, her petition would have been denied. Gil didn't refute the guidelines, he simply made an exception. He had armed himself with a raft of defensive arguments – Ann Coulter was well known to him professionally and personally, her husband was an attorney, albeit rather poorly remunerated; the Coulters were an old San Francisco family, the essence of stability – but none of them proved necessary. Since Gilbert Cooley was normally so cautious, no one seriously thought to question his judgment.

Ann's heart almost stopped later that day when the secretary told her that Gil was on the phone.

'Tell me quickly,' she cried. 'Yes or no?'

'Yes.'

Ann couldn't speak. 'Oh, Gil!' she finally said. 'Thank you!'

'It was the least I could do for you, Ann,' he said quietly. 'Good luck.'

Phillip took the news calmly. 'Congratulations, Ann. I just hope you haven't bitten off more than you can chew.'

Ann refused to let his pessimism affect her attitude. She was going to succeed if she had to plumb, wire, and plaster the whole of Hampton House herself.

The loan included $1,500 over the purchase price, earmarked for renovation. Ann had already calculated the cost of the appliances and building materials, and as she had told Phillip, she had found a nonunion contractor. Guido Verona worked for his uncle, who owned a large Italian grocery. Ann had discovered him when his uncle bragged to Ann about Guido building a new storeroom practically for cost. 'That Guido. He know everything.'

Ann had been doubtful, but when she talked to Guido, she discovered that he spoke English fairly fluently and that he really was handy, not only at carpentry but at plumbing and electrical work too. Already he had a brisk business and someday soon he planned to get a contractor's license.

When she asked Guido if he'd work on Hampton House, he looked over the property and then quoted her a price which was so low, she protested.

'When you buy more buildings, I want you to come to me.' He gave his rare, slow smile. 'Then I'll charge you more.'

Guido was a find. He worked ten hours a day, his

brawny arms making short work of the massive renovation. Of course, neither of them knew much about
restoring old Victorians, but Guido proved to be a
genius at ferreting out cheap period materials. Sometimes he even got them free at wrecking operations.

Ann did most of the painting and wallpapering.
Every afternoon after finishing work she rushed over
to the house. Even when she was exhausted, she dog-
gedly pushed herself to keep going, knowing that
every week the property stood vacant, they were
losing money.

She said as much to Phillip when he complained that
she hadn't cooked dinner in a month.

'Well, if you can't handle it, that's your fault, Ann. I
told you you were biting off more than you could
chew.'

'It's only for a little while, Phillip. I'm sorry about
dinner, but as soon as we're through with the renovations, I'll make it up to you all.'

Working together constantly, she and Guido soon
became close friends, despite the differences in their
backgrounds. He had a wealth of common sense, and
unconsciously Ann began to depend on his judgment.
With Guido's help and unstinting approval, she began
to feel that she could do anything she set her mind to.

As the weeks passed, Ann noticed with surprise that
the young Italian, with his dark liquid eyes and smooth
olive skin, was even more handsome than she had
thought when they first met. When he lifted a stack of
lumber, the strong muscles of his back rippled underneath his thin T-shirt. Yet despite his muscularity, his
body was lean in the close-fitting Levi's he usually
wore, and he moved with the unconscious grace of an
athlete.

One day he looked up and saw her watching him.
Embarrassed, she dropped her gaze. When she raised
her eyes, she saw his slow smile. 'You are quitting
already?'

She had jumped up quickly. 'No, no.'

One Friday evening, Ann had gone over to work on the house after dinner. Ann was surprised to find Guido still there.

'You shouldn't be here Friday night, for goodness sake! You need to go out, have a little social life. I don't mean to work you into the ground.'

'It's okay,' he replied. 'I want to fix the fireplace before I go.'

'Still clogged, huh?'

They worked together in companionable silence for a while. Then Guido called out, 'Ann – the one-pound hammer, please? If I fix the damper, it will be finished, I think.'

Ann was using the hammer to pry up the baseboard molding. As she crossed the room she tripped over a two-by-four. She tried to save herself, but her legs, cramped from stooping, moved too slowly.

She heard Guido call, 'Ann!' as she fell. Then there was a sharp blow to her head. When she regained consciousness, Guido was holding her, murmuring, 'Cara mia. Anna, cara mia. Speak to me!'

Ann allowed herself to lie without moving in his arms for a moment. Then she opened her eyes and saw his face, drawn with concern, close to hers.

'Guido?' she whispered.

'Anna – you can speak! Grazie a Dio!'

She nodded weakly. Her forehead throbbed horribly, but somehow she didn't mind the pain. It was so delicious just to lie there. She knew she should try to get up, but Guido's arms were so strong, so gentle. And she was so tired.

When Guido spoke again, his voice was so soft that it was a mere breath: 'Anna . . . cara.'

When he kissed her lightly on the mouth, she made no effort to resist.

He drew back and looked at her, his eyes roving hungrily over her delicate features. It had been torture for him working near her and not being able to touch her – not being permitted to make her happy.

171

He kissed her again, this time more urgently, moving his lips over hers in a kiss so sensual that Ann's desire flared into life. It was beautiful and exciting – yet frightening at the same time. She knew she had to stop before she did something she'd regret. And she didn't want to hurt Guido.

Gently, she placed her hand on his chest, pushing him away.

He didn't seem offended. As she tried to get up, he placed a supporting arm behind her and helped her to her feet. Regaining her balance, she moved to the window and stood staring out at the rainy gray night. All day, the city had been blanketed with fog, and toward evening it had been replaced by a heavy, monotonous downpour. Through the rain, a halo glowed steadily around a streetlight. But none of it registered. The dripping of the rain emphasized the very stillness of the room, and she was intensely aware of Guido as he came up behind her. Feeling his warm breath on her neck, Ann knew that he was about to embrace her. And then, as his arms slipped around her waist, she closed her eyes and leaned back, unable to help herself.

Slowly he turned her around, and they faced each other.

'*Cara mia*,' he said softly. 'Anna, I love you and I want you. You don't know what hell it is for me to be so close and not tell you. You love me too, Anna. Tell me that you do,' he commanded softly, cupping her chin in his hand and pressing hard against her.

Ann wanted him – wanted him badly, but she knew that afterward she would have to go home to Phillip and Evie, and she knew she couldn't go through with it.

'Guido, we can't do this—'

Guido interrupted her roughly. 'Anna, I see it in your eyes. I feel it in your lips. You love me too.'

'Maybe I do. But don't you see? It's impossible. There are other people in my life whom I would hurt badly.'

'But you do not love your husband,' he accused. 'You live with him, but you do not love him. That is a sin!'

172

Ann was sorry she hadn't stopped him sooner. She should have recognized his growing interest. He was a man, after all – kind, warm, tender – but a man nonetheless. She was grateful for his love. It was wonderful to know that she was still capable of arousing desire, even though it could never be consummated.

'Guido, I think that we must try to forget that this ever happened. I'm not sure whether I'm happy or sad about it . . . a little of both, maybe. But I want so much for us to be friends. I need you in my life. Do you think that's still possible?'

Hearing Ann's plea in a voice that revealed her loneliness and frustration, Guido was torn. It was difficult to imagine repressing his feelings; at this moment he wanted her, wanted her so much that his body ached. But Guido was also a true romantic, and he knew he couldn't let down any woman who trusted and needed him the way this one obviously did.

He took her hands and said, 'I will be your good friend, Anna. May I kiss you just one more time?'

'Yes, Guido. You may.' As he held her close, Ann wondered where she had found the strength to say no.

That night, Ann lay in the bed she shared with her husband, thinking of Guido. She had done the right thing, the only thing, but just for tonight she allowed herself to fantasize about what might have been.

Twenty-Eight

Finally, the day came when the house was finished. Guido had painted the outside white. Red geraniums and blue lobelia bloomed in the newly planted beds. Each apartment had its own green door with a shiny brass knocker.

Simon, Phillip, and Evie all came over to look, and Ann waited nervously for their verdict as they inspected the gleaming floors and woodwork, the dark-patterned wallpaper, the newly cleaned fireplaces, and the small but efficient kitchens. Simon was unstinting in his praise. 'It's amazing, Ann. You did all this for fifteen hundred dollars?'

'Well, it cost just a bit more. About seventeen hundred, to be exact.' She glanced at Phillip apprehensively.

The truth of the matter was that it would have been nearly three thousand dollars except that in the end Guido refused to take any payment at all. 'No, *cara mia,*' he had said a little sadly. 'There is so little I can do for you. I will not take money from you.'

They had argued and argued, but in the end Ann had acquiesced. She had no idea where she would have gotten the money to pay him anyway. Phillip had been right. The renovations had cost twice her original estimate, but how could she explain that Guido had worked for nothing? It was impossible and Ann just smiled guiltily when Phillip commented, 'You've done a wonderful job.'

'It's beautiful, Mommy,' Evie enthused. 'Can we come and live here?'

Ann caught the little girl up in her arms and kissed her, grateful for her enthusiasm 'No, silly goose. We have a house of our own.'

The ads went into the paper the next day.

That evening there were no calls. The next day, Ann received one, but the woman hung up as soon as Ann told her the address. 'Western Addition? No, thank you.' The next day was equally frustrating, and by the end of the week, Ann was more than discouraged, she was downright frightened. What if the apartments didn't rent? She was asking $75 per month, which was cheap for the apartment, but expensive for the neighborhood. She was grateful for Phillip's silence. She didn't want to admit that perhaps she had miscalculated.

At the end of two weeks, Ann ran a second ad. She changed the wording slightly and dropped the rent to $70 – which just about killed her. She was becoming desperate. The next mortgage payment was due shortly, and there was no rent money coming in at all. She dreaded having to confess to Phillip that her plan was floundering.

Somehow she had to let the world know that her apartments were at least worth considering. If people saw them, they might appreciate their attractive layout and convenient location. In the end, she decided to give an open house. It was going to be expensive, but she had to make one last effort.

The invitations went out the next day for a champagne party in showplace Victorian flats at the former home of tycoon James Hampton. Ann included everyone on her client list, as well as all her friends.

When the first guests arrived Saturday morning, they found the Hampton house sparkling. Guido, looking handsome in his rented tuxedo, circulated with champagne, while his cousin Gina played a violin softly in the background. In less than three days Ann had even managed to furnish one of the apartments with a few charming pieces borrowed from friends' attics. She had talked to some of her friends in the Marina and found clever little accessories to fill in the gaps. Simple lace panels hung in the bay windows, and as a finishing touch, she had rented big Victorian parlor palms.

The result, coupled with the champagne and the music, was so inviting that the people entering the apartment wondered why they had never considered a remodeled Victorian before – and they were so close to downtown. By evening three of the four flats were rented, and a young Chinese couple was going to let Ann know the next day about the last.

Ann's triumph would have been complete if Phillip had only stayed to share it. He had stopped by earlier in the afternoon, but soon left, and when Ann recounted her success that night he merely nodded and said she must be relieved. Ann realized she would have to enjoy her success alone. It wasn't as much fun, but it was still rewarding.

She continued to study hard for her brokerage exam and began thinking about opening her own office. Then, one day in May, she heard that the house next door to Hampton House – as it was now called – was up for sale. While working on the renovation, Ann had occasionally gone over to use old Hazel's phone, and had seen most of the interior. It consisted of four apartments, somewhat smaller than those in Hampton House, but considerably less dilapidated. They had been unattractively modernized, but in her mind's eye, Ann was already seeing the ugly paneling stripped from the walls, the fireplaces restored to working condition, the cheap modern fixtures replaced by pedestal sinks and claw-footed tubs.

Hazel informed her that the owner had died and the estate was being liquidated. Ann quelled her rising excitement. This was not like a foreclosure, where a house could be had at a bargain price. Unless the beneficiaries were in immediate need, they could afford to hold out for their price in an estate sale. And any beneficiaries of this Mr. Coleman were probably already well-to-do.

But just thinking about the house made her eager to try her hand at another renovation, even though she knew she didn't have a spare penny to invest. Still, she started looking around the neighborhood again and a week or two later, found another Victorian for sale. It was painted an awful purple, and it was in terrible shape, but it had been foreclosed, so it might be had for a song.

Gil Cooley raised his eyebrows expressively when Ann came into the bank the next day and began describing the property, extolling its hidden potential.

'You're determined to become a tycoon, aren't you, Ann?'

Ann's face fell. 'Well, I'm not really looking seriously, Gil, of course. We're pretty much stretched to the limit with the payments we have.'

Gil rocked back in his chair. 'You know, Ann, I was thinking about you the other day and wondering if you had considered rolling over Hampton House. Have you had the property appraised?'

Ann shook her head.

'Well, I suspect the value has appreciated considerably. Remember, rental property is essentially valued at a multiple of the rent. When you bought the house, it was renting two apartments at fifty dollars each. Now, it's – what? Seventy-five times four?'

'Seventy.'

'Okay, seventy times four is two hundred eighty a month.' He calculated briefly on paper, murmuring, 'Three thousand three hundred sixty a year. You could probably sell it for twice what you paid.'

'Oh, I don't want to sell it yet, Gil!' Ann said, startled.

'Okay. You're probably right; after all, you're getting most of the interest deduction the first few years. But how about leveraging? Get a second mortgage on Hampton House and buy something else.'

'Could I, Gil?'

He looked at her pretty face, alight with enthusiasm, and for the second time, swallowed his usual banker's caution. 'I think so, Ann.'

Phillip hit the roof when Ann broached the topic. 'Goddamn it, Ann! We already have one nice piece of rental property. Isn't that enough for you? Look, I'm willing to admit that you were right about Hampton House. It's turned out well for us; our taxes – I'll admit it, it's *our* taxes now – will be lower this year because of your deductions. And it looks like we'll make money when we eventually sell. But now you want to take our security and throw it out the window once again! This crazy pyramid scheme could bury us in debt.'

'Phillip, I don't know why you're so unwilling to take a few chances! I keep telling you that we don't *have* any real security yet!'

For several weeks, Phillip angrily refused to consider the matter, even though Ann patiently explained the leveraging concept that she and Gil had worked out. One night as they were going to bed, the tension thick between them, Phillip snapped, 'All right, Ann. I've heard enough. You know how I feel. You make your own decision and let me know.'

They went to sleep without another word. Phillip thought, even though he was not the kind of man to tell his wife, 'I forbid you,' that he had made his stand perfectly clear. Surely Ann would abandon the project.

Consequently, when she told him the next day that she had applied for the loan, he stared at her in disbelief. 'You went ahead, despite my saying I was opposed?'

'Phillip, it's just too much of an opportunity to pass up. Your objection didn't make sense. Please don't be angry.'

But Phillip had already decided that Ann was so consumed by ambition that she no longer cared if she hurt him. It was too late to argue. He bit back the harsh words that sprang to his tongue. He would keep the last remnants of his dignity intact. 'As you wish,' he finally said in a cold voice.

Three weeks later, the purple mansion was theirs and Guido and Ann went to work again, stripping, sanding, painting, and fixing. With all their experience, she expected the renovation to be finished faster, but nearly three months passed before she could schedule their open house.

This time the response was tremendous. Restored Victorians were coming into fashion, and the five apartments at $65 a month were taken by the end of the week.

Ann's eye next strayed back to the empty house next to her first investment. She was surprised to find that it was still on the market, and decided that the cheap modernization which had destroyed most of the gingerbread trim kept buyers from seeing its essential charm. Still, she hesitated inquiring again until Gil Cooley called on her at the office one day to ask, 'Your units are still rented, aren't they, Annie?'

He was the only one who had ever called her Annie.

'Yes, Gil. With no problem at all. Why?'

'Well, the people who inherited the house next to the Hampton are getting pretty restless. Two of the units are vacant, and they're sick and tired of playing landlord. I think they will take almost anything to get it off their hands.'

'How much?'

'Hey, Annie.' Gil laughed. 'Are you ready to take on more debt?'

'Won't the bank go for it?'

'I don't know.' He looked at her curiously. 'Correct me if I'm wrong, but don't you already have two apartment houses to manage, a job with Violet Cunningham, and a husband and child? Isn't your time already pretty well filled?'

'How much, Gil?'

'You're a glutton for punishment!'

'Gil, look at how well the other two houses have turned out! I just raised the rent on Hampton to seventy-five, eliminating the negative cash flow there. We're actually making money on Guildford, and that's not even taking into account the tax benefits for Phillip and me.'

'You are turning out to be one heck of a businesswoman, Annie Coulter. Before you know it, you're going to own half the property in town.' He waved his hand. 'Buy the property. I'll get the bank to back you.'

'Thanks, Gil. You're a good friend.'

She wished Phillip had as much confidence in her judgment. They certainly were doing well thanks to her investments and hard work, but he almost seemed to resent her success. Maybe someday she wouldn't care so much about his approval, but right now his lack of praise really hurt. In her depressed or angry moments she sometimes even dreamed of telling him off: *How can you be content with so little? Don't you care anything about your daughter's future, or mine?* But she couldn't bring herself to make the bitter accusation. She had married him in 1941 for better or for worse– and Phillip was a man who had been crippled by the war in ways far more devastating than his limp or the scar on his cheek. A piece of his soul still dwelt in the leech-infested jungles of Bataan and Burma, among horrors she couldn't even imagine. Since he'd come back to the States, he'd done the best he could. In fact, better than Ann might have expected. Some of the men who were liberated in Burma were still in Letterman Hospital.

On the way home Ann picked up steaks and Phillip's favorite – artichokes. She washed the dishes and brought him coffee before she broached the subject of the house.

'Phillip,' she said, hesitating. 'You know the Victorian for sale next to Hampton House? Gil tells me it can be bought for a song and that the bank would finance almost one hundred percent. What do you think we should do?'

The request had a familiar ring to it, and she was sure Phillip would again respond angrily. But when he replied, she got the shock of her life.

'Darling, I don't think you should ask me. Your instinct has proved golden. At this point, if you think it's right, go do it! Whatever you do, I'm with you all the way.'

Ann wondered if Phillip noticed her jaw drop. Was there a note of resignation in his voice? Quickly, she admonished herself. *Damn you, Ann Coulter, you're always looking for ghosts to chase. Can't you be satisfied?*

She got up, sat in his lap, and put her arms around his neck. 'I love you, Phillip.'

'And I love you.' Ann knew that Phillip wasn't really happy about buying another house, but at least he'd agreed. He was probably as tired of fighting as she was.

That night they made love for the first time in a month. Bells didn't ring and the earth didn't move, but the feeling of closeness seemed more meaningful than just sex.

Twenty-Nine

When Ann approached the owners of the house, they were as anxious to get rid of it as Gil Cooley had suspected. With Gil's help, Ann was able to start her third renovation by early spring.

Phillip was as good as his word. He listened to Ann when she described how she and Guido were getting along, but made no disparaging comments, and nights or weekends when she was busy, he went out of his way to keep Evie amused so she did not miss her mother.

By the time the new house was finished, Ann decided the whole family deserved a treat, and on Labor Day she planned an elaborate picnic.

Armed with blankets, pillows, and a huge basket of food, they drove up the steep, winding road and parked the car near the top of Mount Tamalpais, from where they could look out over the Bay Area. The bright sunshine, Evie's joy at the outing, Phillip and Simon's relaxed pleasure, all conspired to make the day a special one. *We're a family, and a united one*, Phillip thought, and as he and Ann looked down at the city below, he put his arm around her waist, pulled her close to him, and told her how happy he was.

He was taken totally unaware when she said, 'Oh, Phillip, I'm so glad you don't mind my working anymore. Now that I've finally got my broker's license, I want to go out on my own. But I was afraid you'd disapprove.'

Phillip didn't know what to say. He hated to ruin their holiday, but he had hoped that with her three houses all fully rented, Ann would finally be content. He had tried over the past year not to resent her success, but each new triumph underlined his own sense of failure.

'Do we need to discuss it now?' he said, holding her tighter. 'It's so peaceful here. Look . . .' And he pointed in the direction of the Pacific.

Ann too hated to break the spell, but she had waited so long to approach Phillip, and she felt pressured by the fact that a rare vacancy had come up in a storefront on Chestnut, two blocks from Violet's. It would be perfect for what she had in mind, and if she didn't grab it, someone else would doubtless snatch it up, on a long lease.

In Ann's opinion it was definitely the moment to strike out on her own. A lot of exciting things were about to happen in real estate. She decided to test Phillip's mood.

'Honey, I've been thinking about leaving Violet ever since I passed the broker's exam. My certificate came in the mail last week.'

Phillip was silent. Once again, Ann hadn't confided in him. She had gone ahead and made her decision without him.

'It's always nice to be your own boss,' he said, trying to maintain a neutral tone. 'What plans have you made?'

'There's a great location on Chestnut available. I think it would be ideal for an office, don't you?'

Phillip had no illusions that she was soliciting *his* advice. 'I'm sure you know what you're doing, dear. You usually do.' But despite the edge to his voice, Phillip really couldn't begrudge her the satisfaction of being her own boss. Heaven only knew, he would have loved to have his own law practice – had he been able to make the grade. No, it was a dream come true for her. And there was no reason in the world to doubt that she would be a success.

Ann studied his face. She wasn't so wrapped up in her career that she had failed to recognize the conflicting feelings that tormented her husband. She knew that her business triumphs disturbed him profoundly; threatened him even. And she loved Phillip and couldn't bear to watch the rift that was forming in their marriage. But she had an idea.

'Phillip – why don't you leave Kenny and help open the real estate office with me?'

To Ann, the plan made sense. Phillip had no future

with Kenny, or in the law, for that matter. Ann had begun to take Kenny's measure. On the surface, he was affable and easygoing, but underneath was a barely concealed hostility and ruthless competitiveness. In the end, no one counted with Kenny Newman but Kenny Newman. And Phillip was being victimized by him. Ann held her breath, waiting for Phillip's answer.

Slowly, Phillip's arm dropped from her waist. He didn't need more than a moment to reflect: *Ann needs me just about as much as Kenny does.* 'No, thanks,' he said coldly. 'There's no house big enough for two mistresses.'

Ann felt a knot in her stomach at his flat rejection. *It was my fault – maybe I should have phrased it differently.*

As they walked back to Simon and Evie, Ann hoped that he might eventually reconsider. They could still be a team. Maybe they would even be happy . . .

Thirty

Standing on the curb, Ann watched the sign painter putting the finishing touches on the name, ANN COULTER REALTY.

'There it is, lady. All finished.'

'Finished?' Ann asked. It was only the beginning. 'It looks wonderful, Mr. Petroni.'

She and Guido had been working like demons. People had been demanding his services ever since they had seen his work on Ann's houses, but he had shoved aside his other projects to do Ann's new office. As they worked, other merchants in the area dropped by to welcome her. Their support helped make up somewhat for Violet's hostility. She had become resentful ever since Ann announced she was leaving. Seeing Violet's cold expression, Ann had impulsively reached across the desk and clasped the older woman's hands.

'Violet, I will never be able to thank you enough for giving me my first job. You were the first person to have faith in me. You gave me my chance. I'll never forget it, or how much I've learned from you.'

Violet had tried to control her envy. Good God! Little Ann Coulter was about to become her primary competitor. And to think that when Ann had applied for the job, she had been an insignificant housewife in a dowdy, pale pink suit, clutching her handbag as though she were afraid it would be snatched from her. Violet sighed. She never lied to herself. Ann had always had the magic touch. If she hadn't hired her, someone else would have.

'I'm happy to have helped you, Ann,' Violet was finally able to say. 'I just hope you're not making the mistake of your life.'

Ann had just smiled pleasantly. 'Thank you, but I don't think so.' Afterward though, she was happy to be so busy working with Guido on the office that she didn't have time to dwell on Violet's anger. Now, looking at the new gilt sign, she felt nothing could dampen her happiness.

'Guido,' she called. 'Come look at this.'

He emerged from the back, brushing plaster from his Levi's.

Usually, his eyes sparkled at the sight of her. But today he seemed sober and preoccupied. After admiring the sign, they went inside and he sat down at the battered oak worktable.

'Doughnut?' she asked.

'No, thank you.'

'What is it?' she asked, noticing his stare. 'A smudge on my nose already?'

'No,' he said gravely, 'I was just thinking how beautiful you are, Anna.'

'Guido . . .' Ann said, shaking her head. Since that night at Hampton House, Guido's behavior had been meticulously correct, and Ann was careful to avoid any subject that might incite him. Only occasionally had she surprised a wistful look on his face, but today she saw that his eyes were dark with yearning.

'What is it?' she asked, hoping to defuse his mood.

'Anna.' He reached across the table as if to take her hand, then stopped, letting his hand slowly fall an inch short of hers. 'Anna, I must tell you something. I am getting married next month.'

'Guido! Married? Why – why that's wonderful! To whom?'

'Maria. I think you've seen her around my uncle's store. She works for him sometimes now. Dark hair, not very tall . . .'

Ann remembered a shy Italian girl she had seen at Verona's recently, who spoke not a word of English. Maria just smiled and shrugged her shoulders helplessly when Ann asked her a question. She had a pretty face and an incredibly voluptuous body. Even Ann couldn't help but notice. And she was young, magnificently young . . .

'Well – that's wonderful,' Ann repeated, wondering why she suddenly felt bereft. She didn't want Guido's attentions, did she?

'Anna.' The word was like a caress. 'I don't love her, you know. I don't think I could ever love someone else as I love you.'

'Guido, you must not say these things to me!'

'Why must I not? They are true.'

'Because—'

'I know, it is impossible. But you know in your heart that I will always love you.'

'Then why are you marrying this girl? Someday you'll meet someone and really fall in love.'

Guido thought back to the evening, several weeks before, when he had told his uncle that he was remodeling Ann's office. Something of what he felt for her must have shown in his tone of voice, the excitement in his eyes, for his uncle had said, 'My nephew, I must tell you. This woman is not for you.'

'Giuseppe! You insult Mrs. Coulter!' Guido sprang to

his feet. 'There is nothing, nothing whatever, between us!'

'I know,' Giuseppe said heavily. 'What I tell you now is, there will never be! You must find a wife for yourself. It is time. It is not good for a man to be twenty-six and have no wife. You need to get married, have some bambinos. Then you will be happy.'

Guido paced the room angrily. Giuseppe watched him for a moment, then said, 'How about you go out with Maria Spinelli? She is young, beautiful, and she likes you.'

'Maria? No thank you, Giuseppe. Don't worry about me. I will find a wife when I am ready. When I fall in love.'

'No, Guido. The best way is to get married, *then* fall in love. You want a woman to cook, clean, have your bambinos, share your life with you. Maria, she is Italian. She understands you. She will make you a good wife.'

'It's not enough that she cooks and cleans! There is more than that to marriage.'

'Guido, never get married for *amore*. That way leads to unhappiness. It does not last.' Giuseppe had continued to argue and threaten until Guido shouted, 'Okay. I will take Maria out once. Just to make you happy. But that will be it, do you understand?'

Maria was a traditional Italian girl newly arrived from Milano. She was more than ready to fall in love with the handsome, successful Guido. On his part, he found it unexpectedly pleasant to have a girl who looked up to him with such adoration.

He took her home for a family dinner and she got along well with his relatives. She helped his Aunt Rosa make the pasta and ladle out steaming marinara sauce. Slowly, his resistance weakened. What did it matter? He could never have Ann Coulter anyway.

Looking across the table at her now, he said, 'I must have someone, *cara mia* – and I cannot have you.'

There was still a question in his words, but Ann could not answer it. It was right that Guido marry Maria.

Undoubtedly he would make a woman very happy. And he was going to be even more successful. Still, there was no denying that Guido's unqualified admiration was something she would miss. He had stirred feelings that had long since disappeared from her marriage.

She and Phillip attended the nuptial Mass as well as the rollicking Italian reception in the church basement. The bride, flushed and happy, clung to Guido's arm throughout the evening. There was only one moment, as Guido, darkly handsome in his tuxedo, turned away from the altar, when his eyes met Ann's. It seemed in that moment that he was conveying to her all the hopes and dreams he was renouncing in taking Maria as his wife.

Ann too felt the loss of inchoate hopes and dreams. But later, when she thought about it more logically, she knew that there never could have been anything between the two of them. It had been just a silly romantic yearning.

When she opened her office four weeks later, Ann had no time left for dreams. She barely had time even to enjoy the room she had decorated to please herself. The walls were robin's-egg blue, the woodwork a pristine white. The carpeting was a deeper shade of blue, setting off shiny black lacquered desks and comfortable modern chairs upholstered in glove-soft leather. On the back wall was a spectacular papered mural of San Francisco, showing a cable car climbing a hill.

The only trouble was that she had so many clients that she was out showing houses almost all day.

Thirty-One

On the surface, life continued pleasantly at the Coulters' after the opening of Ann's office. Phillip tried to pretend things were no different than when his wife was working for Violet, and Ann still tried to have dinner on the table when he got home. A major worry was that Simon was becoming crippled with arthritis. Several times lately he had been unable to manage to pick Evie up at school, and the little girl had had to walk home alone.

Evie was independent, but Ann found herself nervously glancing at her watch these days around three, knowing that her daughter was getting out of school and hoping Simon had been able to make it. In the end she hired a young Mexican girl, Consuela, to come in around one, do a little cleaning, and pick up Evie if Simon wasn't feeling well.

One morning Ann woke up to one of those days when everything went wrong. First, she had a flat tire and by the time the AAA came and fixed it, she was already late for her first meeting. Then, just as she was ready to dash out the door, Consuela phoned to say she couldn't come in. Simon had a bad cold, so as Ann hustled Evie out of the car in front of her school she said, 'Listen, honey, I'll pick you up today, okay?'

'Okay, Mommy,' she agreed, giving her mother a hug.

Ann drove off, hoping to salvage what was left of her early appointment. It would be tough to get away from the office that afternoon, but she couldn't think about that right now. She had so much to do. She was so rushed all day that she skipped lunch and never noticed the dark clouds that had blown up as she raced to see her two o'clock client. A moment after she arrived at the house she was closing, an icy, driving rain began. The closing was a tricky one, but she couldn't concentrate. She knew that it must be near three, and breaking off for a moment, she asked to use the phone, which was luckily still hooked up. It seemed an eternity before anyone at the school answered. 'Hello?'

'Hello. This is Mrs. Coulter – Evie's mother. Could you please tell her to wait? I'll be a little late, but I'll pick her up.'

'I'm sorry, Mrs. Coulter,' came the reply. 'All the children have already left.'

'But I told Evie to wait for me.'

'We had an assembly today, and school let out at two-thirty. We sent a notice home with the children Monday.'

Ann had forgotten all about the crumpled slip of paper. 'I see. Well, do you think you could just check and see if Evie's sitting out in front?'

'I was just outside, Mrs. Coulter. Evie's not there.'

'I see. Thank you.'

Ann hung up, on the verge of tears. That meant that Evie must be caught in the storm.

Quickly she phoned home, and as she listened to the steady ringing, admonished herself, *Don't be nervous. Evie's probably there already.*

Finally Simon answered, his voice wheezing with congestion.

'Dad . . . is Evie home?'

'No, Ann. I thought you were going to pick her up.'

'I was – but I got a little mixed up on the time. How's the cold?'

'Fine, honey.'

He didn't sound fine at all, Ann thought. Oh, Lord, what a day. There was really nothing to do. Evie had no doubt gotten tired of waiting for her, and realized that Mommy had forgotten about Assembly Day. She shouldn't have walked in that rain, but Ann hoped she would have enough sense to come straight home and then dry off.

She went back to the living room, saying forcefully, 'I think this is the best price you're going to get. Doesn't it seem a little foolish to quibble about a few thousand dollars over the long haul?'

She ended up making the deal, but she was so worried about Evie that she barely knew what she was doing. As soon as she could, she rushed to her car and carefully followed the route Evie took from school. That way, if, God forbid, she were still on the street, Ann would see her.

At last she turned into her own driveway, switched

off the ignition, and ran up the steps.

'Evie? Evie, are you here?' she called as she slammed the front door behind her.

'In here, Mommy,' came the blessed reply.

Ann threw off her coat and started toward Evie's bedroom when, to her surprise, Phillip came out.

'Where the hell have you been?' he shouted.

'I forgot that Evie got off school early today,' Ann said, fighting to control her temper. 'And what, if I may ask, are you doing home?'

'Dad telephoned me at the office,' Phillip told her. 'He said that you had called, asking if Evie had come home. He was worried, so I went to look for her. Okay?'

'Well, obviously you found her. Is she all right?'

'She's home, at least – no thanks to you.' He wondered if Ann had any idea what he'd been through.

When he'd called her office, he'd merely been told that Ann was seeing a client and they couldn't reach her. They had no idea if she was on her way to Evie's school. Looking out at the storm, Phillip had decided to see if he could find Evie himself. It had been half an hour before he spotted his daughter, huddled miserably, almost out of sight, in a doorway. By that time he was half crazed with worry.

Seeing Ann standing calmly before him, omnipresent briefcase still in hand, he exploded. 'Goddamn it, Ann! Don't you care at all about Evie? Is your career so important to you that you're willing to risk your child's safety?'

Ann couldn't have been more shocked had Phillip hit her between the eyes. Usually she tried not to react to his snide remarks about her career, but today she had been just as frightened about Evie as he had. And she was tired of apologizing for her work.

'Just who the hell do you think I'm working for if not for your daughter and your father? What luxuries do I ever buy for myself? I drive an old heap of a Chevrolet and I don't buy fancy clothes. I never eat out. I don't take vacations. And I've had enough of your sniping.

There was a time when you were going to take care of me, remember? You wouldn't even have your little clerking job with Kenny if it weren't for me!' The moment the words were out of her mouth, Ann would have sold her soul to have recalled them. She wasn't afraid of Phillip's anger, but she couldn't bear to see the pain she had inflicted so clearly etched on his face.

Phillip was stunned. So Ann had been responsible for the unexpected job offer from Kenny. He had always wondered why it had come so out of the blue.

'So you persuaded Kenny to give me a job . . .'

Ann couldn't reply. She heard Evie cough and said, 'I have to go in to see her. She needs me.'

'She *needed* you an hour ago. Too bad you didn't think of her then. She's okay now. I've already toweled her off and put her to bed.'

Ann no longer was listening. She walked down the hall and locked herself in the bathroom. Without turning on the light, she stumbled to the washbasin and braced her hands against the edge to stop the trembling. Hot tears streamed down her face. *Stop it*, she told herself. *You don't have to cry. You've got to work things out with Phillip. And you certainly can't let Evie know anything is wrong.*

With that, she washed her face and applied a little lipstick. It wasn't going to be easy to pretend to Evie, but when Ann peered in her daughter's door, the little girl was all smiles.

'Hi, Mommy!'

'Honey, why didn't you wait at school as I told you?'

'I waited and waited and you didn't come. So I thought that maybe you had forgotten.'

Sitting down on the edge of the bed, Ann smoothed a lock of Evie's hair off her forehead. It was still damp.

Poor little thing. Phillip's harsh words still resounded in Ann's ears. Evie had a mother who forgot her promises. *You deserve better, kiddo*, she thought bitterly, knowing that there was a modicum of truth to what Phillip had said.

191

'I forgot you were getting out at two-thirty. I'm sorry.'

'Well, I got all wet and kind of scared, but it's okay. Daddy came and got me.'

Evie didn't mention the fact that at first she had thought it a great adventure to walk home in the rain. The puddles were enormous, the one at the corner of Gough and Lombard like a small lake, and Evie hadn't missed one of them, blithely ignoring the water sloshing in over the tops of her boots. But then it had grown windier, and she had felt so cold.

'I took my clothes off and put them in the hamper in the bathroom.'

'That's a good girl, Evie. Well, stay in bed and keep warm. I'm not going back to the office today.'

'That's nice. Daddy and I are going to play a game of cards.'

'Great, honey. Let me talk to Grandpa for a moment and then I'll make us all some hot chocolate. How does that sound?'

'That's okay, Mommy. Daddy already made me some.'

Ann would have given anything to just crawl into bed herself, but she fixed dinner and first served Simon a tray in his bedroom and then fixed another tray for Evie and Phillip. When she placed it on the nightstand, she hoped Phillip would indicate she was forgiven, but he didn't look up from the game. Later, when Evie went to sleep, he settled himself on the living room sofa.

Ann lay in bed, tossing and turning. She finally drifted off around two, only to be awakened an hour later by the unmistakable sound of a sick child coughing.

She got up and put on her robe. As she came out into the hall, she almost collided with Phillip, who had also heard Evie.

As Ann switched on the light, Phillip sat on the edge of Evie's bed and felt her forehead with the back of his hand.

Her skin was burning hot. 'Sweetheart,' he whispered softly, 'how are you feeling?'

'Daddy, it hurts,' Evie croaked.

'Where, honey?'

In response, Evie indicated her throat.

'I'll get the thermometer,' Ann said.

Phillip nodded, then bent over and lifted Evie into his arms, cradling her gently and murmuring, 'I'm sorry you're not feeling well, Princess. We'll get something to fix you up. Probably too many card games, huh?'

The remark didn't even raise a feeble smile.

Ann returned with the thermometer and said, 'Open up, sweetheart.'

Evie's temperature was 104. Ann was suddenly frightened. True, children's temperatures could go up very high, but this had come on so suddenly, and her guilty conscience increased her sense of dread. What if Evie were really ill? It was all her fault.

'Ann, I think we should call Doctor Stein.'

It seemed to take an eternity for the exchange to locate him. For a half hour, she had kept her eyes pinned to the clock, while Phillip sat with Evie.

When the phone finally rang, Ann said, 'Doctor Stein, thank God you're back. Evie has a temperature of 104 and she's coughing violently. She says her head's splitting. She got caught in the rain yesterday and got chilled, I'm afraid.'

'Ann, it's probably nothing, but I've just got back from the emergency room. I'm still dressed. Why don't I run over and check her out?'

Ann immediately felt better, but by the time the doctor arrived, Evie's temperature had climbed to 105 and she was screaming that her headache was so bad she could barely see. After examining her, Stein said, 'Look, it could be just a very bad virus, but I think we should run her over to the hospital anyway.'

Ann felt as if she were trapped in a nightmare as they bundled Evie up and drove to Mount Zion Hospital. Dr. Stein took her off for a battery of tests, saying that Phillip and Ann could see the little girl as soon as they were through.

'Meningitis,' he said shortly when he returned to the waiting room.

'Oh, my God,' Phillip cried. 'Will she be all right?'

'I think so,' Stein said, 'but it's a nasty illness. We have her on antibiotics, and the crisis should pass in a couple of days. Until then things can be a little frightening.'

For the rest of the night Ann and Phillip sat by Evie's bedside, listening to their daughter's agonized breathing, saying nothing.

If anything happens to her, Ann thought, she wouldn't be able to go on living. To think that she was responsible for this horror . . . The doctor could say that Evie's agony was caused by a bacillus, but Ann knew it was her fault. Phillip certainly thought so – his angry accusations still echoed in Ann's ears.

Phillip's reflections were no less anguished. Evie was the only worthwhile thing he had created in life. She was the only person in the world who needed him. The idea of losing her was intolerable.

The two parents sat by their daughter's bedside, isolated in their grief. It was as if they had become two strangers, no longer able to give to each other, even in this crisis.

Day broke, but neither was aware of it. As Evie's condition worsened, they prayed for her to live, each silently acknowledging the fact that without her there was no reason to go on.

Finally the nurse came in again and told them they would have to wait outside while they did some more tests. In the corridor Ann suddenly remembered her office.

'I have to call and let them know that I won't be in,' she said. 'Do you want me to call for you too?'

'Later,' Phillip replied indifferently. He knew it didn't really matter.

Ann reached May Brubeck at the office, an older woman with no family. She was thoroughly reliable, and had keys to everything. 'Don't you worry about a thing,' May told her. 'Just concentrate on getting that little girl of yours better and I'll keep things running smoothly here.'

'Thanks, May,' Ann said weakly. As she hung up the phone, she thought, *Today, for all I care, the damned office can burn down – with my client files in it.*

Going back to the waiting room, Ann saw Phillip's eyes were closed, but it was impossible to tell if he was awake or not. Well, so what? They had nothing to say to each other at this point anyway.

All day, they alternated between Evie's room and the hall. Ann wanted nothing to eat or drink; she felt that if she tried to swallow anything, she would choke. Phillip was pacing up and down like a caged animal.

Evie's condition remained the same. At seven, they called Simon. 'No change, Dad. We're going to spend the night.' At some point after midnight, Ann fell asleep on a plastic-covered chair. When she awoke, it was just beginning to get light. All around her she heard sounds of the hospital coming to life, but in her fatigue and terror they sounded threatening rather than reassuring.

She decided that she could use some coffee, and she got some for Phillip, too. Waiting for the elevator to take her back up, she thought, *I've barely thought of Phillip in all this. It must be as hard on him as it is on me.*

He was still asleep when she returned to the waiting room. His face was gaunt, the skin tightly stretched over his cheekbones above a two-day growth of beard. All at once, her heart went out to him. *Oh Phillip, why, when we need each other so desperately, can't we just reach out? Why do we seem to have nothing to give each other?*

Swallowing the lump in her throat, she touched his shoulder gently. 'Phillip, darling.'

He opened his eyes, and for a moment had no idea where he was. Then he sat up and ran his fingers through his hair in an ineffectual effort to smooth it.

'Coffee?'

'Thanks,' he said, taking the lukewarm cup.

'Phillip?' she said, sitting opposite him. 'Can't we at

least talk to each other? For God's sake, no matter what's happened between us, we're both Evie's parents. We need each other. Or, at least, I need you,' she finished forlornly.

Phillip looked at her silently. Ann's hollow eyes and ravaged face bore testimony to the agony and self-reproach she had been suffering. He no longer blamed her for leaving Evie out in the storm. Meningitis wasn't caused by a chill: Dr. Stein had been quite clear on the subject. Ann wasn't a negligent mother. It was unfair of him to have said so.

He wasn't even angry anymore that she had interceded to get him a job. It was all so long ago . . .

Just then Evie's nurse came out into the hall.

'Any news?' Ann cried.

'No, Mrs. Coulter. Her fever is still hovering around 106. The doctor is coming in to check her.'

Ann turned back to Phillip, her face devastated.

'Oh, Phillip – it's all my fault. If only I had been on time to pick her up from school. Oh, Phillip. What if – what if she dies?'

Her voice broke on the last word, and she buried her face in her hands, her body shaking with sobs.

Phillip's heart suddenly melted. Without thinking, he got up and took her into his arms, rocking her back and forth like a child. 'It's all right, darling. It wasn't your fault, Ann. We'll just do what we can to help her.'

Ann shook her head. 'Why couldn't I have been content with our life? Why did I think I had to work?'

'Ann, please don't keep on punishing yourself.'

'But, Phillip, I've come to the conclusion that I've just about ruined our lives. And now Evie's—' Her voice broke.

'Don't think about that, Ann. It doesn't help anything.'

'I *have* to think about it! I'm going to sell the agency. It's just not worth what it's doing to us.'

'Let's talk about these things later. Right now, let's just help each other through this.'

The sound of his deep voice soothed her. Phillip was still there for her. He had not let her down.

'I love you, darling,' she whispered.

Side by side, they walked down the hallway to Evie's room. The door stood open, but a curtain was pulled around the bed. Several nurses were rushing to and fro with instruments, while Dr. Stein hovered over the little girl.

Stricken anew with fear, Ann grabbed the arm of one of the nurses. 'What's happening? Please tell us!'

'Her fever is still rising. The next couple of hours will be critical.'

They were allowed one glimpse of Evie. She had ceased to toss and turn; instead, she lay very still under the oxygen tent.

Fresh tears came to Ann's eyes. 'Come on, honey,' Phillip said, 'we're just getting in the way in here. They'll call us the second anything happens.'

The waiting room was like a prison now. Ann paced distractedly, unable to sit for more than a minute or two, jumping nervously every time a nurse or doctor passed by. All she wanted to do was to stand by her daughter's bedside, watch her breathe, touch her hand – but they wouldn't let her. Phillip stood at the doorway, smoking cigarette after cigarette.

Suddenly Dr. Stein appeared. 'Good news, folks. It looks as though she's turned the corner. Her fever is starting to drop.'

In a voice so soft as to be almost inaudible, Phillip breathed, 'Thank God. Thank God.'

After Dr. Stein left, Phillip turned to Ann, saying, 'I want you to forgive me. I don't need anything except you and Evie, alive and well. That's all I want. I know I'm not easy – I allow my own stupid frustrations to get in the way of our relationship. But I'm grateful to you for all that you've done, proud of you. And, Ann – I do love you.'

Thirty-Two

After Evie came home from the hospital, Ann spent several days devotedly tending her, content to play wife and mother. But soon her obligations at the agency began to pile up. Phillip didn't mention her vow to sell the agency, and now Evie was well Ann knew it wouldn't be easy to change their lives. Phillip couldn't afford even their own rent without her earnings, and anyway it was out of the question to simply close up shop; she had a long lease and people working for her who depended on her. For a while she swayed back and forth between her conflicting impulses until one day, when she was speaking to Gil Cooley, he said casually, 'Here's a deal, Annie. Live like a prince for peanuts.'

'No more deals, Gil.' Ann smiled wanly. 'I'm even thinking about giving up the agency.'

'That doesn't sound like you. The old Annie would have been champing at the bit, demanding to know what I had in mind.' He tapped some papers he was holding. 'It's on Marina Boulevard.'

'Marina Boulevard? Oh, well, I couldn't afford it anyway.'

'This one you just might be able to.'

In spite of herself, Ann had to laugh. 'Gil, what are you trying to do to me?'

'Take a look,' he said, tossing her the packet.

Ann scanned the closely typed pages, taking in the essential details in a glance. The house in question was a sixteen-room French villa, with six bedrooms and elaborate parterre gardens and a stunning view of the Bay.

She looked up. 'It's obviously a beautiful house. So what? I'd like to own Buckingham Palace, too, but it's not exactly within my means.'

'What if I told you that you could get this place for nothing down?'

Seeing that Ann was hooked, Gil told her the story. For many years, the house had been inhabited by an elderly lady, along with her two pampered pug dogs and her unmarried son. At the excellent age of ninety-three the old woman had died, leaving her estate divided between the pugs and the son, now seventy-two. Unfortunately, the son had terrible emphysema and had just been waiting for his mother to die to move to the south of France. All he wanted was for probate to be granted, and the house sold, so that he could spend what years remained to him in peace. He figured he didn't have many left, so he wasn't going to waste a lot of time holding out for a price.

Ann felt the old, familiar excitement rising in her. 'Gil, do you think we could swing it?'

Gil regarded her with amusement. 'Face it, Annie – you've got this business in your blood.'

Ann debated whether or not to take the plunge. It would mean selling at least one of the Victorians, but houses in the Marina were blue-chip investments. The area would always be valuable if only because of its proximity to the Bay.

After checking with Phillip, who told her to do whatever she felt best, she put Hampton House up for sale, since it was the most valuable of the three rentals she owned.

Meanwhile, the house in the Marina went on the market at $55,000. Ann was almost frantic, waiting for bids on Hampton House, afraid that someone else would snap up her find.

Three weeks later a buyer surfaced for Hampton House, and, miracle of miracles, qualified for the financing. Ann more than doubled her original investment. The minute the papers were signed, she bid $40,000 for the Marina house. It was the only bid to date and, after no more than a day's hesitation, the owner signed. Since the house had such a high appraised value, the bank gave her a loan of $37,000 at 5½ percent for thirty years – almost 100% financing.

Within days Ann Coulter – the former Ann Pollock who had never had more than three dresses at a time to

199

her name – owned a house on Marina Boulevard. For a moment she fantasized living there herself, but she knew it was just a dream. The house was strictly an investment. If the market appreciated in the next couple of years the way Ann anticipated, it could make their fortune. For the time being she leased it to an engineer from Chicago. He almost balked at the huge security deposit Ann demanded, but houses such as this one were almost impossible to find and he soon gave in.

It was Ann's last thought of closing the agency. Evie had fully recovered, and Consuela was coming in every day and staying to start dinner. Even Phillip didn't seem to expect his wife to change, and in fact, since Evie's illness, went out of his way to be nice to Ann. It was as though he had finally stopped opposing her, and the result was that she found herself loving him with the same intensity that she had in those first, all-too-brief early days of their life together. More important, she *liked* him again. The only problem was that Ann totally misunderstood the reasons behind Phillip's change of attitude. She thought he had become adjusted to her career; to her success. The truth was that he no longer cared.

When Evie was sick, he realized that his resentment of Ann's achievements, his feelings of inadequacy, didn't really matter. Only Evie was important, and all Phillip wanted to do was live with her in peace. If the way to achieve peace was to stop interfering in Ann's life, then he would. He could even admit that he loved her and admired her.

As Phillip became more content, life for everyone in the Coulter household improved. And in the happier atmosphere Evie grew and flourished. She danced her way into high school: pretty, popular, and well-adjusted. She took ballet and piano lessons and talked endlessly on the phone.

Ann couldn't have asked for more in a daughter. She rationed her time so as to give Evie the best of it. She bought tickets to the ballet, the symphony, and the theater, and even bought extra tickets so that if she couldn't make it herself, Evie could go with a friend.

The only cause for sadness in these years was Simon's increasing frailty. He suffered a series of small strokes which left him so weak that he couldn't get out of bed. His speech was affected, he couldn't feed himself, and the worst indignity was he became incontinent.

It was almost tragic that Simon's mind remained as sharp as ever. He cursed his weakness, he hated being dependent, and for the first time in his life he became irritable and unreasonable. In the end Ann and Phillip were relieved when Dr. Stein said it was no longer safe for Simon to remain at home. They put him in a nursing home, and Phillip and Evie visited him several times a week. Even Ann, busy as she was, went once a week, and as the country moved into the booming sixties, Ann was busier than ever.

Shortly after Kennedy's assassination, while the country was still in mourning, Ann received an unsolicited bid for the house on Marina Boulevard – $150,000. She didn't need a crystal ball to see that America was entering on a new decade of expansion. She began to review the citywide real estate listings with exhaustive intensity. There were small office buildings available in the outlying districts, but she kept coming back to a particular downtown property on Post Street, between Grant and Kearny. It was an old building, in poor repair, eight stories, with storefronts below.

At first she balked at the $850,000 price tag. It was astronomical, considering what such buildings had gone for a few years before. But she had a clear profit of over $100,000 from the Marina Boulevard property. The real question was whether she could get financing. The sum was out of Gil Cooley's league, and he had to take her to another bank, but in the end her solid balance sheet won the day. With the $100,000 down, the office building was hers.

Within a year she sold it for $1,250,000. With the profits, she bought another office building on Sansome

Street for a little over a million. This time, five months later, she sold it for $1,750,000. Real estate was like wildfire, prices flaming higher and higher, and Ann continued to buy and sell at a frantic pace.

One day she discovered that she was a millionaire – and she continued to speculate. She never stopped to think whether a particular move was brilliant; she just followed her instinct. The first time she heard herself acclaimed as a real estate tycoon, she was amazed. All she had been after was a secure financial future for her family.

Yet, by December 1964, even Ann realized she was riding the crest of the wave. That morning, she had sold one of her buildings in the Potrero District for close to $1,500,000 and for the first time since she went into business, Ann wondered if it was time to spend some of her hard-won savings on her family and herself.

They still lived in the modest house on Bay Street, still drove secondhand cars, still shopped at the Emporium. She owned no jewels or furs. Of course Phillip didn't seem to care about luxuries, but they might be fun, and Evie was old enough to appreciate living in a nicer neighborhood.

Ann was still mulling over the possibility of moving when once again fate stepped into her life.

There was a house she had been shown several years before. At the time she had thought that the couple who bought it were the luckiest people in the world. Now, miraculously, it was for sale again. Ann no sooner heard the price than she was on the phone to the agent.

Built in 1922 by an eccentric millionaire, the house was a delicate off-white brick with a gray slate roof. In front of the French windows on the third floor were hand-wrought iron balconies which had been brought from a château near Versailles. The entrance was guarded by antique filigree iron gates, and the broad steps to the house were flanked by a pair of stone dogs.

When the door was opened by a Chinese houseboy, she handed him her business card and said, 'I am Mrs.

202

Coulter. Mr. Cook, the agent handling the house, is expecting me.'

The servant bowed her in and shut the door behind her as Ann stepped into the foyer. An oval Aubusson rug lay in the center of the room, whose floors were the same creamy marble as the entry stoop. The walls were rose-colored silk, and magnificent paintings lined the curving staircase. A stained-glass skylight flooded the foyer with brilliant hues.

'The elevator is this way,' the houseboy said, moving silently over to what appeared to be a closet.

As soon as they were inside, he touched a button and the grille moved back into place. Then the elevator rose to the third floor.

As it opened, Ann caught a glimpse of the Bay through the broad windows before the boy led her to the library where Don Cook was waiting. The elegant room was book-lined with a beautiful Louis XV marble fireplace.

'I'm Ann Coulter. You must be Donald Cook.'

Cook was pleased that the well-known realtor was apparently looking to buy the place herself. If half of what he had heard was true, she had the money.

'Let me take your coat,' he said. Then: 'I know you must be anxious to see the interior. Why don't we take a little tour before we start talking business?'

They went back down the hall to the foyer, then passed through an archway into the drawing room. It was a spacious, well-proportioned room, one entire wall of which had been replaced by glass doors opening onto a terrace which had the same spectacular view of the Bay as the windows on the landing.

'It's – lovely,' exclaimed Ann, unable to be blasé.

Don Cook smiled. 'You know that the house was extensively renovated. The current owners put the drawing room here to take advantage of the view, and installed the French doors and built the terrace. So it's not absolutely in period.'

Ann shrugged, too thrilled to quibble. The doors and

terrace only added to the beauty of the house. She stepped out and admired the white wrought-iron table and chairs.

As the two of them walked around, the plan of the renovations became apparent. The previous owners had gutted the third floor, which had originally contained maids' quarters, and put the main living rooms there, because of the view. In addition to the drawing room and library, there was a master suite, and two more bedrooms, one of which could be Evie's.

Below, on the second floor, was a dining room, sitting room, and kitchen. Much of the ground floor was now taken up by a two-car garage. However, the renovations had been beautifully done, preserving the magnificent foyer and virtually all of the architectural moldings and paneling, as well as the fireplace mantels, different in every room, and the Tiffany glass.

Ann wandered about in a dream. The house was perfect. She could move in without changing an ashtray. She came to a decision immediately.

'Mr. Cook, if my husband agrees, I am prepared to make a bid for the house, complete with furnishings. Two hundred thousand dollars – cash.'

Don Cook was taken aback. 'Well, as you know, the house alone is being offered for one ninety-five. I can't imagine that the owners will take two hundred thousand and include the furnishings. There are some priceless antiques here.'

'You may as well know that I've looked into the situation pretty carefully already. The owners are going through a nasty divorce, and the wife is anxious to get rid of the place. From what I hear, she will be glad to dispose of all reminders of the marriage. Now, two hundred thousand dollars may seem low, but I'm offering cash. Why don't you see if the owners agree?'

'Yes . . . I'll convey your offer to them,' Cook murmured uncertainly. Mrs. Coulter's pretty face apparently concealed a steely determination as well as a sharp mind. But as Ann sat back in the comfortable, silk-covered armchair, she began to tremble. What if Phillip didn't agree?

This time she didn't make the mistake of rushing down to his office. She waited until they were going to bed that night before describing the house and explaining how they could afford it.

'Can you come with me to see it tomorrow before you go to work?' Ann finished.

'I don't think that's necessary,' Phillip said with an odd smile. 'I'm sure I'll love it, Ann. You never make a bad move. Why don't you just go ahead and bid. If you get it I'll look at it then.'

Ann put in her bid the next day and began to pray, but it was seventy-two hours before she heard from Mr. Cook, and those three days seemed like an eternity. The more she thought about the little jewel-box house, the more she wanted it.

As the days passed, Ann became almost frantic with worry, convinced that this time she had miscalculated, aimed too low. That house, with contents, was worth at least $250,000, probably much more. Someone else would snap it up. She had lost her chance.

Then, when she was ready to give up hope, the telephone rang.

'Ann Coulter speaking.'

'Mrs. Coulter, Donald Cook. I've spoken to the owners, and they have made a counteroffer. They're willing to accept two hundred twenty-five thousand dollars in cash.'

Relief coursed through her. It didn't matter what they demanded, she would pay it! Gripping the receiver tightly, Ann exclaimed, 'That's fine! I'm ready to sign the papers as soon as they're ready.'

When Ann opened the door and Phillip and Evie walked into the soaring foyer, bathed in rosy light, Evie squealed, 'Holy smokes, Mom, are we going to live *here*?'

Ann answered, a lilt in her voice, 'I guess so, honey. I'm just hoping you and Daddy like it.'

She was watching Phillip closely, anxious to see what his reaction would be. Feeling her eyes on him, he looked over at her, a funny half-smile on his lips. 'It's magnificent.'

He began to wander about the foyer, taking in the marble floors and the silk-covered walls, the beautiful furniture with its faint smell of beeswax, the airy, swirling staircase. He had almost forgotten that he had been born in a house even more imposing than this one. For a moment, he felt he had been transported back to Sea Cliff. He was brought back to the present by Evie's shout. 'Oh, keen – an elevator! Does it really work?'

They all stepped in, and the elevator glided to the third floor.

As they walked into the drawing room, Phillip and Evie stopped short, overwhelmed by the view. It was even lovelier than it had been the day Ann had first seen it, the panorama of the Bay and the Golden Gate Bridge glittering brilliantly in the late afternoon sunshine.

'Isn't it gorgeous, Phillip?' Ann whispered.

'Yes, honey.'

'Do you think you could be happy here?'

He looked at her. 'As long as you are, Ann.'

'Well, of course I am. But don't you think it's the most wonderful piece of luck that we could actually buy it?'

'Yes, honey. I'm very proud of you.'

Ann remained calm. Phillip's enthusiasm didn't seem to quite match her own, but perhaps that was only natural. Women were usually interested in their homes more than men.

Evie's enthusiasm, on the other hand, was all that Ann could have wished for. Just wait until her friends saw the house! 'Which room will be mine, Mom?'

'I don't know, honey – whichever you like. The blue room has twin four-posters, which would be nice when you have friends over to spend the night, but the white one has the big canopy bed with the organdy ruffles.'

Evie thought for a moment, then announced, 'I'll go look at them both again!'

She ran off down the hallway, and Ann and Phillip were left alone. She tried to divine what Phillip was really thinking. She wasn't sure that he liked the house, despite his reassurances. All she wanted was for him to be happy here.

She took his hand and they slowly walked out onto the terrace. The short winter day was ending, and even as they watched, the lights of the Golden Gate Bridge began to twinkle.

We're going to live here, with this view, every night of our lives, until it becomes as natural to us as Bay Street, Phillip thought. *Too bad I wasn't able to give her all this. Instead, she's giving it to me.*

He was careful to keep any trace of self-pity from his voice as he told her again how much he liked the house. After all, she deserved to live here. He was lucky to be along for the ride.

Ann tried to believe that Phillip meant what he said, and that he no longer cared whose money had bought the house, but she couldn't help asking one last question.

'Phillip, you don't mind that I bid on the house without asking you to see it?'

Phillip turned to her, smiling gently. 'Ann sweetheart, you always do what is best for us. How could I possibly mind that?'

Thirty-Three

The day they moved in, Ann felt that she would never ask anything more of life. Evie was happy, Phillip actually seemed content, and she herself came home from work with a sense of joy and renewal.

Although she didn't have time to entertain much, she did throw one big housewarming party for their friends. While chiding herself for the petty triumph, she couldn't help smiling at the astonished expressions on Ruthie's and Kenny's faces when they were ushered into the foyer. Then she remembered that whatever Kenny's faults, Ruthie was a good friend and she had her own problems these days. Kenny had been fooling around with his receptionist, and from Ruthie's drawn face it was possible that she had found out. Ann hugged her and walked her over to the bar.

Still, she couldn't help but be proud tonight, in her own lovely home, with her handsome husband by her side.

Life soon fell into a pleasant pattern for the Coulters. Phillip no longer seemed bitter about his mediocre career or jealous of Ann's success, and both parents were happy to see Evie growing into a lovely young woman. She was happy in her new school, and the house was constantly filled with her friends.

It was just after her sweet sixteen party that the nursing home called to tell them that Simon was dead. He had seemed the same the last time they had visited, but looking back, Ann realized that he had adopted a new air of tranquillity. It was almost as if he welcomed the end.

Much as they loved him, it was impossible for either Ann or Phillip to wish him back; he had spent his last years trapped in a body which had betrayed him. Evie, however, reacted differently. Ever since Simon had been put into the nursing home, she had visited him faithfully several times a week. There had been times when neither Ann nor Phillip could make it, but Evie had hardly missed once in the two years her grandfather had been there. In fact, she had seen him just the day before he died.

When she heard the news, she stared at her mother in horrified disbelief. 'No! He can't be dead! He simply can't be!'

Ann had put her arm around her, saying sympathetically, 'I know it's a great shock to you, honey, but you know, Simon is far happier this way. He was ready to go, darling.'

She squeezed Evie's shoulders comfortingly, but there was no response.

Finally, Evie said, 'Okay, Mom. I understand what you're saying. I think I'll go to my room for a while.'

Ann frowned. She had thought Evie was prepared for the inevitability of Simon's death. But this was Evie's first experience with death, so she was bound to be upset. Maybe some cocoa would be comforting. Ann fixed a tray with a steaming mug and a plate of Oreos. Knocking gently at her door, Ann called softly, 'Honey, I've brought you some hot chocolate.'

Turning the knob, she pushed the door open. Ann had expected Evie to be weeping; instead, she sat near her window, staring into the night.

'No, thanks,' Evie murmured as Ann set the tray down.

'Why don't you try to eat a little something, sweetheart? It might make you feel a little better.'

Evie shrugged. Ann touched her shoulder. She couldn't think of what to say to ease the pain. After a minute she left the room, hoping Evie would feel better later, but she refused dinner and spent the night in her room, saying she was tired.

Evie went to school the next day, but when she came home, she went straight to her room and flung herself down on the bed. When her parents came home from work she heard them talking in the living room. She knew that they were worried about her, but somehow she couldn't reassure them. They thought that she had prepared for Grandpa's death, just because he was old and sick, but she had had no idea how totally final death was. The idea that she would never again see his face or hear him say, 'My little Evie,' devastated her. *If Grandpa could die, one day Mom and Dad could die, too.* It was a notion that Evie was unwilling to face. The three of them were so close, Evie knew she wouldn't survive if anything happened to either of them, and she was terrified.

Ann came up later with some supper, but didn't try to force her daughter to eat. Instead, she put down the tray and handed Evie a little package wrapped in candy-striped paper.

'Sweetheart, I know you will miss Grandpa a long time, but I thought this present might cheer you up a bit.'

Evie tried to smile. 'Gee, thanks, Mom.'

'Well? Open it, darling.'

Evie unwrapped the box to find a lovely pale-pink angora sweater. A lump rose in her throat as she stared at it, then at her mother. All she could think was, *Someday you're going to die too – and I won't be able to bear it!* Tears rolled down her cheeks.

Ann sighed. Poor Evie. Maybe they were taking the wrong approach. She tried a rallying tone.

'Evie, honey – please. You must not carry on like this. You know, Grandpa wouldn't have wanted you to feel this way.'

But Evie's tears at that moment were not for Simon.

The next day was Saturday, and although Evie came out to breakfast, she picked at her food, saying little, then retreated to her room.

Ann usually worked Saturdays, but today she hesitated to leave. She went in to see Evie and once again tried to comfort her. 'I know how much you loved Grandpa, Evie. We all did. But his time had come, don't you see that?'

Evie just nodded.

Ann came out and sat down across from Phillip at the table. 'I don't know, Phillip. Nothing I say seems to help. I don't know what to do for her. I had been planning to go in to the office, but I don't like to leave her. Maybe she would like to go to a movie or something. What do you think?'

'I don't think a movie is quite what she's in the mood for. Listen, Ann, if you need to go to the office for an hour or two, why don't you go? I'll be here, and maybe I can talk to Evie.'

'I don't know . . .' Ann protested, but in the end she decided that an hour or two wasn't going to make much difference. She would stop and get scallops for dinner on her way home. Evie loved those. And maybe a chocolate cake as well.

When Ann had gone, Phillip put aside his paper. Knocking on Evie's door, he said, 'Princess? It's Daddy. May I come in?'

'Yes,' came the muffled response.

Evie was lying on her bed. Phillip sat down next to her without saying anything. The misery and loss reflected in the clouded violet eyes pierced his heart. He longed to pick her up and cuddle her as he had when she was little, but she was no longer a little girl.

'I'm so sorry, baby,' he whispered.

It was the sorrow in his own eyes as much as the sympathy in his voice which shattered her defenses. Her lower lip quivered, and at the sight Phillip forgot that his daughter was almost grown up. He reached over and pulled her to him, cradling her gently.

'Oh, Dad, it's so awful!' she wept.

Rocking her back and forth, Phillip murmured over and over, 'It's going to be all right, sweetheart. Daddy's here.'

It was all Evie could do not to sob, *It's not just Grandpa, Daddy. It's you and Mom. Please don't die, don't die!*

As the storm began to subside, Phillip spoke softly. 'I know how much Grandpa meant to you. You and he were buddies, weren't you? When Mom and I were both working, he took you everywhere, didn't he? School, and the playground. You know, Mom and I had kind of forgotten how much time you spent together when you were little. It's no wonder that you feel sad.

'Now, I'm not going to try to talk you out of feeling that way. Right now I'm sure you don't want to hear that someday you'll feel lucky that you had him for as long as you did. But it's true.

'And you know, Evie,' Phillip continued, his voice tender, 'you were the most important thing in the world to him. More important, even, than I was. It was as if he got Eva, your grandmother, back when you were born. I remember how happy he was that day.'

Evie heard her father's voice tremble on his last words and, wrapping her arms around his neck, she whispered, 'Daddy, I love you so much.'

'I know, honey,' he whispered. 'And I'm still here for you, even if Grandpa's not.'

Thirty-Four

Somehow, through some divine Providence, life got back to normal in a fairly short time after Simon's death. Evie was feeling her old self again, and for that Ann was greatly relieved.

Life at the office was as hectic as ever. It seemed everyone wanted to buy a house or trade into a bigger one. It was after a particularly lucrative November that Ann sat at her desk and pondered a proposal sent in by a broker friend in the city.

The sound of it intrigued her: an invitation to participate in a series of real estate syndication deals, put together by a consortium based in New York. They took unimproved parcels and created office parks and suburban shopping centers all over the country.

It was relatively safe, because the risk was dispersed, yet the potential gain was enormous. Ann had studied similar proposals before, but had always held back, unwilling to dive into something over which she would have no direct control. It took a fair amount of financial savvy to sift the wheat from the chaff. The real estate field, like any other, has its share of shady dealers and outright con men.

But each passing year had bolstered her confidence, and now she felt she was ready to take a closer look. Adam Gayne was the man behind this syndication, and her broker friend had assured her he was tops in the field – a lawyer, investment adviser, real estate financier. 'It would be impossible to list all the pies he has his finger in, Ann,' her friend had said. 'You have to meet him – he's quite a guy.'

Well, why not? Ann thought, intrigued. She had dealt with most of the big names in San Francisco; there shouldn't be anything so very different about this New York attorney. She had money to invest and clients who would follow her advice. She would just have to see what it was he was proposing.

Ann was happy that Phillip was spending so much time with Evie these days: it would make it easier to be away from home for a while. When they saw her off at the airport, Ann felt she could leave them with an easy heart.

New York was exhilarating. The discomfort of the December chill was offset by deep blue skies and clear, pale sunshine. Ann left her suite at the Plaza and walked down Fifth Avenue, then east, to her appointment, excited by the prospect of her first syndication deal. The properties were in a boom area – Dallas – and seemed virtually fail-safe.

As she stepped into the soaring atrium of the steel and granite skyscraper, she felt a tingle of anticipation. Today she would meet Adam Gayne. She pictured him as a man of medium height, portly, with thinning gray hair and steel-rimmed spectacles. He was probably quiet and self-effacing; contrary to popular belief, real estate tycoons tend to be the opposite of flamboyant, though there are notable exceptions.

The doorman showed her to a green-carpeted elevator, which shot silently and swiftly to the 47th floor. For a moment Ann's heart hammered against her chest and her hands began to perspire. She would have liked a few extra minutes to compose herself. Squaring her shoulders, she stepped out into a cold-looking, uncarpeted foyer. Above the only doors appeared the name ADAM GAYNE, ATTORNEY.

The atmosphere of the office itself seemed strangely charged, but Ann reproached herself for having too much imagination. After all, she had dealt with many high-powered lawyers and speculators in the past few years, so why should this one be any different? And the name Ann Coulter was one to be reckoned with in real estate circles, wasn't it? Still, something about this office made her take a firmer grip on her briefcase when she walked up to the receptionist.

'Mr. Gayne will be with you in a few minutes,' the woman murmured. 'If you would care to take a seat?'

Ann had barely sat down and unlocked her briefcase when a door opened and a tall, lean, athletic-looking man impeccably dressed in a navy blue three-piece suit strode up to her, his hand extended.

Ann was so dumbfounded that she stumbled a little when she got up to shake hands. *This* was Adam Gayne? She took in the handsome features, the thick, wavy black hair with just a hint of silver at the temples, and the riveting black eyes.

'Mrs. Coulter . . . I'm happy to meet you at last,' he said with a disarming smile.

'Mr. Gayne . . .' Ann managed to say as she pulled herself together.

'Shall we step into my office?' Gayne said softly.

Ann was very aware of his nearness as she walked past him and took a chair.

He seated himself at the large ebony desk opposite her and smiled. 'Shall we get down to business? I trust you have the copies of the agreement I mailed you.'

His neutral, businesslike tone and the familiarity of the legal documents allowed Ann to order her thoughts. She retrieved the relevant papers from her carefully organized case and began: 'Mr. Gayne – I have a number of questions regarding page seven . . .'

From then on, it was all business, Gayne explaining the ins and outs of the syndication in question with such lucidity that Ann could immediately see why he was considered one of the foremost experts in the field. They got into the details of a particularly thorny tax question, and before Ann knew it, the afternoon was half gone. They had been talking for over two hours.

Glancing at her watch, she exclaimed, 'Oh, my – it's

nearly two o'clock. I'm sorry to have taken up so much of your time.'

'Don't mention it,' he said, tossing the papers aside. 'I wanted to make sure you were all clear on the various ramifications.'

'In any case,' Ann announced, more abruptly than she had intended, 'I guess we're about finished. I won't keep you.'

'You're not keeping me,' he murmured.

Barely hearing him, Ann shuffled her papers into her briefcase any which way, and began to get up.

'Mrs. Coulter – haven't you missed lunch?'

She looked at him inquiringly. He seemed amused.

'No,' she said hesitantly.

'You have other plans?'

Ann flashed him a rueful smile. 'Actually, I have no plans at all.'

'Good. Let's go.'

In front of the building, Adam hailed a cab. 'Russian Tea Room,' he said before recalling himself and asking, 'Is that all right with you?'

'Fine,' Ann answered coolly. Now it was her turn to feel amused. Plainly, Mr. Adam Gayne was not in the habit of consulting anyone's wishes save his own, although he covered it adroitly with that graceful manner of his.

He was the perfect escort. Doors flew open, he was given a well-positioned table, waiters scurried to do his bidding. And all the while his attention to Ann never wavered. He asked her about her life in San Francisco – how she had gotten started in the business, what pitfalls she had encountered.

Occasionally he offered entertaining comments and asides, and Ann found herself laughing more than she had in years. They finished their Strawberries Romanoff and sat over cups of Viennese coffee until Ann said, a trifle anxiously, 'I'm afraid I'm keeping you from something.'

'Nothing,' he assured her. 'I had nothing scheduled

215

this afternoon, and if I did it would be too late. It's already five. Time for cocktails, don't you think?' There was a twinkle in his dark eyes.

Two very dry martinis later, Ann gave up worrying about what she suspected were Adam Gayne's neglected afternoon appointments. She just let herself enjoy his company and his wit until Adam startled her by suggesting dinner.

'Goodness – didn't we just finish lunch?'

'Several hours ago,' he laughed.

Ann had never known time to pass so quickly.

'Perhaps you'd like to go back to your hotel and change?' he asked.

'I really should say no . . .'

'Why?'

Ann reflected for a minute. *Am I feeling guilty just because I'm having such a good time? Does the fact that I'm married – happily married – mean I can't spend an evening with a business acquaintance – even an unquestionably attractive one?*

She looked up to see one of his eyebrows lifted in a look of amused inquiry. Embarrassed now by her inhibitions, she laughed and said, 'Why not? Just give me an hour or two to get ready.'

'Great. We'll go to Lutèce.'

Ann returned to the Plaza filled with a delicious sense of anticipation. No matter how many times she told herself not to be so silly, she couldn't calm down. *New York is exciting – that's it*, she had told herself several times. The electricity that seemed to be coursing through her was due to her having finally arrived in America's financial capital . . .

Glancing at the bedside clock, she remembered that she had only an hour and a half until Adam picked her up.

What in the world am I going to wear? Going over to the closet, she realized she had only brought two very businesslike dresses and a pale blue knit dress she had thrown in because it didn't wrinkle. She eyed it with disfavor. It looked so dowdy. She was about to take it off the hanger when an image of a very chic looking shop right in the Plaza flashed through her head. She had glimpsed a stunning black dress there. On an impulse, she dialed the operator and asked for the shop. An elegantly nasal female voice answered: 'Maison Mendessolle. May I help you?'

'Yes, please. Would it be possible for you to send three or four cocktail dresses, size eight, up to my room? I need something for tonight and I just don't have time to come down.'

Ten minutes later, the intimidatingly chic owner of the nasal voice appeared, bearing an armful of cocktail dresses. Without ceremony, Ann held them up to choose. There was a sea-green one with paillettes, a little too glittery; a white one that would have been appropriate for a dance; a red one that was entirely too vivid; and finally the black one Ann had seen in the window.

It was the last one she tried on, an elegantly draped black silk crepe with a slender bodice and a dropped waist. There was just the right amount of black jet beading at the neckline, and the shirred skirt swirled excitingly about her legs.

She poked her head out of the bathroom. 'I'll take the black. Can you please add it to my hotel tab?'

'With pleasure, madam,' said the saleslady, secretly wondering why her customer was so shy about emerging from the bathroom. It looked as if she had a lovely figure.

Ann had never felt so reckless, but at least she would be decently dressed. From a business point of view, it wouldn't do to let Adam Gayne think that she was either too poor or too provincial to dress appropriately for dinner.

Quickly, she ran a tub, throwing in a packet of bath salts thoughtfully provided by the hotel, and lowered herself into the deliciously scented hot water. She closed her eyes and lay back, letting the soothing warmth relax her tired muscles. When she took up the thick cake of soap to wash herself with her usual efficiency, she found her movements had become drugged, languorous. Experimentally, she ran her hand over her shoulders, feeling the satiny texture of her skin. She let her hand travel down over her breasts, almost caressingly. *They're still as firm as a young girl's,* she thought, surprised. She tried to make herself hurry, but her brain seemed strangely slow to respond. Her body, by contrast, felt unusually alive. *That's enough,* she told herself. *Adam will be here in half an hour. You can't be in the tub when he arrives!* She rinsed quickly, first hot and then cold, and stepped out of the tub.

Donning a lacy, clinging slip, Ann applied a little more makeup than usual, accenting her violet eyes with a smoky charcoal shadow and mascara that Evie had given her on her birthday. Ann had brought it along principally to avoid hurting Evie's feelings, but tonight it was going to come in handy. Her hair was still up from her bath, and Ann looked in the mirror. Swept off her neck, it showed off the line of her throat. No, she was being absurd. She never wore her hair up. Perhaps if she just swept it back a bit with two combs . . .

She tugged on sheer black nylons; black, high-heeled shoes; and then slid into her new dress. When she turned back to the mirror, she was astonished. An elegant stranger stared back at her, a luminous creature with silky dark curls, sparkling eyes, and a wild-rose color in her cheeks. Her dress clung seductively to her breasts and hips, and the short skirt made her legs seem very long and slim.

She was just stuffing her wallet into a small black leather clutch when a knock sounded on the door.

'Hello,' she said tremulously, opening it.

For an instant his glance flickered over her body, and his eyes widened. But when he spoke, his voice was composed. 'Ann . . . you look lovely.'

'Shall we go?' Ann asked abruptly. She didn't feel up to coping with his compliments.

'May I get your coat first? It's winter, you know, and that charming silk dress isn't going to keep you very warm.'

All Ann had was her black coat – too casual, but thank God it was black.

Lutèce lived up to its reputation.

'You've never been here?' Adam asked.

'No. I've never been to New York before. And I suppose you find my provinciality shocking.'

'Not at all,' he said. 'No one is as provincial as the average New Yorker. But I hope I'm not that bad. As a matter of fact, San Francisco's one of my favorite cities.'

'You go there often?' Ann asked, then flushed, afraid he would think she was taking too personal an interest in his comings and goings.

'I've begun making business trips every couple of months. Maybe they'll be more frequent now that I have more connections there.'

Without taking his eyes from her, he asked the waiter for Dom Pérignon – two fluted glasses were placed before them and the waiter poured the clear, straw-colored fluid.

Adam Gayne raised his glass and touched it to Ann's. He started to say something, then seemed to change his mind. When he spoke he just said, 'To a successful partnership.'

As Ann slowly relaxed, she found that, just as at lunch, there were a thousand things to talk about. She scarcely noticed what he ordered for the two of them, although later she retained a confused memory of Escargots Endive, Roast Quail, exotic imported wines that added to her impression that she was dreaming. Nothing seemed real, not the incredible food and decor or the man sitting across from her – least of all herself. Every time she shifted her position in her chair, she could feel silk caressing her skin, reminding her of her unfamiliar glamor. Even though their conversation occasionally touched on business topics, Ann felt nothing like her customary clear-thinking, efficient self.

After she had finished the last spoonful of a succulent Coupe aux Framboises, Adam insisted on ordering Armagnac.

The rare brandy came in gently warmed balloon snifters. Ann took a deep breath and looked up delightedly. 'It's lovely! Like Cognac, isn't it?'

'Different region of France,' Adam commented, smiling at her enthusiasm.

Ann took a sip and felt an odd, melting sensation. Deciding she had better not drink too much, she put her glass back on the table. When she looked up, she caught Adam's eyes on her.

'You are beautiful,' he said abruptly, watching the rise and fall of her full breasts under the thin black silk. Her eyes avoided his admiring gaze.

'Mr. Gayne—'

'Adam. Call me Adam.'

'Adam, I—'

'I'm sorry. I didn't intend to make you uncomfortable. You *are* beautiful though – a hundred men must have told you that before.'

Ann shook her head.

'No? Then maybe San Francisco males need glasses.'

Ann laughed. She looked at his strong, tanned hand resting on the tablecloth and fought an inexplicable urge to grasp it. What in the world was happening to her? She should really go home and get some sleep – this evening's madness would wear off by daylight.

'Shall we go?' Adam echoed her thoughts.

As he helped her with her coat, his hand brushed her neck and she could feel the electricity.

She flinched, and Adam moved away instantly.

The night was bitterly cold as they waited for a taxi. Ann sat stiffly in her corner, more aware than she wanted to be of his arm on the top of the seat behind her. Her hotel was only a short ride, and when they arrived, Adam got out of the cab without comment and walked her up the steps of the Plaza.

As she turned to say good night, Ann saw that the

gleam of amusement had returned to his dark eyes, and as they stood at the door, she half feared, half expected, that he would kiss her. But instead he drew her hand from her coat pocket, bent his head, and she felt the light touch of his lips on her fingers.

'It's been lovely, Ann. Good night.'

'Good night, Adam,' Ann returned in a high voice completely unlike her own.

Then she turned and fled into the safety of the crowded, brightly lit lobby.

Adam turned back to the waiting taxi. Suddenly he changed his mind and, handing the cabbie a five-dollar bill, waved him away. It was a long hike, but he would walk home. Perhaps the icy air would chase away the spell Ann Coulter seemed to have cast over him.

He had expected an officious, frumpy, middle-aged virago in a badly fitting pants suit. Well, Ann Coulter certainly wasn't that. She was beautiful, sexy, utterly charming. She could have easily exploited those qualities if she had chosen to, but there was no trace of that in her manner. Maybe that was what really set her apart – her sincerity and honesty. He had heard rumors that Coulter was one of the most respectable in the business. And smart, too. Obviously. He had been impressed by her quickness. She could instantly grasp the essentials of a deal and pinpoint the weak links. No one was going to put anything over her.

As he continued to walk along Fifty-seventh Street, past the glittering shop windows, he tried to talk himself out of his fascination: *So she's beautiful and brainy. She is also happily married and lives clear across the country on the West Coast.*

But the memory of the sparkling, violet eyes; the rueful, sweet smile; the mercurial sense of humor refused to dim. Lost in thought, he almost walked past his building.

The doorman, noticing him, waved wildly, then opened the door and called out, 'Mr. Gayne. Where are you going?'

'Don't ask, Freddy,' Adam said rather sheepishly as he turned back and walked inside.

Usually Adam felt a sense of peace and comfort whenever he entered his apartment, but tonight he couldn't shake off his nervous excitement. When he glanced out the window, the lights of Manhattan seemed dimmer than when they had framed Ann's head at Lutèce.

In his bedroom, his silk robe lay folded on the polished mahogany bed, the sheets turned down, while a decanter and glasses stood ready on the table near the fireplace. Faithful Gaston – what a treasure. 'Better than a wife,' he murmured to himself, but as he climbed into bed he wondered what Ann Coulter would look like with her dark hair tumbled on that pillow, her slender body bare.

Good God! he thought savagely. *Am I going to fantasize all night about a woman I hardly know?* Yet the image persisted.

This is ridiculous. It was late and he had to get some rest. He had all those appointments he'd put off from today. Throwing back the covers, he got up and poured himself a stiff brandy. After downing it in two gulps, he went back to bed and drifted off into a restless sleep.

When he woke, his first conscious thought was of Ann. He had overslept. In his unsettled state of mind, he had forgotten to set the alarm or leave a note for Gaston. Even though he was late, he thought of calling her at the Plaza. Then he remembered that she had mentioned a nine o'clock flight. Even now, she must be at the airport, waiting for takeoff.

Irritably, he called out for coffee and turned on the shower. San Francisco had never seemed so far away.

Thirty-Five

Ann, on the other hand, was grateful for every one of the three thousand miles that separated her from Adam. She forced herself to plunge back into work and tried to spend her free time planning expeditions with Evie. But her daughter was busy now with her own friends, and weekends when Ann was alone with Phillip she couldn't help remembering the electric tension she had felt with Adam. Safe at home, she was able to label it truthfully as desire. She had wanted Adam Gayne even though she knew she couldn't have him. From time to time they spoke on the phone about business, but Ann kept the calls short. Time passed, and Ann began to feel as if she once again were in full control of her emotions.

Then, almost a year later, Adam unexpectedly called to announce that he had put together another syndicate. Was she free to come to New York to discuss the details with the developers?

Ann had temporized, saying that she would call him back. But in spite of her conflicting emotions, she couldn't bring herself to ignore the opportunity. The first syndication had been highly profitable for all concerned, and perhaps this one would be, too. In any case, a woman in her forties should be well past the age of schoolgirl crushes, so there was no real danger.

She had her secretary leave word with Gayne's office that she would be there. Then she reserved a suite at the Plaza. Seized with a feeling of recklessness, she decided to be in New York a day early and do some shopping. Apart from the black cocktail dress she had bought on her last trip, Ann owned only clothing necessary for her work, casual attire to wear around the house, and two modest dresses for occasional business socializing. *Why not indulge myself?* she thought. *God knows I can afford it*.

Once settled in at the Plaza, Ann set out like a child on her way to see Santa. The store windows were filled with holiday merchandise; the air was ringing with Salvation Army bells.

Ann had never been to Bergdorf Goodman's before, but a friend had told her they had one of the best designer floors in the city.

For once in her life, she was going to treat herself and not think of the cost. She would refuse to listen to the cautious inner voice of little Ann Pollock, who still monitored most of her shopping expeditions.

Approaching a black-clad saleswoman, she forced herself to say confidently, 'I was wondering if you could help me. I'm looking for a number of things . . .'

Two hours later, Ann had made a substantial number of purchases, and was debating whether or not to buy a dreamy rose-pink Mollie Parnis cocktail dress. The skirt was made of yards of finely pleated chiffon, while the ruffled neckline, demure enough in front, curved daringly low in back. Refusing to consider the cost, she nodded to the delighted sales clerk and changed back into her own clothes.

Too excited to have anything sent, she staggered across Fifty-ninth Street to her hotel. Back in her room, she tore open the bags. The colors of the dresses and suits formed a rainbow in the large walk-in closet as she hung them – a sapphire-blue dress with matching jacket; a flowing, coffee-colored crepe-de-chine; an off-white raw silk suit; and the beautiful pink chiffon. She had also bought slender alligator pumps and handbag for the coffee silk, lovely burgundy shoes to contrast with the blue dress and jacket, a pair of silvery satin high-heeled sandals, and a beaded evening bag.

When everything was put away, Ann walked to her window and looked out at the park. Suddenly she felt very lonely. All these beautiful clothes and nowhere to wear them. What could she do with the rest of her day? Maybe she should go over the papers Adam had sent her once again, but she was too restless.

Play hooky, Ann, a little voice said. *It wouldn't hurt to indulge yourself just a bit more. Perhaps a haircut? It's time you got rid of that girlish page boy . . .* She picked up the phone and dialed the hotel beauty salon, but there were no stylists free. Leafing through the phone book, she recognized only one name, Elizabeth Arden. It was close by, so Ann dialed the number.

Yes, they had an appointment available.

'Would you like the Maine Chance, Mrs. Coulter?'

'What?' Ann asked, bewildered.

224

'That's our mini-spa special package. It includes a haircut, set, manicure, pedicure, massage, facial, and makeup.'

'Yes,' Ann found herself saying. 'Yes, that's exactly what I would like.'

She loved every minute of it, from the moment she had stepped through the famous red door and was taken in hand by a smiling young woman. She was pampered in a way she hadn't dreamed possible. The biggest transformation was her hair. They cut it so that the natural wave became an asset rather than a liability. It curved under in a shining bell, while gently tousled bangs emphasized her dark-lashed violet eyes.

When she saw her reflection in the store windows as she walked back to the hotel, she felt as if she were looking at a stranger. And though she knew that the transformation was in part to please herself, it was also to impress Adam Gayne . . .

The clock in the lobby said six, and Ann realized that she had skipped lunch. For a minute she considered an early dinner in the Oak Room, but she couldn't summon up the courage to sit there by herself. Instead, she went up to her room and ordered room service. *What a waste*, she thought as she looked at herself in the mirror.

The Boeuf Burgundy and the Château Cos d'Estournel were superb, but she was too depressed to enjoy either. She put down her wineglass with a sigh and lit an unaccustomed cigarette. Then she waited by the window until sufficient time had elapsed to call home.

She had hoped to speak to Phillip, but Consuela answered.

'I am very sorry, Mrs Coulter. Mr Coulter took Evie out to dinner and the movies. Do you want me to give them a message?'

'Just say that I called – and that I love them . . .'

She hung up and looked out at Central Park. The city seemed to have lost some of its magic.

225

She opened her briefcase and took out the syndication papers. *Listen, my friend*, she admonished herself. *You came here on business – remember?*

But her heart was beating wildly when she stepped into Adam's office the next morning.

'Good morning, Mrs. Coulter,' the receptionist said. The note of admiration in her voice was unmistakable. She didn't see that many chic, beautifully coifed women executives, and she was smiling widely as she showed Ann into the conference room as if it were her personal triumph. A dozen men of various ages were seated around a large conference table. All of them seemed to be from Texas. The smell of cigar smoke hung heavily in the air. Their pleased and surprised looks were evidence enough that they too were impressed with Ann's appearance. Only Adam kept his expression carefully guarded as he indicated her chair.

After a few moments of subdued laughter and conversation, they got down to business. At first, Ann had trouble keeping up with what was happening. It was a huge deal, involving a strategically located parcel of land near Houston. The proposal was for a high-tech office park with adjoining apartments, condominiums, hotels, shops, and arcades. It appeared to be a plum investment, and the developers waxed eloquent over the potential gains. But as the meeting wore on, Ann realized that her confusion wasn't the result of her own lack of experience. The developers appeared to be omitting several important specifics. She could think of at least two important tax consequences that they had failed to mention.

When there was a pause in their presentation, she broke into the discussion, posing the question to the developers' attorney, an overweight man with a nervous, unpleasant laugh. He seemed almost surprised by her inquiry, obviously thinking that the 'little lady' shouldn't worry her pretty head about such things. But Ann was not about to be brushed off, however courteously, and the room grew silent as she gently but inexorably pinned the attorney down.

'Thank you,' she said at last. 'You've made it very clear . . .'

The men around the big conference table eyed her with new respect. Observing their expressions, Adam nearly laughed aloud. They had tried to dismiss her, but instead, she had turned the discussion on its ear, with questions they hadn't even thought to ask. Adam was enormously proud of her, almost as if she were his protégée.

The remaining business was taken care of with dispatch, and the developers, as if on cue, began to stuff their papers into their briefcases, congratulating one another on their own efficiency and cleverness in arranging the deal.

'Texas-size,' was the comment of one of the syndicate partners as he smugly relit his cigar.

'Well, then,' Adam said. 'I take it that there are no further questions. You'll be receiving the papers within the week.'

'This calls for a celebratory lunch, wouldn't you say, boys?' drawled one of the Texans.

'Bourbon and branch, Fred?' boomed another. The rest of them laughed so uproariously that it was obviously an inside joke of some sort.

'Ma'am – would you do us the honor of joining us for lunch?' one of the older men asked. 'We're already reserved.'

'I'd love to,' Ann said, smiling. And the herd – Ann couldn't think of the group, containing so many in cowboy boots, any other way – made its way across town to the Café des Artistes.

The Texans looked out of place as they entered the elegant little restaurant, but beneath their aw-shucks façade, it was obvious that these men had the ability, like kings of old, to be at home anywhere. Ann found herself more and more drawn to them, liking their genuine warmth and friendliness. Now that business was finally over, they were more than ready to pay tribute to her as an attractive woman. One pulled out her chair as another rushed to help her put on her jacket. Adam sat quietly at the table, his dark eyes never leaving her face. The men argued good-naturedly over who would sit next to Ann, until Ann, who thought she was hardened to being the only woman in countless business meetings, started to blush with embarrassment over their gallantry.

'So tell me – how on God's earth did a pretty little 'Frisco gal like you get into this big, bad business?' one of the men asked, then laughed uproariously. Ann couldn't take offense: the crudely phrased question was obviously meant to be a compliment. She parried an avalanche of similar questions, her glowing face reflecting their unconcealed admiration for her appearance and her business acumen.

As the waiter took their orders for cocktails, she noticed that, in contrast to the wide smiles and general good humor that surrounded her, Adam looked decidedly glum. Catching her eye, he smiled briefly at her, then continued to watch her silently as the lunch, fueled by plenty of beer and Jack Daniel's, began to get somewhat raucous, though in Ann's honor obscenity was carefully avoided, in spite of the charmingly risqué murals that looked down at them. When Adam refused all of Ann's attempts to draw him into conversation, she concluded that she probably bored him. She had been foolish to read anything into a few hours of chatter in a restaurant, followed by a swift kiss on the hand.

Finally, after much back-slapping and hilarity, the party broke up. Outside, they headed for Central Park West, the Texans yelling for cabs with their bullhorn voices. Ann stood on the curb, smiling, as they said goodbye. It had started to snow heavily.

Suddenly Adam stood at her side. 'Where are you off to?'

'I thought I'd walk back to the Plaza,' Ann returned uncertainly. 'It's not that far.'

228

He raised an eyebrow, then pointed toward the overcast sky above Central Park. 'Those dainty little pumps hardly look to me like snowshoes.' He flagged down a cab, helped her inside, and directed the driver to the hotel.

She should have been annoyed, but she wasn't. Instead, she found it curiously refreshing to have a man make decisions for her – even one as trivial as this. She arranged herself carefully on the edge of the tattered seat as, minutes later, they stopped in a tangle of gridlocked cars and blaring horns at Columbus Circle.

'You might as well sit back and relax,' Adam said lazily. 'This is just typical Manhattan traffic.'

Ann put her hands over her ears.

'Good God – what a racket!'

A grin touched his lips. 'I forget that you come from a civilized town.'

Ann laughed. 'Town? Adam – are you implying that I'm a hick?'

'Good heavens, no! After this morning, those tough birds will treat you like a born New York real-estate maven.'

'Really?' Ann asked hesitantly. 'I hope that my question about the new accelerated depreciation schedules didn't upset them.'

'Look, if you hadn't mentioned it, I would have.'

Ann began to relax as the conversation continued along strictly business lines. She had been foolish to imagine that Adam had a personal interest in her.

'I think I already have at least three-quarters of my investors lined up,' she said, 'but I'll let you know by the end of next week.'

Despite his earlier resolve, Adam heard himself asking, 'How long are you staying in New York?'

'Just until tomorrow morning. I've been here since Wednesday.'

'Oh? What have you been doing to entertain yourself?'

'Shopping,' Ann admitted sheepishly, as if woman

229

executives were supposed to be above that sort of thing.

'Well, it's nothing to be ashamed of. It's usually a female's favorite occupation.' He bit his lip at what he realized was a stupid remark, but Ann ignored it. They were almost at the Plaza, and he realized he couldn't just let her go.

'Have dinner with me tonight,' he said abruptly, hoping he didn't sound as desperate as he felt.

Apart from the dig about shopping, his conversation had been so unexceptional, and his manner so pleasantly impersonal, that Ann found herself thinking, *Why not?* She hesitated for only a second. 'Yes, I'd enjoy that, Adam.'

'Would eight o'clock be all right?'

'Perfect.' She opened the door and got out of the cab before he could help her. 'See you at eight.'

The day had been a full one. Ann returned to her room exhausted. In spite of the weather, she would have liked to explore the city more and really see the sights, but even the thought of it tired her.

Instead, she browsed through the Plaza boutiques and wound up picking up some trinkets for Evie, an imported meerschaum pipe for Phillip, and the latest *Vogue* for herself.

Back in her room, she drew a warm bubble bath, then lay back and luxuriated in the suds. Inevitably, her thoughts drifted to Adam. Tired as she was, she found she couldn't wait to spend the evening with him.

But even her anticipation made her feel guilty. She closed her eyes and sank further down into the tub. They were going out to dinner together, she told herself. They were business associates and that was all. It was perfectly natural that they go out to dinner while she was in town . . .

Toweling herself off, Ann walked to her closet and considered the full wardrobe. She had had a lot of decisions to make in her lifetime, but which dress to wear had never been one of them.

There was the mocha silk, the ivory brushed linen –

and the black silk dress Ann had purchased for this same occasion – dinner with Adam – nearly a year before. Finally she settled on the pink Mollie Parnis with the deep ruching of chiffon at the neck. The plunging back was a little bold, but after all, Ann told herself, this was New York. What she thought of as bold would hardly turn heads here.

She turned in front of the mirror. There was no question: the dress was a tad risqué. But however daring it seemed, however daring she felt, she decided that for this evening, she would just be herself: Ann Pollock Coulter.

Yet, for all of her brave resolve, Ann discovered her heart was pounding when Adam arrived. She felt the warmth rush to her cheeks when Adam said, 'You look lovely.' His admiring gaze confirmed his sincerity.

It was all the same as it had been almost a year ago, yet then again, it wasn't. The weight of the year that separated their first evening together and this night lay upon them both. They were no longer the strangers they had been then. They were as at ease with each other as if they had known each other a long, long time.

As they settled themselves into the back seat of the cab, Adam turned to her and said, 'Ann, please feel free to say no, but I was wondering if you would care to have dinner with me at my apartment.'

His apartment? Ann had fantasized about being alone with him, it was true, but even in her dreams she never thought it would happen. And now that it was about to, she wasn't so sure how good an idea it was. She tried to maintain her composure.

'I just thought that after that session at des Artistes today, it might be more restful than a restaurant,' he said. 'Quite frankly, I found those cowboys pretty damned wearing. I thought it would be nice if we could have someplace quiet to talk. Would you mind, or was your heart set on dining out?'

Would I mind? Ann asked herself. If he only knew how much a part of her wanted to say yes . . .

Adam sensed her hesitation, and his next words were chosen carefully to calm her fears. 'Gaston is a marvelous chef. He's French . . . and he's the soul of respectability.'

'That sounds fine, Adam,' Ann said, both reassured and disappointed.

The lift glided noiselessly upward to the penthouse and they stepped out into the foyer. The floor was creamy Carrara and serpentine marble. Adam took out a delicate, ornate gold key, unlocked the pedimented double doors, and stood aside so Ann could precede him.

She stood in Adam's sanctuary.

Polished sconces cast a soft light onto rich mahogany paneling, and the air bore a faint scent of leather, wool, and beeswax. When he took her coat, his hand brushed her bare back and she shivered, hoping Gaston would arrive soon to serve dinner.

As Adam moved to hang up his own coat, Ann turned, then gasped as she looked out the windows, which soared two stories high and ran the full width of the huge living room. Manhattan lay at their feet, the teeming commotion of people and cars and buildings reduced to a million glowing fireflies. Through the light drizzle, it was overpoweringly beautiful, mysterious, and ethereal.

Adam interrupted her reverie and gently guided her down the marble steps into the room. Despite the vast expanse of glass and the high ceilings, it had a feeling of intimacy that was accentuated by the Georgian fireplace, in which the fire crackled, sending flickering light through the room. Persian rugs covered the parquet floors and set off the palest beige raw-silk covering the walls. Several Picassos and two Edward Hopper cityscapes had been spotlighted by a master hand, and Chippendale and Queen Anne pieces added to the charm of the room. It was irresistibly inviting; everything seemed to have a life of its own. The tables were conveniently placed; the Sèvres vases were filled with flowers. It was a room well loved and well used.

Ann was startled by the sound of Adam's voice at her ear. 'Would you like to see the rest of the place now or would you like to have dinner first?'

'Could we have dinner?' Ann murmured.

The dining room was more brightly lit than the living room. An antique chandelier cast hundreds of reflections on the mahogany table and the cut crystal. A silver epergne brimmed with orchids and iris.

The table was set for two. Adam sat at the head; Ann at the foot. The service was formal, and Ann was delighted by the Irish damask napkins, handsomely wrought Tiffany silver, and no fewer than four Baccarat goblets of different sizes and shapes for each of them.

The menu lived up to the decor. They began with oysters, with a tangy Sancerre rouge to go with them. She ate and drank slowly, savoring every moment of the feast.

Adam was amusing and charming, but the elegant setting had subtly changed the atmosphere between them, from the beginning of intimacy to an almost awkward formality.

Ann put down her fork. 'Tell me, Adam, what's the history of this building? It's exquisite, but I don't recognize the style.'

He told her. It had been created as a pied-à-terre for very wealthy New Yorkers around the turn of the century. Stories had been added during the twenties. For some three decades it had slowly deteriorated until it had finally gone co-op in the early sixties.

'I did the legal work on it, and they gave me the top floor – penthouse if you prefer – in lieu of a fee. Like it?'

In lieu of a fee! Good God – his charges must be astronomical. Ann thought of poor Phillip, in his shabby little office, researching accident claims. She forced her mind to the present. Tonight was a lovely dream, and she would enjoy it as such – nothing more. Adam would remain distinct from the reality of her life; from the practical, loyal wife and career woman she

233

would become again tomorrow. She looked across the table at Adam. She couldn't decide whether he looked more like Gregory Peck or Cary Grant, with the silver at his temples. She picked up her fork and concentrated on the soufflé.

As Gaston refilled her wineglass, she realized she was getting a little tipsy, but when he poured champagne with dessert, she didn't refuse. The dessert was a masterpiece: tiny succulent raspberries in a delicate crust, with crème Chantilly that was flavored with a delicately scented almond liqueur. Afterward came wafers of bittersweet chocolate.

'Oh dear,' Ann sighed, wondering where she would find room for more food. And then, after finishing the dessert and several chocolates, 'Oh dear,' as Gaston refilled her champagne glass.

Adam studied her face for a moment, then nodded at Gaston. The servant left the room, then returned with a dusty bottle of precious Marquis de Caussade brandy and two Venetian glass snifters that seemed too airy and fragile to be real. 'Ça suffit,' Ann heard Adam tell his servant. 'Maintenant, bonsoir!'

And they were alone.

'Shall we have our drinks by the fire?' Adam said.

As they got up from the table, Ann asked with a giggle she couldn't suppress, 'Is this the way you eat every night?'

'If I did, I'd be a real tub, wouldn't I?' Adam laughed, guiding her gently to a love seat and settling himself beside her.

Ann looked at him. She had to remind herself again that this handsome and vigorous man was in his fifties, for only the gray at his temples and a few lines around the eyes betrayed his age. She felt drowsy and contented. It was all unreal ... Then she gathered her strength and whispered, 'Adam ... it's been marvelous. But it's time to go now.'

'Not before you've sampled the brandy. It's sixty years old. It's for very special occasions.'

'And how many special occasions do you have?' she murmured.

'Not many. Not many at all.'

For a long, long moment, there was silence between them. Adam didn't know what to say, and he was rarely at a loss for words. Ann was the loveliest woman he had ever seen. He had invited her to the apartment with every intention of making love to her, but he realized now he wanted much more than to sleep with her. She fitted into his home as if it had been created with her in mind. It was as if, without knowing that she existed, he had planned it for her. He wanted her, yes. But not just in his bed. He wanted her in every aspect of his life. He wanted her to be his wife.

Although he didn't know how she felt about him, it seemed impossible that she too wasn't aware of the bond between them. Looking at her gravely, he said, 'Ann, you know why I asked you here.'

Ann realized that until now, she had been able to enjoy the fantasy without having to deal with the reality. But before she could answer, he continued. 'I wanted to make love to you. But now I realize that I'm in love with you.'

Ann was too shocked to answer. He reached out and gently took the glass from her hand, setting it on the coffee table. Then he took her hand in his.

Ann could neither pull away nor respond. This was beyond anything she had imagined.

'Adam, I don't know what to say.'

'I think you are as drawn to me as I am to you. We've both been playing games with each other for the last year. Isn't that true?'

Ann was too honest to deny it. 'All right, Adam, it is true. I've been – infatuated – with you from the very beginning. It has been hard even to talk to you on the phone. And being with you this trip . . .'

She broke off and took a deep breath. 'But, Adam, dreams are just that. This is reality, and I can't let myself fall in love with you.'

235

'Why not, Ann?' he asked softly.

Ann's eyes were bleak. 'Because I'm married.'

'You don't love your husband, Ann. I don't think you'd be here tonight if you did. You're not just looking for a cheap thrill.'

She looked at him for a long, silent moment. 'Adam, don't you see? This is just not going to work.'

'Because you're married.'

'Of course – because I'm married.'

'If you don't love your husband, don't you think that's just a little hypocritical?'

'You don't understand. I may not love my husband, but he loves me, and ultimately, that's more important. He trusts me.'

'Ann, people get married for a million reasons, but if it no longer works, it's like a bad business investment. You get rid of it.'

'I know a lot of people think that way these days. But I don't. For me to betray the people who love me – to take my happiness at their expense – I just couldn't live with myself.'

'Just tell me one thing. Do you love me?'

Tears welled up in her eyes. 'More than you know.'

That was enough for Adam. Taking her into his arms, he kissed her with all his pent-up passion. She kissed him back, wanting nothing more than to be able to give herself up to his embrace.

Then he lifted his lips slightly and, holding her very close, whispered, 'I love you, Ann.'

No one would ever know how hard it was to push him away, but she couldn't erase the images of Phillip and Evie from her mind. Maybe she was a fool. Maybe she was passing up the chance of a lifetime. No doubt she would regret it later: cry over it. But she just couldn't do this.

'I'm so sorry, Adam. I wish things could be different, but they're not.'

He frowned, then turned away, adjusting his tie and running his hand over his hair tiredly.

'Shall we finish our drinks?' The suave, assured mask was back in place.

But when he returned home after dropping Ann at her hotel, he paced his bedroom until dawn, chainsmoking. For all his intelligence, good looks, and social graces, Adam knew that he'd never had much luck with women. Poor Felicia, his former wife, had been a disaster from the beginning – and now Ann, too, was lost to him.

Thirty-Six

The next day, on the plane, Ann was stricken by a terrible sense of loss and emptiness. For one rebellious moment she imagined herself taking the first flight back to New York and telling Adam, 'To hell with both of them – I'm staying!' But how long would her resolve sustain her? Not only would her own guilt come between them, but there was the consideration that Adam didn't want a casual affair either. He wanted to marry her – and that of course would mean a confrontation with Phillip. And quite aside from the dreadful wound her betrayal would inflict on Phillip, if she divorced him, she would run the risk of losing Evie entirely. Evie would never forgive her for hurting her father.

Ann knew that she had made the only possible decision. Furthermore, she swore to herself that from the moment of her arrival in San Francisco, she would do everything in her power to rekindle the love she and Phillip had experienced for each other when they were first married.

That night, before getting into bed, Ann put on a delicate nightie she had bought in New York. She snuggled up against Phillip, put her lips next to his ear, and whispered, 'Phillip . . . darling . . . do you know what I'd like?'

'What?'

'I'd like to take a week or so off and just go off somewhere – Carmel, or Baja California, or some other nice place. Anywhere you'd like.'

'Of course, honey. But you pick it – I don't care.'

Ann reacted to his indifference as a challenge – she was now all the more eager to win back their old passion – if not that night, then on their belated honeymoon.

'Then how about Carmel? We could stay at the Del Monte.'

'Sure honey – Evie would love it there. She could ride horses along the beach.'

Ann was dismayed. Didn't he understand that this was to be just the two of them?

'Darling . . . I really thought it would be fun to take a vacation alone.'

'But who is Evie going to stay with while we're gone?'

'A friend.'

'Oh, darling, you know how I feel about that. I don't like her spending more than a night away from us.'

'She's a big girl now, Phillip.'

'I know, Ann. But with all those drug fiends and hippies over on Haight-Ashbury, I'm nervous about leaving her.'

Ann sighed. 'Well . . . if you really want her to come along, I guess it's okay with me.'

Evie insisted on bringing her best friend, Pamela. The four of them piled into the old Chrysler station wagon and puttered slowly southward along the beautiful coastal highway.

The Del Monte Lodge was charming, their rooms perfect, and the seafood couldn't be faulted. It was too bad Phillip and Ann had to sit and watch the others dance, but Phillip's leg had begun to bother him lately.

It was a perfect vacation except that nothing changed between Phillip and Ann. No new fires were lit. After a week of relaxation they returned to San Francisco no more than good friends.

This apparently was the price Ann had paid for her career. For several years, she had assumed that Phillip had adjusted to her success. She now realized that he had not; he had simply stopped opposing her. He had caved in. He no longer gave a damn – about his career *or* hers. The only person he truly cared for was his daughter, Evie. Seeing them together in Carmel, Ann had to acknowledge their closeness. Without intending to, they somehow excluded her. They loved her, true, but she was not the center of their lives, as she had thought she was.

A part of her wondered miserably whether they might get along just as well without her. After all, she wouldn't be the only woman ever to leave her husband and child. But Ann could not escape that unsatisfied need that had haunted her since childhood – the need to belong. It was what really kept her from leaving Phillip. It was not just that he loved her. It was that for so many years, she had been able to console herself with the knowledge that no matter what happened, she had a family that belonged to her, and she to them.

No matter how much happiness might lay elsewhere, the thought of abandoning that safe harbor and launching herself into unknown waters was impossible. But she would have to do something, or she would never find tranquillity anywhere. She would have to try even harder with Phillip, bring him to love her as he once had. That was where her security lay.

This summer, she decided, they should try to take a whole month's vacation. It was impossible to make any real changes while she still had all the pressures and responsibilities of the business. And it was Evie's last summer before college. The timing was perfect; she would devote herself to Phillip and Evie.

But when she described her plan to Phillip later in the week, he seemed skeptical. 'You mean you'd leave your office for four whole weeks?'

'I'm not even going to use a telephone, Phillip. I'm going to put May Brubeck in total charge of the agency, and the property managers can deal with most of their problems on their own.'

Phillip almost smiled, but it was not entirely a smile of humor. Secretly, he knew that Ann Coulter could never spend an entire summer away from business.

'Okay, honey. If you say so. I certainly won't be missed at *my* office . . .'

On July 5, bright and early, Phillip, Ann, Evie, Pamela, and Consuela loaded their things into the station wagon and set off on the beginning of what Ann felt would be their most glorious holiday in over twenty-five years of married life.

It would be a new beginning for Phillip and her; she knew it in her heart.

The elegant redwood cottage she had rented was in Nevada, on Lake Tahoe. There was a tiny private beach and an outboard motorboat. For the first two weeks, Ann was true to her word, and took not a single phone call from work. They went on hikes and picnics, boated and fished, barbecued ribs out on the flagstone terrace, and generally enjoyed themselves.

Then, insidiously, business began to intrude. One of Ann's managers quit unexpectedly, a loan needed to be rolled over, May Brubeck had questions that only her boss could answer.

At first it was only a call or two a day, and she was still able to participate in all the lakeshore activities. But as July waned, the calls increased in number, and before Ann knew it, she was spending most of the day talking to San Francisco.

Consuela packed lunches for Phillip, Evie, and Pamela, and the three of them spent long days cruising aimlessly along the lakeshore.

Often, when they returned, they would find Ann still on the phone. She would look up, cover the receiver, and whisper, 'I'll be off in a minute.' But things did not get entirely out of control until August, when an urgent call came from Ann's secretary.

'Mrs. Coulter, Mr. Gayne's office has been calling and calling from New York. A crisis has come up with the

240

new syndication. You're to telephone immediately.'

Ann called, heart pounding at the mere mention of Adam's name. But her excitement was replaced by anxiety when Justin Roth, Adam's partner, came on the line and told her the bad news. There was no choice; she had to fly to New York immediately.

Just then, Phillip appeared at the head of the stairs carrying his fishing rod and a tackle box.

'Phillip? Would you come here for a moment, please?' Even before she spoke she knew what his reaction would be.

'Honey, I just talked to New York. They've apparently discovered a fraudulent omission in the seismological survey down in Florida, and all the partners are meeting in New York tomorrow to discuss what can be salvaged of the project. I'm afraid I have to go.'

Phillip's expression was unreadable. Then he shrugged and replied in an even tone, 'It's your life, Ann.'

Later that day, they drove her to the airport. As they neared Reno, she tried again to apologize. 'I'm so sorry, Phillip darling. I hate to leave you, even for a day. But that's all it will be, I'm sure. A day, or at most, two.'

Phillip nodded. 'We'll see. Have a good trip.'

She felt a brief stab of anger. If Phillip had been a successful lawyer, he wouldn't feel guilty if he went to New Orleans to plead a case. Did any husband apologize to his wife as she packed his bags?

'I love you,' she called as she entered the plane, feeling increasingly guilty.

The ride into Manhattan from the airport seemed terribly exhausting, and her weariness didn't lessen even after she had settled into her room at the St. Regis, where the office had finally managed to book her. Kicking off her shoes, she sank onto the bed, fighting off the desire to call Adam. Instead, she called room service and ordered a steak sandwich and a pot of black coffee.

After she had eaten, she placed a call to Phillip. When he answered, Ann said in her most conciliatory tone, 'Darling, how are you?'

'I'm fine. How was the trip?' he asked, but it was obvious he didn't really care. Well, she didn't blame him. She had left him high and dry. Why should he be concerned?

Ann hung up almost wishing she hadn't called. There was an odd note in Phillip's voice she had never heard before.

Thirty-Seven

Phillip, too, regretted Ann's call. Something inside him had snapped when she left this time. He knew he was being unfair, even irrational, but he felt that she had deliberately deserted Evie and him. Her work would always come first. And it wasn't the need for more money, or for security, that drove her these days. It was sheer competitive instinct. The lust for power.

Phillip suddenly felt an anger toward his wife that surpassed any he had experienced in all their years together. He thought his chest was going to burst as he paced his room. Then he decided: *To hell with it all – I'm going out on the town.*

He put on his navy cashmere blazer and caramel flannel trousers, adjusted his horn-rim glasses, and examined himself in the mirror. *Not bad. Not bad for fifty-two.* Ann liked to tell him that he looked like Robert Taylor. But no – that wasn't so. He stared hard at his reflection. *No, what I really look like is Mr. Ann Coulter, husband of the famous San Francisco real estate tycoon.* He looked down at his gold Patek Philippe watch, then at his tasseled Gucci loafers. Gifts from Ann. As was the Mercedes parked outside. No, he certainly wasn't Robert Taylor. A kept man, perhaps. A gigolo. Some used the word 'pimp.'

He choked back his rage, adjusted his tie, and marched into the living room, where Evie and Pamela were watching television.

'Evie, honey – I'm going down to the South Shore

for a couple of hours. Don't wait up for me.'

Evie looked at her father with approval and winked. 'You look gorgeous. Don't do anything I wouldn't do, Dad.'

Phillip smiled at her: his self-assurance had returned. 'I won't, honey. Don't worry.'

God bless you, Evie, he thought as he stepped out the door.

Even the limp didn't bother him tonight. He walked a little faster to the car and set off down the unlit, winding road that led to the other side of the lake.

Switching on the radio, he began to hum along with the country-music station. Before he knew it, the neon lights of the Stateline casinos lined the road. He picked the second one and pulled into the parking lot.

As he threw the dice, he decided tonight would be his lucky night. He was concentrating on the game, which seemed to be running in his favor, when he heard someone speak his name.

'My God! Phillip Coulter. I can't believe it! What are you doing in this den of iniquity?'

Phillip looked up, annoyed. At first he didn't recognize the woman standing at his elbow. Then he remembered he had met her at a fund-raiser somewhere. He searched his mind, then remembered. Her name was Linda Holt and she'd sat next to him at a black-tie dinner at the Mark Hopkins. He remembered finding her sophisticated, charming, witty, and above all, appealingly feminine.

He smiled. 'And what is a lovely politico like you doing in the wilds of Nevada?'

'Trying to soak up a little Wild West atmosphere,' she drawled, then laughed.

The croupier interrupted their conversation. 'Ladies and gentlemen – place your bets, please.'

Phillip shook the dice and threw . . .

Linda had bet along with him, and when they finally went to cash in their chips, Phillip felt like a conquering hero. Together they had won over three thousand dollars.

'You're a positive genius!' Linda said, laughing. 'I don't know what your system is, but I started with only twenty dollars tonight, and look at all this loot! I've never won anything before in my life.'

Maybe that's what I needed, Phillip thought. *To win for a change.*

'Haven't rattled the ivories since college,' he said. 'Maybe you were Lady Luck.'

'I hardly think so. You were ahead before I came along. Let me at least buy you a drink.'

'Thanks, but to tell you the truth, I'm starved after all that action. Would you care to have supper with me?'

'I'd love to.'

They found a table in the restaurant atop Harrah's, looking out over the midnight-blue lake. The starlit sky, the flowers, and the dimly lit room made Phillip feel even more buoyant and young. Admiring Linda's blond good looks, he began drawing her out, listening to her life story with close interest.

Linda had married right after being graduated from Bryn Mawr and had moved to Washington, D.C., where her husband had worked for the Securities and Exchange Commission. Even though they'd been unable to have children, she had been more than content to be a wife and homemaker, and they had been happily married for nearly fifteen years.

Then, without any warning, her husband had dropped dead on the golf course, leaving only a small insurance policy. She had almost broken down from the shock, but after two painful years, she had pulled herself together. An opportunity had come up to work for a large brokerage house in San Francisco, and the geographical change had been just what she needed.

'. . . And this is my first vacation. Now, what about you?'

'There's not a lot to tell. I graduated from U.C., went to law school there, got married, spent a little time in the Pacific, came home. Ann and I – Ann's my wife – have a daughter named Evie. I've been with the same law firm since after the war. Now, I don't think they could make a musical comedy out of that, either.'

Linda laughed. 'I don't think it would be so bad – if the music were right.'

They continued to chat as if they'd known each other for years. By the end of the meal, Phillip decided that Linda was not only entertaining, but just what he needed.

'How long are you staying in Tahoe?' he asked casually.

'I'm up here for another week.'

'Would you have dinner with me tomorrow night?'

She hesitated, but only because he was a married man. That was a rule she didn't want to break, no matter how attractive Phillip Coulter was and how much she would have loved to see him again.

'I really don't think so. But thanks so much for the wonderful evening. And for all that loot!'

He didn't speak again as he walked her to her car, but back in his room he lay awake for hours thinking about a way to change her mind. Tonight, for the first time in years, he had felt like a man. It was not a sensation he would give up easily.

By morning he had made up his mind. At nine o'clock he called Linda's hotel, hoping she was already awake.

'Listen, I would really like to take you out tonight,' he said without preamble. 'Why are you hesitating?'

'Phillip, you're married.'

'Linda, please. All I want to do is buy you dinner. My wife is away on business, and I would simply like the pleasure of your company.'

'Well, if you put it that way,' Linda said, suddenly deciding that rules were made to be broken. 'We can always talk politics.'

That was why Phillip wasn't at home when Ann called to say she would have to stay in New York a few more nights. The developers were being difficult.

'Oh, Mom, you don't have to tell me why,' said

Evie, who answered the phone. 'I should have known better than to expect you.'

'Darling, this is one of those impossible situations that—'

'—that comes along once in a lifetime. Right, Mom? Okay, what do you want me to tell Dad?'

'Let me speak to him myself, Evie.'

'He's not here.'

'He's not? Where is he?'

'Gee, Mom, I really don't know. Dad has a life of his own. He's a grown-up man, you know, and I think he's entitled.'

'Stop being so fresh.'

'Well, Mom, it's the only way I can show you how upset we are that you broke your promise.' Evie hesitated, knowing she was being unfair. In a more conciliatory voice she added, 'Listen, Mom, I know it's tough for you to be an all-around great person and still be a tycoon.'

Ann laughed. 'Thanks for understanding. I really mean it, dear.'

'Well, that's a measure of my maturity,' Evie said mischievously. 'Now why don't you tell me what's happening?'

'Well, as I started to explain, things just aren't going the way we had hoped. It's so complicated, I can't really get into it, but we have a terrible engineering problem with the Fashion Island complex in Florida.'

'How long do you think you'll stay?'

'I really don't know, honey. I'm going to have to fly to Florida tomorrow.'

'Okay. Where can I get in touch with you if the canary should die?'

'I don't know, honey. I'll call you as soon as I get a hotel there.'

If Phillip had been home to speak to Ann, he would have felt even less guilty about his date with Linda than he did. As it was, he was careful to keep the conversation with Linda on neutral topics. But at the end of the evening, both knew that some barrier had been broken. When he asked her for the next night, she nodded.

After that, they spent all their time together. Phillip told her she made him happier than he had ever been in his life. On Linda's last night at Tahoe, he said, 'Let's go to Rusty's and hear the country and western singer they have there.'

When the two of them were seated in the bar, sipping bourbon and listening to a Glen Campbell song, he reached over and took her hand. 'Linda, I want to go on seeing you.'

'What do you mean, Phillip?'

'I think I love you, Linda.'

'But you're married,' she said sadly.

Unconsciously, he must have been preparing for this moment, for he said without pause, 'I'm not planning to stay married.'

'How long have you felt this way?'

'Truthfully? Since I met you.'

'I don't want to take that responsibility, Phillip.'

'You don't understand. My wife is an extraordinary woman, whom I admire greatly. But our marriage hasn't been a good one for a very long time. She and I have stayed married for all the wrong reasons, Linda. You have given me more happiness this week than Ann has in twenty-five years. But – maybe I'm assuming too much. Do you care about me?'

When she looked up, her eyes were filled with tears. 'After I lost Richard, I just couldn't imagine ever wanting anybody again. I've been a widow for ten years, and you're the first man who has really interested me. But are you sure you're ready to break up your marriage, Phillip? What about your daughter? How do you think she'll react?' There was a slight edge of fear in her voice.

'Evie will love you. She's going off to college; she's old enough to understand these things. Although we have never spoken about it, she knows that I haven't been happy with her mother. The important thing, Linda, is how I feel about you.'

247

'Oh, Phillip, I can't believe that this is happening. I've been falling in love all week and trying not to admit it.'

Phillip stood up and drew her into his arms. Oblivious to the amused glances of the other customers at the bar, he kissed her deeply and passionately.

'Let's get out of here,' he said urgently.

When they got to her hotel room, Phillip asked room service for a bottle of champagne. For one brief moment he was reminded of his honeymoon. Then he fiercely dismissed all thoughts of Ann. This was his night and he refused to let her intrude.

He pulled Linda close and kissed her again. 'I love you, Linda.'

'I love you, too, Phillip. I never thought I would say that to someone other than Richard.'

He turned off the lamp, so that the room was dark except for the moonlight shining in from the balcony.

They stood clinging to each other, then Phillip reached around and gently drew down the zipper of her dress. Picking her up, he carried her to the bed.

He had never known such happiness. He took her over and over again, and afterward they fell asleep in each other's arms.

When they woke the next morning, he felt as if they had been together always. He had told Evie he'd an appointment in town before he'd left the evening before, so he didn't have to rush to get back to her.

He ordered room service so that he and Linda could have more time alone. Reaching across the breakfast table, he took her hand. 'Darling, do you really have to go home today?'

'Unfortunately, yes.'

'What am I going to do without you?'

'You're going to have to take a lot of cold showers,' she said teasingly.

'They won't do any good.'

They spent the rest of the day in bed. When it was time for her to drive back, Phillip walked her downstairs.

'I'll call you later tonight,' he promised.

Phillip waited patiently for the vacation to end so that he could return to San Francisco and Linda. Meanwhile, he concentrated on showing Evie a good time. They swam in a nearby pool and boated, and after Pamela went home he took Evie out for dinner. But no matter where he was, he called Linda several times a day. He tried hard not to think about Ann, and was relieved rather than angry when she called to say she would have to meet them back in San Francisco. She couldn't leave Florida any sooner.

Phillip's first night back he told Evie he had to catch up at the office. He left the house and drove directly to Linda's apartment. As he held Linda in his arms, he said, 'Darling, as soon as Ann returns, I'm going to tell her that we've fallen in love and that I want a divorce.'

Linda was at a loss for words. Of course, she was happy, but she couldn't help feeling sorry for Ann – and just a little guilty.

'Would you consider living with me? I'll rent an apartment,' he asked.

'Phillip, sweetheart, of course I will. But what's wrong with my place? I've never shared it with anyone else . . .'

In answer, Phillip took her in his arms.

The next night he and Evie picked Ann up at the airport. Seeing her again was more painful than he had expected, and he was happy that in the bustle of getting Evie ready for college they had no time to talk. But once they'd driven her over to Berkeley and seen her settled in, Phillip knew he couldn't postpone confronting her any longer.

Glancing over at her on the drive home, he became conscience-stricken. She really didn't deserve this. Ann took his silence as anger at her long absence and tried to be particularly affectionate. Adam had sent a partner to the Florida meeting, so at least she had not been tempted by his presence there. When she finally got back, home had never seemed so precious. After the strain

249

and anxiety of the last few weeks, it was a safe, tranquil harbor.

They reached the house and after parking the car, Phillip went into the study and fixed them each a martini. Ann sat down on the sofa, took a long sip, and sighed contentedly.

'You know, Phillip, this last trip has made me realize that I don't want to be involved in any more of these syndications. They're too stressful and time-consuming. I'd much rather have the time to spend with you and Evie. There's so much we haven't done together. I was thinking maybe we could take a cruise. Maybe to Mexico. How would you like that?'

Phillip stared at her. From the tone of her voice, he could almost believe that she meant it this time. But it was too late.

'Why are you looking at me like that, Phillip?' she asked as if divining his thoughts.

'I guess I was thinking about the strange paradoxes in people's lives.'

'What are you trying to say?' Ann said, suddenly frightened.

'In the past, Ann, I'd have done anything if you had made such a commitment. But for too long a time now, you've had no time for me or Evie.'

'And now?'

'And now I think it's too late.'

A strange tightness began to grow in her chest. 'Late for what, Phillip?'

'Well, when people aren't happy with each other, they . . . separate.'

Ann couldn't believe what she was hearing. 'You mean get a divorce?'

'Yes – unfortunately – I think it's the only way. I just can't continue our charade of being a happy couple. Evie's off at school and it just isn't fair to either of us to stay together any longer.'

'But, Phillip—'

He continued as if she hadn't spoken. 'You're still an

attractive woman, Ann. I know that there's someone out there for you who will really make you happy. I don't. I never really did.'

'I've never complained!'

'Not in so many words . . . but I've never made much of a contribution to your life. We both know that.'

'That's not true! You've given me emotional security all these years. We've had a good marriage . . .'

'But not love, Ann! Love is about sharing. Sure, we get along, but the reason we don't fight anymore is that there's just nothing left between us.'

'Phillip,' she asked slowly, 'are you seeing someone else?'

He didn't want to hurt her, but there was no other way. 'Yes, I am.'

'How long have you been seeing her?'

'Two weeks.'

'Two weeks? And you're planning to divorce me. Do you plan to marry her?'

'Yes.'

'Phillip – you're leaving me for someone you've only known two weeks!'

'It isn't a question of time, Ann! It doesn't matter how long you've known someone if the chemistry is right.'

'I can't believe it. How can you do this to me, Phillip! Replace me, just like that!'

'Frankly, I wouldn't have believed that this could happen to me, either. But whether you're aware of it or not, I've been terribly lonely, and loneliness makes people vulnerable.'

'I'm sorry you feel that way. I did the best I could.'

'Ann, I'm not blaming you for anything. I admire you, but I need something more.'

'Are you really in love with this woman?'

'Yes, I really am.'

She had asked the question, but she wasn't prepared for the answer. Even though Phillip had said he'd found someone else, she couldn't believe that he actually meant it.

'I haven't been oblivious to our problems, Phillip. But I just didn't know how to solve them. And I did ask you to come into business with me. Isn't that true?'

'Yes. But I couldn't and keep my self-respect. Other men might have made a success of it, but I don't have a hell of a lot of self-esteem, Ann, and the little I have left would have been destroyed if I had accepted your offer.'

'Are you saying that I deliberately put you down?'

'No, of course not. Let's not blame each other. But the truth of the matter is that I can't live in your shadow any longer.'

Ann put down her drink and looked hard at her husband. *My God – he really means it.* She had always been the one to apologize, to justify her decisions, to promise to change – and she had always been able to bring him around to her point of view. But now there was an unmistakable ring of finality in his voice.

There was no point in begging. Ann got up and went down the hall to her bedroom, where she burst into sobs.

Listening to her weep, Phillip was overcome with pity. He followed her to her room and sat down next to her on the bed.

'Please don't cry, Ann. I know this is a very difficult time for both of us, but please try and be brave.'

'I just don't have any pride where you're concerned, Phillip. I love you. The thought of losing you just hurts too much. I know I haven't given you the attention I should have, but I need you. And I think you need me.'

She clung to him, burying her head against his chest. 'Just knowing that you were always in my life, that you were always there, made me feel safe. I love you, Phillip, I truly do!'

'I know, Ann. But we're just not right for each other.'

'Don't you think we could try again?'

He looked at her slender body, racked with sobs, and almost wavered. Then he reminded himself that nothing would really change. 'I don't think so, Ann.'

Nearly hysterical, she pushed him away. He went to

the bathroom, got a washcloth, and then came back and gently wiped her face. 'Come on, dear. Let me help you get into bed.'

'Are you leaving tonight?'

'I think it's best that I do.'

She put her arms around him and wept, but more quietly. 'I do love you, Phillip. I do . . .'

Gently, he released himself from her arms. 'Try to get some rest. I'll speak to you tomorrow.'

On the way to the car, he knocked on Consuela's door. When she opened it, Phillip said, 'I'm going away for a little while. Mrs. Coulter is upstairs in her bedroom and she isn't feeling very well. I'd like you to look in on her.'

Consuela nodded, understanding without being told. 'Yes, I'll do that. And . . . God bless you, Mr. Coulter.'

Thirty-Eight

Ann didn't shut her eyes that night. She paced the floor endlessly, smoking cigarette after cigarette. Toward two, Consuela brought her some warm milk and brandy, but there was such a lump in her throat that she couldn't swallow. For the first time in over twenty-five years, she was completely alone. The devastation she felt after her mother's death came back to haunt her. And how could Phillip have left her the very day Evie went to college?

She looked at her lovely bedroom with a feeling akin to loathing. What did it matter, the beauty of this house? Without the people she loved, it was nothing but an empty shell. Worse, it was a symbol of the security and affluence she had toiled for all these years. Well, now it was hers. But what security was there in a world that didn't contain Phillip?

'Phillip, darling,' she moaned. 'How could you? How could you?' She needed desperately to talk with someone. Evie? But it would be unthinkable to ruin Evie's first venture into the world. With a faint leap of hope, Ann considered the possibility that Phillip would suddenly come to his senses. Evie would never have to know. And Phillip had met this woman only two weeks ago – that was really no time at all. Perhaps it was merely a physical infatuation . . . But the image of him in bed with another woman twisted her heart.

Ann tried to think logically. She must wait, and hope that the affair would simply run its course. Lots of men went through a midlife crisis, had affairs, and then came home to their wives. But then she remembered the unfamiliar look of resolve on Phillip's face, the calm determination in his voice, when he spoke of this woman whom he said he loved.

I've got to find someone to talk with.

When Phillip had been in the Pacific, she at least had Ruthie, but it had been years since they had been really close, though their children saw one another frequently and the Newmans' younger son, Peter, had been like a big brother to Evie.

At about five, Consuela, who couldn't bear to hear Ann still crying, came in and sat by her bed, quietly holding her hand until Ann finally sobbed herself to sleep.

The next day Ann could barely drag herself out of bed. About ten, she had Consuela call the office and tell them that she would not be in.

Late that afternoon Evie rang. Ann could barely speak, but luckily Evie was bubbling over with news and didn't seen to notice anything amiss.

'Home early, Mom? I guess you must still be tired from your trip. I have so much to tell you!'

Ann managed to murmur the right words as Evie went on and on about her roommates. Leslie and Kim were the greatest! Leslie was from Los Angeles. Her father was a neurosurgeon, and they had a fabulous mansion in Beverly Hills. She knew a lot about boys – which was Evie's way of saying that she had a delicious fund of carnal knowledge. Kim had been to school in

Switzerland, and vacationed all over the world, but she wasn't sophisticated in the same way as Leslie. Evie just adored them both.

'And, Mom! I don't know how I could have forgotten to mention it. Our room is gorgeous! Those beautiful roses on the curtains and bedspreads. Everyone has been coming by and just freaking out. How did you manage to do that?

'I arranged it from New York, honey. Just a little surprise for you.' It seemed like a hundred years ago that she had made all those urgent calls.

'Well, thanks a million, Mom – I love it. Oh, and guess what, Mom? Guess who I saw on campus? Peter Newman!'

'Well, that's not so surprising, Evie,' Ann murmured weakly. 'He must be a senior there by now.'

'Yes, and he asked me to go with him to the first game, against Oregon, this Saturday! A senior, Mom! Leslie and Kim were pea green with envy. Oh, listen – the bell's ringing for dinner. I have to go. I love you. Ciao!'

'I love you too, Evie,' Ann said, holding back the tears until after she had replaced the receiver.

She was happy that Peter Newman was still keeping an eye on Evie. He had always been around, teasing her, giving her tennis lessons, and, later, reluctantly squiring her to cotillions and dances while complaining that she was just a kid. Phillip would be pleased if they actually started to date. Peter was as clean-cut a young man as Evie was wholesome. That was something, in these times of drugs and rebellion. And, of course, he came from a good family and family was so important.

In the days that followed, Ann sank deeper and deeper into a state of depression. She was unable to get out of bed, let alone go to the office or do any work. The very thought of food was repellent, and she lost so much weight that Consuela began to eye her worriedly.

Phillip called several times, but their conversations were stilted and awkward. He was having his mail forwarded. Was there anything she needed him to do for her?

Numbly, Ann replied, 'I'm fine. No. Nothing, thanks.'

Evie called often. She was pretty sure that she would be bid by the sorority she favored, and she was hoping that Leslie and Kim would be too, so that they could all be together. Peter had taken her to the game, and then out for a pizza. He was so handsome – well, didn't Ann think so?

When Evie asked, 'Is Dad there, Mom? I'd like to talk to him,' Ann could barely respond.

'I'm sorry, Evie. He's not here.'

'Boy, he's never home anymore. What is it, another one of his boring political shindigs?'

'Yes, I think so,' Ann lied. She couldn't bear to tell Evie the truth, and obviously Phillip hadn't yet done so.

'Well, it's no big deal. I talked to him yesterday.'

'Oh? So he's called quite a bit?' Ann asked dully.

'Oh, yes. All the time. I just thought of something to ask him. Well, bye-bye, Mom. See you soon. Ciao. Love you!'

Ann's heart sank. Sooner or later, someone would have to tell Evie, but doing so would give the separation a dreadful air of finality.

Phillip knew that he would have to be the one to do it. Though they had never discussed it, Evie had always been much closer to him than to Ann. When she had gotten her first period while at school, it was Phillip she had called, and he had been the one she had come to with stories of her first crushes. He wasn't blaming Ann; she had always been so busy. But he must be the one to tell Evie about the divorce.

Deciding he would have to do it in person, the next time Evie called, he asked, 'When can I see you, sweetheart? I'd like to meet Leslie and Kim. This weekend maybe?'

But Evie had answered, 'Gee, Dad, I'd love it, but until Rush is over, I have parties and teas every single day. Can you wait until next weekend? Then I can show you and Mom around campus and you can see my sorority house – that is, if I get in. Here's hoping! Ciao!'

It was Friday morning of the following week, and Ann lay listlessly on her bed, not even trying to read the newspapers. She didn't care a damn what real estate prices were doing. When the phone rang, she almost didn't bother picking it up.

'Hi, Mom, guess what! I got my bid! I'm in!'

'Oh, honey, that's great.' Ann tried to rouse herself. 'What about your roommates?'

'Leslie and Kim made it too, and we're all going to room together in the house!' Evie waxed enthusiastic for a few more minutes before saying, 'Well, I have a class. I just wanted to let you know about the sorority.'

'Thanks, honey. I appreciate it.'

When Ann hung up, Evie sat for a minute, worrying about her mother. It wasn't anything Ann had said. She just sounded totally beat. Evie would have thought her mother was just working too hard, except that she was home so much during the day, which was in itself unusual. As she got ready for class, Evie made a decision.

Late that afternoon there was a knock on Ann's closed door. 'Come in,' she murmured, thinking it was Consuela.

The door opened and Evie came into the room. An incredulous look crossed her face as she took in the closed draperies, the unmade bed, the bottles of Valium and sleeping pills on the bedside table. But the biggest shock of all was her mother's face, which was thin and wan, with dark circles under eyes swollen and red from crying.

'What's wrong, Mom? Are you sick?'

Evie couldn't remember her mother ever having had so much as the flu. She was always so vital and full of energy.

257

'Evie . . . I didn't expect you,' Ann said, clutching nervously at the bedspread.

'I can see that. But I decided to surprise you and come home for the weekend.' She hesitated. 'Mom, you look terrible. What is it?'

At the worried look on Evie's face, the concern in her voice, Ann burst into tears.

'Oh, Evie, it's just awful.'

Evie put her arms around her mother. 'Mom, what in the world is wrong? Please tell me!' she said, beginning to tremble with sudden fear. 'How long have you been like this?'

Unable to find the words to explain, Ann just shook her head. Terrified, Evie turned and called, 'Consuela! Consuela, come here!'

When Consuela appeared at the door, she gestured to Evie to come outside the room. Puzzled, Evie stared at her, then said, 'Just a minute, Mom. I'll be right back.' In the hall, she whispered, 'Consuela? What is it?'

'It's your daddy, Evie.'

'Something's happened to Daddy? But I just talked to him this morning!'

'No, your daddy's fine. They didn't want to tell you, honey, but your mama and your daddy are going to get a divorce, and your mama's taking it pretty hard.'

'A divorce?' Evie echoed disbelievingly. 'Oh, no. Consuela, you must be wrong. My mother and father are very happy together!'

'Well, all I know is that he moved out the day your mama came home from New York, and ever since, all she can do is just sit in that room and cry. I can't get her to eat one thing, and I just don't know what to do.'

Returning to the bedroom, Evie saw that her mother was still weeping into her pillow. Because Ann had never used drugs before, she was highly affected by them. Instead of calming her emotions, the sedatives and barbiturates heightened them so that her tears were as much a result of the drugs as her depression.

But Evie was not aware of this. All she knew was that her mother was completely unlike herself.

Sitting down on the edge of the bed, she said softly, 'Mom, listen. Consuela told me about you and Daddy.'

Ann's only response was to bury her face deeper into the pillow. Evie patted her shoulder. 'Come on, Mom, please. I know it must be a mistake. Why, it's ridiculous! You love Daddy, don't you?'

Ann nodded, gulping convulsively.

'Well, then, it will all work out.'

'It's not going to work out. He's not coming back.'

'Yes, he will, Mom! Of course he will.'

'Evie, you don't understand. Your father has found someone else.' Her voice trembled. It was humiliating to have to tell her daughter.

Evie couldn't hide her look of horror. 'Another woman? Oh, Mom, no!' She got up and walked helplessly around the room, wishing there were something she could do to ease her mother's pain.

Finally, when Ann's sobs subsided, Evie asked, 'Can I bring you some tea or something?'

'No thanks, honey,' Ann mumbled. But, desperate to do something, Evie brewed her mother a cup of tea and brought it to her with a plate of biscuits. Wordlessly, she sat by her side while Ann sipped listlessly.

Evie was almost as stunned as her mother by Phillip's defection. The only tragedy in her life so far had been her grandfather's death. She was only just beginning to get over that, and now the rest of her family was disintegrating. Her mother looked and sounded desperately unhappy. When Evie thought of her father living with some strange woman, she wanted to cry too.

Tucking the blankets around Ann's shoulders, she left the room and made a phone call. Peter had dropped her off today and had suggested that he pick her up the next day for tennis.

'Peter, I don't think I'm going to be able to play tomorrow. My mother's not feeling well.'

259

'Oh, I'm sorry. Nothing serious, I hope.'

'I don't think so, but I think I'd better hang around in case she needs me.'

'Of course, Evie. I understand. I'll call you tomorrow to see how everything is.'

'Thanks,' Evie almost whispered.

The next day found Ann no better. On the contrary, she seemed sunk even deeper into her torpor, staring at Evie with unseeing eyes. When Peter called, Evie said, 'You'll have to play tennis without me. I'm staying home for another day or two.'

Evie's first thought had been to phone her father. Then it dawned on her that she didn't even know this woman's name or phone number. She couldn't reach Phillip until Monday morning, when he would presumably be in his office.

All weekend, she rehearsed what she would say, but on Monday morning she was so angry and unhappy that she took the car and drove downtown to confront him in person.

Not waiting for the secretary to announce her, she walked down the hall and unceremoniously entered his tiny office.

One look at his daughter's face was enough to tell Phillip that she knew – and that she was furious. He cleared his throat and started to speak, but she interrupted.

'You know why I'm here, don't you?'

'I think I do, Evie. But I don't particularly appreciate the way you came in.'

'Well, I don't particularly appreciate what you've done to Mom. Leaving her for some cheap . . . whore!'

Phillip jumped to his feet, his jaw tightening angrily. 'How dare you, Evie! I forbid you to use that word. Linda is a fine woman in every possible way. How can you possibly judge her when you haven't met her yet?'

'I don't want to meet her! Ever! I hate her, and I hate you for what you've done,' Evie screamed, and then burst into tears. 'Daddy, how could you? I thought you loved Mom!'

Phillip came around to her side of the desk and drew her unresistingly into his arms. He must try to make her understand.

'Sweetheart, of course I love your mother. I want to make you understand. Will you sit down?'

He took her hands in his. 'Sweetheart, your mother and I tried. I would have done anything in my power to have prevented this, but the fact of the matter is Ann and I were never really happy together. We just weren't compatible. Now I have found someone whom I really love. And your mother will find someone, too. Someone who will make her happier than I ever did.'

'Dad, how can you say you've done everything in your power? All you have to do is stay with Mom. I *know* you and Mom were happy until this other woman came along.'

A hysterical note crept into her voice. 'Dad, please – can't you come home? Mom is in a terrible state; she still loves you so much! Can't we be a family again?'

Phillip looked away. The hope on Evie's face tore at his heart. It cost him all his strength to say gently, 'I'm afraid I can't, Evie.'

Abruptly she pulled her hands away from his and stood up. 'Can't? You mean won't! You prefer this woman you're sleeping with to my mother. Well, Dad, I don't want to see you again. Not until you leave her and come home.'

Phillip started to say, 'Evie, please—' but she was already out the door and down the hall.

By the time she got home, Evie's rage had turned into depression. She had hoped that all she would have to do would be reason with her father and everything would be okay. Now it was apparent that there would be no magic solution.

Meanwhile, her mother needed her. For the next few weeks, Evie commuted back and forth to Berkeley in her mother's old Volkswagen. Sorority initiations came and went, as did parties, football games, and dances, but Evie had no heart for any of it, spending all her available time with Ann.

Peter had finally gotten the truth from her and was both outraged and sympathetic. He volunteered to drive into the city and take her out when she felt up to it, but Evie wasn't interested now. The initial stirrings of love he had awakened were numbed by her mother's agony. Evie was too young to recognize that in attempting to supply all her mother's emotional support, she was dangerously depleting her own resources.

Evie was even more upset when May Brubeck called to say that they couldn't get on much longer in the office without Ann.

'Look, honey,' May said, 'will you please tell me what's wrong with your mom? Consuela won't tell me a thing. We're almost frantic down here. Is Ann sick or what?'

'No, May. I guess you may as well know. Mom and Dad are getting a divorce.' Evie's voice quivered on the word.

'Oh, honey – I'm sorry.' May was silent for a moment. 'Well, that's really too bad. But still, Evie, we've got a business to run and your mother is the only one with the authority to make certain decisions. She's just going to have to pull herself together and see me.'

'May, she's just not able to do that, at least not yet.'

'Well, honey, I'm sorry to say it's not a question of able. She has to, and that's all there is to it. Deadlines are deadlines, no matter what is happening in your personal life.'

Evie knew that May spoke from experience. Her husband had died an alcoholic and her son had died of an overdose at age eighteen. Still, loyalty to her mother made Evie say, 'May, she's just going to need a little more time.'

'She doesn't have it,' May said tartly. 'And what about you, young lady? What are you doing hanging around the house? Aren't you supposed to be enrolled at Berkeley?'

'Oh, I'm still going,' Evie said. 'I'm commuting for the time being.'

'What time do you have to be there, for goodness sake?'

'Eight in the morning.'

'But that means you must be getting up before six! That's just plain ridiculous! And you sound mighty tired. Now listen to me, Evie Coulter. You head right on back to school and leave your mama to me. Tell her that I expect to hear from her this morning, without fail.'

May's message was relayed in edited form to Ann, but all Ann said was, 'The office? Just tell May to do the best she can.'

A contrite Evie was on her way to a lecture when the Coulters' bell rang to announce May's arrival.

'Hello, Consuela. Now, don't you try and stop me. Where is she?'

Consuela had reached the point where any help was welcome. Stepping aside, she said, 'Upstairs in her bedroom.'

May marched up like an avenging angel. She had known Ann Coulter a long time. They had opened the business together, slaved over figures late into the night, held each other's hands in difficult times. Ann had helped her go on living when her son died, and now May was going to help Ann whether she liked it or not.

When May first entered the room, she couldn't believe that the thin, gray-faced woman lying so still under the bedcovers was the vital Ann Coulter she knew, but May hadn't grown up in Missouri for nothing. She launched her attack without preamble.

'All right, Ann. Just what the hell are you doing in that bed in the middle of the afternoon? You're not sick, so don't try and pretend. What in the hell has happened to you? Where's the woman who thought she could take this city with one hand tied behind her – and did?

'Now you listen to me. I know how hard it is to lose a husband. But it's not the end of the world. You're not the only woman in this universe who's gotten divorced. Where's your gumption, Ann Coulter?'

As May took a breath, Ann said miserably, 'But, May, you don't understand! It's awful ... I'm a failure.'

'A failure? It's not a failure when two people who don't belong together get a divorce. So you fell on your face. Big deal. Get back up on your feet.'

'But, May, Phillip would never have taken up with another woman if I hadn't driven him away.'

'Ann, do you really and truly think that the only reason you and Phillip split up is another woman? Let me tell you something, as an outside observer. Phillip is a nice guy, Ann, but the two of you are from two different planets. He stayed behind while you forged ahead. It's not a question of balance. You're just two people who are wrong for each other.'

'But, May, I love him!'

'Stop saying "But, May." Of course you do. You can't throw away twenty-five years of marriage in a day. But at least you're still young. Be thankful you aren't like me! I hung on with Al until it was too late for me. It was only a year or two after I divorced him that he got to be so sick that I ended up nursing him until he died. You've got your health, plenty of money, and a daughter who loves you. You're lucky to have Evie. I'd give anything in the world to have my Jack back again.'

Fiercely, she blinked back the tears which had sprung to her eyes at the thought of her dead son. 'Now, we're going to get you out of that bed, get some food into you, and see if things don't look a bit brighter. And next week, after we get caught up at the office, you're going to take a plane to New York, because you have one gorgeous guy waiting for you there. None of this is going to seem quite so bleak when he holds you in his arms.'

Startled, Ann sat up, heart pounding. 'What do you mean, May?' she asked slowly. She had never told anyone.

'What do you think I mean? I mean Adam Gayne, of course. Or did you think it was a deep, dark secret how you felt about him? He must really be pretty special for you to eat your heart out over him all this time. Well, now you have your chance.'

Without further ado, May reached over and threw back the covers. 'Now, out of that bed, kiddo!' She marched into the bathroom, turned on the tub. Once she saw that Ann was safely luxuriating in the warm water, she searched the bedroom for every pill she could find – the barbiturates, the tranquilizers, even aspirin. Ignoring Ann's protests, she flushed them all down the toilet and tossed Ann's faded housecoat into the hamper.

Then she opened the door and called out, 'Consuela, you go fix a mess of scrambled eggs and bacon, and lots of hot coffee. We're going to have a party.'

By evening's end, Ann was indeed seeing things differently. May had made her realize that she wasn't a failure and that she hadn't driven Phillip away. And there was Adam, who had wanted to marry her. Ann felt a stab of fear at the thought of seeing him. All the time she had been in New York and Florida, she had braced herself for a confrontation, but he had scrupulously confined their dealings to the phone, sending one associate or another to the endless meetings.

Would he see her now or was he still too angry? Even worse, perhaps he no longer cared. She thought of calling him, but was afraid he might hang up. Face to face, she would have a better chance of making him understand. He could hardly slam the door on her.

'Consuela, I'm going to New York this week,' she said. 'Will you call Mr. Coulter tomorrow and tell him I have to go away on business and that I'm feeling much better?'

That night, when Evie came back from Berkeley,

Ann and Evie sat up late after dinner, talking.

'Honey,' Ann said, 'I want to apologize to you for the way I've been indulging myself, lying around wallowing in self-pity. You've been wonderful about taking care of me, but I'm much better now. May was right. Going back to the office will take my mind off things. Now it's time for you to move back into the sorority house and stop worrying about your old mother. I'm even going to make a quick trip to New York. I've got a lot to catch up on with the syndication.' She got up and hugged Evie, who could feel the renewed strength in her mother's arms. Ann looked alive and happy once again.

At first, Evie hoped that her father had had something to do with the change, but as it became apparent that no such miracle had happened, a wave of fear and misgiving swept over her. If her mother was accepting the divorce, it truly was final. Evie cried herself to sleep, and in the morning could barely control her tears as she said goodbye. Driving back to Berkeley, she felt as if she were going into exile.

Early Friday evening, May drove Ann to the airport. Just before boarding, Ann hugged her friend, saying, 'My God – how did I ever get so lucky as to have someone like you?'

'That goes both ways, kiddo.'

May hid her mild envy. Not everyone had an Adam Gayne to go to.

Thirty-Nine

When Ann checked into the Plaza, she found that the management has sent her a huge basket of fruit, and May had sent champagne. The card read: 'It's only begun – make the most of it, baby. Love, May.'

In the morning, Ann put on her white suit and spent nearly an hour fussing over her hair and makeup. She knew that Adam was in town because she had checked with his office, using an associate's name.

She took a cab to his building and sat trembling in the waiting room as the receptionist announced her.

Adam was shaken when he heard her name. 'She'll have to wait a few minutes,' he told the receptionist. He needed time to pull himself together.

Ann. Ann Coulter. The thought of seeing her made his chest tighten. As the shock of hearing her name wore in, that shock turned to anger. How the hell could she show up now, just when he'd finally come to accept his life without her? Did she have any idea how much he had suffered, and all because of her? Did she know what he'd been going through? Did she care? All last summer, he'd avoided her. He'd sent Jeff Cohen to Florida in his place just so he wouldn't have to see her. He couldn't. Not on her terms. Yet here she was, on his doorstep. She must be more heartless than he'd ever imagined if she could come back now after leaving without a word.

Adam went to the bar and poured himself a double scotch, which he then downed in a single gulp. He never drank in the middle of the day, but he really needed this one. He had to contain himself, and his fury. He had no idea why Ann had come to see him. Well, he'd just calmly hear her out, and then tell her exactly what he thought of her – which was something he'd been wanting to do for a while.

Out in the waiting area, Ann was as anxious as Adam was angry. Even after the receptionist told her that he would see her, she stood for a long contemplating moment with her hand poised on the knob and swallowed very hard. Now that she was finally here, she scarcely knew how she would handle it. Almost trembling, she took a deep breath and walked in.

Adam was seated at his desk, reviewing what looked to be some sort of legal brief. He didn't look up at her when she came in. Did he hate her? Had he already found somebody new? His eyes were like Arctic wastes. Ann stood in the middle of his office for what seemed like an eternity. Finally, he looked up. 'Please have a seat, Mrs. Coulter.' His icy tone sent a chill down Ann's spine. Could he really have so little feeling for her?

'Adam, please don't be angry,' she blurted out.

'Don't be angry? Angry? I've just gotten over you and now you show up as though nothing had happened.' His voice was ragged. 'What's the matter, Ann? Is life getting a little too dull out in San Francisco?' This was not what he'd meant to say, not how he'd meant to come across, but he was just too furious to say anything except exactly what he thought.

In spite of his fury, Ann felt a surge of hope. Surely he wouldn't be this angry if he didn't still care.

'Well, am I right?' he demanded harshly.

'No, Adam. That's not why I'm here—'

'Why, then? A little shopping spree, perhaps? Saks is uptown aways, you know.'

On the verge of tears, Ann said, 'Adam, I know that you're angry, and I suppose you have every reason to be.'

'Oh, I do? Well now, that's mighty big of you, Ann. But I'm not in the mood to play games.'

'I'm getting a divorce.'

Adam froze. When he finally regained his composure, he told his receptionist to hold all calls, and without another word he rose from his desk and took her into his arms. They stood holding each other for several minutes. Then he pressed the intercom again. 'Do I have anyone coming in for the rest of the day? Just my lunch date? Please cancel it and say I've been called away. I'm afraid I won't be available until tomorrow.'

He took Ann's hand and they went down the elevator to the street, where they caught a taxi to Adam's apartment. A few blocks before they got there, Ann asked, 'Can we walk the rest of the way? It's just beginning to snow.'

'Of course,' he said, his dark eyes twinkling.

Adam took her elbow as they emerged into a swirl of large, soft flakes. Ann's high heels were totally ill-suited to the wet sidewalk. Each time she slipped, Adam used it as an excuse to pull her close to him. She was dizzy with excitement when they finally reached his building and took the elevator to his penthouse. After opening his door, Adam suddenly swept her up in his arms and carried her over the threshold.

The apartment was very still. Kissing her gently, Adam put her down. 'You're all snowy.'

Almost breathlessly, she answered, 'Am I? I hadn't noticed.'

Helping her off with her coat, he hung it next to his own in the closet. Ann's hair was dripping.

'Let me get you a towel.' With infinite gentleness, he dried her face and rubbed her hair.

'It's Gaston's day off,' he murmured. 'Luckily we're all alone.'

Adam took her face between his hands and lifted it upward. Their lips met. Ann felt a quiver of joy run through her body. For a long moment, she neither thought nor spoke. She only felt.

Instinctively, her arms reached around Adam's neck, drawing him to her. With an inarticulate sound, he again covered her mouth with his own, gently parting her lips and insistently exploring her mouth with his tongue.

As she ran her fingers through his hair, she felt his hands travel hungrily down her back, burning through the thin silk of her blouse. Slowly, he unbuttoned it, cupping her full breasts. She loosened his belt, feeling him tremble in response. Never had he wanted a woman so desperately.

Ann, too, could wait no longer. She wanted him to make love to her, needed his thrusting strength inside her.

Unable to postpone the joy a minute longer, they pulled off their clothes and lay on the bed.

'You are so beautiful,' he whispered.

Every nerve in her body thrilled to his touch. As he entered her, she knew that there would never be anyone in the world for her except Adam.

For a long time afterward they lay in each other's arms. Then he began making love to her again. It was less urgent than before, and this time they whispered all the sweet things that lovers say.

Eventually they fell into a contented slumber, and when some hours later Ann opened her eyes, it was to find herself pressed against Adam's body.

A slow smile curved his lips. 'Hi, sleepyhead. How are you?'

'Wonderful,' Ann said, tears starting to her eyes at the loving note in his voice. 'Just – wonderful.'

'I love you, you know.'

'I love you too, Adam.'

'Do you mean that?'

Hearing his uncertainty, Ann pressed her lips to his. 'With all my heart, darling.'

Stretching, he got out of bed. 'I hate to say this, but I'm starving. Do you have the energy to go out? We missed lunch, but we could get an early dinner.'

'Why don't I just fix us something here?' Ann said.

'All this and you can cook too? How did I get so lucky!' he said, putting on his robe.

Ann sat up and was about to push away the covers when she realized her clothes were scattered from the living room to the hall. Grinning, she said, 'I hope you have something I can borrow.'

He started to open drawers, but she shooed him out, saying, 'I think I can manage.'

A little while later she came into the kitchen wrapped in an enormous maroon silk robe, her feet swimming in fur-trimmed slippers that flopped as she walked.

He slipped his arms around her waist and nuzzled her ear. 'I thought you were starving,' Ann laughed. 'Food first.'

Rummaging about, she found eggs, a small jar of caviar, and some sour cream. Twenty minutes later, they sat down to delicious scrambled eggs and chilled champagne.

Adam ate hungrily. 'You're a hell of a cook,' he said, looking at her with new respect.

'Not as good as your Gaston, I'm afraid.'

He looked at her mischievously. 'Ah, but you have so many other talents to offer.' They washed and dried the dishes, pausing every few minutes to kiss.

'Okay.' Adam smiled. 'It's time for the cook to relax.' He led her to the huge jacuzzi, and afterward he kindled the fire and they lay on the carpet, staring into the flames.

Ann knew that this was where she belonged. Strangely, it was Phillip who had given her this gift. She would never have had the strength to break up her marriage, so now she was filled with gratitude toward her husband.

Adam too was thinking how lucky he was to be given a second chance with Ann.

All his life he had been searching for the right woman. It surely had not been Felicia, whom he had married far too young, or any of the women who had come after her. But with Ann next to him, he knew real happiness for the first time. He looked at her as she gazed into the fire and hoped she shared his contentment.

'Penny for your thoughts,' he said, hoping to be reassured.

But when she turned to him she said with unexpected curiosity, 'Adam, tell me about yourself. I want to know everything about you from the time you were a little boy.'

'It's not very exciting.'

'It will be to me.'

Adam got up and poured two snifters of brandy. Then, gazing steadily at her, he began.

There was nothing to indicate that Avrum Gnetsky would achieve great fortune, but his mother, Leah, knew that there was something extraordinary about this baby. Of course she had thought that about her older three, too. She already referred to them as the Doctor,

271

the Dentist, and the Lawyer. Obviously, there was nothing left for Avrum but to become the first Jewish President of the United States of America. Nothing could convince her otherwise as she lay in her bed in the flat above the bakery on Slotkin Street.

Inhaling the familiar smell of bread, she felt a great sense of peace. What a joy he was, that husband of hers. Yankel had run up and down those stairs a hundred times that morning just to make sure that the midwife was doing a good job. He couldn't understand how his wife could be so serene, but to Leah, giving birth was a miracle and the pain was nothing.

Three days later, after having fed Avrum from her more than ample breast, she left him in his little basket, went downstairs, and took her usual seat on the high stool in front of the cash register. By eleven o'clock that morning, she had seventeen dollars in the till. Pleased with the morning's take, she went upstairs and once again took Avrum to her breast, singing a lullaby which her mother had once sung to her.

It was in that aura of love that Avrum had grown up, in a family devoted to one another. When he began school at age six, there were many things about the world Avrum did not know. Among them was the fact that there were people in the world who were not Jewish, who ate peanut butter and jelly sandwiches, and who had yellow hair the color of cornsilk.

He also discovered that in this strange world he was called Adam. But it really didn't bother him. He loved his teacher, and more important, he loved to learn, a desire his mother did everything to encourage. Leah spent all their extra money on books and music lessons for the boys. Each afternoon she would leave the bakery to make sure they practiced on the old upright piano. When they complained that they would rather play ball, she fed them milk and cookies and forced them to continue.

The only time that the boys were permitted to escape practice was on Friday nights when, bathed and dressed in their best, they went to the tiny *shul* three blocks away, where they worshiped with their father.

As the years passed, Adam's brothers went on to college, where they fulfilled their mother's dreams. The excellence their parents demanded began to pay off, as Max became a surgeon, Irving an engineer, and Morris an orthodontist. Leah's only remaining goal was that Avrum become the next Clarence Darrow.

He arrived at Columbia University during the early days of the Great Depression, and, just as little Avrum had been astonished to learn that not everyone in the world was Jewish, so young Adam was appalled to discover that Jews were not welcomed with open arms at Columbia. In spite of what he was reading in the papers about events in Europe, he hadn't really believed in the existence of systematic anti-Semitism. Now he wondered if he could cope with this threat. His older brothers quickly reassured him.

'You bet it's tough being a Jew,' they told him. 'But it's never stopped us. We just have to work harder, and the result is that we're better off for having been put through the extra tests. You know something? We should thank the bastards!'

One day he met a senior named Jerry Moss, who admitted that he was born Abe Moskowitz.

'Why did you change it?' Adam asked him.

'Look, Adam,' Jerry explained patiently. 'A name like Moskowitz – or Gnetsky, for that matter – makes it just that much harder to hack it, particularly if you're trying to get into a Gentile law firm, like I am. I don't look Jewish – and neither do you. Why make things tougher than they are? So I'm not a hero. Sue me.'

Adam still wasn't convinced. 'Isn't that like cheating? We make it and other Jews don't?'

'Wake up, kid. I know they say that anyone in America can become President, but I don't see any Gnetskys or Moskowitzes in the White House. Make your own decision, but I'm staying Jerry Moss.'

Adam slept badly that night; he had never really

273

thought about being a Jew. Finally he shrugged off Jerry's warnings, deciding that changing his name would be a betrayal of his parents. But, after graduation – he had gotten his degree in record time – he reconsidered. He was beginning law school, times were bad, and he knew that with the exception of a few firms, the New York law offices refused to hire Jews.

In a quandary, he asked his brothers for advice. They agreed that theoretically it was desirable to remain Adam Gnetsky, as they had, but given Adam's situation, it might be better to change his name. It would be possible to do this without abandoning his faith.

So, when Adam registered at law school, it was as Adam Gayne. And, whether it was because of his elegant new name or possibly guilt over having relinquished his original name, he worked even harder than his classmates, graduating with honors and as editor of the *Law Review*.

In spite of his extreme youth and the Depression, he had an excellent choice of jobs. He finally settled on Williams, Stein and Brown, one of the best corporate firms in New York. He quickly acquired a host of new clients from all over the city, for besides his legal knowhow, he was interested in everything – politics, charity, the arts – and he mixed well with people.

The law firm was delighted. Adam Gayne was exactly what they needed. He was shrewd, discerning, and at ease in any company. How he got his polish was a miracle, but he was in demand at parties as an excellent mimic, and his brothers had given him lots of good advice on the social graces. He dated frequently but had no strong desire to marry.

One of the partners in the firm, Daniel Brown, was especially interested in the new young associate. A widower for twenty-five years, Brown had no children of his own, but he was devoted to his sister's only child, Felicia. Felicia was extraordinarily beautiful. As she grew into womanhood, though, he had begun to worry about her future. Painful as it was, he was forced to admit that the girl was also flighty and immature: even infantile. She needed a strong, levelheaded husband to look after her, but while many young men asked her out, none became serious.

And so it was that Daniel found himself taking an appraising look at young Adam Gayne. One day Daniel invited Adam to spend a weekend at his estate on Long Island. Adam had thought that he could no longer be impressed by money. But he gasped with wonder as he drove his second-hand Buick through the wrought-iron gates, up a driveway lined with lovely oak trees, and parked in front of an exact replica of a sixteenth-century French château. Upon entering, he was immediately surrounded by young men in tuxedos and beautifully dressed women: the cream of what remained of the international set. The Great Depression hadn't reached the home of Daniel Brown.

It was in that somewhat dazed condition that Adam first saw Felicia, floating down the immense black marble staircase in white silk. Adam immediately concluded she was the most beautiful girl he had ever seen.

After dinner there was dancing, and he found himself leading Felicia on to the floor. As he took her into his arms for a waltz, he couldn't help comparing her to an exquisite Meissen figurine he had recently bought for his mother. When the music stopped, he took her hand and led her to the garden.

There, under the flickering Chinese lanterns, they stood and watched the moonlight play on Long Island Sound.

Felicia was very quiet, and Adam found himself doing all the talking. Her comments, uttered in a childlike voice, were extremely brief, and were always accompanied by her high silvery laugh. To Adam, her reticence lent her an air of sophistication.

He had never met anyone quite like her, and soon managed to convince himself that what seemed to be shallowness was simply an amusing pose, that she had been brought up to let men do the talking. And she was so tiny, so lovely, such good company . . .

Adam had no way of knowing as he fell asleep that night dreaming of Felicia that she had been carefully tutored by her mama and her Uncle Daniel. She was to say little, stay away from the punch bowl, smile her enchanting smile, and agree with absolutely everything Adam said. They were determined not to let yet another eligible young man get away. If Felicia would only refrain from chattering in a way that revealed to all her utter lack of comprehension of what was being discussed, she just might land Adam Gayne.

Felicia was the sole heir to her father's pharmaceutical company, and to her Uncle Daniel's personal fortune, so neither her mother nor her uncle felt any qualms about their tactics. Adam would thank them one day. After all, beautiful young heiresses weren't a dime a dozen, and the Depression was still on, wasn't it? One never knew.

Adam soon found himself being invited to parties, receptions, and elaborate dinners at Felicia's apartment overlooking Central Park West. He never quite knew how they became officially engaged. Everyone seemed to expect it, yet the odd, frustrating thing was that they were rarely alone; protective relatives always seemed to be hovering about. Nonetheless, still dazzled by the aura of great wealth, he almost convinced himself that he was in love with her . . .

They were married at the Hotel Pierre, in one of the most lavish weddings of the year. Adam's parents were there, as well as his brothers and their wives. Leah looked regal and Yankel slightly intimidated by it all. Daniel, and Felicia's mother, were so delighted to have married off Felicia that they managed to be cordial to the Gnetskys, who returned to Brooklyn believing that their Avrum had found the perfect bride.

Adam and Felicia honeymooned in Europe, at Daniel's expense. London, Venice, Rome, the Riviera – there was no lack of things to do and see, and the dollar was king. Adam was delighted with his new bride – she was like an adorable, playful kitten.

The first incident occurred at Monte Carlo.

They were playing bacarrat and chemin de fer. At first he laughed when he saw her betting recklessly, a wild, unfamiliar gleam in her eye. But as time passed, he became increasingly alarmed. Felicia refused to leave the tables, and she had already lost over two thousand dollars. She had also switched from champagne to Pernod on the rocks, and was knocking back these potent drinks at an amazing rate.

Finally, when her losses hit twenty-five hundred dollars, Adam touched her on the shoulder and gently suggested that it was time to go home.

Whirling on him, she said loudly, 'I'll go home when I'm damn good and ready.' Then she went to the bar, ordered another Pernod, and returned to the tables.

Adam took her arm. 'Felicia – let's go home.'

'You let go of me!' she shrieked, and the people near them turned around and stared.

Adam's face flushed with humiliation, but he continued to hold her arm. 'Felicia – either we walk out quietly or I'll carry you out.'

'Stop that!' she screamed. 'I'm going to tell Uncle Daniel about this and he'll fire you for being mean to me!'

This was followed by a stream of threats and insults, at which point Adam picked her up in his arms and carried her out of the casino to the amused or shocked comments of the other guests. They drove to their hotel in silence.

There was more to come. Adam discovered that when Felicia was crossed, she would fly into infantile rages, pounding him with her tiny fists and screaming hysterically. Worse, he began to understand that she had a fondness for the bottle – a penchant which her mother and her uncle were undoubtedly aware of. For Felicia was drinking far too much in restaurants and night-clubs, and often seemed tipsy even in their hotel rooms.

Loathing himself as he did it, one morning Adam went through her luggage and found several bottles of gin. Felicia had obviously been taking nips whenever he turned his back.

Confronted with the evidence, she responded with denials and threats to call her uncle. The honeymoon had turned into a disaster. They sailed for home three weeks early. Pacing the deck of the liner, Adam wondered what he had gotten himself into. Then he reflected that he was being unfair. Felicia had been spoiled since the minute she was born. He had to give her a chance to grow up. For God's sake, the poor girl was so pathetically young . . . He resolved to do what he could to help. With understanding and patience, there was no reason that Felicia couldn't mature into an exemplary wife and mother.

He spent the rest of the voyage trying to patch up his shattered marriage. They were established in their new Park Avenue apartment for only six months when Adam finally had to admit that his wife – the woman he had pledged to spend his life with – not only had an uncontrollable temper, but a second-rate mind as well. No, that was far too kind. The truth was that Felicia was simpleminded.

He felt deceived, trapped, humiliated. Her family must have known about her failings. He investigated and learned that she had never gone to school beyond the fifth grade. The stories of tutors with PhDs and elegant Swiss schools were lies; she couldn't speak a word of French. In addition, she was emotionally unstable and unable to assume any kind of responsibility.

Now he realized why her family had been willing to settle for Adam Gayne from Brooklyn, and he bitterly resented Daniel's part in the sordid plot. Adam's first thought was divorce. But, as if divining his intent, Felicia announced she was pregnant.

Nine months later, Michael was born. In spite of everything, Adam thought the world of his son, who

278

seemed to have inherited his father's intelligence. He lavished on the little boy all the love he was unable to feel for Felicia, and personally saw to his care and well-being. It was fortunate for little Michael that Adam did, since after the birth Felicia went completely to pieces. She became sickly and hysterical, refusing to get out of bed or to share that bed with her husband.

Adam vowed that there would be no more children, but then fate intervened. To keep up appearances, Adam and Felicia had gone to the wedding of Felicia's cousin in Lake Placid. The famed resort was a winter wonderland, and many of the guests were staying for the weekend to enjoy it, but Adam, claiming a pressing workload, insisted on driving back to New York. Shortly after leaving, it began to snow heavily. Adam motored grimly on, but after an hour they skidded around a curve and stalled their car in a drift. The heater stopped functioning, and, even bundled in her sables and fur-lined boots, Felicia was soon shivering. When she realized that they were really stuck, she pressed her tiny body against Adam and cried, 'Adam – I'm afraid! We're going to die here – I just know it.'

Adam tried to calm her, but nothing helped. The wind howled through the bare trees, and even he was becoming alarmed as the snow continued to pile up around the car.

He strained his eyes through the windshield and finally noticed a light.

'Felicia – there's some sort of building out there. Can you make it if I carry you?'

'Please, Adam,' she begged. 'Please.'

As Adam slogged through the drifts, Felicia kept repeating, 'When will we be there? When will we be there?'

After about two hundred yards they stumbled up the front steps of a small country inn and were greeted and given hot tea by the sympathetic proprietor. Felicia stood in front of the pot-bellied stove, trying to get warm, while Adam signed the register. Then he took her arm gently and guided her up the steep wooden steps.

Their room was small but cheerful. There was an old-fashioned four-poster with a faded down comforter on it. The rough muslin sheets scratched Felicia's delicate skin as she climbed under the covers in her slip, shivering and sobbing, near hysteria.

Adam, totally exhausted, undressed, climbed in beside her, and turned his back to her, ready for sleep. But as the wind continued to howl and sleet pelted the rattling windows, Felicia pleaded, 'Adam, please hold me. Kiss me, I'm scared. I'm scared . . .'

Adam groaned, then turned and put his arms around her, moved in spite of himself. At first he had no intention of making love to her, but it had been a long time, and he found it impossible not to respond. He was shortly to curse his weakness.

Nine months later a daughter was born, a blond, blue-eyed cherub whom they named Renata. She looked so much like Felicia that Adam could not immediately bring himself to love her. She was a tangible reminder of his folly.

Felicia became increasingly withdrawn and unmanageable, leaving the children entirely in the care of the nanny Adam had hired for them. They stopped entertaining altogether. She drank more and more heavily, and all she could say when he tried to talk to her about it was, 'I can't cope, Adam! I simply can't cope with it all.'

The outside world terrified her, and at the thought of leaving the house, she became hysterical. One morning she tried to throw herself off the balcony. The maid stopped her just in time. It was then that Adam summoned her family, who agreed that she might benefit from a few months in a sanatorium.

The institutionalization was just the first of many, leaving the children entirely to Adam's care. He was a good father, learning to love Renata as much as her brother. He felt that it was up to him to try to give them a sense of stability despite their mother's problems. After all, they hadn't asked to be born.

But when Michael had turned twenty and Renata eighteen, Adam had decided that it was time to consider his own needs. Even Uncle Daniel didn't object, possibly because he felt guilty about the entire situation. Adam had just gone through the preliminary motions of divorce when Felicia signed herself out of the sanatorium near Boston where she had been for some months. Friends picked her up and drove her with them to the airport, where they took off for Greece.

They apparently hired a yacht, because several days later, after a long, drunken dinner, Felicia fell overboard. She was not missed until morning, and by the time her friends were sober enough to call Adam, her diminutive body had washed ashore at Mykonos.

Adam was deeply saddened when he heard the news. He had long since stopped loving Felicia, but he had certainly never wished for her death. He flew to Athens and made arrangements to have her remains sent back to America.

After the funeral, he was somewhat startled when a lawyer reminded him that he was her sole heir. They had never revised the will drawn up at their marriage.

Shortly afterward he transferred most of the money to the trust funds he had set up for Michael and Renata. To his amazement, both children objected violently to the gesture. Worse, Michael began to act as though he hated his father. Apparently the boy had felt closer to his pathetic mother than Adam had suspected, and had spent considerable time with Felicia even though Michael was officially under the care of others.

Michael had secretly blamed his father for Felicia's mental breakdown; now he blamed him for her sordid death. Adam could keep his money; Michael was going to India with some friends. He refused to say what he would do there.

Renata was more tolerant. She said she knew that Adam had basically cared about Felicia, but she still refused either his money or his affection. She was going to live with an art teacher in New Hampshire. They would get by somehow.

Adam was appalled when she brought her boyfriend home. He was shabby, wore his black, greasy hair in a sort of pigtail, and spoke an almost incomprehensible English. Adam pleaded, cajoled, threatened. Why couldn't she wait a few years? Renata was doing well in school – why did she want to drop out? But he failed to dissuade her. 'I'm sorry, Daddy. I love you very much, but it's my life and this is what I want.'

Since then, his children had almost vanished from his life, and the only recognition they accorded him was a Christmas card or a birthday telegram from time to time.

Forty

Ann had listened to Adam's story spellbound. 'Darling,' she said finally, 'let me pour you a drink.'

He looked up, startled to be back in the present. 'I'm sorry I burdened you with all that, Ann.'

She reached over and took his hand. 'Nothing is a burden if it concerns you, Adam. My God! I never could have imagined that you've been through all that. It makes my problems look pretty small.'

'We all have our share of troubles, I guess.'

'That's true – but you handled yours with courage. And I love and admire you for that.'

Their eyes met. It was time to put the ghosts of his past to rest.

'Enough of the past,' he said, his tone changing. 'Let's get dressed and go out. I'll tell you what – I'm going to take you to a disco and we're going to dance until dawn.'

'But, Adam – I don't know the new dances.'

'You'll learn, darling. I'll teach you. Now, come here.'

When she sat on his lap, he said, 'You won't ever leave me, will you?'

'Never,' Ann replied simply, and she believed it. But she had forgotten that Thanksgiving was approaching and Evie would expect her home. Or perhaps at that moment she didn't want to remember.

For several days she did nothing but devote herself to Adam. She would wake up thinking of him, spend the day waiting for him to return from the office, and every night invent new ways to satisfy him. But at the end of the week she was not only fielding calls from May, she knew she had to return to see Evie. Her daughter would never understand if she wasn't home for the holiday. Ann wondered how she would be able to leave Adam, even for a long weekend, when she was having difficulty even being away from him for a matter of hours.

The thought of telling Evie terrified her. She had retained her suite of rooms at the Plaza in case Evie tried to call, but once back in San Francisco, Ann knew she'd have to confess the truth. Remembering how Evie had reacted to the news about Linda, Ann knew she would regard Adam with equal distress. Evie kept hoping her parents would get back together, and the mere mention of other people in their lives enraged her.

Sensing her distress, Adam was extra loving as Ann packed to go back to San Francisco, heartsick at leaving.

'Darling, what will I do without you?' Ann asked.

'It won't be for long, thank God.'

'What will you do?'

'I'll be with one of my partners. Next year we'll all be together. Evie, too.'

She looked at him with tears in her eyes. 'Do you think that's possible?'

'Not only possible, but a certainty.'

'Oh, Adam,' she sighed, touched by his strength. 'You could move mountains if you wanted to.'

He laughed. 'Maybe not mountains, but surely one eighteen-year-old Berkeley coed with her mother's violet eyes. I think I'm a match for her.'

But once she was on the plane, Ann was filled with fear of what was to come. When the cab drew up in front of her house, she was shaking so badly she couldn't fit the key into the lock. Finally, she got the door open and called out, 'I'm back.'

Wiping her hands on her apron, Consuela came out from the kitchen. 'Oh, Mrs Coulter! I'm so happy to see you! You're looking wonderful.'

'And I'm happy to see you, Consuela. Did Jurgensen's bring all the groceries I ordered?'

'Yes, they did. And I already have the pumpkin pies baked for tomorrow. Would you like a piece?'

'Maybe later. Have you heard from Mr. Coulter?'

'Yes, he's called once or twice to see if I needed anything. He's a nice man.'

'Yes, he's a very nice man.' And she meant it.

Slowly, she walked up the stairs to her room and gazed around. She had worked so hard for all of this, but as she surveyed her possessions, she realized that none of it meant a tinker's damn. Money without love was worthless.

When the phone rang she picked it up expecting Adam, who had promised to call to see if she had arrived safely. But the voice on the other end was Evie's.

'Darling,' Ann lied. 'I was just about to call you.' The truth was that she hadn't decided what to tell Evie.

'I figured you'd be home by now,' Evie said with unmistakable coldness.

There was a long, awkward pause. 'You sound angry, Evie. What's the matter?'

'I don't know, Mom. I guess I'm mad at the whole world. You kind of walked out on me, you know. One day you're a basket case and the next you're flying off to New York. Everything's fine – you've decided to accept the divorce. Well, where does that leave me? You sure kept it a secret that you didn't care about each other.'

Ann let her get it all out of her system.

'Dad always said I was the apple of his eye, but now he has a lady friend who takes all his attention. I'm sure one of these days he won't even remember my phone number. And as for you, you're so busy you don't even know that I exist!'

'That's not fair, Evie,' Ann answered, but she knew the accusations held a modicum of truth. Although she had in fact called Evie, she still defended herself. 'You know, I've always tried to do my best for you, Evie. I wasn't working just for myself.'

'Oh, I know how noble you've been. But the fact is that I have no mother, no father, and no home.'

'You still have a home, Evie.'

'Last week when we talked, you said that you were thinking about putting the house up for sale.'

There was a bitter taste in Ann's mouth as she heard the hurt and betrayal in her daughter's voice. 'Look, Evie, I don't blame you for being upset. We'll have to see about the house. But I want you to understand something. Your father and I didn't mean to deceive you. We never did argue much. You know that. Perhaps that was part of the problem. Anyway, we both still love you – it's just that our relationship to each other has changed. We can still be a family, Evie, if we try to be a little more understanding.'

Evie laughed. 'Sure. A family – plus one.'

'Evie, please! You're a woman now and it's time for you to grow up.' Ann suddenly realized that she was talking to herself as well. 'When you fall in love, your father and I will try and respect your choice. Your father has found someone he wants to spend the rest of his life with. Be happy for him, Evie, just as we'll be happy for you.'

'Sure, Mom. That's easy for you to say, since you know I'm dating Peter Newman, who you think is just perfect for me. But I'll bet you wouldn't be so happy if I brought home a rock singer.'

Knowing Evie was trying to hurt her, Ann tried to remain calm. 'Listen to me, Evie. Come home tonight and you and I can spend the evening together. And tomorrow, we'll have a lovely day, the three of us. Try not to be bitter, and to forgive your father. We have forgiven each other.'

Evie had finally run out of things to say. She had no alternative but to capitulate. Her mother was right. The two of them were all she had.

Ann felt drained when she hung up. The phone rang again, and this time she was sure it was Adam, but Phillip's voice greeted her instead.

'How are you?' she said with more warmth than she had felt since the day he left. 'I'm happy to hear from you. I think it might be a good idea for us to celebrate Thanksgiving together. You know, Evie is very angry at us both, and I thought a family dinner might help cheer her.'

'I don't know. I've spoken to her every day and I've just about run out of things to say. She's been refusing to see me – so maybe you're right about tomorrow.'

'We'll have to be patient with her, Phillip. She's terribly opposed to the divorce, to say nothing of our finding new partners. We'll just have to take it a step at a time. She'll have to accept that, unfortunately, couples do grow apart. It's painful growing up, but it's more painful growing old, isn't it, Phillip?'

He sighed. 'How right you are.' Then, as if just hearing her, he added, 'What was that you said about new partners? Is there someone new in your life, Ann? You stayed a long time in New York.'

'Yes, Phillip, there is someone.'

He felt a twinge of, what – jealousy? Probably that was to be expected. Ann had been his wife for twenty-five years. 'Well, I think that's wonderful, Ann,' he managed to say. 'If anyone deserves happiness, you do.'

'Thank you, Phillip. It means a lot to me to have you say that. I'll see you tomorrow.' She hung up, wishing she might have felt the kind of passion for him she did for Adam. If she had, he might never have left. She would never have let him go.

The next day the three of them sat at the dinner table as they had at every holiday since Evie was born, but this time the tension was so thick it could have been cut with a knife. Evie refused to give an inch.

Watching apprehensively as Phillip carved the turkey, Ann wondered what he was thinking. Certainly Evie's mood must be as upsetting to him as it was to her.

'Evie, would you like light or dark?' he asked.

Evie sighed irritably. 'You know I only like white, Daddy. Have you forgotten so soon?'

Ann looked on, hardly believing the situation had deteriorated to this in so little time. This wasn't their Evie, who always bubbled with cheerful chatter about her friends and school. But, damn it, how could they reach her? Ann decided it would take a miracle and, as none seemed likely, she was happy when the day finally came to an end and Peter came to drive Evie back to Berkeley.

Grateful that Ann, if no one else, seemed to understand, Phillip left the house shortly afterward, eager to see Linda. Linda's holiday had been equally bleak, spent dining with acquaintances who, like herself, had no families to visit. She was careful not to complain, however, and was sympathetic with Phillip when he told her about Evie.

Phillip felt both relieved and slightly guilty when he left the house, feelings that were shared by all of the adults involved where Evie was concerned. They said nothing, but were all secretly relieved when she was back in Berkeley studying for her exams and too busy to make trips home.

Ann spent the weeks between Thanksgiving and Christmas flying back and forth to New York, trying to get ready for the holiday, seeing Adam, and still not getting too far behind at work. She wondered whether she would have to close her office when she married him. Well, she could postpone making that decision. In the meantime there was a much harder task to be dealt with. When Evie came back for Christmas, Ann would have to tell her about Adam. She had no choice. He had insisted on flying west on Christmas Eve. Adam wanted

Ann to be his wife, and both he and Ann saw no reason not to tell Evie as soon as possible.

Although it bolstered Ann's courage to have him with her for the holiday, it did force the issue.

'Darling, do you really think this is a good idea?' Ann asked the night before he flew out.

'It's not a question of good or bad. There's no alternative. Your daughter has to know that I exist, that you and I are going to be married, and that she is not going to come between us. It won't be easy, Ann, but if we approach her honestly she will eventually accept it. Trust me, darling.'

She did trust him, but then again, Adam didn't know Evie. They had decided to meet at the Fairmont and spend some time alone before driving over to the house. Ann just told Evie she had some last-minute shopping.

Adam arrived promptly at five and insisted on ordering champagne, saying that there was nothing better than fortifying yourself before a difficult scene.

Ann's hand trembled as she accepted the glass. 'She's going to hate me, Adam. I just know it.'

'No, she won't.'

'But what am I going to say to her? I have to warn her. I can't just bring you home.'

'Ask her to join us here. Say you want to talk to her. If things don't go well, I'll stay here tonight.'

Ann took a deep breath and dialed. 'Evie, I'm so tired, maybe you'd join me downtown for dinner. We can meet in the lobby of the Fairmont.'

'Okay, Mom. Anything you say.'

'I need to talk to you—' Ann began, but Evie interrupted.

'I love you, Mom. We'll have all night to gossip. Ciao!'

Ann hung up and thanked God. Evie sounded more like her old self.

It was Evie's roommate Leslie who was responsible for the improvement. By the time Evie had come back after Thanksgiving, Leslie had gotten sick to death of hearing about Evie's problems: her unfaithful father, her absent mother, and her grandfather's death, until finally she let Evie have it.

'Look,' she exploded, 'you're not the only kid whose parents are getting divorced. The truth is that you're luckier than most because they stayed together until you went off to college. What the hell are you griping about? I walked in one day and found my father in bed with the maid. And my mother has been married three times and I liked all my stepfathers just fine. Wake up, Evie. You have your whole life ahead of you. Start living it.'

Evie hadn't been ready for all of Leslie's advice, but it did make her wonder just how much she really could change her parents' lives. And with that realization, she began to lose her belligerence. Instead, she began to feel helpless, though Ann took her change of mood as a more hopeful sign than it really was.

They sat across from each other in the Cirque Room. Adam was waiting upstairs. Ann's courage almost failed her, but finally, fortified by a double martini, she said, 'Evie, darling, I know that all of this has been a shock, but would you really want your father and me to live unhappily together until you gave us permission to do what we really wanted?'

Evie twirled the straw in her glass. 'What are you trying to tell me, Mom?'

'The truth is, Evie, that I've met someone too.'

There was no mistaking Evie's stunned expression as she stared at her mother. How could a woman who had professed to love her husband for twenty-five years find a new lover in less than a month? *Or has it been much longer than that?*

'I hope you'll be very happy,' Evie said in a cold, flat voice.

'Do you really mean that?'

'Sure, Mom. If that's what you want, I'm not going to stand in your way.'

'It's going to be wonderful, Evie,' Ann said. She was

crying softly now. 'Please believe me – it's going to be wonderful.'

Evie didn't believe her. Evie didn't believe that anything was ever going to be right again. Their family had been destroyed. But if this was what her parents wanted, so be it.

'. . . love him,' Ann was saying.

'What?' Evie snapped. 'I didn't hear you.'

'You're going to love Adam.'

'Oh? His name is Adam. Sounds rather Biblical,' she said, trying to keep the bitterness out of her voice.

Evidently she succeeded, for Ann continued with genuine enthusiasm. 'Darling, I want you to meet him. He's flown out for Christmas and he's waiting upstairs for you.'

'Oh? Well, that was nice of him.'

'You don't know how happy you've made me. Now let's go up.'

As they rode the elevator to his floor, Evie wondered why she was going along with this. Standing before Adam a few minutes later, an artificial smiled affixed to her lips, she knew she would never accept the fact this man was sleeping with her mother. And when they got married, what was she supposed to call him: Dad? Mr. Gayne? Adam?

'We're going to be very good friends, Evie,' Adam was saying. 'And I always want you to come to me if you need something.'

I won't! she wanted to scream. *You're not my father and you're not my friend. You're just my mother's . . . gigolo. And I don't like you – not one little bit, even if you are Mr. Bigshot.*

But she didn't say any of that. Her answer was an almost inaudible 'Thank you.'

Christmas Day went unexpectedly well. A very polite and subdued Evie had lunch in Chinatown with Ann and Adam. The next day she finally met Linda and chatted with her in the lobby of the Fairmont while Phillip stood by, waiting for an explosion that never came.

Evie seemed delighted with her presents. Just before New Year's, she cheerfully packed up to join Leslie and her roommate's new stepfather in Vail for some skiing.

The moment she left, Ann and Adam decided to fly east for New Year's. Adam went a couple of days early to arrange a party to introduce Ann to his friends. When Phillip called to say goodbye, Ann was able to wish him a happy New Year with all her heart. For the first time it really seemed as if things would work out. They knew that Evie had not totally accepted the divorce, but she was no longer overtly hostile and they hoped with time she would realize they all were better off this way, and that Linda and Adam would in fact enrich her life.

Ann flew to New York with a light heart to find Adam's apartment decorated for a gala New Year's Eve celebration.

For the party, Ann made herself more glamorous than she had ever dreamed possible. Adam had taken her to Valentino's, where she had bought a stunning black velvet sheath with one shoulder drawn up into a wide, pink satin ruche. She had her hair done that afternoon by Mr. Kenneth himself, who had just finished doing Jackie Kennedy's.

The evening was a grand success, and Adam's friends accepted Ann not just as Adam's fiancée, but for herself.

At twelve, the little orchestra broke into 'Auld Lang Syne,' and Adam pulled her into his arms, kissing her as though there were no one else in the room.

'Ann, dearest – you've made me so happy,' he whispered in her ear.

At last the future seemed to be in their hands.

Forty-One

Across the country, Evie Coulter was immersed in a drama of her own – one with far less hopeful prospects. She and Peter had arrived home from Vail late New Year's Day, and, refusing to go home, Evie had insisted

291

that he drop her off at the sorority house. Peter had been trying to get her to come to a party at Chuck Swanson's place in Berkeley – all their friends would be there – but Evie just didn't want to go out after what she had been through at Christmas. At the last minute, Kim and Leslie insisted, and Evie dressed without enthusiasm and went downstairs to meet Peter.

From the moment he picked her up, Evie was silent and withdrawn, and she sat as far as she could from him in Peter's car. Peter wondered if he had made a mistake sending the two girls up after her, but justified his action by telling himself that it was stupid for someone to spend her life mooning about the breakup of her parents' marriage. A few drinks and some laughs would do her good.

The party was well under way when they arrived, and the first thing Peter did was to force several glasses of champagne on Evie, reasoning that this was what she needed to get in the spirit of things. It did the opposite: Evie retreated to a corner of the huge living room, next to the bar, and remained mute.

Peter tried to be gallant, then told a few jokes. Nothing helped. Finally he lost his temper. 'Evie – as far as I'm concerned, you're acting like an idiot. Your parents have a right to their own lives, just as you do. It's about time you grew up – God knows I don't want to marry a sulky child.'

Evie slammed down her champagne glass. 'Don't give me any of your stupid advice!' she screamed. 'I've had enough to last me a lifetime. Anyway, who ever said I was going to marry you? I'm *never* getting married – understand?'

She had totally lost control of herself. 'Here's to marriage!' she screamed, and threw her drink in Peter's face. Then she turned and fled up the stairs and locked herself in the bathroom.

Kim followed her up and angrily rattled the door-knob. Fortunately the party was so noisy that only a handful of guests had noticed the scene. 'Let me in, Evie.'

'Go away.'

'Evie, open the goddamned door and stop acting like a brat.' With a sigh of relief, Kim heard the lock turning. Evie was sitting on the edge of the tub. Her eyes were red and swollen, and her hair was strewn over her distraught face.

Kim's heart went out to her friend. She took Evie's hand. 'I know we've all been a little rough on you, Evie. But we're trying to help. We just want you to accept the situation with your parents. And Peter really loves you – he's just a little gauche, that's all.'

'I know,' Evie sobbed miserably. 'I acted like a bitch. I just don't know what's happening to me.'

'I do, I think,' Kim said. 'All these upheavals – your grandfather, the divorce, learning about Adam and Linda – they've really gotten to you. But give Peter a break – he feels rotten about the whole business.'

Evie swallowed hard. 'I guess you're right – I'd better shape up. Let me fix my face and I'll be right down.'

Fifteen minutes later, when an outwardly composed Evie returned to the party, Peter was nowhere in sight, and no one seemed to know what had happened to him. She couldn't blame him for disappearing – he had every right to despise her, didn't he? But how could she stand to lose him? He was the one remaining constant in her life.

At a loss what to do next, Evie went over to the buffet table, picked up a glass of champagne, drank it down, and refilled it.

An hour and several glasses of champagne later, she was still in the same spot, swaying slightly in an almost agreeable haze, when the host, Chuck Swanson, sauntered up and stood close by her. He was dressed in a beautifully tailored velvet tux and was holding a glass of scotch.

'You look a little lonely,' he said quietly.

'I am,' Evie said. 'I am a little lonely.'

'Aren't you a friend of Kim's?'

Evie nodded.

He hesitated. 'Evie Coulter – I remember now.' He gently took her empty champagne glass from her hand. 'How about a refill?'

Evie had seen Chuck several times on the Berkeley campus and at football games. He was, by unofficial vote among the coeds, the prize catch of the year: from a wealthy Bay Area family, good-looking, an excellent dancer, and headed for Yale Law School after graduation. His attentiveness was balm for her bruised spirit.

She tried to think of what to say next, but she felt only anger and defiance. *So Peter's gone. Well, then, to hell with him. Too bad for Peter.*

She lit a cigarette, then quickly put it out. She looked at Chuck and smiled. 'Yes, Chuck, I'd love a drink. But bring me what you're having. I'm tired of all these bubbles. Happy New Year . . .'

The next morning Evie came to with a horrible headache. At first she thought she was back in the sorority house, but then she realized that she was lying in a strange bed in an unknown bedroom, and that she wasn't alone. Lying next to her, in red-and-white candy-striped pajamas, snoring placidly, was Chuck Swanson.

Evie almost screamed, then stopped herself. *Dear God . . . did I spend the night with him?* She closed her eyes and tried to concentrate, but she couldn't recall anything very clearly. It was obvious, however, that she had lost her virginity like some teenage tramp drunk for the first time on cheap beer and looking for a nice way to end the evening. It was probably a blessing that she couldn't recall anything. She couldn't even remember this man's name.

If it had only been Peter.

She tried to slip out of bed, but Chuck awoke and reached out for her. Evie knocked his hand away.

'What's the matter?' Chuck asked. 'You didn't act like that last night.'

Evie's eyes filled with tears. 'What do you mean?'

'Just what I said. You came on like Gangbusters. Forgotten already?'

Evie closed her eyes. The room suddenly began to spin. 'I think I'm going to be sick . . .'

She rushed to the bathroom, bent over the toilet, and vomited until there was nothing left. Then she sat on the edge of the tub, half naked, and wept softly, more over the possibility that Peter would find out than for what had happened the night before.

When she returned to the bedroom, it was empty. She put on her soiled and wrinkled party dress and her pumps and went downstairs. Chuck was in the kitchen, opening a can of Budweiser. The house seemed to be deserted.

Evie finally remembered his name. 'Chuck . . . listen. I had way too much to drink last night. I . . . well, you'll keep it quiet, won't you?'

He put down the can of beer and looked hard at her. 'That depends. You were pretty damned good. A tiger, I'd say. Maybe someday I'll want a repeat performance.'

'Chuck . . . please.' She stopped, knowing that begging would be useless. 'I'd better go home now.' She took her topcoat from the hall closet.

He didn't bother to see her to the door.

Evie stumbled out into the winding streets of the Berkeley hills with no real idea of where she was headed. The important thing was to get away – from the house, from Chuck, and from her own intolerable thoughts. After an hour she found herself in downtown Berkeley. There was a coffee shop open, so she drank two cups of strong black coffee, smoked a cigarette, and walked to the bus stop.

An hour later she was home.

Another empty house greeted her – Consuela was off for the day – but this time it was a sanctuary. Evie ran upstairs, tore off her party dress, and stuffed it in the wastebasket. Then she took the hottest tub she could stand.

She went down into the living room in her bathrobe and stared bleakly out the window at the winter fog. Whom could she talk to? Not her mother, who was in New York. Phillip, perhaps? She reached for the phone. Linda answered, and all Evie could bring herself to say was, 'Hi, Linda . . . it's Evie . . . I just wanted to say Happy New Year.'

'Why, thank you, Evie,' Linda said. The warmth in her voice was obvious. 'Let me get you your dad.'

'No, no . . . Just tell him I called. Bye.' She hung up, her courage gone. She had been about to tell her father that she had given herself to an older man she hardly knew, at a drunken party – she, who had assumed such a high moral tone about her parents' indiscretions.

Evie realized that she couldn't confide in her mother, either. Ann was, in spite of her relationship with Adam, a highly moral person, conventional even, and always had been. She had always, by word and example, conveyed to her daughter that physical intimacy was a gift that could be all too easily squandered. Still, Evie reflected, if she just heard Ann's voice, she would feel better.

For the second time a parent failed to answer.

'How nice of you to call,' Adam said. 'Before I get your mother, tell me – did you have a good New Year's?'

'Fine, thank you. I went to a party,' Evie said woodenly.

'Well, I wish you'd been here. Your mother was the belle of the ball. I hardly had the chance to dance with her once.'

There was a pause while he handed the phone to Ann.

'Evie, darling – Happy New Year!' Ann's voice rang with happiness. Evie dutifully answered her questions, feeling like a hypocrite. Yes, I went to a great party in Berkeley. Yes, I had a great time. Leslie and Kim did, too. While all the time she wanted to throw herself into her mother's arms and tell her what had happened. But

Ann was in New York, and Evie knew she couldn't bring up the subject on the phone.

She was in tears when she hung up – speaking with Linda and Adam had only intensified her isolation. Her mother and father had found new lives. When she had tried to do the same thing, the result had been disaster. She couldn't bear to think about Peter. How could she face him now? Above all, what would happen if he found out?

The renewal of classes provided some solace. Evie plunged into her studies with a fierce determination that astonished her sorority sisters. A couple of them who had been at the party tried to question her about the scene with Peter, and about how she had gotten on with Chuck, but she somehow managed to defuse their curiosity. Apparently they suspected nothing.

Peter phoned several times, but Evie refused to take his calls. Finally one morning he waited in front of her sorority house and waylaid her on the way to history class. Taking her arm, he said, 'Evie – I've got to talk to you.'

She shook him off. 'Peter, we don't have anything to talk about.'

'Evie, all these years I thought we meant something to each other. Don't you think you owe me some kind of explanation?'

Taking her silence for assent, he led her over to a low stone wall and made her sit down, then sat beside her.

'Well – what is it?' he asked point-blank.

'It's nothing, Peter,' Evie said sullenly, staring at the ground.

'Nothing? Evie, you know how it's been between us. We've been together since the day you started college. Sudddenly it's over? Why?'

'It just isn't going to work out, Peter.'

'Evie, look at me!' He took her face between his hands and said more gently, 'Evie, I'm in love with you. Now look at me and tell me you don't love me!'

Evie clenched her fists at her sides as she looked up at

Peter's dear face, so concerned, so full of love. It was intolerable to hurt him, but how could she explain what she had done on New Year's Eve? She must simply end it, once and for all.

'Peter, I don't love you anymore.'

His eyes were wide with disbelief as he searched her face. Then he dropped his hands to his sides and stood up. 'Well, that's that, isn't it? Excuse me ... I didn't realize ...' He made no attempt now to conceal the bitterness in his voice.

'I'm sorry, Peter.'

As she watched him walk away, Evie, for the first time in her life, wished she were dead.

Forty-Two

Adam took the week after New Year's off from work. It was a magical time for Ann, who had never really had a vacation with nothing to do but play. It was as if they were the only two people in the world.

Adam fell deeper in love with her each day, and Ann's love for him knew no boundaries. One of the most surprising things about Adam was that, mature as he was, he brought a marvelous spontaneity to everything they did. She was catapulted into a vibrant world that she had never known existed. Over and over, she thanked God for sending her Adam. She reveled in the maturity of their love. Things that would have bothered her ten years ago no longer mattered.

Adam's energy amazed her. He had so many interests outside his work and still found time to swim, ski, and play tennis. More important for Ann, he had never forgotten his roots.

One Sunday he drove Ann over to Brooklyn to show her his parents' bakery. 'You'd be surprised how large that tiny flat looked to me when I was a child,' he reminisced.

Ann remembered the dreadful day Phillip had taken

her to meet Eva and Simon. Dear God, how nervous she had been. But today she couldn't wait to meet Adam's parents.

When they arrived, Leah was wearing her best dress in honor of her Avrum's lady friend, and nothing could have been warmer than her greeting. For a moment Ann felt as though her own mother had returned, and as she hugged Leah she knew that someday Adam's mother might fill the lonely space in her heart.

As soon as they were seated, Leah put the teakettle on and brought out some homemade strudel and several sumptuous-looking cakes. Then she led them into the old-fashioned parlor, and over Adam's laughing protests, proceeded to drag out all his old baby pictures.

'This was Avrum at four . . . and at his Bar Mitzvah . . . and on graduation day.'

Leah urged Ann to come back as soon as she could. 'And don't bother to bring Avrum if he's working.'

Over the next three months, as Adam and Ann kept up their bicoastal romance, Ann decided that the fact Evie came home so little meant she was settling down to enjoy college. She would have been less sanguine had she known the truth.

When Evie first missed her period she felt a stab of fear. Then she reminded herself she had always been irregular, especially since she left home. But several weeks later, when she began waking up too sick to face breakfast, she suspected the worst. She stayed in the bathroom nearly an hour, and when she emerged and sank wearily onto her bed, Kim came over and said with concern, 'You must be coming down with the flu, Evie. Why don't you stay home. I'll get your French notes, and Les can give you hers from math and Chinese history.'

'Okay,' Evie had mumbled.

Later that day she had felt much better and hoped it was indeed the twenty-four-hour virus. But the next morning, as she sat miserably on the floor of the bathroom, she admitted the other signs she'd tried to deny – the extra weight, the sore, tender breasts.

When she finally staggered out, she looked at her two roommates and burst into tears.

'How long has it been since you had a period?' Leslie asked shrewdly.

'Leslie! Evie's a virgin, remember?' Kim exclaimed.

'Then she's the first pregnant virgin in two thousand years. Evie,' she said as her friend tried to bury her face in the pillow, 'sit up! This isn't something you can fool around with. Is it possible that you're pregnant?'

'Yes.'

'You haven't had a period lately?'

Evie shook her head.

'Since when, Evie?' Kim asked. 'You told me you haven't seen Peter in months.'

'It wasn't Peter,' Evie cried. 'It was Chuck Swanson. You know, on New Year's? I got drunk, I guess, and I went to bed with him. I can't remember one thing about it, but that's when it had to be.'

'Evie, for God's sake – this is March! What have you been waiting for? You're over three months pregnant!' Leslie exclaimed.

'I don't know,' Evie whispered brokenly. 'I just don't know. I wish I were dead.' Visions of her parents' disgusted reaction brought a fresh burst of sobs. She had thought sleeping with Chuck was the most horrible thing that could happen. Now she realized that this was a million times worse.

'Damn it, Evie, pull yourself together,' Leslie said. 'Stop carrying on like a grade-B movie heroine. There's a simple solution to all this: you'll have an abortion.'

'How?' Evie moaned. 'I can't just go to our family doctor.'

It was very simple, Leslie explained. It wasn't legal, strictly speaking, but all you had to do was find a doctor who was willing to certify that the health of the mother would be endangered by carrying the baby to term.

Thousands of abortions were done every day.

By the time Leslie finished, Evie had made up her mind. There was really no choice. She couldn't have Chuck Swanson's baby – worse, she couldn't disgrace her mother and father.

A few days later, Evie found herself sitting next to Leslie in a dingy waiting room in an outlying district of Oakland. Leslie reached over and patted her hand. 'Relax, Evie. You're as pale as a ghost. It will be all right – you'll see.'

'It's not going to be all right, Leslie. I can feel it. I'm scared.' Her voice was so low that Leslie could barely hear her.

Frightened by Evie's pallor, Leslie got up and walked over to the receptionist's area. She rapped smartly on the closed panel. 'Nurse!'

Nothing happened. Then, after about five minutes, the window opened a couple of inches and two sleepy-looking eyes peered out. 'Yeah?'

'I need a glass of water for . . . Mrs. Smith.'

The nurse looked at Leslie and sighed, then slammed shut the partition. Leslie had just about decided that her request was going to be ignored when the nurse opened the partition again and shoved through a paper cup filled with tepid water.

It was better than nothing. Leslie brought it to Evie and urged her to sip it. She was terribly worried. Evie seemed to be taking this so hard. She had barely eaten anything for the past week, and several times Leslie and Kimberly had been wakened by her screams as she had nightmares. Every morning the dark circles under her eyes seemed bigger. She was smoking incessantly, and drinking cup after cup of coffee.

Leslie had gotten the name of an abortionist from a boy she had been dating, who said that several of his frat brothers had sent their girlfriends there. The doc was very cheap and no questions would be asked about her marital status.

Evie knew that she couldn't go to any of the reputable

practitioners in San Francisco because they might know one of her parents. But Oakland was more anonymous, and, as promised, the doctor asked no questions. The operation would take thirty minutes and cost only three hundred dollars: less than half the going rate.

Evie and Leslie had been taken aback by the untidy office and the coarse, gum-chewing receptionist, but everyone said that the man knew what he was doing.

Finally the receptionist opened the door and called out, 'Mrs Smith – the doctor will see you now.'

Summoning what courage remained, Evie stood up, smiled at Leslie, and walked through the doorway into the operating room. The doctor was a thin, bald little man in his late fifties. Evie immediately disliked him, even though she had to admit that, unlike the waiting room, both he and the operating room were scrupulously clean.

He asked her politely to disrobe and lie down on the table, where he put her feet up in stirrups, then left the room.

Evie was perspiring and trembling, trying not to cry. The feeling of terror and humiliation – of total mental and physical exposure – was something she could never have imagined. The nightmares she had been having were nothing in comparison.

She had almost lost her nerve and was starting to get up when the door opened and the doctor returned, together with a nurse whom Evie hadn't seen before. The nurse was black, and her look betrayed without the need for words what she thought of rich kids who got pregnant and couldn't cope with having a child.

She stood by and calmly studied Evie's body as the doctor rattled off a list of the risks involved in having an abortion, speaking so quickly that Evie could barely comprehend what he was saying. Finally he thrust a pen into her hand. 'We'll need you to sign and date this form . . .'

It was at that moment that Evie fully realized what was going to happen to her. But it was too late to back out. She had to go through with it. She couldn't endure the

thought that otherwise she would be betraying everything Ann and Phillip stood for.

She began to write: 'Ev—', then scratched out the
letters and wrote, disguising her handwriting, 'Mrs C.
Smith' and the date. Then she lay back on the narrow,
uncomfortable table while the doctor began work. He
picked up a metal instrument that looked like clippers.
Then Evie felt the slight prick of a needle as she was
injected with a local anesthetic.

She heard the doctor say, 'Hold on now,' and then
there was a pain that seemed to start in her loins and
spread throughout her body. She twisted her body,
trying not to scream. The doctor shouted something at
her, but her ears were ringing and she couldn't hear him.
She knew she was going to die. How would they find out
who 'Mrs. Smith's' next of kin were? Leslie would tell
them . . . Leslie would tell Ann and Phillip. . .

The pain seemed to flow away. She opened her eyes
and saw the doctor leaning over her. He patted her hand
and said softly, 'That's it – all taken care of.'

The nurse took Evie's arm and said, 'Put on this robe
and follow me, miss.' Evie was shown to a cot in a
darkened room. The room was hot and airless. There
were two other women there, both lying motionless.
'You lie down now, honey,' the nurse ordered. Evie
thought the woman seemed a little more sympathetic now.

The pain had returned, but no one came with medication or even a cup of water. One of the women was
moaning quietly. After what seemed days, but what was
in fact exactly one hour, the receptionist came to the door
and said, 'Mrs. Smith – you may go home now.'

Evie allowed herself to be dressed and was given pads
to absorb the bleeding. Then she was taken back to the
reception room, where Leslie was waiting. The woman
held out her hand. 'That will be three hundred dollars
cash, please.'

Leslie picked up Evie's purse, opened it, and carefully
counted out the money.

*

Back at the sorority house, Evie fell onto her bed and was asleep within seconds. Kim, who had an important exam and couldn't go along to the abortionist's, was waiting in the room the three of them shared. 'Is she okay?' she asked Leslie in a whisper.

Leslie shrugged. 'I guess so. What can I tell you? Go get some pain-killers – the doctor didn't give her any – didn't want her passing out in the street, I guess.'

Kim was wakened in the middle of the night by Evie's moans. She switched on the light and went over to her friend's bed.

'Evie – what's wrong?'

There was no response.

She put her hand on Evie's forehead; it was feverish. Her eyes were open but glazed and unseeing. Her head and shoulders were soaked in sweat. Her breath was rasping.

'Les – wake up!' Kim shouted. 'Evie's sick. We've got to get her to a hospital.'

Leslie sat up in her bed and thought for a moment. 'Don't be in too much of a hurry. Evie wanted this kept quiet, you know. Maybe we should wait.'

'Les – for God's sakes look at her!'

'Okay . . . maybe you're right. She looks pretty bad. We'll take her over to old Doc Cheng as Mrs. C. Smith. That's the name she used today at the clinic.'

When Kim pulled back the covers, she screamed. 'Oh, Jesus – look!'

Evie was lying in a pool of blood.

'I'll call an ambulance,' Leslie said decisively. 'Take her pulse.'

While Leslie was dialing, Kim said frantically, 'Les – I can't find it!'

Although it seemed like hours, it was only minutes before they heard the ambulance screaming up Piedmont Avenue. It stopped in front of the sorority house and two men in white jackets jumped out. Several girls sleepily put their heads out their windows, then returned to bed. Evie was carried out on a stretcher.

Half an hour later, Kim and Leslie paced the waiting room at Herrick Hospital. The nurses had rushed Evie into the emergency room and called one of the attendants.

Twenty minutes later a doctor emerged, grim-faced. 'Who's here with Mrs. Smith?'

Kim and Leslie stepped forward. 'We brought her in,' Leslie said. 'Is she all right? We're friends of hers.'

The doctor hesitated. 'I really need to speak to the family. Is her husband available?'

Leslie swallowed hard. 'No, he's not.'

'Well, she needs to go into surgery immediately, and we need consent from the next of kin. If she has parents – anyone – they should be called.'

The two girls looked at each other helplessly. Evie had made them swear to secrecy, but surely that didn't apply now.

But Mrs. Coulter was in New York this week, and Mr. Coulter was living God knows where with his girl-friend. 'She has parents – but they're not available either,' Leslie announced defiantly.

The doctor looked at her very hard. 'Ladies, I wasn't born yesterday. That is a very sick young lady in there. She might not make it. Do you want to take that responsibility?'

They stared at him mutely.

'All right. If that's the way it's going to be, we'll have to proceed without consent. But I would advise you to rethink your position, if *Mrs.* Smith is truly your friend.'

'We have to get in touch with her parents!' Kim said once the doctor had gone. 'What if something happens?'

'Forget it! Evie would never forgive us if we told them.'

'It's gone way beyond that. We can't keep this to ourselves.'

Looking at Kim's terrified face, Leslie weakened. 'Where would we get their phone numbers?'

'I think Evie carries a little phone book in her purse.

You brought it along, didn't you? She must have them written down.'

But as soon as they had fished the small leather volume from Evie's purse, they realized their predicament. They knew the names 'Adam' and 'Linda,' but unfortunately had never bothered to find out the last names. Their only hope was that Mr. Coulter would be in his law office that morning.

Hour after hour they waited outside the surgical suites. Every time they saw a nurse emerge, their hopes rose, but as dawn broke, Evie was still in surgery. Finally it was nine and a hollow-eyed Leslie went to the pay phone and dialed Phillip's office.

'Mr. Coulter? This is Leslie Winston.'

'What is it, Leslie?' Philip asked, knowing immediately that something was wrong.

'Oh, Mr. Coulter, it's Evie! She's in the hospital, and she's been in surgery since four-thirty. We couldn't call you because we didn't have your number at your girlfriend's.' After hours of intolerable strain, Leslie began to cry.

'What are you saying, Leslie? Has she been in an accident?'

'I can't explain over the phone, Mr. Coulter. Pease come right away. It's Herrick Hospital in Berkeley. Do you know where it is?'

'Yes, yes. I'll be there as soon as I can.'

Not even pausing to grab the topcoat he had just taken off, Phillip rushed out, leaving the receptionist staring after him, open-mouthed.

When he arrived at the hospital, he raced up the stairs to the surgical floor, but the waiting room was empty.

He grabbed a passing nurse. 'I'm looking for my daughter – Evie Coulter.'

She stared at the obviously distraught man. 'Was that the emergency case we just had? Young girl, looks about eighteen?'

'Yes, yes, that's her.'

'She's just come out of surgery, but she's still critical.

They've taken her directly to intensive care.'

He found Leslie and Kim huddled together outside the ICU. His face was like death as he cried, 'Is Evie in there? Can I see her?'

'They told us we can't go in yet.'

Phillip reached over and grabbed Leslie's shoulder. 'Now you tell me what's happened to her, young lady!'

The two friends looked at each other guiltily. At the sight of Phillip's grief, all at once they realized the enormity of what they had done. They had encouraged Evie to have the abortion with little thought as to the consequences, and now they saw the agony of a parent who might be about to lose his child.

Taking a deep breath, Leslie was about to speak when the ICU door opened and a doctor emerged, tiredly rubbing his neck.

Seeing Phillip with the girls, he walked over and said, 'Are you Mrs. Smith's father?'

Seeing his hesitation, the doctor added, 'Evie's?'

Slowly, Phillip nodded.

'Well, I'm Doctor Neilson, the surgeon. Have the girls told you anything yet?' When Phillip shook his head, Neilson said, 'Your daughter had an abortion. Unfortunately she seems to have gone to a real butcher. The placenta wasn't completely removed. That's why she began hemorrhaging in the middle of the night. She lost so much blood that she went into a coma. We've given her transfusions and managed to stop the bleeding, but she still hasn't regained consciousness.'

Abortion . . . blood loss . . . coma . . . Phillip couldn't believe they were talking about his daughter. Yet Leslie and Kim were there, and their expressions told all. It had to be true.

'May I see her, doctor?' he said stiffly.

'Just for a moment.'

The sight of Evie's motionless body, hooked up to an array of machines and tubes, almost made him faint. 'Oh, God,' he whispered.

'She has a good chance,' the nurse murmured. 'We

just have to monitor her very carefully.'

Phillip nodded wordlessly and allowed himself to be ushered out.

Once out in the waiting room, he sank into a chair and buried his face in his hands. The furthest thing from his mind was the fact that Evie had needed the abortion. Not for a moment did he think of blaming her. All he cared about was that she lived. When he looked up he saw Evie's roommates sitting across from him, their faces drawn with fatigue. It was Kim who, in a choked and trembling voice, told him of their role in arranging the abortion. Phillip didn't have the heart to be angry.

'Girls,' he said quietly. 'Go home. There's nothing more you can do for her.'

When they had gone, Phillip dialed Ann's number in New York. He hesitated to call Adam's apartment, but he had no choice. Ann had to be told. The phone rang and rang, but no one answered. In desperation, Phillip knew that he would have to call Adam's office. Maybe Ann was even there.

But again, he was stymied. 'Mr. Gayne is out for the day. May I give him a message?'

Wearily, Phillip replied. 'Yes. Please tell him to have Ann Coulter call this number. It's an emergency.'

Phillip hung up. There was nothing more he could do. Hour after hour he walked the floor. There was no change in Evie's condition. It was 7.00 P.M. when he remembered Linda. *Good God, she must be frantic!* They were expecting dinner guests and he'd promised to be home early to help cook.

Linda answered the phone in an anxious voice. She'd called Phillip that morning to ask him to pick up some wine on the way home, and his secretary had told her he had run out the door without telling anyone where he was going.

All day, while Phillip had been trying to reach Ann in New York, Linda had been calling Phillip's office, hoping to hear some word of him. At six o'clock, she decided something terrible had happened to him. She called off their dinner and sat down to wait.

When she heard Phillip's voice, she started to sob from sheer relief. 'Phillip – where in God's name are you? What happened? I've been sick with worry!'

'Linda, sweetheart. Forgive me. I'm sorry to have been so inconsiderate. I just now remembered the dinner party.'

'Phillip, it doesn't matter at all. Just tell me what's wrong.'

'It's – Evie. I'm over in Herrick Hospital. She's in intensive care.'

'What—'

'She's had an abortion, Linda,' Phillip said emotionlessly.

'Phillip, I'm so sorry. Shall I come over?'

'Would you please? I need you so much.'

When he saw her coming down the hall, he wondered why he hadn't called her the minute he found out.

As they settled themselves on a couch to wait for the next bulletin, Linda tried to reassure him. 'Phillip, if no one is coming out and telling you anything, that probably means she's stable. If there were a change for the worse, they'd let you know.'

'I suppose so. It's just that I've seen a lot of doctors running in and out over the last hour.'

Linda squeezed his hand, and after a moment, he returned the pressure. But he couldn't help thinking that no one who wasn't a parent could really understand.

'I have to call Ann again,' he muttered. 'I've been trying her all day and there's been no answer.'

'Of course. I'll stay here and wait in case there's any news,' Linda said quickly, trying to hide the pang his words gave her. All day long he had been calling Ann – and hadn't once thought of her. *But Ann's Evie's mother*, she tried to tell herself.

Phillip dialed Adam's apartment. He'd done it so many times that he'd memorized the number. Ten o'clock – that meant it was one in New York, on a weeknight. They had to be in, for God's sake! If Adam Gayne were half the businessman everyone said he was, he would have to be at work early. The bastard had to sleep, didn't he?

Ann had just turned off the light when the phone rang. It had been a glorious day. Adam had finally convinced Ann she would have to close her office for good. They had spent the day in Connecticut looking for a place they could rent for the summer. Funny, after all these years of grinding away, suddenly he had acquired a new perspective on success.

They had fallen in love with a rambling old house high on a hill. It had started as a farm, but a later owner had gutted and remodeled it as a summer retreat. Behind the welcoming veranda lay spacious rooms flooded with sunshine, with wide floorboards and fieldstone fireplaces. Yet, despite its aura of timeless charm, there was every modern convenience, and behind was a huge swimming pool.

Despite the bleakness of the late-winter day, Ann could visualize the trees clothed in new leaf, the grassy meadows dotted with wildflowers, and she and Adam, together on long, summer weekends.

'Can we take it, Adam?' she asked.

A little smile hovered on his lips, and she knew that he saw the same picture she did. 'Of course, sweetheart. It's – perfect.'

Now as Ann heard Adam pick up the phone and say, 'Yes, Phillip,' she knew that something had happened to threaten her happiness.

She grabbed the receiver. 'What's wrong, Phillip? Please tell me!'

'You're going to have to brace yourself, sweetheart. Evie's in the hospital – in intensive care.'

'Phillip . . . no! What happened? An accident?'

'Not exactly, darling,' he temporized. How could he tell Ann over the phone? 'Listen . . . it's complicated. All I can tell you is that she's lost a lot of blood and her condition is very serious. They're doing their best, but' – he swallowed – 'I think you'd better come home as soon as you can.'

'Well, of course! I'll be on the first plane west. I'll go straight to the airport and wait for a flight. Oh, Phillip.'

'Now calm down, darling – she's in good hands.' He tried to be reassuring, but he couldn't keep the note of fear from his voice.

Ann hung up, tears running down her face. 'Oh, Evie . . . Evie . . .'

Adam gathered her into his arms. 'Ann, please. Is Evie sick?'

She nodded.

'All right. We're leaving right now. Get dressed and I'll have Gaston call the car.'

'You're coming with me?'

He looked at her, puzzled by the inquiry. 'Well, of course. I wouldn't dream of letting you go alone.'

'But Adam, it's one-fifteen. I may have to wait at the airport all night.'

'Darling, we're going to charter a plane.'

'We can do that?'

'With Evie in the hospital? I should say so.'

'Oh, Adam, I love you!'

Phillip had returned to the waiting room and was sitting next to Linda. 'I got her,' he said with a sigh of relief. 'She's flying right out.'

'That's wonderful, Phillip. Now, how about some coffee. You look all in.'

'Okay. That might be a good idea.'

After Linda left, Phillip slumped back against the couch. He was lighting yet another cigarette when Dr. Neilson came up to speak to him. 'Mr. Coulter, I'm afraid I've got some bad news. Evie is going to have to go back in for more surgery.'

'What's that mean? I thought you'd already done everything necessary.'

'That's right, Mr Coulter, we did. We managed to

311

stop the hemorrhaging. But you must understand that she sustained a good deal of tissue damage from that botched abortion. I'm afraid there's also the possibility we'll have to do a hysterectomy.'

Phillip looked at him blankly.

'Mr. Coulter? Are you all right? I'll need you to sign a consent form.'

Phillip finally nodded. 'Show me where.'

When Linda handed him his coffee, she knew right away that something had gone very wrong. She looked at him closely. His fists were clenched and his eyes were shut. The nightmares of the past were flooding across his consciousness: Bugleman's shattered body, a tortured American soldier, the monkey cage . . .

Linda put her hand on his shoulder but he shook it off roughly. He opened his eyes and looked up at her, not seeming to recognize her.

'Phillip . . . it's me . . . Linda.'

His eyes focused as he jerked back to the present. 'Linda . . . they're taking her to surgery. If she doesn't make it . . . Linda . . .'

She couldn't think of the right words to comfort him.

'When's Ann coming?' he asked.

'I don't know, darling. It might be awhile. You can't always get a flight out to the coast after midnight.'

He groaned and closed his eyes while Linda held his hand in mute, helpless sympathy.

A half-hour later, Evie was wheeled past them on the way to surgery.

When the swift little jet carrying Ann and Adam touched down at Oakland Airport, a car was waiting to rush them to the hospital, where a nurse told them that Evie was being operated on.

'Why don't you go down the hall to the waiting room,' the nurse said, looking curiously at Adam. 'Her father is there.'

Brushing off Adam's hand, Ann ran down the hall. As she rounded the corner, she saw Phillip's familiar silhouette outlined against the window. Without thinking, she flew across the space separating them and into his arms. At that moment, it was as though the word divorce had never been mentioned. They were Evie's parents and no one else could share their grief.

Linda and Adam watched uneasily, knowing that under the circumstances to feel jealous was inappropriate, but unable to entirely help themselves. Finally Adam walked over to Linda, extended his hand, and said, 'Hello. You must be Linda Holt. I'm Adam Gayne.' They sized each other up with polite curiosity.

Phillip had gently seated Ann in a chair and explained what had happened as unemotionally as possible. When he finished, Ann shook her head in disbelief. 'Evie? Our daughter? It's impossible. I've talked with her almost every day since Christmas.'

'I have too, Ann – and I've had no idea that anything was wrong. Darling, I wish it weren't true – but it is.'

Ann burst into tears. 'Oh, God, Phillip – it's my fault. I've been in New York enjoying myself while she needed me here.'

'It's not your fault—' he began, but Ann interrupted him.

'Yes, it is. I knew how miserable she was over the divorce, but as soon as she seemed to settle down at school, I went off to New York and abandoned her. So maybe we sheltered Evie more than we should have when she was younger. But what good does it do to say that now? The fact is that ever since you found Linda, and I found Adam, we left Evie without anyone to turn to.'

Phillip felt the truth of her words like a blow. All he could do was gently pat Ann's hand until she stopped weeping. Oddly enough, now that they had both fallen in love with other people, they were able to give each other the emotional support they needed. While they were living together, Phillip's suppressed anger at Ann had been so great that he hadn't been able to find a place in his heart for her. Now there was no longer any reason for hostility, and they were able to share their common burden of sorrow.

It was awhile before they realized they weren't alone, and Ann went over to sit by Adam.

'I'll do anything, Lord, anything,' she prayed. 'Just save her.'

It seemed an eternity before the doors opened and Dr. Neilson appeared. Sighing tiredly, he said, 'It looks as if Evie's going to pull through, but I'm sorry to say that we had to perform a hysterectomy. There was infection developing in the damaged tissue.'

For the moment, Ann and Phillip brushed the implications aside. All that mattered was that Evie would live.

After she had come out of the anesthesia, they were allowed to see her for a few minutes. Still groggy, she murmured, 'Mom . . . Dad . . . What are you doing here?'

After she had been taken back to intensive care, where she would probably have to stay for several days, Adam turned to Ann and said firmly, 'Come on, now, darling. Time for you to get some rest. The doctors say she's out of danger.'

Ann refused to go far, so they ended up at a chop-house on San Pablo Avenue.

'Not the best.' Adam held up the stained menu and grimaced. 'But food is food.'

He ordered eggs, French toast, juice and coffee for the two of them. 'You need to keep your strength up, for Evie's sake. Remember, you had no sleep last night.'

Ann managed to swallow a few bites, but was too upset to finish.

'What are you going to do, Adam?'

'What do you want me to do, sweetheart?'

'You have to get back to work, don't you?'

'Not if you need me, I don't.'

Though neither would say so, both knew that his presence was superfluous. Now that Evie was through the crisis, her mother would have to stay with her, and

314

Adam knew that Evie would not want him there.

'Look, Adam.' Ann tried to choose her words care fully. 'I know you've taken off a lot of time since Christmas. Perhaps you should go back. It's not that I don't want you here, but—'

'I understand.'

'You'll call me, won't you?' she asked.

'Of course, sweetheart. Every day. And I'll pray for Evie's speedy recovery.'

They checked back at the hospital to learn that Evie was sleeping peacefully. Ann accompanied Adam to the airport. There was note of desperation in her farewell. 'I love you,' she whispered as she kissed him.

Back at the hospital, Ann felt a stab of jealousy when she saw Phillip and Linda seated close by each other. They were still together. Then guilt overwhelmed her again. *It's only right that I feel lonely. This is God's way of punishing me for being so happy. Decent women don't run off and abandon their children.* Much as she loved Adam, at that moment Ann wished that she had never met him.

Late that afternoon, one of the doctors told the weary trio that Evie was doing much better. 'There's no reason you can't all go home and get a little rest. She's out of the woods now.'

Linda took Phillip aside. 'Honey, you heard the doctor. Won't you please come home and get some rest? You can have a shower and some supper. I'll run you back to the hospital later. Okay?'

'I suppose I should,' he said, looking at Ann. Linda followed his gaze. Ann looked so pitifully alone.

Impulsively, Linda said, 'I know that your house isn't open. Would you like to come back with Phillip and me? I could make some dinner and you're very welcome to stay with us.'

Ann was touched. It was an extraordinarily kind and generous offer. But after a moment's thought she replied, 'That's very sweet of you, Linda, and I appreciate it. But I think it will be easiest all around if I just take a suite at the Claremont. That way I'll be close to the hospital and I won't be a bother to anyone.'

'Of course, if you prefer. But can Phillip and I drive you? We have our car here.'

'I'd appreciate that, Linda. I'm exhausted.'

At the Claremont, Phillip helped Ann with her bags. Then he said quietly, 'Evie's going to be all right now. Try to get some rest. And, Ann – please call if you need anything. Even if you just need to talk.'

Almost too weary to reply, Ann smiled weakly. 'Thanks, Phillip.' He was so sweet, so kind. She wondered tiredly how the two of them had been so angry with each other.

Later that evening she went back one final time to see Evie. The anesthetic had worn off, but the other pain medication made her very sleepy. After murmuring, 'Hello, Mom . . .' she fell back asleep holding Ann's hand.

Ann felt someone tap her shoulder, and the nurse said gently, 'I'm afraid you're going to have to leave now.'

As she was leaving the hospital, Ann was startled to see Leslie and Kim standing out in front.

'Hello, girls,' she said wearily.

Phillip had told her of the role Evie's roommates had played in getting the back-alley abortion, and Ann couldn't help feeling that if it hadn't been for them, Evie would have probably come to her with her problem. On the other hand, she told herself, if the girls hadn't discovered Evie when they did and called the ambulance, Evie might have bled to death.

'How is she, Mrs. Coulter?' Kim asked timidly.

'They had to operate, but she seems to be improving. If all goes well, they'll move her into a private room tomorrow. You'll be allowed to visit then.'

'That's terrific!' Leslie said. 'When do they think she'll be able to come back to school?'

'I don't know. I expect she'll need to convalesce for a while.'

Then she faced the girls squarely. 'Leslie, Kim: I'm

not blaming you for what you did. Evie's a big girl, and responsible for her own actions. But do you know why she didn't tell me she was in trouble? She must have known I would do anything I could to help her.'

They looked at each other uncertainly before answering. Finally, Kim said, 'Mrs. Coulter, I don't think Evie herself knew for very long. But you and Mr. Coulter had your own problems, and she probably didn't think it was fair to burden you with hers.'

'Then why did she go to an incompetent butcher? Surely she could have found a better man.'

Kim realized she was being backed into a corner. She thought quickly and replied: 'Evie would have been afraid to go to a reputable doctor, even out of town. He might have said something to someone. The one in Oakland wouldn't dare. Don't forget, Mrs. Coulter, you and your family aren't exactly unknown around here – your pictures have been in a lot of local newspapers and magazines – and in other parts of the country, too.' She paused, then sighed. 'If you insist on knowing the truth, Mrs. Coulter, Evie was afraid of compromising you.'

But Ann knew what the whole truth was. She suddenly pictured Evie, alone with her burden of guilt, convinced that both her parents had abandoned her. No wonder she had jumped at the first solution that was proposed to her. Ann's eyes filled with tears. She turned her head away and whispered, 'I deserted you . . .'

The next day Evie was transferred to a private room. When Ann arrived, carrying flowers, her daughter was sitting up in bed. Evie made things easy for her. 'You know, don't you, Mom?' she whispered.

'Yes, honey – the doctor told me.'

'I'm sorry.'

Ann put her arms around her daughter and drew her close. 'I'm the one who's sorry. I wasn't there when you needed me.'

317

'No, Mom, don't say that. It was my fault.'

Evie seemed fairly composed, and Ann suspected that the doctors hadn't mentioned the hysterectomy.

They were allowed only a short time together. Afterward Ann sought out Dr. Neilson.

'You haven't told her yet, have you?'

'I wanted to wait a day or so until she's a little stronger.'

'Well, let me know when you plan to speak to her. Her father and I should be here. I'm afraid she's going to be very upset.'

'Yes, it's a difficult thing for a young girl to accept.' He shook his head. 'Such a pity. Well, if you can come in tomorrow morning, I'll tell her at ten.'

The following day, Ann and Phillip paced the hall anxiously while Dr. Neilson spoke to Evie for what seemed a long time.

Finally, he emerged, his face set. 'I've told her,' he said. 'I'm afraid she's not taking it well. You'd better go in.'

She was sitting up, staring out the window.

'Evie, darling?'

There was no response. 'Evie!' Phillip cried. 'Sweetheart, say something.'

He walked over and stood in her line of vision, but she still remained mute.

Ann bent over and stroked Evie's forehead. 'We know about the hysterectomy and we're very sorry. But it's not the end of the world. You're alive and that's the important thing.'

Evie still remained silent. Phillip cajoled and begged her to speak to them, but Evie acted as if she didn't hear. It was as though she were in trance.

Finally, Ann looked up and whispered, 'Phillip, I'm scared. I'm going to get Neilson.'

She went to the front desk and had the operator page the doctor. 'What did you tell that girl?' Ann almost shouted when he appeared. 'She seems practically catatonic.'

318

'Mrs. Coulter, please calm down. All I told Evie was the plain truth: that we had to perform a hysterectomy on her.'

'How did she react?'

'Well, she was pretty calm at first, asking what that meant.'

'And?'

'I told her that of course she couldn't bear any children of her own, but that there wouldn't be any other side effects. Then I started to tell her that many couples adopt children. But she didn't seem to be listening to me so I decided she needed time to get used to the idea and left.'

'Well, what should we do? You saw her. We can't leave her like this!'

'I'm afraid that psychological problems aren't my province. But I can refer you to a psychiatrist.'

A psychiatrist . . . Evie? The idea of Evie having mental problems was as unreal as all the other events of the past days. But there appeared to be no alternative.

A short while later, a pleasant-looking middle-aged man appeared and introduced himself as Dr. Frankel.

Phillip and Ann waited while Frankel introduced himself to the still silent Evie. Then he turned and spoke softly. 'It would be best if you waited outside.'

After a little while they heard Evie's voice rise shrilly, then the sounds of sobs. Phillip was just about to charge in when Frankel came out. 'I'm going to prescribe a sedative. She's hysterical.'

'Can we see her?'

'It would be best if you didn't for the moment. Tomorrow she will hopefully be calmer and we can discuss what treatment she should have.'

Ann and Phillip left and Evie sank into a drugged sleep. But early the next morning the sedative began to wear off. Evie woke with the doctor's words ringing in her ears: 'You won't be able to bear children, Evie. I'm sorry. . .'

It was like a death sentence. All her hopes and

dreams for her future were bound up in marriage and family – a big, happy home filled with children. An only child, she had always longed for brothers and sisters and she and Peter wanted at least four kids. Now she had not only lost Peter, she would never have children at all. She was no longer a woman. She was an empty shell.

She lay in bed for a while, going over the events leading up to the abortion. She couldn't absolve herself. Abruptly, she came to a decision.

Swinging her legs from the bed, still woozy from the sedative, she stumbled to the bathroom. Picking up the water glass, she brought it down viciously on the rim of the basin. Glass fragments sprayed the floor, leaving the jaggedly broken base in her hand.

She gritted her teeth and with two quick, decisive movements she slashed her left wrist, then her right, with long, lengthwise strokes. As the blood spurted, she was overcome with nausea. The glass dropped from her fingers as she slowly crumpled to the floor.

It was the sheerest luck that the floor nurse checked Evie's room a few minutes later. Evie was not in her bed and the nurse looked in the half-open door of the bathroom. A glance told her what had happened. She rushed to the door and called, 'Sandy – STAT!'

The LVN ran in and gasped at the sight. 'Oh, Jesus – I'll call the resident.'

Within seconds, the doctor arrived. 'Tell surgery we're bringing her up.'

'I already have, doctor,' the nurse said.

She had stopped the flow, but Evie was unconscious from shock and loss of blood. For several desperate minutes the resident was afraid they were too late. There was an agonizing delay before the nurse could start the IV, but finally she said, 'The pulse is steadier.'

The doctor heaved a sigh of relief. 'Okay. Now let's get her onto a gurney.'

Once again, Evie was raced down the hall and through the white-enameled doors.

*

When Evie woke, she was completely disoriented. She tried to look around in the dim light. She was in a small, bare room. The windows were shadowed by narrow bars. It was dark outside, and she didn't know what time of day it was.

I want to get out of here.

She tried to scream, but her throat was tight and sore, and all that emerged was a hoarse croak. She couldn't seem to move her arms. Then she realized that her wrists were heavily bandaged, and memories flooded back. Dr. Neilson . . . the hysterectomy.

Why didn't they let me die?

When the nurse opened the door, the shaft of light from the corridor blinded her for an instant. She heard Ann's voice.

'Evie, darling . . . Daddy and I have been waiting to see you. You've been asleep for a long time.'

If I pretend to be asleep, they'll go away.

This time Phillip spoke. 'Evie, sweetheart – Mommy and I want you to know how much we love you.'

She felt her father's presence close to her and tried to turn away as his lips brushed her cheek.

'I suppose you don't feel much like talking,' Ann said, 'but Daddy and I will be here, so you just tell the nurse when you want to see us.' She touched Evie's shoulder hesitantly. 'We love you so much, honey.'

The next week was like a nightmare for Phillip and Ann. Evie had been moved to the psychiatric unit at Herrick, where the halls resounded with moans and screams. Evie, by contrast, remained mute.

Linda had to return to work, so Ann and Phillip kept up the vigil alone. Adam sent Evie huge bunches of flowers every day and called Ann every night for news. But all Ann could tell him was, 'She's no better. They're suggesting that she go to a sanatorium.'

'Will you send her?'

'We have no choice. I'd open up the house and take care of her at home, but Frankel feels that would be counterproductive.' She paused. 'Adam, darling, I'm really sorry to be away so long. But I just don't feel I can leave Evie.'

'I wouldn't dream of asking you to leave at a time like this. Now tell me, where's she going to be staying? In the city?'

'No, Doctor Frankel has recommended a place up north called Rolling Hills.'

'Okay. I'll tell you what I'm going to do. I'll take a suite of rooms for us at the Huntington. You can stay there and I'll fly out as often as I can.'

'Oh, Adam, could you? You're sure it won't be too hard on you? Can you leave your office? God knows my business is barely surviving. If it weren't for May, I'd have to close up completely. I've been neglecting it so.'

'My office will be just fine if I take off long weekends,' said Adam. 'Don't worry about me. Just take care of yourself.'

'I love you, Adam,' Ann said, 'and I'm too selfish to tell you not to come.'

So Adam took a suite in the Huntington and arranged to be in San Francisco from Friday morning to Sunday afternoon. He was at the stage in his career where a great deal of routine work could be delegated, so some weeks he even stayed longer.

Forty-Three

Evie was installed in a private room at Rolling Hills, and for a nerve-racking week, Phillip and Ann were not allowed to visit her. When they finally entered the pleasant nursing home surrounded by beautifully kept gardens, they were appalled by her appearance. She was incredibly thin. The nurse told them that she simply refused to eat.

She was no longer catatonic, but she seemed distant, detached from everything. Although she responded politely and intelligently to her parents' questions, her eyes remained vacant. Phillip and Ann deluged Dr.

Frankel with questions, but all he would say was that Evie's recovery would take time, and they would have to be patient.

One evening when Adam was in San Francisco, Ann came back to their suite, crying. 'Oh, Adam – she's never going to get better!'

He gathered her into his arms. 'Of course she will,' he said firmly. 'She's basically very healthy. This was just too much for her to take all at once. She'll come out of it. You'll see.'

Across town, Phillip and Linda were also discussing Evie. 'Ann agrees with Frankel – that we should go to see Evie only once a week, but I told her that we should go every other day. I don't care what Frankel says – she's my daughter and I think I know her best.'

He looked up. 'Do you need another drink? Oh . . . you've already got one.'

'While you were talking.'

'I'm sorry, honey. I know I've been going on and on. But it was really rough today because Frankel wanted to limit our visits.'

'Ours? Yours and Ann's?' Linda asked slowly.

'Well, yes, honey. At this stage it seems best that we go see her together.'

'And just where do I fit in?'

Phillip didn't seem to notice the edge in her voice. 'What do you mean, honey? At this point she's not seeing any visitors.'

'That's just what I mean, Phillip. Visitors – outsiders. I suppose it's natural that you and Ann need to support each other, but I'm beginning to wonder what role I play.'

'What role? Linda, you can't resent my time with Ann while Evie's so sick!'

'I don't, Phillip. It's just that I feel so helpless. I can't do anything for you and I can't do anything for Evie. When we fell in love, I thought we were going to be partners – sharing the bad times as well as the good.'

'That's what I want, Linda.'

'Well, it doesn't seem like it!' Linda cried, all the frustrations of the last few weeks finally exploding. 'You see your wife constantly, your daughter doesn't want to see me, and I feel as if I have no part in your life!'

'I love you,' Phillip said evenly, 'but for the time being I have to put Evie's needs ahead of yours and mine.'

'That's obvious.'

'For God's sake, Linda! We're talking about Evie's future. She tried to commit suicide! What kind of parent would I be if I turned my back on her now?'

'Phillip, I've tried to understand, I really have. Maybe it's because I never had children of my own, but it seems to me as if there's never going to be room in your life for anyone except Evie. And I just can't take it, Phillip!' She buried her face in her hands.

The sound of her bitter words lingered in the silent room. Phillip was unable to reply. A part of him cried out that if she left he would lose the only person in the world who could make him happy. He wanted to tell her that she would always come first. But was that really true? No one would ever come before Evie in his heart. Perhaps if this crisis hadn't happened, he would never have faced the issue, but it had and now it was too late. Linda would either have to accept the situation as it was – even his need to see Ann until Evie was better – or they could not continue together. It was up to Linda to decide.

Quietly, he asked, 'Shall I move my things out?'

She smiled sadly. 'That won't be necessary. I think I'll be going back to Washington. I got a job offer there a few weeks ago.'

'Linda—' Phillip moved toward her, but she stepped away.

'No, Phillip. Don't touch me. I don't think I could bear it.'

'It's a funny thing about love,' he said. 'It's the most fragile thing in the world. Like a soap bubble, lovely, buoyant. And then one day it bursts and it's as though it never existed.'

*

324

Three weeks later Phillip stood at the window of the air terminal, watching Linda's plane taxi into position on the runway. For a short while he'd had a glimpse of Eden. Now it was lost to him forever. He waited until the plane disappeared into the distance, then turned and walked back to his car.

It was late in May when Dr. Frankel asked Ann and Phillip to stop by his office after seeing Evie.

'Evie's problem is not just what happened with the abortion,' he said. 'It's become obvious in therapy that your separation traumatized her badly. As an only child, she derived a great part of her identity from her family. First her grandfather died. Then Phillip moved out and she learned you were both in love with other people. According to Evie, she had never heard so much as a cross word between the two of you. She thought that you were the happiest couple in the world.'

The doctor spread his palms expressively. 'She now says she has lost not only the close family she thought she had, but also her chance to have a family of her own. She believes she has nothing left to live for.'

'Will she get better, doctor?' Phillip inquired huskily.

'I still expect her to recover, but I'm afraid it's going to take some time to work through her problems. It's very important for you to continue to see her together. It gives her a sense of stability. And it would probably be best to avoid mentioning your other – interests – around her.'

Ann and Phillip were silent on the ride home, each lost in thought. Phillip was full of self-recriminations. He was the one who had started all this. But Ann couldn't face the implications of Frankel's analysis of the situation – that Evie was devastated because her mother and father had found other partners. She loved Evie with all her heart, but how could she contemplate life without Adam?

What if it came down to choosing between the two? What then?

Over the next months Ann felt as if she were living in limbo. It was even harder on Adam, for the constant flying back and forth had exhausted even his almost boundless vitality, and San Francisco simply wasn't his city. His social life – and his business life – were in Manhattan.

Although he did his best to be sympathetic, Ann's constant anxiety was a terrible strain on him. She was so emotionally drained by her daughter's condition that she had very little feeling for anyone else. Many nights she was too tired to make love, and Adam started to skip his weekend flights to San Francisco to see her.

But Ann was too depressed to protest.

One morning she woke up and immediately felt even worse than usual. For a moment she couldn't understand why. Then she remembered: it was September 9, Evie's birthday. And it had been six months since Evie had had the abortion. She rolled close to Adam, grateful for his presence.

'Morning, sweetheart,' he murmured.

Ann said nothing, then: 'It's Evie's birthday.'

He was fully awake now. 'So you're going up there to see her?'

'Later. When Phillip can get away from work.'

Adam digested this announcement in silence, refraining from suggesting that he go along. He had stopped questioning Ann on this point, since it was obvious that Evie didn't want to see him. At first he told himself that this was temporary, that when Evie got well, she would not only be able to appreciate how happy her mother was with him, but also would come to like him for his own sake. But as time passed, it had become harder and harder to believe this. The brutal truth was that Ann's only child wanted no part of him.

As if guessing his thoughts, Ann said, 'Adam – I know what you're going through, too . . .'

He put his arms around her and held her close. But he couldn't banish the misgivings that were passing through his mind.

*

The cook at Rolling Hills had made Evie her favorite chocolate cake, and Ann and Phillip sang 'Happy Birthday.' They had brought a pile of gaily wrapped presents and Evie dutifully opened them.

There was a frilly new robe and nightgown, and several books, as well as cards from Leslie and Kim. Phillip had picked up an Imari ceramic cat contentedly curled up on its own satin pillow.

'A kitten,' Evie said softly. 'I've never had one.'

'Well, I know you can't have a real cat here, sweetheart.' Phillip smiled. 'So I thought you might like this.'

'Thanks, Dad,' Evie said, stroking the little figure as if it were real.

Then a look of infinite sadness crossed her face and her gaze returned to the window.

After leaving Evie, they insisted on seeing Dr. Frankel. With uncharacteristic irritation, Phillip refused a chair. 'Doctor Frankel, would you mind telling us just what you're doing to help Evie? It's been six months and I don't see any progress at all.'

The psychiatrist regarded Ann and Phillip thoughtfully, as though turning something over in his mind.

'We just would like some assurance that Evie is making progress,' Ann added.

Frankel seemed to come to a decision. 'Sit down please, Mr. Coulter.'

When Phillip had seated himself, the doctor continued. 'I'm going to tell you the conclusion I reached after many sessions with Evie. She is a lovely, bright girl, but very sensitive and perhaps not as resilient as she might be.

'There has been some progress. She is slowly overcoming her feelings of disgrace and shame. Time has softened the raw edges of the memory.

'Unfortunately, the central problem remains: Evie feels she's lost her place in the world. I cannot tell you how intensely she mourns the breakup of her family. Without that security in her life, I believe she doesn't want to get well. She knows that as long as she is like this, she can stay at Rolling Hills, where she's safe. And until we break that barrier, she simply is not going to get much better.'

'What can we do, doctor?' Ann asked, dreading his response.

'Well, I hate to suggest it, knowing your situation. But I think that if Evie saw the two of you together again, it might set her on the road to recovery.'

Neither Ann nor Phillip would look at each other.

'What do you mean, Doctor Frankel?' Ann asked sharply. 'Pretend that we aren't going to get a divorce after all?'

He nodded.

'For how long?' she cried.

'For as long as it takes, Mrs. Coulter. I wouldn't have suggested such a course if I didn't think it was absolutely necessary. This episode was a serious trauma for Evie, and it hit her at a crucial stage in her development. What you do now may affect her for the rest of her life.'

'But, doctor . . .' Phillip began.

'Can't you, as parents, put your personal lives aside for the time being? For the sake of your daughter?'

They stared at him helplessly. What choice did they have? Phillip knew that for him it would be no hardship. But as for Ann . . . He knew how happy she was with Adam, but Gayne didn't look like the kind of man who could be put off indefinitely. How would he react to Ann's moving back in with Phillip?

'Phillip?' she begged him for a solution.

'It's up to you, Ann.'

She nodded and turned back to Frankel. 'All right. When do you suggest we tell Evie?'

'The sooner the better. Right now, if you like.'

As Phillip and Ann walked back down the hall to Evie's room, Ann felt as if she were marching to her death. She couldn't allow herself time to think. Once they had told Evie, she would have no chance to reconsider.

Evie was surprised to see her parents back. She listened quietly as Phillip started to talk. But when he said, '. . . and so, you see, your mother and I have decided to move back into the house,' she interrupted him eagerly.

'You're getting back together? You're not going to get a divorce after all! Oh, Dad, Mom – I can't believe it – you're both terrific! I love you!'

Hugging her daughter, Ann thought, *Adam – forgive me. I had no other choice.*

As they were leaving, she said, 'We'll be back to see you as soon as we can, darling. Remember: we both love you very much.'

In the car she asked, 'What do we do now, Phillip?'

He sighed. 'I wasn't going to tell you this yet, but Linda and I have broken up. She couldn't stand the strain of living with me while Evie was so sick.'

'Oh, Phillip' – Ann paused awkwardly – 'was it just Evie? Don't lie . . . please.'

'Evie . . . and other things. The situation.'

'You mean your spending so much time with me. Phillip – I'm sorry.'

He shrugged. 'Well, it's over now. She's back in D.C.'

'I wondered why she never seemed to answer anymore.'

Phillip cleared his throat. 'And what about you? How's Adam going to take this?'

'I don't know. So far he's been very understanding – wonderful, in fact. But I'm afraid he's not going to like this idea one little bit.'

Phillip hesitated, then said, 'Ann, if you'd like me to, I could go see him. Try to explain that this little charade is for the sake of our daughter, that you and I aren't going to—'

'No! Don't do that. Thanks, but it wouldn't help. I'll just have to try to make him understand.'

Adam's eyes were dark and unreadable as he paced the living room. 'Let's hear this once again. You're moving

329

back in with your husband? For how long, if I dare ask?'

'I don't know, Adam. Until Evie is okay, I guess.'

'That's pretty nebulous, isn't it?' His voice rose angrily. 'What you are proposing is that we simply put our relationship on hold until some unknown date when Evie recovers. Is that it?'

'Adam, you don't understand. Phillip and I aren't going to live together in any real sense. It's just that for our daughter's sake we have to pretend to be reconciled. Until she's strong enough to face reality on her own.'

'Come on, Ann. Be serious. We're adults now. Christ! Do you actually think I'm going to spend my nights lurking under your balcony, waiting for you to come to the window, like a character in some old Spanish play?'

'Adam, please try to understand. It won't be forever. Frankel says that Evie is already improved. It can't be that long.'

Adam took a deep breath as he fought for control. He was fed up with the situation already, but had hoped it was nearing an end. Now it would get even worse. He wanted to scream, *To hell with your precious sick daughter! Think about me for a change.* The idea of Ann sharing a house – if not a bed – with Phillip made him nauseated. He wanted to strike someone; kill someone. But he couldn't give up Ann.

'All right. All right. You win,' he told her in an even voice. 'But I've waited a long time for you. And I'm running out of patience . . .'

The next day Ann called Consuela. The previous year, when Ann had announced her intention of selling the house, Consuela had moved in with her sister in Sacramento, but she readily agreed to come back to the Coulters'. Within three days she had opened the house, aired the rooms, made up the beds, and stocked the pantry.

Phillip moved out of Linda's now empty apartment. He moved his clothes back into his spacious dressing room, where a single bed had been installed.

The day they picked up Evie was brisk and sunny, without a cloud in sight. They waited while she bade goodbye to the smiling nurses and to Dr. Frankel, whom she had come to love and trust. Phillip carried her suitcase out to the old Chrysler station wagon and they drove southward toward San Francisco and home.

On the way, they stopped off in Sausalito and had a seafood lunch at a restaurant that overlooked the Bay. An old favorite of Evie's.

Watching her parents over the lunch table, Evie wondered fleetingly what had become of Linda and Adam, but was afraid to bring up the subject. *If Mom and Dad are getting back together, they've broken up with their lovers.* There could be no other explanation. *But was it for my sake?* The thought was intolerable. Evie tried to study their faces as they walked to the parking lot, but all she could detect was their delight in having her back with them. *No, it couldn't have been for me. They've come to their senses, that's all. They know that we belong together, the three of us, just like it's always been . . .*

Like all human beings, Evie believed what she wanted to believe. Phillip and Ann still loved each other. They had learned from their folly. If she had been the catalyst, so much the better.

Moving back into their house as though nothing had happened proved much harder than either Phillip or Ann had expected. Phillip had to renounce any ideas he might have had about following Linda to Washington, while Ann detested having to sneak calls to Adam and seeing him for a brief hour when he flew in for the weekend. And there was always the terrible risk of discovery.

The first few weeks, Evie seemed unwilling to let her mother out of her sight and followed her about the house like a two-year-old. Then, just as Ann had decided that Evie was worse than she had been at the sanatorium, she suddenly seemed to get better. She began going out, called her friends, and made plans to go back to school the following semester.

Ann began to hope again that she could resume her life with Adam. As a temporary measure she asked Frankel if Evie was well enough for Ann to spend a week in New York. She had some pressing business.

Frankel told her that it might actually be good for Evie – and of course Phillip was there if the girl needed anything.

Ann thanked God for Frankel's blessings. By now she was desperate to see Adam and reassure herself that he still loved her.

Forty-Four

Adam met her plane, but during the ride into Manhattan both of them felt far too inhibited to say more than a few polite words. Each was afraid of wounding the other; of opening a breach that might never be closed. For a moment Ann wondered if coming to New York was a mistake. She remembered his cold anger. Did she dare bring up the subject of Evie? She didn't ask him where they were headed, but knew it was his apartment. She was almost afraid.

As soon as he had closed the door behind them, he took her in his arms and kissed her. Still not daring to speak, they went into the bedroom.

Afterward, Ann turned toward him and sighed. 'I must be depraved. No one could want a man as much as I want you.'

He kissed her gently on her shoulder. 'Ann . . . You can't imagine how I've missed you. I know you've got plenty of burdens already, but I can't take this separation much longer.'

'I promise you – it will be over soon.' At that moment, lying in his arms, if he had ordered her to abandon her daughter and move in with him, she would have said yes. But he didn't. She dug her fingers into his wrist. 'Love me, Adam.'

As their week together wore on, they could feel the tension building. Neither Ann nor Adam had so much as mentioned Evie's name, but the sick girl was like a third presence on their shopping excursions, in the restaurants and theater, and even in bed.

Their conversation grew increasingly guarded lest the forbidden subject somehow be raised.

When they kissed goodbye at the airport, Adam said, 'Ann – I mean it. This can't go on much longer.'

Her eyes were filled with tears as she clung to him. 'It won't – I swear it.'

Neither Phillip nor Evie asked Ann much about her week in New York, and life continued as before. Every day Phillip and Ann told each other that their daughter was looking more like her old self. But they weren't really convinced. Even though Evie was seeing some of her old friends, and Frankel had cut her sessions to one a week, Evie experienced moments of panic and withdrawal, and sometimes she became very nervous when either Ann or Phillip mentioned leaving the house for any length of time. She frequently cried late at night, and she refused to mention Peter. Ann read the latter as an especially unhealthy sign.

Peter himself had realized after the terrible New Year's Eve party that he had behaved very badly. But wasn't Evie at least partially responsible? She had consistently refused to consider him more important than her parents' marital squabbles, so how much could she have ever really cared for him? She had thrown a drink in his face. And then one day she had told him bluntly that she didn't love him anymore. What more proof did he need?

Nonetheless, when he heard that Evie was sick and had dropped out of school, his old affection for her had overcome his pride. He had sent her flowers and cards. He had even finally written her letters, begging her forgiveness and asking if there were some way they could work things out.

But there had been no reply, and as time passed, Peter decided that her silence meant that what she had said was true: she didn't love him. Still, he begged Leslie and Kim to tell him how to contact her. When they refused, he finally gave up and flung himself into his studies. He was graduated magna cum laude, and various engineering firms bid for his services. For most of the summer, he flew all over the country on interviews, and in September he had finally accepted an offer from Bechtel. As he was signing the contract, he wondered again if he could see Evie at least once before his new firm sent him overseas. He cornered Kim one last time and dragged the information out of her. 'She's not back at school, Peter. She's . . . ill.'

'Still? What in God's name is wrong with her?'

His voice was so anguished that Kim felt herself weakening. After all, this was Peter, whom Evie had been so crazy about. She took his hand and said quietly, 'She's not physically ill, Peter. She's been . . . depressed. She was in a sanatorium.'

Peter was staggered. All this time he had been trying to harden his heart against Evie, calling her immature and fickle, while she was in fact alone and desperately ill.

'You said was. Where is she now?'

'Well, the Coulters have gotten back together and Evie is staying with them at the old house.'

'Do you think she would see me?'

Kim hesitated, not wanting to hurt him. She didn't think Evie would ever be able to face Peter again, let alone tell him the truth.

'I don't know, Peter. Maybe, just maybe. It might be worth a try.'

The next day he parked his old Corvette across the street from the Coulters'. Maybe she really didn't love him, but if that were so, he was going to hear it once again from her own lips before he left for overseas.

Taking a deep breath, he pressed the bell. Consuela opened the door and looked him up and down critically.

'Is Evie home?'

'She's home, but I don't know if she's seeing anyone today—'

She started to close the door, but Peter stuck his foot out, stopping her. 'I think she'll see me, Consuela. I'll announce myself.'

He was already past her when he saw Ann coming down the stairs.

'Peter – I'm so happy to see you!' she said, extending her hand. 'I suppose you want to see Evie.'

He nodded.

'Well, you'd better come into the drawing room so we can talk a little first. Tell me what you've been doing, Peter.'

'Well, aside from agonizing over Evie, I've been hired by Bechtel. They're sending me to Norway on a year-long project. I'll be leaving next month and I couldn't go without trying to straighten things out with Evie. Do you know why she never answered my letters?'

'Peter, you have to understand,' Ann began uncomfortably. 'Evie has been very ill. She had a nervous breakdown. And the doctor said it was best that we not give her any of your mail. Please . . . try to understand.'

Peter's expression betrayed his horror and incomprehension. 'Mrs. Coulter – why didn't you call me? I had a right to know. Evie wasn't just a casual date – we'd talked about getting married.'

At that moment it dawned on Ann how selfish she and Phillip had been in their preoccupation with Evie. Not once had they considered the feelings of this young man.

'Peter – I don't know what to say. Forgive me. I knew how Evie felt about you, but she was so ill . . . so unhappy. We were half out of our minds with worry and we could only think about protecting her. We were wrong. Can you forgive us?'

Peter's expression softened. 'Mrs. Coulter, there's nothing to forgive. Just tell me how she is. When can I see her?'

Ann reflected as she studied his face. *That's a good question, Peter. When?*

Peter was too distracted to notice that Ann was obviously at the breaking point herself. After the first elation of having Evie home again had faded, she had to acknowledge that her daughter's recovery would be a longer process than she had anticipated, and the strain had gotten worse rather than better.

The decision seemed to come from nowhere: at that moment Ann knew that neither Evie nor herself could continue to keep the world from Evie's door.

She turned to Peter and smiled. 'Peter . . . I'll go tell Evie that you're here.'

Her legs almost gave way as she marched up the staircase, went into the library, and found the packet of Peter's cards and letters. She pulled out the most recent one and went to Evie's room.

Evie looked up from her bed listlessly. Her breakfast tray lay untouched beside her. 'What is it, Mom?'

Ann took a deep breath. 'Peter is downstairs.'

Evie pushed the tray to the floor. 'No! I don't want him here. Tell him to leave!'

In that split second, Ann realized that if there was any hope for her daughter at all, this would be the turning point. Evie would have to confront the events that had led to her illness. Relying on her instincts, which had stood her in such good stead over the years, she took Evie by the shoulders and held her still while she said, 'It's going to be all right, Evie. You must trust me – it's going to be all right.'

Evie got up, adjusted her robe, and sat down in a wing chair facing her mother.

'Evie,' Ann continued, 'I want you to know how much your father and I love you. But the truth is that we are no longer the basis of your problem. You have to stop blaming yourself for what happened. Until you do, you will never get well. And seeing Peter now is part of getting well. You don't have to marry him, sweetheart – just face the past so you can get on with the rest of your life. Your father and I will support any decision you make. But give him – and yourself – a chance.'

She handed the thick envelope to Evie and held her breath as her daughter slowly extracted the closely written sheets and started to read.

The first few pages were conventional enough – news of school and the fraternity, expressions of sympathy for her illness. Then she turned to the final page.

... Evie, darling, I have been debating whether or not to try once again with you. For months I've fought this battle within myself. But no matter how hard I try, I can't stop loving you. Is there still any chance for me?

I tell myself that you made it perfectly clear that it was over as far as you were concerned. But somehow I just can't believe it. It was so right between us, wasn't it?

I knew from the very first moment I saw you that day on the campus. And I was so happy when you said that you loved me too. It just seems impossible that love like ours could die.

No matter what has happened between us, Evie, I still love you with all my heart.

Is there any possibility that I could see you? If the answer is no, I won't force myself on you. But I'm hoping that the answer will be yes.

Love,
Peter

Ann waited, watching Evie's face. By the time Evie finished reading Peter's letter, tears were pouring down her cheeks. Every word underlined Peter's steadfast, unselfish love – a love of which she was totally unworthy.

Finally Evie looked up and said, 'I'll see him, Mom.'

Peter shot up the stairs three at a time. When he saw how thin and pale Evie was, he sobbed and covered his face with his hands.

'Evie, darling,' he said softly and took a step toward her.

'No, Peter! Don't come any closer!' She pulled her

337

robe tight around her body and shrank back into the chair.

'Evie, darling,' he repeated, in a daze. He looked into her wide, frightened eyes. Then, in spite of her protests, he picked her up from the chair and drew her close, cradling her like a child. Evie shuddered, then, in spite of herself, responded to the joy of being held by him again. The icy shell that had grown around her heart began to melt. He was so good, so strong . . . She had always felt so safe with him.

Then she remembered what she had done. She was sterile. Damaged goods. She had no claim on Peter and there was no future for them together. She pushed him away. 'Please leave now, Peter. Thank you for coming to see me.'

'Leave? I love you, Evie. What's happened? Evie – tell me!' His voice sounded almost angry now.

But Evie turned her back to him, unable to reply.

Peter could stand it no longer. Spinning her around, he caught her roughly in his arms. Throwing caution to the winds, he shouted, 'Evie, just what kind of a game are you playing? Are you going to tell me what's wrong or am I going to have to drag it out of you? Maybe you don't understand how many sleepless nights I've spent worrying about you. I asked around, but nobody would tell me anything about your illness. You just dropped out of my life. How the hell do you think I felt? But you're better now, so why can't we get together? Tell me.'

'All right, Peter. Just give me a minute. Please . . .' She looked out the window as she tried to collect her thoughts. It was too late to turn back now. She would tell him and he would leave. It had suddenly become much easier.

'I do love you, Peter. I always have. But I don't have the right to. Not after what happened.'

'Evie – how can you say that? How can you even think it?'

'I betrayed your trust. I didn't mean to – it just

338

happened. What I did can't be made right again.'

'Evie, I can't imagine one thing you could have done that I wouldn't forgive.'

She swallowed hard. 'Peter, this might be that one thing. Listen. Remember that New Year's Eve party . . .'

When she had told him everything, she was surprised to discover that she felt somehow relieved, even though she knew that Peter would despise her. She waited for his reaction, but he said nothing.

She took his hand. 'You must hate me.'

Peter finally collected his thoughts. He was furious, but not with Evie. It was Chuck who was to blame for taking advantage of Evie's loneliness and naiveté. And Peter blamed himself, too. He should have known better than to abandon Evie at a drunken party with a well-known operator like Swanson.

'I love you, Evie,' he said. 'And that's all that matters.'

She didn't have the courage to look directly at him. 'But Peter – don't you understand? We can't have children.'

'Evie . . . darling . . . it doesn't matter.'

'But we wanted a big family – remember?'

'I know, Evie. But if we feel like it, we can adopt. It's you I care about.'

Suddenly all the horror and anguish of the past seemed to vanish, and Evie almost laughed out loud at the thought that not so long ago she had wanted to die. Not only wanted to, but had actually tried to do something about it!

She turned to Peter: 'Peter, you step outside for a minute. I'm going to get dressed. It's almost time for lunch. I'll ask them to set an extra place . . .'

That afternoon, over coffee, they told Ann and Phillip that they wanted to get married before Peter was sent to Norway. 'I know it'll be a rush, Mom,' Evie said, 'but we just need a small wedding – family and a few friends.'

Ann was about to agree when she remembered that

339

her daughter was sick. Did her bright, hopeful eyes and suddenly glowing cheeks mean that she had already recovered? It all seemed so abrupt. Things were happening too fast . . .

'I do think you and Peter both should discuss your plans with Doctor Frankel. If he feels Evie is up to moving abroad, then you certainly have our blessing.'

Frankel's opinion was that marriage to the man she had always loved was just what Evie needed to complete her recovery. The only problem left was for her parents to tell Evie that they still planned to go ahead with the divorce. Surely now she had a stable and happy future of her own, she would no longer be so upset . . .

Ann agreed to be the one to talk to Evie the next day. That night she went to bed determined to make her daughter understand that her mother and father would always be there for her whether they lived together or apart.

When she was ready for bed she glanced at the clock. It was one o'clock in New York, but she was too excited to wait until morning to call Adam.

'Darling,' she said. 'I hope I didn't wake you, but—'

'What's wrong?' Adam asked, sitting bolt upright in bed and reaching for a cigarette.

'Nothing. Everything is wonderful. Evie's a thousand times better. And Adam, she's going to be married!' Adam didn't say a word. Their long separation was over. Ann could sell her business and move to New York.

'Adam, are you there?'

'Yes, darling. Tell me what happened.'

Ann told him about Peter's visit and ended by saying, 'I just thank God, Adam. You've been so patient. There were times I thought I'd lose you.'

'Never, Ann. You'll never lose me.'

'Darling, can you come to the wedding? It will be very soon since Peter has an assignment in Norway.'

'You know I'll come. But are you sure Evie will want me?'

'I'm positive, Adam.'

Ann wasn't quite as certain as she sounded.

The next morning she confronted Evie at breakfast.

'Evie, your father and I think you are well enough now to hear the truth. We still feel great affection for each other, but we are no longer in love with each other. If we had been, then there would have been no room in our lives for Linda or Adam. Do you understand what I'm saying, darling? We cannot choose who we will love. It just happens. And, Evie – just as you want to spend the rest of your life with Peter, I want to spend the rest of mine with Adam. Can you accept that, darling?'

Evie thought for a moment. She would have loved to have her parents spend the rest of their lives together. But her mother was right. On some level she had always known that the reconciliation had been a charade put on for her benefit.

'I think I can,' she said. 'I want you to be happy, Mom. And Adam is . . . attractive.'

Ann jumped up and kissed her daughter on the cheek. 'Thank you . . . thank you, Evie.'

The next three weeks passed in a frenzy of activity. Invitations had to go out, the wedding lunch planned, clothes bought to replace Evie's wardrobe, which despite a healthy weight gain was still too large.

Evie's dress arrived barely in time for the ceremony, but as Ann watched her twirl about in the eggshell lace, she thought her daughter couldn't look more beautiful if the dress had been designed with Evie in mind.

Kim and Leslie had arrived the night before, delighted to see their friend finally well and happy. They admired everything, particularly her handsome bridegroom, and they couldn't resist telling Evie how lucky she was to be getting such a gorgeous stepfather.

Tears had gathered in Evie's eyes. 'God, I don't know what I would have done without the two of you.' She tried to smile. 'You both look so beautiful today.'

Kim laughed. 'We do?' She took a closer look at

herself in the mirror. She was wearing a beautifully draped peach silk dress with a matching flowered hat her grandmother had bought in Paris in the thirties. As Grandma had always said, Lilly Daché certainly knew how to make a hat.

Next to her, Leslie appraised herself critically. Hyacinth blue was certainly her color. She looked more sophisticated than her two friends in her crepe sheath with a flapper-style ribbon around her head.

Smiling at each other, the three girls knew their love and friendship would last a lifetime.

In the space of a few short weeks, Evie had regained her bloom. As Ann stood drinking in her daughter's beauty she could not help remembering her own wedding back in the 1940s.

Ann had longed to be a bride in white, walking down the aisle to the *chuppa*, with yards and yards of floating train. And here Evie had chosen a wedding as simple as Ann's own had been. What irony.

The ceremony was in the rabbi's study. Vows were timeless but, as was common in the sixties, Evie and Peter read from *The Prophet* by Kahlil Gibran as part of the ceremony.

> *And stand together, yet not too near together:*
> *For the pillars of the temple stand apart,*
> *And the oak tree and the cypress grow not in*
> *each other's shadow.*

Adam was deeply, deeply touched by the beauty of those words. They were much more spiritual than any sermon could have been. Taking Ann's hand in his, he looked at her, his eyes filled with love. It was a moment so poignant, so full of hopes for their own future, that it was as though, standing here in this sacred place, their own union had already been blessed.

At the luncheon Ann and Ruthie smiled tearfully across the table, remembering Ruthie's wedding that long-ago spring.

'Who would ever have dreamed,' Ruthie said, 'that someday our children would marry?'

Looking past her to Phillip, Ann said a little sadly, 'We never know what will happen in our lives, Ruthie.'

After Evie and Peter cut the cake, Phillip got up to make a toast. 'To my son-in-law. I have already given you my most precious possession. Now I wish you all the happiness in the world.'

Later, when the newlyweds left for the airport to spend a few days in New York before flying to Oslo, Phillip watched Ann and Adam drive off. He wondered what had happened to all his dreams. His hopes of a brilliant legal career had faded years ago, and now he couldn't even look forward to a future that included Linda. He was happy Evie seemed so well, but as he drove home, he kept thinking of his own wedding day and all his bright expectations.

At the Fairmont, Ann and Adam were celebrating the fact that Ann was finally free. For the first time Adam pressed her to rush through her divorce.

'I've already spoken to Max Friedman about it. He doesn't think there will be any problem dividing our property, and Phillip won't obstruct proceedings in any way.'

'The only one you're going to have problems with is me. Because six months from now, I expect you to be a free woman.'

The next day, Phillip insisted on driving them to the airport. While Adam checked in, Ann and Phillip had a few minutes alone.

'Phillip, what are you going to do? Don't you think that you should call Linda?'

'Well, it's been a long time. I don't know if she'll want to see me.'

'I think you should try anyway. Women don't fall out of love that quickly. Besides, things have changed, haven't they?'

'Yes, that's true,' he said. 'I wonder . . .'

'Don't wonder. Just call.'

He looked at her with admiration. 'That's always been the difference between us, Ann, hasn't it? You're always willing to take a chance, and I always hesitate. Maybe this time I will take a leaf out of your book and phone her.'

'Phillip . . . do it,' Ann urged gently. 'I hope it works out for you.' Impulsively, she reached up and kissed his cheek. 'Goodbye, Phillip. I wish you all the luck in the world.'

Back in Ann's lovely house, which he knew would soon be going up for sale, Phillip decided to take her advice. He picked up the phone and dialed.

'Linda . . .?' There was a long silence when she recognized his voice. 'I know you weren't expecting to hear from me, but I had to call. I know you must still be angry, and you have every right to be. I'm not going to try to defend myself except to say that Evie was so ill. But the situation has changed. She's better now. In fact, yesterday she married her childhood sweetheart.'

'Phillip – I'm so happy for you.'

He took a deep breath and said in a rush, 'Linda, I still love you. Do you think there's a chance for us?'

'I'm not sure, Phillip. It was so hard leaving you. I've been numb for so long that I don't know what I feel anymore.'

'Is there someone else?'

'No, Phillip. There's no one. I just need time . . .'

'I understand. But could I fly out and see you in a couple of weeks?'

'I don't know.' She paused. 'Don't you see, Phillip? I couldn't bear to be hurt a second time.'

'But I can call you?'

'Yes – of course.'

'Tomorrow,' he promised.

That same evening Ann and Adam were dining at Lutèce. As they lingered contentedly over coffee and Cognac, Adam said, 'Darling, there's something I want you to have.'

And he took a small, velvet case from his pocket.

Inside was a Cartier diamond. He slipped the ring on her fourth finger. 'For my wife,' he said huskily.

That night was supreme.

It was six the next morning when Consuela's call wakened them. *Oh God – something's happened to Evie,* was Ann's first thought.

Her housekeeper's voice was shrill with fear. 'It's Mr. Coulter – he's had a stroke. A very bad one.'

Ann was shaking so hard that she almost dropped the phone. She suddenly knew that she was being punished for some terrible sin. She had been so incredibly happy these last weeks – and now this.

'Where is he, Consuela?' she said, finally recovering her voice.

'Mount Zion Hospital.'

'Have you reached Evie?'

'Yes. I called Peter. He said he'd tell her, and if you want, they'll fly home.'

'Listen, Consuela. You go stay with Mr. Coulter. I'll be there as soon as I can.' When she hung up, she was beyond tears.

Adam had already guessed the situation from hearing Ann's end of the conversation, but still he asked, dreading the answer. 'What is it, Ann?'

She didn't know how to tell him. Adam had stood by her so faithfully, but how much more would he be willing to take?

For the first time, she had a moment of doubt. Was she wrong for Adam? Here she was, bringing him so much unhappiness . . .

'Phillip had a stroke.'

Adam didn't answer. For the moment, all he felt was murderous rage.

'Adam – what should I do?'

'What should you do? Well, I'll tell you. Just pack your bags, call the airport, and fly home to your Phillip so you can play Florence Nightingale.'

'Adam . . . please.'

'So why are you waiting? You've already made up your mind, right?'

In misery, barely able to speak, Ann begged, 'Adam, please. Don't be angry. He doesn't have anyone else.'

In spite of his fury and disgust, Adam's heart went out to her. There was something about Ann that never failed to evoke his compassion – and his admiration. He knew that she was torn between her love for him and her sense of duty.

He sighed. 'All right, darling. Let's go. I'll take you to the airport.'

Forty-Five

When Ann saw Phillip at the hospital, she was horrified by his condition. He couldn't speak, and his left side was paralyzed. She sat by his bed and took his hand.

'Phillip, darling . . . I'm so sorry. It's all so unfair. I love you, Phillip, and I'm going to see to it that you're taken care of. You're not alone now.'

She remained by him until visiting hours had ended. Kenny and Ruth insisted that she stay at their place, and Ann was grateful for the invitation. To have been alone through all this would have been intolerable.

'I feel so bad for Evie,' Ann told Ruth the next morning. 'Even if Phillip's condition improves, I don't want her to come home. Her place is with Peter.'

Evie called later in the day, and Ann was heartened that she took the terrible news so calmly, saying that she would wait a day or two before deciding whether or not to fly to the West Coast.

But Ann had forgotten to notify one important person. In Washington, Linda was worried that Phillip hadn't called her. She knew him to be dependable and sensitive, not the sort to forget such things, and she guessed that something was wrong.

She waited one more day, then called his office. The call was transferred to Kenny.

'I'm sorry to have to be the one to tell you, Linda, but Phillip's had a stroke. The doctors hope that with the right therapy, he'll eventually recover some of his speech and perhaps a little of his movement. But at the moment he's completely incapacitated.'

Linda sat numbly, clutching the receiver. 'I'll come back. I've got to see him,' she finally managed to say. 'He needs me.'

There was a pause as Kenny searched for the right words. 'I know Phillip would appreciate it, Linda, but I must tell you: Ann is already here. She flew back right away from New York. Evie's in Norway but she may come back. We'll know her plans soon.'

Linda understood only too well what Kenny was trying to tell her: Phillip may have loved her, and he still might love her. But these people were his family. *If only he hadn't called me that day . . .*

In a composed voice, as calmly as she could manage, she said, 'In that case I would only be in the way. Phillip doesn't need three women in his life.'

And Kenny had no answer for that.

Between the therapy and his fierce determination to get well, Phillip was able to go home after a week. The library was turned into a hospital room of sorts, and Ann arranged for nurses 'round the clock. Two days after he came home, Evie flew to be with him, though her mother still felt it unnecessary that she return.

'I'm coming, Mom,' Evie had announced over the phone from Oslo. 'Peter understands.'

'No, Evie,' Ann said firmly. 'Your place is with your husband now.'

'And where is your place, Mom?'

Evie's question echoed in Ann's ears. Where was her place, indeed? Legally, she was still Phillip's wife, but beyond that, she felt responsible for him. Who was going to care for him if she didn't? He had no one else. It was unthinkable that Evie stay. The only solution Ann could see was to persuade Adam once again to accept a compromise.

It was with that thought in mind that she headed back to New York for the weekend. She prayed that she could make Adam understand, but her hopes were rudely shattered five minutes after they were in his apartment.

'Let's hear that once again – I want to get it straight,' he shouted. 'You're proposing that we just sit around and wait for Phillip to recover before we get married? I love you, Ann – more than I've ever loved anyone in my life. But this time I've had it up to here.' He paused, then said more quietly, 'You're going to have to choose, Ann – me or your family.' His voice rose. 'And let me warn you. If you say it's your family, then by Christ, we're through!'

'Adam . . . you can't mean that.'

'If you really loved me, you wouldn't even consider leaving again.'

'But I'm not leaving you, Adam.'

'Really? Not leaving me? How odd. You said you're going back to your husband, didn't you? And how long is a "short time"? Look – the discussion just ended. I put up with it when Evie was sick – she's your only child, and I could understand – but I am not sharing you with your husband. I'd be better off getting you out of my life once and for all.'

'Adam . . . how would your life be better with me cut out of it?'

'You want to know? I'd be free! I wouldn't sit by the phone, hoping you could spare a moment from your family to talk to me. Once again: if you walk out of this apartment tonight, we're through.'

'Adam . . . don't do this to me. Just give me some time.'

'Ann, you've got your time. I'm going for a walk. If you decide you want to go back to California, be so good as to be out of here by the time I get back in thirty minutes.' He glared at her, put on his coat, and left the apartment.

Adam, no . . . her heart cried out. She ran to the door,

ready to follow him, to tell him she would stay. Then she stopped. Phillip was weak and ill; Adam was strong. Phillip needed her more than Adam did. If she abandoned her husband, he would probably die. Wouldn't her guilt then destroy her love for Adam?

Fifteen minutes passed. Ann picked up the phone and dialed airline reservations. When she hung up, she knew that her life with Adam was over – he was not the man to make idle threats. He had been wonderfully understanding during Evie's illness, whereas Linda hadn't been able to deal with the strain. He had stood fast. And this time, when he had told Ann to choose between him and her family, the issue was equally clear.

Weeping softly, Ann picked up her bag and walked to the door.

Forty-Six

During the months that followed, Ann willed herself to think of nothing but the present. If she let herself wonder about the future or dwell on the past, she knew she would soon find herself standing on the Golden Gate Bridge, ready to jump. Concentrating instead on each of Phillip's small gains, she could keep her sanity.

When she was planning to move east, she had sold her office to another realtor who had promised to make May a partner. Now, without her business, she had little to do to occupy the long days. A solitary outing to Muir Woods or a lunch in Chinatown was an event; a letter from Evie, who had finally returned to Peter in Norway, was an occasion.

In time, Phillip recovered his speech, though it remained slurred and hard to understand. And he began to walk again, first leaning on Ann's arm, then later with a heavy cane. Despite these improvements, he began spending his days looking up at the sky, strangely withdrawn. Ann realized that he needed more than just physical therapy. She began to give him small errands – to the post office or the grocery store – anything to keep him busy and out of the house.

Her new plan triggered another problem.

She would send him for one thing and he would come home with something different, often wholly inappropriate. Or he would come home empty-handed. And he would be devastated, knowing that he had gotten it wrong. He would beg Ann to forgive him, tears of frustration welling up in his eyes.

After this happened several days in a row, Ann became alarmed. She called the doctor, who said to wait a little longer and see if Phillip improved. Unhappily, he did not. He began to answer questions out of context, and he repeated himself often. He could remember exactly what had happened on the day of the Great Crash, but not where he had laid his trousers. Sometimes he would even forget what he was saying in the middle of a sentence. And one horrible morning, he hadn't seemed to recognize Ann.

At that point, Dr. Cohn took him into the hospital for a battery of tests. Afterward, he asked Ann to come in for an appointment.

'He has Alzheimer's disease, Ann,' Dr. Cohn said. 'I thought I noticed a change the last time I examined him. It's what most people call senility.'

'Oh, my God! But Phillip's only fifty-four!'

'It isn't a natural part of aging. We don't know yet if it's genetic or if it's caused by a virus.'

'Isn't there any cure?'

'Unfortunately, Ann,' he replied gently, 'there isn't even any treatment, at least not yet.'

She stared at him, horrified. 'Will he get worse?'

'It's usually progressive. Frankly, from what you've told me, he's deteriorating rapidly. I don't know if you'll be able to care for him at home much longer.'

Shaking her head resolutely, she said, 'There's no reason he should have to be institutionalized. I know how to care for invalids; my mother-in-law had a severe stroke and I cared for her at home until the day she died.'

Dr. Cohn eyed her somberly. 'A stroke is one thing. Alzheimer's is another. Phillip may become very difficult to handle. And it's best that you be prepared. It's not a question of being willing to care for him. Eventually you won't be able to, and I don't want you to feel guilty.'

Ann looked away, her eyes brimming with tears.

Finally she took a deep breath and squared her shoulders. 'How long do you think I'll be able to handle him?'

'That's hard to say. Maybe a few months, maybe a few years.'

Ann left in a daze and spent several hours driving aimlessly around San Francisco, trying to gather the courage to return home. How could she face Phillip with this terrible new knowledge? Desperate for someone to talk with, she pulled into a service station and found a pay phone. But whom could she call? She thought a moment, looked at her watch, then dialed Adam's office.

The receptionist answered.

'This is Ann Coulter. May I speak with Mr. Gayne?'

'I'll see if he's in. One moment, please.'

Please be in, she wanted to scream into the phone. *Please be in. Please.*

Adam was surprised by how unnerved he felt when his receptionist announced the call. He had achieved some degree of inner peace by banishing Ann from his thoughts, and by God he wasn't going to lose it. He had longed for her and had lost her enough times already, and he wasn't strong enough to go through it all again. Despising his weakness, he told his receptionist, 'Marie . . . please tell Mrs. Coulter that I'm not available.'

When Marie relayed the message, Ann gripped the receiver until her knuckles turned white. She thought she was going to faint. She hung up, then dropped to her knees in the tiny steel and glass booth and whimpered like a wounded animal.

That was the last time she had tried to call Adam. Even on the dreadful December day when she had placed Phillip in a nursing home, she kept her grief to herself. In the end, it hurt much less.

Although she didn't need the money, she opened a new real estate office in nearby San Mateo and buried herself in her work. Her only self-indulgence was a weekly phone call to Evie in Norway – Peter's contract there had been extended – to reassure herself that Evie and Peter were still as happy as ever. They were.

It was nearly eleven one rainy night when Ann returned exhausted from a tax-shelter seminar to find a worried-looking Consuela waiting up for her. 'Mrs. Coulter – the nursing home called. They want you to call right away.'

Her heart pounding, Ann dialed the number. Had Phillip fallen? Injured himself in some way? But the news was far worse: he had died in his sleep earlier that evening.

Epilogue

After the funeral, once the mourners had left and Evie and Peter had gone upstairs to pack, Ann sat alone in the living room and made a decision. She couldn't go back and change the past, but she could try to take charge of her future. It had been over a year since she had last seen Adam, and six months since he had refused to accept her call.

This time she would try him at home.

She looked at her watch. Her hand hesitated over the receiver. This was the moment of truth. Did she have the courage to reach out for whatever chance she might have remaining for her happiness? It was a gamble, but she had to take it.

'Operator, I want to place a person-to-person call to New York . . . to Mr. Adam Gayne . . .'

Summer
in the City
of Roses

Also by the author

All of Us with Wings

Summer in the City of Roses

Michelle Ruiz Keil

Published in the United States by Soho Teen
an imprint of Soho Press, Inc.
227 W 17th Street
New York, NY 10011

Library of Congress Cataloging-in-Publication Data
Names: Keil, Michelle Ruiz, author.
Title: Summer in the city of roses / Michelle Ruiz Keil.
Identifiers: LCCN 2020052760

ISBN 978-1-64129-386-0
eISBN 978-1-64129-172-9

Subjects: CYAC: 1. Brothers and sisters—Fiction. 2. Supernatural—
Fiction. 3. Social action—Fiction. 4. Musicians—Fiction. 5. Punk rock
music—Fiction. | Portland (Or.)—Fiction.
Classification: LCC PZ7.1.K41513 Sum 2021 | DDC [Fic]—dc23
LC record available at https://lccn.loc.gov/2020052760

Interior design by Janine Agro, Soho Press, Inc.
Rose illustration: © elenavlas/Shutterstock
Printed in the United States of America

10 9 8 7 6 5 4 3 2 1

For Luciana & Angelika

Summer
in the City
of Roses

ACT I

Whoever drinks from me will become a tiger

1

THE FIRST
ACQUAINTANCE
WITH A PART

I t's the middle of summer, but of course there's rain. Clouds race past, covering and uncovering the moon. Iph's high heels squish with water, insult to the blistered injuries that are her feet. Her mother's cashmere sweater, already two sizes too small, is now a second skin. She stops at a wide, busy street that might be familiar if she'd remembered her glasses. But those, along with her purse, are far away, sitting innocent and hopeful on the white tablecloth in the hotel banquet room.

A guy across the street beams a glance her way and walks backward a few steps so he can keep on looking. She concedes a point to Dad. Earlier tonight, when she swanned into the living room in her white movie-star dress, he nodded approval at the first impression—glamorous but appropriate—followed by a jaw-drop of horror when his eyes reached her chest. Iph turned without a word and got the sweater out of her mother's closet—oversized and beachy on gamine Mom, not-quite-button-uppable on Iph. Although Mom has trained Dad against the sexism of policing his daughter's clothes, Dad insists on a basic truth: *Men are malákes.* Disgusting. A wolf whistle follows her around the corner, bringing the point home.

   Iph turns away from the busy street—Burnside, she thinks,
squinting at the blurry sign—and walks back the way she came.
A car drives by a little too slow. More men, more eyes. This
never happens in Forest Lake. She isn't scared . . . but maybe
she should be? "The trick to bad neighborhoods," Dad once told
her, "is to act like you belong." She was twelve or thirteen then,
brought along to pick up a load of salvaged building materials
from a part of the city people called Felony Flats. Staring out
the rain-spattered window of his truck at the small houses with
their peeling front porches and dandelion gardens, Iph wondered what exactly made a neighborhood bad.

   An older woman wearing a blanket instead of a raincoat shuffles past on the other side of the street. A car whizzes by, blasting
the Beatles. "Yellow Submarine" to go with the weather—a childhood road-trip favorite. Iph would give anything to be in that silver Volvo now, sharing a pillow with Orr in the back.

   She stops. She can't think about her brother. Can't stand here
crying in the rain with no coat.

   She takes a deep breath and starts walking again. Each step cuts
like her gold heels are the cursed shoes of a punished girl in a fairy
tale. She passes an alley. The same creepy car that slowed down
before is turning in. A group of kids, some who look younger than
her, are leaning against the wall, smoking. Iph hurries by. The scent
of wet asphalt and urine wafts toward her on the wind. Iph wills
her nose to stop working. So yeah, this neighborhood is probably
what her father would call bad. She should go back and face him.
Find some way to make him change his mind. But there's no making Dad do anything, not when he thinks he's right.

   It's humiliating how useless she is out in the real world. Like
a jewelry-box ballerina waiting to be sprung, she's dreamed
her life away in her pink suburban bedroom, sleeping as much
as possible, rewatching her favorite movies, and rereading her
favorite books. She always thought she'd be one of those kids
who got their driver's license the day of their sixteenth birthday so she could drive into Portland whenever she wanted. Like

Mom, she loved the city. But sixteen came and went without even a learner's permit.

Once, years ago, Iph heard Mom talking on the phone to her best friend. "If I'd have known how white it was in Oregon," she said, "I would've made Theo transfer to NYU and raised the kids in Brooklyn."

City-girl Mom made the best of it. Portland was still mostly white, but more liberal and diverse than Forest Lake. She'd taken Iph and Orr into Portland weekly since they were little—for Orr's cello lessons and Iph's theater camps, trips to museums and plays and record stores and summertime Shakespeare in the Park. Most often, they go to Powell's, the enormous bookstore downtown that covers an entire city block. The streets around Iph look a little like those.

But really, all the streets in downtown Portland look like this—art deco apartment buildings crowded next to the sooty turn-of-the-century low-rises Dad calls brickies; parking lots next to Gothic churches; nondescript midcentury offices and newish high-rises, shiny with rain-washed glass. In Portland—or everywhere, really—Iph has been content to let Mom do the driving, the thinking, the deciding. They all have. And now, after two weeks without her, their family is broken, and Iph can't imagine a fix.

She stops at an intersection and squints at the sign. The streetlight is out, so it's only a blur. Something hot is oozing from her heel. Her fingertips come back bloody. Blood has always made Iph feel faint. Sometimes, she actually does faint. She looks for somewhere to wipe her hand.

On the corner is a box with the free weekly paper. She rips the cover page in half and does her best with the blood. Doesn't see a trash can and settles for folding the sullied paper and sending it down the storm drain—a lesser form of littering, she hopes. She breathes through the pain in her feet. She needs a break. A plan. She leans against the nearest wall. The stucco snags Mom's sweater. What a waste. And for nothing. The whole outfit, the whole evening, was a con.

Iph cringes at her three-hours-ago self, proudly walking into that hotel on Dad's arm. When the band began "Fly Me to the Moon," he even asked her to dance. They waltzed easily, him singing the words so only she could hear them. When she was little, they'd bonded over Ol' Blue Eyes, which is what Dad calls Frank Sinatra. He twirled her and dropped her into a dip, a routine from their father-daughter dance in middle school. His co-workers smiled, and Iph remembered what it was like when she and Dad were close.

"Sweetie," he said as the song ended, "I need to talk to you about something."

2

SENSING
THE HUNTER'S
FOOTSTEP

Orr sees stars. Thinks about the phrase, *He saw stars*. Words for a cartoon head injury, a cast-iron pan to the head. He gags—a sudden rancidness. The scent of an unwashed pan. The way the kitchen smells when Dad's away and Mom leaves the dishes in the sink all week. But this isn't kitchen grease. Or a dream. It's the smell of the men pulling him from his bed.

A sack covers his head. His arms ache where hands grip him, lift him. The upstairs hall tilts by in the shadow world outside the thin black fabric. Orr remembers to scream. He flails, knocking into a chair, the countertop. He reaches out to the bumpy plaster wall of the entryway and claws at the worn spot next to the phone, but the men yank him away.

The alarm beeps its familiar goodbye as the front door slams shut. Orr quiets. Listens. The night is cool and smells like rain. He is strapped into a vehicle. Like Agent Scully on *The X-Files*, he is being abducted.

His sockless feet are clammy in his shoes, tied too tight by his kidnappers. His breathing is shallow. A meltdown builds. He reaches inside for the ghost in him, the thing Mom calls *tu alma*—his soul—but the ghost is gone, hiding or fled.

With his index finger he traces the map line of the West Coast on his leg, from British Columbia to Baja California. Questions form: *Where am I? Where are they taking me? And why?*

He breathes a little deeper. Wiggles his toes, tells them it's okay. Waits for the world to settle.

He is in a large car, possibly a van. The cracked vinyl seat is a fanged menace under the worn flannel of his too-short pajama pants. Summer rain hisses under the tires. The radio switches on, a sports station blaring. Orr reaches for music—his battered *Klengel, Volume 1* with its old-world yellow cover and pages of punishing drills he's grown to love. He recalls every detail of the slick round stickers his teacher placed on the fingerboard when he was a beginner. He remembers the deep cramping of new muscle in his wrist and hand. His right elbow crooks around an invisible bow. His legs shape the cello's curves until he can almost feel its purr.

The radio drones on and on. *Baseball.* Orr knows more than he cares to about the game. For Dad's sake, he's tried to love it. The announcer's voice is deep and comforting. The rhythm of *thwack, cheer, talk* surprisingly helps Orr think. Details coalesce. The silent house, the men. The way he never heard them enter. The alarm's familiar sequence of beeps, because . . . because . . .

They knew the code.

They *knew.*

Orr narrows his eyes in the solitude of the hood. Fucking Dad. That's what Iph would say. This whole ordeal is because of Dad and that awful brochure.

The van stops. Orr is unsure how much time has passed.

"Okay, kid," a voice says, and the sack is pulled from Orr's head.

The waxing moon is bright as a bare light bulb in the star-exploded sky. Crickets chirp. Frogs harmonize in the deep forest hush. The gravel parking lot is a stark landing pad in a tree-circled compound. Orr nods. This has been a long time coming.

Finally, here he is: a prisoner at the Fascist Reeducation Facility

for Inadequate Specimens, also known as the Meadowbrook Reha-
bilitation Center for Boys.

Boot camp.

He's heard of it, of course. A place for kids who do drugs or
kids who fight—kids with something they need to change. What
is Orr supposed to change? He doesn't get into fights. Has no
interest in drugs. He's quiet, but silence is part of him, heads to
the tails of his music.

The driver closes the van. Another man guides Orr toward a
building that looks like some sort of lodge. A third walks ahead.
This one is taller than the others, with a back like a bull's. One
second, Orr is fine. Then he's not. He sees now that his calm in
the van was only his mind's clever ruse to protect himself and
fool the men. Sound boils in the tar pit of his stomach, but Orr
won't let it out. It's an experiment, an untested suggestion from
his therapist: *Contain the meltdown without dissociating. Talk to it.
Make it your friend.*

The lodge looms closer. The mountain silently watches. Orr
morphs the meltdown into a tactical step. Sound transmutes
to animal knowing. He feigns a slip, a twisted ankle. The man
releases his arm and bends down.

After that, Orr doesn't think. He just runs.

3

FUNDAMENTALS
OF ART MATERIAL

A pay phone beckons at the corner. Iph keeps thinking about last winter—her and Dad finding Mom crying at the kitchen table, the acceptance letter from the residency in one hand, a pack of contraband cigarettes in the other.

"Theo," Mom said, handing him the letter, "it's three full months."

"He'll be fine," Dad said, pulling Mom up and wrapping her in a hug.

"It's just the summer," Iph said.

And she believed it then. She would take care of Orr. Dad would take care of her. But she hasn't. And Dad certainly hasn't. And now what? Call Mom and tell her that Orr, who's never lasted the night at a sleepover, is in a militaristic boot camp for wayward boys? Iph is at the phone, hand on the receiver. She picks it up. The streetlight goes dark overhead. A sign?

Something warm touches her ankle. A soft breath. A dry little tongue.

"Scout!"

The small, stocky dog pulls away and sits at attention, looking up. Iph follows the yellow gaze to a mohawked boy on a beat-up ten-speed. No, not a boy. Or . . . maybe not?

"I'm George." A boy's name, but not a boy's voice. "This is Scout." The miniature brindle pit wags its stubby tail. "Are you okay? Do you need help?"

As if in league with the pair, the sky clears and the moon appears. Iph shakes her head. Is that . . . a bow and arrow slung over George's shoulder?

George pulls an index card from a back pocket and reads. "Are you in need of medical attention?"

Iph looks down and shakes her head. Her feet are bad, but Band-Aids will fix them.

"Are you being pursued?"

She shakes her head again. Dad didn't follow her when she stormed out. *Why* didn't he follow her?

"Are you a victim of trafficking or domestic violence?"

Does lying count as violence? How about betrayal? If so, maybe she's as guilty as Dad. Iph shakes her head. "No, I'm fine."

Scout whines and quivers for attention. Iph bends down in a weird sideways twist, constrained by her dress, to stroke the dog's brindle fur. "So soft!" she says. "She's adorable!"

Scout vibrates with happiness.

"And knows it," George says.

Close enough now to defeat her nearsighted astigmatism, Iph takes George in: bear-brown mohawk, bright black eyes. Well-shaped ears with five earrings in the right lobe and three in the left. A silver septum ring in a small, slender nose. Crisp white shirt, ankle-cuffed jeans, and oxblood Oxfords. A sort of dandy archer with an adorable mini pit-bull sidekick. They look like they belong in a story that starts with, *Once upon a time* . . .

"Thank you," Iph says to Scout, who's licking her ankle above the worst of the blisters. "I'm feeling much better now."

The dog offers her paw. Iph takes it and laughs.

"Are you sure there isn't something we can do?" George's skin is pale olive with hints of gold. Iph wonders but would never ask. She hates the question herself—the inevitable *What are you?* Maybe George is like her—a little of this, a little of that.

Iph stands, wobbly in her demon shoes. "I was at a work thing with my dad. We had a fight and I ran out. I left my glasses there. I'm lost without them."

It's an oversimplification of the ugly truth. In reality, Iph had a tantrum and ran away instead of staying to fight for her brother.

"Do you feel . . . safe going home?" George is being careful, like maybe it's common to find girls in sensitive situations alone in the city at night. Is that what the bow and arrows are for? Iph flashes back to the alley, the smoking kids. The men in the car.

"It's not like that," she says. "My dad—he did something awful, and I found out about it."

George's eyes widen. Even Scout is at attention.

"No, I mean, he's not . . ." Iph can't find the words for what Dad is or isn't. Not after tonight. "Look, if anyone needs to worry about their safety at my house right now, it's probably my dad."

"I see," George says, nodding like of course Iph is a powerful angry goddess whose father should fear her. "Can I help you get home, then?"

"It's far," she says. "Way out in Forest Lake." The second she says it, she wants to take it back. To most people, Forest Lake means money and white people and Republicans.

George just nods. "No bus out there this time of night."

"My dad's probably still somewhere around the hotel, looking for me. Could you give me directions back?"

"Of course," George says with a formal bow. "I'm at your service."

Iph can't help smiling. "Thank you kindly," she says. "I'm Iph."

"If?" George grins, then furrows, then drops to one knee and begins to recite.

> *O, if a virgin,*
> *And your affection not gone forth, I'll make you*
> *The Queen of Naples.*

Iph laughs. It's familiar, but not *R and J*. Not *Two Gentlemen of Verona* or *Twelfth Night*, either. "Ha!" she says, tapping her forehead. *"The Tempest!"* She should've known right away—she stage-managed the play last year. "Ferdinand to Miranda."

"Wow!" George grins. "No one ever knows what I'm blathering on about. But seriously, your name is If?"

"I-P-H. Short for Iphigenia. We're named after our dad's side— he's Greek."

"We?"

"Me and my brother."

"Why not your mom's side?"

"Good question." Mom's side of the family is a no-fly zone— even nosy Orr has learned to back off about Mom and her past.

"What hotel is it?" George adjusts the bow and arrow so naturally, it's clearly habitual.

"The one with the fancy doormen? With the breeches and big hats?"

"The Heathman," George says. "It's not too far."

Iph takes a step forward and hisses in pain—standing still for so long had been a mistake. Scout runs to her and whines.

"Blisters?" George asks.

Iph nods. There's no getting around it. She has to take off her shoes. She reaches down, but George stops her.

"If you take them off now, you'll never get them back on. They won't let you into the hotel without them. I have alcohol wipes and ointment, but only two Band-Aids—I need to restock my first-aid stuff."

Iph looks around for a place to sit where her dress won't be completely ruined. White seemed like such a great idea at the mall.

"Let me," George says. "We can at least do the heels."

"It's so gross," Iph says. "There's blood."

"I have gloves." George produces a pair of latex gloves and a first-aid kit from a well-worn messenger bag.

"So you just . . . ride around at night, helping lost maidens and shooting ne'er-do-wells and dressing strangers' wounds?"

"Yep," George says. "Lift your foot up, but not all the way out." The cleanup and bandaging is gentle and precise. "There we go." George takes off the gloves and stows them in a Ziploc bag.

"Thank you," Iph says. "That's way better."

George smiles. "It's nothing." In a fluid motion, the messenger bag and bow and arrows are back in place.

"Have you ever shot anyone with that thing?"

"Once." There's a beat, a shift. Iph notes it and files it away. She's always on the lookout for these in-between moments where everything breathes. "Find them onstage," Mom's director friend from New York once said, "and you can make magic."

Iph waits. George breaks the silence with a gesture at the ten-speed leaning against the wall. "Why don't I take you? If you sit sidesaddle on the rack and hold on, I think we'll make it. It's not far."

"Are you sure?"

George grins, one hand holding up the bike, the other holding open the flap of the messenger bag. Like a tiny gazelle, Scout leaps in. Even though it's the worst night of her life, Iph laughs.

"Milady," George says, gesturing to the bike like it's a chariot. Iph hobbles over and wriggles on. The relief of getting her weight off her feet is sweet enough that she doesn't even care about her butt, which is far from comfortable on the narrow metal shelf. George stands to pedal, calf muscles impressive as they work.

Iph grips the sides of the rack, careful to hold her feet away from the gears. Her shoes twinkle in the streetlights, cruel but pretty with their shiny gold leather straps and chunky four-inch forties heels. She found them in a box of Mom's old stuff and brought them with her when Dad handed over his credit card and told her to get something nice for the party.

The white cocktail dress saw Iph coming with its retro vibe and thick damask satin with the perfect amount of stretch—a necessity for serious boobs and hips. The wide straps hid her bra, and the sweetheart neckline did something amazing for her waist. When she put the shoes on and stepped out to look in the big three-way dressing room mirror, the saleslady whistled.

"Just like a Spanish Marilyn Monroe!"

Spanish. Mom has always hated being called that. The Spanish were, in Mom's words, *"pendejo* colonizers." She also hates *Hispanic,* which she considers basically same thing.

Still, Iph knew what the saleslady meant and took it as a compliment.

She held on to that good feeling all week. Which made it so much worse when Dad told her the real reason for the evening out. He didn't invite her because he wanted her company. She was there so strangers could come into the house and kidnap her brother without her braining them with a cast-iron skillet.

Take care of him, mija.

That was the last thing Mom said when she left. Orr was too upset to come to the airport, so Dad and Iph were the ones to see her off. There had been a scene the night before. Mom almost didn't go. Iph found her after Orr was asleep and Dad had retreated to his den, frozen in front of her closet, still not packed.

"You have to," Iph told her. "It will be me next year. Show me how to be brave."

Mom's eyes cleared. She nodded. They held each other tight. They had been a team for so long, taking care of Orr. Making sure the world didn't break him. "I've got this," Iph told her. "He's going to be fine."

Iph's spine straightens. She opens her eyes to the now-clear night. She will find Dad. She'll convince him. They'll drive straight to that boot camp and get Orr back. Mom can stay at her residency, and Dad can deal with her fire-spitting fury when she gets home at the end of the summer and finds out what he did.

George sits to coast down a small hill. The clean wind cools Iph's face. She holds out her arms for a second, perfectly balanced. Scout peeks out of the messenger bag and grins. Even if everything else about tonight is abysmal, being rescued by these two is undeniably great.

4

THE
SMOKE-BLUE
FOREST

O rr lies on a thin mattress that feels slightly better than nothing. Rocks press cold into his bones, but the pressure is oddly painless. Is this what it feels like to be dead?

He rubs the thick paste stuck in his lashes but doesn't open his eyes. He imagines he is Uncle Marcos on the Greek side of the family, who would open one eye to light his first cigarette of the day and only open the second when it was smoked down to the filter. Marcos sat propped against his pillows and drank coffee for cigarette number two.

One eye is all Orr needs to see that it's very dark. He hears the woods around him, fur against fir, frog song, the rustling of dreaming birds. The second eye is easier.

He's in a tent. A dirty-sock-smelling sleeping bag is draped over him.

He sits up. Something is wrong. It's a static in his ears, something missing. A sting on his earlobe where the clippers have cut.

Orr remembers now: the barbed-wire fence that stopped him, being dragged back to the lodge with its wood-fire common room and silent, watching boys. The adults were the ones from the van.

The Minotaur man kept him still, his muddy boot resting on the chair an inch from Orr's crotch.

There was a string of words meant to unnerve him. Things he heard in middle school, names people called him. Words Mom said no one should ever use. Orr pans out on the memory, adjusts the angle. It's one of his tactics, maybe his best. He can turn the sound of any memory on or off. He can pause, rewind, fast-forward.

He zooms in on the scene in the lodge. The men holding him look less like men and more like older teenagers. College age at most. They're in charge, though. Of him and all the other boys.

One of them, maybe the one who drove him here, is saying the worst things. He's angry Orr ran, angry he won't stay still. Maybe Orr hurt him with his flailing. He keeps the sound on at first. The driver is holding his shoulders, calling him *dirt surfer*. This is a new one—probably a slur for hippie, referring to Orr's long hair. It's a dumb insult and easy to reject. Orr and his hair are always clean.

The sound goes off. He knows what's coming next—a bad word for someone who is Chinese, also inaccurate when it comes to his ethnicity. But Orr is used to being misclassified. The whole Santos Velos family has a look Dad's New York family jokingly calls "mystery ethnic." Mom and Dad both dislike the term but let them say it anyway. "It's not the worst thing I've been called," Mom always says.

"We're American," Dad counters, raising his thick eyebrows at Mom like he's daring her to disagree. "As American as anyone."

"Ha!" she says. Then she sighs. "I don't know, my love. The kids are *mestizo*, right? Mixed."

But Orr doesn't like that one, either. It makes their family sound like cake batter.

Orr knows the Meadowbrook guys don't care what he is, not really. They want to find his weak spots. The worst one wants to punish him.

Orr fast-forwards to a slur for a gay man or boy, something Orr has heard countless times since elementary school. It's a throwaway in terms of insults. Mom's dancer friends visit a few times a year from New York and use that word with affection or neutrality. But Mom never uses it, so neither does Orr. He's still not sure if it applies to him. Mom says he can decide when he's ready.

The final insult is kind of ironic. Another elementary school taunt with roots in one of the best things about being half-Mexican—Mom's creamy, perfect refried beans, the ones she says are like her *abuela*'s. Not that he would know. He's never met a single person on Mom's side of the family, and she refuses to talk about it. Ever. "I took the food and left the rest," she always says. "It was the one thing worth taking." Orr wonders now, like he always does, why that's true. Why nothing and no one from Mom's past is worthy.

By the time Orr thinks that one through to its logical end, he's not angry, only hungry. Or he would be, except he's not in his body anymore. Just floating around like a big naked brain in a giant pickle jar. This is Orr's way. He can spend full days in his head uncoupling sense from sensibility. It takes time and precision, like disarming a bomb. But now, in this cold, lonely moment, Orr needs to do something real.

He tries a formerly rejected calming exercise of Mom's to make it safer. He lies back down. The ground is there, holding him. He sends a cleansing breath in through his nose, past his heart, solar plexus, belly, and root chakras, down into the molten core of the earth.

In. Out. In. Out.

Images emerge, abstract at first. Ordinary moments at home. Dad. Iph. Mom.

Mom. The night before she left. Her suitcase. Clothes piled on the bed.

NO.

Orr shakes his head like it's an Etch A Sketch he's erasing.

He goes back to the van, his attempted escape, the lodge.

The chair, the men, the silent, watching boys. The memory stops.

He rewinds a little. Presses play.

Metal bites his neck. The Minotaur-man moves him like he's a puppet.

That's Orr's crime, the reason he's here. His father wants a real boy.

"*Bad Pinocchio,*" Dad says, "*believing that fox was your friend.*"

"*Bad people,*" Mom says, "*villainizing the fox. It's men who lie, not animals.*"

"*Corvids can.*" Dad grins. "*Crows, ravens, and jays. They're smart enough to lie.*"

When Orr was little, he was afraid of everything: the vastness of the sky, the weight of a roof over his head, the grating sounds of machinery, the feel of certain substances on his skin. But Mom had been there. Mom and Iph.

From the start, he understood that they were a team. When Dad was home, he always pushed. He wanted his son to throw and catch, to ski, to snowboard, to golf.

Dad called it love, but it wasn't love.

Dad pushed so hard, it was almost like he wanted to prove Orr's unworthiness. In the end, Orr's high-pitched keen always exposed Dad for the fake he was. He would yell and slam doors. Things the kids were never allowed to do.

To be fair, when Orr was three, four, even five, the wailing upset Mom, too. It probably upset the entire county—it was that loud. Sometimes, back then, Mom covered her ears and rushed to her room and closed the door. A few times in the car, she even cried. Orr hated upsetting her but was unable to change. Then Mom read a book about sensitive people and various coping methods, which she passed along to Iph and Orr. They made a game of it, spotting freak-outs before they erupted. They learned calming yoga poses. They meditated. They all learned to be kinder, gentler. Even Dad. But instead of laughing, he would go silent. Instead of meditating, he escaped to his den and shut the door.

As Orr got older and started running, he freaked out less often. Now he hardly ever does. But when he was little, it happened almost daily. Mom protected him, but for important things—things Orr needed to learn no matter how hard they seemed—his mother endured.

Whatever happened, Mom knew what to do. When kids called him a girl for his long hair, she took him to the mall to get a tiny gold earring. When his father complained, she brought home romance novels from the grocery store with long-haired, muscular, earringed men on the covers to put on Dad's bedside table. Mom knew Orr's hair was important. He needed its weight against his back, its rosewater curtain of protection around him wherever he went.

Mom taught him everything he knows about love. About being good. So he knew what to say when the letter came, inviting her to a prestigious residency in California to finish the epic dance piece she'd been working on since he and Iph were toddlers. Iph kicked him under the dinner table to make sure he said congratulations like he meant it.

Leading up to the residency, Orr tried to tell himself it would be like her other trips, just longer. In the past, he'd made it through by reading a book a day and buying and rationing a party-size bag of M&M'S. Doable, if just.

This time, she would be gone for three months.

That was ninety books. Eighteen jumbo bags of M&M'S.

Mom was worried, too, so she made lists and printed them out at Dad's office. A daily schedule with reminders and little jokes. She thought it would help, but it didn't.

Orr is sobbing now, his stress level rising fast. Tears run down the sides of his face and sting his nicked scalp. He reaches to rub them away and finds that his wrists are still bound with plastic ties. His body seems to exist in parts. Are his legs even attached? A wiggle of his toes tells him they are. Now that his eyes have adjusted to the dark, he sees the shape of the tent around him: small, too short to stand in. In the corner, there is a pile of something soft—his hair!—and in it, a small breathing something.

He crawls to the foot of the mattress and lies on his stomach. A mouse has made good use of his shorn hair, tucking her brood of children into the silky pile. Orr smiles and thinks of the *Red-wall* books with their poetry and ale-loving rodents. He makes the tiny sounds his neighbor's guinea pig, Estelle, prefers, but a little softer in deference to the mouse's smaller stature.

The mouse mother meets his gaze. She rises from the pile of nursing children and comes closer. She is a brown mouse, proof that *mouse-brown* should never be used as an insult. Her coat is the color of softness. Of late afternoon. Of small, warm safety.

Orr holds his breath.

On her hind legs, she sniffs the zip ties on his wrists and looks at him again. With her tiny hands braced on either side of Orr's right wrist, the mouse begins to nibble.

Orr thought Mom was the one who had a way with animals. The family of feral cats that live on the wooded edges of their half-acre yard allow her alone to pet them. Last fall, they found an injured falcon on the highway. Mom was the only one who could go near him. She's saved countless songbirds and more than one baby squirrel. Dad calls her a wood witch. The Lady of Beasts. Now it seems that Orr has some of her magic.

Orr smiles at the feel of mouse breath on his sensitive inner wrist. The mouse mother makes quick work of the right tie and moves to the left. She's so careful, he never once feels teeth.

The metal-on-metal sound of the tent zipper makes the metal in Orr's fillings ache. It's cold outside. Mountain cold. One more clue about where he is.

The lights are out in the building that houses the boys. The row of cabins under the stand of firs is also dark. He holds very still.

Even though Orr is fifteen, he doesn't often go places alone. In fact, the only places he's ever gone without Mom or Iph are the country roads around their subdivision. But of course he recognizes the white cap of the mountain behind him. Out-of-town business associates of his father's always *ooh* and *ahh* at the postcard perfection of Mount Hood, visible from the city on clear days. Iph always scoffed at it. "A little much, don't you think? Like it knows everyone's looking."

This always made Dad laugh. "A mountain can't be conceited."

"Umm, tell that to poor Mount Saint Helens," Iph said, pointing to the mountain's cropped top, her peak flattened when the volcano inside her bubbled to the surface.

Orr swears he remembers the day it happened, even though he wasn't quite two. They'd woken to a pale dusting of ash over everything. *Fairy snow*, Iph had called it, padding to the deck in her footie pajamas.

The mountain is much closer now, less a postcard than a sentinel. Meadowbrook must be in the forest at its feet. If Orr walks with the snowcap at his back, he will eventually find his way home.

The thought stops him.

Home.

His heart races, his breath a warm cloud in the air.

Home. To Dad. The person who'd authorized his kidnapping, his shearing, who was probably paying a lot of money to transform Orr into someone he wanted to call his son.

Orr is dizzy. He feels for pockets, but his pajamas don't have them. No vial of homeopathic anxiety medicine. No EpiPen.

He opens his mouth to call out . . . to who? Mom, all the way in California? Iph, who's probably so freaked out she's snagged one of Mom's sleeping pills?

There is no one.

He falls to his knees.

He lies down on the ground.

Pine needles lisp above him, mocking the tic of his grade school years.

He closes his eyes and gropes for the hologram of home that he carries inside himself. It's something he made to sustain him on the long days at school before Mom decided to keep him home. It never changes in his hologram world—always summer, always twilight, that perfect moment five minutes before nightfall when the sky turns indigo, a color his mother calls "our blue" because she and Orr love it equally.

Sobs gather in Orr's belly. The hologram can't help him. Nothing can.

Something cold touches his face, then something warm.

A nose, he guesses. A tongue.

He opens his eyes. Amber gleams down into his brown. Moonlight shines in a mouthful of teeth.

He sits up.

The coyote sits down.

If Orr had been raised by someone besides Mom, he might have been afraid.

The coyote whines, a high, soft sound. Orr searches her face, marked as if with makeup—dark liner around the eyes and a black star on a pale gold forehead. She moves a step closer and stops, sits, lowers her head.

Orr reaches out slowly, slowly, to touch the fur on her chest. Softer than he expected.

A heart beats under his hand, steady.

The animal is not afraid.

His own heart steadies.

The coyote rises, looks back at Orr, and trots west, away from the camp. Pulling his hood up to cover his shorn head, Orr follows her down the mountain.

5

STAGE
CHARM

George parks the bike under an awning around the corner from the hotel entrance and looks Iph up and down. Not checking her out or anything, but Iph blushes.

"We should clean you up a little."

Scout whines in the bag.

George shushes her but lets her out, setting the bag on the bike rack. "Okay if I get some of the smudges off?"

"Sure," Iph says.

From a pocket, George produces an actual handkerchief, clean and white and neatly folded. Very Prince Charming. "Close your eyes."

The cotton is soft and comforting. Iph realizes how tired she is. Her eyes fly open when the cleanup moves to her grime-splashed ankles and shoes. George is kneeling in front of her, intent on the work at hand. So gallant!

Rummaging in one of the messenger bag's outside pockets, George comes up with two tubes of lipstick. The red one is opened, discarded. George shows Iph a medium pink.

"Not mine," George says. There's a story in those two words. Maybe more than one. "My friend always brings both. She says pink is for innocent but classy. This might be a little light on you, though." George leans in close to apply the lipstick. It smells like cotton candy. Iph holds still, mouth open slightly for the second coat. She has done this so many times for actors as part of the costume crew, but no one's ever put makeup on her.

George tucks a few stray curls back into Iph's updo and steps back. "Yeah, that'll work. I see what she meant about the pink for certain missions. It does something red just can't."

"Missions? I'm going in there to find my dad, not abscond with state secrets."

"Lady," George says, "no disrespect intended, but you look a little . . . undone? There are a lot of street kids around here. Scammers. You know."

Iph doesn't know. She's nervous now as George steps back and nods. "Just go in there like you own the place. I'm gonna wait out here."

"Oh." Iph had imagined them going in together.

"You're better off on your own in there. Trust me."

And maybe she's an idiot for the second time tonight, but she doesn't think so—she does trust George.

"Thank you," Iph says, bending to touch Scout's silky head for luck. "Both of you. I'll be right back, whether he's in there or not. Will you wait?"

"I will if you're really coming back." Something crosses George's face—there and gone, like lights from a passing car. Iph wonders again about the bow and arrows, the index-card list. She reaches into her memories of *The Tempest* and whips out some Ariel.

> *My lord it shall be done!*
> *I drink the air before me, and return*
> *Or ere your pulse twice beat.*

"Excuse me," Iph says to the person at the front desk. "I'm looking for someone?" She'd blown easily past the doorman in his incongruous British tower guard uniform and large-brimmed, rose-wreathed hat. But this clerk seems like the kind of person Mom calls Born Skeptical. He's young, with longish droopy hair and an unsuccessful mustache. He looks up from his newspaper, eyebrows raised.

"He's tall," Iph says. "With dark hair. Was here earlier for the Theodore Velos party?"

"I can't help you, miss. There are no events happening now." His tone is smug and final.

"Did someone turn in a gold-beaded clutch purse?" Then, at least, Iph would have some money to make a call. "And a pair of glasses?"

She finally has the man's attention. He looks her up and down, and not in the concerned way George did. "Why don't you try finding your party at the bar?"

There is something condescending about the way he says *bar*. That and the disdainful look. Iph tries to flip her vision, see herself with his eyes. A little montage—the tight cocktail dress, Dad's horrified look, George's insistence on pink lipstick over red. Suddenly, she gets it. This man has added up the cut of her dress and her smudged eye makeup and rain-frizzed curls and decided she's a call girl. Rude! And so what if she *was* a call girl? This guy's clearly a jerk who needs a taste of his own snotty medicine.

Iph lets her eyes go wide and puts a tiny wobble in her voice, a teaspoon of angry in a cup of seriously offended. "The bar? How old do you think I am?"

The clerk looks confused.

"I'll tell you how old. Seventeen. So the bar isn't an option. But how about you go in there and find my party for me? And tell him his daughter is waiting for him."

"Oh, I see. I'm sorry, miss. What event did you say it was?"

"Velos Design."

"And you are?"

"Iphigenia Santos Velos." She actually taps her foot. She's having too much fun altogether, considering the situation.

The clerk magically notices the note his co-worker left at the desk and hands it to Iph. Dad's scrawl. *Looked everywhere. Worried sick. Call home* makes her ache for the warmth of his car, the dark of her room. She will fix this. Persuade him to go get Orr. Everything will be okay.

Her "Can I use the phone?" is met with a fast "Of course," but all Iph gets is a busy signal. She tries again and again. "I can't imagine who he's talking to," she says after the fourth try.

Her stomach drops. What if it's Mom? Iph imagines her in the big wooden common house in the Santa Cruz Mountains, pacing back and forth with the phone, twisting her long hair around her finger until it turns blue as Dad confesses.

"Call the operator," the clerk suggests. "Ask for an emergency breakthrough."

"You can do that?"

The clerk smiles, and the world shifts back into place. Iph is a kid, the clerk an indulgent grown-up. But the reason that's happening is because Dad left the note. What if he hadn't?

"Here, write down the number and I'll do it." The clerk speaks to the operator. No one is on the line. The phone is off the hook. Iph's eyes fill with tears.

"Is there someone else you can call?"

Iph shakes her head. She has no real friends at school. Not anymore. Mom has no family—at least no one she speaks to. Dad's family is all back east or in Greece. The only number Iph has memorized besides the video store and pizza place is their neighbor Mindy's. But Mindy and her family are out of town until next week.

"No," Iph says. "My dad and I had an argument. I ran off and got lost. I left my purse. My glasses. Everything."

"You can keep trying." The clerk's voice is gentle now. His eyes have gone kind, like maybe he understands problems with parents. That's the thing with people. They're both sour and sweet. Like Dad. In his misguided, messed-up way, he was trying to do the right thing. Iph calls again. He has to notice the phone sooner or later. "Maybe he'll turn up back here. Why don't you have a seat? We can call again in a few."

"Thank you so much." The plush sofas look like heaven. Except, there's George. Iph finds what she hopes is the right smile. "I ran into a friend who helped me find the way back here. I'm completely lost without my glasses." Iph does her best to channel innocent, nearsighted Marilyn in *How to Marry a Millionaire* without being too over the top. "Would you mind if we waited in here together? Just for a little while?"

The clerk's brow furrows. "Where is this friend?"

"Right outside." She opens her eyes a little wider.

Iph sees him weighing her boobs, his own sympathy, her father's status, his customer service training against some loitering rule, and she feels a little sorry for him. He's just here for the paycheck, biding his time to put food on the table. That's what Mom always says about cranky service workers. Still, Iph promised George.

He sighs and rolls his eyes. "Just for a few minutes," he says.

6

CHARACTERS
AND TYPES

Iph and George had been waiting together in the lobby with Scout concealed in George's bag for all of ten minutes when the manager walked in, took one look at George, and booted them all. Iph batted her eyes at the clerk, but he just shrugged. Now if Iph's dad got upset, it was on his boss's head, not his. This is the kind of thing that makes Mom say, *Capitalism wrecks everything*, and makes Dad call her his little Bolshevik and kiss her, which in turn makes Iph and Orr chorus *Gross* when what they mean is, *Our parents love each other and that feels good.*

Out on the street, the rain is finished and the sky is completely clear. "I'm sorry," George is saying as they head back to the bike, locked to the metal security door of a men's haberdashery half a block up. Before they get there, the doorman in the ridiculous outfit is calling them back.

"Hey," he says. Something about him suggests *Alice in Wonderland*—and not just the big floppy rose-crowned hat that is part of the hotel uniform. He's holding a cardboard box. "Sorry about that. It's the manager. He has it in for teenagers. But here—you can look for your stuff in the lost and found." He hands Iph the box and motions to the large doorway of the closed shop next to the hotel, set back from the street. There's someone sleeping in the other end of the alcove.

"We should be quiet," Iph whispers.

"He can't hear us," George says. "Takes his hearing aids out when he sleeps."

"You know him?"

"Everybody down here knows him." George kneels and hunts through the box so Iph doesn't have to bend over, which is a good thing because she's pretty sure she can't. Her dress dried out completely in the hotel and is now as stiff as paper. Apparently, there's a reason for the DRY CLEAN ONLY tag.

"Sorry," George says. "No purse."

The doorman ushers a handsome older couple into a cab, then ambles over on huge feet. "No luck? It's okay—take whatever you need. No one ever comes back for that stuff. Here"—he pulls out a huge Portland Trail Blazers hoodie from the box—"I almost took this myself, but the sleeves are too short. They had to order my uniform special." He sticks his long arms out like Frankenstein's monster and grins. He has braces, complete with an elaborate lacing of rubber bands.

"Thanks," Iph says. She puts on the hoodie and it's heaven. Soft and clean-smelling and warm.

"Thanks, man." George slaps his arm like maybe they know each other, then sorts the contents of the box methodically, taking a pair of leather gloves, a yellow Walkman, and a pair of pink fuzzy socks with the tag still on them. Last are a pair of round gold-framed glasses and a heavy black old-man pair. "Either of these yours?"

Iph shakes her head.

"Wanna try them on anyway? Maybe one of them's close enough to help."

The gold John Lennon glasses are crazy—bifocals, it turns out. The doorman tries them on after Iph. She's gotten used to the uniform, but the addition of the glasses skews it late sixties, very Sgt. Pepper's. He strikes a pose, surprisingly graceful.

"Do you dance?" Iph asks.

"Basketball," he says.

Iph tries the black glasses. Stronger than her regular prescription, but pretty good. She turns to the others. "What do you think?"

"Punky," the doorman says.

"Very cute. And look!" Two quarters shine in George's hand. "Okay if we take these, too?"

"Totally," the doorman says.

"Where's the best pay phone, do you think? 7-Eleven?"

"That one's always gross. Try up at PSU."

"Thanks," Iph says. "And thank the desk guy for sending out the box!"

"No problem. Take it sleazy!" The doorman flashes them a peace sign and hurries the lost and found box back inside.

IPH AND GEORGE ARE alone again, and the street is quiet. No people, except for the old man sleeping in the alcove. No cars. Iph feels a sudden vertigo. Everything is too sharp with the new glasses. Too clear.

"Milady?" George bows again.

"Are you sure? You've done so much already. Maybe I should . . ." But Iph doesn't know how to finish the sentence.

"I don't abandon my missions," George says. "Let's go find that pay phone."

THE PORTLAND STATE CAMPUS is quiet. A few people pass as Iph calls home, but the phone's still busy. What's Dad's deal? Why hasn't he tried calling the hotel? Why did he leave in the first place? "I still can't believe he went home." Iph says. "If that's where he even is. I mean, I don't know. I think I would've waited."

"Me, too," George says. "If it was my kid? I'd have waited all night."

"Well, in his defense, I was kind of horrible."

Iph's chest aches. She yelled and cried. Made such a scene. Heat rises from her clenched stomach to her face. Her feet throb. She sits on a wet bench, hoping her dress won't rip. At least the rain has stopped. Scout leaps up between Iph and George, settling her head in Iph's lap. The wind blows the big trees in the park that runs through the city campus. The sound is soothing. Like being at home.

"He sent my little brother away to a boot camp," Iph finally says. "He had him taken against his will. Orr . . . isn't a boot-camp sort of kid. If anyone is."

"Those places can be rough. I think some parents don't get what they're like."

"Have you ever . . . seen one?"

"Not boot camp," George says, "but something similar."

George gets up and leads Scout a few paces away for a bathroom break. Iph compares the buildings on either side of the bank of phones. One is a concrete structure designed in what Dad calls the "prison-yard school of architecture." The other is an old white Renaissance Revival hall, sturdy and elegant, the way a college building should look.

"Okay, here's the deal," George says, coming back to sit by Iph. Scout leaps back to her spot on the bench between them. Her ears feel like the silk lining of Iph's lost purse. "I have kind of a weird living situation. An apartment—but it's a secret. No one can know I live there."

"All right, but . . . I mean, how old are you?"

"Seventeen," George says. Iph's age. And living alone? "My mom's gone, my stepdad's out of the country. I was supposed to stay with my cousin, but that didn't work out. I decided to do some urban camping till he gets back and everything is sorted."

"Like squatting?" Mom has some great stories about her year squatting in Amsterdam.

"It's more like . . . haunting? It's my nana's old place. I come in late at night when I'm sure the neighbors are asleep, and I leave after they go to work. Sometimes I have to stay in all day on the

weekends because they never leave. Then I'm up all night 'cause
I've been cooped up so long."

"And that's when you ride around rescuing lost maidens?"

George grins. "Exactly."

"So are you inviting me to stay at your top-secret hideout?"

"I am."

"Is there a phone there?"

"Sorry, no." George takes out a pocket watch and studies it.
"We can try stopping at pay phones along the way. We should jet,
though. Downtown's dicey after midnight."

7

IMAGINATION

The sign on the building is shaped like a curvy bull, midnight blue, with a starry flank and horns like crescent moons. Under golden hooves, TAURUS TRUCKING is lettered in faded retro script with the ghost of an *F* over the *T*, a bad joke someone made and someone else scrubbed away.

"Your nana was a trucker?"

George laughs. "I mean, yeah. I guess you could say she was. Drove Ethel till she was in her seventies."

"Ethel?"

"Her tow truck," George says. "By the end, it was Ethel the Fourth."

They're on Division Street now, in Southeast, the sleepier part of the city. To get here, George and Iph rode over the fairy-lit Hawthorne Bridge, stopping at four Plaid Pantries along the way, but the phone was busy every time. Iph takes the street in, opening all her senses as wide as she can. The sidewalk is clean and smells of summer rain. The street is lined with shabby little houses with overgrown yards and weedy parking strips planted with sunflowers and rosemary and lamb's ears that spill over onto the sidewalks. Roses are everywhere, climbing the telephone poles and clinging to fences and front porches cluttered with gardening shoes, children's toys, and boxes of recycling. The odd little stores across the street seem barely plausible as businesses—a washing machine repair shop, barbecue supply outlet, and a barber shop with a sheet of plywood over a broken window and an actual barber's pole out front.

It seems fitting that if Orr must be alone in a new world, so should she. Cut off from her family and home, this little neighborhood is Iph's whole reality. George, a stranger two hours ago, is the only person she knows. The thought is a little revolution. Iph's chest expands, lets in so much air she's a little dizzy. Something akin to relief runs like a feather down her arms. Guilt follows, right on cue.

They enter through a side door. Iph feels the dark container of the garage around her. An old game she and Orr used to play was listing their three favorite darknesses. Whoever had the best answers won. Currently, Iph loves the fur of panthers, Maybelline black eyeliner, and the black velvet coat with black satin lining she stole from the costume closet at school but is afraid to wear anywhere but alone in her room at night. The darkness in Taurus Trucking is excellent, soft and deep, with bits of light wavering in like she and George are inside some massive underwater animal. The square building's giant metal garage door and concrete walls distort the sounds of the neighborhood outside.

Iph thinks of Orr's favorite childhood version of *Pinocchio*, the illustrations done with photographs of puppets. In the scene where the puppet maker/father figure, Geppetto, is stranded inside a whale, there is a whole living room. A table. A lamp. There, he mourns the loss of Pinocchio. Maybe Dad is doing that now—drinking whiskey, the empty house sighing around him.

"Sit tight," George says, a little louder but still conscious of volume. Scout's nails click against the floor. Iph peels off her shoes: pain, then pleasure. Or maybe just relief. They are so similar, she thinks, in the same way pain is caught up with want. Scout is at her feet sniffing her injuries, offering a soft lick. George is moving around the room. Spots of light bloom in the darkness as George turns on a series of flashlights that beam toward the high ceiling, tracing the shape of the empty garage.

"No trucks?"

"Not anymore," George says. "Sold to pay the property tax. My nana left this place to me. Some people in my family think that isn't fair. They want to, like, 'help out' and 'run the business' till I'm an adult." George's air quotes say it all. "My stepdad's in charge of the estate. Tells you something that it wasn't anyone blood-related. Anyway, he mostly got them off my case before he went back to Iraq. Now I'm sitting here waiting to turn eighteen."

George is like Mom, Iph realizes. A complicated history and a lot under lock and key. The flip side to this amazing place is that George lives here alone and in secret with no adults around to help—and still rides around at night, helping other people. Iph's stomach does a disappointed-in-herself drop. That's the problem with being young. You're immature, insufferable. And then you realize it and think, *Why? How could I be that self-absorbed?*

"So, um . . . welcome to my humble abode?" George says.

There's a hay bale with a canvas bull's-eye target stuck to it in the corner and a tire swing hooked to the rafters by a stout rope. In the other corner is a hammock. "Scored it on the street," George says. "And uh, maybe you want to turn around. One sec, I'll grab you a flashlight."

Iph turns back to the garage door. It's completely covered in painted images. "Oh!" She covers her mouth as the syllable bounces around the room, her flashlight illuminating a nearly life-size painting of George as both twins in Gemini, one with waist-length hair, the other with a short-cropped buzz. There are birds and flowers and animals, mythical and real. Trees. Constellations.

Iph moves closer to the Gemini twins, tracing the clasped hands of the two figures with her index finger. "It reminds me of this painting . . ."

"*The Two Fridas*?"

"Yes! I love Frida Kahlo," Iph says.

"Me, too. I call mine George and Georgina."

Touching the long-haired figure, Iph wonders if this is how George once looked. "Are you still both?" Iph asks, hoping it's not the wrong thing to say. "Or just George?"

"Good question," George says.

Iph moves the flashlight across the art-covered walls. There's a sort of cubist rendering of Scout chasing a squirrel that makes her laugh. A bear as high as the warehouse ceiling with its arms open to catch a school of starry fish. A figure—half man, half badger—holding a machine gun. An old woman in a sky-colored kimono flying with a great blue heron. Iph pauses again, this time at a large portrait of a naked blonde girl holding a golden apple. "Who's this?"

"This?" The word is a soliloquy of unrequited feeling. It is a perfect example of Iph's favorite thing: a true reveal. It's a Santos Velos term, something Mom and Dad made up to describe their favorite element in all kinds of art. A building could have a reveal. Or a dance, a play. A song. It starts with a particular kind of noticing. This heightened attention, Dad says, is performed by the noticer but initiated by the art itself, like a siren song calling you to see it. The true reveal is the moment you heed the call and slip into the artist's secret world.

Iph's brain goes where it usually does—she's onstage in London playing Antigone and whips out the sound of longing George has jammed into the tiny throwaway word about the girl in the painting. The theater is silent and electric, but . . . no. Iph shakes it off. The play dissolves. She might write a play with a moment like that, even direct one, but star in one? Not likely.

Last year, when she fired all her fake theater friends, she resolved to stop wanting the things she'd never get. The world is what it is, and Iph is what she is—medium height, medium brown with bombshell boobs and a butt that hasn't fit into a single-digit dress size since she was eleven. Since puberty, she has been the girl with "such a pretty face," a red pouty mouth and big brown eyes and Mom's skin and Dad's ridiculous lashes. Even she can admit to liking her freckles, and her cheekbones are legitimately great. Sometimes, if she is brave, she lets herself look in the mirror after a candlelit bath and see herself as beautiful. If this were the Renaissance and she could learn to sit still, she'd have a promising career as an artist's model. But it's not. Models today look like the girl on the garage door—slender, with high breasts and sculpted abs and thin, waifish limbs. She traces the golden apple with her finger. "I thought it was the snake who tempted Eve, not the other way around."

"Oh!" George's eyes open wide. "I never knew why I painted her like that. You might be onto something."

Iph is silent, waiting for more about the girl. It doesn't come. "So," she asks, "what are the rules of this lost-boy hideout, please?"

George grins. "The governing principle is to avoid detection."

"Who's detecting us?"

"Pirates. Grown-ups. The tricks are few. We come in late and leave when the neighbors aren't around. We don't use flashlights upstairs except for navigation—too many windows."

"Upstairs?"

"There's a whole apartment up top," George says. "We'll sleep up there. It gets cold in here at night and super hot in the morning. Upstairs is insulated."

Iph follows the beam of George's flashlight up a narrow staircase.

"We have water. The city never turned it off. But it's cold. The bathroom window has a shade that's pretty tight, so we can use a little light up there if we're careful. C'mon, Tinkerbell. I do think we should go up and take a better look at those feet."

Upstairs is shadowy, but Iph's eyes adjust. The streetlight seeps between the cracks in the drapes. Kitschy fifties paneling lines one wall of an oddly situated living room. The other wall is a muddy green. They pass a scratchy-looking plaid sofa and matching La-Z-Boy recliner, both a little big for the room. Iph follows George to a narrow elephant-themed bathroom.

"It's like a time capsule," Iph says. There's even a pink elephant soap dish and matching cotton-ball canister.

"Nana redecorated in 1964. After that, she said why mess with perfection."

"That's valid," Iph says, touching the shiny wallpaper with its pattern of champagne glasses and round, tipsy elephants.

"Sit." George puts the pink fluff-covered toilet lid down, grabs something from the medicine cabinet, and squats in front of her, reaching for her ankle. She allows this without protest, even though her feet are truly gross, crook-toed and bony. Iph sighs as her feet are washed with a cold cloth and dried with a soft towel, and antibiotic ointment and Band-Aids are expertly applied, along with the fuzzy socks from the hotel lost and found box. She is already used to George taking care of her.

"You could be a doctor," Iph says.

"I want to be a nurse."

"You'd be awesome at it."

"I'm also pretty good with a hot plate. Want some SpaghettiOs?"

8

MOON-FROTH
COVERED HER FACE

The coyote leads Orr down the mountain. The night has turned clear. He shivers, ears painfully exposed without his hair. Aside from the quarterly trims Mom did in the kitchen, always during a full moon because she said it was good luck, his hair had never been cut. All these years it worked, shielding him from germs and sounds and, lately, from the aliens haunting his dreams, beaming him to their glaring spaceships and returning him home, unable to place the tracker in his neck as they did with Agent Scully.

Mom is dead, he keeps thinking. He knows that's not true, but she *feels* dead, unreachable hundreds of miles away in the Santa Cruz Mountains.

Before she left, she showed him pictures so he could imagine her there—the cottage where she'd sleep, the dance studio with its meadow-flung windows and shiny wood floors, the sprawling wooden common house with the fireplace in the kitchen where she would hang out and eat with other artists—but the moment she drove away, the pictures began to fade. After five days, they were gray in his mind, like newsprint left in the rain. After a week, they were gone.

At first, she called every other day, but her voice sounded wrong, and Orr began to worry she'd been replaced by someone else. It was a weird thing to think. He knew that. He told her calling once a week was better. He told her he was completely fine. It was his first truly successful lie.

After that, he trudged through the motions of summer. Video marathons—sci-fi when he chose, Marilyn and musicals when Iph did. Brunch competitions with Iph and their neighbor Mindy, a Dungeons & Dragons–playing twelve-year-old aspiring chef. At his age, he was supposed to be considerate. Self-sufficient. But every night he tossed and turned until dawn, and every day it was harder to get out of bed.

Now he follows the coyote, probably a mother herself, to a dirt road that eventually leads to Highway 26.

Orr loves maps. Because of that, he knows this road. He walks it for a long time. Hours. He isn't sure how many. As the sky begins to purple, he looks back and sees how thick the forest is, how lost he might have been without the coyote's help. But she's brought him straight to this road that leads, fork after fork, mile after mile, right to his own tree-lined street. To his long gravel drive and the wood and glass house his father built his mother to get her to marry him.

Orr goes there in his mind as his body trudges the roadside. Inside the rustic-planked doors are soft, bright Mexican carpets in the colors his mother loves: magenta, cherry, gold, and parrot green. There are seventeen light switches with plates he and Mom and Iph had collaged using animal images from the Audubon calendar. There are forty windows, all looking out on something beautiful and green. There are fifteen stairs to the upstairs hall, where a window frames a fig tree named Fiona, her large fruit lusted after by his mother's favorite troupe of cedar waxwings— Bowie birds, she calls them, because of their Ziggy Stardust hair and makeup and their love of getting high on fermented fruit. At the height of the fig frenzy, some of them eat so much they fall off the tree, too drunk to perch. Iph and Orr used to collect the stunned party birds and place them carefully in towel-lined shoe-box drunk tanks, waiting for them to sleep it off.

At the top of the stairs is the family room, an open, octagonal space jutting over the living room like the crow's nest in a ship. This is where movies are watched, board games played. Down the hall are the bedrooms. The third door on the left is Orr's.

His room is sanctuary blue. His bed is narrow and canopied with an Indian tapestry of leaping deer that Mom used as a bed-spread when she lived in New York. Orr can smell the just-right scent of the lavender sachets his mother places in his drawers. It's as if he's come back from an early-morning trip to the bathroom. He sees it all so clearly—the droppers of flower essence tinctures in their perfect line on his bedside table: Rock Rose for bad dreams, Cherry Plum for depression, Rescue Remedy for freak-outs.

He's imagining climbing into bed when he realizes the coyote has stopped. She's sitting a few feet away, patient.

She waits for him to catch up to the truth.

Home is a thing of the past. As long as his father is there, Orr can never go back.

The coyote crinkles her furry lids to comfort him.

He trembles so hard, he thinks maybe it's the earth. A quake? The landing of a spacecraft so large it's shaking the snow off the mountain?

But no. Only him. Him and the first hint of birdsong and the fur-jacketed lady coyote who blinks at him, waiting for him to do the thing humans are supposed to do—think.

Orr could call his mother. If he were home, he would. The number is written in Sharpie on the notepad by the telephone in the entryway. Maybe he could find the number some other way. Information. 411. He could tell them the name of the residency. All he needs is to find a phone.

He thinks of his calendar, the X'd-out days until his mother comes home. Sixteen down, seventy-three to go.

There's no way he can survive in the woods for even a week on his own. He's read *My Side of the Mountain*, about the boy who left home to live off the land in the Catskills, taming a per-egrine falcon to hunt for him. But even with his coyote guide, Orr knows he's not tough enough. He has allergies. Gets head-aches. Is vegetarian. Neither he nor Iph have ever eaten meat, although Dad sometimes used to dare them. "Fifty bucks," he would say when they drove past a McDonald's.

Satisfied that Orr knows what is what, the coyote scratches and gets up, trotting to where the road widens. In the light, he can see she is shedding, fur rising in unkempt tufts on her rusty haunches. She glances down the road toward a sign: REST STOP. She and Orr walk side by side until they reach it.

A water faucet, a bench, a bathroom . . . and a phone! Orr picks it up, but there's no dial tone. He turns to look for the coyote, but she is already trotting off into the tree line beyond the parking lot.

Orr panics. But then he stops. He is alone. More alone than he's ever been. He can't rely on Mom or Iph, only himself.

He laps water at the faucet, a little at a time, until he feels bet-ter. He goes into the bathroom. The women's, he realizes when he sees the tampon machine. But it doesn't matter. No one is here. He uses the hand dryer to warm himself even though the roar hurts his ears.

Outside, the sky is paling and the birds are waking up. Orr walks the way the coyote had. The trees open to a rocky beach along a river. A scrub jay caws from a tree and flies down-stream. Orr follows until the beach widens. Ahead is a large canvas tent, the bigger version of the place where he'd woken up with his hands tied and hair shorn. In front of the tent is a campfire, and tending the fire is a young woman with a ciga-rette in one hand and a hot dog on a stick in the other.

Orr stops and the woman looks up. For a moment, he thinks the coyote is back. That's what her surprised face seems to say. But it's Orr she is staring at.

"Hey there," she calls, as raspy as Orr's Greek grandmother. "Where'd you come from?"

"I escaped from some kidnappers," Orr says.

"No shit?" The girl blinks. "Seriously. Are you shitting me? 'Cause I'm a little hungover for boyish pranks."

"I'm not shitting," Orr says. He likes her swearing. It reminds him of Mom.

"Were you hitchhiking? I know you're a dude, but it's still not safe. Pervs are pervs, babe. You gotta watch out."

"I don't think they were pervs," Orr says. "It was a boot-camp place. They came to my house and put a hood over my head and put me in a van and took me there." He points toward the mountain.

"You escaped from Meadowdouche? What are you, like, a boy wizard?"

"I had some help." Orr grins. Why is he smiling at this strange woman? He only does that with family. And Mindy, their neighbor.

"You okay?"

"I'm hungry," Orr says.

"Here," she says, holding out the hot dog. Orr's mouth literally waters. Not a figure of speech after all, he realizes.

"I shouldn't," Orr says.

The girl laughs. "I don't bite." This is another expression Orr had needed to parse when he was little—just a joke, and no one expected other people to bite them. Except when it came to Iph, who was known to bite when provoked and occasionally when she was overcome with love.

"I'm a vegetarian," Orr says.

"Well then." The girl stands up and walks toward Orr with legs that are not in long pants as Orr first thought, but in cutoff shorts and covered in tattoos. "It's your lucky day. This is prime tofu wiener, my friend. Burned to a perfect crisp." She grins, showing a gap between her two large front teeth.

Orr's smile widens.

"C'mon, kid," she says, turning back to the fire. "Have a seat. We've got five packs of these puppies—I'll get us some ketchup. You want a beer?"

9

DICTION
AND SINGING

I ph can't sleep. At home, there's a Jacuzzi tub for this in the pink
bathroom attached to her bedroom, lined with vanilla-scented
candles and lavender salts. There's her stereo and the pile of
sleep mixes she and Orr trade to battle their insomnia, plus the
guided meditations they borrowed from the library for their summer project of learning how to lucid dream. There's the stash of
sleeping pills she's pilfered carefully from Mom and the vibra-
tor—marketed as a neck massager—she shoplifted when her
"friends" ditched her in Walgreens last year and took the bus to
the mall without her. In winter, there's the rain on the roof, and
now, in summer, there are crickets and tree frogs and the grove of
plum trees behind the house, full of sleeping birds.

Here, there's the occasional car, the buzz of the streetlight,
and a too-soft mattress that is an odd size between a double and
a twin and smells faintly of menthol cigarettes. Her bed at home
is a queen, a present for her tenth birthday with a headboard
and footboard that Dad made himself, with hand-carved roses and
gilded thorns like something out of *Sleeping Beauty*. "For my
princess," he said.

This was before the fissures had formed, before it had become her and Mom and Orr against Dad, a truth none of them wanted to admit.

"What's this?" she asked Orr about the brochure on his desk— when was that? Last night? The night before? It feels as if days have passed.

"Boot camp for Bonzo," Orr answered, making a monkey sound.

"Oh, you're definitely a menace," she said, flopping onto his bed. "All those *Redwall* books and the classical music. Not to mention the chess."

"Dad's having buyer's remorse," Orr said, scooting his foot away from hers.

When they were little, Iph used to tease that he'd never be able to get married if he couldn't stand a little footsie. Orr maintained that foot-to-foot contact was vile. Iph still finds it funny to push it a little, scooting her always-cold feet toward his always-warm ones.

"He thinks he can send me back to the factory and exchange me for a real boy."

"Real boys are overrated," Iph said, getting up and grabbing fresh Walkman batteries from his desk recharger. "Want me to talk to him?"

Orr didn't reply. Since he was a toddler, he simply ignored the things he wouldn't consider doing. You knew by his silence what was a no-go. But Dad has been blown off one too many times. And now Orr is paying for it. They all are.

"I'm telling Mom," Iph yelled at Dad mid–Frank Sinatra. She hadn't raised her voice to him since she was four. It was about Orr that time, too, the first and only time Dad had ever tried to spank him. She didn't just yell back then. She bit, right on the spanking arm.

"We have to go get him," she said, pulling Dad from the dance floor. "Right now!"

But Dad shook his head with maddening calm.

It was then that Iph pushed him, pushed her *father*, pushed away the image of Orr being touched by strange hands, Orr without his Walkman and headphones, without his EpiPen, his anxiety pills, his special pillow. She pushed him and yelled, "What were you thinking?"

"Lower your voice," he said. He never yelled anymore. Not even at home. He'd taken classes for that.

"How could you?" Iph cried. She always cried. He wasn't looking at her, but over her head at the cluster of wives watching them. He sent them a look that said, *Teenagers—what can you do?* with his tan handsome face. The look he got in return made Iph want to barf. Women were always like that with Dad. Not that it did them any good. They could be as shiny blonde and jazzercised as humanly possible and Dad would never give them a second glance, because none of them were Mom.

That was Iph's thought when he asked her to the party. She'd go in Mom's place, a worthy understudy. In the dress, she really felt the part. What was that saying Mom hated? *Pride goeth before a fall?* There was a babysitter at some point, an after-school lady so Mom could take a dance class in Portland, who said stuff like that all the time and tried to teach Iph and Orr stories from the Bible. Mom fired her after four-year-old Orr started rambling about Adam's rib and the curse of Ham and pride before falls.

"Pride is good," Mom said, raising Orr's little fist.

"Brown power!" she said.

"Brown power!" Iph and Orr had chorused.

"Brown power!" Dad said in solidarity.

That's the thing with Dad. Iph knows he wants to do what's right. But sometimes, his version of right seems so wrong to the rest of them. The truth is, things have mostly been done Mom's way: no spanking, no yelling, no forced eating of hated foods. Mom grew up in a controlling religious family. Iph and Orr have pieced that much together. She was determined to do things differently with her own children. Iph felt sorry for Dad. Sometimes it felt like he was only along for the ride. Seems like he finally got sick of it.

After Mom left for Santa Cruz, when Orr stopped talking, Iph tried to explain it to Dad: Orr needed some time. She should have tried harder. And tonight—what if she hadn't flipped out? Maybe she and Dad would be in the car right now, speeding to Orr's rescue.

As it is, she's the one who's been rescued, and Orr is someplace far away in the care of adults whose job it is to kidnap and institutionalize unwilling teenagers.

Iph is sick with the wrongness of it. It goes against everything her family is supposed to be about—they are antiwar, feminist, democratic. Iph shakes her head even though there's no one there to see it. She balls her fists and presses them to her stomach. How could Dad betray them? Had he wanted a different family all this time? Normal kids, a regular wife? The kind of family who went to sporting events and knew all the words to the national anthem?

Iph remembers a fight her parents had years ago, before couples therapy taught them to disagree instead of battle. As always, the fight was about Orr.

"You sound like my father," Mom said in the coldest voice Iph had ever heard her use with Dad. "Don't you have any compassion?"

Dad's bitter laugh ran through her, even now. Karma for listening—she still wishes she never heard this fight. "Sometimes I feel like you don't even see me," he said. "Like all you see is the past."

Iph doesn't remember Mom's response.

Her throat clenches. For a second, she's worried she needs her inhaler, far away in the jumble of her nightstand drawer at home. Then she realizes it's not her asthma at all. It's that her family is falling apart.

Iph is standing. How did that happen?

She has to get to a phone. There has to be a way to fix this.

She fumbles for the thick-framed glasses. It's so dark in the hallway, Iph lets her hand trail the wall. The textured wallpaper is sticky in places, rough in others. She turns the corner to the main room. It's dark, too, but there are windows. A streetlight does its best to get in through the blinds. Everything, even the light, takes on a furtive feel.

George is on the sofa, covers kicked off. Scout is splayed on the rug, paws in the air, snoring. Iph takes the flashlight from the coffee table and walks backward into the bedroom.

The nightie she's wearing was Nana's. It's thin and a little pilled, see-through even in the dim apartment, but it will have to do. Iph finds her bra and hunts in the closet for shoes. She finds a neat row of canvas sneakers, all sized for the tiniest feet. Right as she's giving up, she notices a backpack in the corner, a beat-up green JanSport like the ones most kids use for school. Inside is a copy of *Shakespeare's Sonnets* and a pair of boots. The flashlight shines a *ta-da* light on the miracle of them—Doc Martens, size eight, black, adorned with hand-painted roses. Iph is a seven and half, but with the fuzzy socks, they feel great. Her blisters only hurt a little. She's sure George won't mind. A long crocheted cardigan completes the outfit. In the mirror on the closet door, she looks greenish and strange in her getup, with her wild curls and rose combat boots and old-man glasses.

She tiptoes past George and Scout, down the stairs and out. It's a little before daybreak, a time of day Iph knows well as an insomniac, though it's different being outdoors on her own. *These boots are made for walking*. The song repeats in Iph's head as she picks a direction that feels right. It's a favorite of Mom's, one that appears on most of her housework mixes. The tune of it marches Iph down the empty street. The rain has come and gone again. Everything is clean. It's dark, but the sky is showing signs of morning around the edges. Here and there, an early bird chirps, then quiets.

She passes a few houses, inhaling the sweetness of their jasmine-clotted porches. There is a Japanese restaurant and a few empty storefronts. A hardware store. An incongruous adult theater next to a new-looking coffee shop. Finally, the corner of a large street with the occasional car and a gas station. A pay phone! She still has the quarters from the lost and found, taken from the kitchen counter and slipped into Nana's nightgown pocket.

She's shaky as she puts the coin in its slot. She needs to keep it together. To find the magic words that will make Dad relent.

The phone rings. The answering machine clicks on. It's Dad's deep voice instead of Mom's usual greeting.

"Hello, you've reached the Santos Velos household. If this is Iph, sit tight and leave a number where I can reach you. I'll call as soon as I can. Anyone else, please leave a message."

She imagines the night that led up to this—Dad trying to act normal at the party, then finally giving in to his worry and heading out to look for her. Yanking his tie loose in a familiar pissed-off gesture that says, *You kids never face the consequences of your actions.* She imagines him giving up, heading home, thinking maybe Iph got a ride with someone from his office, speeding toward Forest Lake half-ironically praying to whichever Greek Orthodox saint keeps you safe from getting a ticket. At home alone, he'd last an hour, maybe two, his leg jiggling as he tried to distract himself with *Star Trek* reruns. Finally, he'd discover the off-the-hook phone, call the hotel, and learn she'd been there and gone—and totally freak out. He's probably downtown right now. Or at a police station.

Iph can't remember how long it's been since the answering machine beeped. She has no phone number and even if she knew the address, she can't have Dad bursting into George's secret hideout. She hangs up and instantly regrets it—yet another instance where she acts before she thinks. When will she stop being such a drama queen? She should at least let him know she's safe, that she'll call again in a few hours.

She goes to slide her last quarter into the slot, but misses. It drops and rolls under an ice machine, totally out of reach. She's furious. Predictably, she starts to cry.

A little bark stops her.

"How did you know I was here?" Iph crouches and holds out her hand.

The dog's eyes are the exact color of maple syrup. Her coat is a mix of mink brown and ink black. She tilts her head as if she intends to speak.

"What?" Iph says.

Scout play-bows, circles three times, and trots over to the ice machine. Flattening into a small brindle pancake, she does an awkward scoot like something a seal might do on land and pushes herself underneath. She grunts as she scoots back, a movement she seems to manage with her whole body at once, and emerges, clearly pleased with herself, popping up like a jack-in-the-box to reveal Iph's lost quarter under her chin.

"You're a genius," Iph says. She's dropped any kind of dumbing-down she was doing before for the dog's sake. "Thank you so much."

She bends to pick up the coin and gets a surprise kiss attack. Scout seems determined to lick up all traces of her tears. After leaving a semi-sane-sounding message on her home answering machine, Iph takes a second to breathe. The sky is rosy pink and feels a little closer to earth than it does at home.

Scout's shoulders twitch as she trots up the block in a different direction than Iph came. Iph follows. They walk less than half a block up Southeast 39th and turn onto a narrow street crammed with tiny houses and outrageously lush gardens. What kind of story would you set in a place like this? What would her story be like if she'd grown up here, with neighbors so close you'd have to close the curtains to get dressed and whisper if you wanted to talk about them?

Scout zigs, then zags, taking them in what feels like the direction of Taurus Trucking with a few detours so they can see the best yards. The birds are in full morning mode. Chickadees sing their names to each other from the tops of wide-hipped maples with leaves as big as Iph's head. A hummingbird dives face-first into a fat purple flower. Iph wants to dive with her, to taste what the tiny bird tastes.

From a house ahead, a small stucco bungalow covered in pink climbing roses, piano music spills from an open window. Iph stops in the middle of the street to listen. A line of crows bob above her. Scout dances around her ankles. Iph is still, trying to will the peace of this morning, the joy of this music through the ether to Orr. She's crying a little and laughing a little at the crows because it seems like they're laughing at her. "Tell Orr I'm coming," she tells them softly. "Don't forget!" she calls as they caw at her and fly away like maybe they understand.

The piano music swells. A jazz standard, something familiar. A window down the street slams shut—not a morning person, perhaps.

Who plays the piano this early? Probably an insomniac like her who sleeps best at sunrise. Iph knows that if she lived here on this narrow street in one of these dollhouses—maybe the cream one on the corner with peeling paint and a tilting porch that seems to be held up by thick vines of passionflower and clematis—she would never be angry at the early-morning music. She'd let it slip into her sleep. Let it move her, change her, the way art is supposed to.

10

UNITS AND OBJECTIVES

George is waiting, sitting at the top of a staircase leading directly to the apartment, when Iph follows Scout up a side street to the small parking lot behind Taurus Trucking. There is no mention of Iph leaving or Scout bringing her back, just a quick glance down at the boots she borrowed and a brief nod.

"They're never up this early on weekends," George whispers, nodding at the small house that shares a back fence with the lot. "Normally, I use the side door closer to the street." It takes Iph a minute to remember about the neighbors and the need for secrecy. "C'mon." George motions her inside.

There are three phone books on the kitchen table beside a piece of binder paper and a pen. George and Iph search for Meadowbrook in the cool light seeping through the yellowed window shades. Either Iph isn't remembering the name on the brochure correctly or the place isn't listed in metropolitan Portland. In any case, George woke up with a plan, and the phone book is only phase one.

It's too early for phase two, so they doze on the sofa, Scout between them, and wake up in the heat of early afternoon. It's so hot a cold shower feels good. George has given Iph the okay to raid Nana's wardrobe. She finds a pair of overalls good enough to fight for if someone else tried to nab them at a thrift store. The denim is worn soft and paper-thin. The legs are loose and hit Iph at the ankle. With an undershirt of George's, her hair piled in a bun on top of her head and secured with a pair of take-out chopsticks, and the clunky black glasses, Iph has managed to be both on the lam and actually cute. Not that it matters. She shakes her head at herself in Nana's vanity. *Pretty is as pretty does*, she tells herself. Or maybe Nana's telling her that, because it's not a thought she remembers having before.

The wait for the neighbors to leave is a metal-on-metal grind Iph feels in her intestines and back teeth. What is Orr doing at boot camp? Surely he's been up for hours. Maybe the place isn't so bad. Maybe they're hiking or trying to force Orr to do crafts. Maybe they will let him do a trail run. He loves to run through the forest.

The street below Taurus Trucking is quiet. The businesses in the neighborhood don't seem like they've ever been very busy. It's the back neighbors George worries about, a nice family of four who might be concerned about a lone teenager squatting at the vacant tow truck place. So they wait, George narrating the family's exodus.

"They load the kids up first. Mom will get in and remember the stuff she forgot. This happens between one and four times before she's good to go. The dad blasts the tunes on his way home from work in the evening, so when the mom turns the car on in the morning, it's like a rock concert—Red Hots, Bad Brains, Fishbone. The mom turns it down and switches it to NPR, but the kids make her change it back so they can sing. They know all the words. It's pretty cute."

Iph laughs, watching Scout's ears telegraph the steps a second before they happen. Kids in, a mumbled swear from the mom, screen door slamming open, screen door slamming shut. The music blast—Nirvana this time. Iph misses Orr even more hearing the kids scream-singing the words to "Smells Like Teen Spirit" out the open windows as their mom drives away. Nirvana was Orr's first independently discovered teenager thing. Iph sort of misses the owlish little classical music snob he used to be.

In the bright heat, Taurus Trucking shows her age: blue paint faded to white in places, duct tape over the cracks in a window, rust on the metal garage door. Gripping the seat while George stands to pedal is easier since Iph ditched her party dress and can straddle the bike with these Rosie the Riveter overalls. She's getting used to the Orr-shaped pain in her stomach, and the hunger, too. George offered her Cheerios with bananas and soy milk, but Iph could barely manage a few bites.

Southeast Portland is thick with crows and roses and families out walking their dogs and toddlers. They fly down side streets and over the Hawthorne Bridge, pacing the seagulls, the river sparkling summer blue below. Iph puts a hand on the messenger bag to feel Scout's solid body. Downtown, they stop, and Iph hops off a second before George does, almost graceful.

They walk together, pace for pace. Today George wears jeans cut off at the knees, a short-sleeved shirt buttoned all the way up, and a mustard cardigan, even in the heat. Iph recognizes Pioneer Square. Once at Christmas, they'd come to Portland, all four of them, to see the massive tree lit up and have dinner at a restaurant at the top of a bank building.

Today the square is empty except for a group of ragged shirtless hacky-sack boys and some shopgirls drinking iced coffees on their cigarette break. Even without the bow and arrow, George heads into the square like someone who patrols the streets at night to protect wayward girls. Scout whines to be let out of the messenger bag and runs over to a black lab Iph hadn't noticed dozing in the shade. The two frolic with the boys, who play their game around them, a laughing mass of dog and boy and summer.

One of the players waves when they get closer and lobs the hacky sack to his friend, pulling a shirt from the pile and yanking it over his head, not seeming to notice it's inside out. He bows to George, then to Iph, doffing an imaginary top hat.

"Hey." George grins. "Iph, this is Josh. Josh, this is my friend Iph."

"If?" Josh says. He leaps to the bandstand, still set up from some weekend festival, and falls to his knees, clutching his heart.

> O! if, I say, you look upon this verse,
> When I perhaps compounded am with clay,
> Do not so much as my poor name rehearse;
> But let your love even with my life decay.

George snorts and Iph applauds. "From one of the sonnets?"

"Seventy-one," he says, getting up to take a bow.

"Bravo!" Iph laughs.

"If you go in for that sort of thing," George says like it's an old joke between them. How do these two know each other? And why do they both quote Shakespeare? "My man," George says, "we're here on business. Iph's brother got nabbed."

"Cops?" Josh leaps off the stage easy as a cat.

"Boot-camp mercenaries," George says. "A place called Meadowbrook, she thinks, but we can't find it in the phone book. Iph needs to call them and check in on him."

"Won't talk to her. Parents only. And they're all named like that—faux-wholesome nature-sounding crap. I've been in several." Iph looks closer at him. Pretty, sandy hair, hazel eyes. Something around the bridge of his nose, the memory of a fist or a rock—but Iph is probably imagining that. It happens sometimes, the outlandish image of some detail from a stranger's life. "Overactive imagination," her dad had said when, as a little girl, she worried that someone was hurting her third-grade teacher.

"It's Meadowbrook," Iph says. "I'm pretty sure. I saw the brochure."

Josh shakes his head. "Not ringing a bell. But wait—" He takes Iph's hand gently in his, running a finger over her long, glossy gold-painted nails, freshly manicured a lifetime ago. "A *lady*, I see," he says in his decent English accent. "So . . . are we talking Ritz-Carlton rehab? Is there money involved?"

Iph nods slowly. Her family *does* have money. Dad has been very successful. "Yeah. It would be expensive."

"I'm not your gent, then. It's institutions for the likes of me. But our friend Georgie knows someone who might be able to help." Josh drapes an arm around George, who shrugs it off, but not in an angry way. These two are playing their roles at full stage strength. For Iph? Another game with Orr is people as ice cream flavors. Together, these two are definitely Lost Boy Ripple.

"I could take her there, old chap, if it's too much for you." Josh says in the English accent again, and Iph imagines him dressed in jewels and a fur cape, like pictures she's seen of Oscar Wilde. But wait—is George pawning her off on this boy? He seems nice enough, but George and Iph are a team. At least, she thought they were after yesterday. This always happens. Why is she such a side-kick? Ever since preschool she's glommed on to a more outgoing or capable friend, usually an alpha girl who undid her elaborate braids at recess and insisted she do embarrassing or servile things to prove her loyalty. Last year, when Iph renounced this practice and gave up on the limited stock of potential friends at her small school, she glommed on to Mom. And now, on her own for the first time ever, she's immediately glommed on to George.

Iph sighs as George gestures to the side of the bandstand and pulls her over.

"There is someone who can probably help us."

Iph can't help it—she smiles a little at the *us.*

"She might not be thrilled to see me. But I'm worried your dad isn't picking up. Something feels off. We can at least use her phone."

"You've done so much already. Are you sure it's not too weird?" Iph leaves the real question—*Why is it weird?*—unspoken. It's a Mom trick, and like always, it works.

"Cait . . . is my ex. It ended because of me. I cheated."

This is certainly a new data point in George's backstory. And a confirmation. George dates girls.

"You know how I was kind of weird for a second this morning?"

Iph nods. When Iph got back from the gas station with Scout, there was a moment—something about the boots. It's interesting that George noticed Iph noticing. George looks down at the flowered Docs Iph borrowed. "They . . . belonged to the girl I cheated with. I painted them for her. She's the reason I go out with my bow at night. Why I know what it's like to need to find someone."

"Oh."

"But it's okay. Cait and I are all right now, pretty much. And she'll definitely want to help you with this."

When they go back to Josh, he's sitting on the steps with a love-crazed Scout wriggling belly-up in his lap. "It's settled, then? You're taking your chances with the queen?"

George grunts and opens the messenger bag. A little girl in a pink leotard and leopard-print rain boots trailing her quick-stepping Birkenstocked mother sees Scout's leap and claps.

Josh gives George a quick, back-slapping hug and takes Iph's hand again, briefly kissing it. Close up, he smells like the boys' locker room. Iph knows because she'd had to go in there more than once to collect a melting Orr in middle school before Mom, to Iph's enormous relief, decided to keep him home.

The smell is strong, but backing away seems impolite. For all his charm and prettiness, Josh looks like the kids Iph used to see panhandling outside Powell's, the ones Mom always made sure to give whatever cash was in her wallet. He's probably homeless, Iph realizes. And without the secret hideout at Taurus Trucking, maybe George would be, too. They both know boot camps. Institutions. Maybe if Orr is lucky, he'll find a few kids like these at Meadowbrook, kind and wise in a way he and Iph have never had to be.

Gripping Josh's hand, Iph steps back into a curtsy, full prima ballerina. Pre-blood and boobs, Iph had been set on being a dancer like Mom. Her moves can still impress a layperson. Josh and George are wide-eyed in a way Iph likes, and again she's confused by the pleasure-pain of this day and last night and all the things that have happened since Orr was kidnapped and she ran away.

"Farewell, milady," Josh says. It's nice on his lips. George scowls and Josh grins.

Are they . . . competing? Over her?

"Farewell," Iph says. "And thank you."

11

THE SEAGULL

The bus climbs into the hills above the hospital. Iph has been to this part of Portland countless times for Orr's quarterly appointments with his psychiatrist. The medicine was a blessing. Before it, there were times when Orr's body went so rigid with tension, he would worry his limbs had turned to wood. The same doctor treated Iph last year during the worst of her existential crisis. She took the pills for several months until she felt stable enough to stop.

Iph notes the change in neighborhood as they climb. As the kid of an architect and a socialist kitchen witch, she perceives a city by its building style, garden aesthetic, class dissection, and degree of magic. Iph used to wonder what other parents talked about while driving their kids around.

This area was developed later than the tiny Victorian cottages, English Tudor revivals, and Craftsman bungalows in the other parts of Portland—probably constructed in the sixties or seventies, clean-lined geometric houses built for doctors and lawyers when everyone was talking about space travel, modern art, and the future. Ugly, but made of quality materials with at least some aesthetic in mind, they are her least favorite sort of Portland house. Some of her earliest memories are of Dad driving around the West Hills showing her examples of midcentury architecture or into Northeast to find a perfect example of an Old Portland foursquare.

The bus slows on a curving road that borders the city forest. They pass a familiar stretch that leads to a trailhead. Mom used to bring Orr here before his appointments so he'd burn enough energy to sit still. Iph would walk in the pagan cathedral of the trees slowly enough to lose sight of them, loving the illusion of being alone.

"Is Forest Lake like this?" George asks, speaking for the first time in a while. Maybe worried about the ex.

"Kind of. Not so wild. There's lots of trees, but they're more spread out and intentional looking. My mom always tells people it's east of the sun and west of Boring."

"Next door to the troll princess?" She and George clearly read the same books when they were kids.

"Just a type A, twelve-year-old aspiring chef," Iph says. "And more trees. And Republicans."

"I'm an Idaho kid myself. Or, was. I lived there when I was little. I'll never forget the day I learned Boring, Oregon, was a real place." In the light of day, Iph notices how crooked George's bottom teeth are. She commands herself not to stare. In her world, crooked teeth are quickly straightened.

At the top of the hill, they get off the bus and turn the corner. Iph pants up a tall set of cement stairs. The day has settled into true summer, in the high eighties at least. The entry of the glass-fronted house looks more like an office building than someone's actual home.

Our house could have been like this, Iph realizes. Her dad is into modern architecture and worships Frank Lloyd Wright, but instead of a cold, angular box, their house has a feel Dad calls organic, its tall sides clad in shingles faded to the sheened gray of lamb's ears in late summer. There were magazine profiles of it when it was first finished. The best was headlined, MODERN

BOHEMIA: WUNDERKIND ARCHITECT AND FLOWER-CHILD BRIDE
MAKE FIRST HOME IN ELEGANT PORTLAND SUBURB. A framed photo
of the cover shows Iph's parents, Mom barefoot and bangled with
silver earrings and a white sundress and shaggy-haired Dad in
jeans and sneakers, standing in the entry, backlit by sun streaming
in through a line of slatted windows in the high ceiling—what Orr
always called the house's gills. "It breathes sunlight," he'd insisted.

This had bothered Iph. "What happens at night, then?" she'd
asked.

His answer hadn't made her feel any better. "At night it holds
its breath."

Iph pulls the stray hair off her neck and knots it on the top of
her head, repinning the chopsticks. The doorbell's echo hints at an
even bigger house than the imposing façade suggests. George is
suddenly a stranger beside her.

The girl who answers the door makes her feel both worse and
better. Harmless, probably, but so fine-featured, blonde, and thin
Iph has to fight the impulse to turn around and walk away. Suddenly, Nana's overalls are too snug. The not-quite-right glasses
press a headache into her temples.

The girl tries to keep a straight face but smiles at George anyway, little lightning bolts of sun flying off her perfect cheekbones.
"You're like a million hours too late, man. The party's over," she
says. "The cleaners left half an hour ago. I'm locking it down. My
parents will be home at four."

"Cleaners? Really?" George is smiling, too, and Iph feels the
spark between them. Suddenly it's like every other day, demoted
from principal to chorus girl just like that.

"Leave no trace," the girl says. Her golden hair falls over her
eye, and she makes no move to shift it. Iph notes for future reference: in the truly beautiful, there is no such thing as a misstep or
malfunction. Everything falls as it should.

"We aren't here for revels, milady. We come to request a boon."
George bows low and turns on the charm, the same British schtick
as Josh.

"You can take a shower," she says like it's grudging. "I have that shampoo you like." Cait moves aside for George, still not addressing Iph. Well, she's used to that treatment from pretty girls. *Conventionally pretty white girls*, she hears Mom correct. At school, Iph sometimes feels like she can smell the fear seeping out from under their deodorant, their worry that Iph's soft belly and thick thighs are contagious. Cait hugs herself, cupping the sharp tips of her elbows in her delicate hands. Black nail polish, chipped. Silver rings on every finger, even her thumbs.

"I'm the reason we're here," Iph says. "My brother is in trouble. George thinks you can help."

"He got nabbed," George says. Iph shivers at the fairy-tale finality of the word. "I wanted to ask you—what were the names of the first few places they put your sister? The outdoorsy ones?"

The look on Cait's face tells the missing part of this story. Iph thinks about that—how one look, one reaction, can say more than hours of dialogue.

"They kidnapped him," Iph tells her, looking her right in the eyes. "Last night."

The girl's eyes widen and change from pale blue to watery gray, and Iph knows that whatever monster is after Orr has already taken this beautiful girl's sister.

"Please," Iph says, "can you help me?"

12

LIKE METAL
IN ROADS

A nother day, another van ride. The Columbia flows by on the right. The gorge is a dream landscape of forest and rock formations and spinning raptors and the wide powerful river.

There are two girls—women?—in front, and Orr and the tattooed tofu wiener girl are riding in back. Jane? He thinks it's Jane. She looks like a Jane. They stopped for breakfast at a diner that served perfect fried eggs over medium and almost-perfect pancakes because, as the girl driving said, "Woman cannot live on wieners alone." Now it's three in the afternoon, and they're headed for Portland.

Orr holds his hands over his ears. Probably-Jane snores on the bench seat beside him, sleeping through the mix blasting out of the low-quality speakers.

At a stoplight in the outskirts of the city, Jane wakes up. "Don't like Dead Moon?" she yells.

"I like it," he yells back. "It's just loud. And these speakers suck. No offense!" he remembers to add.

"Huh." She grunts and leans into the front seat, practically in the lap of the girl on the passenger side, a medium-tall, plump redhead. Orr has always loved red hair, even the dyed-red kind like hers. Not love-love. Orr isn't sure where he stands in that department. His mother asks him a few times a year, making sure he knows it's totally okay to be gay or bi or something else altogether that is specific to him. But at fifteen, Orr can't decide.

He knows a few things. He likes looking at certain parts of certain people—a boy's slender, long-fingered hands, a girl's high-arched feet and seashell ears. He prefers plumpness to thinness and darker skin like Iph's and Mom's and the girl driving the van's to lighter skin like Jane's, which is as white as binder paper under her colorful tattoos. He has always been able to tell Iph honestly that the shape of her body is good, fine. A valid shape for a body to be. He knows, of course, that the Overall Messaging for girls is particularly harsh on these attributes. They've talked about it, he and Iph and Mom. Although Mom is slimmer than Iph, she was told when she was young that her body was too sturdy for ballet, her breasts too big for Broadway. She tells Iph this when Iph feels bad about herself. Because of the patriarchy, they hear this story a lot.

Orr's own body is slim to bony and requires a lot of movement. He runs every morning at dawn because he must. It's been this way since he was eleven and the world began its slow press inward, like the trash compactor in the Death Star in the first *Star Wars* movie.

Mom went running with him at first because back then he was still prone to getting lost. But it was hard to wake her some mornings after she'd had wine or a sleeping pill the night before. So Orr studied maps. First his street and neighborhood, then the suburbs and freeways, then the streets of Portland and the surrounding mountains to the east and the coast to the west. When he knew he wouldn't get lost, he ran by himself. Not tethered to Mom's lesser stamina and slower pace, Orr galloped the surrounding country roads. His arms and legs, exposed in the tank top and running shorts Mom got him along with his running shoes, had turned the golden brown of Dad's Mediterranean skin in summer. He found a long, circular route, almost ten miles total. He ran it every morning and sometimes again before bed. Probably part of why he was able to keep up with the coyote, he realizes. Almost as if he's been training for this.

"Here, kid," Jane says, placing a small plastic bag in his hand. Inside are two little foam blobs, orange as safety cones. Orr can't decipher their purpose.

"Dude. They're earplugs." Jane laughs, opens the bag, takes one out. "Take your hands away, babe. One at a time." Orr likes clear, direct instruction. He likes being called babe. He does as she says.

The blobs are squishy and glove-compartment hot going into Orr's ears, but once there, he can hear the music without pain. The scratchy speaker noise and road sounds are gone.

The next song is from a band he hasn't heard before, all jangled and falling apart with a husky girl singer. The song goes perfectly with the big rattly van and the gray city outskirts and the summer-blue sky.

"How do you like this one?" the redhead yells from the front.

"It's great," Orr says. "Who is it?"

"It's us!" the girl driving says. "The Furies."

"The Furies rock," Orr says.

He grins at Jane.

Jane grins back.

13

TOWARD A PHYSICAL
CHARACTERIZATION

The phone in Cait's room is pale blue to match the wildflower wallpaper peeking out between pages torn from magazines, postcards, photographs, and band posters. Cait has surprising taste—mostly seventies punk with some Björk and Tori Amos thrown in, and a vintage poster of Janis Joplin with a frame of dried marigolds pinned carefully to its edges that squeezes Iph's heart.

Dammit. Why isn't this girl more hateable?

Iph almost forgets to care about acting when she imagines directing someone like this. Cait doesn't even bother to put her body in character, as Iph surely would have had to do to make the phone call she's making. This girl is used to being obeyed. A fan of brochures filched from a filing cabinet in her mother's study sits on the bed next to her. None match the exact one Iph saw in Orr's room, but these are all from a few years ago, the font sort of hokey and the kids' clothes a little outdated. Iph is sure it's Meadowbrook, though. The lodge looks right, the position of the mountain in the background the same as in the brochure on Orr's desk. Cait tries it first.

Draped across her king-size canopy bed in baggy sweats and

a cropped Hello Kitty tee and smoking a clove cigarette, she sounds like the world's most bougie Euro-mom. "I'd like a progress report on my son. Orestes Santos Velos," she demands in a clipped, sexy growl. The rationale behind the accent is clear when she says Orr's not-American-sounding name. In Cait's mouth, it communicates "diplomatic corps" and "Spanish aristocracy" and "owns a Greek Island"—a strange opposite to Mom's California lilt and occasional Spanglish, which used to make people wonder if she was Iph and Orr's babysitter.

"What?" Cait's accent almost drops. She sits up. "Are you joking?"

Something is wrong.

"Has his father been informed?" she sputters as if genuinely affronted, the accent thicker now. Iph can hear the faint hiss of words on the other end of the phone. Cait nods and puts the receiver down in its cradle.

14

THE PERIOD
OF EMOTIONAL
EXPERIENCE

Iph tries Dad every ten minutes until they have to go.

"You could stay and keep trying," Cait says. "It's just George. Persona non grata. My parents would have a fit."

"No worries." Iph meets Cait's eye easily now. They are definitely going to be friends.

Iph picks up a photo on the nightstand: two blonde girls in swimsuits at the beach. There's so little margin between where Iph is now and where Cait lives every day as an only child. She may have supermodel cheekbones and mile-long legs, but her sister—her *sister*—is dead.

Cait rummages through her purse. Vintage Coach, simple with a brass lock. A smaller version of Mom's favorite bag, one she bought new in the early seventies with her first paycheck from an off-Broadway show.

"Here," Cait says. "Take my phone card. Run it up all you want. My dad's accountant pays it; my parents will never see the bill." She slips it into the front pocket of Iph's overalls with a packet of travel tissues.

At the bus stop, she and George are silent. The heat feels good after the air-conditioning at Cait's. It's when Iph goes to blow her nose, stuffy from crying, that she discovers the twenty-dollar bills Cait tucked in her pocket. They get off the bus on Hawthorne in front of Burgerville. Iph tries Dad. He doesn't pick up, and the machine is full.

After a Gardenburger Iph can barely swallow, she tries again while George stays in the cool restaurant with Scout. Like most people, the manager is a Scout fan and allows her to sit discreetly in a corner booth lapping water from a cup while George feeds her a child-size burger and fries.

It's boiling at the pay phone. Iph remembers why she hates summer. This time, Dad picks up on the first ring.

"Iph." Dad sounds like he's swimming underwater.

"Did you find him?"

"There was a search team," Dad says. "With dogs. Wait, how'd you know he was gone?"

"Is he okay?" The last time they went camping, Orr had to go to the emergency room for a wasp sting. Without help, he could have died.

"He's fine, sweetie. I know he is."

"You had him kidnapped. Now they've lost him. That doesn't sound fine."

"There's a waitress who swears she saw him yesterday with a bunch of tattooed girls."

"Dad! That doesn't sound like Orr."

"Eggs over medium, extra hash browns, add cheddar."

"Sub pancakes for toast," Iph whispers.

"Hot chocolate, lukewarm." Dad's voice breaks. "It was him. He must have hitched a ride."

Iph's mouth is hanging open. She shuts it and closes her eyes.

"The waitress said the girls looked like punkers from Portland."

Iph stands up straighter. He knows *punkers* is outdated. The cute dorky Dad routine isn't going to work. "Good thing there are so few tattooed girls in Portland. Finding him should be a breeze."

"Iph, come on. Where are you?"

"Don't worry about me. I'm fine."

"That's not what I asked." There it is—Dad's *I'm an Olympian god and you're a peon mortal* voice. "Iph?"

"Portland," Iph says. "With friends." Mom would have jumped right on this—she knows Iph's friends, if you could call them that, and none of them live in the city. "What about you? I called like a thousand times."

"How kind of you," Dad says. "That really helped when I was out scouring the streets."

"I came back to the hotel. You were gone."

Dad exhales. Iph feels him letting go of the rope. That's what he and Mom call it when one person realizes a fight is going nowhere. "When I got back, someone said Bill's daughter left early. I thought you must have gotten a ride with her."

"You thought I was with Mackenzie? Our last sleepover was in second grade. She thinks Phyllis Schlafly is a feminist icon. We've hated each other for years."

"I assumed you hated me more." Dad's gone quiet. Like Iph, his temper rises quickly and falls as fast. "I went to call you over there when you didn't come home. The phone was off the hook."

"I know," Iph says. "The hotel guy called the operator for me."

"That guy!" Iph can picture Dad shaking his head. "Couldn't answer a simple question. I had to lean on him pretty hard. A big tip helped. Apparently, you left with some boy."

There is a beat. A weighted silence.

"Dad, I told you. I'm perfectly fine."

Another beat. She can hear him shifting in his seat. "I called the police. They told me to call back if you were gone more than three days. I got home at four in the morning, and a few minutes later, Meadowbrook called. I drove straight there." Dad stops, takes a drink of something. "Iph," he finally says, "are you sure you're all right?"

"Dad. I just ate a Gardenburger."

"Really? That's good. You left your purse, so I was worried." He exhales like a horse, a thing Iph used to love when she was little enough to ride on his shoulders. "I still can't believe it. Your brother ran away."

Is that *pride* in Dad's voice? Running away is exactly the sort of thing he would admire. He's always telling stories about his adventures with his brother—pranks and misdemeanors, outsmarting neighborhood bullies. It would be just like him to spin Orr's disappearance into some sort of Huck Finn adventure. The fact that this is the only kind of bravery Dad can see is the whole problem. He's always underestimated Orr.

A group of squealing toddlers swarm the outside tables. Iph plugs her free ear.

"Did you call Mom?"

He hesitates. "I want to find him first."

Iph has never considered the possibility of her parents breaking up. They aren't just married. They're in love. They walk hand in hand. Stay up late talking politics and art. It's a common occurrence to enter a room and find them holding each other silently and breathing like they are each other's air. But if anything could break them apart, it's this.

"Dad, why? What were you thinking?"

"I'm his father." Iph hears ice cubes clinking in a glass. Is Dad drinking? That was a thing when Iph and Orr were little, Dad drinking a little too much every night.

"It's iced coffee," he says. As much as he blows off Iph's intuition, he's the other one in the family who seems to share it. "I know things are a mess, Iph. I'm not resting until I figure this out. I'm sure he'll call home soon. He hates sleeping away . . ." Dad trails off, perhaps stopped short by his own hypocrisy. Mom was going to have his guts for garters.

Iph shivers. *Someone walked over your grave.* That's what Mom always says about those weird spasms. The shiver and the saying became a part of her dance piece. She spent hours in the studio behind the house working variation after variation of it—that moment of cold or premonition or possession.

The working title of Mom's three-part modern ballet is *El*

Mundo Bueno/El Mundo Malo, from a favorite book of hers—*The Fifth Sacred Thing*, a utopian alternative history by an ecofeminist witch. *The good reality and the bad reality exist side by side*, Mom wrote in her application for the residency, *imperceptibly separate, like the scrim between waking and sleep. The trick is knowing where you are. Is the bad reality a dream that you only need to wake up from? Is the good reality lost in a single moment, like falling asleep at the wheel?*

Iph wonders now if the two worlds are not separate, but simultaneous. Or what if there is a space between them, a no-man's-land where things are good and bad all at once? Orr at boot camp and now lost is a living nightmare—but this otherworld she's found in Portland is the stuff of impossible dreams.

In just two days these strangers feel more like friends than the kids she grew up with. Even though they have every right to judge her, pickled as she is in her spoiled suburban childhood, they've been nothing but accepting and kind. Maybe time in *El Mundo Malo* marks you. Maybe George and Josh and Cait saw it before she did—that her life will never be the same.

Dad's ice clicks like he's draining the coffee. "Iph? Are you still there?"

"I'm here."

"I did a lot of research. Visited several places. Your mom and I talked about it last year, but she didn't think it was a good idea. He was just so depressed with her gone. I wanted to help him find his power."

"Waiting for Mom to come back without freaking out *was* Orr exercising his power. He needs to shut down sometimes. If you were ever around, you'd know that. But you're always at work or in your study or out on a date with your precious wife. You don't even know your own kids. I hope you're happy."

There is a hiss of breath—the sound of Dad expelling his own monster, the temper she'd inherited. In and out, three times. Then, "The camp has an investigator who's on it. The police will start looking if they don't find him by tomorrow."

"The police? Dad, oh my god." Iph will never forget the day

she found Mom doubled over in the kitchen, a copy of some magazine at her feet. There was an article about a kid who sounded a little like Orr, a brown-skinned boy who was melting down. There were cops and a gun and it was too close to home.

"Dad, we don't need the cops. There's no way he'd sleep on the street. And if he's in the city, he's definitely not lost. Every time we're in Portland, Mom tests him, asks which way to go and he always knows. And I mean, at least it's girls who have him. They sound like kids, right?"

"College age," Dad says. "The waitress said they were rowdy but harmless. Talked about music and castrating rapists." There's a little uptick in Dad's tone. He's all about that Greek-tragedy level of revenge. Told Iph when she was ten that if any guy even tried to touch her against her will, kicking him in the balls was her birthright. "And you're right," he says. "We'll find him. Come home, *kuklamu*."

Kukla. Dad's special nickname for her—"little doll" in Greek. Iph gets a wave of Dad: his bear-deep singing voice and cedar aftershave and honey shampoo. The world quiets, and it's him and Iph on a silent stage, their fast-beating hearts pounding over the sound system.

Dad needs help. Needs her. And yes, of course Iph wants to go home to her obscenely soft bed and enormous bathtub and full refrigerator and house that is shined weekly by a team of housekeepers. But can she?

Suddenly, she's not mad anymore. "Where are you?" she asks. "The deck?"

His voice catches as he says, "Treehouse." Orr's treehouse. The special place Dad made for him in the days when he was still trying to have an actual relationship with his son. He installed a phone up there, extending the landline from the second floor to the majestic linden at the bottom of their property where Orr retreated when things were too much. He could be alone there with Mom just a phone call away.

Dad sniffs. Is he crying?

"Let's go find him, Dad. Let's find him together."

"I'll come get you."

I'll stay if you come back. That's what George said when Iph went into the hotel.

Now, after all they've been through, Iph can't just say goodbye at this Burgerville. There has to be something more she can do. Some small way to pay George back for saving her. She'll have to be crafty. George was not happy when Iph discovered the twenties from Cait.

"She knows not to pull that with me," George said. "Unless Scout's going hungry, I won't take a handout. Of course, she left the larder open on purpose, knowing I don't mind nicking a few things from her robber-baron parents."

"Who says *larder*?" Iph laughed. "Who says *robber baron* and *nick*?" Then she saw what was in the backpack—a full bottle of gin and a six-pack of tonic water, several limes, and a carton of cigarettes. "And who needs all this?"

George quoted Shakespeare again, this time from *King Lear*. "*This cold night will turn us all to fools and madmen.*"

"Dad? Are you still there?"

"I'm here."

"We need to make flyers," Iph says. "My friend here is an artist who could totally make one. Like those police sketches." Maybe George will let Dad pay for that, like a commission. It's worth a shot, and maybe a better option than the few outdated snapshots they have of Orr, who hates being photographed. "I'm in Southeast. There's not a phone, but I can meet you—"

"Iph?" Dad's tone is suddenly cautious. "There's something else. Before you make a flyer." Dad clears his throat. "Honey, they cut Orr's hair." There is a beat that goes on a breath too long. "They shaved his head."

Anger has always been fleeting for Iph, there and gone faster than an ice cream headache. What she feels now is something else. It's muscled and clear-eyed and huge. *This tiger-footed rage.* Padding, soft, calculating. She shakes with it.

Her father is forgotten. She is nowhere, no place at all. Or some-place between atoms, some other dimension, sent away in a Hail Mary play to save life on earth because she's about to explode, and it will be nuclear.

Something is hot. Metal. The outside of the phone booth. She stumbles forward. There is a wall. She manages a pivot, the stucco rising to meet her back. She slides down to the hot pavement and clamps her hands over her face, not wanting anyone to hear the sound she is going to make. She weeps until she's sick with it. As if it is work she is being forced to do.

She gasps for breath and opens her eyes. The women herding the birthday party toddlers are making a quick exit, careful not to look at her.

She wipes her face. Finds one of the tissues from Cait. Blows her nose. The phone dangles on its metal cord like the Hanged Man in Mom's deck of tarot cards. She will get up any moment to hang it up. Sever her connection with Dad. She presses her back into the burning wall. She closes her eyes.

Scout pushes her sleek head under Iph's hand and presses her body into Iph's lap. Iph holds her. George reaches out a hand to help her up. Iph thinks of Mom, how she always wants to talk through every little thing, and for the first time ever she's glad to be away from her. The world is large and airy without her parents and their epic love affair and beautiful house and worry for Orr.

She and George walk into the quiet of Ladd's Addition, a neighborhood right off Hawthorne laid out around traffic circles full of roses. The Craftsman homes here are stately and square, made for large prosperous families. The massive trees—oaks and maples and cherries, the same vintage as the houses—touch fin-gers in the middle of the street like a line of couples waiting for a minuet to begin.

Scout scampers ahead to sniff, then waits for them to catch up. Iph likes the feel of George's hand in hers. She doesn't remember when it got there, but they're walking together like they do this every day. They emerge from Ladd's Addition at Division, and

Iph is pretty sure if they go left, they'll be back at Taurus Trucking. But even though they're tired, they can't go back, not yet. It's the weekend, so the neighbors could come home anytime.

They cross Division and walk aimlessly, changing sides of the street to follow the shade. Iph likes this modest neighborhood even more than grand Ladd's, with its mix of smaller bungalows and low-slung fifties garden apartment buildings and varied yards, some with unwatered lawns the color of toast, others psychedelic with bloom. They pass a house with a porch dressed in yellow roses that look and smell like cupcakes. There are two rust-flecked red tricycles and a pair of muddy clogs on the porch. Another house has dandelions gone to seed, a resplendent passionflower vine, and a peeling porch flanked by jasmine and purple hydrangea lounged upon by five fat cats.

"Come on," George says, turning the corner and breaking into a run. Scout darts to catch George, then shoots back to Iph, who does not run unless she is made to, and only then if she is wearing a sports bra over a very supportive underwire in a temperature below fifty degrees.

This street is shaded with lindens and cherries framing houses that are set up from the street with sidewalk-chalked cement staircases leading to their wide front porches. More cats. More kids' toys. And in the middle of the block, a little oasis of a park. "Scout's favorite," George says. "A pocket park for a pocket pit."

There is tender grass and glorious shade. In the center is a little elevated playground, bordered by a low brick wall, pungent with fresh cedar chips and shiny clean from yesterday's rain. George has already climbed to the top of the slide with Scout.

Iph sinks into the grass. A giggle, children's voices. The lovely rise and fall of George's voice directing Scout through her repertoire of tricks. The calliope sound of an ice cream truck in the distance. Iph closes her eyes, too exhausted to worry about anything.

She wakes at sunset to a melted-popsicle sky. George and Scout are crashed out beside her, both of them softly snoring. The air is still, and the playground is empty of children who are surely being put to bed, upset because it's still light outside.

Iph wanders toward the play structure. She sits on a swing, languid at first, then pumping her legs. Now she's flying alone in the sky. Crows roost in the tallest trees. Streetlights come on a few at a time.

Iph feels for Orr, imagines him swinging next to her. For years they've been honing their psychic powers, practicing ESP and, since last spring, lucid dreaming. They'd always treated it like it was a game, but maybe it wasn't. Maybe somehow, they knew something would happen and were training for this separation.

The rhythm of the swing is perfect for self-hypnosis.

> *How do my hands feel when Orr is swinging next to me?*
> *How do my legs feel when we do the thing where we sync*
>   *the swings and pump in time?*
> *How can my heartbeat match Orr's heartbeat?*
> *How can my breath mirror his breath?*

Iph slits her eyes and sees a small blue window high in a wall, the indigo moment right before dark. The exact color Orr and Mom have claimed as their own. A square, closet-size room. A velvet nap of dark hair on a delicate egg of a head on a faded zebra-striped pillow. It's probably just a comforting daydream. But sometimes, these weird daydreams of hers turn out to be true.

Clairvoyant is what Mom's New Age New York chorus-girl friend pronounced Iph when she predicted who was calling when the phone rang three times in two days. Dad says it's coincidence, especially when he does it, and maybe it is. It's never anything big. What's for dinner, what color someone will be wearing. Who's about to call. And usually no more than a few minutes into the future. Close enough that they've always laughed it off. Except sometimes, it's something bigger. Like when Iph had a nightmare that Yai-Yai fell on the ice. Or when Mom applied to the residency and Iph knew she would get it. So there is a chance that somewhere in this city a few minutes from now when the sun has just set, Orr will be snuggled in some safe zebra-cushioned nest, fast asleep.

She sends him a hug, her love. Pumps harder, swings higher.

Now George is beside her, swinging in rhythm.

In sync, they slow down.

Iph holds out a hand. George takes it.

Together, hands clasped, they jump.

15

MOTHER,
MY MOTHER

Orr wakes as the streetlights come on outside. The last thing he remembers is sitting on the sofa with a coverless copy of *Dragonsong*, lent to him by Mika—not reading, just listening to the comforting sound of the Furies' whispered talk and the almost-silence of their bare feet as they padded around the cluttered house. Now they are in their rooms. Allison, Mika, and Jane. Music and TV and cigarette smoke seep out from under the cracks of their three doors and sneak down the stairs.

Orr is so tired. He curls into himself, but the living room is too open, the door unseeable behind the cat-smelling sofa's back. Where is this cat? Orr barely remembers Dad's famous Maine coon, Agamemnon. Even though they all love animals, they haven't had a pet since then. It's too hard for Dad, Mom says. Their shorter life spans. The loss.

This sofa smells like several cats and, if he's honest, something like Mindy's house, where there are four guinea pigs, three indoor Abyssinians, and a rude parrot that reminds Orr of Iph when she has PMS.

Iph. He's barely thought of her since his escape. Can only stand to do it now for a minute or two. He usually thinks of her often. When he reads, he notes things to tell her. When he runs, he arranges playlists or new songs he will learn on the cello to stump her in their games of Name That Tune. So what's going on now? Memory erasure? Mind control? Orr indexes *X-Files* episodes, cross-referenced with *Star Trek*. Maybe the people at the boot camp were aliens in disguise. Or humans working for aliens. Or for the government. Maybe they put a tracker in his neck like they had with beautiful, badass Agent Scully.

He touches his head. Could his hair have already grown back a little? How many months would it take to reach its former length? And even if it did, would it ever be the same?

There is a story he tells himself at night. His hair features prominently. That, like so much else, will have to change. Not even in fantasy can Orr have long hair anymore. Its taking was too brutal, his transformation too extreme.

In the old story, Orr was a hero in his own personal X-File. Because his hair shielded him, he was able to sneak into the spaceship, sabotage the aliens' experiments, and free the people who'd been abducted, helping them recover their memories and heal from the violation of being taken unknowing from their beds every night for months, or in some cases, years. In the end, both Agents Mulder and Scully fell in love with him. Orr could never decide which one to kiss.

Now, will anyone ever want to kiss him? Like Jo March in *Little Women*, he considered his hair to be the one thing that made him beautiful. He still hasn't looked in a mirror to see if that's changed. Tomorrow, he promises himself. Standing before the mirror is a practice of his. The boy in his reflection is his old friend—himself, but not him. A boy trapped in the room inside the mirror. It's a silly game from when he was very small, but still. Routines are grounding. Ritual makes daily life sacred, according to Mom. She told him that when she was packing for the residency. She'd been trying to get him to write out a daily schedule for himself for when she was gone.

"Ritual creates boundaries," she said, holding a red dress against herself in the mirror.

"Bring it," Orr said. "It's one of your best."

"Boundaries are containers." Mom folded the dress into her suitcase. "Like a glass jar. Nothing special—till you think about what they can contain. All sorts of ambient intangibles."

Ambient Intangibles is the name Orr gave an imaginary paranormal investigative agency in a series of stories he was writing last winter. The whole family adopted it as shorthand for the inexplicable or vast—space, time, consciousness, the afterlife.

"I keep imagining a big invisible spider I'm trying to trap in a mason jar so I can take him outside," Orr said, fiddling with the zipper on Mom's suitcase.

"Sorry." Mom touched his hair, running a strand of it between her two fingers from his temple to where it ended below his shoulder blade. "But maybe it's not a spider. Or maybe it's a nice one."

"Maybe."

Mom stopped in front of him with a pair of socks in her hand. "Actually, I think the metaphor is good. Like, what if this ambient intangible gets out of control? Invisible spiders running rampant in your bedroom. Then what do you do?"

"Freak out?" Orr was kidding but also serious.

Mom laughed. "That's right, *mijo*. You freak the fuck out. And then you have to learn. You need a procedure. I'm asking you to think about what intangibles create chaos in your life. And what rituals could you create to contain them?"

Orr understood a little, but not all the way. "Bring this," he said, holding up one of Mom's most prized concert tees, thin now and faded from red to pink, from the second ever Bread and Roses Festival. They'd driven all the way to Berkeley for the three days of concerts. Iph says it's her first memory—the sound of Joni Mitchell's voice under the moon.

Orr remembers none of it but loves to hear Mom and Dad tell the story of that trip—camping on the Rogue River on the way down, staying with a friend of Dad's in Berkeley and an old hotel in the redwoods on the way home. All of them cozy in the car together. Mom and Dad realizing they could still have adventures even though they had kids.

Mom took the shirt, squinted at the pinholes along the hem, rolled it up, and tucked it inside a chunky brown ankle boot wedged in the corner of her suitcase.

"Three months is a long time," Orr said.

"That's what I'm trying to tell you, love. Think of it like beads on a necklace. Each chunk of time is a bead you string on the wire of the day. Be aware of this and you will calm down—"

"—because repetition is inherently calming." Orr finishes for her. They both know repetition's power from direct experience, Orr from music and Mom from dancing. They tried an experiment once: Orr wrote a song and Mom made a dance where nothing repeated. Neither piece worked.

Mom's eyes go darker and brighter. "When you slow down and make these daily activities conscious, you begin to see the beads differently. They start out plain. Boring. It's more about accumulation at that stage, like checking off days on a calendar or doing pliés at the bar. But after a while, the beads get shiny. Like by touching them again and again, you polish them into gems. That's when you know you're getting close."

"Close to what?"

"*El Mundo Bueno*. Life as art."

"How do you know all this?"

"I learned it the hard way, *mi amor*. The way I do everything." She was laughing, but there was also sadness.

"Why?" Orr was pushing now. "I mean, I learn this stuff from you. Didn't your parents teach you?"

Mom was silent at first, matching pairs of socks. Orr thought she was, as usual, blowing him off. Then she said, "There has to be trust for that, *mijo*. But I did learn things from my parents. I learned who not to be and what not to do. And that's something, right?"

She folded her second-best jeans in half, then rolled them

up. Orr didn't like to see them tucked away. Mom was quiet again. Orr saw her trying to decide what to tell him. She did that a lot. With Dad, the stories flowed. They'd heard about his childhood exploits hundreds of times. With Mom, they came out very rarely, like deer in the yard in winter.

She took a breath. "I was a little lost when I first had Iph. Then you came along so soon after. I was overwhelmed for a while. Your dad had to do everything. For a little while I even stopped nursing you. He fed you bottles. I stayed in bed. Then one day he burst in with a kid under each arm and plopped you both down next to me and stalked to the bathroom to take a shower."

Orr can see Dad doing this. And Mom still gets sad like that sometimes, but usually only for a day or two.

Mom patted Orr's hand and smiled. "You two were staring at me with your big black eyes in your creepy alien baby heads like *What now?* So I brought you down to the kitchen and put you in the playpen. You were standing in there with your hands on the bars like little jailbirds in your white onesies and sticking-up hair. I went to make some tea, but the kitchen was disgusting. That's how you know your dad was losing it.

"I don't know why I thought to do it, but I set the egg timer for ten minutes and tidied till it dinged. Then I went to the hall bathroom and washed my face. A pair of earrings was there on the shelf. I hadn't worn dangly earrings since I'd had Iph. The midwife told me I'd have to give them up because babies pull on them. I can't believe I listened to that. As you know, I might as well be naked without earrings."

He knew. Mom went nowhere without jewelry. It was her armor.

"So I put them on and kept doing that every day after washing my face. Then I'd go downstairs and set the timer for ten minutes. Then I'd have my tea. Like a little ritual—see where I'm going with this? If one of you interrupted the routine, I started where I left off. That timer was my lifeline, *mijo.* A little container of time. It wasn't fast, but after a while I learned to string the beads together like spells—dishes, garden, dance class, carpool. They all became sacred."

"Why are you leaving, then?"

"You know I'm coming back, right?"

"That's not what I asked."

Mom sighed and spoke to her reflection in the mirror, head cocked to one side. "I have to work again, my love. You and your sister are growing up. I need to grow, too."

She handed him the packet then, printed and comb-bound at Dad's office. Each day, a list. Little notes from her. Reading it, he became aware of a growing sensation of cold.

He stood up. "This isn't for me," he told Mom. "It's for you."

"I thought it would help. Just little reminders . . ."

"This isn't about me," he said. "Just admit it."

"You don't have to use it." Mom's face was red. She looked like she might cry.

"I won't," Orr said. And he took the little book and pulled it apart, ripping out its guts like a wild animal.

"Orr!" Mom's voice was hard. "You don't have to use it, but don't be an ass."

"I'm an ass?" Orr was shouting. "Me? You do so many things that are supposed to help me, but really, they just help you. Headphones? Great, now I don't flip out and embarrass you at the store. Telling me my hair is pretty? Good, now I'll take a bath so people don't say your kid stinks when you take him to school. This is the same. You did this so you don't have to worry. How about this? Just don't worry at all. Just go there and forget us for the summer. We'll be right back here when you come home. Just like always!"

Orr shakes to remember what he did next.

The things from the suitcase went everywhere.

Something small and hard—maybe Mom's green box full of earrings—flew out and hit Mom under her eye. But Orr did not stop.

The Bread and Roses shirt was thin from so many washings.

It ripped easily, right down the center.

Orr threw it in Mom's face and ran out of the room.

Climbed up to the treehouse.

Didn't come out until everyone was asleep.

A MOTORCYCLE WITH A terrible muffler zooms past the Furies' house. Orr wipes his eyes. He sits up. The wood floor is gritty under his bare feet. He flops back on the cat-smelling sofa. Maps the house on his bare right leg. Allison lent him loose basketball shorts and a Bikini Kill T-shirt. Iph loves Bikini Kill, but Orr prefers Nirvana. Their music is almost painful to listen to, but it's a good, productive sort of pain, like having sore muscles from running. More memories rise—Mom coming in to kiss him before she left for the airport. The silence of the house when everyone left. Orr presses hard on the stop button to end the memory. "No more," he says out loud, his voice small in the quiet house. He rolls on his back and hums "Come as You Are" softly to himself.

Kurt Cobain is another one that's confusing—does Orr want to kiss Kurt or *be* him? He starts from the beginning and goes through the A side of *Nevermind* and feels a little better. The truth is, there's no way he's going to be able to sleep on this sofa. And if he doesn't sleep, he can't function. He tiptoes to the hall, less for quiet than because he doesn't want to place his entire foot on the floor. Even when surfaces are clean, Orr doesn't like much skin-to-skin contact with the floors of other people's houses.

In the hall by the front door is a closet. Orr has to pull hard to open it. As he suspected from the footprint of the house, it is large and square. The small high window is a nice surprise. It's later than Orr thought, early evening. The closet is full of junk, a sediment of coats and shoes. On arrival, he noticed some boards leaning in the corner of the porch, sharp with tacks. He removes them using the nail clippers he found on the coffee table under a pile of *Willamette Week* newspapers and Burgerville wrappers. This works surprisingly well on the soft wood. A hunt with a flashlight in the backyard unearths a few cinder blocks. There are crickets here, like at home, but too faint to hear from inside the house. There is jasmine and some other night-blooming flower that smells like lemons. Orr is barefoot. *Outside.* He shakes his head and puts his feet out of his mind. His blisters are too bad for sneakers. The whole thing is outlandish. He doubts anything could surprise him now.

He excavates the closet until he finds floor, the same scarred, narrow oak as in the living room. The coats and impractical shoes are not as numerous as they seemed. In the entryway, he uses the boards and blocks to set up a shelf for the shoes, arranging them by size and color and heel height. He rummages for a hammer but can't find one. A hard-soled leopard-print platform sandal his mom and Iph would have loved works fine to bang the nails from the wood scraps in a straight row. A nail for each coat, four more for guests.

After sweeping out the now-empty closet with a broom he found in the questionable space between the refrigerator and kitchen wall, which is also stuffed with paper grocery bags, he takes the slippery cushions from the sofa and lines his nest. The cat smell is stronger here. He puts the cushions back and remembers the camping gear the girls dumped in a pile on the front porch. Out again, his feet cringing on the splintery wood, it takes three trips to bring it all inside.

He finds the first aid kit Mika used for his feet, an old Converse shoebox with Band-Aids, rubbing alcohol, and ointment. He disinfects the blow hole on the Therm-a-Rests and blows up all three. They fit almost perfectly into the square space of the closet. He opens two sleeping bags and puts them over the camping pads and snuggles into the woodsmoke and girl smell. His heart pounds the first notes of the fear song. Orr is always anxious before sleep.

He thinks of Iph, asleep in her rosy bedroom, her pedicured foot peeking out from the pile of light down quilts.

Thinking about someone causes missing.

Missing causes crying.

Orr isn't brainwashed; he's smart, rationing the things he can't control.

He girds himself and reaches for his sister now, mind-to-mind, a trick they've been practicing for years. A game, really. But maybe this time it will work.

He follows the bread-crumb trail of memory—first her face, her voice, then deeper, down to the ghost in him. Mom used to correct him. "I think you mean your soul, *mijo*." But he means more than a soul.

He'd gotten the idea from a song Mom used to play a lot from an old mixtape Dad made her. He could almost see his ghost with his eyes closed tight, a soft mist of a thing like shower steam or cotton candy. Iph has one, too—a ripe, bright yellow that feels the way an oven-fresh lemon bar both tingles and is sweet on your tongue after a glass of ice-cold water.

He settles in now to call Iph's ghost, a process he and Iph call *tuning*, where you think of the other person while checking your body one part at a time. All summer, they'd been using this to try and contact one another in dreams, and so far had come up with similar imagery seven nights out of twenty, according to Orr's detailed notes. Maybe the missing ingredient had been necessity. Orr needs his sister. Needs her to know he is safe.

He rolls to his back. The window is bluing, almost his favorite shade but not quite.

Hello, feet. If Iph were here, how would you feel?

"Scared," his feet say. "Scared of her gross clammy toes."

Hi, knees. How do you feel when your sister is with you?

"Soft," say his knees. "Less achy."

Hands, remember how you feel when Iph is beside you watching a movie?

"Worried," say his hands. "She'll steal the popcorn if we aren't careful."

Nose, what do you smell when Iph is around?

This one is easy—vanilla, sugar, amber. "You are what you

eat," Mindy always said to get Orr to eat more of her baking. Iph needed no encouragement to eat sweet or spicy things.

He checks in with his neck. His ears and eyes.

At his scalp, he has to stop and start over again.

His missing hair is still so hard to integrate. What does his head even feel like? He has no idea. It's like they cut his whole head off with his hair.

His heart is pounding, and his head feels hot.

Hot! That's how his head feels. Like a ball of fire.

That's what he imagines it looks like now—a burned meadow, the only thing left an inch of charred grass.

He feels like crying again. From sadness, but also relief. Like a Nirvana song.

Somehow, he got away from Meadowbrook and found these kind girls.

The moon rises in the window, smaller here—the window and the moon—than at home. Mom is under the moon. Dad, too. *Fucking Dad.* And Iph.

Orr's eyes are heavy.

He is so tired.

He sleeps and dreams.

Iph, flying through the evening sky in unfamiliar boots.

Iph, laughing. A boy in a yellow sweater holds her hand.

A tiger in miniature.

Anger, a phrase. Tiger-footed rage.

A dangling pay phone.

A crucified man.

Tarot cards falling from the trees like rain.

Iph, flying higher,

A crow winging past

The tops of trees,

Dollhouses golden with bedtime.

Tiny cats out to prowl the blue twilight.

Iph flies higher and higher.

Then she jumps!

16

ATTEMPTS
IN OPERETTAS

The pillow tastes like mothballs, but Iph keeps it shoved against her mouth because she can't stop laughing. Scout whines, nosing around to find her face.

"I have to smoke," George says. "Because drinking."

"Don't leave me!" Iph giggles. "You have to stay with me, George." Gin is her drink. The perfect alcohol. She sees now why Mom told her she wouldn't like it. Reverse psychology, because Iph more than likes this buzz. She is crushed out on it. On everything. Even herself. And, of course, George. Dapper, beautiful George with those crow-black eyes and perfect rose macaron mouth.

"Iph! I'll be right back. I don't want to give you asthma." George, impressively, stands up straight.

"You're a good drinker," Iph says, and they both laugh again, stuffing pillows into their faces, George kneeling. When did that happen? Wait—now George is up again, so easy. Standing, pulling Iph up.

"Come with me then." They are face to face, but the kiss doesn't happen.

George looks down and away.

"You're thinking about the lost girl, right?" She should be bummed, but the gin takes away the sting.

"Yes," George says, grabbing the big flashlight.

Iph stops herself short of rolling her eyes and stomping her foot. It's not George's fault for being in love. "Ugh," she says. "Fine. Let's go down to the garage. You can tell me all about her."

Downstairs, the cement floor is cool under Iph's feet. She plops into a rusty lawn chair with a faded floral cushion. "So, what's her name?"

George settles onto the tire swing and lights the cigarette, careful to blow the smoke away from Iph. "Lorna."

"In real life, is she strawberry blonde? With pale-blue eyes?" In George's painting, her hair is lavender and her eyes are gold.

"How did you know?"

"I don't know," Iph says. "It's how I imagine her. Delicate-looking, like in your painting, but tough in person. A little bit of a mean girl? But not all the way through."

George stops swaying around on the tire swing and shines the flashlight beam at the painting of Lorna with lavender hair and gold earrings and the Gustav Klimt–like suggestion of a halo. "Wow. Yeah, that's Lorna. You're exactly right." George sucks on the filter hard, blows the smoke out in a quick hot puff. Iph likes the smell. It reminds her of Mom.

"Hmmm," Iph says. She has a big crush on George, of course, but the gin seems to leave little room for being maudlin about it. "Let's have another gin and tonic, darling," Iph says in her best flapper voice. "But first, tell me the sad part."

"Oof." George mimes taking a hit to the gut and falls to the floor. When Iph offers a hand up, she's pulled down instead. The concrete is stained, but relatively clean. Deliciously cool.

"Well," George says, lying back, eyes closed. "It's all sad, if you want to know. I heard something on the street one night. It was Lorna. Someone was attacking her."

"Is that when you used your bow?"

"Yeah," George says. "I was too late. The damage was already done."

"Whoa," Iph says. "I'm so sorry. That's horrible."

"Yeah."

"So you rescued her and fell in love?"

"Something like that," George says.

They're quiet. A dog barks somewhere in the neighborhood. Scout's hackles rise.

"Leave it," George says.

They lie still, their hands a few inches apart. Iph can feel the heat coming off George's skin. She inches her pinkie closer. She pulls it back.

"C'mon," she says. On her feet she sways a little and holds out her hands to pull George up. Static sparks between them, the result of some explainable phenomenon that Dad has tried to teach her about on many occasions to absolutely no avail.

George's hand snaps away. "Whoa!" Then, with much heart clutching, "*My drops of tears I'll turn to sparks of fire.*"

Stop it. Stop being so adorable, Iph thinks. Her brow furrows. *Sparks of fire . . .* What play *is* that from? She sticks her tongue out at George.

"Queen Katherine," George says. "*Henry the Eighth.* Duh."

"Who knows that play? Who even reads the histories?" Iph's consonants are mushy, authentically drunk-sounding, something that is surprisingly hard to act. She turns on her mental tape recorder and hopes for the best. "How did you learn all this Shakespeare, anyway?"

"Shakespeare in the Shelter, milady. They had it at Outside In. Anyone could do it. You didn't have to live there," George adds quickly.

"Is that how you know Josh?"

"Yep," George says. "And Cait. She was a volunteer."

Cait. Lorna. George is way out of Iph's league.

Upstairs is still sweltering, the godlike effect of the gin is wearing off, and Iph feels like crap about Lorna and Cait and all the girls with leading roles. More gin doesn't help, partly because the bag of ice they put in the kitchen sink has melted away, and warm gin and tonic isn't nearly as nice as cold. But also, Iph is basically a monster, because Orr is gone and needs to be found, but all she seems to care about is George's stable of exes. Then again, maybe sitting in her personal lovelorn drama is easier than contemplating the spectacular fall of her own once-perfect family.

Lovelorn. Love Lorna.

Oh well. This is familiar, at least.

"You're tripping," George says, tapping Iph's forehead. "I see you in there."

Iph's eyes narrow. "Um, no. You see girls like Cait. And Lorna. And whatever other *Sassy* magazine models you hang around with."

George groans and leans forward in the plaid recliner, head in hands—the same pose Dad assumes at the start of a fight with Mom. This new alternate reality has such odd moments of symmetry to life at home. Same shapes, same sadness.

Are she and George fighting now? Iph used to think her temper was an essential part of her character, like hating watermelon or loving books, but lately she sees it as a habit, exhausting and so stupid. She can almost grasp this other, better version of herself that keeps her temper and does the right thing, but almost doesn't count. She's always apologizing. Another familiar thing. What's one more?

"I'm sorry," she says. "Please ignore me. I don't care about your girlfriends. I'm upset about my brother."

"Dude, no. It's me. I'm toxic. For real. Like . . . contagious." George is bright red. Takes the bottle and swigs. "Girls totally love me. I'm not being conceited. They've always loved me. You know that nursery rhyme? Well, it's basically my life."

Nursery rhyme? Iph scrunches her face. She sees her *Mother Goose* book like it's right in front of her. What's that damn rhyme? She needs to lie down. Nana's green shag carpet is dusty and smells a little like feet. Her own feet still hurt, so she puts them up on the sofa. The breeze wafts in, jasmine and mock orange. "You have to tell me. It's driving me crazy."

"Don't make me say it," George says, plopping down on the sofa with the bottle of gin, knees an inch from Iph's feet. "And don't you say it, either. I hate that thing."

"Tell me," Iph says. "It's killing me. It's on the tip of my brain."

George laughs. "Your brain has no tip. You mean your tongue."

The word *tongue* shuts them both up for a second. And then Iph has it. *Georgie Porgie, pudding and pie. Kissed the girls and made them cry.* She sits up slowly.

"Oh my god. I mean . . . wow. It's like destiny. Like, did your name make you a Lothario? Or is there some inherent quality from birth that causes a parent to name their kid George? A quality that, later in life, manifests in rampant, dramatic love affairs?"

"Whoa. Way to get it on the nose." George sits up and passes the gin to Iph.

"I know," Iph says. "I'm very good with summation." And she is. She feels good again. She's a seer, Mom says. A noticer. And lately, there are moments when she almost sees herself. As a woman, she may well be appreciated. A pretty face, a body that looks like it can make babies or fill out a fifties wiggle dress the way the Goddess intended. Womanly stuff. But now, it's girlishness that's wanted. The girls who look like kids the longest—waifish, like runway models—are always considered prettiest. All that was over for Iph by sixth grade. She's had a woman's body since she was twelve. It's what she's got. Who she is. For now, being smart will do. "At least I have my brain, right?"

"Shut up," George says. "I mean, my god, Iph. Look at yourself. Total Gina Lollobrigida."

"Sorry, but I know my movie stars, and she was totally skinny—just had big boobs. Plus, she's Italian, which I'm not. But whatever!"

"To be honest, I don't really know what Gina Lollobrigida looks like. Just, you know, voluptuous. And hot. I like the name. It rolls off the tongue."

That word again.

"Anyway," George says, "what I meant to say is, you look like a fifties screen siren. Especially in that white dress you were wearing."

"Whatever." Iph lies back again.

"Are you mad?"

"I don't think so. But you never know. Either I flip out right away or it happens a few days later. Ask me Wednesday."

"Don't be mad. You have star power, that's all I meant."

"George. I'm not fishing for compliments. But I don't really believe you. I go to this school with a big theater department. They're famous for it. I know I'm as good as some of the girls who get leads, but I can barely get cast as a maid or somebody's mother. I don't look like an ingenue. I don't fit into the costumes."

"Can't they, like, sew?"

"*I* sew! I could make it myself, if that's the issue. When I finally asked my drama teacher, do you know what he said? 'It's the way of world, dear. Some of us aren't leading ladies.' I get it. I'm supposed to, like, be a good sport and not be jealous and accept the things I can't change—but I don't. I can't! I hate it."

"Your drama teacher is an ass," George says. "But I get the jealousy. For me, it's more an envy. I wish I had certain things, you know? Like what you and Cait have. I know money can't buy love or anything, but I've always wished I had it."

Iph wants to say she's not like Cait, but the truth is, she is on the Cait continuum. Goes to a private school. Lives in a big house.

"Is it weird I said that?" George is on the sofa next to her.

"Not at all," Iph says. "I wish you had money, too. I wish everyone did. But I think we're alike in one way."

"What's that?" George meets her eyes. For a second Iph imagines herself leaning in, but she doesn't. She leans away, scoots to the edge of the sofa.

"Work," she says. "We both like a project. Systems. Rules for things. Like here. Most people would have blown it the first week and had a kegger, but you're good at this. You're a planner. A hard worker. I am, too. Everyone thinks I'm lazy, but I'm not. There just isn't anything real for me to do most of the time."

"Wow," George says. "I've been trying to think how to explain the good parts about living like this. That's it! It's real. Not the busywork you're supposed to waste your life on till the magical day you turn eighteen."

"Totally. And George? We're going to be hungover tomorrow, but we need to work anyway. Will you help me find my brother? Be the Ned to my Nancy?"

"I think you mean the Sid to your Nancy. Although I don't know if Sid Vicious was generally known for getting things done."

"No, no! Not Nancy Spungen—Nancy Drew!"

"That's her last name? Like a sponge?"

"My mom knew her," Iph says. "They worked together in New York."

"Wow. But wait, what were you saying? Hangover, work, something, something something?"

"George. You're drunk." Iph giggles. "I said be the Ned to my Nancy. I'm talking about NANCY DREW, for crying out loud."

"Um, is Ned the boyfriend?"

"That's not the point," Iph says. "I'm saying we need to sleuth. There's something afoot, my friend."

"Afoot?" George wiggles a foot in the air.

"George! Focus! My brother is hiding out somewhere in this city. We've gotta figure it out. I wish I had an apropos Shakespeare passage right now, but I don't."

"Is Lothario from Shakespeare?"

"I don't know," Iph says. They're quiet, and then George is laughing again, so hard there are tears.

"What?"

George is gasping and Iph is giggling. Finally, George comes up for air and grabs Iph by the shoulders. "Lothario? Oh my god, woman. Who even says that?"

"If the shoe fits—"

"I'm not wearing shoes." She sees it now. George does want to kiss her.

"I'm already crying," Iph says, "about my messed-up family. So it won't be your fault."

"It will," George says.

After a while George gets up and brings them both big glasses of water. It's late enough that they can drink them on the back steps.

The stars twinkle in a clear sky. It's going to be hot again tomorrow.

"You said you're Greek on your dad's side," George says. "What else?"

"Are you asking me what I am?"

"Well, when I tried to tell you what reminded me of, you got a little miffed. Which I get because I hate that myself. So yes. I am asking."

"Greek from my dad, Mexican from my mom. Hot-tempered and anxious from both."

"I'm Japanese and white on my mom's side and who-knows-what-because-my-mom-won't-say on my dad's."

Iph downs her water. "How about Scout?"

"Scout," George says, "is a pound puppy wonder dog."

At the sound of her name, Scout rallies, whining very quietly to go for a walk.

"Not now, little beast," George says. "Now it's time to sleep."

THE BOY
SHOUTED BACK

Orr is awake at dawn, starving. The girls' kitchen is the filthiest space he has ever seen. The weak light through grease-spattered windows turns the dish-piled whitish Formica counters the color of urine. The refrigerator is Chernobyl. An old model from a former era with the bins inside missing. In their place are desiccated carrots, an empty plastic tub labeled MIKA, and several cans of beer. On the top shelf are two boxes of Chinese takeout smeared radioactive red, a jar of honey mustard, a jar of cocktail olives, and a carton of milk screaming *go to hell* to the entire world with its sour-death smell.

He tries to remember the last time he ate. The night before. Pizza. Normally, he can handle an entire medium pie himself, but he remembered what Mom always said about making sure there was enough for everyone in group dining situations. The etiquette training seemed ludicrous then, but he's gone by many of her axioms since he took up with the Furies. After pizza, the girls had band practice. That had been the best part of the night. He didn't think about Mom or Dad or Iph or the polar ice caps. He didn't think about sex or his brain or how it would feel to contract a horrible disease. All that was in his head were

Mika's drums and Allison's bass and Jane's caterwauling over her badass guitar.

Yesterday, Orr had loved the Furies and their ramshackle pink house. WELCOME TO THE PUSSY PALACE, a sign on the door read in gold. A stylized sixties cat in an odd shade of green looked over its shoulder under the loopy cursive.

"That's your house's name?" Orr had looked back to ask Jane, but it was tiny Mika with the shaved head who answered.

"Yeah, but we usually call her Penelope."

Last night, Orr appreciated Penelope's quirks—the front door you had to slam to make it shut, the windows you had to prop open with moldy encyclopedias. He delighted in the number and variety of things on the dining room bookshelf alone: the encyclopedia set, a bunch of wilted daisies in a Slurpee cup, a discolored glass bong, a green glass ashtray stuffed with matchbooks, an aloe vera plant in a plastic pot, a set of jacks, a framed photo of the band onstage, a rusted metal Slinky, a Raggedy Ann doll with fishnet ankle socks and safety pin earrings, a pack of American Spirit cigarettes, a plastic tub of Red Vines (stale, but Orr eats three), a stack of feminist zines, and five books: *Blood and Guts in High School*, *SCUM Manifesto*, *Bastard Out of Carolina*, *Parable of the Sower*, and *This Bridge Called My Back*, which Orr recognizes from Mom's bookshelf.

Now, in the daylight, the house feels different. Stale, ugly. Sinister. Orr goes to the bathroom and thinks about a shower. The bath mat is soaked and smells like mildew. He curls his toes away and slits his eyes, tiptoeing out.

Back in the kitchen, sitting in the corner by the window in an easy chair with loose stuffing and a not-right pillow, Orr tries to get the feeling from last night back. All his usual ways of coping— hot food, hot shower, dark bedroom, clean clothes, even a run— are lost to him here. His feet are still blistered from the sockless hike. He nursed them the best he could last night, but had a hard time getting the Scooby-Doo Band-Aids to stick after putting on the antibiotic ointment Mika gave him. "I'm always scraping my knuckles on the rim of my drums," she said. "This shit works."

Orr likes Mika with her gruff words and high, gentle voice. He likes Allison's soft body and red hair and tough-guy attitude. He likes raspy, funny Jane the best. Yesterday, he didn't know any of them. Today, is he living at their house? Does he live anywhere?

Orr is shaking. Mom did this experiment with him when he was younger, adding baking soda, spoonful by spoonful, into a glass of vinegar. It was a metaphor for meltdowns—meant to show that you needed to know how many spoonfuls of stress you could take before you started to bubble, how many more it would take to make you blow. At home, he knows exactly where he is in this process at any given moment. But here, he has no idea. He wants to go back to the coat closet but can't remember how. He wants to go *home*! He wants Mom! He needs the white oak outside his window, his Rescue Remedy tincture. He hears a buzzing—what if it's a bee? His EpiPen is miles away!

"Hey! Hey, you okay?"

A voice. It sounds . . . frightened. This makes Orr shake harder. Something, a hand, touching him. Orr flinches, his teeth aching like they do when he touches newsprint, like when he needs to get something out of his head. He puts his fist in his mouth to quiet the nerves in his gums. He knows he's crying too loud, but nothing can be done. He needs three hands: two for his ears, one for his mouth. Four hands, a long arm, octopus limbs to wrap around himself tight.

The girl is saying something, but he can't remember her name right now. All he can do is squeeze himself with his nontentacled arms and wait for Mom to come. He rocks and rolls. Mom calls it that. She plays him Jimmy Page, who can howl almost as loud as Orr.

The kitchen is loud. Led Zeppelin loud. He forgets where the volume control is in his brain. Pinocchio is never never never going to be a real boy. Never never never never never—

Orr gasps.

Gasps!

He's wet!

"I'm wet!" It's his voice! Speaking words!

"Yep," Jane says. "Sorry, dude. I didn't know what else to do." She stands in front of him with an empty glass in her hand. She hands him a towel to wipe the water from his face.

"Janie." Mika says this.

Mika, Allison, Jane. Orr remembers.

"Jane . . ." Mika's eyes are filled with tears. Orr sits at the kitchen table. He knows that look. He's frightened her.

"Mika," he says. "I'm sorry."

"It's cool." Mika tries to smile.

"It was a meltdown," Orr says. "I used to have them all the time. My mom helped me get them under control. Tame them."

Jane grins. "I'm picturing your mom in, like, fishnets and a sparkly leotard and tailcoat. Holding a chair and a whip, you know?"

"Uhh, that sounds kinda wrong in the context of his mom, Jane," Allison says.

"My mom would wear that," Orr says. "She loves costumes. But it's me who needs to wear it. I have to be responsible for taming myself."

"Word," Allison says. She gets up and plugs in the coffee maker. "Look, dude, I don't want to talk behind your back, so I'm gonna say what we're all thinking here. We can't keep you around if you're going to be doing that. I mean, what's the plan here, Jane?"

"We already decided last night," Jane says in a *that's final* voice. She's the one who could tame lions.

"Keep him till his mom comes home?" Mika pulls out a box of cereal and a container of soy milk from a cupboard next to the basement door. "We could get in trouble. His dad could, like, prosecute."

"He wouldn't," Orr says.

"How do you know that?" Allison sits next to Orr. "Look what he did to you."

"That's different," Orr says. "He wants a real boy, not to sue an awesome rock band."

"You think we're awesome?" Allison is smiling now. Orr likes the chip in her front tooth.

"Oh my god," Mika says, plopping an empty cereal bowl in front of Orr. "Allison, you're such a compliment whore."

"We're not putting him out like a stray cat," Jane says, lighting a cigarette and pulling a beer from the fridge.

"Jane!" Mika groans and takes the beer away, replacing it with coffee.

"Fine," Jane says.

"None of us would put a cat out, either." Allison coughs and produces a cigarette from the pocket of her bathrobe. Jane lights it with her shiny silver lighter. It smells like the ones Great Aunt Lolly used to smoke—attic dust and breath mints. Mika frowns and opens the window, propping it up with three encyclopedias. They're silent while the coffee machine slurps like a very rude eater. Orr starts to laugh.

"Your coffee machine," he says between giggles. He's often punchy after a meltdown. "That sound!"

"Like a queef, am I right?" Allison says.

"What's a queef?" Orr asks. This sets them all off laughing. Orr keeps asking, but every time he says queef, they laugh more. Finally Jane sits up straight, folds her hands, and says, "A queef, young man, is like a fart."

"Only it comes out of your . . ." Allison is laughing again, a great sound peppered with little snorts. She's wearing a T-shirt that says PROPERTY OF SAN QUENTIN and fuzzy slippers shaped like Oscar the Grouch.

"I like your slippers," Orr says.

The laughter calms down. Mika gestures for Orr to pour himself some cereal. Cheerios, not cornflakes, but he complies. Soy milk is a Mom food, not preferred but acceptable.

"Do you have any honey?"

"Above the stove," Jane says. Orr gets it down and honeys his Cheerios.

"Out of where?" he asks when they are all crunching their cereal. They look at him askance, as Iph would say. "A queef is a fart that comes out of . . . ?" he reminds them.

"Persistent," Allison mutters.

"Fine," Mika says. "Fine. A queef is a fart that comes out of your . . . Penelope." She bursts out laughing. Allison nearly spits out her coffee.

"You mean vagina?" Orr asks.

The Furies look at Orr like he's a cute stray cat. He grins back at them. Mom always taught him to use the proper words for body parts.

"What are we gonna do with you?" Jane says, stubbing out her cigarette and opening the cooler from yesterday. She gets out the last pack of tofu wieners and stabs one with a fork. Holding it over the open flame on the gas stove, she looks at Orr like he knows things.

"Keep me?" Orr says. "Maybe till my mom gets home?"

ACT II

Whoever drinks from me will become a wolf

1

THE FIRST JOURNEY
TO PETROGRAD

Iph's first act as a profoundly hungover girl detective is to drag herself to the gas station and call the diner in Sandy. The waitress isn't there, but the guy answering the phone claims he was out having a smoke when the group of them—three girls and a boy with a shaved head that had to be Orr—left. "I asked if they were a gang. They said no, they were a rock band."

It's been oddly easy between Iph and George from the moment they woke up back to back on the carpet, heads pounding and parched in the stuffy apartment. Iph couldn't face the bumpy ride on the bike rack. She had bruises, she finally admitted. Black and blue and green ones. So they walked.

Now, at a little vegan diner on Belmont, they share veggie biscuits and gravy and the free weekly paper, reading each other's horoscopes.

"Okay, Gemini," Iph reads, "*It's time to regain the focus you need for the massively ambitious work of the next few years. Review all commitments and connections, especially your closest ones.*" Iph wonders—does that mean Cait and Lorna? Or her?

"Don't look at me like that," George says, taking the paper and reading Cancer to Iph. "*There's power in what you say and hear now. This week brings a flurry of messages and ideas, pushing important pending matters (including relationship decisions) decidedly forward."*

"Hmm," is all Iph says, taking the paper back in the spirit of leaving no clue unturned to read Virgo for Orr.

Focus on gaining the momentum where you can, Virgo, without resorting to road rage. The opportunity here is to become more structurally sound. Relationships are challenged now; you might even feel trapped. Some of this alleviates next week, after the full moon.

She reads it twice but can't find anything useful. The thought of Orr feeling trapped is scary, but maybe the horoscope is referring to Meadowbrook?

Fed and properly caffeinated, they begin part two of George's plan. They hit Showcase Music and Portland Music, asking if people know a band who meets the diner guy's description, with no luck. They also tried Music Millennium, a record store where bands would definitely advertise their shows.

"We still need to make a flyer," Iph says. "Maybe later could you draw Orr for me?" She tenses her body for the blow that comes with imagining his shaved head, but she is stronger today. It feels good to have a plan.

All morning, George has been lugging around a huge backpack full of clothes to sell, including Iph's shoes of pain. Her feet are better now. Have they healed quickly? How many days has she been in Portland? Time feels so strange. It's hard to remember a life before this one.

At 6th and Burnside, Scout runs up to a door and barks. The shabby storefront doesn't look like the sort of place with air-conditioning, but anything is sure to be better than the naked sun. The sign on the door is lettered in pink duct tape:

SHINY DANCER
FINERY FOR THE FINE

A woman in cutoffs and a turquoise tank top is sitting on the counter, acid-green platforms dangling in time with the *toot-toot beep-beep* of Donna Summer's "Bad Girls." She drops to the floor at the sight of Scout, allowing herself to be flagrantly kissed. "Who's my baby?" she asks Scout. "Who's the best girl?"

"Wow," George says. "My dog is such a slut."

"She's come to the right place then," the woman says. After another kiss and then one more, she holds out a hand to be helped up. "Hey, Georgie. And Georgie's cute friend," she says.

"This is Iph," George says. "Iph, meet Glow. She runs this joint."

"Hi," Iph says. The walls are pink and peppermint, and the floors are stenciled with stars in gold and baby blue. "I love this shop! Great feminist reclaiming of pink."

"See?" Glow sticks her hip out at George.

"You're a pinkist?" Iph puts her hands on her hips, too. Glow might be a fellow Latina, by the look of her—light-brown skin and big brown eyes, hair dyed honey blonde.

"Look," George says, "I have a complicated relationship with pink. My mom dressed me like a Polly Pocket until I staged a coup when I was nine."

"Pink was a boy's color till the twenties," Iph says.

"Whoa. That's weird. I mean, it's not a bad color. Roses and girl parts and strawberry ice cream and bubble gum, all good stuff."

Girl parts? Iph closes her gaping mouth, also pink.

"Fair enough," Glow says, laughing. Turning a movie-star smile on Iph, she says, "Nice outfit, Georgie's friend Iph."

Iph is wearing another Nana ensemble, a muumuu printed with little hula girls and hibiscus flowers that hits mid-thigh and may have been originally intended to wear over a bathing suit at the beach. It's thin as onion skin and so light it feels a little indecent. The boots make it an outfit, even if they're basically functioning as foot ovens. Iph imagines her feet in Nana's white ankle socks, a pair of biscuits getting browner as they bake.

"I think I've discovered my new look," Iph says. "Nana chic."

"It's working for you. As for you and that big-ass bag," Glow tells George, "you know the rules, right? Iph, you listen up, too. Word on the street is I only take donations, so this is on the DL. I don't want people trying to sell me the clothes off their backs when they come in here for a health kit. However, since you're a Pippi Longstocking–level thing finder, Georgie my love, I will happily transact with you. But mum's the word. Yes?"

"Yes, ma'am!" George says. "And nice Pippi reference."

Iph eyes George. Another childhood book in common. She's smiling and realizes it when George goes, "What?" Flirting again. But under the flirting, there's always a hint of sadness. Lorna, maybe. Or something deeper, older. In every detective story, the partners getting to know each other's deep dark secrets is always Iph's favorite part.

"Quit mooning and show me your goods," Glow says, feeding Scout a tortilla chip.

While they do business, Iph wanders. Clothing carousels packed with magpie treasures are topped by displays with posters listing statistics illustrating the public health benefits of needle exchange programs, diagrams of how to properly put on a condom, and complimentary travel-size bottles of lube. Iph first encountered the concept of lube recently—and only then because of the terribly uncomfortable conversation she'd had with the nurse practitioner at Planned Parenthood the time Mom took her to get birth-control pills—not for sex, but to help her heavy periods and monster PMS. A sex-ed 101 lecture was the price she had to pay to slow her monthly deluge.

And then there was all the other stuff Mom—*oh god*—told her when she started high school. Lube was probably the only thing she forgot to mention.

"Eww," was all Iph could manage as Mom did a thing with a rubber and a banana. They'd been in the kitchen of all places on a rare Saturday afternoon when Orr had agreed to go on an errand with Dad.

"You need these anytime there's contact with fluids," Mom had said. "Even if it's just a blow job."

"MOM! There are no blow jobs in my near future, I can guarantee it."

"Safe sex is important with women, too."

"Like that's really going to happen in Forest Lake. Can we table this till college?"

"Sometimes you don't see it coming," Mom said.

Mom would certainly approve of Shiny Dancer with its glitter and sequins and high-heeled shoes and radical posters—everything you needed to look hot and be safe and get justice. Iph likes it, too. Except the dildos propped here and there in the displays. They're one of those things you hear about and think you can picture, and then the reality is so much worse. Some are oversize and grotesquely fleshy. Iph can barely look at them. Surely no real penis is that enormous? Even the not-especially-detailed ones in sparkly pink and green to match the walls do not bode well for the real thing. Just . . . *gross*. Maybe Iph is a straight-up lesbian after all.

The far wall of the shop is all shoes. Iph fingers a pair of pink flip-flops with little daisy toppers and wonders if she could use some of the money her shoes bring in to get them. She puts them back. They'd be cool on her toes but terrible for trekking around Portland. Another vestige of her pampered life—not having to worry about practical shoes because your mom will always give you a ride. Iph should have womaned up and gotten her license. This would all be so much faster with a car.

A magazine rack is at the back of the shop with issues of a neon pink zine, also called *Shiny Dancer*, with a blurry black-and-white picture of Glow and a short punk girl on the front, both wearing knee-high boots and feather boas. Above is a sign that says:

SHINY DANCER IS A NONPROFIT THAT PROVIDES INFORMA-
TION, SUPPLIES, AND ADVOCACY TO SEX INDUSTRY WORK-
ERS, DRUG USERS, AND OTHER MARGINALIZED MEMBERS
OF OUR COMMUNITY. OUR PROGRAMS INCLUDE NEEDLE
EXCHANGE; A THRIFT STORE AND COMMUNITY EDUCATION
CENTER; LOCAL, NATIONAL, AND INTERNATIONAL LABOR

AND PUBLIC HEALTH ADVOCACY FOR SEX WORKERS' RIGHTS
AND WELL-BEING; AND A QUARTERLY PUBLICATION. RACISM,
SEXISM, AND HOMOPHOBIA WILL NOT BE TOLERATED HERE.

The only other person Iph's heard use the term *sex worker* is
Mom. Once, when Orr had first learned to read, they'd seen the
word WHORE tagged on the wall of a parking garage. When he
asked what it meant, Mom said, "*Whore* is a mean way of saying
prostitute, honey."

"What's a prostitute?" Orr had asked.

Mom didn't hesitate. "A nice lady who has sex with people for
money."

Iph flips through the zine. She has a small zine collection
herself, things she's picked up from Powell's and others she's
written away for. There is a body positivity one she especially
loves called *I'm So Fucking Beautiful* that has helped her feel better about her big hips and belly and thighs—or to at least question why she feels so awful about them. She also loves the more
personal zines—more like illustrated diaries—like the one about
a girl and her cat and a deeply sad illustrated memoir by a girl
who was abused by her dad. Iph will never forget the look she
saw on Mom's face when she picked it up from Iph's bedroom
floor and read a little. Mom won't talk about her past, but Iph
has always known some sort of abuse was there. She feels it. The
more she learns about the way things can go wrong for kids, for
brown people, for girls, the surer she is that something really
bad happened to Mom when she was younger.

Iph's way of finding things out is often like that—intuitive and
roundabout. She always thinks of the bread-crumb trail in Hansel
and Gretel. People forget that trail was their downfall. They used
pebbles at first, a smart plan. The bread crumbs were what sunk
them—birds and animals ate them up. How do you find your way
then? You find the ghost of the thing, the echo of the trail, the little
tells everyone has to show you who they are. That's theater done
right. In her limited experience, it works for life, too.

Iph takes a copy of *Shiny Dancer* and sits on the pink faux-fur sofa. The low-quality fur prickles, but it's good to be off her feet. The zine is both serious and funny, with a mix of handwritten and typed articles and great cartoons. There are reviews of different strip clubs from the worker perspective, some poems, an article about what to tell your family about your job and how to form a childcare co-op with other sex workers to make sure your kids are in good hands while you're at work. In the back, there's a feature called the Bad Date Sheet. The scrubbed, simple language of it is stunning.

- *Anthony, white male, dark hair, gray beard, heavyset, at least six feet tall. Followed dancer home from Magic Gardens and rang her doorbell for three hours. Police called but never came. Became abusive when bouncers refused to let him into the club after the incident.*

- *White Ford pickup with dent in passenger side near door. White older male, bald, gold aviator glasses. Picked up worker from 82nd and Powell, took to a vacant lot on Columbia Blvd. and assaulted. Injuries required stitches.*

- *White older male. Black late model Cadillac sedan. Violent with male workers. Refuses to pay. Strands workers in remote areas.*

- *Younger male. Brown skin, dressed business casual. Newer Honda Civic with child seat in back. Raped worker.*

- *Kelly, fifteen years old, white, brown hair, green eyes. Missing since May 17th. Last seen in Old Town. Leave any information about whereabouts at Shiny Dancer, 6th and Burnside.*

The missing persons listing has a sketch of the girl, pretty and so young. Iph thinks of George's index card and the story about Lorna. She wonders how George knows Glow. On a table next to the rack is a sign on heavy cream paper with crisp lettering in front of a blue ceramic bowl.

ROSE CITY TRANSMUTATION

PUBLISHER OF FORGOTTEN POETS

HEALER SPECIALIZING IN

DREAMWORK, TRANSFORMATION, TRANSMOGRIFICATION

DISCOUNTS FOR SEX AND SERVICE WORKERS, ANIMAL HELPERS, STRAPPED

WITCHES, TEEN MOMS.

COME FIND US.

Come find us? There's no address. Iph giggles. She's been raised on Dad's old Monty Python reruns and appreciates the surreal. At the bottom of the sign is a stamped hand with a finger pointing down to the bowl with the words FREE POETRY.

The poetry is printed in matchbook-size volumes. Iph squints. The heavy-framed glasses are almost too clear for distance but make it oddly difficult to read close up. She takes them off. The front cover is a meticulously detailed watercolor of a forest. On the back cover is a tiny logo, the letters *RCT* made of climbing roses.

"Ready?" George says.

Iph startles. "Sure." She starts to take a copy of *Shiny Dancer* to the counter, but Mom isn't here with her credit card now. She puts it back but pockets the free matchbook poem.

At the front of the store, Scout is up on the counter eating chips with Glow.

"*Gracias por los tacones,*" Glow says, dangling the shoes in one hand and beckoning Iph to the counter with a twenty-dollar bill in the other. "These are so about to be my lucky work shoes. I can just see those hundreds raining down on the stage."

Ah! Iph had wondered if Glow was a sex worker herself. "You're welcome!" she says, leaning on the counter. Iph loves when people speak Spanish to her but hates that she never speaks it back. She sighs for the gold shoes a final time. No wonder Mom had them in a giveaway box. She and Iph share the same weird feet. Maybe Glow will have better luck.

"*No hablas español?*" Glow says, kicking off her platforms and setting the gold shoes reverently on the floor to be tried on.

"Ugh!" Iph hides her face in her hands. Scout, still happily up on the counter, whines and tries to pry them off with her muzzle. "Kind of? *Pero malo?* I spoke some when I was little. I had this *Sesame Street* book with Spanish words I loved. So, like, if you know any babies or Cookie Monster fans, I can talk to them."

"I learned after college when I lived in Peru—and Spanish was my freaking minor in undergrad. I'm super rusty now. I guess it was the shoes. They moved me."

"These shoes for sure speak Spanish. They used to be my mom's. I wouldn't part with them, but they totally chewed my feet up," Iph says, stroking a gold strap. "I think they run small. I knew when I tried them on, but they were so pretty."

"Hmmm." Glow takes a few steps. "Damn," she says. "Like, they fit, but I know with a little swelling it's gonna be all over. It's one spot right by my big toe. Oh well, some other lucky babe is gonna score. I'm charging an arm and leg for 'em, though. Fleet Week's coming up. High-end vintage is gonna move great." She puts the shoes on the counter next to Scout, who's sitting like a little Buddha propped against the huge antique cash register. She promptly licks each shoe in turn. "Yes, baby, kiss them goodbye," Glow says. Iph blows them a kiss, too.

"You women are crazy," George says. "Those things are little torture chambers."

"It's a deep femme mystery, Georgie my love," Glow says, waving a hand. "The lure of the high-heeled shoe. So, are you coming to see me tomorrow?" Where does she mean? Here? At the strip club? You have to be eighteen to go into those places, right? Or even twenty-one?

"And don't forget the benefit Saturday. I think it's all ages."

"I'll be at needle exchange for sure," George says. "And hopefully the benefit."

Glow hands George the now-empty backpack. "Maybe I'll see you, too, Iph?"

"Sure," Iph says. "I'm kind of just visiting, but if I'm still here . . ."

"Hey, wait a sec," George says. "I almost forgot to ask. We're looking for someone."

"Haven't seen her," Glow says. "And if I did see her at needle exchange or at work, I couldn't tell you."

"No," George says. "Not Lorna. I figured you'd say—if you could."

"But I can't," Glow says, no-nonsense. And wait . . . are they saying Lorna is a stripper like Glow? How old is this ex, anyway?

"Understood, boss. I know I was a pest in the past. Never again, I promise. This time it's actually important. We're looking for Iph's little brother."

They explain about Orr and boot camp and the girl band. "That sounds like this girl Mika's band."

"Do you know how to get in touch with her?" Maybe this is it!

"I met her a few months ago at a self-defense workshop and I've seen her play, but I don't have her number or anything. She seems like a righteous babe, though. Used to volunteer for needle exchange downtown and works at Powell's. I'm pretty sure she's the one who got them to carry our zine."

"What's the name of the band?" Iph's whole body is suddenly one pounding heart.

"The Furies," Glow says. "Rad, right?"

"Thank you so much!" Iph's mind is already outside racing toward Powell's.

"Thanks, Miss Glow," George says. "C'mon, Scoutie. No bag, but you gotta go on the leash."

"Bye, little burrito!" Glow calls to Scout. "You be good, Georgie. You, too, Georgie's cute friend. Hope you find your brother!"

2

UNWOUND HER
HEAVY KNOT OF HAIR

"**W**ake up, babe."

Orr startles. One eye, two eyes. Why is he asleep on the sofa and not in his closet? The last thing he remembers is sitting down to have some tea. The tea is there on the coffee table, cold. Meltdown recovery requires sleep. Usually he makes it to bed, though. Well, things are different at Penelope than they are at home, but—a novel thought!—maybe that's all right.

"C'mon," Jane says. "Get your shoes. We're going out."

He goes to the hall to get his sneakers off the shelf. His feet are better today. He puts on the pair of socks Jane lent him—the ankle kind people wear for sports but rainbow-striped and sparkly. A little small, but workable.

"Orr, dude. This situation is life-changingly rad." Jane is so psyched about his hall organization project. She couldn't stop saying "Dude!" and "Wow" when she first saw it. Mika and Allison like it, too.

Outside, Portland is hot but beautiful. Orr doesn't always think this about the city, but usually he's riding in a car with his headphones on. Today, he and Jane walk. Roses trade scent for sunlight. Lavender sways lightly in the wind. They cross a major street—Belmont, Orr notes. Mom got him a Portland map before she left. She wanted him to start thinking about taking the bus into the city for his cello lessons. "Just consider it," she said when she saw the look on Orr's face. "I'd say Iph could go with you, but honestly, you'd be better off blindfolded. No sense of direction, that girl."

Orr notes how Iph's name slips past his brain's sieve like a tiny minnow through a net. She's probably not even awake. In the summer Iph is almost completely nocturnal.

As for Mom's suggestion that he come into Portland on his own—it seemed absurd at the time, but maybe she was onto something after all. Orr pictures the booklet she made him. He only managed to read a few pages before freaking out. In addition to his daily routines, Mom listed some suggested activities— cleaning out closets full of outdated stuff, spending time outside, going places on his own. All stuff he's actually been doing.

The rest of the memory flares, this time from a different angle. Huh. He lets it play, sound off. Much less upsetting. This way, he sees that even though she'd been onto something about being more independent, he had been a little right, too. What Mom was trying to do defied the laws of physics. There was no way she could be two places at once. Now, instead of being mad at her for it, Orr feels sorry that she was so torn.

Jane is a surprisingly fast walker, given that she is also smoking a cigarette and drinking a Diet Coke. They pass the Bagdad Theater, a beautifully renovated 1920s movie house that serves pizza and the best strawberry lemonade in addition to popcorn to eat while you watch your movie. Iph and Orr love it, even though Dad thinks the place is hideous because it's made to look like a white person's idea of Egypt. "Not to steal your mom's catchphrase, but all I see is imperialism when I look at that place. I'd rather go to the movies in the mall."

Dad! Ugh. Thinking of him is exhausting. Or maybe it's the meltdown hangover. It's suddenly hard to keep his eyes open.

The neighborhood's big-boned Craftsman houses have such wide, inviting porches, like nice ladies with soft laps. A patch of sunlit grass in a side yard beckons. Orr lets them pass and dutifully follows Jane. She won't tell him where they're going or why, but Orr has lost any leeway for protest after this morning, and he knows it.

They finally stop at a once-green house, its paint flaking like the skin of some huge molting reptile. Jane bypasses the front door for a gate that leads to a narrow side yard. Orr runs his nail along a peeling green shingle, pretending the house is a dragon with an itch. The narrow path is dim and cool, a tunnel of faded jasmine with a hint of sweetness left.

Jane gives his arm a gentle pinch. "C'mon," she says. It's the first thing she's said since they left Penelope.

Around the corner the yard is bright with weeds and waist-high wildflowers. If there is a fence, it's invisible, covered in tall roses with wicked thorns that completely obscure the neighboring houses. The yard could go on for miles, Orr thinks, walking around a lacy gingko, like the rose hedge around the castle in *Sleeping Beauty*. A deck is built around the tree connecting the yard to the back of the house.

He follows Jane up the stairs to the back door. A hot tub is recessed into the far side of the deck, smaller than the redwood tub Dad installed for Mom's thirty-fifth birthday. The cover is off, propped awkwardly against the snakeskin siding. The sun is shining like a spotlight on the octagon of water, and first all Orr sees are flower petals and white light. The light resolves into fabric, and the fabric clings around the shape of a person. A girl floats in the tub in a white dress, eyes closed, covered in rose petals and jasmine blossoms, crowned in sunlight, a mane of crimson hair floating around her like blood in the water. Orr looks away. His mouth is suddenly so dry.

"Kids today," Jane says, shaking her head. She sits in a rickety Adirondack chair whose paint has worn away. Orr touches its arm, soft like the paper bags they rubbed together in kindergarten to make buckskin clothing for the Thanksgiving play. Mom had come to help that day and was livid when she read the script of the racist, historically inaccurate skit. The other kids' eyes were wide. They liked Orr's mom. All kids did. The teacher had no choice after she'd told the real story of Thanksgiving but to the change the script on the spot.

Orr is smiling now. Smiling makes him forget where he is, but when he notices again, he sees the girl, her eyes closed in the water, and worries she'll be frightened when she realizes they are there.

Jane lights another cigarette. Orr is suddenly parched, overtaken with the desire to fall to his knees and lap at the water in the tub like an animal. Would it taste like the rose tea Mom gets at her favorite café? Or would it be salty with the sweat of the girl?

Jane blows smoke toward the tub. The mermaid's nose wrinkles. She opens her eyes.

"Hi, Jane," she says, rising ungracefully and heaving herself out the tub. The fabric of the dress molds to her skin, and Orr feels a surprising flair of want—what, exactly, he doesn't know. Still thirsty, he watches her wring the water out of her hair, longer than even Orr's used to be. She has to pull its heavy wet mass over her shoulder to avoid sitting on it.

Settled in the sun on the bare wood of the splintery deck, which has needed to be sanded and refinished for many years now by the look of it, the girl finally turns to Orr.

"I'm Plum," she says. "Who are you?"

"I'm Orr."

"Huh." She takes her thick rope of hair in her hands and wrings it out again. Orr touches the moss-soft velvet of his own skull. His head is throbbing a little. Jane's cigarette, probably. Or the heat.

"I had a Jane's-coming inkling this morning when I woke up and smelled Irish whiskey in the bathroom," Plum says. "I thought it was premonition, but it turned out it was an open bottle someone left in the shower where the shampoo goes. Now I'm thinking the premonition still counts."

"Jimmy partying a lot?" Jane asks, a little frown between her brows.

"The usual," Plum says. "It's more the girlfriend and her friends. But she won't last."

"Well, you would be the one to know, Plum Jam."

Orr notes the look they share, the little nickname, and realizes Jane has known Plum for a long time.

"Jane was my mama's client," Plum says, like she can hear Orr's thoughts. "At Outside In. Then they became friends. She used to babysit me. She even lived with us to take care of Mama when she got sick."

"Your mom is sick?"

"Dead," Plum says gently, as if she doesn't want to scare Orr. But it's too late—Orr is scared. He thinks of Mom dying and cuts the thought short as fast as he can, erasing as he goes. He cannot think about losing Mom. And what about Iph? Why isn't he thinking of her more? She must know he's gone by now. Must've found out the other night when she and Dad got home from the party. She will be so worried. And so, so mad.

The world is spinning. Jane's cigarette, the hot-tub water, the heat. He needs to sit, to lie down, but his body stands there, head untethered in the vast universe, the blue sky stretching too wide above the spinning planet, its cloud countries unmappable.

Something clatters like the keys of a typewriter, and Orr opens his eyes and sees it's the girl, bluish with cold, chattering her teeth.

"Aren't hot tubs supposed to be hot?" he asks.

"Only if the heater works," Plum says.

"What were you doing in there?"

"Acting out a painting," she says. "Waterhouse. *Ophelia*."

"Ha!" Jane says. "This is what happens when you homeschool your children."

"I want to know how it feels to *be* them, okay?" Plum says.

"I'm homeschooled," Orr says.

"Of course you are." Jane puts her cigarette out in an old mason jar.

Plum holds her hand out to Orr from her sunny spot on the deck. "Help me up, fellow uneducated heathen. I need to change before I freeze."

He likes this, of course. Bossiness is one of his favorite qualities in a person. He takes her cold hand in his warm one and pulls.

On her feet, she is almost as tall as Orr.

"I'm off to check on Jimmy," Jane says. "Behave, you two."

"Plum," Orr says, wiping his hand on his jeans, then worrying she'll think it's about germs and not water. Honestly, it's a little bit of both, but Orr means no offense. Plum's face seems to say she hasn't taken any. Still, it's hard to know. "Can I use your phone?"

Plum leads Orr down the basement stairs and pushes through a beaded curtain. "This was my mom's office. I sleep down here now." The low-ceilinged room is dim, painted the color of clover honey. Green light slips past the lemon thyme that grows in front of the ground-level windows across the front of the basement. The air smells of incense and old books. The floor is covered in a pinkish, threadbare carpet that was probably red or purple once. A spinning wheel stands in a corner like a prop out of the illustrated fairy tales Iph used to read to him when he was small. In the center of the room is a table covered in a block-print cloth.

"My mom was an art therapist," Plum says. "She saw her clients here."

"I've done art therapy before," Orr says, remembering therapist number five. "We drew a map of my inner landscape."

"Cool," Plum says. "The phone is there." She points to a table next to a low-slung sofa. "I'm gonna go change."

Orr dials the number. He knows it by heart, of course, but has dialed it himself very few times. Usually, he is the one at home doing the answering.

Dad picks up on the first ring.

"It's me," Orr says.

"Orr!" Dad sounds weird in a way Orr can't place. Not business Dad. Not weekend-energy Dad. Not not-a-morning-person

Dad before coffee. Not headache Dad or date-night Dad. Not even tipsy Dad.

"Son," he says, and all Orr can picture is a desert. Nothing but sand and wind for miles.

"Not the one you want."

"Orr."

Why does Dad keep saying his name?

"Did you really go to Portland with a bunch of tattooed girls?"

"How do you know that?" Orr touches the back of his neck—maybe there's a tracker there after all.

"The waitress. At the diner. Your order was a dead giveaway."

Of course. He always has the same thing at any breakfast place. Still, wow. Orr didn't ever imagine that—a manhunt. Again, life is like an *X-Files* episode. "Did they scour the forest? Were there search and rescue dogs?"

"Yes," Dad says, and Orr knows he's smiling. "Two German Shepherds. Taiga and Tundra. Sisters, the handler said."

"Nice." Orr can't help it—he's softening to this throwback Dad who remembers smiling and shares his love of dogs. This is how Dad always wins. He turns on the warm tan handsome tall money-guy charm. The good-guy routine. You can see it then, why Mom married him. But Orr isn't Mom. He isn't even Iph.

"I'm not coming home, Dad," he says. "Not till Mom gets back."

"That's a long time to be away."

"What do you mean?"

Dad is silent.

"She doesn't know?" Orr had assumed Mom would come home the second she found out. That it was a matter of Dad getting in touch with her. There is no phone in Mom's cabin. She has to use the phone in the common house. Calling in, there's no guarantee someone will be around to pick up.

"I want her to have her residency, Orr. She deserves it."

"Maybe you shouldn't have had me kidnapped by fascists, then."

"Maybe not," Dad says. Orr knows he's thinking about Mom, about how angry she'll be when she finds out about Meadow-brook. "I'm hoping she'll decide to stay. If you're sure you're okay."

"Do you even care?"

The other end of the line goes silent. Have they been discon-nected? Then Dad breathes, so ragged on the exhale, Orr wonders if he's crying. "I was worried about you. You were sleeping so much and not eating. You wouldn't talk to me. I found out about Meadowbrook from Oliver's wife. She's a school psychologist. She highly recommended it."

"I don't care," Orr says. "If it was so good, you should have convinced me. You didn't even try."

"I didn't think you'd listen."

They're silent together—one of the few traits they share. Mom and Iph have debates about who's more stubborn, Orr or Dad.

Finally, Dad says, "I'll come get you. What's the address?"

"What makes you think I would go anywhere with you?" Orr's voice is louder now. "I told you, I'm not coming home till Mom gets back. The girls say it's all good. They don't mind feed-ing me, because I clean."

"You clean?" There he is—the typical, more skeptical Dad. "Have they seen how much you eat?"

Wait. *Wait.* He's sitting here talking to Dad, but what about Iph? "Dad! Why aren't you telling Iph?" He's done it again—for-gotten his sister. "Is she freaked out that I'm missing?"

Dad makes a weird noise. "Iph isn't here. She says she's in Portland. With a friend."

He's lying. Orr knows for a fact that Iph has no friends. Not even in Forest Lake, let alone all the way out in Portland. "Where did you send her? Dad, what did you do?"

"Nothing. God, Orr. Nothing, all right? It's all her—she's there looking for you, kid."

Dad sounds so strange. What is he feeling? What does he want?

"I told her about Meadowbrook. That night at the party. She

was furious. She took off. Left the hotel. I tried to find her. Looked all over. She left a message early Friday morning. I didn't get it because I was driving up to Mount Hood to search for you."

"You lost both your kids?"

"Father of the year," he says, but Orr doesn't feel sorry for him.

"Did she ever call back?" Orr is standing now, pacing, twisting the phone cord as he goes.

"She's fine," Dad says. "We talked yesterday. She won't come home, either. I guess you both think I'm a total bastard."

"Dad. Why did you send me there?"

"I thought it would help."

"Help what?"

"Help you feel stronger. Happier."

Orr stops. "Say that again."

"I thought Meadowbrook would make you feel stronger. And being stronger would make you happier."

Orr takes the words in through his nose, sniffing deep the way the coyote on the mountain had at a hole in the base of a tree. He swallows Dad's words. Listens to them in the hollow of his chest, lets them vibrate like strings on a cello, and now he is crying.

"You thought having me kidnapped would make me happy? Dad, they put a sack over my head and carried me out like executioners. They tied my wrists and stole my hair."

Dad is silent. Then he says, "It was a mistake. I don't know what I thought it was going to be like. I guess I didn't think about that—the means. I was focused on the end result."

"They were racist," Orr says. "Homophobic! It was a bad place." Orr takes a deep breath, all the way down to his tailbone, the way he does when he's getting ready to play a difficult piece. "But, Dad . . . getting away from there? Finding Jane and Allison and Mika and living in Portland? This is what's making me strong. *This* is making me happy. And it doesn't mean I forgive you," Orr says. "I don't know if I ever can."

Dad is silent again. Finally, he says, "Iph is looking for you, Orr. If she calls, can I give her your number?"

"I don't know it."

"Can't you ask?"

Plum is back, changed into leggings and a white button-down shirt that reaches her knees. Her rainbow-striped socks bunch at her ankles in the uncomfortable-looking way Iph always wears hers.

"Do you know the number for Penelope?" Orr asks her.

"Who's Penelope?" Dad asks. "I thought you said the punkers were Mika, Allison, and Jane."

Orr rolls his eyes. "No one says *punkers* anymore, Dad. And Penelope is the house."

"Then who are you talking to? Where are you?"

"I'm at Plum's house," Orr says. "I'm talking to Plum."

"Who is that? Another punker?" Dad's doing this on purpose to make Orr laugh, but it won't work.

"Plum's a friend of Jane's."

Plum grabs Orr's wrist. Her hand is dry now but still cold. She writes a phone number in purple Sharpie on the back of his hand. Orr repeats it for Dad.

"I'll give this to Iph," he says. "Now, how about the address?"

"I don't know it," Orr says and looks at Plum. She mouths *no*—she must be able to hear Dad through the receiver. It's a Dad thing, always being a little too loud on the phone. "I know where the house is. It's on Southeast 35th Street, off Belmont. The pink one on the east side of the street halfway down. I can give you the address later."

"I'd appreciate that."

"Dad, why aren't you trying to make me come home?"

"Because I believe you," Dad says. "I believe you're happy. You sound happy. You haven't been in bed with your headphones on, have you?"

"No. They're still at the house, anyway."

"Not banging your head or not eating?"

"No." Well, he could be eating more, but that's not Dad's problem. Not anymore.

"Is this Plum person nice?"

"She seems nice. Very pretty," Orr says. "She homeschools."
Why is he telling this to Dad?

"Orr, I'm planning to tell your sister this next time we talk. I'm
saying it now to you. I'm willing to evac you anytime for any reason, but if you come home, you stay home. If you stay in Portland,
you're on your own."

"I'm not coming home."

"I won't ever send you back to Meadowbrook, Orr. I promise."

"I don't believe you."

"Fair enough. One more thing, though—I want you to call me.
Once a week, okay? Every Sunday. No matter how much you hate
me. And call me sooner with the exact address."

"I can do that."

"Thank you," Dad says. Orr is surprised by that. He's not sure
why. "I love you."

Orr doesn't say it back and hangs up the phone.

Plum is there with a little frown on her forehead, but the rest
of her face is smiling. Her skin is speckled like a sparrow's egg.
Even her lavender eyelids are freckled. The hair around her face
escapes the top of her bun in corkscrews—curly like Iph's and
Mom's now that it is drying.

"So," Plum says, "you think I'm pretty?"

3

THE OPERA

ph doesn't need a mirror to know her cheeks are red and her hair is crazy. Waiting to cross the street to the movie theater, she puffs out Nana's muumuu for air and gets another whiff of minty smoke. She imagines herself lighting up a skinny white cigarette, enjoying every puff. George said Nana smoked Pall Malls. The dress, it seems, is a little haunted.

She and George hit Powell's downtown and the one on Hawthorne before calling it quits. Glow had been right—Mika does work at the bookstore, but the information desk guy wouldn't tell them which location she worked at or when she would be in next. There was nothing to do but try again tomorrow.

For dinner, they had slices of pizza and endless free cups of water. She wanted to split a salad, but she wanted air-conditioning more, so she and George are going to the dollar movies.

They're early enough that the line is short. The cute green-haired girl in the ticket booth seems to know George and won't take any money. George winks at Iph and waves an extra ticket, pink instead of the red ones for admission. "Free popcorn and a Coke!" George crows.

"I have to pee," Iph says. "I'll see you in there."

The restroom is oddly situated, up a narrow flight of stairs carpeted in a color you never see anymore, the pinkish-gray of end-of-summer hydrangeas and faded velvet sofas. Inside the restroom is an anteroom, an actual place to rest, with a love seat and small tufted stools in front of a mirrored counter. A girl is there putting on lipstick. She is mouse-boned with delicate hands, her vertebrae a dollhouse staircase in her back-baring halter dress. In the mirror, she looks Iph up and down—and down again. She turns and asks, "Why are you wearing my boots?"

Iph rubs her temples where the lost-and-found glasses pinch. Takes in the girl's familiar waifish supermodel brand of pretty.

Of course. The mystery girl in George's painting.

"You're Lorna," Iph says.

"I know who I am," the girl says. "The question is, who are you?"

"I'm Iph. I'm in town for few days," Iph says. Why did she say that?

"Do I look like I care about your itinerary?" Lorna stands, taller than Iph would have guessed. Iph looks her up and down and down again. Gold strappy sandals with a chunky forties heel.

"Why are you wearing *my* shoes?" Iph says.

"These are . . ." Lorna's huffiness disappears. She drops back down to her seat. "Wait," she says. "You're the cute friend. And George, I presume, is here?"

"And you bought those from Shiny Dancer today, didn't you?"

Lorna holds one foot out, tilting the shoe to catch the light like it's a diamond engagement ring at the end of her hand. Her feet are daintily shaped, with red toenails and high arches that mold to the shoes' own curves. She'll probably be able to walk ten miles and then dance all night in them without a single blister.

"George has been looking all over for you." Iph says it like she and Lorna are friends, aiming for disarmament. As much as she'd like to instigate some soap-opera-style manipulation to keep Lorna and George apart, she won't. For whatever reason, it's not in her.

"Georgie Porgie, pudding and pie. Kissed the girls and made them cry," Lorna says. "You crying yet?"

"Did George do something to you?"

Lorna's forehead is high and her eyes are blue, but she's a little more like a real person and a little less like Kate Moss than she was in Iph's head last night. Still, just a little.

"No," Lorna says. "Georgie's fine. It was me." Lorna pinches the bridge of her nose like she's a forty-year-old French woman having problems with her lover. Like someone who talks about the people she's dating using that word. *Lover*—eww. It's probably uncalled-for to hate Lorna for something Iph only imagines she's guilty of, but there is a too-muchness about this girl. And an odd vulnerability.

"Please," Lorna says, "don't tell George you saw me." She meets Iph's eyes, and there it is—the beleaguered heroine. Iph would cast her as Nora in *A Doll's House*. As Queen Anne in *Richard the Third*. As Norma Jean in the play about Marilyn Monroe in high school that Iph is supposed to be secretly writing in her spare time.

"Please," she says again. The lipstick is still in her hand. She puts it in her purse. How old is she, anyway? Her eyes have faint creases at their tips. Her under-eyes are bruised crescents. World-weary, that's how she looks.

"I know it's none of my business, but . . . would it be so bad to go say hi?"

Lorna looks up and to the left—a gesture to access memory. Iph sees her love story with George in that look. Is she about to cry?

Suddenly, Iph is willing to cede any sort of claim she might have on George. It's always this way for her—she's jealous and possessive until the moment she's not. In the end, competition doesn't make sense. Whoever wants the thing more should get it. She wonders, though, does Lorna want it more, or is she just good at looking heartbroken?

"George and I are just friends," Iph says. "If that helps at all."

"For now." Lorna puts away her lipstick. "You are so Georgie's type."

"I think that's more you," Iph says. "Have you seen the painting?"

Lorna nods. Slowly, like the painting is a lot. Which it is. You might think you want that kind of attention thrown your way, but Iph sees it on Lorna's face—that kind of love can be a burden.

"Here's the thing," Lorna says. "Georgie loves to be in love."

"So it was a one-way street?"

"No! I mean, George is amazing. But . . . kind of? I don't know, George made me feel safe. For a while." Lorna looks down at her hands, clasped like she's holding a tiny animal between them. Like she's praying. A tear drops and disappears into the folds of her fingers.

Iph reaches out her own hand like Lorna is a child she's about to help across a busy street. Lorna takes it. They're quiet. The moment is weirdly intimate. Iph's theater brain strains to be let free, to take notes, but something else in her shushes it.

"Maybe I used George." Lorna's grip tightens. "It's hard to know how much you like someone when you need a place to sleep." She looks straight at Iph and takes her hand back.

"That makes sense," Iph says. And for once she knows it's true, not because she has a great imagination, but because she's been there herself. *Is* there herself. But honestly, even if she were riding high right now, Iph would still like George. She's never met anyone she's liked even half as much.

"Be careful." Lorna's eyes are wide open now and pale as a husky's. "George is easy to love."

"I can see that."

Iph can just as easily see how to fall in love with Lorna—just look into her eyes. So big and blue. So much saving to do. Irresistible for a knight like George.

Lorna looks back at the mirror. Takes out a brush and pulls it through her silky hair, then zips up her purse and stands. Awkward, yet elegant. Like Audrey in *Funny Face*. Or Jean Seberg in anything.

"Those boots look better on you than on me," she says. "Just keep them. I'm gonna take off. I've seen this movie a hundred times anyway."

4

LIFE FROM
THE FLOWERS

People crowd the sidewalk in front of the theater. The line snakes around the corner. It's seven P.M. and eighty-seven degrees in the shade, but at least the light is softer now that the sun is lower in the sky.

Even here on busy Hawthorne Street, Orr smells roses from people's yards and the sunscreen everyone uses on children that is synonymous with summer. Most days, he tries to hold sensory input at bay, taking in a little at a time. Not tonight. He wants every possible detail of popcorn smell and snatches of car-radio music and kids bickering and cawing crows to stay in his memory so he never forgets this feeling of waiting in line for the movies on a summer night with such a beautiful girl.

When it comes to looking straight at Plum, though, Orr has decided to pace himself. Out here in the gold-lit world, she is bright as a parrot in a yellow dress that makes her dark red hair look almost magenta. These are Mom's colors in the house, the walls of their living and dining rooms. Here, they are Plum's alone. She wears white rubber flip-flops, and her toenails have chipped purple polish. Her feet are very nice. She originally intended to leave the house barefoot, but to Orr's immense relief, when her dad and Jane found out they were going to the movies, they both insisted she wear shoes.

"Fine." Plum has a way of saying it that sounds like, *You're an idiot, but I'll humor you.* Iph's *fine* is also loaded, but hers is more like, *Screw you.* Orr wonders if this is a universal teenage girl thing.

Now, they wait. Jane gave Orr the dollar for the movies, but Plum has money for popcorn and candy, and Orr, as always, is starving. He wonders if they will give him a free cup of water. He feels like he could drink a river. A lake. A sea.

"Have you seen this yet?" Plum points her fox chin at the marquee. THE SECRET OF ROAN INISH.

"I haven't," Orr says. "Have you?"

"Ten times. It's the only thing that ever plays at this theater. It's, like, a thing this summer. I think it's doing something to the city."

"Something good?"

"Something magical."

"You sound like my mom," Orr says. "She's witchy, too."

"All women are," Plum says. "But not all of us know it."

"What about men?"

"Men . . . oy." Plum rolls her eyes. "Men have magic. Look at little boys! But you squish it down young. You know how in physics, pressure changes things? Like, makes carbon into diamonds? Men's magic is like that. Then they sell the diamonds for something else. That's what ruins it for you guys, I think. The whole alpha-male status trip."

"I'm not like that," Orr says.

Plum cocks her head. What kind of animal *is* she, anyway? A fox, probably. Or a cat. That's an Iph game, figuring out what kind of animals people are. She learned it for acting, to help her get into character. She decided to play Hermia as a standard poodle for a monologue at school. When she practiced it for Orr, she was suddenly not Iph at all, but a completely different girl. It almost frightened him.

Orr sends his sibling tentacles out into the city but feels

nothing. Dad says Iph is here, that she's looking for him. He imagines seeing her in line for the movie. She'd run up to him, jump on him, squeeze him way too tight. He always complained, but really, he liked it. She knew that. But now his body curls away from the image like a poked pill bug. He doesn't want to see Iph. He doesn't even want to see Mom. The only person he wants to see right now is Plum.

5

ADAPTATION

It's stifling in the apartment. The rule is windows closed till the neighbor's house goes dark, but it's too hot to bear. They've taken a risk already, coming home so early. They didn't stay for the movie. George was too upset. Now they have to keep their voices low.

Iph is lying on the scratchy carpet like a starfish, trying to maximize her surface area to catch any hope of a breeze. George is on the sofa. Scout has ditched them for the cooler kitchen linoleum.

"Did she tell you about how she disappeared one day?"

"No," Iph says.

"She's stripping now. Did she tell you that?"

"You sort of did. At Shiny Dancer." It had been hypothetical then. The reality of it is hard to connect with the actual girl. "How old is she?"

"Eighteen as of two weeks ago. She used her stepsister's ID when she started. They probably didn't even look at it."

"Well . . . I don't know. In a perfect world, she'd be taken care of by nice adults, but that doesn't seem like it's happening. I mean, how does she feel about her job? Does she like it?"

"Iph. She takes her clothes off in front of creeps for money."

Iph feels Mom's training rise but sets it aside for now. "Did you two fight about it?"

George groans.

"I mean, I'm sure she has her reasons. Did she tell you why she first decided to strip?"

"Why does anyone?" George flops facedown on the sofa. "Kill me now."

"You don't seem to have a problem with Glow's work," Iph says, rolling over and stretching up into a cobra pose, trying to relieve what riding on the bike rack has done to her lower back.

"That's different. Glow's older. And I don't know—she doesn't seem like she has Lorna's history. I told you how Lorna and I met. I can't believe she'd get naked for strangers after that. It doesn't make sense."

"I don't know. Maybe it's not perfect logic, but I bet it makes sense. Everyone has their reasons," Iph says. "Or maybe you're right and it's self-destructive. But George . . . it's kind of up to her, you know?"

"I drove her away. She wanted to stay here," George says into the mossy deep of Nana's couch cushions. "She kept bringing home weed and Thai food. Kept buying me stuff."

"Sounds terrible."

"It *was* terrible," George says rolling to face the back of the sofa. "I couldn't accept her ill-gotten gains."

Iph sits up and props her back against the sofa. She's trying not to laugh. George slides off the sofa to sit next to her and is smiling a little, too, because it's hard to be melodramatic in a hundred-degree apartment.

Iph shoves George a little with her shoulder. "Ill-gotten gains?" She giggles and George giggles, and it's suddenly more of a slumber party and less of a funeral, but it's so hot that even party-girl Scout just thumps her tail from the next room.

When the laughing is over, they're sitting cross-legged, face to face like they're preparing to do the hand-clapping game Iph loved as a little girl. *Say, say, oh playmate. Come out and play with me.*

Iph leans in and kisses George—a short press of Iph's chapped lips to George's smooth ones.

"It's fine," Iph whispers, "that you still love Lorna. You can love her and like me at the same time. If that's what's happening."

George's eyes glow. "I think that's what's happening."

Iph leans in again, and the kiss is deeper this time. She's never done this before, but already she knows she's good at it. With practice, she'll be really good. An alternative future spools away from the lonely dorm-room microwave-brownie scenario Iph has been inching toward since high school disappointed her. There is sex in her future if she wants it.

George—who is also good at this, whether inherently or from practice—seems lost in the kiss. Iph touches the baby hairs on George's neck with her fingertips. Moves her lips down to those beautiful collarbones. Brushes her eyelashes against George's cheek. Blows cool air on George's sweaty forehead. Lightly bites George's ear. Stops. Looks into George's eyes. Sees herself there, yes. But Lorna's there, too.

"So," she says. "Tell me more."

"About?"

Iph laughs at the look on George's face. "About Lorna. You're thinking about her, right?"

"You're a little scary with your mind reading."

Iph smiles. Everything feels . . . fine.

She reaches out for Orr wherever he is in the city. *Safe* thrums back to her.

Nothing is how it's supposed to be, but everything is all right.

6

OVER THE POOL

Movies are often overwhelming for Orr. *The Secret of Roan Inish* is no exception. There are moments he needs to cover his ears—not because the soundtrack is loud, but because the emotions are so intense. The selkie woman is too lovely, the tiny child in the cradle boat too brave, too alone. The wistful sister longing for her lost baby brother nearly undoes him. It's all too close to home.

And then there's Plum in the seat next to him. Orr is grateful for her contained energy. She seems to expect nothing of him. The first time he put his head down and covered his ears, he felt her noticing. After that, she seemed to get that some parts were a little too much and handed him the tub of popcorn or moved a little to let him know it was safe to emerge. Now that the movie is over, she waits with him till most of the people are out of the theater, almost as if she knows that's the way he likes to do things.

Should he have held Plum's hand during the movie? Should he hold it now? But she is walking in front of him, hands in the pockets of her sundress, hair swishing back and forth behind her like a goldfish tail. Orr hurries to catch up with her.

They are mostly quiet on the way home. The night is still warm, but it's nice after the air-conditioned theater. The scent of night-blooming flowers flavors the air like syrup in an Italian soda. A few blocks from her house, Plum asks, "What was your favorite part?"

"That the boy didn't come home easily," Orr says. "He wouldn't have in real life. He was scared, but his sister knew how to call him. She understood him even after they'd been apart so long."

"Do you miss your sister?" Plum asks, her voice very soft like Orr is the feral little boy in the movie, living with the seals in his cradle of a ship, naked out at sea.

Orr nods. "Do you miss your mom?"

Plum says, "I always cry when Jamie goes back to his family. It's the right ending, I know. But there's a part of me that's a little resentful. It's like the movie version of my favorite book. This girl's dad dies, and she has to overcome it and keep living. But in the movie, it's all a mistake. He's not dead after all. It's like, give us the real story, you know?"

They're quiet for the rest of the walk. When they get back to Plum's, the house is dark. There's a note on the refrigerator door from Jane held by the same wizard magnet that's on Orr's refrigerator at home, a free gift from a box of herbal tea. Jane's out grocery shopping with Plum's dad, the note says. Orr can wait at Plum's or go back to Penelope.

"That's good," Plum says. "Most days, he doesn't leave the house." She must mean her dad. "So, wanna stay and hang out? I'm going to make tea and read. You can join me if you want."

"I'm tired," Orr says. He knows it's from the movie.

"I'll make you a map." She draws a diagram of how to get back to Penelope on the back of an envelope that reads *Environment Oregon*.

Orr prowls the living room, restless and ready to be alone. Plum's house is messy at first glance, full of books and newspapers and empty beer and soda bottles and board games and musical instruments, but clean underneath. Like the Furies' house is now that Orr has moved in.

On the front porch, Plum says goodbye. She does this with a hug and then a funny thing—a head press, her forehead to his. How had she known his head was hot and a little achy? Plum has powers, like Iph.

He finger-traces the map and the digits of Plum's phone number, written on the other side of the envelope, then puts it in the pocket of Allison's basketball shorts. He knows the way. He starts to run, and when he starts, he doesn't want to stop. He flies past Penelope, blocks and blocks. He smells green. He is so fast. His body makes wind that cools his face. Ahead, massive trees touch the black velvet sky where the brightest stars are visible—such a different sky from the one at home, where even a few miles from the city the light pollution is so much less.

Orr remembers his hair, the way his ponytail flowed out behind him when he ran. He is so light now without it. So much faster. How can a good thing come from such a violation? This night would never have happened without Meadowbrook. Orr thinks about the dark theater hour spent shoulder-to-shoulder with Plum and the way fairy tales are sometimes true.

He runs toward the trees, past a playground, and into a park. He senses water before he's even close to the big oval pond. The rancid mossy green surely reeks—but tonight the strong smell is enticing. He thinks of Plum floating in the hot tub, surrounded by flowered water. Here, there are no flowers. Only a neon scrim of algae over black water. Still, he kneels at the water's muddy edge.

On the center island, the ducks murmur. Surely if he drinks here, he will be sick. The moon is so bright, a few days away from full. There are turtles sleeping on a log in the center of the pond. How does he know that? It's a smell or maybe a sound, slow amphibian blood. He cocks his head to hear the roosting herons. Crows sleep tucked in high branches in a stand of Douglas firs around the pond. Little fish swim deep below. The water wears moonlight the way Plum wore her Ophelia dress. Orr's mouth is so dry. His hands are in the water now.

A sound startles him. A growl. A big lab's quick bark rebukes his aberrant behavior. The dog strains on the leash held by a small, hurrying woman. Orr smells their fear, both the woman's and the dog's.

Why is he here at the edge of this pond? The gravel cuts into his knees. Without even drinking, he knows how the water will taste—of pleasure and relief.

But Orr stands and backs away. Listens to the lap of the pond against the shore. Smells pot smoke. Hears voices from the far end of the park. A bat passes under a streetlamp. Orr turns his back to the pond.

You can have all the water you want at the house, he tells this new, thirsty part of himself. After one final look at the moonlit water, Orr trots back to Penelope.

7

HIS FOUR
BLACK HOOVES

There is a man in the kitchen. He is stinking drunk—another supposed euphemism proven. He makes the entire house rank with beer and pee and gross BO. Orr stands over him, cast-iron skillet poised.

"Who the hell *are* you?" The guy has asked this seven or eight times. The emphasis had switched at around the fourth query from "Who the hell are *you*?" to the way it is now, less belligerent and more bemused. "Dude, let me up, man. I wanna get my stuff."

"You don't live here," Orr says. His heart is beating so hard. Like always, he is thirsty. "Will you stay down while I get a drink?"

"These chicks are straight-edge, bro. It's like the Bible Belt up in here."

Orr has no idea what the man is talking about. All he wants is a glass of water.

"We're not straight-edge, asswipe," a voice says. "We hide our stuff from you. Our cash, our smokes. Definitely our beer. We lock our bedroom doors." Mika stands fierce in her tank top and boys' underwear with dinosaurs on it. She told Orr she shops in the kids' department where clothes are cheaper—usually the boys' section, because she prefers the prints. She touches Orr's elbow, and he sets down the pan. It's funny how long he was able to hold it without shaking. His bicep is a small hillock of rock—when did that happen?

The guy shifts like he's going to stand, but Mika puts up a hand. "Don't move." She grabs her camera from the counter and snaps. "For posterity," she says. "Now get out, or I'm getting Allison."

"Jane," the guy shouts.

"Shut up!" Mika says. "She's not here."

"Janie!" the guy yells, lumbering to his feet. "JANE." Mika starts kicking him, but her feet are bare. She gets in a few good ones, but he just laughs. He's so drunk. Orr has never seen someone this intoxicated in real life. "*JANE!*"

Mika gets a dish towel and goes to stuff it in the guy's mouth as he tries and fails to stand up, singing as he stiff-arms Mika with one hand and snatches the dish towel away with the other. Orr knows the song—"Kung Fu Fighting." Mika makes a little shriek and pulls back her arm to sock him. Then Jane is there, pulling Mika off and pulling the guy up. Once he's standing, she shoves him and bursts into tears. Then he's holding her.

Orr doesn't like this one bit. "Jane, who is this guy?" he asks. But Jane isn't listening.

"Come on," Mika says and pulls Orr into the living room. Jane is still crying, and the guy is slurring something.

"I can't watch this," Mika says. "Porch?"

Outside is cool and perfect. The wind slides over the trees like a loose-strung bow. "Want to go for a run?" Orr asks Mika. But Mika is resting her head on her knees.

"I hate that guy," she says. "He's awful for Jane."

Orr thinks of Dad. Is he bad for Mom? Are he and Iph bad for her? Part of the reason she needed the residency was because of her sadness. It's why Dad encouraged her to dance more, to go into Portland for the classes that left them eating pizza three nights a week. And the way Orr acted when she left . . . no wonder she wanted to go away for so long.

"Awful how?" Orr asks Mika.

"In every way possible," Mika says. "I can't deal with this. Not again." There's a note in Mika's voice that makes Orr understand how temporary his own stay at Penelope will be.

"That song," Orr says.

"Racist dickhead."

Orr is shaking. It must have started before, when he thought the guy was there to kill the Furies in their sleep. He sits on his hands. That stupid song is stuck in his head now.

"Why's Jane with him?"

"They went through some hard stuff together when they were young. Jane got over it, but Red never did."

They're quiet enough that the background sounds of the neighborhood move to the front. Voices rise and fall in the house. The crickets sing and the neighbors across the street laugh at something they're watching on TV. Someone next door turns on a shower. A baby cries, then quiets. Unlike his neighborhood at home, the houses in Southeast Portland are close together and no one seems to have an air conditioner—hence all the open windows. A car passes, then a trio of laughing bearded guys on bikes.

"People always teased me for being Asian when I was a kid," Orr says.

Mika looks closely at Orr. "Huh."

"I'm not Asian," Orr says. "They didn't know what I was, so they guessed."

"They knew you were something," Mika says. "So, uh . . . where are you *from*?"

The way she says it makes Orr laugh out loud. "My mom hates that."

"Don't you hate it?"

"Oh, no," Orr says. "I love it. I get to tell them I'm from the galaxy QRT 9987 in the Orion sector. Or sometimes I say I'm a fugitive surfing the space-time continuum. Or, you know, keep it simple. Say I'm from Mars."

Mika is smiling now. The grin makes her face into a pointy triangle like the face of a cat. "Can I borrow that?"

"Are you a Martian, too?"

"I'm thinking more like a vengeful time-traveling demigod."

"People will definitely believe that," Orr says. "Especially if they ever hear you drum."

Mika turns red when he says it, and that makes Orr blush, too. They're quiet again. Mika punches him softly on the arm. "Wait here. I'll be right back."

The door makes the tiniest squeak as Mika opens it. Orr inhales deeply. Something sweet blooms on Penelope's street at night. Mika returns with both their sneakers. She plops Orr's on the porch and sits on the top step to lace up her own.

He pulls on his shoes over bare feet. It doesn't even bother him now not to have socks.

"Race you to the cemetery!" she says and takes off.

Mika is faster, but Orr's legs are much longer. They are both straining in the final blocks, bursting past the cemetery gates neck and neck. At the last second something gathers in the muscles of Orr's legs and rockets him past Mika. He's halfway down the path before he can stop.

Mika trots up, laughing. "You're a freaking centaur, boy! I thought you had hooves for a second there."

They stagger to a moonlit patch of grass and collapse.

8

FAITH AND A
SENSE OF TRUTH

The heat is an asshole. Iph misses the rain. She's gone through all of Nana's clothes, and the only clean things are a huge boxy T-shirt with a sea lion on the front from the Newport Aquarium and some unflattering, baggy shorts. Just lovely with her undereye circles and frizzed-out curls.

George woke up quiet and distant, and Iph the bohemian adventuress of the night before was gone like yesterday's makeup, leaving her in the familiar Land of Almost. Almost pretty. Almost cool. A party guest earnestly mumbling *peas and carrots* in the chorus.

Being a protagonist is infinitely better.

There is a thing Orr always said about the kids who were nice to him at school. That he was their "human credential." Like, *Look, I'm so kind and open-minded, I'm friends with the boy who meows in class when he's bored.* It was like that with Iph's friends, too, although it took her longer to realize it. She knew how to make herself socially useful in a way Orr never figured out. But by sophomore year, Iph got tired of it. She experimented with eating lunch alone in the library and not calling anyone for a week. After a month without diminishing herself to fit in, she was stronger.

She boxed the sporty, brightly colored clothes she'd never liked and had Mom take them to the women's shelter.

She'd decided on her new uniform and started wearing it: old dress shirts of Dad's, knotted at the waist. Straight-legged jeans and men's white tees and vintage penny loafers. Pencil skirts and sweater sets. She offset the classic fifties coed vibe with Yai-Yai's loud costume jewelry, mixed with little things she made from party favors from the toy store—mismatched earrings and bracelets made of tiny plastic animals and a growing collection of Barbie shoes. She was never without lipstick, dark red or hot pink with nails to match. A sort of method-acting, student-era Marilyn Monroe going to a rave. A few of her old friends had been interested in her transformation—at first. A few boys seemed to notice, too—but that meant nothing unless she was down for clandestine sex. There would be no actual dating in high school for Iph. Teen coupling was all about status, and Iph's body type and brownness counted her out, at least in Forest Lake.

"Ugh," George says, pulling the bike out. "Portland is not supposed to be this hot."

"Does she have a name?" Iph asks about the bike as they wait for Scout to do her business.

"Ethelette," George says. "I'm a dork, okay?"

"No," she says, straddling the bike rack. "That's perfect."

As crappy and insecure as she feels this morning, she'd rather be here than anywhere else. Bouncing on the back of the ten-speed is what Iph does now. George has even fastened a throw pillow to the rack with a bungee cord in deference to Iph's bruised butt.

Last night, post-kiss, George had been chivalrous, offering Iph Nana's room like crashing in a pile on the sofa together suddenly wasn't proper. Except neither of them wanted to separate. They'd stayed up talking till four in the morning instead and took Scout for a pre-sunrise walk. It was dawn when they went to bed and three in the afternoon when they finally woke up. Now the bones of the Hawthorne Bridge tower above them. George's calves are glorious as they push the bike through the hottest part of the afternoon.

George is busy today. A stop in Old Town. A stop in Southeast. Then meeting Glow at her needle exchange site. After Old Town, Iph will be dropped off at Powell's to wait like a child.

You're a detective, she tells herself, *looking for Glow's friend Mika.* But before the thought is complete, she shuts it down. The whole girl-detective thing is a game. She can't actually find Orr. Is she even trying? What about flyers? Ads in the paper? If she was serious, she'd go back to Dad and get his credit card and plaster every telephone pole in Portland with images of her brother. She'd make Dad hire a real investigator. Use her supposed psychic powers to find him herself.

Once off the bridge, they veer right and cross Burnside, passing under the red lion-guarded gate to Chinatown. George gave her the downtown tour the day before, and surprisingly she's retained some of it. It's different exploring without a car. Slow enough for her brain to catch up with her body.

George locks the bike kitty-corner from an old hotel called the Gentry, telling her it's known as the Entry on the street. "It's a joke," George says. "Gallows humor. The Entry is like a portal. Once you go through, it's hard to find your way back."

Iph has never been on this street. Its narrowness and the age of the buildings hint at earlier eras of white settlement. She always wonders what it was like for the indigenous people who lived here before colonization. There are so few traces left of that world. When people talk about Portland history, they tell you which settlers the streets are named after and how the city almost washed away in the 1894 flood. Some of the bars around here probably still have basements that lead to the so-called Shanghai tunnels below the city that were used for shipping and as speakeasies during Prohibition. There were even rumors that poor white sailors and racial minorities were kidnapped and kept there to be indentured to ships' captains when they came into port.

Then and now, the population in Portland is mostly white.

Mom used to supplement the history they learned at school. It was from her, not the teachers, that Iph learned Oregon was the only state to explicitly exclude Black people at its founding. Even though that law eventually changed, the sentiment is baked into the city's segregated neighborhoods. It's a regret of her parents' now, that they settled in a place with so few Black and brown people.

"You should probably wait outside with Scout," George says, checking and rechecking the bike lock. Iph rolls her shoulders back and knots her hair on the top of her head. If she had a pair of scissors, she'd cut her T-shirt into a tank top right here on the street. Even Scout looks cranky.

"Stay close—I'll be quick." George hands Scout's leash to Iph. Maybe George is getting sick of her. They've spent almost every moment of the past four days together.

The street smells like pee, and Scout is very busy checking it out. A man is having an angry conversation with himself. He passes Iph and turns a red face to her. He is clearly in pain, his head fiery with things he sees and she doesn't. But he's also scary, filthy in a layered, long-term way, with filmy, unfocused eyes. Iph thinks of the word *unhinged* and how this describes not just his possible mental state, but the way he's holding his body. His arms are too loose, his knees too mobile. Maybe he's drunk, but Iph doesn't think so.

"GO AWAY!" he roars. Iph steps back. Sweat drips from her forehead to her nose. Her glasses fog. She wipes them, puts them back on. Like the first time she wore them, everything looks too bright.

"GO AWAY."

This time, he is roaring at her.

Scout moves between Iph and the man and bristles.

An insect halo is swarming the man's head. It's not really there . . . is it? He swats around his ears. He's stomping now. People cross the street to get away from him. "GO. AWAY." He's in tears. The insects buzz louder.

Iph wipes her glasses clean again with her T-shirt. She can see them now. Winged red ants with little angry human faces and mouths full of pointed teeth.

"Hey!" Iph says. "Hold on for a second." Scout barks to get the man's attention, ready to go along with Iph's improv. The man stills. Listens. "I have some insecticide in my bag." She gestures to a bag that's not there. "You'll have to close your eyes to protect them. Maybe you should cover your face, too."

The man is startled. "The bugs?"

"Yes, those red ants. They're awful. Let me get them."

He tenses, afraid, she realizes.

"I'm going to stay back and spray from here. It's a strong propellent, so it should work all right."

His eyes widen. "Give me some warning," he says. "Count to three."

"Okay! Here goes." She braces herself and pretends to pull out a heavy can of bug spray. She feels the efficacy of the spray will depend completely on her commitment to its reality. She uncaps the canister and puts the cap in the bag. She shakes it and holds out her arm. "Here it comes," she says. "One, two, three!" She presses the nozzle, making the *shhhhh*-ing sound of liquid spraying out.

"Keep your eyes closed! They're dropping," Iph says. "I'm gonna spray the ones on the ground to be sure."

When Iph stops spraying, he opens his eyes one at a time. He turns in a circle, nodding as he goes. He presses his hands together like he's going to pray, bows a little in Iph's direction, then walks away, still nodding.

Iph rubs her temples, the sweaty back of her neck. She feels drained now and a little like crying. The door to the Gentry opens, and a crusty older version of one of the Pioneer Square boys emerges. His energy is sticky as ground fruit, sweet and false. There is violence there. Iph shivers in the heat. Steps back. She's raw from the red-ant man, she realizes, too open.

She used to get headaches from going out in crowds when she

was younger. Mom said she was like a sponge and taught her to close her receptors. "Like a little psychic raincoat," she said.

Iph's been spongey all day. Skinless. Maybe kissing George has opened her up. And that, of course, is the danger of sex. The reason why there might be less of it in her future than last night's flagrant kissing promised. She is exposed now. Fatigued from seeing and being seen.

"You going in?" the guy asks. Before she can say no, Scout shoots through the open door, dragging Iph inside. Scout may be tiny, but she's strong enough to pull a sled.

INSIDE, IPH LOOKS FOR a sofa to rest on, but it's not that kind of hotel. There doesn't even seem to be air-conditioning. The desk clerk is a head and torso in a plexiglass box, like those animatronic fortune-tellers they had in the awesome pizza place in downtown Forest Lake before it was torn down to build a Wal-Mart.

Scout barks a sharp little hello.

"Scout!" The lady adjusts her Dolly Parton wig and slips a bejeweled hand out of a slot in the plexiglass, wiggling two manicured fingers. Scout hops up to lick them, then sits for a treat. The lady obliges with a cackle, tossing it out the slot into Scout's jaws.

"George is on the third floor. Take the stairs, sweetheart. There's a mess in the elevator. If it opens, hold your nose."

Iph follows the extended red claw to a door that reads STAIRS and climbs. Can the elevator smell worse than this? She wills her nose shut and follows a perfectly cheerful Scout up two flights.

The third floor smells better, but still not remotely good. There's a cafeteria scent mixed with wet gymnasium and some sort of toxic cleaning solution. Iph hesitates, but Scout pulls her down the hall. There's a weird vibe in the place that Iph can't quite pin down.

Scout tugs her onward and stops at the final door on the left. She scratches and whines until it opens. "Sorry," Iph says when she sees George's face. "There was a guy. Scout brought me here—"

"It's all right, doll," someone says. "Come on in." It's a woman. White, older, hard to say how old. She's wearing a pink kimono trimmed in balding ostrich feathers, and her hennaed hair is piled high on her head and stuck through with three red chopsticks. Another woman leans against the headboard, eyes closed. This one is light brown, graying and handsome, eyelids fluttering like she's in the middle of an intense dream. Iph turns away, trying not to stare. The woman is high, Iph realizes. Probably on heroin.

"This is Velma," George says. A rotating fan clicks in the corner like a metronome. Iph turns her face to meet the breeze.

"I'm Iphigenia." Iph smiles. Something about this woman's old-timey glamour makes Iph want to give her full name.

Velma's eyebrows raise. Maybe she knows her Greek tragedy. "Well, hello there," she says like they're all in a forties comedy and there isn't someone nodding out right next to her. "George tells me you're an actor. And clearly quite the dish."

"Why, thank you," Iph says, smiling like a silver-screen inge-nue. It's nice being referred to as an actor. And it's the first time anyone's ever called her a dish.

"Don't mind Pete," Velma says.

"I'm so sorry for barging in." Iph's eyes have adjusted, and she sees that Velma is older than she thought. She has great skin, but her hands, absently stroking Pete's arm, are wrinkled. Her neck is, too. She's probably at least sixty. That explains the name. No one is called Velma anymore.

"Velma's a poet," George says. "Pete's a jazz man."

He, Iph mentally corrects herself in relation to Pete. "I love poetry," she says. "And my dad's a big jazz guy."

"What poets do you like?" Velma leans forward like she's dying to know.

"Anne Sexton," Iph says. "Theodore Roethke. Sylvia Plath. Emily Dickinson. Shakespeare. Tennyson. Sappho. Blake."

"That's an excellent list. It's so nice to see young people still read," Velma says. "Shakespeare certainly improved George. You should have seen the hell-raising before the bard came along."

"Velma!" George shakes a finger and Scout dances as Velma laughs.

"I won't keep you kids." Velma rubs the cuff of Pete's white shirt, a long-sleeved button-up that's surprising in this heat. "And George, if they have anything in the van for Pete's leg—"

"Velma"—George's voice lowers—"you might want to get over to the ER. I'm worried. I think it's got to be lanced."

Velma's eyes fill. "Pete won't," she says. "Not after the way they treated us last time."

George exhales, short and fierce. Sometimes Iph sees the ghost of the bow and arrow even when George isn't wearing it.

"So lovely to meet you," Velma says. Her voice is soft and slow. Is she high, too? Iph has never considered this—older people addicted to drugs. But of course it happens.

"You, too," Iph says. "I love your kimono."

"Oh, this old thing?" Velma smiles, winking like a showgirl. "You two be good, now."

IN THE HALL, IPH stops. Something's pulling her back into the room. She looks at the door. For a second, she sees water flowing out from under it, a wave on the beach of worn brown carpet.

"George, what's wrong with Pete's leg?"

George sighs. "An abscess. Probably an infected injection site. I wish Glow was here. She knows how to lance them."

"How do you know Glow, anyway?"

"I lived around the corner from the needle exchange site a few years ago. I'd go bug her over there, asking to help out."

There are so many things left out of what George shares. Iph is getting used to that. She imagines what's missing. The dark apartment. The missing-in-action mom. Lonely George with long braids like the ones in the painting at Taurus Trucking.

"Why weren't you more freaked out in there?" George asks. "It's pretty intense."

They've started toward the stairwell. Iph stops again. "I don't know. My mom, maybe? She had a friend, her best friend Rob, that died of an overdose. I've heard a lot of stories. Mom was kind of wild back in the day."

"How wild are we talking?"

"Like, *lived at the Chelsea Hotel with a rock star* wild," Iph says. "Like, there are famous naked pictures of her in photography books that this woman took when she lived there."

"What rock star?" George is hooked. Everyone loves Mom's stories. Everyone loves Mom.

"She won't say. Says it's for Dad's benefit, so it doesn't wreck the guy's music for him. Dad says she's making it up to make him jealous. I'm not sure, but I think it might have been Jimi Hendrix."

They're quiet for a moment. Then George says, "Can we go back and try to help Pete? I think I could probably deal with her leg with what I've got in my bag."

Her, then. Good to know.

"I can't look, but I can keep Velma distracted. I'm squeamish."

"Definitely don't look. And I'm going to open a window before I start. There might be a smell."

"No problem. I'm very good at turning my nose off when necessary. I babysit."

"Of course you do." George takes her hand and squeezes, and together they walk back down the hall.

9

EMOTION
MEMORY

Velma and Pete's bathroom is small and stuffed with beauty products. A sticky layer of what is probably hairspray covers the sink and mirror and walls. There's a thing Velma said while George worked on Pete's wound that Iph can't get out of her head.

"They treated us like dirt last time Pete went to the clinic with an abscess. The nurse was so rough. When I asked her to be gentle, she made this sound—I swear to God, honey, it was like a wicked witch cackle with a little snort at the end—and said maybe next time, Pete would learn her lesson."

"Do they treat smokers with lung cancer like that?" Iph asked, squeezing Velma's hand.

"That's a good point, sweetie," Velma said, wiping her eyes.

What George did for Pete was amazing. Not just the skill of it, but the bedside manner. Shame and fear drained from the wound. Like a day in endless Portland January when the sun comes out and everyone feels awake for the first time in weeks. Now Pete is laughing in the other room at some story George is telling. Velma is singing jazz standards to Scout.

Iph puts the toilet lid down and pulls the phone cord taut.

She is procrastinating. It was George who suggested she use the phone to call Dad, and Velma who sent her to the bathroom for privacy. She dials.

"Iph!" How does he know it's her? It really must be Dad she gets that intuition from. "He called me!"

Everything seeps out of her till she is boneless. She grabs the side of the tub for support.

"Let me talk to him." Iph is shaking. From the next room, she hears Pete laughing again.

"He's not here," Dad says. "He decided to stay in Portland."

"What . . . do you mean?" Iph is dizzy—probably needs to eat. Dad is saying something. The world has changed so fast. Without the gravity of Mom, they've all spun off so quickly.

"He's having a good time with the punk chicks. Jane and Allison and . . ."

"Mika," Iph says. "I think the third one is Mika."

"You found him, too?"

"Almost," Iph says.

"He met a girl," Dad says. "Said she was pretty, so maybe he likes her. I told him he can come home whenever he wants. All he has to do is say the word. But once he's back, he's back for good. The same goes for you."

Iph is silent. Dad as the villain has shifted into some other thing that is still sneaky, but also a little brilliant.

"Do you want his phone number?"

"Yes," Iph says. "And the address. I can't believe this." She cradles the phone against her shoulder and turns on the cold tap. Lets it run over her hot, sticky hands.

"I don't have an address. He didn't know it. He called me from the girl's house. Some kid who's a friend of the band. They're called the Furies. Which is . . . well, kind of perfect. The house is in Southeast Portland off Belmont, and they call it Penelope. You should call him and go see for yourself. I bet he'll be happy to hear from you."

"He's really okay?"

"More than okay. He sounded great."

Dad sounds smug. Why didn't he make Orr give him the exact address? Iph slurps a little water from her cupped hand and dries it on her shorts. There is a stack of brown paper towels by the sink. Iph grabs one and an eyeliner pencil and writes down the number.

There's a silence. Dad is fiddling with something. He never could stay still.

"Iph," Dad says. "I'm sorry."

"For what?"

"You were right. I underestimated him."

"Yeah," Iph says. "You did. I'm assuming you haven't told Mom." Iph imagines her mother flying home from Santa Cruz, Wicked Witch of the West style. She's glad she won't be around for that fight.

"Not yet," Dad says. "I'm going to try and convince her to stay. Can I have her call you? She'll want to hear your voice herself."

"My friend doesn't have a phone," Iph says, basically daring Dad to freak out with the deadpan way she says it.

But he stays cool. If his blasé attitude is part of some overall strategy, Iph can't figure out what he's planning. "That's okay. Not everyone can afford one. I remember those days. Is there somewhere I can leave a message? In case I need to reach you?"

Iph thinks. "There's a store. Shiny Dancer. On East Burnside. You could probably call there. I'm assuming it's in the phone book." Iph wonders what, exactly, the Yellow Pages listing for Shiny Dancer will show. Will there be an ad with a little cartoon stripper?

"Thank you," Dad says. "Will they let you use the phone sometimes? Or can you get to a pay phone once a week? I told Orr he has to call in on Sundays. Would you do that, too?"

"Sure," Iph says, suddenly missing him. "I'll talk to you soon."

"I love you, Iph."

Iph opens her mouth to say it back, but the words won't come. She puts the phone in its cradle and folds the paper towel into a small, thick rectangle, feeling . . . what?

This part of the story is so unexpected, so surreal. Orr, living with a punk band in Southeast Portland. Iph . . . here, in this seedy hotel that feels normal in a way school never has. She's at home in this world of George's. Why does she feel this way?

She taps the phone with her index finger. The polish is still intact, a relic from another world. She knows she should call Orr. But she's not going to. She doesn't know why, or if it's right or wrong. Their trajectories have fractured. Their lives are suddenly separate. Iph rips the paper towel into little pieces and confettis the toilet bowl with them, a celebration of something. Then she opens the bathroom door to George and Velma and Scout and Pete.

"This is for you, doll." Velma is sitting at a book-piled desk with a slim volume open to the title page, fountain pen in hand. "Spelled like Agamemnon's daughter in *The Iliad*?"

"Just like that," Iph says. Not many people catch the reference. "Is this your book?"

"It's so good," George says.

"I didn't know you read poetry," Iph says. "You've been holding out on me."

"Writes it, too." Velma winks. "Damn fine poetry, if you ask me. The one time I got to read it."

"That was a fluke. I don't write much anymore."

"Hmm," Pete says, "that notebook you keep in your back pocket tells me otherwise, my friend."

Huh. Come to the think of it, Iph *has* seen a little notebook tucked under George's wallet and keys on the kitchen counter at Taurus Trucking. She's noted how George always puts it in the same place, right after coming in the door. Dad is like that. Orr, too. Good at regularity and habits. Iph and Mom are another story, always losing their keys and never able to find the mate for a sock or shoe or earring.

"Here you go, sweetheart." Velma hands Iph her book. It's a thin, elegant volume with a matte cream cover and a foiled circle—or no, it's a snake. A silver-green snake eating its tail. The title reads: *Ouroboros*.

"What does it mean?"

"It's the name of the snake symbol. It came from Egypt and spread to the alchemists in Alexandria and ancient Greece. It's an image of wholeness, of the way we transform and circle back into ourselves. It's also a fertility symbol, but self-contained. How we self-create, how we contain the parts we need to be whole."

Iph turns the book over. A familiar symbol—RCT, in rose vines. Like the little matchbook poetry book she found at Shiny Dancer.

"I've seen this before," Iph says. "RCT Editions."

"Rose City Transmutation. They do great work," Pete says. "All kinds of stuff. Poetry collections. Experimental theater and little one-off matchbooks with out-of-print poems. I met the pub-lisher at one of my shows. She was there looking for Velma. Had an old collection of hers. Wanted to see if she had anything new. That's how the book came to be."

Pete is an old-school looker, with thick cropped hair, huge dark eyes, a soft wide mouth, and a smoky voice with a mild Southern accent. The wound Iph saw from the corner of her eye—she tried to give Pete a little privacy, even in the small room—was a devasta-tion, a screaming plea from Pete's body for relief. There must be a reason for it, Pete and Velma's addiction. Some reason, some solu-tion. It's the kid part of her that's begging for this, she realizes. The same part that used to think if Mom told her about her past, Iph could find a way to fix it. Like with Mom, there probably isn't an answer here. Not a simple one, anyway. Most things are like this, she is beginning to understand. Most things and most people.

Iph smiles at Pete and Velma, at George and at Scout, snuggled into Velma's lap like she's never planning to leave. "Thanks for the book. And for inviting me in. It's been great to meet you both. Pete, maybe sometime I'll get to hear you play."

"I'd like that," Pete says. George's smile is sunlight in the dim room.

"Hold your horses, you two." Velma is rummaging in the room's small closet. She appears with a large slouchy rose velvet shoulder bag, something that would work as well for a play set in the 1620s or the 1920s.

"Be right back," she sings, heading for the bathroom.

When she returns with the bag, she presents it to Iph with a flourish. "I've tucked in a few goodies. You can look later."

She ushers them to the door like they're leaving a grand apartment, not a stuffy run-down SRO. She takes Iph's fingers in hers, an old-fashioned ladylike farewell handshake Iph finds brilliant. "Charmed," she says, then leans over to kiss George on the cheek. "Off you go now, sweet young things."

Iph wonders if she'll ever see Pete and Velma again.

"YOU'RE A GOOD EGG, Iphigenia Santos Velos," George says, grabbing Iph's hand and holding it tight until they reach the stairs.

In front of the Gentry, Iph feels like crying but won't. She hasn't told George about finding Orr. She's not ready for this to end. There's more for her here—she can feel it.

"It's too hot to bike," George says. "I'm gonna leave Ethelette locked up here. You sure you don't want to bus over to needle exchange with me? We can still go to Powell's after and check for Mika then."

Iph surprises herself by saying, "I think I'm gonna head to Powell's on my own. I need a nice bookstore visit. And air-conditioning."

"Fair enough. They have free water in the café," George says. "You were pretty great in there. Pete and Velma are crazy about you. You should have heard them when you were in the bathroom."

"I did nothing," Iph says. "That was all you."

"You did the most important thing," George says. "You didn't judge."

"I didn't—but I did wonder. Why are they doing that? Can they stop? Don't they want to?"

"They've tried. I hope they'll try again. Even with all the stuff they're dealing with, they really helped me when I was losing it,"

George says. "Pete's the only person I've ever met who's like me. I mean, none of the words feel quite right. Queer? Sure. But there's something else. Butch sort of gets at it, but then . . . I don't know. Pete's the same way. Says we're peas in a pod. Plus, dude, such a style icon."

"They both are."

Iph closes her eyes and sees a Japanese mother that looks like George alongside a stocky white man. Sees George with a freshly buzzed head and a red puffy face. Sees the stuffed backpack and rolled-up sleeping bag. Sees George at a bus stop, all alone. Iph knows she's probably making it up, imagining a story to fill in the blank spots George isn't ready to share. But another part of her knows these images are close to the truth. She takes off her glasses. They actually feel like hers now. She wipes them clear.

George leans in and kisses her forehead. Marking it, like Glinda the Good. "You know how to get to Powell's, right?"

"No." Iph laughs. "I would lie to save face, but it's too hot to get lost again."

"Let us walk you," George says. "I'll catch the bus from there."

10

THE STARS
WOULD GAPE

Orr sits on the sofa tuning Jane's acoustic guitar while the band fights in the kitchen.

"For fork's sake, Allison!" Jane is angry because Allison broke her hand and can't play bass until she gets the cast off. They've also decided to not to swear so much in front of young Orr. A joke, considering who raised him. "Why'd you have to hit him so hard?"

"I don't do dick in the wild," Allison says. "He, like, whipped it out of nowhere. I didn't think—I just clocked him."

"You should've kicked him in the balls," Mika says. Her high voice and small body make her look as young as Orr. In reality, Jane, Allison, and Mika are all twenty-four. The age Mom was when she had Iph.

Mom. It's weird thinking about her here in this living room with its wallpaper of band flyers and postcards and rough wood floors prickly with staples the girls didn't bother to remove when they pulled the carpet up after one too many cat accidents. Orr still hasn't seen the cat that made them.

"He's a lounger agent," Allison told him when he asked about the housemate responsible for the smell. Finally, he realizes who she sounds like—the girl from *Clueless*, one of Iph's favorite movies. It makes sense. Allison says she's a real-life Valley girl, born and raised in LA.

"He's for sure some sort of spy," Mika says. "Does nothing but lie around for weeks, then goes off on some secret mission out of nowhere. Clearly, it's when his handlers activate him. Comes home dirty and exhausted and sleeps for days."

"Either that, or he gets locked in people's garages. He's a little . . . decorative," Jane says. "Not the brightest kitty in the caboodle, if you know what I mean."

The girls deny you can still smell the cat pee, but they've let Orr scrub every floor in the run-down, hundred-year-old house, happy to buy him the Murphy's Oil Soap he asked for and watch as he dumped pail after pail of black water into the backyard to quench the summer-dry jasmine.

"The issue remains," Jane says, carrying two Slurpee cups full of iced tea into the living room—one for her and one for Orr—and settling beside him on the sofa, which Orr has covered with a paisley tapestry he found in the basement. "We finally have a chance at a decent gig, and now we can't even do it. I mean, you guys, Dead Moon! And it's a benefit for the hos!"

"I know that girl—from Shiny Dancer? Kind of a babe," Mika says.

"It sucks that the Meow-Meows broke up." Allison lights up a cigarette. Mika instantly jumps up and opens a window. "But dudes, their loss has got to be our gain. We can't afford to pass this up."

"You don't mind if someone else plays bass?" Mika says. "Be honest."

"I mean, ego-wise, a little. But band first. I mean, I can at least shake a tambourine while I do my vocals."

The girls start making lists of possible substitute bass players. Orr tunes out, noodling around on the guitar. He plays a chord progression—something vaguely familiar. He slides into something else—a version of a song he heard the band play over and over again the night before, when Allison still had the use of both her hands. He sets the guitar on its end like it's a cello or a tiny upright bass, thinking about Mom and Iph and Dad and what it felt like when they used to go camping and why, even if he tries, he still doesn't feel homesick. When he finally looks up the girls are frozen and staring straight at him.

Jane is the first one to thaw. "What the hell was that?"

"What?" Orr looks behind him toward the white-flowered tree in the yard framed by the large front window, sparkling after Orr cleaned it that morning with newspaper and white vinegar.

"Play that again," Jane says.

Orr does.

"You know our songs?" Allison's mouth makes a perfect cartoon O.

Of course he knows them. The Furies have been rehearsing every night since he arrived—he's heard their set at least twenty times.

"Come." Jane's pulling him down to the basement. The girls follow. Jane turns on some equipment, and Mika gets behind the drums.

"Here." Allison puts the strap of her bass guitar over Orr's head. "Do you know how to use this?" Orr shakes his head no. The basement isn't his favorite place, with its lack of windows and mildew smell. Allison flips a switch on the bass's side and shows Orr the volume and effects knobs.

When everyone's ready, Jane gets on the mic. Then she stops, smacks her forehead with her hand, and tears up the stairs, returning with Orr's orange earplugs. He squishes them into his ears. Jane grins at him, and Orr grins back. She gets him.

Back at the microphone, Jane cocks her hip the way singers do on MTV, and Mika counts off the beat.

"One, two—one two three four!"

11

SWALLOW
THE WELL

O rr is in his closet warding off the start of a headache. Last
night, he managed to decouple the little window from
the layers of old paint that stuck it to the sash. Now, the
closet is perfect, blissfully cool and comfy since Allison brought
him a thick piece of foam from her boyfriend's recording studio. It
was being used for sound absorption but makes an excellent bed.

In the other room, voices rise and fall, a gentle chirping like the
tree frogs outside his bedroom window at home.

His neck is sore from banging his head in a way that always
looked so affected when he saw guitarists do it on MTV but turned
out to be a natural movement in the context of actual rock and
roll. Maybe that's what's causing the headache. He's so tired, but
his body is tense the way it gets when he needs a run. There are
simply too many things to process from playing with the Furies.
And then there's Plum.

At the thought of her, heat surges through his body, but there's
no erection. He hasn't had one since he left home and wonders if
it has something to do with his hair being cut.

At the beginning of the summer, constant arousal plagued
him. The desire was never directed at or stimulated by another

person. When he lay in bed and touched himself, he thought of running through beautiful terrain, places he'd seen in the pages of *National Geographic* or even the woods that bordered their town. Sometimes, the feeling built up as he ran. He'd sprint home and climb into the treehouse, feeling a little resentful afterward about the strength of his body's call. The pleasure was almost a pain, too intense.

When he was younger, he imagined that desire would bring him close to another person, help him find some reason to get to know someone besides Iph and Mom, but the confusing power of it had isolated him further. When he turned twelve, Dad tried to talk with him about girls. Finally, he even tried talking about boys. Orr was silent for both, and Dad seemed happy enough to give up.

But the other day, when he called home from Plum's house, there was something in Dad's voice. Almost . . . satisfaction. Maybe even approval. Are these the kinds of adventures he always wanted for his son? Midnight escapes, van rides with punk bands, a redheaded girl who looks like a painting? Orr thinks yes, they probably are. Even so, Dad didn't even try to imagine a life like this for Orr. All he could think of was a place like Meadowbrook.

Late afternoon sounds drift past Penelope. Kids rolling down the sidewalk on skateboards and scooters. Cars driving by, windows down and radios on. Orr knows he is crying because the shaking hurts his head. He is weeping like a puppet might, limbs floppy, torso jerking up and down with the rhythm of this unidentifiable emotion. Panic rises, but he sends it a song—something in Spanish Mom used to sing.

Whatever this feeling is, it's linked somehow with memory. He shudders to recall his childhood foolishness. So many misunderstandings. Outbursts he couldn't control, rules he could never intuit. The tsunami of stimulation from the other children—their smells and colors and accessories and, worst of all, their energies. It was like living in a vat of primary-colored poster paint. All the edges were hard and the textures unpleasant. But these are old memories, situations already cried over and gone. What's left is this strange . . . sorrow.

Orr weeps for the boy who wanted his mother to stay so badly he overturned her suitcase and ripped her favorite shirt. For the boy who was stolen in sleep, innocent in a way he will never be again. He weeps for Dad, maybe most of all. At heart, Dad is admirable. Like a TV dad, he is wise in so many ways. But what he's done, this level of his betrayal—handing his son over to bigots. Having him kidnapped from his own bed. Orr can't ever forget. Dad found and lost his son in the wrong order. Can it ever be right between them again?

Orr's headache is getting worse. He rubs his temples. Sleep is the thing that will stop it from turning into a migraine. He hums Mom's lullaby to himself.

Ai, ai, ai, ai! Canta y no llores. Sing, don't cry.

12

WHEN ACTING
IS AN ART

ph drops a dime into the violin case of the busker outside Powell's, sorry it isn't more. The temperature inside the bookstore
is deliciously just right, not over-air-conditioned like the mall,
where Iph always ends up with a summer cold. Just cool enough
for the relief-pleasure loop to activate.

And then there are the books. A whole city block of them.
Room after room. Floors and floors. Iph and Orr used to fantasize about being locked in Powell's overnight, their version of
the brother and sister in *From the Mixed-Up Files of Mrs. Basil E.
Frankweiler*. They'd strategize about how they would hide, but
more importantly, how they would spend the precious hours
between the store's 11 P.M. closing time and when it opened
again at 9 A.M.

As always, Iph starts in the Blue Room at the drama shelf.
Today, she finds a sweet old edition of *An Actor Prepares*. Stanislavski was the Russian creator of "the Method" and mentor
to Lee Strasberg, who passed along this physical/psychological
approach to Broadway and Hollywood actors. Iph had learned
about Stanislavski because of her favorite version of Marilyn
Monroe, all dressed-down and bespectacled in her New York

acting student days. When Iph had asked about method acting in her high school drama class, she was told it was old-fashioned and too complex for high schoolers.

So she studied it herself, learning the techniques in secret and trying them out in class. Some were good, basic tune-ups for an essentially physical art. Some of the exercises felt clunky, more academic than useful—like the sense memory technique where you recalled physical details of something in the past to evoke the emotion called for in a scene.

Iph's approach is more visceral, like a dancer's. In dance, the movement and music should be enough to evoke the feeling. Iph feels like the text and relationships should do the same in a play, at least when you're onstage. But before that, during preparation, Stanislavski is very useful. She grabs *An Actor Prepares*, which at this point is a comfort read, and heads to the café for a nice sit and several gallons of free water.

There are ghost prints of Iph's childhood everywhere in this place. On the maps they offer at the big info desk, she can trace her own development from the toddler-size tables in the picture book section of the Rose Room to the middle-reader stacks she haunted and adored until she got the theater bug and became a professional lurker in her special section of the Blue Room.

Ever devoted to his *Redwall* books, Orr had stayed in the Rose Room until last year, when he started making forays into the Gold Room for fantasy and sci-fi. Iph closes her eyes against tears for the millionth time today. She must be premenstrual. What had she been thinking, ripping up Orr's number and flushing it away? If she had it right now, she'd be outside at the pay phone with her second-to-last quarter.

Clearly, Powell's has undone her. She misses Orr. And Mom. Even Dad. But how can she go back? Even with the sweetness of their shared language and familiar bodies and beloved faces, she can't imagine the old life being anything but suffocating after her days in the real world with George.

Her heart beats hard. A sign of dehydration. The tables in the café are all occupied. Tourists with stacks of books and shopping bags. Moms with little kids. Street people drinking the free water like she is—except she can't forget, for her this is a choice. She gulps a final cup of the cold water and heads for the bathroom. It's when she's alone in the stall that she remembers Velma's velvet bag slung over her shoulder.

She reaches inside. Silk chiffon. Her fingers know without looking. She pulls the fabric gently from the bag. A scarf? No, a dress. An antique treasure that surely Velma should have kept. Its provenance is likely late twenties or early thirties, with a painterly scattering of wildflowers on a ballet-pink background. It has short, barely-there sleeves, a low ruffled surplice neckline, and a flowing bias-cut skirt. Iph's chest burns with disappointment. With want. This is exactly the sort of dress she wears in her leading-lady daydreams, but, as always, there is no way it will fit in real life. The best vintage clothes, like so many other things Iph covets, are made for the slight and slender. So sweet of Velma, though. She folds the dress carefully and slips it back in the bag, pees, and heads out of the café for a favorite bench of hers next to the section for small-press poetry and zines. Maybe when Mom comes home, she will give the dress to her.

Before she sits to read, Iph looks for books by Velma Smith and finds nothing. She checks big-press poetry, too, but no luck. She settles on the bench and wishes hard for five bucks. Iced tea and a chocolate croissant sound like heaven. After that, a nap. Iph looks around. The section is empty. She lies back on the bench and closes her eyes.

Pssst.

She sits up too fast. Dizzy. Now that she's cooled off, she feels how hungry she is. She lowers her head between her legs like she does when she's worried she might faint.

Psst.

She looks up. Is someone talking to her? Is she imagining things?

Psst.

The sound seems to be coming from a cylindrical rack of books. There is a sign on the rounder: PORTLAND PRESSES.

A deep-green hardbound book seems to be emitting some sort of glow. It's often like this at a bookstore, where a title seems to call to you from its place on the shelf.

Keep telling yourself that, says a little voice in Iph's head. (It *is* in her head, right?)

She gets up and walks to the rounder. Picks up the shiny green book. The source of light is the book itself—a figure on the cover embossed in gold, a riot grrrl mohawked Artemis with a bow and arrow and a dog at her heels. Basically, the patron saint of George. There is no title.

The first page reads, *Stratagems, Poetry, Plans*.

It's a journal. Each page has faint bronze lines on one side, with a blank page opposite. The perfect thing for a Renaissance artist like George. Poetry on one side, sketches on the other. Iph thinks of the beat-up spiral-bound notebook and the way George's energy flickered when Velma mentioned writing. George deserves a book like this. Maybe even needs it.

Iph fingers the smooth spine. Sniffs the pages—fresh paper and fir trees.

She turns it over. Stamped in the same gold as the front cover are the initials *RCT* with its vine climbing the *R* and *C*. This time, there are little wings sprouting from the top of the *T* in *Rose City Transmutation*.

The price tag reads $9.99. It might as well be a hundred. Iph puts the book back. Rejoins Stanislavski on the bench. The section remains empty, so she risks lying back again and closes her eyes.

What would the book's patient teacher, Tortsov, a stand-in for Stanislavski himself, advise in this situation? If it were an acting exercise, what would Iph do?

She wants to give this journal to George. But how to obtain it? In the theater and out in the world, a character's trajectory is never perfectly smooth. In every play, even every scene, there must be an obstacle. Here, the obstacle is money. How can Iph get some? She relaxes, lets her body melt into the part of Girl Who Wants to Buy a Present for Her Sweetheart.

She lets her mind wander. A song peeks out like a rabbit in the underbrush. A jig played on a fiddle.

Iph sits up. She hides the journal behind another book to prevent anyone else from buying it. All the water she's had in the café has gone right through her, so she stops at the bathroom on the way to the exit. Drying her hands after washing them and splashing water on her face, Iph feels around in the bag, almost like she's worried the dress will be gone. She pulls it out again.

In the larger space of the empty ladies' room, she notices that there is no zipper. It's a wrap dress, an adjustable style that often works for curves. She also remembers how oddly stretchy silk can be when it's cut on the bias. How many times has she succumbed to a beautiful vintage dress's siren song only to crash into the rocks in the dressing room when she realizes she can't get the thing past her neck?

Girding herself, she sets the velvet bag on the metal ledge above the sink, checks under the stalls for feet, then whips off her shirt and slips on the dress. It goes around her, at least. Under the cover of the skirt, she turns her back to the mirror and takes off Nana's baggy shorts and stuffs them into the bag. The skirt has a sewn-in slip of smooth silk that's cool against her legs. Her bra is totally visible in the front, but untying, adjusting, and retying the dress at her waist actually fixes that. She turns slowly, not ready to believe. But, oh! The mirror reveals the truth. Velma is a sorceress.

The dress is perfect. Iph is both voluptuous and somehow light. A girl of summer, sylphlike and young. An ingenue. A leading lady.

Rearranging her shorts and bulky T-shirt so they fit in the velvet shoulder bag, Iph finds a little packet at the bottom. An envelope of rice-paper blotters, a sweet old-fashioned beauty trick. Iph uses one on her face. There is a small sample lipstick, the kind in a fingernail-size pink tube from Avon. Mindy's mom used to sell these and let Mindy and Iph have all the unused samples. Iph puts on the berry-pink shade and pulls her hair up off her neck. This whole situation seems to call for an updo. Of course, there's an ivory hair comb in the bag. And finally, a pair of delicate gold chandelier earrings. Looking at the entire ensemble, Iph smiles. She's always been the kind of actor who comes to life in costume. Her plan is totally going to work.

THE FIDDLE PLAYER HAS moved around the corner from the entrance, following the shade. What now? She remembers her training and takes a beat, leaning against the building a respectable distance away. He finishes the song and takes a break to drink some water.

Iph's intention is to persuade—but maybe she needs a better verb. What she wants is to join forces with this guy.

"Hey," she says. "Thanks for the music."

"Anytime!" He grins. He's actually kind of gorgeous, with dark shoulder-length hair and elegant wrists covered in jade bracelets. "It's been so slow. It's the heat, you know? I keep thinking if I figure out the right song, it'll shake loose. It's like that sometimes—you get a few tips and then the rest rolls in." He plays a few notes of a mournful flamenco.

"I have an idea," Iph says. "And it's totally fine if the answer is no. But I think people may need something unexpected in this ridiculous heat. And to be honest, I could use a little cash."

"Do you sing?" The guy looks excited.

"A little," Iph says. She can carry a tune, but that's not what she has in mind. "I'm more of an actor. And I was thinking a little Shakespeare accompanied by music could be just the thing."

He looks at her, and maybe he thinks she's flirting. Guys usually don't interest her, but this one's exceptionally pretty. Besides, her objective must be achieved! They will join forces.

"I'm Iph," she says.

"Simon." He puts his hand out. Iph takes it, knowing she's won. "What should I play?"

"Anything you want. I'm going to start with Emilia from *Othello*. She has an excellent feminist rant in Act Four in defense of cheating wives. That should stir things up!"

"Sounds good. Just wait one sec, though. The lights are about to turn red, and then all those people will be a captive audience while they wait."

"Pro advice. You got it."

The violin begins a few moments before the light changes, priming people to listen and look. Iph takes a step away from the building into the sun.

For a moment, she is lost. She knows the words to the monologue but has forgotten whatever preparation she did before performing it last year in class. Besides, this isn't a stage, and these strangers haven't signed up to watch a show. She steps back, then realizes. She will join forces with *them*.

Diaphragm engaged, Iph begins.

> But I do think it is their husbands' faults
> If wives do fall.

People are stopping, smiling. They definitely want to hear what these errant husbands have done.

> Say that they slack their duties,
> And pour our treasures into foreign laps,
> Or else break out in peevish jealousies,
> Throwing restraint upon us; or say they strike us,
> Or scant our former having in despite;
> Why, we have galls, and though we have some grace,
> Yet have we some revenge.

A crowd has gathered. The fiddle is underscoring her delivery perfectly, egging her on and adding an edge of humor that is perfect for Iph's objective.

> *Let husbands know*
> *Their wives have sense like them: they see and smell*
> *And have their palates both for sweet and sour,*
> *As husbands have. What is it that they do*
> *When they change us for others? Is it sport?*
> *I think it is: and doth affection breed it?*
> *I think it doth: is't frailty that thus errs?*
> *It is so too: and have not we affections,*
> *Desires for sport, and frailty, as men have?*
> *Then let them use us well: else let them know,*
> *The ills we do, their ills instruct us so.*

Iph concludes to a huge round of applause and a bark. George and Scout! How did they get back from needle exchange so quickly? Several people have dropped money in the open violin case, but the crowd hasn't dispersed. To Simon, she whispers, "Play something romantic."

Looking straight at George and then away, she begins the balcony scene from *Romeo and Juliet*. After swearing that a rose by any other name would be as sweet, she has a quick wonder about her objective here. But then she knows. It is beguilement. She slows for the final lines of the monologue.

> *Romeo, doff thy name*
> *And for that name which is no part of thee*
> *Take all myself.*

From the audience, George answers, striding forward.

> *I take thee at thy word:*
> *Call me but love, and I'll be new baptized;*
> *Henceforth I never will be Romeo.*

The crowd goes crazy as George moves to the open sidewalk and falls to a knee, kissing Iph's hand. She pulls George to stand, and they finish the scene, hands clasped, Scout gazing up at them like a trained dog actor.

Money floods the violin case, and people head around the corner to Powell's thanking and complimenting the trio as they go.

"Here," Simon says, handing Iph a wad of cash. "That was badass. Can I call you sometime? Both of you," he rushes to add, looking sideways at George, who is giving him the evil eye. "I'd love to try that at Saturday Market."

"Can I grab your number instead?" Iph says. "I'm not quite settled right now." Saying that is weird, like Iph is channeling a future self that might have the sort of bohemian situation her answer suggests.

He hands her a slip of paper with his number and packs up his case. "Time for a beer," he says. "Thanks, Iph. And you, too."

"It's George."

"Yeah, man. Thanks."

George turns to Iph with a face like fairy lights.

"Wait here!" Iph says.

"Iph!" George calls. *"Parting is such sweet sorrow."*

"That's my line," Iph says.

13

COMMUNION

Iph and George leave Powell's at dusk with the crows. They cross the river with a tailwind and hit all the green lights on Hawthorne. Flying past Mount Tabor, they blow a kiss to Pele, goddess of volcanos, because that's what Mount Tabor is—a little volcano in the center of Portland. Orr did a report on it in the third grade.

George stops at an apartment building called the Lindy Sue. It's baby-shit brown and a little run-down with those Brillo-pad evergreen shrubs with the chalky blue poisonous berries people planted by the thousands in the seventies. Dad considers them a scourge. Scout hops down and swaggers up the stairs to the second-floor apartments.

"Scout really can pull off Big Pit when she wants to," George says. "Like, any ne'er-do-well would think twice, even though she's the size of a piece of sushi."

"Don't even say the word *sushi*!" After she bought the journal, they took what was left of their share of the busking money to gorge at the Sushi Train. "And also—who says ne'er-do-well? Tell me that."

George laughs and pulls Iph up the cement staircase with a rusted wrought-iron railing. The night ahead thickens between them. A whole long, beautiful night. It's cooling off, and Iph wonders if they can spare fifty cents for a bag of ice for the rest of Cait's gin.

George's cousin Julie opens the door. You can tell she was once as pretty as George described her, but now her beauty is faded—no, more than that. It's drained.

"Hey." Julie's voice wobbles like a tape deck in a bumpy car. She does not look pleased to see Iph.

"Just dropping something off for you," George says. Clean needles, alcohol wipes, little metal containers Iph thought were some sort of portable votive candleholders when she looked in the brown paper bag at the sushi place. Really, they are used for cooking heroin. And maybe other drugs? Iph isn't sure of the procedure. The thought of it makes her a little faint.

"This is Iph—the girl I told you about. I'm actually wondering if you'd loan her your bike." Julie believes George is staying with a girl and her roommates in Northeast Portland. Iph is to play the girl.

Julie smiles and steps aside to let them in. That smile changes everything. She's clearly related to George, with thick-lashed dark eyes and long silky hair. Iph recognizes her now from a photo collage in the upstairs hall at Taurus Trucking.

Inside, the apartment smells like garbage. George gathers the trash, takes it out to the dumpster. Scout is kissing Julie's face on the sofa, trying to make her laugh. "Come sit down," Julie says, patting the seat next to her.

"Thanks," Iph says. The living room isn't so bad. Cluttered, but there was clearly a recent attempt at tidying. There are pictures on the wall. A black-and-white photo of a wolf. An Ansel Adams print and a framed drawing of a mermaid that looks a lot like Julie.

"Did George do that?"

"The family genius." Julie smiles, clearly proud of her cousin. Her nails are painted a deep blue, perfectly done and pretty against her pale skin. "It's cool of you to let George stay with you," she says, right as George comes back with the empty trash can.

"Yep," George says. "I'm lucky she isn't sick of me yet."

"George isn't so bad," Iph tells Julie. "Makes a mean can of SpaghettiOs. And this one"—she reaches over to pet Scout—"is a sweet little angel muffin." Scout enjoys baby talk, even though it drives George nuts.

"Yes, she is!" Julie joins in. Her laugh is light and young, even though her smile is a little sad. George says she has a terrible boyfriend.

"How are you?" George perches on the arm of a ripped gray chair, leg jiggling—not comfortable here, Iph realizes, but pretending it's all okay.

"I'm good," Julie says.

"Liar."

"I'm getting there. Like Nana used to say, it's not over till it's over. But when it's over, run." They say this last line together and laugh.

"Seriously, Jules. I worry about you."

"Soon," Julie says. "I'll be done soon." Are they talking about the drugs or the guy? Maybe both.

They're silent for a minute. Iph has kind of missed TV. Julie's watching a nature show for kids, Scout splayed out like a tiny beached hippo in her lap.

"I'm sorry," Julie finally says, meeting George's eyes. For what? Maybe picking the drugs and the guy over George.

"Here," George says, handing Julie a brown bag. "I put in a flyer with some resources, too. Don't be mad."

"George, you know I can't have that around here."

"I'll put it in the pile with the bills," George says. "I know he never looks there."

"Oh, he's interested in my mail these days," Julie says. "Ever since Dale sent me a birthday card. He thinks we're running away together." To Iph she says, "Dale was my first boyfriend."

"Dale was nice. Maybe you should write back," George says.

"Maybe." Julie stands and pulls George in for a hug. Iph sees the love. Thinks of her own family. Their first story together is over. What will the next one be?

14

THE SECOND
REVOLUTION

The wind molds Velma's dress to Iph's legs. Julie's purple ten-speed is a perfect fit. She imagines Velma in the dress, pear-shaped and pink-cheeked, riding a bike in some European city, a loaf of bread in the handlebar basket and Pete on a bike ahead.

It's been years since Iph has ridden. What happened to the happy days of flying around the lake on her princess-pink Schwinn, pumping hard to keep up with Dad? When does the past become the past? It can happen slowly, the way her childhood has faded, the way the daylight is fading now. Or it can happen so fast, the way it has for her family.

She pedals harder, lungs so generous in this life. Maybe her asthma lives back in Forest Lake with the unkissed version of herself. Maybe, like in a fairy tale, George's kiss has cured her.

George signals left, and Iph follows, coasting down the hill to Plaid Pantry. The guy there knows George and gives them ice and two candy bars for free.

They pedal lazily now. Apartments give way to houses, snug little sun-faded family homes with sensible cars parked outside and children's toys in the yards. They turn onto Southeast

Division and swoosh up to Taurus Trucking. There is a light on in the basement of the neighbor's house. George shrugs, and they risk it, golden and untouchable.

Nana's apartment is reasonably cool. George gives the bag of ice to Iph. From the kitchen, Iph hears music. Ella Fitzgerald on very low, a splurge of expensive battery use. A song about beaming smiles that could so easily be about George. Iph runs cold water over her wrists and splashes her face and heads to Nana's room.

She carefully takes off Velma's dress and hangs it on a padded satin hanger. There is some rose water in a mister on the dresser. The droplets are deliciously cool on her skin. Riffling through the drawers, she spots a slip she's overlooked. It's tight—probably something from Nana's younger days. The white cotton is moony in the dark room. Iph's curls spill onto her temples and around her forehead. She tamps down the impulse to turn sideways and chide her stomach for not being flat. She won't allow a single despairing look at her ass. She smooths the slip with her hands, the thin fabric soft against her softness.

In the living room, George has bathed early—wet hair, scrubbed face. Their drinks are on the coffee table, and Iph can feel the ghost of Nana and her third and favorite husband on a hot summer night dancing cheek to cheek in the space between the window and dinette.

They sit and rest and drink their drinks. Ella sings on. George stands and offers a hand. Iph accepts. She is shaking; this is different than before. She has seen George's secrets. They slow dance like they're in a movie. Of course, George can actually lead. Iph goes loose, follows the press of the hand on her back, the knees against her knees. They're belly to belly now. Iph instinctively shrinks, always trying to hide this part of her, but George tells her it's okay with a gentle press on her back. They dance until the tape clicks off.

Iph steps away, reaches for her drink. Takes a sip for courage. George does the same. They move together again, no music but breath.

Scout whines. Runs around the room. They pull apart. Laugh. Come back together in their silent dance. George is kissing her neck, pulling down the strap of her slip. There is a sound, and George jumps back as the door that leads from the garage below opens. Iph expects a meth-loaded relative, but it's so much worse than that.

"Sorry," Lorna says. "I still have my key—"

She stops. Sees Iph. And George. Together.

"Well," she says, setting down a duffel bag that surely contains her work outfits, "let the crying begin."

15

SCATTER
HIS BONES

Someone is sobbing. Orr stands up in his closet before he's even awake. He ducks when his scalp connects with one of the brass hooks near the door. Too late. It throbs. He's walking before he sees the blood from his head on his hand. The sounds are getting worse, deep and ugly. Is this how it feels for people to hear him melt down?

There's a light in the kitchen. It bounces off the freshly waxed avocado linoleum and turns the whole room green. Even Jane looks green kneeling there on the floor.

Orr knows he should hide before he knows why. He crouches in the dark hall to see Jane better. She doesn't see him. She's looking at Red.

Jane reaches for Red's belt buckle. He smacks her hand away. "Get off, bitch." His voice is incinerating. Orr looks for the imprint of Jane's charred skeleton in the air. *Dragon man. Evil Wyrm.*

Orr stands and walks in. "Get out of here," he says.

"What the hell?"

"Leave!" Orr yells.

Red says something but all Orr hears is Jane. She's back to life, furious. *Furious.* With . . . with him?

"Orr," she says, standing. "Get out. Now."

Red smirks. His face is pale as a pancaked clown's, his red-dyed mohawk an ugly joke.

"Get out, Orr," Red mimics in a high, silly voice.

Orr hates that. Hates mimicking so much. When he and Iph were kids, it was the one thing she could do that made him lose his cool. That and her icy feet.

"Get out now!" Red says again. His stupid cartoon voice is nothing like Jane's.

Orr steps between Red and Jane. "You called her a name. You made her cry. *You* need to go."

Red moves closer. So close, Orr can smell him. He smells like sex, Orr thinks. How does he know this? There's a movie Mom loves, *The Unbearable Lightness of Being*. The wife smells another woman on her cheating husband's face, in his hair. That's what this fight is about.

"You lied to her," Orr says. "You're a cheater."

Red pushes. Orr stands his ground.

Red lunges. Orr's fist shoots out. Red is on him. A fist to his face. Spit in his eyes. Orr's hands balled up, hitting back. Not stopping.

Hands clawing, pulling at his back. Orr shrugs the weight off his shoulders, a heavy cape of fur. His forehead throbs in twin points of pain. He bucks, turns, pushes. Jane! It's Jane. She flies across the kitchen, lands at Mika's feet.

"Get out." Jane is crying. She's not talking to Red, who is doubled over by the refrigerator. She's talking to Orr. She's rubbing her head, cradling her arm.

She is hurt.

Orr has hurt her.

"*Leave*, Orr. And don't come back."

16

MY GRAVEYARD
ANTLERS

Orr is Jane on the ground, the buckle on Red's belt, Red's spit running down his own face. He is the word *bitch*. He is his fist against the bone of Red's skull. He is his own skull beating like a heart, and his bone-hard bare feet hitting the sidewalk stride after stride, running away from Penelope.

He flees to the cemetery to hide among the graves.

The moon reserves judgment.

The grass is cool.

His sister is somewhere in the city.

His sister.

His mother.

He lowers to all fours and retches.

He curls in a ball and rocks. Shame has fallen on his house, and now he is houseless.

Dad.

Fucking Dad.

Red.

Orr presses his head to the flat stone marker, its marble as cold as the moon.

He rubs his cheek back and forth on the gravestone as his

breath slows. He bangs his head there, too, but gently. He sits. He aches but can't cry. This pain is not for him, but for Jane. For the wrongness of her groveling before such an inferior person.

Jane on her knees.

The image is attached like a leech, somewhere loathsomely deep inside his body.

He sits up and braces his back against the headstone.

He reaches for something real. Digs his fingers into the grass. Planting himself.

The trees of Lone Fir Cemetery hum.

They hold him in a lattice of root and dirt.

They acknowledge him, a fellow soul, breathing in the summer night.

Animal, boy.

Animal boy.

Animal desire.

Arousal like hunger.

Like the thirst Orr has for the wrong things: pond water and hot tubs, the droplets on the pink tiles of the bathroom at Penelope after one of the Furies has taken a shower.

Like being vegetarian, you can choose the right thing and reject what's wrong. After a while, even the thought of meat will choke you. If he can suppress this want long enough, maybe it will go away.

But Orr is thirsty. And so, so hungry.

Just today, he's eaten half a loaf of bread and the remaining peanut butter at Penelope and slurped a quart of chocolate milk. Even if Jane forgives him, it's wrong to ask for more. He sees that now, what they've all given up to take care of him.

The trees whisper their approval. They know that sometimes a sacrifice is needed.

He reads the gravestone where he's lying: ANNE JEANNE TINGRY-LE COZ. She died in 1885.

"I'm sorry," he tells her and lies with the damp grass under his back, hands folded like hers might have been in her coffin. Unlike

Anne Jeanne, Orr can look up and see the sky. He tries to see it for both of them.

His eyelids grow heavy. He will sleep here with the moon and the dead.

He will send his soul to comfort them instead of dreaming.

He will wake in the morning and call his father.

He will go home.

17

THE OPERA STUDIO

"Truth or dare?" Lorna calls from the kitchen.

"I'm not playing," George says.

Lorna comes back into the living room with two gin and tonics. She sets them on the table and goes back for the third. How she's seized power by serving them is something Iph is going to have to study later. Right now, she's still stuck in the perfection of half an hour ago, no Lorna, slow dancing with George. At least the genius of Stanislavski's sense memory technique is finally obvious. It's all about having good enough physical memories. The feel of George's hand on her back, the shiver of hip against hip—that could fuel an extended run on Broadway with even a lukewarm leading man.

Lorna settles on the floor on the other side of the coffee table with Scout in her lap. She is such a slut. Not Lorna! Iph is a feminist, even in jealousy. It's Scout who spreads herself around like peanut butter on crackers. Not that there's anything wrong with that. Certainly some people would say Iph is a slut. She's known George for—how many days now? If Lorna hadn't come in, who knows what they'd be doing?

"How about you, Iph? Truth or dare?" Lorna's face is freshly scrubbed, and she's wearing a white baby tee, pink shorts, the gold shoes, and a ponytail. She looks like a fourteen-year-old runway model.

"Truth." It's what Iph always says—the only way to survive this game, which should rightly be called Sex & Misdemeanors.

"Hmmm." Lorna is pretending to think. It's true: when you're that pretty, you don't have to be able to act.

Me-ow, Iph thinks. *So much for my inner feminist.*

"Lorna, no," George says. "Come on. Don't be like this."

"I'm playing. Trying to, you know, make the moment less awkward. But I can go now." She stands. Iph would bet her last ten bucks from busking that Lorna is bluffing. "Sorry for the interruption." Lorna says *interruption* like it's the title of a porno.

"I didn't say you had to go," George says. "I'm just not in the mood for games."

Go, Iph thinks. *Go, go, go!*

Lorna's face slides from femme fatale straight into girl next door. Maybe she can act after all. "You're right. I'm sorry. I barged in. I came to talk, but if it's a bad time . . ."

Is she being honest or manipulative? And when is she going to leave? Not that they'll ever get the mood back. One look at George is all Iph needs to see that.

"We can talk . . . we'll go have one cigarette, okay?"

Iph's body fills with poisonous gas. She will expel it and kill them all. Except, of course, because of the patriarchy and her own passive personality, she won't kill anyone. She will swallow it. Swallow the poison, her own tongue, until her stomach balloons. Her eye whites will turn saffron, and her skin will follow. And no, she doesn't think this is overdramatic.

Iph stands. "Don't leave on my account," she says. "I'm going to bed."

"Iph!" George stands, too, as if suddenly remembering she's there.

Iph wills her face to be still. Wills her body to the bedroom. Except she isn't going. Her face is contorting. Her eyes sting.

NO!

No no no no no no no.

She's crying.

In front of George. In front of *Lorna*.

"Oh my god!" Lorna says. Yet again, her face is different. This one seems closer to the real girl. "I'm such a dick. Wouldn't you know? It was me, not George! I'm the one who made you cry."

"Not just you," George says, grabbing Iph's hand and pulling her back to the sofa. Everyone breathes and drinks and listens to the bus clacking along outside.

"Things have been so weird since that night I met you at the movies," Lorna finally says. "It almost feels like it's the shoes. I keep wanting to go to the train station to visit my mom in Tacoma, except we're not speaking. I left work early tonight and started walking to the opposite side of Burnside. I didn't even know where I was going. I figured it out when I got off the bus and starting walking toward Division. And here"—she hands George a key—"I should have left it when I bailed."

George takes it. More silence. Iph sniffs. There's Kleenex in a mother-of-pearl tissue holder that is one of Iph's favorite things in Nana's house. It's such a sweetness, to make this thing used for colds and crying a pretty part of the decor. She takes a tissue and blows her nose, not worrying herself about dainty Lorna.

"I kept thinking about you," Lorna is saying. Wait—she's talking to Iph. "How nice you were. How decent. I could tell how much you liked Georgie. You could have done ten different things besides try to get me to go down and patch it up. But you didn't."

"If you and George want to be together, that's what you should do," Iph says. "I'm going home soon anyway."

"You are?" George's eyes are wide.

"Orr called my dad. He's fine."

"So wait, you're leaving, then?"

"I can leave now. Or I can stay. My dad doesn't care what I do." That's not quite true, but Iph can't stop her own pity party. There's one way to be sure of the outcome here, and that's to beat them to the punch. She folds her arms and refuses to look at either of them.

"All right, that's it." Lorna is surprisingly versatile. In this mode, she could easily be cast as the older sister or a young mom. "George, come on. You're totally over me and into Iph, right? Be honest! I can take it."

George's open mouth is classic. It's weird how responses considered cliché onstage feel natural in real life. "You want to talk about this now?"

"Yes," Lorna says. "I think it's only fair."

"Fair to who?" Iph is surprised to hear herself asking.

"To you," Lorna says to Iph, wrinkling her adorable nose like that's the obvious answer. "I mean, I came in drama-ready. You were an innocent bystander."

"I guess some things never change." It could have been an insult, but George says it like it's the opposite. These two have some serious history.

Lorna smiles for real, and of course she has dimples. "So, out with it, George. Just how over me are you?"

George laughs outright. Iph finds herself . . . smiling. The whole thing is oddly not embarrassing. Just interesting. Her kingdom for a notepad. Or a video camera.

"Last week, it was hovering at fifty percent. But the last few days . . . I have to admit, it's closer to ninety. Maybe eighty-five. I might always love you a little, okay? But I see how I put a lot on you. We didn't even know each other that well. We never really talked that much."

"Oh my god, you guys. I don't need to hear about your sex life." Iph can't believe she's joking now, but every time she tries to buy into the drama of this love triangle, something else happens instead.

Lorna is laughing. George is laughing, red. Iph is laughing so hard she sneezes. Lorna hands her another tissue.

They all reach for their gins and sip on cue.

"So, Lorna," Iph says. "Truth or dare?"

18

IF I WERE
TO GO BACK

Orr can't fall asleep in the graveyard. The dead are buried too deep to be any company, and the moon has traveled somewhere behind the trees. He's waited as long as he can for something to happen, an *X-Files*–worthy brush with aliens or the occult, but there is only a pair of fat raccoons.

Orr has been thinking about the baby squirrel Mom found last year. They first saw it sitting preternaturally still on the driveway down to their house. Mom stopped the car and jumped out, knelt, held out her hand. "I don't know how," Mom had said, "but I knew she'd trust me."

They called the Audubon Society, but the person on the phone decided that because it was born so late in the season, it must be a red squirrel, not native, and therefore ineligible for rescue.

Undaunted, Mom called the library information line, where the librarians would look things up for you on their computer. A squirrel rescue was found. The lady there knew exactly what to do. She held out her cupped hand and took the little thing, stroking it with her finger until it stretched with pleasure. "This is no red squirrel," she said. "This is a Douglas pine squirrel. It has every right to be here in Oregon. *Every right!*"

They'd all loved that so much. Even Dad. Every once in a while, one of them would say it out of nowhere. "This is a Douglas pine squirrel! It has every right to be in Oregon. *Every right!*"

Would they ever say it again?

That squirrel lady was so much like Jane, so calm and assured and easy to relax around. But unlike that little squirrel, Orr is no orphan, and his right to be at Penelope is tenuous at best. Even though he was trying to protect Jane, there's something off about what happened. In what he did. He wishes he could figure out what.

Mom always says love is complicated—usually when he bugs her for stories about her family. There is something bad in Mom's past, a love there she doesn't think she should feel. And a terrible, destroying hurt. She cries sometimes, and Dad holds her. Once, Orr saw her curled up in Dad's lap like she was child. He rocked her back and forth the way he used to with Orr before the melt-downs and freak-outs hollowed out the love between them.

That's what Jane needs. Someone who loves her the way Dad loves Mom. But Orr can't make her hold out for that. Maybe it's something she needs to figure out for herself.

And then there is the violence. Orr knows he needs to think about that. Once is an anomaly. Now there is a pattern.

The worst was the thing that happened when Mom was packing. The way he pushed her suitcase off the bed. The way the green silk earring box flew out and hit her below the eye. Orr never meant to hurt her, but the box left a mark. Orr saw it when she came to say goodbye.

Tonight, it was Jane he hurt, even if he hadn't meant to. But Red—he'd meant to hurt him. Orr had never used his fists that way before, not on a person. It was a little like a meltdown, a sort of fugue state. The worst part is that Orr liked it—being stronger than Red. Making him fall. Defeating him.

Orr gets up and brushes off his butt. Why his bare feet aren't killing him is a mystery, but they feel normal. Portland has tough-ened them.

It's close to sunrise, and he knows where to go. He stretches and begins a slow trot. Out of the corner of his eye, a white flash of something. A ghost? No, ghosts probably aren't so cliché. He runs again, a little faster.

Again, a flash. He stops. Nothing. Starts. Stops.

Finally, he sees them. A slinky white dog, tall as a wolfhound with the legs of a gazelle, and a smaller pure-white wolf dog about the size of Orr's friend, the lady coyote, running together on the far side of the graveyard. Orr crouches. They bow. Orr bows back. They charge, stopping a few feet away from him, tails wagging.

The big one approaches first, sniffing Orr in an almost maternal way. Her cool nose on his forehead erases the last of the throbbing headache. The smaller dog, her protégé by the look of things, bounds over, unable to wait any longer. This one must still be a pup. Orr romps with him in the grass, then races the ghost dogs out of the cemetery. They pace him to the exit and trot alongside as he heads down Stark Street toward Plum's house. At Southeast 30th, they part ways. Orr's trot falters. He's tired now. And very hungry.

Two blocks away, he tastes Plum on the air—dandelion greens, hot sauce, and honey. He also smells a cigarette. Closer, he sees the red glow on Plum's porch.

It's Jane, sitting on the front steps.

He slows to a walk. Stands on the sidewalk—looking respectful, he hopes. He waits for her to say something first.

"Orr." Jane's face is all worry and mascara. "I'm so sorry."

"I'm sorry," he says. "I've never done that before. Never hit anyone."

"Whoa," Jane says. "You cleaned Red's clock, babe. He'll certainly think twice before pissing off the next skinny fifteen-year-old."

Orr is shaking, so relieved it tells him how scared he was. Jane pats the step beside her. He sits, close but not too close.

"Jane," he says, "you deserve someone good."

Jane closes her eyes. "Red used to be different."

"Different how?"

Jane cocks her head and looks at Orr. "I'm trying to think." She laughs. "Actually, he was drunk then, too. We met in a train yard. He showed me how to ride the rails."

"Like a Woody Guthrie song?" This is stuff Dad likes, Depression-era old-timey freight-riding troubadour stuff. That and Sinatra.

"More like don't get killed, don't get raped. Traveling with a guy was smart."

"Red doesn't seem smart, Jane." Orr lets a twinkle show in his eyes so Jane knows he's teasing her.

"Nope. That hasn't changed, that's for sure." She sucks on her cigarette and blows some feeling out with the smoke. Sitting up straighter, she says, "If I'm honest, nothing about him has. He wasn't different back then. I was. Now he's just a bad habit. One I gotta break."

"I have those, too. I think that's why my dad wanted to send me somewhere."

"Some people think you need to break to heal. Not me, man. I think that's bullshit. I think joy is what heals you."

"Me, too," Orr says. "You helped me so much, Jane. I wanted to help you back."

"Oh, you did!" Jane says. "Tonight was the last straw, kid. Mika and Allison told me I'm the one getting kicked out if I let Red in again. They're making me pay to change the locks."

"I don't want them to kick you out!"

"No—babe. They're messing with me. We had a good talk. Those girls, the band, it's the first time I've felt part of something real. I got kinda messed up after Plum's mom died. She meant a lot to me."

The sky is turning to roses. A snore sounds from somewhere on the porch. Orr stands and pads up the stairs toward it.

Plum is lying across the porch swing like a drooping poppy in a yellow nightgown, her hair in a pile on the blue floor. She opens her eyes.

"I told Jane," she says. "I knew you'd come here."

"Are you playing a painting again?"

Plum stretches, laughs. "No, crazy man cub. I'm sleeping."

"If I'm the man cub," Orr says, loving the *Jungle Book* reference, "then which one are you?"

"Me?" Plum thinks. "Definitely Kaa," she hisses, making her eyes snakelike.

"You're not Kaa." Orr is thinking about the girl at the end of the Disney version. The beauty who lures Mowgli to the village.

"I'm not that girl." Apparently Plum is reading his mind again. "I'm not any of them. Just a girl cub you met in the jungle."

"Hey," Jane says, coming up onto the porch. "Does the Paradox Café still open at six? I'd roll a nun for some vegan biscuits and gravy about now."

"I'm pretty sure," Plum says. "Maybe you should go see if my dad's up. Just yell from the bottom of the stairs. My goal is getting him out of the house at least three times a week. Remind him of the cornmeal pancakes."

Jane leaves and Orr sits next to Plum on the porch swing.

"I'm going home after tomorrow night," he says. "But it's not far—will you ever visit me?"

"I might." Plum says it like it's a yes.

The sky is hibiscus tea and honey now. The wisteria climbing the purple trim on the lizard-green house stretches all the way to the porch roof.

"You did look like a painting when you were asleep, you know," Orr tells her. "It's called *Flaming June*. It's in one of my dad's art history books. There's a beautiful redhaired lady sleeping in a long orange dress sort of half sitting, half lying down with her hair flowing down to the floor."

"Orr?" Plum says like she's going to laugh. "Are you doing it again?"

"Doing what?"

"Calling me beautiful."

"Yes," Orr says. "I am."

19

FIRST EXPERIENCE
AS A DIRECTOR

"**D**are," Lorna says.

Iph takes her time. Something is happening here—or maybe something needs to happen. There's a space for change. She thinks about her drama teacher's litany: *Make the most dramatic choice.*

"I dare you," Iph says, "to show us your favorite move from work."

George's mouth hangs open again. Mission accomplished.

The one virtue of this stupid game is that it's good for airing certain truths. Iph shouldn't hate it so much. It was Truth or Dare that helped her realize she liked girls when it devolved, as it always did, into a directive brand of spin the bottle.

Lorna laughs. "I mean, we don't have a pole, so—"

"You said you were no good at pole tricks." George's tone is petulant, trying for a fight.

"Practice makes perfect, right?" Iph says. Her light tone is both a dare and a rescue. She's seen Mom remind people of their manners this way before. Like, *Are you going to make this situation worse with your bad behavior? Or are you going to save face and grab this rope and pretend you were joking?*

"Well, in that case, I guess Lorna's probably going to win an award, considering she spends all her time at that disgusting place." Clearly, no. The rope has been bypassed, and George is going full-on jealous ex. So much for that eighty-five to ninety percent. George is not over Lorna at all.

"Wow," Iph says. "That was rude."

"I'll say." The calm in Lorna's voice belies her tense posture, the way a cat is silent before it pounces and rips your face off.

Iph giggles, not because it's funny, but because she's nervous, and also because it reminds her of four-year-old Orr's confusion about the term *spitting mad*. He thought it meant that instead of yelling, a person would literally act like a cat to show displeasure—growling, spitting, arching their back. The family had been pretty confused when he whipped that out to protest bedtime.

"Is this funny to you?" George asks Iph.

"No! No, not at all. I'm remembering this thing from when my brother was little. He didn't get euphemistic language—"

"What does that mean?" Lorna asks.

Ugh. The game is doing its evil. With one word, she's exposed her life in a house full of books with a family who enjoys Scrabble tournaments and the *New York Times* crossword puzzle every Sunday. Her vocabulary was something she used to get teased about. Other kids thought she was being stuck-up when she used archaic words from the old-fashioned books she preferred. She felt powerless then. Later, when Mom helped someone in the store who didn't speak English or a classmate couldn't make heads or tails of Shakespeare, she realized language was a route to power. And now she's made Lorna feel stupid.

"It just means, like, a metaphor. Like, right now, you look spitting mad. My brother used to take stuff like that literally—he really expected people to spit."

"I can't make any promises," Lorna says with a look Iph can't decode.

George looks down. Everything is off.

"Well," Lorna says, getting up. "Here you go."

"You don't have to." George says it like a plea.

Lorna takes a chair from the dinette and places it in the center of the small living room. The moon is her spotlight. Her hair glows with it. She walks deliberately to the tape deck, takes out the Ella Fitzgerald, and pops in another cassette in its place. It's Billie Holiday. "Ain't Nobody's Business." *Ha!* After being so judgy about Lorna's business, it's totally the song George deserves.

Lorna stalks a circle around the chair, her hand running along its back like it's the jacket of a man in a three-piece suit. She flips her hair, arches into a spin, and sits, crossing her legs into a pose worthy of a fifties pinup.

"Wow!" Iph says. The move is very Bob Fosse, something straight out of *Cabaret*.

"Why do you wanna do that?" George says. "For those gross perverts?"

"They're not all like that."

"So you actually like the table dances, Lorna?"

"We've all done things we don't love to get by," Lorna says. "Including both of us."

George folds up like a broken-down cardboard box. Iph's glasses are acting up. She takes them off, wipes them. Back on, it's clearer—George isn't breaking down, but squaring up to fight.

Lorna is sitting in her chair, holding her pose, face tight. There is something so familiar about her locked-together knees, the way her spirit seems to have left her body. And then Iph sees it. Lorna is like Mom. The pieces click into place like a Rubik's Cube she's been trying to solve her entire life.

This is why Mom gives money to homeless kids every chance she gets, making sure to get cash from the ATM in Forest Lake before they drive into the city. This is why she knows to say *sex worker* instead of *prostitute* or *whore*. Why she's always made sure her kids knew not to judge. Mom was that kid, once. On the street, alone. Doing what she had to in order to survive. Like Lorna. Like George.

Iph gathers her mother's secret life into her body like a treasure.

She will hold it there and never say a single word unless Mom wants to talk. But she's right. She knows it. And even though there's nothing she can do for teenage runaway Mom, maybe it's enough to help these two.

"Can I ask something? What are you guys really fighting about?"

George glares at Iph. "Why did you ask her to do that?"

"I'll tell you what we're fighting about," Lorna says. She walks over to the sofa and sits, owning the room. She must make so much money at the strip club. "George is judging me. We can't all rise to your level of moral perfection, okay?"

"What are you talking about? I'm not perfect." George's eyes close, and Iph sees how perfect George wants to be. How perfection is George's way of surviving, no better or worse than living as Lorna does, this girl equivalent of a Siamese cat.

"I'm not like you." Lorna hugs her knees to her chest. "I don't like urban camping. I don't find it charming or fun. I don't like having to sneak around and worry all the time. You know what happened to me on the street. You're the one who picked up the pieces. But I have an apartment now, George. Did you even wonder where I was staying?"

"I assumed with some guy."

Lorna heaves a pillow at George and misses. "Go to hell." She takes a breath. "After living here, I needed space. I live by myself, you self-righteous little pill."

Scout whines into the silence. Wags hopefully at George and Lorna and Iph. Iph pulls her close and comforts her.

"What's your apartment like?" Iph asks. "Is it nice?"

"It's just a dinky studio in one of those old buildings near the library."

"One of the ones from the twenties? With those medallion things on the roofline?"

"Kind of," Lorna says. "I think it might be older than that. The kitchen and bathroom have that black-and-white tile, like a checkerboard. And there's these ledge things over all the windows and doors. There's no reason for them—they're just pretty. I hung Christmas lights on them."

"Crown molding," Iph says. To Lorna's raised eyebrow, she says, "My dad's an architect."

"My bed is right under the windows—what are they called? When three windows meet and are, like, pushed out from the front of the building?"

"Huh. I don't know. Picture windows? That doesn't sound right."

"No, I think that's it. Anyway, they're super tall, so I bought these long white lace curtains at Fred Meyer, and it's so pretty with the wind blowing in. I love to just lie there with the windows open. I feel like a girl in a book."

"I'd love an apartment like that."

"I mean, it's nothing special," Lorna says. Iph knows this need to downplay; if you shine too much, the gods might get jealous and take it all away. "But I've got my routine—go to work, come home. Make food. I actually cook! I have a wok. I drink tea at night. There's this herbal tea that's supposed to be relaxing. With the bear on the front?"

"Sleepytime," Iph says.

"Yes! I make that and run a bath. I put on music. I thought I'd get a TV right away, but I love it without. Life at Taurus Trucking taught me to entertain myself." She looks at George, who is staring down at the floor. "I'm starting at PCC in the fall. I took all the placement tests and applied for financial aid."

"That's amazing," George says, finally looking at Lorna. "I want you to have all that. I just wish you didn't have to do this to get it."

"Maybe I'm not supposed to admit this, but I like my job." Lorna sits up straighter. "I like performing. I love the other dancers. Even the mean ones. The unstable cuckoo ones are kind of my favorite. I've made friends. I feel . . . at home there."

"Maybe that's not healthy, Lorna. Did you ever think about that?" George's voice is low, already defeated.

"I'm not working at another restaurant, George. I've had enough grease in my hair to last a lifetime. Enough minimum wage. And what about all the times I've had to do stuff for free? Take a number I don't want, smile on the street so I don't get harassed. It feels good to get paid. At least at the club, there's a bouncer. There are rules. I leave with what I used to make in a week in one night. Tell me that isn't better."

"Those guys don't deserve you."

Lorna rolls her eyes. To Iph she says, "Ever wonder what a Gemini with a Taurus moon *and* a Taurus rising looks like? Here it is!"

"George?" Iph touches her foot to George's. Even with all this drama, there's still a little spark. "Have you thought about what Lorna deserves? She sounds happy."

"I am." Lorna gets up and heads for the gin in the kitchen. She brings back the bottle and sits back down on her chair.

They're all quiet. Scout makes the rounds to each of their laps in turn as they finish off the gin.

"So," Lorna says. "Now you, Iph. Truth or dare?"

"Dare," Iph says like a crazy person.

"Ha!" Lorna sits back in her chair like she's not onstage but in an audience. "Excellent choice."

There is a pause, but Iph knows what Lorna's going to say.

"I dare you," she says, "to do what you were doing five minutes before I barged in here."

TIME STOPS AS IT always does when the game turns transgressive. Iph knows how this plays out—she and George kiss. Then Lorna and George. And finally, Lorna and Iph. Maybe Lorna's been wanting to do that since she first saw Iph at the Roan Inish theater. Maybe Iph thought about it then, too, or earlier, when she first saw the painting. Maybe George wants this, although that's the least likely possibility. It will end with someone crying, Iph or Lorna. Odds are it will be Iph, sitting there, waiting for George and Lorna to stop, for the game to continue. But it won't, and Iph will run off like she did at the hotel with Dad.

"No," Iph says. "We have to stop."

"What? I did your dare."

"Lorna. You just want to compare our chemistry to yours. That's still us competing for George. And I'm probably going to lose. But either way, this is beneath us."

Lorna's face is blank for a second, but she finds her footing quickly. "Oh, I'm so sorry, do they not play truth or dare in the West Hills?"

"Lorna," Iph says, "do you want George back?"

The room is silent and still, down to Scout. "Does it even matter?"

Now George breathes out, an exhale that's almost a whinny. On the back of the bike, Iph enjoyed thinking about how like a centaur George was. Lorna and George finally lock eyes. Iph's chest aches as she watches. What are they acting out, and why?

It's not simple teenage relationship drama; that much she knows for sure. It's deeper, about their parents and their child-hoods and the things they've seen too young. These two will do this over and over again, Iph realizes, until they've hurt each other so badly there's nothing left to salvage. Something has to change.

"I dare you both," Iph says, "to do exactly what I say right now."

Lorna laughs. "Now who's the boss?" she asks Scout.

"Fine," George says. "But I'm drinking the rest of my gin first."

"No more gin," Iph says. "Stand up, both of you."

Lorna looks surprised but does it. George obeys only when Iph holds out her hand.

"Close your eyes."

First, Iph moves George a little closer to Lorna. Then she moves Lorna into George, as close as Iph was an hour before. Their hip bones collide. Iph adjusts Lorna until they fit together. They stand like that, arms at their sides. "I want you to be aware of your body right now," Iph says. "Focus on your breath, your heartbeat."

She turns on the tape. She places George's hand on the small of Lorna's back and Lorna's on George's shoulder. "Listen to the music. Open your senses wide. What do you smell? Do you still

taste the gin? How do your legs feel? Is there tension in your face?"
She waits, watching them both pretend to follow her instructions
at first, then fall into the tasks. "Breathe," she reminds them. She
fits Lorna's free hand into George's. "Now dance."

The two sway and stumble. Feet are an issue. And shoulders.
And knees. "Lorna, lean your head on George's shoulder and take
a deep breath. What's the first thing you notice?"

"Rose soap," Lorna says. "George washed up for you."

"What else?"

"The breeze on my neck feels good."

"And?"

Lorna stops swaying. "I feel . . . sad."

"How about you, George?"

"For the last three months, this was all I wanted," George says,
eyes open and on Iph. "But now it feels weird. I'm worried about
you."

"George? I don't want to know how you feel about your
breakup with Lorna or anything about me. I want you to tell me
how you feel right now, in this moment. And close your eyes!"

After a beat or two, George says, "I'm sad, too."

Iph lets them dance for a while. "Spin her," she says. And,
"Don't forget to breathe."

The two of them dance to the end of "My Man" and through
"Stormy Weather," gliding around the living room gracefully
now, eyes open. The song changes to "Don't Get Around Much
Anymore," and they're looking at each other once in a while,
smiling now. If this were a play, Iph would start the scene here:
they're both so present, in sync with each other, simultaneously
happy and sad. They stop. Step back a foot, no longer touching.

"We're done, aren't we?" says George.

"Yeah," Lorna says. "We are."

They hug as Scout dances around their feet, and then they stop
and open their circle to Iph. She hesitates.

"We're friends now," Lorna says. "All of us. Promise me,
you guys. I don't have too many people I can be real with. I

think that's why I was so scared to lose George. Why I couldn't let go."

George nods. "You know that stuff you said when we had that fight on Hawthorne?"

"I said a lot of things."

"Well, at least one of them was true. It's sort of a life mission of mine—to be someone's person. Their protector."

"I said that?"

"You said I loved being in love," George says.

"That's what she told me in the bathroom at the movie theater," Iph says, stepping back.

Lorna laughs and plops to the floor, pulling them both down with her. They're in a circle now, cross-legged, knee to knee.

"Is that what it is with us?" Iph asks George. "A rescue drama? The prince and the maiden?"

"Iph." George gives her a look she doesn't understand. "Let's talk about this later."

"What do you mean, later?" She knows she's whining, but it doesn't stop her.

George laughs. "How old are you right now?"

"I feel about thirteen," Lorna says. "Also, forty-five."

"I meant Iph," George says.

"Huh," Iph says to Lorna. "That's what I thought when I first saw you. You have a spooky old-young thing going on."

"I do," Lorna says. "But tonight, dancing with George, I felt my age. Like the age I was at that very second. It was wild."

"That's presence," Iph says. "It's what actors do. You're good at it. I think you could act if you wanted."

"You think?"

"Um, yeah," George says. "But Iph? So can you. You're so smart and shiny." George presses a shoulder into Iph's.

"So is it later now?" Iph is teasing, but she's also human. The director in her has left the building and all she wants to know is if George still likes her.

"What I am," George says, dark eyes wide, *"and what I would,*

are as secret as maidenhead; to your ears, divinity, to any other's, profanation."

Iph's whole body contracts. She sees George seeing it, lips parting into a pretty *O*.

"That's what?" Lorna says. "Shakespeare again?"

"Ask Iph," George says.

"I don't know what it's from." Iph wonders if she's blushing.

"Twelfth Night," George says.

"All I know is *Romeo and Juliet,*" Lorna says. "And you're perfect for that. Noble family, super smart. All bright-eyed and pretty."

"You really think so?" It's like Iph is ten years old, maybe eleven, at an epic sleepover.

Lorna looks at Iph like she's a problem that needs solving. "Are you still in high school?"

"I'll be a senior," Iph says.

"Well, I'm sure you're headed off to college or Broadway or whatever after that, but if you ever needed the cash, you would clean up at my club."

"Really?"

"Oh my god, yes, and I'm not even into girly-girls. Plus, say all you want about the strip club, but high school is seriously toxic." Lorna winks at her.

"Hey!" George says. "Don't put that idea in her head."

"Don't worry," Lorna says. "She's not going to take me up on it. No offense, Iph, but I have the feeling girls like you do internships and summer jobs abroad."

"None taken," Iph says, thinking about Mom and the daughter Lorna might someday have. About money and healing and love.

THE SKY IS ITS earliest-morning pale, and the neighborhood is hushed. Not a car or person in sight. They walk in a hip-and-shoulder-bumping mass toward Clinton Street and end up at Piccolo Park. Scout races off-leash in the cool grass as George easily crosses the monkey bars. They converge at the swings, three in a row with Iph in the middle, pumping in unison into the rosy sky.

"When does Cup and Saucer open?" Lorna calls from her swing.

"We're broke," George says. "We blew our busking money on sushi and presents."

"It's on me, dummy," Lorna calls.

"I don't want your ill-gotten gains, woman," George says.

"Oh, George," Lorna says. "I made a stupid amount of money last night. Let me spend it on you two."

"Do they have French toast?" Iph's mouth is already watering.

"Yes," Lorna says. "It's excellent."

"Let's jump off together," Iph says. "On three!"

They grab hands, and together, they fly into the dew-dropped summer morning.

Lorna's hand slips from Iph's, but Iph and George land together, feet on the tan bark, hands clasped.

20

THE CHERRY
ORCHARD

Iph rubs the crust from her eyes and stretches out on the sofa. She's been curled tight into herself, too crashed to realize she needed a blanket. The apartment is chilly, and the sky is pinking. Dusk or dawn?

She sits up. George is on the floor, snoring lightly. Kicked-off covers reveal curves of breast and hip that are usually hidden. Mink lashes skim delicate cheekbones. Scout is cuddled at George's feet.

After breakfast with Lorna, on their own again on the walk back to Taurus Trucking, George told Iph Nana's story—how her father came to Oregon to work the railroads and how her grandmother had been a picture bride from Japan. When Nana was fifteen, her family was uprooted and sent to a Japanese American internment camp in Minidoka, Idaho. George stopped at that part—stood still, eyes down. "She told me before she died. From what she said, it was like a prison. Growing up, my mom barely knew about it. Like, she knew it happened, but not anything else. My great-aunts don't talk about it, either. Like they're ashamed. Like it was their fault."

"I never heard about it in school," Iph said. "I only know because of my parents."

"I got like one paragraph in middle school," George said. "I don't know why, but I didn't connect it with my own family."

"What happened after the war?"

"She stayed in Idaho a while, got married to a louse at seventeen who left her after two years, then a nice but boring guy who died six months later. After that, she swore off husbands and became a truck mechanic—the one woman in her trade-school class. That was how she met her true love. She helped him fix a stubborn carburetor."

George said Nana wore orange lipstick with her grease-covered overalls and got a manicure every Friday after work, even though it was usually wrecked by Monday night. Nana's third husband, George's grandpa, was also called George. Nana and Grandpa George had George's mom, an only child. There was a typical George-style silence at this part. "My mom won't tell me who my dad is. She married my stepdad when I was three. Her drinking got bad when he deployed. In rehab, she found Jesus. Met husband number two. And suddenly, it was clear who my dad must have been."

They'd gotten home by that point and were in the bathroom together, brushing their teeth. How had that become a thing? "Wait, who's your dad?"

"Well, if I'm as evil and degenerate as my mom seems to believe, it can only be one man . . . "

"Ah, Satan! I see." They laughed the way you laugh about abortion protesters and Republicans who think condoms in schools make kids into sex fiends. But George didn't bother to hide the hurt there, the bitterness.

Now Iph has to pee. She tiptoes around George and peeks out the window—it's evening, not morning. And there is an ugly brown pickup pulling into the Taurus Trucking parking lot.

"George!"

George bolts up and is at the window in an instant. Car doors slam shut. Feet pound up the unused back stairs.

George pulls jeans and a T-shirt over heart-printed boxers. Voices bounce up through the open windows. A woman's. A man's. Too late, Iph remembers that she, too, should get dressed, but the door is opening. She grabs the afghan from the floor.

"Georgina Marie!" The woman is shorter than George and almost as pretty, with dark bobbed hair and a pink cardigan— total PTA president. Or based on what George said last night, the church-lady equivalent.

The man is wearing cowboy boots, a baseball cap, and a gross mustache. Iph is certain there is a combed-over bald spot under the Oakland Raiders cap and a Bush-Quayle sticker on his over-compensatingly large truck.

"What are you doing here?" George says. Scout is on edge, doing her big-pit routine.

The man notices Iph. George's mom turns to her a split second after. When you ask people what the most important element of a play is, most will say writing or acting. Yes, those are essential. The set, too. But more than all of this, Iph has always been a firm believer in the power of costume.

If she were to set a scene where she wanted to show two worlds colliding in the most disturbing way, she would have dressed George's mom and stepdad exactly the way they are dressed and put herself, the surprise element, in the thin white slip that is so much more transparent in daylight than it was in last night's dark apartment. She would have styled her curls into a wanton mess. Even Iph's bare feet somehow scream *lesbian sex*—even though she and George only talked before falling asleep that morning in separate nests.

"Hi," Iph says, channeling one of her favorite characters from the dated collection of plays on her drama teacher's bookshelf—the free-spirited hippie Jill from the sixties dramedy *Butterflies Are Free*. She bats her eyes and smiles.

George shoots her a look. Panic retreats. Understanding dawns. This is their show. They can direct it. Iph has George's back.

"Georgina, did you break into Nana's apartment?"

"It's *my* apartment, Brenda. Remember the will?" George's tone is even. So far so good.

"That will is still being contested," George's mom says.

The man is leaning in the doorjamb with his armpit exposed. It's a pose that says *I'm releasing my stink on all of you, and there's nothing you can do about it.* "Your nana was a little senile there at the end," he says.

"No, Gary. She wasn't. And I'd appreciate it if you'd both leave."

"So you can party all night in poor Nana's house doing God knows what?" George's mom stares at the empty gin bottle like she might set it on fire with her eyes.

"Brenda," George says, "that's pretty rich coming from you. But whatever. You still need to go."

The husband pushes past Brenda and George with a leave-the-women-to-fight-it-out look and heads purposefully toward the door leading down to the garage.

"What do you think you're doing?" Scout's accompanying growl tells Iph all she needs to know about how pissed George is.

The man doesn't answer but goes on his way.

"Why are you here?" All of George's untold stories are distilled in the question that is actually a warning.

Brenda tucks her hair behind her ears and shifts in her pristine white mules. "Bob wanted to borrow a few tools from downstairs, is all. To work on the truck."

"Did he lose his job again?" George's voice is a notch softer.

Iph knows from growing up with her dad that tools are worth a lot of money and easy to sell secondhand.

Brenda picks up the gin bottle from the coffee table. Sets it down again. "I can't believe you'd desecrate Nana's home." In the movie version of this, Brenda's tone would be nasty. Here, it's shaky, sad, and afraid. Then her eyes slide to Iph, and there it is—judgment. Maybe even disdain?

Iph's breath catches. Being branded with a scarlet *A* is both awful and strangely exhilarating. Hester Prynne is a role that's always interested her.

"Get out." George's voice has taken the register of Scout's low growl. It's a new side of George, a little scary. "Brenda, you don't want to mess with me. I promise. I still know things Gary doesn't."

Brenda pales and backs away before turning to head out the door, her steps clicking like animal claws down the wooden stairs. George watches the parking lot. Iph hears a car door slam.

"Go get dressed, but stay up here," George says. "I'm going down to deal with Gary. He's not taking my tools—*Nana's* tools—because he lost his temper and got fired from another shady car lot."

"Just a second." Iph grabs a Nana sweater from the recliner and shoves her bare feet into her boots. "You're not going down there alone." But George doesn't wait. Iph struggles with the laces, then the arm of the sweater. She pounds down the narrow staircase. The light in the garage is diffuse. Gary is fumbling in a toolbox, his back to the stairs.

George is standing, feet apart, bow and arrow ready, waiting for him to notice.

Iph opens her mouth to say something. Physical violence was not part of the danger she considered here. But looking at George, at Scout, even the way Brenda left and got in the truck, violence has always been a part of this scene. It's come to Taurus Trucking with this man.

Gary glances up and goes straight back to digging. There's already a pile of tools on the workbench.

"Gary, get off this property. I'm warning you."

"Shoot me and you'll go straight to juvie. Maybe even grown-up lady jail. Or wait, I guess they have to send you in with the men, *George*. The rest of the guys are gonna love you."

He turns, neck out, head cocked, like this is the wittiest thing in the world. Scout barks . . . and lunges for the asshole's ankles. Before Iph or George can move to grab her, the man has pushed Scout away with his boot and then, though she doesn't lunge again, kicks her across the room.

Iph is there a moment before Scout lands, or is it the moment after? The timeline is scrambling and she's both holding the dog and running toward her, unsure how badly she's hurt. Scout's high-pitched scream of pain bounces off the walls for longer than it seems like it should. Like there are multiple keening animals in the room. The sound mixes with the man's profanity—ostensibly English, but Iph can't understand it; she can only perceive the singe of Scout's pain and her own fear for all of them. In less than the space of a breath, Iph understands why George goes around with the bow and arrows.

Scout is in her arms, and she turns just in time to see it—the muscles in George's back flexing like wings, the arrow flying in slow motion through the dim garage, the sound like scissors cutting hair when the arrow pierces the Oakland Raiders cap and pins it to the wall.

The head is balder than anticipated. Blood trickles down. A nick.

Everything stills.

Then, all at once: movement. Scout wriggles out of Iph's arms and is at George's side again, barking. Gary is shouting. Iph understands the words now. A river of acid—the most misogynistic, hateful rant she's ever encountered. The sound bounces off the painted metal walls. The side door to the garage unlocks and opens.

A woman stands in the doorway with a toddler on her hip and a baseball bat in her hand. It's the neighbor lady. A man holding a newspaper follows her in, trailed by a little girl.

"Oooh!" the girl says, seeing the painted walls. The oohs turn to squeals when she sees Scout.

"Is there a problem here?" The man moves his daughter behind him. She peeks out around his legs.

"Just a family disagreement," Gary says. George is pale. Iph knows exactly what to do. What Mom would do. She ignores Gary and speaks to the neighbors.

"This man is here uninvited and attempting to take tools that don't belong to him." Iph lowers her voice so that the daughter, who's being licked all over by Scout, doesn't hear the next part. "He kicked my friend's dog. He needs to leave. We don't have a phone here. Can we use yours to call the police?"

"Iph," George hisses. Iph ignores it. The mom of this family is like her mom. These people are not on Gary's side.

"This building belonged to my wife's mother. I came over here to check on things and found these kids. They must have broken in."

"That's not how I understand it," the mom says. "I'm Ellie Crawford Ford, by the way. Civil rights attorney and mother."

"John Crawford Ford," her husband says. "Public defender. And, uh, dad to these hooligans." He smiles toward his kids and extends a hand to George. "A family friend of yours, Kyle Murphy, asked us to keep an eye on this place while he was out of the country. Said it was willed to his stepkid and some relatives weren't happy about that. Gave us this extra set of keys in case."

"Murphy did that?" George is shaking.

"Yep." The woman smiles. Laugh lines form around her dark eyes. The toddler pulls on her cornrows and puts the beaded end of one braid in his mouth.

"Kid's underage," Gary tries.

"I'm almost eighteen," George says.

"It's a gray area." Ellie Crawford Ford smiles. "You, however, have no legal right to be on the premises. And I have to say"—she hands the baby to her white, long-haired, spectacled husband—"I didn't like the language I heard coming in my kitchen window a few minutes ago. I was concerned an assault was taking place over here. Which is why I brought my bat." She swings it lightly. Her bicep is impressive. George is grinning now. "This one is such a quiet neighbor. We never hear a peep. So you can imagine how worried we were."

The man looks at all of them now, and Iph sees it click. This interracial lawyer couple and their kids. George and Iph and Scout. They're what he's afraid of. The change he goes to church and the rifle range to keep at bay.

He shakes his head in a fake-pious, *I'll pray for you but you're going to hell* way and takes his time walking out.

The air in the room brightens. Or maybe it's Iph's glasses, which she's taken off and cleaned with Nana's sweater.

The little girl hugs Scout around the neck. "I don't like that man," she says.

"Me neither." Iph smiles at her.

"Smart kid," George says.

"You knew I was here?" George asks the Crawford Fords.

"Were we not supposed to know?" Ellie furrows her brow. "Wait, have you been living here?"

George takes an unconscious step back. John steps in to stanch the fear in the room. "It's fine," he says. "Murphy said you were staying with a relative, but this is your place. I don't see why you shouldn't stay here."

"When do you turn eighteen?" Ellie puts a hand on George's shoulder. Iph suddenly realizes George is still holding the bow.

"May." George looks down. "Almost a year from now."

"Well, you could have a great case for becoming legally emancipated. I'm not sure if that would secure you the right to manage your inheritance—that's not my area. But I have a friend I could hook you up with. They owe me one—I'll make sure it's pro bono."

"Wow," George says. "Thank you. Should I . . . come by and ask about that later?"

"Sure," she says. "Or I'll stop by when I find out."

"Are you like Robin Hood?" the little girl asks, looking up at George with wide excited eyes.

"Yes," Iph says before George can answer. "Just like Robin Hood."

21

LIKE A
WILD ORCHID

Orr wakes in his little closet from a dream of running with the ghost dogs. Today is cooler, and because of that, he has slept a little too long. His forehead aches like two beating hearts. There are bumps now, one on each side. He hoped he was done with the head thing. It upsets everyone so much. But he's not trying to harm himself. It's something he needs to do to readjust. To process what has happened and figure out what to do next.

As always these days, he is hungry and thirsty. And a weird mix of bouncy and tired. When Orr was little, this mood boded poorly for his coming day at school. He'd do the wrong thing, either accidentally or on purpose. Either way, it had been exhausting for the entire family. What a relief it had been to leave that behind and stay home with Mom.

But this past year, even at home, he's had the bouncy-tired feeling most days, and there's been nothing to do about it except run and sleep. He's even fibbed to Mom sometimes about how he spends his days when she takes classes in Portland or spends hours out in her studio. Most of it was watching *X-Files* episodes he'd taped on the VCR, living a life of purpose as an FBI agent investigating the paranormal through Mulder and Scully. It was almost enough.

In the living room, Mika is doing push-ups. On the coffee table is a stack of the zines she made to pass out at tonight's show. The cover is a blown-up picture of Red's face. Mika wasn't kidding when she said she'd plaster Portland with it. It's titled *THE FURIES*. And below that is the excellent subtitle: *Assholes to Avoid: Portland's Worst Boyfriends.*

"You know it's funny you guys are the Furies, right?"

"Huh?" Mika puffs out the final set. She is such a badass.

"In Greek mythology, the Furies are after Orestes. They want to kill him."

"Why?"

"Well, you know—Greek tragedy stuff. He killed his mom because she killed his dad because he killed their daughter, Iphigenia. Same name as Iph. Only the daughter didn't die. She got a last-minute save from Artemis."

"Whoa. That's twisted. Why'd your parents name you guys after such a bloodthirsty family?"

"I don't think they're bloodthirsty. Just tragic. The names are from Dad's side of the family. His brother, who died young, was Orestes. And his grandmother, who was, like, his favorite person in the world, was Iphigenia. He and Mom decided the real people were more powerful than the mythical ones."

"Orestes—that's what Orr is short for? I thought it was iron ore or something volcanic, since you said your mom's kind of a hippie." Mika sits up and stretches. She has a whole preshow workout. "The Furies *did* try to catch up with you last night, you know. You should run track. I left maybe twenty seconds after you bailed, but you totally smoked me."

"I did?"

"Yeah. And Allison went after you in the van."

"Oh."

"Orr. You're a great kid. If I had a little brother, you're the one I'd want. We all would."

Orr looks away and fights the urge to walk over to Mika and press his head into her shoulder. She's not big on physical affection. "I am someone's little brother," he says softly. "But it's like my sister and I both forgot."

"I'm a twin," Mika says. "My sister and I go weeks without talking. We used to be together all the time. When she went away to college, I was devastated for, like, months. But then I started making zines and got into playing drums. Last year I met Allison and Jane. Now I love my life. And I don't know if I would've found it if Layla hadn't made the break for both of us."

There's something so true in this. For the whole family, maybe—him and Iph and Mom and Dad. "When do we leave for the show?"

"Like, now."

"Already? I need to eat first, but then I'm ready. Sorry, though. About eating so much. I'm always hungry."

"Consider tonight's bass service payment in full. Also, you're not ready. Plum's styling us. We were supposed to be at her house twenty minutes ago."

Orr stuffs down a PBJ and drinks the last of the soy milk. Mika's already on the front porch. "Wanna run there?" she says. "Race you!"

JANE AND ALLISON ARE in Plum's basement, looking like great and terrible goddesses in blood-red togas and fishnet stockings and big chunky boots. Allison's hair is braided into a thick crown around her head with several plastic snakes woven through it. Jane is wearing an ivy crown with a wine-colored band of paint across her eyes and the same color on her lips. "Mika, yours is in the bathroom," Plum says, taking a pin from her mouth. "It's the sturdiest one. I didn't want you busting out of it like She-Hulk the second you hit the drums." Jane stays very still as Plum removes the rest of her pins. "I have to sew them onto you guys," she tells Orr. "It's the only way we can make it stay. Next time, please tell me you want costumes before the day of the show."

"But we didn't know until you had the idea at breakfast," Jane says.

"And anyway, Plum, you're totally pulling it off," Allison says. "You're a wizard."

"That's witch to you," Plum says. She is wearing her white men's shirt again, this time belted as a dress. Her legs are long and beautifully freckled. There's a delicate silver chain around her left ankle with woodland animal charms hanging off it—a skunk, a rabbit, a deer. Plum catches Orr looking. "It's from Disneyland," she says. "From my mom. Bambi was her favorite . . . I know"— Plum stabs the pins into a tomato-shaped pincushion—"Bambi's mom and all. Ironic. But back then, we didn't know." Plum's basement is a riot of costume supplies. "Take your shirt off and stand still."

Orr hesitates.

"Chill," Plum says. "I'm a professional." She takes a red length of fabric and pins it on him, then sews the pinned spots to secure them. "It will rip if you take it off, so there's no going back. But it should be fine for the show. And here." She hands him red-and-black striped leggings. "These are mine, but you'll wanna wear them to be decent. I only had enough fabric for a short toga for you." She stands back and observes him. The basement is cool and green, with garden light through the open door and ground-level windows. Plum takes his hand in hers. He wants to lick it. *It will be salty*, he thinks. *It will be sweet*. She sits him in a chair to do his makeup.

"You're so blinky," she says. Then, gently, "I know this feels weird. Raise your eyebrows like you're surprised and make your face sort of stiff."

Plum's breath smells like lemons and sends quivers down his back every time she exhales. If they were alone, Orr might kiss her.

Her lips are pursed as she tickles his face with a large fluffy makeup brush. She touches the bumps on his head with a fingertip. "Did this happen last night?" She's talking about the fight with Red, but Orr nods. "Do they hurt?" Orr shakes his head, but Plum kisses both spots anyway, so quickly it could have been a moth flying by. When she smooths color onto his lips with her fingers, Orr pulls away. Even good things can sometimes be too much.

She steps back. There's a feeling growing between them like the wisteria vines on her porch. Orr watches her know what he knows. Her cheeks turn pink and her freckles darken.

"You're fabulous," she says. "Let me put your crown on, then you can go change into your leggings and report back."

ORR STANDS IN FRONT of the bathroom mirror for several minutes. The boy in front of him seems to know him, maybe better than Orr knows himself.

He tilts his head to see how he looks from different angles. The ring of black around his eyes makes them bigger and darker. The red lipstick gives him the look of a classical cupid. The wreath of fresh roses around his head makes him look like some sort of god. All he has for shoes are his sneakers. Plum was adamant in her veto of them. He will be barefoot onstage.

"Come out," Jane says behind the bathroom door. "Plum insists on painting your nails."

ACT III

Whoever drinks from me will become a roe

1

GIVEN
CIRCUMSTANCES

The bus huffs and puffs down Burnside. It's after eight, but the day gleams on with its buttery light, still and hot. Iph rests her head on George's shoulder. They pass Music Millennium, the Laurelhurst Theater, and Shiny Dancer, heading for the bridge. Iph hums something soft and low to Scout, who has her head out of the messenger bag for pets. Iph smiles, realizing what she's singing—a lullaby she and Orr used to call "*Ai, ai, ai*" for the first line of the chorus. "*Cielito Lindo*" is its real name. Pretty Little Heaven.

The river is full of sailboats. At the end of the bridge the neon stag rises from the Portland sign like it's leaping away from Old Town into the blue-green Willamette. Mom's husky voice floats through Iph's head. *Ai, ai, ai, ai. Canta y no llores.* Sing, don't cry. After everything that's happened, the timing is right. Iph is ready to find her brother.

They have John Crawford Ford to thank for this confluence. Clearly an agent of fate, he left the weekly paper on the workbench at Taurus Trucking, open to the live music listings. And there it was, in big block letters:

FRIDAY NIGHT AT THE X-RAY CAFÉ
DEAD MOON
CAUSTIC SODA
THE FURIES
WITH A SPECIAL BUCK MOON INVOCATION
BY THE SCARLET LETTER PERFORMANCE COLLECTIVE
3 DOLLARS
ALL AGES
NO ONE TURNED AWAY FOR LACK OF FUNDS.
PROCEEDS TO BENEFIT SHINY DANCER

IPH FEELS CUTE IN Nana's minidress muumuu, worn this time with drugstore fishnets and a ninety-nine cent red lipstick. In the bathroom drawer of Taurus Trucking, she found the stubby end of an eyeliner pencil and revived it the way Mom taught her, by holding the freshly sharpened tip to a lit match. George liked her smoky eyes, red lips, and fishnets so much it led to kissing, then painting each other's nails with silver glitter polish. On the way to the bus, George poached some pink roses and tucked them here and there into Iph's tied-up curls. Iph plucked a daisy to thread through the buttonhole in the chest pocket of George's crisp white shirt and two more for Scout's collar.

Because the moon is full and it's a perfect kind of night, the first person they see is Lorna rocking a sixties-inspired Twiggy ensemble with mile-long lashes, white go-go boots, and an ugly-cute loud floral shorts-and-halter set—most likely once a swimsuit—that turns her eyes green. She pulls Iph and George into her spot in line and hugs them. Even though they're cutting, no one seems to mind.

The sidewalk in front the X-Ray Café is packed with every kind of kid. A pair of lipsticked boys in metallic leggings, feather boas, and hair like the guy from the Cure stand behind raccoon-eyed rocker girls in fishnets, cutoffs, and knee-high boots. Unshowered grunge kids in new Converse and holey flannels lean against the building next to too-skinny street kids with the occasional sock

poking through their beat-up sneakers, scarfing falafels provided
by one of the grunge guys. He's older than the others and looks
sort of familiar—like maybe he's in a band Iph's seen on MTV.

A gang of buzz-cut vegan punks with safety pins in their faces,
home-Sharpied MEAT IS MURDER T-shirts, and those World Wild-
life Fund panda-bear patches on their jean jackets pass around
a single clove cigarette. A boy in a top hat rides up on a unicycle
so tall the seat is level with the street signs. He dismounts with
surprising grace to perform a complicated lock-up and is greeted
by a mohawked girl on a normal bike with a pink-haired toddler
strapped into the baby seat behind her. The unicyclist swoops
the toddler onto his shoulders, and the three of them head for the
back of the line. George raises an eyebrow at Iph, like *cute* but also
whoa. Iph nods. Those parents look about their age.

A trio of tween girls in kindergarten dresses and plastic bar-
rettes coo at the toddler and flirt with skater boys doing tricks
at the curb. Interspersed like sparrows among Bowie birds are a
surprising number of normal-looking teenagers who might've
come straight from the library or soccer practice—or even, like
Iph, from Forest Lake.

The line moves fast. Inside is dim and smelly but buzzing with
energy. Sitting at tables with the posture of regulars are a mixed-
age group of what Dad would call career misfits for their well-
marinated quirkiness. Some look like they're in their twenties.
Others are older, maybe even her parents' age. In a corner in the
back, Iph spots the guy who had ants buzzing around his head
that day outside the Gentry. He looks better today, showered and
in clean clothes with clear eyes and a relaxed face. He's younger
than Iph thought. He sees her and gives her a thumbs-up.

"What was that about?" Lorna asks, blowing bubblegum
breath in Iph's ear.

"Nothing," Iph says. "Just a friend."

UP FRONT THE DIN is fantastic. George is swamped by a pack of kids
who've spotted Scout in the messenger bag, and the pink-haired

toddler climbs onto the stage and jumps off into her dad's arms. Baby Orr would have been a howling puddle after five minutes here. Even Iph has to fight the urge to cover her ears. It's not the volume so much as the chaos—thrash punk over the house speakers mixed with talking-yelling-laughing and someone onstage doing a sound check that involves an unreasonable amount of screaming feedback. Then, all at once, the X-Ray quiets.

A *sssss* starts somewhere in the back of the room, and the Scarlet Letter moon priestesses begin their snaking procession through the small, packed space. Their silver outfits and metallic kohl-lined eyes are a knockout combination of silent film goddess and science fiction robot queen. They wear identical black Cleopatra wigs, chain-metal bras, low-riding liquid-silver harem pants, and space-age moon-phase headpieces. One of them, at the head of the sinuous line, has a fat albino boa constrictor draped over her shoulders and around her waist. All of them are tattooed: mushrooms and mermaids, waves and fire, flowers, birds, foxes, bats. One of the few brown priestesses looks a little like Mom with a machine-gun Guadalupe on her forearm and what looks like a vintage educational chart of all the kinds of sacred hearts on her back: hearts on fire, hearts with wings. Knife-, arrow-, and sword-pierced hearts. Hearts wreathed in roses and golden light. Broken hearts wrapped in garlands of thorn.

"I heard about them at work," Lorna whispers to Iph. "They're a coven of sex worker poets. They came up from San Francisco."

A ritual cup passes, lip to lip. "Magic mushrooms," Lorna says, drinking. Iph takes the vessel and sips the bitter forest tea. George passes it along, not drinking.

Iph has never taken psychedelics before, but both her parents have. "It was the seventies," they used to say when Orr, who's never seen the point of drugs of any kind, not even caffeine, scolded them for it. It's how her parents met, at an East Village party thrown by Dad's musician brother. Mom knew the punch was spiked, but poor straightlaced Dad, visiting from college in Oregon, did not. According to family lore, Mom found him wide-eyed and freaked out, hiding in the bathroom. They spent all night talking on the roof, a conversation that's still going.

George pulls Iph close as the procession speeds up. Scout peeks her head out of the bag to give Iph a tentative lick. She's not sure about these priestess-snake-women. "It's okay," Iph says. "We've got you, girl."

The hissing line resolves to a linked circle in the center of the crowd. Hearts pound. Drums beat. Or is it rain in an ancient grove? Maybe it's both—drums calling rain from the clear summer sky. *Sympathetic magic* is what Dad calls it, Mom's religion of tarot cards and candles and feathers and pine cones and stones. What exactly are these witches calling?

As the rhythm reaches an apex, the snake grows arms, a bejeweled kraken rising from the deep to partner the crowd in a dance. As if instructed, everyone joins hands to move in a spiral, chaos to order, like the folk reels Iph learned in preschool. She and George are linked for a moment, but George's hand is jostled away and another takes its place, calloused, belonging to a woman whose round, high-cheekboned face changes age in the flickering light—twenty, fifty, twelve. The hissing thickens as tongues kiss teeth throughout the room. On the stage is a large bowl full of gleaming coals. One by one, the priestesses peel away from the crowd and drop branches of rosemary onto the fire. The smoke curls through the air, another kind of snaking, and the spiral slithers faster.

Then, in marvelous unison, the collective snake of them stops. The hiss sheds its skin, becomes song. An elfin blonde onstage is singing to the moon. She plays a strange instrument, a gold electronic-looking box with an antenna sticking up from either side. Moving her hands between the two metal poles, she seems to bend space into sound. The word *theremin* forms in typeface in Iph's mind. The woman's head tilts, almost as if she was the one who sent it.

"Who is that?" Iph asks George, whose rose-soap sweetness is somehow extra thrilling in this crowd where only Iph really knows it. Well, Lorna knows it, too. And did Iph see Cait back near the door? She flashes back to the ticket girl at the movies. Probably there are more of George's exes here. It's that kind of crowd. She leans in close to hear George's answer, inhaling.

"Are you smelling me?"

"Yes."

George moves closer, lips to Iph's neck. "What were you saying?"

"The singer." Iph is grinning. Ridiculously crushed out.

"Right," George says. "She's from some San Francisco band. Why can't I think of the name? You're distracting me, woman."

"I'm just standing here," Iph says.

"You guys are gross," says Lorna, reappearing from wherever the dance landed her. "She's from Lady Frieda. They're in town for a big show. Oh, she's from the same band." Lorna gestures toward a woman with blue mermaid curls and light-brown eyes who has joined the theremin player. They sing together, their harmony breaking the room like an egg.

"Swoon in moonlight," they sing. *"Fall into the arms of fate."*

Iph closes her eyes, giving into the woodland magic of the tea.

In the still moment of synchronized breath after the song is over, Iph feels him.

Orr.

Her brother is very near.

2

SPOKE TO THE SONGBIRDS

There isn't really a dressing room, but there is a patchwork curtain at the back of the stage and a small space behind it with a few folding chairs. After one look at Orr when they first walked in, Jane led him here, handed him a fresh set of safety-orange earplugs, and said to wait while the girls went and smoked and the witches did their thing.

It's taken him the better part of half an hour to calm down, but now that his heart's stopped racing and he's used to the noise, it's kind of great. Iph is so right: backstage darkness is one of the best kinds, even though in this case the stage is more a platform in the middle of a café and its darkness is broken by tiny beams of light coming in through the curtain's irregular seams.

The hairs raise on Orr's arms when the hissing in the café stops and changes to a weird wordless song that sounds like an old record Dad has of singing humpback whales. There is also music. What instrument? Orr could get up and look but doesn't. The words morph from sound to language.

"Compass your blood to your desires," a witch sings. *"Swoon into the arms of the moon."*

Orr pulls Allison's bass onto his lap. If his family knew about this, they would be here, cheering in the front row. He closes his eyes and tries to feel them, but all he sees are Jane and Mika and Allison—or really, mental portraits of them in their red costumes with golden auras around their heads like the saint candles on Mom's altar.

"Classic transference." Iph said this when he was eleven and fell in love with his third therapist. Or wait, had Thao been the fourth? Either way, what he's done is clear—substituted Jane for Mom and the girls for Iph. And in this version of mathematics, people aren't important beyond meeting Orr's needs. Maybe Portland has changed him into some sort of monster. Or no, it's the same kind of beast he's always been. The one who made his mother cry the night before her residency started and pretended to be asleep when she left for the airport. In this way, he is like Red. Selfish, no self-control. A terrifying, giant man-baby-monster.

He tries to concentrate on this, teach himself to change, but as always, his thoughts turn to Plum. He doesn't even have to try to conjure every detail of her snapdragon hair and lake-colored eyes. She's always there, hovering like a swarm of honeybees, a constant buzz in the back of his brain. She'll be in the front row tonight. She promised. Even if he doesn't deserve her, Orr's heart gallops.

Coming offstage, a woman with white-blonde hair and a slight English accent is saying, "Someone was passing this around, and I have to say, I don't approve."

"Haven't they heard of germs in this town?" another woman says, laughing. "I think it's pretty weak. But yeah, not cool at an all-ages show."

"Oh," the small blonde one says, noticing Orr. "Hello. Are you in the opening band?"

"Yes," Orr says. He is!

"Stage fright?" The other woman sets a blue ceramic bowl the color of her curls on the graffitied head of a dented tom-tom that seems to function as a backstage table. "I still get it myself," she says. "It's all good—just energy. Your body getting ready for something big!"

He smiles at them. He likes the smaller woman's pointy ears with their many silver studs and the bluish-green curls and maple-syrup eyes of the curvy one who looks like a mermaid, and how they talk to one another like they're sisters.

"Have a great show!" the blonde woman says. "You look amazing, by the way. I love your toga."

"Love and luck!" says her blue-haired sister. They leave, and before Orr can think about what they've told him, the blue-haired one is back. "That bowl should be dumped out—like down the drain—but we have to go. Can you tell somebody?"

"What is it?"

"Mushroom tea," the woman says. "Don't get rid of it outside. I heard about someone doing that and feral cats getting to it. It really messed them up."

3

NEON GLITTER

"It's time," Jane says.

Orr's mouth is still contracted from the bitter tea in the blue bowl and Plum's strawberry lip gloss. He was thinking of her when the thirst came on, worse than ever before. Did the bowl really glow? Did the tea actually call to him? When Plum found him, he was licking the bitter dregs.

"Jane's on her way, crazy boy," Plum said. "I wanted to give you this for luck." Orr held out his hand, but Plum pushed it away, standing on tiptoe to kiss Orr on the mouth. His ears had filled, wings beating, hoofbeats, blood. When he opened his eyes, she was gone.

Now he follows Jane to the stage and waits at her heels. He can see the crowd from here. So many people!

Allison is on the mic brandishing her cast. "So he whips his dick out," she says. The crowd is roaring. "Who knew his dumb face would be so hard when I hit it?"

"Next time aim lower!" someone yells.

"That's what we told her," Jane yells back.

"All right, animals!" Allison says. "Simmer down. I wanna introduce my new friend Orr! This boy genius started playing the bass like five days ago, and he's already got me out of a job. Give him a warm Portland welcome!"

Jane pushes Orr up front and he feels it then: the forest swelling toward him, sweet pitch, wind in his face. He's supposed to be moving into his spot in front of the drum set, but he's standing there, staring at the crowd. Jane laughs and leads him to the amp. Allison plugs him in while Jane greets the audience. Then there's a fizzing moment of silence before Mika counts out the beat.

"One, two—one two three four!"

4

CHARISMA

The minor sparkle of the mushroom tea is nothing compared to this boy. Her brother.

Orr is stunning. The lead singer of the Furies, impressively tattooed and legitimately hot with a Joan-Jett-meets-an-avenging-goddess vibe, is reduced to a bit player, singing the words so Orr can bounce them back to her with effortless notes from the bass while he stands there in his eyeliner and red toga and rose crown, looking like a young god visiting from Olympus or Chichén Itzá.

"Your little brother is a total rock star," Lorna yells into Iph's ear.

All Iph can do is watch, mouth open like she's trying to drink the music. Like that will somehow explain this phenomenon. This human who she's bathed with, who slept in her bed until he was five, who's needed so much from her his entire life, is thriving without her. In this chaotic space, Orr has found balance. His rhythm is generous—steady and loyal, like he is. Iph is crying. She always cries. Love and loss mix and cleanse. The bread-crumb trail has finally led her back to Orr. Soon, this chapter of their story will be over.

"You okay?" George's mouth is on her ear. Iph turns her face to meet those lips. George pulls her closer. Tears, tongue, a hand to her neck. It's a light kiss that knows there are many more to come. Iph takes a deep breath and smiles to show George she's all right.

"I'm taking her out," George says.

Iph touches the messenger bag to feel Scout inside. Her little body is tense.

They talked about this earlier. That for Scout's sake, George would probably listen from outside. That they wouldn't leave without each other, no matter what happened with finding Orr. "I'll find you or you find me," George says, giving her one last kiss.

Iph turns to look for Lorna, but Lorna is gone.

Alone in the crowd, she imagines that Orr is gone as well. "The tea was strong after all," she'll say later to George as they sprawl upstairs together at Taurus Trucking. "Maybe we'll find him tomorrow." As the traitorous thoughts unspool, Iph tries to wind them back. But there are no do-overs here. The truth is, she's not quite ready to be anyone's big sister again.

"I abandoned him," she says out loud to no one in particular. "I abandoned my brother for lust."

The guitar solo eats her words and flings them back to her. There's no room for recrimination now. Lust is fine with this music. And if she abandoned Orr, look who picked him up! A pack of tween girls have commandeered the front of the stage and are dancing like dervishes. Little trails spark from the tips of their fingers and the ends of their hair as they spin. They crash into one another, laughing, drunk from the movement. Just like that, Iph lets go. Mind off.

And here is Lorna, shimmying around like a baby horse on her long graceful legs. She isn't slinky here, but awkward in a way that is a gorgeous contrast to her it-girl perfection. For a second, Lorna's just-rightness wraps around Iph, and every move she makes is glorious. A split second later, Iph sinks into herself, so heavy she can't move.

She will never be beautiful like that. Never so light and lithe.

So perfect. *Never*, her heart wails. *Never ever!* The mushroom tea plays cat's cradle with the string of thought. *Never. Never ever.*

Iph can usually tame these voices with Mom's rabid feminism or the wise words she's read in riot grrrl zines. But it takes energy. And so much precious time. It seems like it will never end.

The song is reaching a distorted crescendo. The audience screams. Iph screams with them and feels a little better.

The next song creeps in as the band is tuning up with a sneaky drumbeat and slow simple bass. The X-Ray Café inhales, a dumpster-dive creature made of glitter, trash, hormones, and magic markers. Jane whisper-sings into the mic.

> *Don't be sorry*
> *Don't say sorry*
> *Don't be sorry*
> *Don't say sorry*

Iph steps a few feet back from the stage because Jane is up there reading her mind. The music builds and the front-loaded chorus repeats, getting louder each time. Iph is singing with her now. The entire audience is.

> *Don't upologize*
> *Blood in his eyes*
> *I'm not sanitary*
> *Not your Virgin Mary*
> *Look at me*
> *A delicacy*
> *It's that time babe*
> *You can eat me*

Orr yells this last line with the rest of the band and the crowd yells it back, and someone pogos into Iph, and she's laughing and dancing. Orr is dancing, too, headbanging with Jane and Allison and the joy onstage is a slow-motion firework, sending tails of light out into the crowd.

The Furies are Iph's new favorite band, her brother her all-time favorite bass player. Their music is hard like punk but a little slower, with a bluesy feel that takes hips into account. The lyrics are total riot grrrl, personal and political. The songs pile up one after the other with almost no breathing room in between. After the friend breakup and abortion and period songs and a very short song the drummer dedicated to someone named Red that is basically the band playing the *Batman* theme but screaming *Fuck You* every time you'd normally say *Batman*, there are two longer songs. One is slow, about a friend dying—just Jane and her guitar and the rest of the band humming behind her, a container for her sorrow. Here Jane shines, and Iph can see the craft she's put into this lo-fi, seemingly thrown-together show. She is open-eyed and breathtakingly present. *This*, Iph thinks, *is how you do it*.

They wrap up with a surprising slow-funk seventies groove and announce that people can make an extra donation to Shiny Dancer at the table in the back. Glow comes onstage in a pink plastic raincoat and monster silver patent leather platforms and shares the mic with Jane to do an excellent rap about stripping.

> *She walks right up to those neon lights*
> *Gonna make her rent in just one night*
> *She's knows it's not her clothes or her smooth young skin*
> *It's how she moves with what she's in*
> *She shakes it hard, she's got a plan*
> *You know that she knows what the men don't understand*
> *You call her a slut, call her a ho*
> *But she knows a little secret that you don't know*

The audience is howling. The song ends, and Orr scans the crowd. Iph jumps up and waves. "Orr!" she shouts. But he's not looking her way.

No, her brother is looking stage left, smiling like a googly-eyed cartoon character. Iph follows his gaze. Dad mentioned a girl, and this has got to be her. The entire family has wondered for years if Orr would ever have a type, but if they'd just stepped back and pictured it, it totally would be someone like this—waist-length wavy dark-red hair worn with a Halloween devil-horn headband, a black leotard under a frayed denim miniskirt, black Converse, sparkly striped knee socks, and a furry blue Cookie Monster backpack. Iph already loves her.

5

STAG OF THE
STONE FOREST

Orr's playing is like breathing. One long breath sipped from Plum's lips, a radiating warmth, a sure path through a grove, a roving, ramping lust.

It is the belly of a bear. He is a beast being born.

His shorn head buzzes with a crown of bees, and Plum in the front of the crowd is the honey.

When the music finally pants to rest, he is sweating and thirsty, and the room is a mush of color and muffled sound. Then he sees the Furies. They are haloed as he imagined them before the show. Allison, Patron Saint of Knuckle Sandwiches, is holding him as they jump up and down together. Even Mika comes to join the hug. Jane waits for the others to step away.

"Babe," she says. She means, *You were good*. She means, *I am proud*. She hugs him.

People worm into their pack with more hugs and congratulations. The next band is setting up. The Furies scatter. Orr stands alone on the stage.

Where is Plum? She said she'd find him. Fear sprouts. His head twinges a migraine warning above each eye.

"Orr!"

He looks around the room, but there are too many possible sources.

"Orr!"

The stage tilts and begins to revolve, a slow orbit around the throbbing pulses in Orr's head. The singer for the next band, a slight pale girl with big dark eyes and curls like Iph's, comes over to adjust the height of a mic stand. He moves out of her way to stand at the edge of the stage. Where is he supposed to go now?

Then, somehow, with no warning at all, his sister is standing on the stage beside him.

Iph? Is his mouth moving? Did he say her name or think it? His heart is racing. "Iph, I'm kind of spinning."

She smiles. "You, too?" She puts her hands on his shoulders to steady him.

"Hi," she says.

"Hi," he says back.

Iph. It's Iph.

"You were beautiful up there." Her face is shining. Her curls are full of roses. She smells like herself but different.

"Iph?" Orr says. "Is the stage tilting?"

"Little brother," Iph says in a bad British accent that means he's stumbled onto one of their many private jokes. "Did you, by chance, drink any of that tea?"

"Iph," Orr says, "we're on drugs. Are you even here right now?"

She laughs and Orr's head stops pounding.

"We have to get off the stage," he says. "I need to find Plum."

"I'd be offended that finding some girl is all you can think about after this crazy week, but I have to find someone, too."

"A boy?" Orr asks. "A girl?"

"Yes," Iph says. "Named George. And a pocket pit named Scout. Now take my hand. We're gonna walk to the edge and jump off together."

Hand in hand, they're laughing like hyenas. That's what Dad always says when his children get started and can't stop.

They jump on the count of three. The distance is short, but time stretches and they land softly, like the floor of the club is a pile of September leaves.

When Orr looks up, Plum is there. He looks from her to Iph. He should say something out of politeness, blah blah blah. He's laughing again. Plum's face is slow-motion starting to frown. Iph saves him because she's his big sister.

"I'm Orr's sister," she says. "Iphigenia." Why is she giving her full name? Orr swats away the thought of alien abduction in favor of mushroom tea. Or maybe this week has changed Iph as much as it has changed him.

"I'm Plum," Plum says, and Orr can only think of kissing her again. "And that," she says to Orr, "was fantastic. FANFREAK-INGTASTIC. I'm almost mad at you, it was so good."

"Why mad?"

"Because you're a maniac rock-star man cub, that's why." Plum grabs his shoulders and shakes him a little. "How did you learn to do that?"

"Iph," Orr says, "we're not on TV." Iph is standing there staring, like she's watching *Bringing Up Baby* or *My So-Called Life*. She has that same smile.

"Sorry," Iph says. "Do you want to come outside and meet my friend George? And I'd love to meet the band—"

Feedback screeches, penetrating Orr's earplugs. Nails on a chalkboard amplified all the way up. *Up to eleven*, Orr thinks—Dad's dumb joke from some old movie. It squeals again, and the crowd seems to double. Orr remembers, something about the next two bands. They are popular, better known than the Furies. Iph is talking to Plum, who is pointing out Mika. Orr puts his hands over his ears. Where is backstage? Is there a quiet place here? Allison warned him about the bathroom—too gross even for her, she says.

Orr does a therapy technique, looks for the corners of the room. Velvet-painted Elvises and glamour girls stare back. A table of poker-playing dogs look suspicious as he tries to scan the room's perimeter. His head hurts. He needs air.

Then Plum is there, leading him outside, around the corner. "Your sister's going to meet us out here," she says. It's still loud, but quieter. The moon is high and the cool is good. Plum leans against the building. Orr looks down at her. When did he get so tall? He touches her hair, something he's longed to do. Bunches it in his hands.

She closes her eyes, lifts her face. They are kissing now. A real kiss. Plum is pulling him closer. A car speeds by, honking. He startles, pulls away. Plum laughs, but her face is distorted like she is underwater. Orr's head aches. It hurts so bad. He's holding it. He is so thirsty. He presses his forehead to the side of the building. The rough brick is a poultice. He's tapping now, rhythmic hits against the bricks. Plum is saying . . . something. Pulling at his arm. Everything is hushed except for the sound of his forehead hitting the wall.

"Orr!" Iph says. "Stop it!"

Your sister is in charge. That's what his parents always say when they go out. *Listen to your sister.*

"Stop it right now!"

Dad's voice.

No, it's Iph channeling Dad. And it's enough. He stops. Turns. Plum is crying.

Humiliation falls like poisoned rain. Or is he drenched in sweat? He won't look at Plum. Can't bear to. Can't even look at Iph as she pulls him away from the wall. Then he sees it in the glass of a shop window.

The boy in the mirror is gone, and so is Orr's pain.

In their place is a tall lanky creature with two small mossy horns peeking from his forehead.

He stomps his foot. Once, twice, three times.

This is not a place for him to be. Not anymore.

Orr steps back, clear of Iph and Plum. Then he runs.

6
INNER
PSYCHOLOGICAL
DRIVES

Iph is in front of the X-Ray yelling her brother's name, but he is so fast. She wishes for George, for the bikes. She can barely see him now, already blocks away and still running down Burnside.

"Iph!"

She turns. Not George, but Josh—no Shakespeare now, all business.

"Cait's getting her car. I'm gonna run ahead and see if I can at least keep sight of him."

How are Josh and Cait here just when she needs them? She remembers hearing people call Portland a big small town. Josh takes off fast, but not as fast as Orr. Iph squints to see the red toga now. And where is George?

Plum takes her arm. "What can I do?"

A honking BMW sedan turns the corner. "My friend is here somewhere. George—with dark hair and a mohawk, carrying around a little pit named Scout."

"I saw them earlier! I'll tell George where you went," Plum says. "Do you want to meet somewhere later?"

"Back at Taurus Trucking," Iph says. "George will know."

CAIT PULLS UP IN front of the club. Iph climbs in the back seat. Somehow, Lorna is in the passenger seat. "Thank you, Plum," Iph calls out the open window. "Tell George I'm sorry!"

The car is silent as Cait drives down Burnside. Iph doesn't see Josh or her brother. Cait speeds up. There, on the corner in front of Powell's, is Josh, doubled over. Cait pulls into the bus stop, and he gets in the back with Iph.

"Your brother is hella fast," he says, panting. "He went that-away." Josh points past Powell's. "Down 12th."

"Thank you," Iph says. "I didn't even know you were at the show."

"I got there late. George heard your brother ran off and sent me." He leans forward, hands on the two front seats. "Greetings, George's exes."

"Shut up," Cait and Lorna say in unison.

Cait drives several blocks. They stop to ask a guy on a bicycle if he's seen a barefoot boy in a red toga running past. *Barefoot.* Iph has a moment of certainty that this is all a dream. There is no reality in which tender-footed, easily grossed-out Orr would walk barefoot anywhere, let alone run.

"He went up Lovejoy," the guy says. "Is he training for the Olympics or something?"

"Thank you," Cait says and takes off.

The streets in this part of the city behind Powell's are alpha-betical. Iph checks them off as they pass. On Lovejoy, Cait floors it. At Overton, she stops again to ask a group of smokers out-side a restaurant. "I saw him," a guy says. "He was headed that way." The man points toward Northwest 23rd.

They keep driving, but Orr is nowhere in sight. Cait pulls over to regroup. Iph's hand goes to her pocket. Matches? No, it's the little book of poetry she picked up at Shiny Dancer. The moon comes out from behind a cloud, illuminating the inside of the car. Iph opens the tiny cover. On the title page it says:

Fragment from Ferenc Juhász's
"The Boy Changed Into a Stag Clamors at the Gate of
Secrets"

On the next few tiny pages she reads:

He stoops over the pool
stares into the moonlit water —
a beech tree with the moon in its hair
shudders — the pool reflects a stag!

Iph can't breathe. She flashes for a panicked second on her inhaler, left in her nightstand drawer. Her quiet, empty, messy room. She needs air. Gets out of the car.

"You all right?" Lorna is beside her.

"I'm scared."

Lorna takes her hand. "Think about him. You know him. Where would he go?"

Iph hands Lorna the matchbook poem. Lorna nods as she reads it.

"Is there an entrance to Forest Park around here? Maybe a trail with a creek?" she asks through the car's open windows.

"On Thurman," Josh says. "The trail to the Witch's Castle."

7

JOURNEY TO
THE PROVINCES

I ph waits alone in the dark forest, sitting on the steps of the Witch's Castle. Cait, Josh, and Lorna offered to stay, but she sent them back to Taurus Trucking to update George. She has the flashlight and blanket from the trunk of Cait's car. The butterflies in her stomach—well, maybe bats, considering her location—tell her Orr is close by.

The air is sweet with the breath of trees who tower over the tumbledown stone house like whispering giants in fringed pine-needle party dresses, their limbs silvered in moonlight. The Witch's Castle was once part of an 1880s homestead, then a rest stop for hikers, Cait told them. Now it's a burned-out stone structure layered with graffiti and moss that glows highlighter bright in the beam of Iph's flashlight. She runs her hand over the springy stuff and tries to send a psychic message to Orr. He is in this forest; she knows he is.

She draws her knees up and makes herself small. The forest is singing its midnight litany of *swish* and *woosh* and *chirrup* and *snap*. Iph looks up, hoping for stars, but the branches are too thick above to see more than a few patches of sky, a grayer black than the forest's darkness. Iph leans against the mossy wall and closes her eyes.

SHE'S WALKING THROUGH THE *lavender light of the predawn forest. A lanky white hound, the sort of regal beast you'd see on a Medieval tapestry, is a bend ahead. Every time the path curves, Iph sees the feathery tail flick and disappear.*

The path follows a creek, which ends at a wide, deep pond. Iph must cross it. She undresses. Takes off the rose-painted boots. Wades into the pond, deeper and deeper. The cold is profound.

The still water ripples with her approach. A court of swans, moon-white and black-beaked, surround her. She crouches until her chin grazes the water, digging her toes into the slime. She gathers herself and rises, winged now and powerful. She flies from the pond, wings spread over the wood, and lands in a meadow. The grass is dew-damp and sun-warm under her wide, webbed feet. She stretches like a fern unfurling—tall, then taller still, wings to forelegs, webbed feet thickening to large, razor-tipped paws. She ambles to a tree to scratch her back, fur against fir, like Baloo from the movie The Jungle Book. *She drops to the ground and shambles forward on all fours. Comes to a gate.*

Inside is a beehive, a siren on the rocks promising every sweet thing she could ever want. She rambles forward, works the gate handle, and reaches for the gold. Honey to tongue, throat to heart, and she is shrinking like Alice, folding into herself until she is a golden unit of pure desire. She flies over the meadow fragrant with wildflowers that glow psychedelic with sunrise.

A stone cottage peeks from behind a copse of trees. The flower world buzzes with morning work. Iph flies through a glittering cloud of pollen to land on a sunlit dais, velvet-draped with the scent of summer. Here, she sleeps.

Waking, she rises on her two feet again. Slowly, processionally, she makes her way toward the large dark shapes in the shady border where the meadow ends and the forest begins.

There, in the midst of a sleeping family of deer, is her brother.

The toga is gone. He is wearing a pair of torn red-and-black striped leggings and somehow still has the crown of roses he wore onstage. His head is leaning against the haunch of a large doe half-hidden in the trees' shadow.

Iph takes a step closer. The deer are awake. Have been since she began her approach. One step more, and the deer rise. Orr awakens. The stately animals walk slowly away, leaving Orr in the meadow, shirtless and barefoot, roses twined between his newly budded antlers.

8

WHERE THE
BONE-BRANCHES
BUDDED

"Iph, where are your clothes?" Orr's voice sounds different to him. He's surprised the words make sense when they come out. He touches his ears. The earplugs must have fallen out when he ran. The morning sun is so warm. He is so tired.

Iph spins in a circle. "I . . ." she says, scanning the meadow. "I'm sorry. I don't know what happened." She sits and pulls her knees to her chest, hiding her body.

"I don't care," Orr says. "Just pretend we're at the hot springs. Anyway, it's kind of the least of our worries." His ears twitch. As in, actually move. He feels for them. They're in the same location and the same shape as always—just keener and more mobile. He reaches up to touch his forehead, but he isn't ready. He knows this. Knows he must wait to confirm such an outlandish, impossible change.

At the far edge of the meadow is a flash of white. It moves closer. A single dog, the smaller companion to the leggy hound from the cemetery. Orr is certain it's the same animal—he knows it by smell. The thick-ruffed dog is a little larger than the coyote Orr met on the mountain, with a long snout and the golden eyes of a wolf. He—this is another thing Orr knows from the smell—is carrying a basket, handle in his mouth. He trots a respectful distance from Iph, sets the basket down, and bows, playfully wagging. Iph puts out her hand, and the dog comes eagerly forward, pressing his blocky head into her shoulder.

Orr picks up the basket and brings it to Iph. "My clothes!" She pulls out a dress and her underwear, bra, and socks. There is a blanket folded in the bottom of the basket. And a flashlight.

"This stuff looks like it came straight from the cleaner," she says, turning her back on Orr to dress.

The dog bows and bounds off, returning quickly with a pair of boots in his mouth. Dropping them at Iph's feet, he races around the meadow like a puppy, clearly pleased with himself, then speeds away again into the woods.

"Orr," Iph says. Her voice is shaking. "What happened last night?"

Orr stands, paces. Twitches again, the animal sounds around him distractingly loud. The squirrels scold. Birds forage for their fledglings. And the deer. The deer breathe a few bounds away, hidden in a cluster of salmonberry bushes inside the dark, fragrant grove.

Last night.

Last night.

How to even think about it?

Last night wasn't the ending he'd meant it to be—a graduation from this adventure and a way to take responsibility for himself. No longer a burden to the Furies. No longer hiding from his family. In that way, it had been an end. But in a vast and terrifying way—he can't explain it—it was also a beginning.

"I saw myself in the glass," he says to Iph. "I ran."

"Right," Iph says. "But Orr, those deer . . . "

Orr crouches in the dewy grass, clipped short by the deer who were sheltering him. "I don't know how, but I knew where to find the forest. I didn't stop until I came to that stone structure. I was panting and crying. I was so thirsty. Then I felt them, all around me. Quiet until they were close enough to touch. But I didn't move. I was scared! They're so big. Iph, they've been living right here. Animals in the city with us all this time."

"Right?" Iph says. "There are all kinds of things happening we never imagined tucked away in Forest Lake."

Orr is pacing again. "They have a hierarchy. The one in charge—her granddaughter came to inspect me first. Then her daughter. Then, finally, the oldest deer came over. Touched her nose to my nose. Then licked me." He stops, remembering the sweetness of it. "My headache . . . it went completely away. And now, I feel . . . right, but also not right."

Orr is shaking. He is so exhausted. He drops onto the grass beside his sister. Lies down. She folds the blanket into a pillow, and he rests his head in her lap.

She touches his shorn hair. It has grown into a short, thick pelt in the week since the men on the mountain sheared him. Her cool, strong fingers find the place on his neck where the migraines start. Her hands are as familiar as his mother's. Since the moment he took his first breath of air, Iph has been there. She was never a jealous sister, never a judgmental or rejecting one. She begged Mom and Dad for him. Lobbied for him. Loved him before he even existed. His first memories are of her holding him. Holding his hand as he toddled around the house. Holding his foot when he rode in his car seat. Memories so early he's not supposed to have them—but he does. Not of Mom. Not of nursing or riding in a sling. But of Iph, curled around him in their puppy pile of sister and brother.

Now she traces his forehead, fingers running over the substance that has mossed the skin there. "It's so soft," she whispers. "I'm going to press down a little—is that all right? I want to make sure you're not hurt."

Iph is always gentle with him.

"Orr," she says, "what do they feel like?"

"Before they came out, they felt achy, like a loose tooth. Now there's a little pressure, but it's sort of . . . a relief."

"Orr, these look like they're antler buds. I think they call this stuff around them velvet. They seem like they've grown since last night." Her words are calm, matter of fact. It's the same voice she uses to help him figure out the source of a meltdown. Orr has always appreciated her talent for being able to see the big picture and finding a way to talk about it that makes sense.

"I think you should touch them," she says. "Mostly for me. I want to be sure this is real."

Orr grabs Iph's hand so it covers his. This is how he learned to hold a crayon, then a pencil. He touches the velvet first. It is so soft and sensitive, the way the inner part of his forearm and earlobes are, but more. Then he touches the antlers, only single horn buds at present, one by one. The right is slightly larger than the left, but both are about two inches long. They are like teeth, he realizes, growing in the bed of velvet on his forehead like teeth grow in gums.

"I'm so scared, Iph. But also . . . I kind of love them."

9

CONCENTRATION
& ATTENTION

Stroking Orr's forehead, Iph is filled with purpose. The chaos last night after the mushroom tea is one thing. It is morning now, and they are here. Her brother is changing, and he needs help. Things could have gone so badly for her alone on the street that first night when she ran away from Dad. It was luck, maybe fate, that she met George when she did—but it was also Iph. She's learned to trust herself more over the past year.

She extricates herself gently and stands.

"Orr," she says. "Come on."

"Where are we going?"

"Over there." She points to the cottage.

THE PATH LEADS THROUGH the meadow and into the copse. Iph feels comforted among the trees. Last night's dream is still looping through her mind—swan, bear, bee. Lying on the path is a long, curved white feather. She picks it up and puts it in the basket, then continues out of the fir trees into a small grove of cherries with gnarled trunks and rustling leaves. At its heart is a bright cottage garden, meant to look wild but carefully tended. The garden path curves to reveal a small stone house, constructed similarly to the Witch's Castle, but as maintained and tidy as the castle is derelict.

Iph grabs Orr's hand. Together, they approach. The red-painted door is slightly ajar.

"Hello?" Iph calls. The place is silent and feels empty. But it's warm inside, and Iph is chilly after the walk through the dark grove. She pulls Orr in behind her.

Iph has always loved the sort of house Dad calls fairy-tale rustic. They often stayed in cabins or beach houses with a handmade whimsical feel when they traveled, but those all pale in comparison to this cottage. This is the real thing.

Inside, the entry is made of two miniature linden trees, white with blooms growing up through the stone floor to create an arched corridor, a miniature of the one Iph and George strolled through in Ladd's Addition. Farther inside is a large woodstove glowing with a crackling fire, a pillow-stuffed window seat, and several worktables.

At the longest table are a typewriter and three stacks of materials. The largest pile is made of various unopened envelopes, the middle one a stack of manuscripts, presumably unread, and the third pile, the smallest, is made of manuscripts marked in red and held together with large brass paper clips. In the typewriter is a blank piece of stationery with a familiar letterhead—*RCT*, vined with roses and shaped around the silhouette of a leggy white hound.

Iph steps back and keeps going until she's sitting on the window seat. There in the corner under the opposite window is a letterpress. In the middle of the room is a table piled with matchbooks—the source of the matchbook poetry Iph found at Shiny Dancer. At another table is a large embosser. Iph recognizes these archaic machines because Orr did a report on print methods for Mom as part of his homeschooling. He'd been obsessed with the *Terminator* movies and wanted to be prepared to foster the revolution after artificial intelligence took over and digital technology had to be abandoned.

"Orr, I know these books. I've been seeing them all over Portland." Iph gets up and runs her hand over the creamy paper in the typewriter. "Orr?"

Where is he? She rushes from the workroom through a dining room and a large living room into a hallway, longer than it should be given the footprint of the house. The third door on the left is open. Orr is there in a modest twin bed, snuggled under a feather comforter and patchwork quilt.

"I'm so sleepy," he says, then closes his eyes and starts to snore.

Iph backs away. Trapped in a fairy tale—well, she's not going to sleep. She will explore. She'll find the next clue. There has to be one. In stories like this, there always is.

She retraces her steps to the workroom. A dim corner opens into an alcove she didn't see before. She walks in and the lamps turn on. It's a library. She reaches for a random book.

Over here, says a very small voice.

She turns, but no one is there.

She moves closer to the shelves and sees they're labeled. FICTION, FAIRY TALE, POETRY, MYTH, MEMOIR, POLITICAL SCIENCE, MUSICOLOGY, SHAMANISM, RADICAL PSYCHOLOGY, PERFORMANCE STUDIES, ALCHEMY, etc. She yawns again.

Pssst, says the voice again.

Oh! Like at Powell's, a book is calling her.

Of course it is.

She takes a breath and listens. Touches a possible source of the call. No. She knows somehow. Not that one. She tries again, but it's for sport. Given the logic that is surely behind this situation, she knows her third choice will be the correct one. She pulls the book from the shelf.

Case Studies in Transmutation

What is that supposed to mean? A sound like a window closing draws her attention to a large dictionary on a stand, lit up by a perfectly placed sconce. The sound she'd heard must have been the book opening. She reads:

TRANSMUTATION, noun.

TRANSFORM, METAMORPHOSE, TRANSMUTE, CONVERT, TRANSMOGRIFY, TRANSFIGURE: *to change a thing into a different thing.* TRANSFORM *implies a major change in form, nature, or function ("transformed a pile of scraps and snippets into a book of poetry").* METAMORPHOSE *suggests an abrupt or startling change induced by or as if by magic or a supernatural power ("the silver-haired woman transformed into a tall, lanky hound").* TRANSMUTE *implies transforming into a higher element or thing ("the alchemist transmuted lead into gold").* CONVERT *implies a change fitting something for a new or different use or function ("converted the ruins of the cabin into a snug forest home").* TRANSMOGRIFY *suggests a strange or preposterous metamorphosis ("the boy was transmogrified into a deer").* TRANSFIGURE *implies a change that exalts or glorifies ("wonder transfigured her face").*

Well, then. Iph is definitely in the right quadrant of the enchanted forest. She opens to a page that reads:

Transmogrification has been reported to occur as the result of a curse or as an intentionally developed skill. We are not referring to either manifestation in this chapter, but rather the occurrence of temporary or permanent physical transformation as a result of psychological trauma.[1]

In such cases, the course may be reversed by enacting a psychonarrative change such that the affected person is able to release and/or incorporate the elements and/or experiences in such a way as to render the physical transfiguration unnecessary. This operation requires: [2]

1.   *A willing subject*
2.   *A trusted psychopomp*
3.   *Trained ritual participants*

At the bottom of the page are footnotes:

1.   See the tales "Tam Lin" and "The Girl Who Trod on the Loaf."
2.   See ancient Greek dream theaters—*Asklepion*.

Iph knows "Tam Lin"—the story of Janet, whose lover is taken by the Fairy Queen. To get him back she must grab him and hold on no matter what as he morphs into a succession of terrifying beasts. The other one with the weird name she's never heard of. And what the hell is a psychopomp?

She needs paper, and of course there is a stack of index cards and a box of small, perfectly sharpened silver pencils at the end of the shelf—the enchanted cottage version of the scrap paper and golf pencils they keep by the lookup computers at the library and at Powell's. After writing down *The Girl Who Trod on the Loaf*, she goes to the dictionary, unsurprised to find it already opened to *P*.

PSYCHOPOMP, *noun*
plural noun: psychopomps; noun: psychopompos; plural noun: psycho-pompi (in Greek mythology) a guide of souls to the place of the dead.
*   The spiritual guide of a living person's soul ("a psychopomp who stays by her and walks in her dreams").*

Iph thinks back to last night's dream—if that's even what it was—and the white dog who led her into the forest. Not the Malamute who brought her clothes to her, who is clearly a minion, but the regal moon-colored hound. Definitely a psychopomp.

She carries the book to the workroom window seat. On the wide sill is a cup of steaming black tea, flavored with roses and pale with the perfect amount of cream. She sits and reads.

She closes the book when she hears singing from the library, something that sounds vaguely like doo-wop or Motown. Iph finds several books with spines sticking out an inch or two, asking to be chosen. She takes her stack back to the window seat.

A Feminist Reimagining of Jodorowsky
The Theater of the Oppressed
Individuation in Fairy Tales
Flying Ointment: The Witch's Book of Depth Psychology
Women Who Run with the Wolves: Myths and Stories of
    the Wild Woman Archetype
Grimm's Fairy Tales with an Introduction by Carl Jung
The Pan Within: Transmuting the Masculine
Radical Intuition: Lessons from Baba Yaga
In My Mother's Garden: The Somatics of
    Intergenerational Trauma

There is too much to read. Too much to learn. The stakes are too high.

She puts her head down. There is a sound, little clicking hoofbeats. She looks up. Like a player piano, the typewriter is moving on its own.

The message reads: *Bibliomancy: foretelling the future by interpreting a randomly chosen passage from a book.*

As Iph reads the sentence, another forms.

You can do this.

There is a yellow legal pad Iph didn't notice before and a cup full of tall pencils, this time licorice black.

Back at the window seat is another steaming cup of tea and a plate—a golden grilled cheese and tomato sandwich, carrot sticks, and sliced strawberries. Now her throat aches, because this is Mom's special lunch for her. Her favorite. Maybe there's a phone in this house. Maybe she can call Mom. Get help. But what would she say? The ache turns to laughter. She must be hysterical—a word she hates, but if the laughing/crying/hyperventilating fits . . .

She looks around the room. Curtains embroidered with forest flora blow in the breeze. The creamy stucco walls are rough and peaked like meringue, covered in small paintings, etchings, and shadow-boxed objects—a little plastic doll, a spool of red thread and thimble, a rusty military medal on a purple ribbon, a shiny brass bullet casing and a playing card, the ace of hearts; a baby's white sock, a red-capped mushroom, a pressed pansy, a diminutive silver spoon. Ordinary, sentimental objects that somehow in this context don't seem ordinary at all. This whole thing is both magical and surreal. Like the Brothers Grimm meets Theater of the Absurd.

What Iph needs now is fairy-tale logic. She is desperate for her mother. She tries to imagine her now, in her residency studio surrounded by redwoods. Iph suddenly wishes she could see the sky.

A CROW CAWS OUTSIDE the window. *They know things,* Mom always says. Iph heads to the back door she noticed earlier in the kitchen. Outside is a creek crisscrossed with bridges. The most delightful things! Little replicas of Portland's bridges across the Willamette. Iph is drawn to them—but which to cross? The familiar Hawthorne? The industrial beauty of the group, the Steel Bridge? Over the Burnside Bridge replica is a miniature of the famous Portland sign with its retro neon leaping stag. This seems like the most likely candidate until she walks toward the creek and sees it around a short bend: the St. John's Bridge, Portland's pale jade empress. Memories of summers past wash over her—the years they had the boat, before Dad started working so much. They would sail down the river from the Forest Lake boat club all the way to Cathedral Park, right under this bridge, Dad's favorite.

Iph crosses in a few steps and walks down a narrow path to the tallest tree she's seen outside California.

The redwood is as thick around as the linked arms of at least ten children playing ring-around-the-rosy and so tall she can't see the top. She approaches slowly and touches the bark. The comfort is instant, like a hug from someone who loves her. She wraps her arms around the tree. She falls to her knees. The ground is spongy and sweet-smelling, dotted with mushrooms. She digs like an animal until she's buried her hands to the wrists. She lies on her side, fetal in the womb of the forest. *Mom*, she thinks, sending her thoughts to the roots of this tree, imagining it sending out a tendril to its neighbor, on and on through the forested lands of the West Coast to the redwoods in Santa Cruz, a kids' cup-and-string telephone-style SOS. *We need you. Help us!*

She closes her eyes and maybe even sleeps. After a while, she rises and turns back to the cottage. Behind the kitchen is a garden, fenced against deer. Beyond it, she sees large dark shapes moving in the trees. The wild animals who have cared for her brother. Her brother, asleep, his body changing in a way Mom's puberty talks and embarrassing illustrated books would never have anticipated.

Iph returns to her window seat. The grilled cheese still looks as if it came out of the pan and is almost too hot to touch. She eats the strawberries first. She'll save the carrots to munch as she reads. Eating and reading at the same time is a primary pleasure of hers, the ultimate comfort.

She looks down at the note, which she must have pulled from the typewriter because here it is, tucked inside *Artemis's Arrow: Performance Practice and the Reclamation of Wildness*.

Bibliomancy? Well, she'll try it. She opens to a page: *Instinct is the primary tool of the artist*.

She takes up the next book, *Ritual for the Modern Witch*, and opens to: *The drum is ritual's heartbeat*.

She sips and reads and makes her notes on every book in the stack. There is a rhythm to her work, like creating a collage. An idea is forming, a plan where none seemed possible.

10

ONLY THE
VOICE OF A STAG

O rr's body is a castle with stained glass windows for eyes and jeweled caverns for intestines. His toes are secret coves at the edge of a warm blue sea.

Red-haired girls in yellow dresses dance on the sand, none of them Plum. They laugh and whisper and run away, looking back now and then as if daring him to follow. He shadows them to the entrance of a cave that is barnacled and covered with slime. A briny wind from deep inside the rock formation blows his hair behind him like the robe of a king. It is long again, longer than ever, all the way down to his waist. His walk slows, as befits his royalty, understanding the paradox of simultaneously walking into and being the stone castle, the cliff, the beach, the girls, even the sea.

The cave narrows for a long, dark stretch, then opens wide. He is not inside his own body now, but the body of a whale. A whale inside a book about a puppet inside a dream, like a Jungian Matryoshka doll.

The puppet maker's chair is empty and on the little table sit three frogs. One is Plum. Orr knows this. One is Iph. One is Mom. He must kiss them to find out who is who, but he can't bring himself to touch their green-brown warty skin. They croak, singing. Their frog song pitches higher, and the frogs are transforming. They are birds now, *little brown sparrows. They fly away and leave Orr alone. He weeps for them, all of them. But he knows: in this moment, none of them are the right choice.*

He sits in the chair and waits as his hair grows longer. He is restless. He moves around the little room. There is a dresser with three drawers. The first has a mirror inside it. The second, a pair of scissors, and the third, a fat carrot with a feathery green top.

Orr looks into the mirror. A three-eyed deer boy with tall antlers looks back. He blinks. Three eyes blink back. He takes the scissors. He cuts his hair, first in big chunks, and then in careful snips so it is close to his head. He gathers the hair and places it in a large pot filled with water on the round-bellied woodstove he now notices. He makes a fire. The pot boils, and the air smells of roses and patchouli and rotting leaves. He remembers the carrot. It is still there. He eats it, savoring the greens on top. Looking in the mirror now, his face is covered in a fine down, and his third eye is closed, concealed by furring.

The hair soup on the stove is singing like a kettle, but it's not a kettle. It's the woman from the X-Ray, the blond sylph. She rises with the steam and turns into a cloud. The cloud dissolves the whale cave, and Orr is on an island. His mother approaches from the end of the beach. "I'm coming," she says, but never gets any closer. "Wait for me!"

Orr is gazing at his reflection in a puddle collected in the smooth bowl of a boulder and sees himself, a long-haired boy waiting for his mother. His face tightens and shrinks. The hair grows down his forehead to cover his eyes, his nose, his mouth. He is mummified by hair.

He is back in his bed at home. He dreams of Plum and music and sex, but the world is too loud. He steps out of the boy in the bed and observes him.

He is onstage after the show at the X-Ray, looking for Plum.

The stage is revolving, turning him away from the people in the club, pointing him toward the forest.

He is running through the city, keenly aware of every danger with his mouth and nose and ears. His eyes work even faster than his legs, so well it's like he's able to speed up time. He always knows what's coming.

He reaches the forest and doesn't stop running until he sees the stone building. There is the long-legged white dog. No, it's a woman. Long-legged, white-haired, tall, and slender in silver earrings and a green sweater. She whistles a low call Orr feels in the newly hardened soles of his feet.

The deer come, crowding around him.

11

THE SUBCONSCIOUS
AND THE ACTOR'S
CREATIVE STATE

ph sleeps and dreams in black and white. A movie musical starring her and George. They meet and the dialogue sparkles. They dance and are light as air. They kiss and the sky opens, drenching them with rain. They bicker and make up. They are in danger and save each other. The movie ends and Iph rewinds.

12

THE UNFAMILIAR VOICE

hen Orr wakes from his deep-dreaming slumber and stumbles into the main room of the cottage, Iph is asleep in the window seat. There is food on the table in the cheerful kitchen. Fruit and a salad of tomatoes and corn. Eating makes Orr want to move. As the sun sets into the blue hour, Orr hears them. Looking out the window, he sees them. Not the does who sheltered him the night before, but bucks with budding antlers and strong musks.

Orr itches to go outside, but memory stops him—playground children promising joy that always turned to cruelty or confusion. He closes the curtains. Closes his eyes.

A melody sounds from somewhere in the cottage. It is coming from the tree-arched entryway. From the front door? Then he sees that its source is the doorknob, shaped like a hare's head, with tall ears and a slender snout. The brass animal's mouth is open, and it is singing. The song is familiar. It takes Orr a while to figure out how he knows it. Finally, he connects the sweet, high voice of the surreal brass hare with the buzz-saw punk-rock anthem Iph blasted last year after she divorced her awful friends. She played it so loud and so often it drove the whole family crazy:

I will resist with all my breath
I will resist this psychic death

He didn't understand it back then. It sounded like noise. Now he gets it, and it gives him courage. He takes off the striped leggings that belonged to Plum and leaves them on the floor. He walks naked into the meadow. The ground is still warm underfoot from the just-set sun. The grass is sweet, with a lemon and ginger sharpness. Orr bends, pulls a blade from the ground. Puts it on his tongue. It tastes the way it smells. Better, even.

The largest buck snorts. Taps the ground with a gleaming hoof. The tails of the three others twitch. Their scent is heady and terrifying. The night glows so blue it blues Orr's skin. Or is it hair—hair or fur? The air is cool. The moon is rising huge and gold above the tree line. He looks down. His skin is brown. Skin or fur? He moves forward. Lowers his head and settles his shoulders into a posture of respect.

The lesser bucks snort as well. One dances. Orr's heels ache to dance back. He does it, a little three-step gambol. The largest buck meets his eyes, twitches his nose, and runs. Orr chases, muscles straining, body singing, foot to hoof to bone to antler into the dark wood.

13

THE
SUPERTASK

Iph is on her knees on the porch of the cottage, Orr's striped leggings in her hands. She doesn't have to search the house to know that he has left to run with the deer. She buries her face in the gross leggings and lets loose. And suddenly, someone is nosing under her elbow. Someone is squirming into her lap. A wet nose pushes her hands away and a soft little tongue licks up her tears.

By some miracle, here is Scout. And George, who says nothing, just holds her, which is the exact right thing. Scout barks, and Iph looks up to see Lorna and Cait and Josh and Plum and the members of the Furies carrying their instruments through the gate.

"How?" Iph is laughing. The relief of them. The reality of them! If she is delusional, it's a shared hallucination. Introductions are made. Then explanations.

"It was this one," Jane says, scooping up Scout. "She started howling like a little werewolf."

"She totally did," George says. "Good thing we don't have to worry about being quiet anymore."

"She made us all get off our asses and get in the car," Josh says. "We figured she wanted to come find you."

"Dude," Allison says. "What is this place? We were on the

path, and then it was like the path was never there. I didn't even have any of that tea last night."

"Well, it's a fairy-tale cottage in an enchanted wood," Plum says. "I mean, obviously."

Everyone laughs at that and goes inside, exclaiming over the cottage. Plum hangs back, picks up the leggings.

"He was here?"

"Here and gone," Iph says. "He slept for a long time. I meant to watch him, but I fell asleep myself."

"Did you, like, touch the antlers?" Plum looks exhausted.

"They're really there," Iph says. "I mean, if you're losing it, I am, too."

"What should we do?"

"I have an idea, but he needs to come back first."

Plum nods. "I'm assuming there's an awesome bathroom in there?"

Iph laughs. "If you don't come out in an hour, I'll assume you decided to move in."

"I'm just going to pee," Plum says, oddly forthright. "I brought my tarot cards. I think I'd better take a look."

Iph sits still again, like maybe if she doesn't move Orr will come back.

Scout sidles into her lap, a warm dose of chamomile tea in dog form, nosing her and meeting her eyes. There is so much awareness there. Iph's been too busy mooning over George to notice.

George comes out of the house with a glass of water for each of them and a little bowl for Scout. They drink.

"I missed you," George says.

"I missed you, too." Iph runs her hand over the shaved part of George's head, which is nearly as soft as the velvet around Orr's antlers.

Orr's antlers.

Scout makes a playful little growl-bark and picks up the leggings in her mouth. She shakes them and drops them at Iph's feet. Iph gets it. "I don't want you going out there alone, girl."

George offers Iph a hand. So warm. Scout presses next to her on the other side. The pair of them make her strong enough to think this through. "She wants to go get him," Iph says.

"If anyone here can bring him back, it's probably her."

"Aren't you worried?"

George crouches down to look Scout in the eyes. "Are you sure?"

Scout whines, spins in a circle, and sits. Waiting for George's word.

George puts the leggings under Scout's nose once more. "This is him."

Scout inhales and sits again.

"Okay!" George says.

Before the word is out of George's mouth, Scout shoots out of the cottage and into the trees.

14

THE DRAMA OF LIFE

As the night deepens, things happen on their own in the cottage. Lamps light. Windows open to let in the cool evening air. Fairy lights turn on in the garden. Plum discovers the laden table first.

"Everyone come out here!" she calls.

Mika looks up from a conversation with Lorna. Holds out her hand to help Lorna off the deep-cushioned sofa in the corner. Iph shoots a look at George and gets a raised eyebrow back. Jane and Allison are swearing their appreciation at the wooden table in the garden piled with food.

"Holy shit!"

"Hell yes!"

There are kebabs of grilled vegetables and tofu, shiny with olive oil and green with fresh rosemary. There is a salad of spinach, strawberries, and feta cheese. There is *elote*—corn on the cob Mexican-style, grilled with butter and chile and squash blossom enchiladas. There is seashell pasta, bright with moss-green pesto and studded with forest mushrooms and tiny yellow flowers. There is a bowl of whipped cream, a platter of blackberries, and five kinds of pie.

They sit and eat. Plum is next to Iph.

"I kind of wondered why he didn't talk much about you. I figured it was either because you guys were super close or not close at all."

A little bit of guilt drains away. Iph is always surprised how much she has stored in her well. The Furies' song plays in her head. *Don't say sorry. Don't be sorry.* She's trying.

"He's perfectly fine out there, you know," Plum says.

"Trust her." Jane has a kebab in one hand and *elote* in the other. She looks like Caesar, still dressed in her red toga from the show. "She's hella uncanny. Her mama was a fortune teller."

"It's true." Mika nods. Mika is also wearing the toga, but under the Trail Blazers hoodie Iph and George got from the Heathman's lost and found. It goes past her knees.

Iph likes Mika. She's a curious combination of reserved and a little shy without seeming insecure. And Iph isn't the only one who's curious. Lorna is across from Mika looking almost better after being up all night than she did in line for the show. She lowers her lashes at Mika, whose eyes widen.

"Are we talking séances? Should I be scared?" Cait asks. Iph notes her seating choice—right next to Mika. She's subtler than Lorna but possibly even more devastating. Her barely-there smile has everyone smiling back.

"Maybe a little," Mika says. "But I'm pretty sure Plum uses her powers only for good."

"How about you?" Lorna says, meeting and holding Mika's gaze. "Do you use your powers for good?"

Mika is bright red. She touches her cheeks. "It's the wine," she says, raising her glass to take another gulp.

"Did your mom have one of those Psychic Reading shops you see around?" Josh asks. He has been silent since they sat down to eat, already on seconds. He looks skinnier than he did a week ago. Iph wonders—where does he sleep? "My mom used to go to one when we lived in Oakland—" He stops. Iph can't tell if it's the mom or the psychic Josh doesn't want to talk about.

"No shop. My mom was a therapist," Plum says. "But also a great tarot reader. My deck used to be hers."

"Used to be?" Iph catches her eye. Plum is so pretty, with those gorgeous freckles and fox-fur brows. Orr has excellent taste—in girls, of all things! Iph's guess had been boys for her brother, but maybe she was projecting her own queerness onto him. Or maybe he likes boys, too.

"Cancer," Plum says. "Don't be sad, Janey." She reaches across the table for Jane's hand. "I've been feeling her lately, you know? She wants us to move on."

Jane wipes her eyes with the backs of her hands and presses her palms onto them, rose tattoos where her eyes were.

"Your eyes just turned into roses," Iph says. Maybe this place will change them all.

"How bad did they hurt when you got them?" George asks.

"A lot," Jane says. "But they're my favorites."

"So, Iph," Allison says, "what's going on? It seems like nothing has been the same since Orr found us that day. What's the story with your family?"

Iph tells the group their story: Mom and Dad meeting at the party, falling in love. Writing letters for two years while Dad finished college and secretly started building Mom their house. How the two of them shared a tiny trailer in the meadow until the house was finished, and how they got married under the hawthorn tree where Orr's treehouse is now, just the two of them and a pagan priestess in a white robe and motorcycle boots. How things got hard. How they went wrong.

"It sounds like you all really love each other," Plum says.

Iph sighs. "Love isn't the problem."

They're silent now, just eating and drinking and listening to the crickets.

Finally, Cait says, "Um, I keep wanting to ask this. If you guys knew someone." She looks at Mika, Allison, and Jane. "My sister was in a band a few years ago. In Olympia. The Athenas? Have you ever heard of them?"

Jane stands up, knocking a fork off the table. "Cait, is your sister Britta?"

"Yeah," Cait says, barely audible.

Jane sits. "I should have seen it the second I met you. You look just like her. I was in her band when they were the Grizzlies. Right before I moved back to Portland." To Plum, Jane says, "That was the friend who died right after your mom."

"That was a horrible year." Cait puts her fork down.

"I knew Britta," Mika says. "Just a little. She dated my roommate for a while when I lived in Seattle. I played at her memorial show."

"She was a kickass bass player," Allison says. "I was such a fan. Dude, you do look just like her."

"It's wild that you all knew her," Iph says.

Jane nods. "That's the music scene. Especially coming out of Olympia."

"Not many girls," Mika says. "We tend to know each other."

Lorna reaches across a plate of berries to touch Mika's hand. Josh puts an arm around Cait. George raises a wineglass. "To our beloved dead."

"To your nana," Mika says in the after-toast quiet. "I loved being at Taurus Trucking last night. It's so cool that she came back after internment and did something so badass. My family was first generation, all in Hood River. Half of them were sent to a camp in Idaho and half to California. Those two parts of the family don't really know each other now." Mika takes a long drink of water. "They had a fruit market, but it was taken from them. They never came back here."

"To Nana," Iph says. "And Mika's family."

The ruby liquid in their glasses is somewhere between wine and ambrosia, whatever that's supposed to taste like. It's cool going down Iph's throat but warm in her belly.

"To Britta," Josh says.

"And my mom," says Plum.

They raise their glasses and drink again.

There is a silence filled with the whispers of the dead, other losses too sore in their hearts to mention. Parts of themselves they buried long ago.

"To the ghosts in all of us," Iph says.

All glasses are raised.

They return to the food. The talk dissolves into twos and threes. People drift from the table.

"Plum," Iph says, "can we consult your tarot cards? Like, maybe just a three-card reading? I have an idea, but I need some sort of structure to start."

"Structure. Huh," Plum says. "That's a nice way of thinking about the tarot. Do you read?"

"My mom does," Iph says. "She uses it like this—that's what made me think of it. She's a choreographer and sometimes when she's stuck, she'll draw some cards to get her going again."

"My dad used to do that," Plum says. "When he played music. He has this weird deck from the seventies called *Oblique Strategies* by this musician guy—what's his name?"

"Brian Eno," Jane calls from across the room.

"Yes," Plum says. "Eno. I'll go get my backpack. I left it someplace around here."

To Josh and Cait and George, who are clustered around a firepit that is now burning brightly inside a circle of Adirondack chairs, Iph says, "Do you guys have any training in improv?"

"Yes!" Josh says.

"Yes, *and*." Cait laughs.

"Good answer," Iph says. "Sit tight. Plum and I have some witching to do."

15

BITS & TASKS

Indoors, the cottage flickers with candlelight. The workroom is rearranged with the tables pushed up against the walls, leaving an empty space in the center of the room. A large round carpet takes up most of the space with its forest pattern of red-capped mushrooms and stylized banana slugs on a background of deep green and pale gold. Iph and Plum sit in the center. Plum unties the moth's-wing silk scarf wrapped around her cards. These, too, are round, their colors and card backs echoing the carpet, the forest, the room's gold glow. Plum shuffles and hands the deck to Iph.

Iph grounds herself the way Mom taught her—rooting her energy down past the carpet, past the foundation of this old house and the worm-rich soil beneath it, deep down to the roots of the surrounding trees. *Orr*, she thinks. *What does he need?* She holds the deck. It feels good in her hands. She shuffles and chooses— once, twice, three times.

Plum turns over the first card. Death. "So," she says. "The way I read them, the cards tell a story. So Death is like the 'once upon a time' of the reading."

Iph must have a look on her face that betrays what's happening in her stomach, because Plum grabs her hand. "I know it's not literal," Iph says, squeezing back.

"It's about transformation." Plum's voice is high and sweet. It's an odd combination, this woman-level wisdom and forthright girlishness. "The snake in the foreground—that's about change and rebirth. The tree, too. Birches also shed their skin. The skeleton on the card—it's what we need to mourn to really change. Sometimes you have to let stuff go to make room for something new."

Orr *does* need to release something. And according to the books Iph just read, the only way to stop him from transforming so radically is to find the fork in his path that allows another choice.

Plum turns over the next card. "The Four of Discs," she says.

"Does that look a little like the inside of this house to you?" Iph squints to get a better look at the card. There's a woman in a white robe inside a cozy room with a fire and open beams along the roof. Art on the walls. She is holding on to the door—to open or close it, it's hard to tell which.

"It does!" Plum says. "It's about being in a safe place where you can decide something. We're at a pause point—a time where we can either open the door to something new or close it against something unwanted."

"What about the third card?"

"Another four—interesting. The fours are about the completion of a cycle. In the *I Ching*, the fourth hexagram is called Youthful Folly. In this deck they're having some sort of party. Plus, it's the Wands—power, energy, will, sex. To me, this says Rite of Passage. It says ritual. So yeah."

"That's good, right? It feels like we're on the right track. We need to do some sort of ritual, some rite to help him." There is a word for this from one of the books—a word that is a combination of ingesting and incorporating. Like a snake eating its own tail. Iph flashes on Velma's book of poetry, the snake image on the front. The title—*Ouroboros*. Integrate. That's it!

"He needs to integrate it—whatever energy he has right now that's manifesting as a deer. Then it can become a part of him without taking over. Does that sound right to you?"

Plum pauses and wrinkles her nose. Iph likes her more and more by the second. After a lifetime living alone with Orr on the island of misfit toys, it's still a shock that they're suddenly out here in the world, their lives webbing with others' lives, making the kind of friendships that vine and flower and last.

"I mean, yes," Plum says. "Integrate sounds right. But Iph—he needs our help to choose what's right for *him*. I mean, have you asked him what he wants? I see this ritual as more of a way to help him decide. Like, this could take him over before he realizes it's happening—and that's scary. He's very impulsive, you know."

Iph does know. She wraps her arms around the ache of it. *What if he doesn't come back?* It's what they're both thinking.

They sit, quiet, for several minutes as the fire crackles.

Plum sighs. "How long ago did Scout leave?"

Iph shakes her head. "Time is weird here. When did you arrive?"

"We left Taurus Trucking at around six, and it only takes about twenty minutes from there to the trailhead. But then we walked forever until Scout found the right trail. It's so dark now. It must be at least after ten." Plum yawns. "Sorry," she says, covering her mouth. "We were up all night." She folds the silk scarf back around her tarot cards. "Deer are crepuscular. Active mostly at dusk and dawn. I have a feeling he'll be back by sunrise. Unless Scout can get him." She gets up and stretches and heads to the window seat. "I'm gonna rest for a few minutes."

GEORGE AND JOSH AND Lorna and Cait and the Furies wander in a few at a time, talking softly. A delicious scent wafts from the kitchen. George goes in and comes back carrying a tray with nine cups of hot cocoa and a plate of fresh-baked almond cookies.

"I'm never leaving this place," Jane says. "Just so you guys know."

"This is the best cocoa I've ever had," Cait says.

"It's Mexican hot chocolate," Iph says. "With cinnamon. The kind my mom makes."

"Not mine," Josh says. "Mine is totally Swiss Miss from the packet with the little freeze-dried marshmallows—my all-time trailer park favorite."

"Mine's a ringer for the kind they make at Stumptown on Belmont," Mika says.

Jane's and Allison's are extra thick with a mint leaf on top—just like at brunch at the Cuban place in Northeast.

The fire crackles as they sip and talk a little, trailing off. Mika and Lorna are on the sofa, curled up together under a blanket. Jane and Allison and Josh and Cait have wandered into the bedrooms. Iph gets an extra blanket and throw pillows from the sofa and lies next to George, who is crashed out in front of the fire. She might rest her eyes, too. Just for a minute.

16

THE LITTLE THEATER

CAIT IS COVERED IN *trash. It sticks to her hair in slimy clumps. To her face. To her dress, which is pink as a piglet. Rotting vegetables and old Kleenex and clumps of dirt stick to her skin. And Cait is happy about it. She finds a pit of mud and rolls in it. She then rolls on the newly mowed lawn of her parents' country club. Dry grass sticks to the entire mess like she's one of those candies coated in chopped nuts. People—her parents, their colleagues from the law firm, her next-door neighbors, her orthodontist and pediatrician—are picnicking on the golf course. She stomps over their blankets to reach all eighteen holes. Inside each plastic cup, wedged into the sod, is a small animal. These she rescues and carries away in a basket. The birds and mice and chipmunks and frogs and little garter snakes all sit prettily together, taking great care not to upset one another with any sudden movement.*

Now she is at the river. She sets the basket down. She sits in the mud at the river's edge, waiting. A person approaches. Britta. She holds out a hand. Together, they walk into the river. When the water reaches their shoulders, Britta dissolves but is still present. Cait's hair grows until it brushes her ankles. She begins to sing.

JOSH IS ON HIS *knees, puking off a bridge. Luminescent fish flop from his mouth into the bay far below, one after the other. He sees them glowing in the black water as they swim toward the open sea. His body is bruised and bloody. He is finished with this life of cold sidewalks and winter shelters, sleeping with his shoes under his head so no one will steal them. Finished with the men in the cars and alleys and the pain in his jaw and the way his hair never ever feels clean. His face is swollen from being hit. His fists are hot from hitting back. He is strong for how skinny he is, for how hungry he is. He stands. The bridge is the color of Cait's nails—the orange of coral reefs, not golden. When did he hitchhike all the way back home? He is climbing the supports like the bridge is a ship and he is a sailor. The breeze throws his scent back at him, and he gags again. His wounds are already rotting.*

Across the bay is the redwood forest. All he has to do is fall into the water and swim.

He hears singing in the bay below, down near Angel Island. The words are in a language he doesn't understand. He opens his own mouth and drinks in the sound. He exhales small green birds. His wounds begin to heal. His stomach feels full of wholesome food. His blood is clean, his skin is clear, his organs are unbruised. He stretches his arms out into the mist, and his hair whips behind him. He smells roses. He smells the sea. He climbs to edge of the support beam and leaps—not down, but up. Josh is flying. He reels and rolls and swoops and floats. Finally, he dives joyfully into the blue-black water.

JANE, MIKA, AND ALLISON *are tending the garden in the back of Penelope. They are singing together. The sun shines down.*

"What are you doing?" *Red says from outside the fence.*

"We're going on tour," *Mika says.* "We need to have enough food."

"We got a record deal," *Allison says.* "We need to get these tomatoes mulched."

"We're getting married," *Jane says, smoothing the wedding dress down over her hips with her dirty hands.* "We need wheat and berries for wedding cake."

Red shakes the gate.

The Furies laugh and sing louder.

Allison gets the hose and sprays Red until he disappears.

Jane twirls in her wedding dress, tattoo sleeves dark against the stark white skirt. She spins and spins. Mika and Allison join her. They twirl until the garden tilts and they all fall down onto the warm tilled earth.

LORNA HAS NEVER DANCED this well, every move more perfect than the last. All the dancers, the bouncers, the bartender, and every man in the audience are rapt. A customer approaches the rack and Lorna's breath catches. A tiger dressed in a three-piece suit places a hundred-dollar bill on the stage.

Lorna is lying on hot rocks near a gentle sea in a state of perfect pleasure. The enormous sandpaper tongue slides slowly down her spine, down each leg all the way to the soles of her feet. She turns her face to see him—the tiger, no suit, but a patch over one eye, like a pirate. "Do you want to wear this?" the tiger asks. "To cover your wound?"

Lorna touches her face and there is . . . nothing. Nothing where her eye should be! Nothing! She screams, but no sound comes out of her mouth.

She's walking up the front steps to her dead grandma's house in Tacoma, wearing the good-luck gold shoes she got at Shiny Dancer, and they refuse to be quiet. "Go on!" they dare her. "Go on!"

"Screw you," Lorna hisses. But she keeps on going, one step at a time.

She feels for the key under the ceramic pig with the chipped snout and real rubber rain boots that once belonged to a doll of Lorna's named Bitty. The pig never got a name. Just Pig.

"If she's dead, she's dead," Lorna tells the shoes, unlocking the door.

The house smells like cat piss and garbage. Home sweet home.

The TV is on upstairs, so you know the power bill was paid and someone was once alive enough to turn the damn thing on. Lorna thinks about hiding the shoes. She knows her mother will try to take them. But when she faces the staircase with its moldy brown carpet, she decides to keep her shoes on and take her chances.

Mom is in bed.

Georgie always thought Lorna was sending letters to an old boyfriend in Tacoma, but this is infinitely worse.

This lady.
Her mom.
A boyfriend would be easier to leave.
Even Georgie, the best kisser in Portland, was easier to leave.
"Hey," Lorna says from the doorway.
Mom barely looks up. "Well, I'll be damned," she says like she's saying hi back. "How many days, Lorna? How many days has it been?"
"I don't know, Mama," Lorna says. "Why don't you tell me?"

PLUM IS IN A *Dublin pub, pregnant with her own grandmother. She drinks a glass of black beer and follows a familiar green coat out the door and around the back of the building. She is kissing a redheaded man for all she's worth. This man is not her husband.*

Plum is in labor in her bathtub in Portland. Her belly ripples as she bears down. It's early in the morning, and no one is awake. If she calls for her father, he won't come. Since her mother died, he needs whiskey to sleep. She crouches now, hands on either side of the tub, and pushes. A large, silver-scaled fish slides out of her body and into the bathwater. It bumps its blunt head against her leg—a greeting and a farewell—and narrows its body to swim down the drain.

GEORGE IS ON THE *back steps of Taurus Trucking with Nana. This is a lucid dream, George knows, downshifting time until it purrs along slow as a summer afternoon. George lifts Nana's beloved hand and kisses it. Nana is in workday mode with unpolished nails, a little grease in her cuticles. George squeezes, and Nana squeezes back. She is very strong.*

George holds close this stolen moment between the worlds, rolling in the warmth of Nana, the fit of George's head against her shoulder; the orange-sherbet-menthol-cigarette-green-tea scent of her. The way Nana's pointy chin presses into George's freshly buzzed scalp. They sit, content, grandmother and grandchild. Every detail gleams with precision, and George doesn't know if this is a visit to Nana's version of heaven or a relived moment from the past or random neurons sparking into a beautiful dream.

"Georgie," Nana says.

"Nana," George says back.

They are silent. Cars pass now and then. Chickadees sing their names from the pine tree in the corner of the parking lot, and crows hop around the asphalt, pecking for the bread Nana feeds them every morning. A baby cries and children laugh. The wind rustles the neighborhood trees.

17

THE
CONSERVATORY

*I*ph is backstage with a team of dressers. She holds her hands up and a garment slips over her head, covering her everywhere. A second skin.

She looks in the mirror, and she is her mother. She isn't Gracia, the girl her mom was on her birth certificate and during the childhood she won't talk about with anyone. She isn't Gracie, the straight-A high school sophomore who dropped out and ran away. She's not Callie, either—the name she says she got from her best friend, a boy she met when she first arrived in New York from California. She is Grace, the girl who came to New York alone at fifteen.

The curtain rises. Lights fade up on a playground.

Grace pulls her sweater tight, sliding lower against the wall. Up high in the little room made by the walls at the top of the slide, she is invisible from below. She knows because she propped her sweater up to her seated height earlier, slid down to the bottom of the twisty slide, and checked every angle.

She curls up and closes her eyes. She's almost asleep when she hears it: whistling. Someone's on the swings. Grace grins. It's a perfect rendition of the doot-do-doots in "Walk on The Wild Side." He whistles the entire song, then moves on to "The Low Spark of High Heeled Boys." She sits up and peeks over the edge of her playground fortress.

Just as she thought—it's the cute skinny blond boy she's been seeing around. No, Grace thinks, skinny is too generous a word. That boy is a swing-set calavero. *A skeleton whistling as he sways back and forth, a bottle dangling loosely from one bony hand.*

"I see you," the boy drawls. He sounds a little like the girl from Kentucky Grace met on the bus. "Saw you go up there. Thought I'd try a Pied Piper approach to get you out." He leaps off the swing, lands solid, and holds up the bottle. "Seems like a shame to drink it alone." His cowboy voice is soft, but it carries.

"You spent actual money on that? Instead of food and cigarettes?" Grace tries not to think about how empty she is now or the Automat cheese sandwich she ate yesterday morning or how she got the money for it. The taste of that is still bitter in her mouth.

"Girl, who says I spent money?" He pulls a salami and a loaf of bread from someplace in his trench coat and walks over to an empty park bench. The other person in the park is an old woman snoring under a layer of newspaper. He motions for Grace to sit. "I'll have you know, though—I am officially employed as of today. That's why we're celebrating."

"Where?"

"Strip joint around the corner. I'm the bouncer, ma'am."

"Who do they think you're gonna bounce? A bunch of rowdy kindergarteners?"

"I'm not questioning their judgment. I'm happy for the cash. Tomorrow night, it's gonna be a hotel room for your boy here. And a shower down the hall."

Grace sighs. She'll probably be in a room tomorrow night, too—she's getting to the point where she's going to have to try and pick someone up. Her hair is stringy. And her period is due any day—for that, she's going to need money for supplies.

"You could dance over there, I bet. You're pretty enough, that's for sure."

"No ID," Grace says.

"You think they're checking? Anyway, that's my job now. Can you dance?"

"That's what I came here to do," she says. She stands up on the bench

286 MICHELLE RUIZ KEIL

and does her prettiest ballet curtsy, then plops down beside him. The skeleton boy hands her a crusty piece of bread stuffed with salami. She picks up the sandwich and raises it in a toast. They clink and wolf down the food and trade gulps from the stolen bottle of Chianti.

"I'm as full as a queen," she says.

"You think you're the queen here?"

"Oh, you're a queen, all right. The queen of thieves!" Grace holds the bottle up in salute.

"I've been called worse. But my mom calls me Rob."

She holds out her hand. "I'm Grace."

"Grace? That sounds like somebody's great-aunt. Where are you from?"

"California," Grace says, chin out, daring him to ask her what she is. Although that doesn't happen much here in the city. Most people assume she's Puerto Rican.

"Hmmm," he says. "That's more like it. That's what I'm gonna call you from now on, so get used to it."

"Get used to what?" Grace laughs.

"Your name. California. Callie for short."

"If you call me Callie, I'm calling you Queen Rob."

"Oh, I insist," Rob says. He gets up and runs to the slide like they're kids at recess.

She runs after him, slides down . . .

. . . and down . . .

IPH IS IN A windowless room. There is a baby on the floor—her mother. Tiny. Maybe under a year. We are born with all our eggs, Iph thinks. The eggs that will become her and Orr are here, dormant for now, inside this brown dark-haired baby in a dirty onesie and saggy diaper. Little gold hoops hang from her ears. She's playing with something on the floor. Behind her is a door. There are noises she doesn't like. A woman, crying. Gracia's mother? Iph's abuela? The dream pans closer, zeroes in on baby Gracia's toy. A severed finger! With a long, yellowed nail and a flaking gold-plated ring, the detached end caked with dried blood. Iph screams as Gracia lifts it toward her mouth.

Iph takes the finger and puts it in the sink. Turns on the water, then flicks on the garbage disposal. Gracia cries for the finger, her only toy. Iph pats her pockets. She's wearing Nana's overalls. She pulls out a stick of eyeliner from one. Gracia reaches for the red pencil, pops it in her mouth. "No," says Iph, taking it away. Gracia screams. Iph's head is pounding. She reaches in her right pocket and pulls out a red-capped mushroom. This she eats herself to make sure the baby doesn't get it. "It's poison for you," she tells her nine-month-old mother.

Gracia reaches out her arms to be held. Iph picks her up, holds her close. The heaviness of the baby head on her shoulder is exhausting. She shifts her to a hip. A little hand reaches into the bib pocket of the overalls and pulls out a ring of golden keys. "Where there's a key, there must be a lock," Iph says. She searches the small room, but it is bare. She turns to the door, which has a cheap dented doorknob with no visible lock of any kind. She sets the baby down to search. As she runs her hands over every inch of the door, minuscule splinters penetrate her skin. Her palms burn. The pads of her fingers begin to bleed. The baby whimpers, then howls. Iph sits on the floor next to her, defeated. Then she sees it. There! On Gracia's pink tongue! A small golden keyhole! A door opens from the cave of her baby mouth, and water pours out. The room fills, faster and faster. Iph stretches Gracia high in the air, away from the water that pours from her eyes and ears, as well as her mouth. Soon, they are both engulfed.

Iph searches the water, *frantic. Gracia is gone. She vomits, and out come the eels, brown and fanged and muscular. They crowd up into her throat, stampeding toward freedom. She gags until she is empty. Numb. She swims toward a light. A boy a little older than Orr is drifting here, long hair and love beads swaying like underwater flora. Iph touches his face. Dad's face! Dad?*

The boy isn't breathing. He is so heavy. The current pulls him away. Iph tries to follow, but the tide takes her to land.

Dad is there on his knees in the sand. His stomach heaves, but there is nothing left inside him. He doesn't see Iph. Doesn't feel her embrace. He is sobbing. The boy in the sea is his brother. His brother who died, who killed himself by jumping off a bridge.

Iph is lucid now and knows what to do. She reaches her hand into Dad's chest. She pulls out his heart and rinses it in the sea. Lifts it to the sun until it is warm as blood. Then she places it back in his chest, holding her hand over the wound to close it.

18

EACH LACE
FROND OF HORN

*H*ome, she said. *Follow me!*

There was a moment in the woods when Orr truly thought the little dog meant to lead him home to Forest Lake. She'd found him after a run with the bucks, his body in an awkward state of almost-transformation, exhausted and alone. At the sight of the humble little brindled animal, a sweet and ordinary creature from the old world, he wanted nothing more than his room at home, with its line of flower-remedy tinctures on his neat bedside table and the sound of his parents laughing while they did the dishes together, listening to Mom's classic rock or Dad's cheesy jazz. Iph would be running the bath in the next room. He'd fall asleep without even the Walkman. He would wake up in his old life.

He wept then. It was the tears that called back his human form, his shape of sorrow. The dog had tenderly washed his face, licking at the spots of blood where the velvet had frayed after his dangerous frolic with the bucks. After a time, he'd become more oriented.

Now, approaching the familiar clearing, he sees that he is still in some enchanted corner of Forest Park. This dog must be Scout, the one who belongs to Iph's friend George—the person who made his sister blush and look so happy. He sits for a moment, and Scout waits at his side. His head is heavy. The antlers have grown. Soon, the velvet will drop from them, leaving the blood-stained bone exposed until the sun blanches it.

This time, the change was exultant and pitiless. Mulder would have loved it. "The Deer Boy"—a case for *The X-Files* if ever there was one.

They are in the clearing now.

Home is where your pack sleeps, Scout says without moving. Then she runs, as tired and paw-sore as she must be, body vibrating with joy at the prospect of reunion.

Orr follows her slowly into the cottage. Already its magic is ordinary, incorporated. Maybe because his own body has already shown him the magic of the impossible world. *I wonder*, he thinks, *did I cross over somewhere, or were things always this way and I didn't notice?*

Orr opens the arched door and stands at the flowery threshold. It's like looking into an enchanted snow globe. He feels large and distant but still deeply drawn to the action in the warm golden realm inside.

Inside, Scout is in George's arms.

Inside, Iph is offering George a small red pot of some sort of ointment. "Poor little paws," he hears Iph say.

Inside, Plum is sleeping. He knows by her smell. He finds Jane and Allison the same way. Mika is asleep on the sofa in the corner, huddled next to a girl who was in the audience at the show.

This is a place for him.

He knows. Most of him knows.

Home is where your people are.

But it feels wrong to enter.

"Orr!" Iph sees him. Grabs a blanket and rushes to put it around his shoulders. Opens her arms. He lets her hug him, because this he knows: his sister will always be able to show him the way home.

She leads him in, and he collapses on the carpet. "I'm so tired."

"I bet." Iph sits beside him. "Do you need food? A glass of water?"

He looks up at her. "I'm fine. I ate and drank with the bucks."

He watches her take that in. All the improv training has made her mind so flexible. Or no—she was always this way. Empathetic and curious. Her natural gift.

"I have an idea," she says. "First, I have to ask—do you want to stop this?"

Want. Orr hasn't considered it in the context of a decision. Want is what calls him to run alongside the herd. But tonight, after a while, even that want faded and changed. There was a time in a deep part of the forest where he made a bed of pine needles and rested alone. He dreamed the seasons changing—a thickening coat, bright leaves, the ground littered with apples. A secret place protected from rain and snow. The quickening spring. And . . . rest. A break from the world of talk and expectations.

"I don't know," he says. "It's lonely there. They let me stay with them. They're curious. But they know I'm different. Even if I change completely, I think they'll know. But Iph"—he takes her hand—"something about it also feels right."

"Maybe my plan can help you decide," Iph says. "That's what Plum thinks."

"Yes," Plum says. She has wandered over, rubbing sleep from her eyes. "Hey," she says to Orr. "How are you?"

"I don't know," Orr says. He is naked under the blanket, which would have embarrassed him once.

Plum settles cross-legged next to them as if this were a normal night and they're all getting ready to play a hand of Uno. Orr smiles. *Uno.* It's good he can still remember these things.

"I want to try a ritual," Iph says. "A kind of . . . psychodrama. It's a thing from ancient Greece—they would act out people's dreams as a type of medicine. I wonder if somewhere along the way, your narrative split. Like a whole part of you separated and went into this . . . other reality? Does that make sense?"

"I was thinking that." Orr nods. He almost topples backward, unbraced for the new weight there. He holds his ears to steady himself. They are softer than usual, beginning to fur. He pulls his hands away and sits on them.

"They must be so heavy," Iph says.

"But also . . . so beautiful," Plum says. Why is she blushing?

Iph laughs. "Oh my god, Plum, do you think my brother's hot as a deer?"

Plum hides her face in her hands. Scout dances over to push her head under Plum's fingers so she can lick her face. "You are so precious," Plum tells Scout in a way that makes Orr a little jealous.

"We need to get ahold of ourselves, people." It's Dad's voice again. Dad's phrase. Orr sits up straighter, stretches. His neck is sinewy in response to the new weight of his head. He has to forget about what's there, or the panic will keep whipping his insides like a black-ops helicopter landing in his stomach. What would Mulder do? Or no, forget Mulder—he needs to channel the smart one. What would Scully do? Or, wait! He smiles. In this scenario, Iph is Scully.

"What?" Iph says.

"You." Orr's smile widens. He feels almost normal.

"No, you!" Iph says.

"You guys are adorable." Plum's voice gets thin at the end.

"Why are you sad?" Orr wants to touch her hand but is suddenly very aware of how naked he is under the blanket.

"Why are you psychic?" Plum sticks her tongue out.

"Now who's adorable?" Iph says.

"Tell us the plan, Agent." Orr sits up very straight.

"That's what it was. I know I'm not Mulder here, so that means I'm the hot one!"

"The hot *smart* one," Orr says. "Yes. Tell me!"

"Fine, but go get dressed," Iph says. "I have a feeling there will be clothes for you in the room where you were sleeping."

19

THE TRANSITION TO EMBODIMENT

The Furies circle with their instruments on the periphery of the carpet—Jane's two guitars, one shiny new, the other battered and plastered with stickers. Allison holds her tambourine, and Mika places the percussion instruments and hand drums she's gathered from the shelves of the cottage.

With Jane, Iph goes to the garden. They snip rosemary, a large basketful. They snip roses, peonies, daisies, lavender, and bright, old-fashioned flowers whose name Iph doesn't know.

"Thank you," Iph says as she and Jane head back to the cottage. "For taking care of him."

"It's been my pleasure," Jane says. "Your mom and dad must really be something."

"Why do you say that?"

"Just . . . with you two. I see it."

"They're all right," Iph says. "Even my dumb dad." She wonders—when will it be time to call them?

Inside, Plum is giving Lorna a tarot reading. Mika and Allison and Cait help Jane and Iph line the edge of the carpet with the rosemary and flowers. Iph keeps back a few stems for the fire.

George and Orr are laughing about something. Scout is crashed on the hearth. *This place*, Iph thinks, trying to reach for what it is or represents, but her thoughts are slippery, and she finds herself staring at the bright coals in the fireplace instead.

"Um, Iph," Jane says.

Iph looks up to find that the round rug has transformed into a woodland stage with moss for carpet and real mushrooms dotting the soft green. There are a few stumps and a rough carved step for entrances and exits. Really, the perfect set for a Shakespearean romp. If only this were *Midsummer* or *As You Like It*. Iph can't forget—the magic that's making all this happen is also swallowing her brother bit by bit. She takes a deep breath and gets to work.

Plum pulls a card from her tarot deck—The Wheel of Fortune. Noting the circular image on the circular card and the circular stage, Iph places Lorna, Josh, Cait, and George in the cardinal directions. Plum sits in the center with her tarot cards in her lap. In middle school they learned about a classic dramatic structure called Freytag's Pyramid. Diagrammed on the board and described, even seventh graders saw the embarrassing parallels in the formula—inciting incident, a series of rising actions, a big climax, and then falling back to rest with the denouement. A few of the boys illustrated with a pencil and exaggerated panting. Iph was incensed. Was there nothing the patriarchy hadn't tried to wreck? She argued that this was only one way for a play to operate. The teacher told her she was wrong. She said he was a misogynist and proposed a vaginal story arc. "What would that look like?" she demanded. "Something new, right? Not the same old play we've all seen a million times!" She may have actually stomped her foot. It was the only time she ever got sent to the principal.

What she sees here, now, is not a rise and fall, but a spiral—circles in circles in circles.

She asks them all to sit. To start by telling their dreams. "Furies," she says, "anytime the mood strikes you, play to the narrative."

"Iph?" Plum asks. "What about Orr?"

Iph planned to let him watch as the stories unspooled, but maybe Plum is right. "What do you think?" Iph asks her brother. "Do you want to sit in the middle with Plum?"

"I want to stay here for now," he says. Scout is in his lap. "If I need to join you, I will."

"I kind of want to sit on the side," Plum says. "If that's all right."

"You guys," Iph says. "This is devised theater. We're making the story together. If I say something, it's just a suggestion. We need everyone's intuition. Everyone's voice."

Allison has her bass in her lap. She plucks the lowest string with her good hand, and now they have a heartbeat.

Iph inhales and exhales. They mirror her, already starting to sync up. Mika's hand drum joins Allison's bass.

One after another, they speak their dreams aloud. There is a theme here Iph is trying to understand, something cathartic and elemental. Jane plays a harsh progression of chords on her electric guitar that resolves to melancholy, even bereavement. Loss is part of this story; that much Iph knows for sure.

Allison sings, her voice shockingly angelic, in a language Iph doesn't know. Maybe Allison doesn't even know it. Iph opens her mouth to take in the high notes; they taste like the purest water.

Something about Lorna's dream makes Iph think of banked coals or a dormant volcano. "You're holding our fire," Iph says to Lorna.

"What about your dream?" Lorna's voice is sharp, but she is fully present for this. Willing, Iph senses, to expose herself in a new way—but only if everyone else does.

Iph sits next to Orr, takes his hand, and tells him her dream of their parents.

"Whoa," Lorna says. "Your mom—I guess it explains the gold stripper shoes."

"Her mom was a stripper?" Allison's whisper to Jane carries like her soprano singing voice. "Sorry!" she says when heads turn. "I always used to get in trouble at church for loud-whispering.

But it wasn't a your-mom joke or anything. I was just curious—
some of my best friends are sex workers."

"Our mom is a huge proponent of your-mom jokes," Orr says.
"She's the queen of them. And I know your dream about Dad is
right. His brother did die, but I didn't know it was suicide."

"It might not be a perfect interpretation of what happened, but
I'm not sure that matters."

"Me neither," Orr says.

Jane picks the guitar up again. She hums a low, simple lullaby. Then the song changes to something familiar Iph can't place.
Maybe it's not usually done on the acoustic guitar.

"Remember, babe?" Jane says in her ten-packs-a-day rasp. For
a moment, Iph sees her and Allison as cigar-smoking old ladies.

"Nirvana," Orr says. He joins the circle with the musicians.
Grabs Jane's acoustic guitar. They play together. Suddenly, Orr
stops. Jane keeps playing, a song that gets soft and sad, like the
wind blowing through an empty house.

"I'm going to tell you about the mountain," Orr says.

Iph rises. Brings Cait to the center. Is it cruel to cast her, with
her lost sister, in this role? She asks Cait, "Are you okay?"

"I'm all in," Cait says.

Orr looks at her. These two haven't connected until now.
"George told me about your sister," he says. "I'm sorry."

"I'm glad you got away from that place," Cait says. "Britta was a
badass, but even she never managed to escape from the girls' side."

Orr directs them. "Lie down," he says to Cait. "The house is
empty. You're in your bed. You're thinking about *The X-Files*."

Cait giggles and it's the cutest sound. Iph realizes it's the first
time she's heard Cait laugh.

The others play the transport team. Someone fetches a pillow-
case, and Iph says, "Scene!"

They go through the motions as Orr describes them: The abduction, the van ride. Arrival. When Orr reaches the part about running from the men, Cait explodes into fury, kicking and screaming
and spitting like a wild animal.

Lorna stalks forward, hunching her shoulders to shape the Minotaur man who shaved Orr's head. George and Josh are the chair that holds Cait as Orr tells of the taking of his dark sentinel locks—his only protection.

He stops there. "Please, do it again."

They repeat.

"Again!" Orr says.

They are switching roles now, rotating until they come back to Cait.

"No, wait," Plum says. How did Iph forget about Plum? "I should do it."

"No," Orr says. "Not you. Maybe Josh can be me this time. You be the mouse."

Plum nods. Jane squeezes her hand.

Orr tells of waking in the tent. Of the mouse, played by Plum. Of the coyote, obviously George.

Iph doesn't have to direct them now; they are choosing their own roles perfectly.

When Orr gets off the mountain and meets Jane at the campfire, Iph signals for them to stop.

"Orr," she says. The music stops suddenly, too. It's as if they all know what she is thinking. "Orr, what about you? Can you do it?"

A bell chimes. Allison has amazing timing. Again, the bell. And again. A little voice calling Orr. Mika's heartbeat drumming resumes. Orr moves to the center, lies down, and pretends to be in bed. Jane is playing the guitar again, peanut-butter-thick blues. Where the movements were fast and raw before, they are now stylized and deliberate, more choreographed dance than theatrical improvisation.

Orr is deep in concentration, a look reserved for the cello. Something flickers at the edge of Iph's attention, but she releases it. She has to be here in every sense. She is the psychopomp. Orr's witness and guide.

Everything goes well until the shearing. George and Josh hold Orr. Cait is weeping and can't wield the imaginary shears. Once again, Lorna plays the villain. The moment she touches Orr's head, the wind whips up in the trees outside, and Orr's body convulses so hard someone screams. Scout barks and barks.

Orr is changing, too rapidly to track.

Deer to brother. Brother to deer.

They are all frozen. Watching.

Deer to brother, brother to deer.

Orr's strobing form flickers with the firelight, transforming faster and faster.

The cycle begins again, so fast Iph worries Orr will fly apart. She throws herself on him and holds with all her might.

He is now the fish from Plum's dream, the embryo in her belly. He is the tiger! The white hound, her arctic minion. A redwood tree. He is teenage Mom on the slide and Dad mourning his brother on the shore.

Iph holds him through every change until finally Orr is still.

The others are holding hands in a circle around them.

Applause sounds from an invisible audience in the house.

A spotlight shines in Iph's eyes.

Orr stands. Holds his hand out to her as if they're preparing to take a bow.

The antlers are gone.

She presses her forehead to his forehead. They stay this way for a long time.

The applause dies. The cottage is silent. The trees are still in the breathless night.

Iph knows before he even moves. Before he says a single word.

"No!" she says.

"I'm sorry," he whispers.

He holds her close again. "I love you," he says.

Then he turns and walks out of the cottage. When Iph reaches the doorstep, there is a pile of clothes on the flagstone path.

Orr is gone.

20

VOICE & SPEECH

ph makes the call from a laundromat on Northwest Thurman, a few blocks away from the trail leading to the Witch's Castle. Being in the real world is decidedly surreal.

"Hello?"

Mom! Iph can't speak. She can only cry.

"Orr?"

"No—Mom! I'm sorry. I'm so sorry."

"Where are you? We're coming right now. I'm putting my shoes on. Theo!" Mom yells, forgetting to cover the receiver. "It's Iph! Get the keys!"

"How are you home?"

"Later," Mom says. "I have to find my other shoe. Here—tell your dad where to go."

"Macleay Park," she tells him. "Bring Orr's cello."

CAIT'S PURPLE BMW AND the Furies' van are next to each other in the laundromat parking lot. Lorna has to work, and Cait is looking rough. The night has been hard on her.

"I don't even know how to thank you guys," Iph says. She has phone numbers for Cait and Lorna. "Where can I find you?" she asks Josh.

"Around," Josh says, opening his arms for a goodbye hug.

"No bardic comeback?" Iph smiles a little.

"Too tired," Josh says.

"Come stay at my house," Cait says to him. "My parents left for Europe two days ago."

"See you soon, Iph." Mika smiles and shakes Iph's hand. She and Allison are cramming into Cait's car, too. Mika also has to work, and Allison needs her pain meds. Her broken arm has been throbbing all night. "Too much bonus rocking," she says, looking like a debauched empress in her disheveled red toga and raccoon eyeliner.

Iph grabs Lorna and hugs her tight. "Thank you for being so strong," she says.

"What do you mean?"

"You held the shadow for us tonight. We needed that."

Lorna rolls her eyes, but she's smiling a little as she reaches into her ever-present duffle. "Here," she says, taking out the gold shoes. "Give these back to your mom. Or maybe they'll fit you now. They don't feel like mine anymore."

Iph looks down at the boots that have basically become a part of her body. "No." Lorna smiles. "Keep those, too. I've got my own."

Iph waves as Cait's car pulls out of the parking lot and turns left into the ordinary world.

IN THE VAN, JANE is smoking. "You all right?"

"Yes, considering."

"I'm gonna go call Plum's dad," she says. Plum and George stayed back at the cottage. "Be right back."

Iph takes one of Jane's cigarettes and lights it. It goes straight to her head. She puts it out, wishing for water.

"We should stop at the store for more of these," she says when Jane starts up the van. "My mom's going to need them."

21

STRUGGLES
WITH OBSTINACY

Iph hears the Volvo before it turns into the Macleay Park lot. She runs from the picnic table where she's been waiting—Iph, who doesn't run. Maybe Orr has rubbed off on her.

Mom gets out before the car has fully stopped. Iph is her arms, heartbeat to heartbeat. Mom's patchouli perfume, her essential Momness—ursine, soft, and fierce. Like something that's tamed itself to love her.

Dad gets out and stops, hesitates. "I'm sorry," he says. Iph has never seen him so pale and stricken. He looks thin and hollow—like the ghost in him fled when Orr did.

"It doesn't matter now," she says, trying not to sound cold. The reenactment of Orr's kidnapping was going to be with her for a long time. To her mom she says, "How come you're home?"

"I had a dream," Mom says.

"Me, too." Dad's voice is trembling. "I don't know what it meant, but it was the same dream. We both had it. Your brother—"

"Turned into a deer," Iph says.

They stand in the parking lot at the border between worlds.

"Mom?" Iph says. "It's like your piece—*El Mundo Bueno* and *El Mundo Malo*."

"Yes," Mom says softly, like she already knows where Iph is going with this.

"*El mundo* what?" Dad says, his terrible Spanish accent a little extra terrible. A tiny joke, a tactic that is the start of them making up. But Mom isn't having it.

She strides toward the path.

Iph's stomach flips, full of dream fish. She's never considered her parents breaking up. Not for even a second. But Mom has never, ever been this mad.

"They're the good and bad worlds—but not exactly," Iph says. "It's the multiverse, sort of. Except we keep going back and forth between the two. You have a chance to choose if you pay attention."

"Iph," Dad says like he hasn't heard a word. He's staring at Mom's disappearing back. "Where is your brother?"

"In the forest," Iph says. "Follow me."

22

VALUE OF
CHILDISH
IMPRESSIONS

Mom has been gone for over an hour looking for Orr. After quickly greeting Jane and Plum and giving a slightly more interested hello to George, Mom asked for a glass of water and headed back out, Scout at her heels. She promised to keep to the trails and not go too far. She didn't speak to or look at Dad, who is now asleep on the sofa. The house took one look at him, produced a turkey sandwich, and lured him to the pillows. George is reading in a chair by the fire. Plum is outside picking flowers and talking to Jane while she smokes.

Iph touches George's sleeve. "I'll be back," she says.

George grabs her hand and pulls her close. Plants a kiss on her forehead. "For luck."

Iph returns the kiss on George's perfect lips. "See you soon." She takes Orr's bundle of clothes and places them in the basket hanging by the front door.

In the woods, Iph wanders. Soon, she hears something—singing. *Mom.* The song Iph hummed to Scout on the bus last night— or no, two nights ago. Or was it three? Iph follows Mom's voice deeper into the woods. So much for staying on the path.

De la Sierra Morena,
cielito lindo, vienen bajando,
Un par de ojitos negros,
cielito lindo, de contrabando.

Iph follows the song to a stream and along the stream past a weeping willow. There, on the mossy creek bank, are Mom and Orr. He is asleep with his head on her lap, and she is stroking his face, now softly furred, and his antlers, which have grown and forked. Sitting there with her long curly hair haloed by a shaft of perfect light, Mom and Orr are a gilded Medieval painting—the Queen and the Stag.

She shifts position and looks around protectively. Now Iph sees Scout, snoring at Mom's side. It's always been one of Mom's gifts, putting babies to sleep. It works as well, Iph supposes, on deer brothers and pocket pits.

"Hey, Mom!" she whispers. "Can we take him back? I have an idea."

23

DON'T SPEAK
OF MY FATHER

Mom. Orr holds her hand as they walk back to the cottage like he is four years old and afraid for his first day of kindergarten. He will stay, he thinks. Of course he will stay. Maybe Iph is right. Maybe Mom's return is the fork in the path they've been searching for. Maybe they will find another cottage with different magic that will help Orr become a human man instead of the thing he is becoming.

He spent the night alone, away from the rest of the herd, although their presence was everywhere in the forest in the scrapes where they'd recently slept and the trees scarred by other new antlers and the rich musk of their hooves and bodies in the wind. He walked at first, his forehead clear of antlers, his legs their normal shape. But then there was a doe. A tilt of her eye, a way she moved. It reminded him of Plum. And he was gone again, farther than ever, as he raced her through the woods. She beat him easily and lost him with as little effort—one moment ahead, melted into the trees the next. Alone again, he'd found a place to rest. He'd slept. Woken up neither boy nor stag. It was then that he heard his mother's singing.

Inside the cottage, Orr stands over his sleeping father. Dad starts and flinches back, bumping his head hard on the window behind him.

"Orestes?" he says.

But Orr is also backing away.

Dad, the brochure, Pinocchio. The hood over his head like he's a hawk bred for hunting. Tamed. Dad trying to talk to him after Mom left. Orr turning his back, damming up, locking down.

"I know what you tried to do," Orr says. "But you shouldn't have trusted those people. I needed you, Dad. Not those strangers."

"They cut your hair," Dad says. Orr sees his reflection in the windows behind Dad and realizes it's a strange thing for him to say, considering the rest of his appearance.

"They hurt you." Dad stands. Takes a step forward. Orr knows this dance—he's learned it from the bucks. Slowly. Head low to show respect.

Orr takes a half step forward and offers Dad his velvet-covered horns, but the moment skin connects with bone, electricity moves through Orr's body.

He is shaking, his abdomen contorting. Something last night— a shifting, rending, dizzy thing too fast for memory to process. It's happening again. Happening now.

Orr's knees buckle, but Dad is here. Holding him.

"Don't let go!" Iph says.

"I won't," Dad says in Orr's ear. "Not until you say so. Never again."

24

OUR HOME
THEATER

Orr is improvising on the cello. His notes soar and break into flower petals that float away on a river, gathering mass as they slither to shore.

Jane plays with him, flamenco runs that start soft but gather in speed to pound like a herd of hooved animals. She's changed clothes somewhere along the way, into jeans and a plain white T-shirt. They are both in the zone, loose and aware.

"She never plays the acoustic guitar anymore," Plum says. "I was surprised to see it at the show."

"She's amazing."

"My mom met her when she was my age, living on the street in Old Town. My dad—well, he used to restore and repair old instruments. He redid that guitar for Jane. She was like, practically a professional as a kid."

"Is she Latina?"

"Argentinian." Plum smiles. "She can dance, too, but she never does it. Says she's so sexy when she tangos, people start calling 911."

"Believe it," Jane calls in her alley-cat voice.

"Like me with these," Orr says, cocking his head to show off the antlers. Are they . . . joking about this?

"Iph." Plum pauses to take a sip of water. "Jane had to leave for a while, too, you know."

"When your mom died?"

"Before that. When she was sixteen."

"What did you turn into?" Orr asks.

"A boxcar kid, babe," Jane answers. "For about a year."

"She really was," Plum says. "But she won't tell me how to hop a train."

"I'll tell you how," Jane says over a sassy strumming pattern. "Go to Union Station. Buy a flipping ticket."

Orr laughs at them bickering like sisters.

Iph's plan was exactly this—being together, playing music, reminding Orr of things he loves. But Mom and Dad are outside fighting, and the music has turned sad. This isn't her brother deciding to stay. This is Orr saying goodbye.

"Jane," Orr says when the song is over, "thanks for rescuing me that day."

"Who rescued who, babe? That's what I want to know." Jane reaches out and touches the tip of an antler. "Drugs, man. They wreck your brain. Make you see shit that's not there."

Orr laughs. Jane lets out a shaky breath like she feels the end coming, too.

"Plum?" Orr says. "Can we go for a short walk?"

"Sure." She squares her shoulders like Jane did. They all know it's coming, except maybe Mom. Orr and Plum go out the front door. Jane waits a bit, then heads out after them. For a smoke, Iph guesses.

Mom wanders in through the back.

"Where's your brother?" There's a familiar squirt of panic in her voice. They used to lose Orr sometimes in stores. It would be too loud or smell bad, and he'd go find a place to curl up.

"Just out talking to Plum."

"Sorry." Mom's been crying, but that's a good sign. She cries when the fight is over, after she and Dad make up. She paces the workroom, stops at the little library. Iph knows her moods. It will be hard for her sit still.

"Did you see George out there? And Scout?"

"Yes, they're out there talking to your dad," Mom says. "So freaking cute."

"Which one?" Iph smiles.

"Both," Mom says, then startles. "What was that?"

"Did a book just go *pssst* at you?"

"Is that what's happening?" Mom squints at the shelves. This year, she's started to need reading glasses.

"It's a self-recommending library," Iph says. "The books choose you."

Mom cocks her head to listen, then takes a slim volume and goes back outside. The sun is getting low. All day, the dream of Mom and Rob in the park in New York has been floating through her head. Why didn't Mom ever tell them about her past? She could have at least told Iph. There were moments—when they gave money and food to street kids, when Iph asked Mom if she thought porn was inherently sexist—when she could have said something. Looking back, Iph thinks maybe there were times she almost did.

Through the front window Iph sees her mother settle in an Adirondack chair with the book. *Her mother.* Maybe that's it—it's like that old *Sesame Street* song. *One of these things is not like the other.* Maybe she didn't know how to be both that girl in the park and Dad's wife and Iph and Orr's mom. Iph sees how hard she has to work to get the family to make space for her dancing. They try, but they are selfish. Not so much Dad, but definitely her and Orr.

Iph lies down on the rug. Earlier, they all tried to figure out when it had morphed back from a stage. The house does these things so imperceptibly, it's hard to catch the moment of change.

The sun refracts rainbows on the walls as it hits the beveled glass windows. It's warm, but not too hot. A perfect Portland summer evening—except that something unimaginable is about to happen.

Plum and Orr come back inside. Plum looks happy and flushed, like maybe they've been kissing.

Orr starts to play another song on the cello—the Schubert from the soundtrack of Iph's favorite movie about elegant bisexual vampires Catherine Deneuve and David Bowie. Iph grins. Orr grins. They've seen the movie so many times and always fight over who gets to marry Bowie. Even though he's shriveled and dying by the halfway point, he's still so hot. In the end, Iph always capitulates because Orr gives her both Catherine Deneuve and a very young Susan Sarandon. "Two for one," he says.

She can't hear this song right now. She stands up, not sure where she's going. Orr stops playing.

Plum is the one who's brave enough to say it. "The sun is going down soon," she says. "Orr, I think Jane and I should go. Where is she?"

"Out for a smoke." Iph says.

"Should I maybe go see if George wants a ride?" Plum's voice is steady. Whatever she and Orr discussed, she seems sure about it.

"I think George and Scout are out somewhere with my dad."

"I'll go with you," Orr says to Plum.

With everyone out of the house, Iph is suddenly exhausted. She closes her eyes for one second. She drifts.

"Iph," Mom says, rushing back into the house. She holds out the book she's been reading like it's turned into a snake.

The book is open to the poem: "The Boy Changed Into a Stag Clamors at the Gate of Secrets." The same poem from the matchbook.

"It's about a mother crying for her son who's changed into a stag and can't come back to her." She chokes back a sob. "Iph. Is he going?"

Iph can't look at her.

Mom drops the book, covers her mouth like she's going to throw up, and runs out of the house. Iph follows, but stops. Across the creek standing next to the redwood where Iph tried to psychically summon Mom is a leggy woman in faded blue jeans with feathery white hair and dangling silver earrings. Is she the cottage's owner? Something about her is familiar. The young white wolf dog is at her feet. She calls out to Mom, but Iph can't hear what she's saying. Mom reaches her, and the woman holds out her arm. Mom takes it, to Iph's surprise. They walk off together on a path Iph didn't notice before.

Iph goes back inside. Her attention is drawn to the cottage walls—the little sock in its carefully constructed shadowbox, the beautifully framed silver spoon. Baby things, but nothing from a child who's grown. Maybe the woman in the woods owns this place, and maybe she has something to tell Mom about loss.

She picks up the book and opens to a random page. It's near the end. She reads.

> *There he stood on the crest of all time,*
> *there he stood on creation's highest mountain,*
> *there he stood at the gate of secrets —*
> *the points of his antlers plated with the stars*
> *and with a stag's voice he cried,*
> *cried back to his mother who'd borne him —*
> *mother, mother, I can't go back*
> *the hundred wounds in me weep pure gold.*

25

THE BOY CHANGED INTO A STAG CLAMORS AT THE GATE OF SECRETS

Blood pounds through Orr's antlers. The boy in the window, the same one who lives in the mirror, strokes the mossy velvet that covers them. Both he and Orr are beginning to know and love the weight of them. Orr almost laughs. He expected aliens, but never this.

The sun is setting.

George and Scout and Jane and Plum are gone.

"It's time," Orr says.

"Can we go out to the meadow first?" Dad asks. "Just for a minute?"

Orr hesitates, and they all see it: the lack of trust, born way before Meadowbrook.

Dad bows his head, bucklike. Orr relents.

They walk together, arms linked like the heroes of *The Wizard of Oz*. First Mom, then Orr, then Iph, then Dad. They hear what Dad made before they see it—a low hum, like the forest opening its mouth to sing.

The desire to find the source of the sound quickens Orr's deeper desire, itching his ankles toward their new shape. He will control it this time, giving in when he's ready—but then he will do what he's been so afraid of all this time. He will fall into it until he's fully submerged. He will know this other self entirely.

Now he walks with his family, who will always be his family. At the top of a small rise are two trees once scorched in a fire, probably years ago. They look dead, but Orr knows they aren't. Under his bare feet, he feels it. Their children, the tall trees that circle them, will feed them as long as they live.

Between these trees, Dad has strung five thick metal wires. "Piano?" Orr asks.

"I was talking to George. We were letting the dog run around, following her, and I noticed something in the bushes over there. There was an old rotting piano that someone must have left out to pasture. I saw these trees. They're hollow—" Dad stops himself. He loves to explain how things are made but worries other people don't care the way that he does.

Orr runs his hand along one tree, then the other. The wind picks up and runs its invisible mane over the strings. Dad has made him a forest cello.

His antlers are tender, so he uses his hands. Later, he won't need to. Already the bone branches are hardening. He and the wind play a duet that rings from the hollowed trees and vibrates the ground as if the song is rising from some deep cathedral.

"Dad," he says. He can't say more.

"Now you can make music," Dad says, "no matter what."

The family gathers around. They hold each other. Night is falling. The forest calls him. He wants to stay but has to go. He pulls away; they let him.

"Iph," he says. "Come to the forest once in a while. Look for me."

"I'm scared I won't know you from the others," she says, so quietly only he can hear.

"You'll always know me," Orr says. "Just like I'll know you."

"Orr?" Iph isn't crying. She is strong. His strong big sister. "I want you to come back. When you're done. You have to remember. It might be hard when things are so different. When you're done, come back to me."

Iph steps away and lets Dad put his arm around her shoulders. Orr reaches out for Mom. When had her hand gotten so small?

"Look," Mom says, "it's our blue."

Linked, they gaze at the sky. The moon is rising.

Mom turns to him, traces his antlers with the palms of her hands. Licks her left index finger. Reaches down to the dirt. Traces a symbol on the back of each hand and one on his forehead. "Protection," she says.

"I'm going into the trees now," Orr says. "I don't want you guys to watch." Orr knows that seeing will frighten them.

"*Te amo,*" Mom says. Love in Spanish.

"*S'agapo,*" Dad says. Love in Greek.

"Don't forget us," Iph says. Love in Big Sister.

Orr can't say anything. The night is pulsing through his veins. His body yearns to meet itself in fur and hoof and strength and speed. He has to go.

Orr walks away slowly until he hits the trees.

Then he runs.

ACT IV

How fares my child? How fares my roe?

1

THE LINE OF
THE FANTASTIC

"This isn't going to work," Iph says, laughing. She's at the basement sink, washing paint brushes while George kisses the back of her neck. "Stop it or else." Iph brandishes a hot-pink paint-covered roller. It took five coats to cover the dining room, but it's totally worth it. The fuchsia looks so decadent with the dark wood built-ins and bookcases.

"Give me one kiss, and I'll give it thee again, and one for interest, if thou wilt have twain," George says, shoving Iph over to help at the sink. "Is everything out of the old house?"

"Almost," Iph says.

Scout was the one to find the new house—they were walking back from the cello spot when she ran off, barking at them to follow. A few blocks from the Macleay Park entrance was a big yellow Victorian—Dad's nightmare and Mom's dream.

"It's your turn anyway," said Dad, lover of modern architecture, clearly hoping to trade this Victorian monstrosity for the doghouse he was still in.

Iph and Mom laughed. You could see the project wheels turning behind his eyes—how to modernize a hundred-year-old house? What would he need from the hardware store?

"Is your mom at the studio?" George has that *Are we alone in the house?* tone that still makes Iph swoon.

"She is," Iph says. "But don't you have to go?"

George is apprenticing with Shakespeare in the Shelter—a paying job that's brought electricity back to Taurus Trucking.

"There's a little time," George says, pulling Iph closer. As always, Scout weaves around their ankles, worming her way in between them. George scoops her up and laughs.

"Tell my mom to get eggs if you see her," Iph says. "And almond milk. And ice cream."

The biggest changes at the end of summer had been Mom's. Since George introduced her to Glow, there's been no stopping her. She wrote a grant and got donations from all the people she charmed at Dad's work events all these years. She found a space in Old Town and opened a movement studio catering to street folks and sex workers. People said it would be vandalized, but Mom put up with the broken windows and graffiti until people on the street started sticking up for the place. When Shakespeare in the Shelter needed a new home, Mom hooked them up.

Iph never returned to Forest Lake High for her senior year. Thanks to a book she found at Powell's, *The Teenage Liberation Handbook*, Iph is unschooling. Mom was for it from the start, but Dad needed convincing.

"It just means taking charge of your education. And that education doesn't only happen in school," she told him. Then she set it out to prove it.

She's teaching with Mom, taking acting classes at the university, and volunteering for RCT Press.

When Iph finally returned to the cottage, it was with Mom, who wanted to have tea with the lanky woman with white hair and her sweet yellow-eyed white dog. She and Mom became friends, and suddenly Iph found herself with a job.

Sylvie is a tough boss, but kind and incredibly well read. Iph proofreads and does deliveries and post office runs now that she has her license. Once in a while, on her way back down the path from the cottage, she sees Sylvie's white wolf-dog and a tall white hound race into the deepest part of the wood.

On less busy days, Iph stays home and sleeps so she can dream of Orr. Lately, though, she's spent most of her free hours haunting the library, researching theater programs, and slogging through applications.

Now that spring is coming, she sometimes takes a sleeping bag to the cello spot and sleeps under the stars. That's where she's going today—not for an overnight, only a quick visit.

She and George kiss goodbye on the front porch. Iph notices the mail. She unlocks the door, throws it on the hall table. A large envelope catches her eye. *American Conservatory Theater.* Her heart pounds. She shoves the envelope in her backpack and hurries into the bright afternoon.

THE PATH TO THE cottage behind the Witch's Castle is easy to find now. The others make the same pilgrimage. At first, no one heard Orr's music. But in the fall, as the weather got cold, visitors to the cello spot often felt the deep resonance through their boots as they tromped up the trail. By the time they rounded the bend and crested the little hill, Orr was always gone.

At the base of the rise, a short way from the forest cello, someone set up an old table with ornate legs and a splintery top under a thick-branched pine. Under the table, out of the rain, is a child's tape player Allison and Mika found at Goodwill—the kind with large simple buttons that might be worked with the tip of an antler or a talented hoof. It was Jane who first started leaving the mixes. First, random stuff she thought Orr would like. Then a two-song Furies demo tape. Then a four-song EP, recorded at a local studio. Now there's an actual full-length release. The Furies are signed to a Seattle label. Soon, they'll be going on tour, opening for Bikini Kill.

Iph sees evidence of Plum in the artful still-life arrangements of forest ephemera on the table. Stuck to the trunk with tree sap are Polaroid self-portraits of Plum as various classical paintings and kiss-printed Post-it notes.

Mika comes more often than Jane or Allison, sometimes over-lapping with Iph. She reads *X-Files* novelizations aloud in case Orr might be listening and leaves fresh-baked pies from the bak-ery where she works and talks to Iph about how difficult it is dat-ing Lorna.

Mom comes less than she used to, but every full moon she is here, doing rituals of protection. Dad has started running again, visiting the spot daily to pour fresh water from his water bottle into a blue ceramic bowl, even though there is a creek so close you can hear it, and placing mounds of organic oats and corn under trees where there are visible hoofprints.

Today under the blue sky, Iph thinks the cello spot looks a little too much like a shrine or a memorial. The copy of the Furies' tape has been there since last week, unplayed. Iph pulls a blanket out of her backpack along with a bag of caramel popcorn and a book—Jung's *Memories, Dreams, Reflections*. Also, a battered pocket copy of *A Midsummer Night's Dream*. She's auditioning for Shakespeare in the Park next week and needs to practice her monologue. The sun feels so good after last week's rain. Iph lies back. Then she remembers—the letter!

How could she forget? She grounds herself, checks in.

Okay—she's scared.

No, terrified.

She takes a deep breath. Asks herself why.

George, she thinks. But ACT is only in San Francisco. She and George have already driven Mom's Volvo down there twice for the auditions. George is saving for a car, too. Dad is making noise about George getting something classic and them fixing it up together. So, no. Not George.

Is she afraid of the program itself? Maybe a little. But in a good way. The way you're scared because it's something you really, really want.

She sits up. *Ugh*. The answer is obvious. It's what she's been afraid of since fifth grade when she realized she'd graduate two years before Orr. She's afraid to leave her brother.

She takes out the envelope and opens it with a long, black-painted fingernail. She doesn't have to pull out the letter to know what it says. Iph feels her path forking, calling her south. She lies back and lets herself read the nice things they say about her audition. She imagines a studio apartment a little like Lorna's, but in a pink Victorian near Golden Gate Park. She drifts, dreamless at first.

Then comes her favorite dream—a deer approaches, hooves silent on the soft turf. A cold nose presses her cheek. She wakes up. She stands—a tip of antler, a flash of white tail. This is not the first time it's happened. As the weather warms, she imagines Orr's memory rousing from its winter slumber.

"Orr," she calls. "I know it's you." The rustling in the bushes stops. Orr has never quite gotten the stealthy, silent deer thing. "See this?" She raises the letter like a white flag. "It's from ACT. In San Francisco. I go in September." She waits, but all is still. "That gives us the rest of the spring and all summer," she says, even though she's pretty sure he's already gone.

She gathers her things. The bag of caramel corn is empty and hoofprints mark her blanket. As she walks down the hill toward the trail she hears a familiar melody. The words of the lullaby rise into Iph's mouth from the forest floor.

> *Cielito lindo, vienen bajando, un par de ojitos negros*
> *Sweet little heaven is prancing down, a pair of little black eyes*

Iph sings in Spanish and in English. At home she'll ask Dad how to say it in Greek. The chorus comes, her favorite part.

> *Ai, ai, ai, ai*
> *Canta y no llores.*
> *Sing, don't cry.*

The notes follow her through the forest and out to the city street.

A NOTE FROM THE AUTHOR

Dear Readers,

First, I want to acknowledge that the land where this story is set, the place I have called home for the past twenty-six years, is stolen land, once home to traditional village sites of the Multnomah, Wasco, Cowlitz, Kathlamet, Clackamas, Bands of Chinook, Tualatin, the Confederated Tribes of Grand Ronde including Molalla and Kalapuya, and many other tribes who made their homes in this green valley and along the Columbia River. It's also important to note that in 1859, Oregon was founded as a "white utopia" and explicitly forbade Black people from living in its borders—the only state to do so.

When I first moved to Portland in the early '90s, twenty-five and pregnant with my first daughter, I wondered where the people of color were. I had a hard time finding stores that carried traditional Latinx foods and strangers often asked if I was just back from Hawai'i because of my winter "tan."

But Portland also met me with midwives and zine makers, sex work activists and unschoolers, misfits and artists both queer and straight—many of them young parents who, like my partner and I, wanted to transform generations-old patterns of trauma into something kinder, healthier, full of possibility and love. Over time, I even found other people of color, some who were raised here, other who are transplants like me, looking for a quiet place to heal. Our stories have rooted here, adding something fertile to a place that has never wholly welcomed us.

At the time when this story takes place, there was a feeling of reinvention in this small uncool Pacific Northwest city, a sense of DIY pride, a feminist and queer resurgence. Still, the term "genderqueer" would only come into use a few years after this book takes place. When I dug into writing the nonbinary character George, I first thought to use the pronoun "they," but doing so felt like an erasure of the experience of a nonbinary person in that era. I reached for a language-based solution that expressed the character's experienced singularity and decided to write George without pronouns, hoping to convey the isolation of growing up with an identity that is unspoken and largely unnamed.

I also hoped to offer a roadmap to readers who are interested in getting to know their own inner landscape. While magical realism is a literary device that lets authors express deep psychological or spiritual ideas in concrete form, for some of us, like me, it's also a way to see the world—enchanted and full of wisdom if you only take the time to look.

There are endless paths to psyche, but these are some that I've found fruitful: the work of Carl Jung and Joseph Campbell, fairy and folk tales, the tarot, the book *Women Who Run with the Wolves* by Dr. Clarissa Pinkola Estés, listening to stories from my elders, reading poetry, exploring diasporic futurism, becoming aware of the cycles of the moon, paying attention to wild animals wherever I go, and writing down my dreams.

A wise friend of mine believes that time is not linear. That by doing our work in the present, we can heal the past—both our own and our ancestors'. My family's journey is the inspiration for this book and my dearest hope is to send some healing to all past/present/future versions of my beloved daughters, my own mother, my husband and my father, who died at age thirty but would have loved this book most of all. I imagine our family line like a battered spine glowing gold, vertebrae adjusting to stack strong, sending us into the future. I wish the same healing for you and the ones you love.

Michelle Ruiz Keil
December 28, 2020

ACKNOWLEDGMENTS

Thank you to the people who inspired this story and whose love and support inspires me every day—my husband, Carl, my beloved daughters, Luciana and Angelika and Kaylib, my sister and the best of friends. To my own parents, Anita Johansen and Patrick Smith, and, as always, thank you to my nana, Luciana Ruiz Dudley. "Cielito Lindo" was her favorite song.

More and more, I find myself telling young writers how much their work will benefit from theater training. I received mine from the famous, fabulous Donna Russell. I will always be grateful.

Lucky for me, the huge bout of writer's block I encountered halfway through *Summer in the City of Roses* was overcome by the radical hospitality of my time in residence at Hedgebrook. The magic of the forest path and my little cottage infuses this story and so does the kindness of my fellow residents, Heidi Durrow, Roja Heydarpour, Jael Humphrey, Diana Xin, Julie Phillips, Liz de Souza and Wendy Johnson. Thank you for sharing your writing, deer sightings and encouragement. The last moments pre-pandemic were well spent with you brilliant women.

Thank you, too, to the writers and readers who answered my late-night Facebook posts about '90s Portland, especially Rene Denfeld, whose experience as a former punk goddess was put to great use in these pages, and to Portland's own Dead Moon for my writing soundtrack.

A massive fan-girl thank-you goes out to the band Bikini Kill, who generously let me use the lyrics to their song "Resist Psychic Death" and to Natalie Garyet of Tavern Books and translator David Wevill, who allowed me to use lines from *The Boy Changed into a Stag Clamors at the Gate of Secrets* to my heart's content.

I wouldn't have known about Ferenc Juhász's poem at all if it hadn't been for the kindred spirit of poet, screenwriter and bruja Stephanie Adams-Santos. I will always be grateful. Thanks also to fairytale expert and tarot alchemist Coleman Stevenson for reading an early draft of this book and for all her inspiration and support. Poets make the fiercest and best of friends.

Thank you to Satya Doyle Byock and the members of the many seminars I attended at the Salomé Institute of Jungian Studies—our conversations are the sea I swam in as I drafted this book. Love and gratitude are also owed to Connor and Sayre Quevedo and Coda Goodrich, who in some deep but indirect way helped me find the boy in this story. And to their mothers, the writers MK Chavez and Talese Babb, who have loved and supported me for all these years.

It was MK Chavez who introduced me to public health and sex worker activism and who connected me with the force of nature known as Joanna Berton Martinez, aka Teresa Dulce, creator of the nonprofit Danzine. Joanna never met a problem she couldn't solve with limitless energy, a movie-star smile and surreal performance art. Thanks for the inspiration and for those Friday nights in the needle exchange van on SE 82nd!

Finally, thank you to my agent, Hannah Fergesen, and the folks and KT Literary and the lovely people of Soho Press for their support of my work, especially Alexa Wejko and Amara Hoshijo. Working with you has been a privilege and a joy.